Seven Contemporary Short Novels

Second Edition

Seven Contemporary Short Novels

Second Edition

Edited by
Charles Clerc and Louis Leiter
University of the Pacific

Scott, Foresman and Company • Glenview, Illinois
Dallas, Tex. • Oakland, N.J. • Palo Alto, Cal. • Tucker, Ga. • Brighton, England

ISBN: 0–673–07971–6

Library of Congress Catalog Card Number: 74-83538

Printed in the United States of America.

Acknowledgments

Slaughterhouse-Five by Kurt Vonnegut, Jr. Copyright © 1969 by Kurt Vonnegut, Jr. Reprinted by permission of the publisher, Delacorte Press/ Seymour Lawrence.

Lines of poetry from "The Waking" copyright 1953 by Theodore Roethke from the book *The Collected Poems of Theodore Roethke.* Reprinted by permission of Doubleday & Company, Inc.

From the "Introduction" by Ira C. Eaker, Ltd. Gen USAF (Ret.) to *The Destruction of Dresden* by David Irving. Reprinted by permission of Holt, Rinehart and Winston, Inc. From the "Foreward" by Air Marshal Sir Robert Saundby to *The Destruction of Dresden* by David Irving. Reprinted by permission of Holt, Rinehart and Winston, Inc. and William Kimber & Co. Ltd.

'Leven Cent Cotton, Forty Cent Meat. Words and Music by Bob Miller and Emma Dermer. Copyright 1929 by Triangle Music Publishing Co. © Copyright renewed 1956 by MCA MUSIC, A Division of MCA, Inc. Used by permission. All Rights Reserved.

Preface

The favorable reception of the first edition of *Seven Contemporary Short Novels* has confirmed our belief that a collection of this kind fulfills a real need among students and general readers alike. We are pleased in this second edition to offer a group of modern short novels meriting rank among other accomplished novellas of the world, past and present, of whatever national origin. Besides their assured stature and vital modernity, these short novels, two of which are new to this edition, have much to offer in scope, subject matter, and technique.

The most significant change in the second edition is the inclusion of Kurt Vonnegut's much-admired *Slaughterhouse-Five,* which is appearing for the first time in any anthology. The novel embraces the middle third of the twentieth century and sheds its peculiar but fascinating light over many of our experiences in a vision that is both tragic and comic. To underscore the diversity and universality of the remaining novels, we have intentionally alternated women and men writers, urban and rural settings, and varying themes and images of contemporary life. The concluding new selection, Flannery O'Connor's fierce and troubling religious novel *The Violent Bear It Away,* verifies the broad range of the anthology.

In our wish to provide an anthology flexible enough for use in the college classroom at any level, we have held intrusive editorial commentary to a minimum. First, we have refrained from tracing the historical development of the genre; nor do we attempt to define the short novel beyond saying simply that it is a type of fiction longer and more complex than a short story and more economical, if not necessarily less intricate, than a novel. We are willing to settle for Vladimir Nabokov's felicitous observation that this genre goes about its business "by diminishing large things and enlarging small ones." So, whether novella, nouvelle, novelette, short novel, we mean simply a novel in which intrinsic brevity and artistic rightness are harmoniously fused. Second, to accommodate the two new works, we have omitted our own critical essays on *Goodbye, Columbus* and *Noon Wine.*

By reducing overt editorial commentary, we have tried to open up the entire anthology to the widely varying responses of its readers and to encourage freer application of its uses. To these ends, the expanded critical apparatus is intended to expose the novels to a multiplicity of interpretations through classroom discussions, analysis, and written assignments. For example, the "Topics for Papers and Discussion," placed at the end of each short novel, offer suggestions for consideration of such essential components of fiction as character, plot, setting, narrative technique, theme, and style. The topics suggest the richness of each work and provide direction and guidance for close textual analysis. Some are better suited for discussion, others lend themselves more readily to written work, especially short essays, and all of them can be used profitably for individual enlightenment.

Like the topics, the "Comparative Studies" and Biographical Notes" at the end of the text have been revised and expanded. They serve, at least cursorily, to introduce the writers, to connect the anthologized novel to the body of their works, and to establish some relationships with fiction other than their own. The "Comparative Studies" are best suited to longer papers, panel discussions, and independent study projects.

We would like to emphasize that none of these aids is a substitute for the enjoyment of reading and the experience of discovery that lie in store in *Seven Contemporary Short Novels.* As works of art, these short novels can be studied and reread with increased appreciation, deepened pleasure, and enhanced understanding.

Charles Clerc and Louis Leiter

Contents

Slaughterhouse-Five

or, The Children's Crusade

A Duty-Dance with Death

KURT VONNEGUT, JR.

A fourth-generation German-American
now living in easy circumstances
on Cape Cod
(and smoking too much),
who, as an American infantry scout
hors de combat,
as a prisoner of war,
witnessed the fire-bombing
of Dresden, Germany,
"The Florence of the Elbe,"
a long time ago,
and survived to tell the tale.
This is a novel
somewhat in the telegraphic schizophrenic
manner of tales
of the planet Tralfamadore,
where the flying saucers
come from.
Peace.

For Mary O'Hare and Gerhard Müller

The cattle are lowing,
The Baby awakes.
But the little Lord Jesus
No crying He makes.

1

All this happened, more or less. The war parts, anyway, are pretty much true. One guy I knew really *was* shot in Dresden for taking a teapot that wasn't his. Another guy I knew really *did* threaten to have his personal enemies killed by hired gunmen after the war. And so on. I've changed all the names.

I really *did* go back to Dresden with Guggenheim money (God love it) in 1967. It looked a lot like Dayton, Ohio, more open spaces than Dayton has. There must be tons of human bone meal in the ground.

I went back there with an old war buddy, Bernard V. O'Hare, and we made friends with a cab driver, who took us to the slaughterhouse where we had been locked up at night as prisoners of war. His name was Gerhard Müller. He told us that he was a prisoner of the Americans for a while. We asked him how it was to live under Communism, and he said that it was terrible at first, because everybody had to work so hard, and because there wasn't much shelter or food or clothing. But things were much better now. He had a pleasant little apartment, and his daughter was getting an excellent education. His mother was incinerated in the Dresden fire-storm. So it goes.

He sent O'Hare a postcard at Christmastime, and here is what it said:

"I wish you and your family also as to your friend Merry Christmas and a happy New Year and I hope that we'll meet again in a world of peace and freedom in the taxi cab if the accident will."

I like that very much: "If the accident will."

I would hate to tell you what this lousy little book cost me in money and anxiety and time. When I got home from the Second World War twenty-three years ago, I thought it would be easy for me to write about the destruction of Dresden, since all I would have to do would be to report what I had seen. And I thought, too, that it would be a masterpiece or at least make me a lot of money, since the subject was so big.

But not many words about Dresden came from my mind then—not enough of them to make a book, anyway. And not many words come now, either, when I have become an old fart with his memories and his Pall Malls, with his sons full grown.

I think of how useless the Dresden part of my memory has been, and yet how tempting Dresden has been to write about, and I am reminded of the famous limerick:

> There was a young man from Stamboul,
> Who soliloquized thus to his tool:
> "You took all my wealth
> And you ruined my health,
> And now you won't *pee*, you old fool."

And I'm reminded, too, of the song that goes:

> My name is Yon Yonson,
> I work in Wisconsin,
> I work in a lumbermill there.
> The people I meet when I walk down the street,
> They say, "What's your name?"
> And I say,
> "My name is Yon Yonson,
> I work in Wisconsin . . ."

And so on to infinity.

Over the years, people I've met have often asked me what I'm working on, and I've usually replied that the main thing was a book about Dresden.

I said that to Harrison Starr, the movie-maker, one time, and he raised his eyebrows and inquired, "Is it an anti-war book?"

"Yes," I said. "I guess."

"You know what I say to people when I hear they're writing anti-war books?"

"No. What *do* you say, Harrison Starr?"

"I say, 'Why don't you write an anti-*glacier* book instead?'"

What he meant, of course, was that there would always be wars, that they were as easy to stop as glaciers. I believe that, too.

And, even if wars didn't keep coming like glaciers, there would still be plain old death.

When I was somewhat younger, working on my famous Dresden book, I asked an old war buddy named Bernard V. O'Hare if I could come to see him. He was a district attorney in Pennsylvania. I was a writer on Cape Cod. We had been privates in the war, infantry scouts. We had never expected to make any money after the war, but we were doing quite well.

I had the Bell Telephone Company find him for me. They are wonderful that way. I have this disease late at night sometimes, involving alcohol and the telephone. I get drunk, and I drive my wife away with a breath like mustard gas and roses. And then, speaking gravely and elegantly into the telephone, I ask the telephone operators to connect me with this friend or that one, from whom I have not heard in years.

I got O'Hare on the line in this way. He is short and I am tall. We were Mutt and Jeff in the war. We were captured together in the war. I told him who I was on the telephone. He had no trouble believing it. He was up. He was reading. Everybody else in his house was asleep.

"Listen—" I said, "I'm writing this book about Dresden. I'd like some help remembering stuff. I wonder if I could come down and see you, and we could drink and talk and remember."

He was unenthusiastic. He said he couldn't remember much. He told me, though, to come ahead.

"I think the climax of the book will be the execution of poor old Edgar Derby," I said. "The irony is *so* great. A whole city gets burned down, and thousands and thousands of people are killed. And then this one American foot soldier is arrested in the ruins for taking a teapot. And he's given a regular trial, and then he's shot by a firing squad."

"Um," said O'Hare.

"Don't you think that's really where the climax should come?"

"I don't know anything about it," he said. "That's your trade, not mine."

As a trafficker in climaxes and thrills and characterization and wonderful dialogue and suspense and confrontations, I had outlined the Dresden story many times. The best outline I ever made, or anyway the prettiest one, was on the back of a roll of wallpaper.

I used my daughter's crayons, a different color for each main character. One end of the wallpaper was the beginning of the story, and the other end was the end, and then there was all that middle part, which was the middle. And the blue line met the red line and then the yellow line, and the yellow line stopped because the character represented by the yellow line was dead. And so on. The destruction of Dresden was represented by a vertical band of orange cross-hatching, and all the lines that were still alive passed through it, came out the other side.

The end, where all the lines stopped, was a beetfield on the Elbe, outside of Halle. The rain was coming down. The war in Europe had been over for a couple of weeks. We were formed in ranks, with Russian soldiers guarding us—Englishmen, Americans, Dutchmen, Belgians, Frenchmen, Canadians, South Africans, New Zealanders, Australians, thousands of us about to stop being prisoners of war.

And on the other side of the field were thousands of Russians and Poles and Yugoslavians and so on guarded by American soldiers. An exchange was made there in the rain—one for one. O'Hare and I climbed into the back of an American truck with a lot of others. O'Hare didn't have any souvenirs. Almost everybody else did. I had a ceremonial Luftwaffe saber, still do. The rabid little American I call Paul Lazzaro in this book had about a quart of diamonds and emeralds and rubies and so on. He had taken these from dead people in the cellars of Dresden. So it goes.

An idiotic Englishman, who had lost all his teeth somewhere, had his souvenir in a canvas bag. The bag was resting on my insteps. He would peek into the bag every now and then, and he would roll his eyes and swivel his scrawny neck, trying to catch people looking coveteously at his bag. And he would bounce the bag on my insteps.

I thought this bouncing was accidental. But I was mistaken. He *had* to show somebody what was in the bag, and he had decided he could trust me. He caught my eye, winked, opened the bag. There was a plaster model of the Eiffel Tower in there. It was painted gold. It had a clock in it.

"There's a smashin' thing," he said.

And we were flown to a rest camp in France, where we were fed chocolate malted milkshakes and other rich foods until we were all covered with baby fat. Then we were sent home, and I married a pretty girl who was covered with baby fat, too.

And we had babies.

And they're all grown up now, and I'm an old fart with his memories and his Pall Malls. My name is Yon Yonson, I work in Wisconsin, I work in a lumbermill there.

Sometimes I try to call up old girl friends on the telephone late at night, after my wife has gone to bed. "Operator, I wonder if you could give me the number of a Mrs. So-and-So. I think she lives at such-and-such."

"I'm sorry, sir. There is no such listing."

"Thanks, Operator. Thanks just the same."

And I let the dog out, or I let him in, and we talk some. I let him know I like him, and he lets me know he likes me. He doesn't mind the smell of mustard gas and roses.

"You're all right, Sandy," I'll say to the dog. "You know that, Sandy? You're O.K."

Sometimes I'll turn on the radio and listen to a talk program from Boston or New York. I can't stand recorded music if I've been drinking a good deal.

Sooner or later I go to bed, and my wife asks me what time it is. She always has to know the time. Sometimes I don't know, and I say, "Search *me*."

I think about my education sometimes. I went to the University of Chicago for a while after the Second World War. I was a student in the Department of Anthropology. At that time, they were teaching that there was absolutely no difference between anybody.

They may be teaching that still.

Another thing they taught was that nobody was ridiculous or bad or disgusting. Shortly before my father died, he said to me, "You know—you never wrote a story with a villain in it."

I told him that was one of the things I learned in college after the war.

While I was studying to be an anthropologist, I was also working as a police reporter for the famous Chicago City News Bureau for twenty-eight dollars a week. One time they switched me from the night shift to the day shift, so I worked sixteen hours straight. We were supported by all the newspapers in town, and the AP and the UP and all that. And we would cover the courts and the police stations and the Fire Department and the Coast Guard out on Lake Michigan and all that. We were connected to the institutions that supported us by means of pneumatic tubes which ran under the streets of Chicago.

Reporters would telephone in stories to writers wearing headphones, and the writers would stencil the stories on mimeograph sheets. The stories were mimeographed and stuffed into the brass and velvet cartridges which the pneumatic tubes ate. The very toughest reporters and writers were women who had taken over the jobs of men who'd gone to war.

And the first story I covered I had to dictate over the telephone to one of those beastly girls. It was about a young veteran who had taken a job running an old-fashioned elevator in an office building. The elevator door on the first floor was ornamental iron lace. Iron ivy snaked in and out of the holes. There was an iron twig with two iron lovebirds perched upon it.

This veteran decided to take his car into the basement, and he closed the door and started down, but his wedding ring was caught in all the ornaments. So he was hoisted into the air and the floor of the car went down, dropped out from under him, and the top of the car squashed him. So it goes.

So I phoned this in, and the woman who was going to cut the stencil asked me, "What did his wife say?"

"She doesn't know yet," I said. "It just happened."

"Call her up and get a statement."

"What?"

"Tell her you're Captain Finn of the Police Department. Say you have some sad news. Give her the news, and see what she says."

So I did. She said about what you would expect her to say. There was a baby. And so on.

When I got back to the office, the woman writer asked me, just for her own information, what the squashed guy had looked like when he was squashed.

I told her.

"Did it bother you?" she said. She was eating a Three Musketeers Candy Bar.

"Heck no, Nancy," I said. "I've seen lots worse than that in the war."

Even then I was supposedly writing a book about Dresden. It wasn't a famous air raid back then in America. Not many Americans knew how much worse it had been than Hiroshima, for instance. I didn't know that, either. There hadn't been much publicity.

I happened to tell a University of Chicago professor at a cocktail party about the raid as I had seen it, about the book I would write. He was a member of a thing called The Committee on Social Thought. And he told me about the concentration camps, and about how the Germans had made soap and candles out of the fat of dead Jews and so on.

All I could say was, "I know, I know. I *know*."

World War Two had certainly made everybody very tough. And I became a public relations man for General Electric in Schenectady, New York, and a volunteer fireman in the village of Alplaus, where I bought my first home. My boss there was one of the toughest guys I ever hope to meet. He had been a lieutenant colonel in public relations in Baltimore. While I was in Schenectady he joined the Dutch Reformed Church, which is a very tough church, indeed.

He used to ask me sneeringly sometimes why I hadn't been an officer, as though I'd done something wrong.

My wife and I had lost our baby fat. Those were our scrawny years. We had a lot of scrawny veterans and their scrawny wives for friends. The nicest veterans in Schenectady, I thought, the kindest and funniest ones, the ones who hated war the most, were the ones who'd really fought.

I wrote the Air Force back then, asking for details about the raid on Dresden, who ordered it, how many planes did it, why they did it, what desirable results there had been and so on. I was answered by a man who, like myself, was in public relations. He said that he was sorry, but that the information was top secret still.

I read the letter out loud to my wife, and I said, "Secret? My God—from *whom?*"

We were United World Federalists back then. I don't know what we are now. Telephoners, I guess. We telephone a lot—or *I* do, anyway, late at night.

A couple of weeks after I telephoned my old war buddy, Bernard V. O'Hare, I really *did* go to see him. That must have been in 1964 or so—whatever the last year was for the New York World's Fair. *Eheu, fugaces labuntur anni.* My name is Yon Yonson. There was a young man from Stamboul.

I took two little girls with me, my daughter, Nanny, and her best friend, Allison Mitchell. They had never been off Cape Cod before. When we saw a river, we had to stop so they could stand by it and think about it for a while. They had never seen water in that long and narrow, unsalted form before. The river was the Hudson. There were carp in there and we saw them. They were as big as atomic submarines.

We saw waterfalls, too, streams jumping off cliffs into the valley of the Delaware. There were lots of things to stop and see—and then it was time to go, always time to go. The little girls were wearing white party dresses and black party shoes, so strangers would know at once how nice they were. "Time to go, girls," I'd say. And we would go.

And the sun went down, and we had supper in an Italian place, and then I knocked on the front door of the beautiful stone house of Bernard V. O'Hare. I was carrying a bottle of Irish whiskey like a dinner bell.

I met his nice wife, Mary, to whom I dedicate this book. I dedicate it to Gerhard Müller, the Dresden taxi driver, too. Mary O'Hare is a trained nurse, which is a lovely thing for a woman to be.

Mary admired the two little girls I'd brought, mixed them in with her own children, sent them all upstairs to play games and watch television. It was only after the children were gone that I sensed that Mary didn't like me or didn't like *something* about the night. She was polite but chilly.

"It's a nice cozy house you have here," I said, and it really was.

"I've fixed up a place where you can talk and not be bothered," she said.

"Good," I said, and I imagined two leather chairs near a fire in a paneled room, where two old soldiers could drink and talk. But she took us into the kitchen. She had put two straight-backed chairs at a kitchen table with a white porcelain top. That table top was screaming with reflected light from a two-hundred-watt bulb overhead. Mary had prepared an operating room. She put only one glass on it, which was for me. She explained that O'Hare couldn't drink the hard stuff since the war.

So we sat down. O'Hare was embarrassed, but he wouldn't tell me what was wrong. I couldn't imagine what it was about me that could burn up Mary so. I was a family man. I'd been married only once. I wasn't a drunk. I hadn't done her husband any dirt in the war.

She fixed herself a Coca-Cola, made a lot of noise banging the ice-cube tray in the stainless steel sink. Then she went into another part of the house. But she wouldn't sit still. She was moving all over the house, opening and shutting doors, even moving furniture around to work off anger.

I asked O'Hare what I'd said or done to make her act that way.

"It's all right," he said. "Don't worry about it. It doesn't have anything to do with you." That was kind of him. He was lying. It had everything to do with me.

So we tried to ignore Mary and remember the war. I took a couple of belts of the booze I'd brought. We would chuckle or grin sometimes, as though war stories were coming back, but neither one of us could remember anything good. O'Hare remembered one guy who got into a lot of wine in Dresden, before it was bombed, and we had to take him home in a wheelbarrow. It wasn't much to write a book about. I remembered two Russian soldiers who had looted a clock factory. They had a horse-drawn wagon full of clocks. They were happy and drunk. They were smoking huge cigarettes they had rolled in newspaper.

That was about *it* for memories, and Mary was still making noise. She finally came out in the kitchen again for another Coke. She took another tray of ice cubes from the refrigerator, banged it in the sink, even though there was already plenty of ice out.

Then she turned to me, let me see how angry she was, and that the anger was for me. She had been talking to herself, so what she said was a fragment of a much larger conversation. "You were just *babies* then!" she said.

"What?" I said.

"You were just babies in the war—like the ones upstairs!"

I nodded that this was true. We *had* been foolish virgins in the war, right at the end of childhood.

"But you're not going to write it that way, are you." This wasn't a question. It was an accusation.

"I—I don't know," I said.

"Well, *I* know," she said. "You'll pretend you were men instead of babies, and you'll be played in the movies by Frank Sinatra and John Wayne or some of those other glamorous, war-loving, dirty old men. And war will look just wonderful, so we'll have a lot more of them. And they'll be fought by babies like the babies upstairs."

So then I understood. It was war that made her so angry. She didn't want her babies or anybody else's babies killed in wars. And she thought wars were partly encouraged by books and movies.

So I held up my right hand and I made her a promise: "Mary," I said, "I don't think this book of mine is ever going to be finished. I must have written five thousand pages by now, and thrown them all away. If I ever do finish it, though, I give you my word of honor: there won't be a part for Frank Sinatra or John Wayne.

"I tell you what," I said, "I'll call it 'The Children's Crusade.'"

She was my friend after that.

O'Hare and I gave up on remembering, went into the living room, talked about other things. We became curious about the real Children's Crusade, so O'Hare looked it up in a book he had, *Extraordinary Popular Delusions and the Madness of Crowds*, by Charles Mackay, LL. D. It was first published in London in 1841.

Mackay had a low opinion of *all* Crusades. The Children's Crusade struck him as only slightly more sordid than the ten Crusades for grown-ups. O'Hare read this handsome passage out loud:

History in her solemn page informs us that the crusaders were but ignorant and savage men, that their motives were those of bigotry unmitigated, and that their pathway was one of blood and tears. Romance, on the other hand, dilates upon their piety and heroism, and portrays, in her most glowing and impassioned hues, their virtue and magnanimity, the imperishable honor they acquired for themselves, and the great services they rendered to Christianity.

And then O'Hare read this: *Now what was the grand result of all these struggles? Europe expended millions of her treasures, and the blood of two million of her people; and a handful of quarrelsome knights retained possession of Palestine for about one hundred years!*

Mackay told us that the Children's Crusade started in 1213, when two monks got the idea of raising armies of children in Germany and France, and selling them in North Africa as slaves. Thirty thousand children volunteered, thinking they were going to Palestine. *They were no doubt idle and deserted children who generally swarm in great cities, nurtured on vice and daring,* said Mackay, *and ready for anything.*

Pope Innocent the Third thought they were going to Palestine, too, and he was thrilled. "These children are awake while we are asleep!" he said.

Most of the children were shipped out of Marseilles, and about half of them drowned in shipwrecks. The other half got to North Africa where they were sold.

Through a misunderstanding, some children reported for duty at Genoa, where no slave ships were waiting. They were fed and sheltered and questioned kindly by good people there—then given a little money and a lot of advice and sent back home.

"Hooray for the good people of Genoa," said Mary O'Hare.

I slept that night in one of the children's bedrooms. O'Hare had put a book for me on the bedside table. It was *Dresden, History, Stage and Gallery*, by Mary Endell. It was published in 1908, and its introduction began:

It is hoped that this little book will make itself useful. It attempts to give to an English-reading public a bird's-eye view of how Dresden came to look as it does, architecturally; of how it expanded musically, through the genius of a few men, to its present bloom; and it calls attention to certain permanent landmarks in art that make its Gallery the resort of those seeking lasting impressions.

I read some history further on:

Now, in 1760, Dresden underwent siege by the Prussians. On the fifteenth of July began the cannonade. The Picture-Gallery took fire. Many of the paintings had been transported to the Königstein, but some were seriously injured by splinters of bombshells,—notably Francia's "Baptism of Christ." Furthermore, the stately Kreuzkirche tower, from which the enemy's movements had been watched day and night, stood in flames. It later succumbed. In sturdy contrast with the pitiful fate of the Kreuzkirche, stood the Frauenkirche, from the curves of whose stone dome the Prussian bombs rebounded like rain. Friederich was obliged finally to give up the siege, because he learned of the fall of Glatz, the critical point of his new conquests. "We must be off to Silesia, so that we do not lose everything."

The devastation of Dresden was boundless. When Goethe as a young student visited the city, he still found sad ruins: "Von der Kuppel der Frauenkirche sah ich diese leidigen Trümmer zwischen die schöne städtische Ordnung hineingesät; da rühmte mir der Küster die Kunst des Baumeisters, welcher Kirche und Kuppel auf einen so unerwünschten Fall schon eingerichtet und bombenfest erbaut hatte. Der gute Sakristan deutete mir alsdann auf Ruinene nach allen Seiten und sagte bedenklich lakonisch: Das hat der Feind gethan!"

The two little girls and I crossed the Delaware River where George Washington had crossed it, the next morning. We went to the New York World's Fair, saw what the past had been like, according to the Ford Motor Car Company and Walt Disney, saw what the future would be like, according to General Motors.

And I asked myself about the present: how wide it was, how deep it was, how much was mine to keep.

I taught creative writing in the famous Writers Workshop at the University of Iowa for a couple of years after that. I got into some perfectly beautiful trouble, got out of it again. I taught in the afternoons. In the mornings I wrote. I was not to be disturbed. I was working on my famous book about Dresden.

And somewhere in there a nice man named Seymour Lawrence gave me a three-book contract, and I said, "O.K., the first of the three will be my famous book about Dresden."

The friends of Seymour Lawrence call him "Sam." And I say to Sam now: "Sam—here's the book."

It is so short and jumbled and jangled, Sam, because there is nothing intelligent to say about a massacre. Everybody is supposed to be dead, to never say anything or want anything ever again. Everything is supposed to be very quiet after a massacre, and it always is, except for the birds.

And what do the birds say? All there is to say about a massacre, things like "*Poo-tee-weet?*"

I have told my sons that they are not under any circumstances to take part in massacres, and that the news of massacres of enemies is not to fill them with satisfaction or glee.

I have also told them not to work for companies which make massacre machinery, and to express contempt for people who think we need machinery like that.

As I've said: I recently went back to Dresden with my friend O'Hare. We had a million laughs in Hamburg and West Berlin and East Berlin and Vienna and Salzburg and Helsinki, and in Leningrad, too. It was very good for me, because I saw a lot of authentic backgrounds for made-up stories which I will write later on. One of them will be "Russian Baroque" and another will be "No Kissing" and another will be "Dollar Bar" and another will be "If the Accident Will," and so on.

And so on.

There was a Lufthansa plane that was supposed to fly from Philadelphia to Boston to Frankfurt. O'Hare was supposed to get on in Philadelphia and I was supposed to get on in Boston, and off we'd go. But Boston was socked in, so the plane flew straight to Frankfurt from Philadelphia. And I became a non-person in the Boston fog, and Lufthansa put me in a limousine with some other non-persons and sent us to a motel for a non-night.

The time would not pass. Somebody was playing with the clocks, and not only with the electric clocks, but the wind-up kind, too. The second hand on my watch would twitch once, and a year would pass, and then it would twitch again.

There was nothing I could do about it. As an Earthling, I had to believe whatever clocks said—and calendars.

I had two books with me, which I'd meant to read on the plane. One was *Words for the Wind*, by Theodore Roethke, and this is what I found in there:

I wake to sleep, and take my waking slow.
I feel my fate in what I cannot fear.
I learn by going where I have to go.

My other book was Erika Ostrovsky's *Céline and His Vision*. Céline was a brave French soldier in the First World War—until his skull was cracked. After that he couldn't sleep, and there were noises in his head. He became a doctor, and he treated poor people in the daytime, and he wrote grotesque novels all night. No art is possible without a dance with death, he wrote.

The truth is death, he wrote. *I've fought nicely against it as long as I could . . . danced with it, festooned it, waltzed it around . . . decorated it with streamers, titillated it . . .*

Time obsessed him. Miss Ostrovsky reminded me of the amazing scene in *Death on the Installment Plan* where Céline wants to stop the bustling of a street crowd. He screams on paper, *Make them stop . . . don't let them move anymore at all . . . There, make them freeze . . . once and for all! . . . So that they won't disappear anymore!*

I looked through the Gideon Bible in my motel room for tales of great destruction. *The sun was risen upon the Earth when Lot entered into Zo-ar,* I read. *Then the Lord rained upon Sodom and upon Gomorrah brimstone and fire from the Lord out of Heaven; and He overthrew those cities, and all the plain, and all the inhabitants of the cities, and that which grew upon the ground.*

So it goes.

Those were vile people in both those cities, as is well known. The world was better off without them.

And Lot's wife, of course, was told not to look back where all those people and their homes had been. But she *did* look back, and I love her for that, because it was so human.

So she was turned to a pillar of salt. So it goes.

People aren't supposed to look back. I'm certainly not going to do it anymore.

I've finished my war book now. The next one I write is going to be fun.

This one is a failure, and had to be, since it was written by a pillar of salt. It begins like this:

Listen:

Billy Pilgrim has come unstuck in time.

It ends like this:

Poo-tee-weet?

2

Listen:

Billy Pilgrim has come unstuck in time.

Billy has gone to sleep a senile widower and awakened on his wedding day. He has walked through a door in 1955 and come out another one in 1941. He has gone back through that door to find himself in 1963. He has seen his birth and death many times, he says, and pays random visits to all the events in between.

He says.

Billy is spastic in time, has no control over where he is going next, and the trips aren't necessarily fun. He is in a constant state of stage fright, he says, because he never knows what part of his life he is going to have to act in next.

Billy was born in 1922 in Ilium, New York, the only child of a barber there. He was a funny-looking child who became a funny-looking youth—tall and weak, and shaped like a bottle of Coca-Cola. He graduated from Ilium High School in the upper third of his class, and attended night sessions at the Ilium School of Optometry for one semester before being drafted for military service in the Second World War. His father died in a hunting accident during the war. So it goes.

Billy saw service with the infantry in Europe, and was taken prisoner by the Germans. After his honorable discharge from the Army in 1945, Billy again enrolled in the Ilium School of Optometry. During his senior year there, he became engaged to the daughter of the founder and owner of the school, and then suffered a mild nervous collapse.

He was treated in a veteran's hospital near Lake Placid, and was given shock treatments and released. He married his fiancée, finished his education, and was set up in business in Ilium by his father-in-law. Ilium is a particularly good city for optometrists because the General Forge and Foundry Company is there. Every employee is required to own a pair of safety glasses, and to wear them in areas where manufacturing is going on. GF&F has sixty-eight thousand employees in Ilium. That calls for a lot of lenses and a lot of frames.

Frames are where the money is.

Billy became rich. He had two children, Barbara and Robert. In time, his daughter Barbara married another optometrist, and Billy set him up in business. Billy's son Robert had a lot of trouble in high school, but then he joined the famous Green

Berets. He straightened out, became a fine young man, and he fought in Vietnam.

Early in 1968, a group of optometrists, with Billy among them, chartered an airplane to fly them from Ilium to an international convention of optometrists in Montreal. The plane crashed on top of Sugarbush Mountain, in Vermont. Everybody was killed but Billy. So it goes.

While Billy was recuperating in a hospital in Vermont, his wife died accidentally of carbon-monoxide poisoning. So it goes.

When Billy finally got home to Ilium after the airplane crash, he was quiet for a while. He had a terrible scar across the top of his skull. He didn't resume practice. He had a housekeeper. His daughter came over almost every day.

And then, without any warning, Billy went to New York City, and got on an all-night radio program devoted to talk. He told about having come unstuck in time. He said, too, that he had been kidnapped by a flying saucer in 1967. The saucer was from the planet Tralfamadore, he said. He was taken to Tralfamadore, where he was displayed naked in a zoo, he said. He was mated there with a former Earthling movie star named Montana Wildhack.

Some night owls in Ilium heard Billy on the radio, and one of them called Billy's daughter Barbara. Barbara was upset. She and her husband went down to New York and brought Billy home. Billy insisted mildly that everything he had said on the radio was true. He said he had been kidnapped by the Tralfamadorians on the night of his daughter's wedding. He hadn't been missed, he said, because the Tralfamadorians had taken him through a time warp, so that he could be on Tralfamadore for years, and still be away from Earth for only a microsecond.

Another month went by without incident, and then Billy wrote a letter to the Ilium *News Leader,* which the paper published. It described the creatures from Tralfamadore.

The letter said that they were two feet high, and green, and shaped like plumber's friends. Their suction cups were on the ground, and their shafts, which were extremely flexible, usually pointed to the sky. At the top of each shaft was a little hand with a green eye in its palm. The creatures were friendly, and they could see in four dimensions. They pitied Earthlings for being able to see only three. They had many wonderful things to teach Earthlings, especially about time. Billy promised to tell what some of those wonderful things were in his next letter.

Billy was working on his second letter when the first letter was published. The second letter started out like this:

"The most important thing I learned on Tralfamadore was that when a person dies he only *appears* to die. He is still very much alive in the past, so it is very silly for people to cry at his funeral. All moments, past, present, and future, always have existed, always will exist. The Tralfamadorians can look at all the different moments just the way we can look at a stretch of the Rocky Mountains, for instance. They can see how permanent all the moments are, and they can look at any moment that interests them. It is just an illusion we have here on Earth that one moment follows another one, like beads on a string, and that once a moment is gone it is gone forever.

"When a Tralfamadorian sees a corpse, all he thinks is that the dead person is in bad condition in that particular moment, but that the same person is just fine in plenty of other moments. Now, when I myself hear that somebody is dead, I simply shrug and say what the Tralfamadorians say about dead people, which is 'So it goes.' "

And so on.

Billy was working on this letter in the basement rumpus room of his empty house. It was his housekeeper's day off. There was an old typewriter in the rumpus room. It was a beast. It weighed as much as a storage battery. Billy couldn't carry it very far very easily, which was why he was writing in the rumpus room instead of somewhere else.

The oil burner had quit. A mouse had eaten through the insulation of a wire leading to the thermostat. The temperature in the house was down to fifty degrees, but Billy hadn't noticed. He wasn't warmly dressed, either. He was barefoot, and still in his pajamas and a bathrobe, though it was late afternoon. His bare feet were blue and ivory.

The cockles of Billy's heart, at any rate, were glowing coals. What made them so hot was Billy's belief that he was going to comfort so many people with the truth about time. His door chimes upstairs had been ringing and ringing. It was his daughter Barbara up there, wanting in. Now she let herself in with a key, crossed the floor over his head, calling, "Father? Daddy, where are you?" And so on.

Billy didn't answer her, so she was nearly hysterical, expecting to find his corpse. And then she looked into the very last place there *was* to look—which was the rumpus room.

"Why didn't you answer me when I called?" Barbara wanted to know, standing there in the door of the rumpus room. She had the afternoon paper with her, the one in which Billy described his friends from Tralfamadore.

"I didn't *hear* you," said Billy.

The orchestration of the moment was this: Barbara was only twenty-one years old, but she thought her father was senile, even though he was only forty-six—senile because of damage to his brain in the airplane crash. She also thought that she was head of the family, since she had had to manage her mother's funeral, since she had to get a housekeeper for Billy, and all that. Also, Barbara and her husband were having to look after Billy's business interests, which were considerable, since Billy didn't seem to give a damn for business any more. All this responsibility at such an early age made her a bitchy flibbertigibbet. And Billy, meanwhile, was trying to hang onto his dignity, to persuade Barbara and everybody else that he was far from senile, that, on the contrary, he was devoting himself to a calling much higher than mere business.

He was doing nothing less now, he thought, than prescribing corrective lenses for Earthling souls. So many of those souls were lost and wretched, Billy believed, because they could not see as well as his little green friends on Tralfamadore.

"Don't lie to me, Father," said Barbara. "I know perfectly well you heard me when I called." This was a fairly pretty girl, except that she had legs like an Edwardian grand piano. Now she raised hell with him about the letter in the paper. She said he was making a laughing stock of himself and everybody associated with him.

"Father, Father, Father—" said Barbara, "what are we going to *do* with you? Are you going to force us to put you where your mother is?" Billy's mother was still alive. She was in bed in an old people's home called Pine Knoll on the edge of Ilium.

"What is it about my letter that makes you so mad?" Billy wanted to know.

"It's all just crazy. None of it's true!"

"It's all true." Billy's anger was not going to rise with hers. He never got mad at anything. He was wonderful that way.

"There is no such planet as Tralfamadore."

"It can't be detected from Earth, if that's what you mean," said Billy. "Earth can't be detected from Tralfamadore, as far as that goes. They're both very small. They're very far apart."

"Where did you get a crazy name like 'Tralfamadore?'"

"That's what the creatures who live there *call* it."

"Oh God," said Barbara, and she turned her back on him. She celebrated frustration by clapping her hands. "May I ask you a simple question?"

"Of course."

"Why is it you never mentioned any of this before the airplane crash?"

"I didn't think the time was *ripe*."

And so on. Billy says that he first came unstuck in time in 1944, long before his trip to Tralfamadore. The Tralfamadorians didn't have anything to do with his coming unstuck. They were simply able to give him insights into what was really going on.

Billy first came unstuck while World War Two was in progress. Billy was a chaplain's assistant in the war. A chaplain's assistant is customarily a figure of fun in the American Army. Billy was no exception. He was powerless to harm the enemy or to help his friends. In fact, he had no friends. He was a valet to a preacher, expected no promotions or medals, bore no arms, and had a meek faith in a loving Jesus which most soldiers found putrid.

While on maneuvers in South Carolina, Billy played hymns he knew from childhood, played them on a little black organ which was waterproof. It had thirty-nine keys and two stops—*vox humana* and *vox celeste*. Billy also had charge of a portable altar, an olive-drab attaché case with telescoping legs. It was lined with crimson plush, and nestled in that passionate plush were an anodized aluminum cross and a Bible.

The altar and the organ were made by a vacuum-cleaner company in Camden, New Jersey—and said so.

One time on maneuvers Billy was playing "A Mighty Fortress Is Our God," with music by Johann Sebastian Bach and words by Martin Luther. It was Sunday morning. Billy and his chaplain had gathered a congregation of about fifty soldiers on a Carolina hillside. An umpire appeared. There were umpires everywhere, men who said who was winning or losing the theoretical battle, who was alive and who was dead.

The umpire had comical news. The congregation had been theoretically spotted from the air by a theoretical enemy. They were all theoretically dead now. The theoretical corpses laughed and ate a hearty noontime meal.

Remembering this incident years later, Billy was struck by what a Tralfamadorian adventure with death that had been, to be dead and to eat at the same time.

Toward the end of maneuvers, Billy was given an emergency furlough home because his father, a barber in Ilium, New York, was shot dead by a friend while they were out hunting deer. So it goes.

When Billy got back from his furlough, there were orders for him to go overseas. He was needed in the headquarters company of an infantry regiment fighting in Luxembourg. The regimental chaplain's assistant had been killed in action. So it goes.

When Billy joined the regiment, it was in the process of being destroyed by the Germans in the famous Battle of the Bulge. Billy never even got to meet the chaplain he was supposed to assist, was never even issued a steel helmet and combat boots. This was in December of 1944, during the last mighty German attack of the war.

Billy survived, but he was a dazed wanderer far behind the new German lines. Three other wanderers, not quite so dazed, allowed Billy to tag along. Two of them were scouts, and one was an antitank gunner. They were without food or maps. Avoiding Germans, they were delivering themselves into rural silences ever more profound. They ate snow.

They went Indian file. First came the scouts, clever, graceful, quiet. They had rifles. Next came the antitank gunner, clumsy and dense, warning Germans away with a Colt .45 automatic in one hand and a trench knife in the other.

Last came Billy Pilgrim, empty-handed, bleakly ready for death. Billy was preposterous—six feet and three inches tall, with a chest and shoulders like a box of kitchen matches. He had no helmet, no overcoat, no weapon, and no boots. On his feet were cheap, low-cut civilian shoes which he had bought for his father's funeral. Billy had lost a heel, which made him bob up-and-down, up-and-down. The involuntary dancing, up and down, up and down, made his hip joints sore.

Billy was wearing a thin field jacket, a shirt and trousers of scratchy wool, and long underwear that was soaked with sweat. He was the only one of the four who had a beard. It was a random, bristly beard, and some of the bristles were white, even though Billy was only twenty-one years old. He was also going bald. Wind and cold and violent exercise had turned his face crimson.

He didn't look like a soldier at all. He looked like a filthy flamingo.

And on the third day of wandering, somebody shot at the four from far away—shot four times as they crossed a narrow brick road. One shot was for the scouts. The next one was for the antitank gunner, whose name was Roland Weary.

The third bullet was for the filthy flamingo, who stopped dead center in the road when the lethal bee buzzed past his ear. Billy stood there politely, giving the marksman another chance. It was his addled understanding of the rules of warfare that the marksman *should* be given a second chance. The next shot missed Billy's kneecaps by inches, going end-on-end, from the sound of it.

Roland Weary and the scouts were safe in a ditch, and Weary growled at Billy, "Get out of the road, you dumb motherfucker." The last word was still a novelty in the speech of white people in 1944. It was fresh and astonishing to Billy, who had never fucked anybody—and it did its job. It woke him up and got him off the road.

"Saved your life again, you dumb bastard," Weary said to Billy in the ditch. He had been saving Billy's life for days, cursing him, kicking him, slapping him, making him move. It was absolutely necessary that cruelty be used, because Billy wouldn't do anything to save himself. Billy wanted to quit. He was cold, hungry, embarrassed, incompetent. He could scarcely distinguish between sleep and wakefulness now, on the third day, found no important differences, either, between walking and standing still.

He wished everybody would leave him alone. "You guys go on without me," he said again and again.

Weary was as new to war as Billy. He was a replacement, too. As a part of a gun crew, he had helped to fire one shot in anger—from a 57-millimeter antitank gun. The gun made a ripping sound like the opening of the zipper on the fly of God Almighty. The gun lapped up snow and vegetation with a blowtorch thirty feet long. The flame left a black arrow on the ground, showing the Germans exactly where the gun was hidden. The shot was a miss.

What had been missed was a Tiger tank. It swiveled its 88-millimeter snout around sniffingly, saw the arrow on the ground. It fired. It killed everybody on the gun crew but Weary. So it goes.

Roland Weary was only eighteen, was at the end of an unhappy childhood spent mostly in Pittsburgh, Pennsylvania. He had been unpopular in Pittsburgh. He had been unpopular because he was stupid and fat and mean, and smelled like bacon no matter how much he washed. He was always being ditched in Pittsburgh by people who did not want him with them.

It made Weary sick to be ditched. When Weary was ditched, he would find somebody who was even more unpopular than himself, and he would horse around with that person for a while, pretending to be friendly. And then he would find some pretext for beating the shit out of him.

It was a pattern. It was a crazy, sexy, murderous relationship

Weary entered into with people he eventually beat up. He told them about his father's collection of guns and swords and torture instruments and leg irons and so on. Weary's father, who was a plumber, actually did collect such things, and his collection was insured for four thousand dollars. He wasn't alone. He belonged to a big club composed of people who collected things like that.

Weary's father once gave Weary's mother a Spanish thumbscrew in working condition—for a kitchen paperweight. Another time he gave her a table lamp whose base was a model one foot high of the famous "Iron Maiden of Nuremburg." The real Iron Maiden was a medieval torture instrument, a sort of boiler which was shaped like a woman on the outside—and lined with spikes. The front of the woman was composed of two hinged doors. The idea was to put a criminal inside and then close the doors slowly. There were two special spikes where his eyes would be. There was a drain in the bottom to let out all the blood.

So it goes.

Weary had told Billy Pilgrim about the Iron Maiden, about the drain in her bottom—and what that was for. He had talked to Billy about dum-dums. He told him about his father's Derringer pistol, which could be carried in a vest pocket, which was yet capable of making a hole in a man "which a bull bat could fly through without touching either wing."

Weary scornfully bet Billy one time that he didn't even know what a blood gutter was. Billy guessed that it was the drain in the bottom of the Iron Maiden, but that was wrong. A blood gutter, Billy learned, was the shallow groove in the side of the blade of a sword or bayonet.

Weary told Billy about neat tortures he'd read about or seen in the movies or heard on the radio—about other neat tortures he himself had invented. One of the inventions was sticking a dentist's drill into a guy's ear. He asked Billy what he thought the worst form of execution was. Billy had no opinion. The correct answer turned out to be this: "You stake a guy out on an anthill in the desert—see? He's facing upward, and you put honey all over his balls and pecker, and you cut off his eyelids so he has to stare at the sun till he dies." So it goes.

Now, lying in the ditch with Billy and the scouts after having been shot at, Weary made Billy take a very close look at his trench knife. It wasn't government issue. It was a present from his father. It had a ten-inch blade that was triangular in cross section. Its grip consisted of brass knuckles, was a chain of rings through which Weary slipped his stubby fingers. The rings weren't simple. They bristled with spikes.

Weary laid the spikes along Billy's cheek, roweled the cheek with savagely affectionate restraint. "How'd you like to be hit with this—hm? Hmmmmmmmmm?" he wanted to know.

"I wouldn't," said Billy.

"Know why the blade's triangular?"

"No."

"Makes a wound that won't close up."

"Oh."

"Makes a three-sided hole in a guy. You stick an ordinary knife in a guy—makes a slit. Right? A slit closes right up. Right?"

"Right."

"Shit. What do you know? What the hell they teach in college?"

"I wasn't there very long," said Billy, which was true. He had had only six months of college, and the college hadn't been a regular college, either. It had been the night school of the Ilium School of Optometry.

"Joe College," said Weary scathingly.

Billy shrugged.

"There's more to life than what you read in books," said Weary. "You'll find that out."

Billy made no reply to this, either, there in the ditch, since he didn't want the conversation to go on any longer than necessary. He was dimly tempted to say, though, that he knew a thing or two about gore. Billy, after all, had contemplated torture and hideous wounds at the beginning and the end of nearly every day of his childhood. Billy had an extremely gruesome crucifix hanging on the wall of his little bedroom in Ilium. A military surgeon would have admired the clinical fidelity of the artist's rendition of all Christ's wounds—the spear wound, the thorn wounds, the holes that were made by the iron spikes. Billy's Christ died horribly. He was pitiful.

So it goes.

Billy wasn't a Catholic, even though he grew up with a ghastly crucifix on the wall. His father had no religion. His mother was a substitute organist for several churches around town. She took Billy with her whenever she played, taught him to play a little, too. She said she was going to join a church as soon as she decided which one was right.

She never *did* decide. She did develop a terrific hankering for a crucifix, though. And she bought one from a Santa Fe gift shop during a trip the little family made out West during the Great Depression. Like so many Americans, she was trying to construct a life that made sense from things she found in gift shops.

And the crucifix went up on the wall of Billy Pilgrim.

The two scouts, loving the walnut stocks of their rifles in the ditch, whispered that it was time to move out again. Ten minutes had gone by without anybody's coming to see if they were hit or not, to finish them off. Whoever had shot was evidently far away and all alone.

And the four crawled out of the ditch without drawing any more fire. They crawled into a forest like the big, unlucky mammals they were. Then they stood up and began to walk quickly. The forest was dark and old. The pines were planted in ranks and files. There was no undergrowth. Four inches of unmarked snow blanketed the ground. The Americans had no choice but to leave trails in the snow as unambiguous as diagrams in a book on ballroom dancing—*step, slide, rest—step, slide, rest.*

"Close it up and keep it closed!" Roland Weary warned Billy Pilgrim as they moved out. Weary looked like Tweedledum or Tweedledee, all bundled up for battle. He was short and thick.

He had every piece of equipment he had ever been issued, every present he'd received from home: helmet, helmet liner, wool cap, scarf, gloves, cotton undershirt, woolen undershirt, wool shirt, sweater, blouse, jacket, overcoat, cotton underpants, woolen underpants, woolen trousers, cotton socks, woolen socks, combat boots, gas mask, canteen, mess kit, first-aid kit, trench knife, blanket, shelter-half, raincoat, bullet-proof Bible, a pamphlet entitled "Know Your Enemy," another pamphlet entitled "Why We Fight," and another pamphlet of German phrases rendered in English phonetics, which would enable Weary to ask Germans questions such as "Where is your headquarters?" and "How many howitzers have you?" or to tell them, "Surrender. Your situation is hopeless," and so on.

Weary had a block of balsa wood which was supposed to be a foxhole pillow. He had a prophylactic kit containing two tough condoms "For the Prevention of Disease Only!" He had a whistle he wasn't going to show anybody until he got promoted to corporal. He had a dirty picture of a woman attempting sexual intercourse with a Shetland pony. He had made Billy Pilgrim admire that picture several times.

The woman and the pony were posed before velvet draperies which were fringed with deedlee-balls. They were flanked by Doric columns. In front of one column was a potted palm. The picture that Weary had was a print of the first dirty photograph in history. The word *photography* was first used in 1839, and it was in that year, too, that Louis J. M. Daguerre revealed to the French Academy that an image formed on a silvered metal plate covered with a thin film of silver iodide could be developed in the presence of mercury vapor.

In 1841, only two years later, an assistant to Daguerre, André Le Fèvre, was arrested in the Tuileries Gardens for attempting to sell a gentleman a picture of the woman and the pony. That was where Weary bought his picture, too—in the Tuileries. Le Fèvre argued that the picture was fine art, and that his intention was to make Greek mythology come alive. He said the columns and the potted palm proved that.

When asked which myth he meant to represent, Le Fèvre replied that there were thousands of myths like that, with the woman a mortal and the pony a god.

He was sentenced to six months in prison. He died there of pneumonia. So it goes.

Billy and the scouts were skinny people. Roland Weary had fat to burn. He was a roaring furnace under all his layers of wool and straps and canvas. He had so much energy that he bustled back and forth between Billy and the scouts, delivering dumb messages which nobody had sent and which nobody was pleased to receive. He also began to suspect, since he was so much busier than anybody else, that he was the leader.

He was so hot and bundled up, in fact, that he had no sense of danger. His vision of the outside world was limited to what he could see through a narrow slit between the rim of his helmet and his scarf from home, which concealed his baby face from the bridge of his nose on down. He was so snug in there that he was able to pretend that he was safe at home, having survived the war, and that he was telling his parents and his sister a true war story —whereas the true war story was still going on.

Weary's version of the true war story went like this: There was a big German attack, and Weary and his antitank buddies fought like hell until everybody was killed but Weary. So it goes. And then Weary tied in with two scouts, and they became close friends immediately, and they decided to fight their way back to their own lines. They were going to travel fast. They were damned if they'd surrender. They shook hands all around. They called themselves "The Three Musketeers."

But then this damn college kid, who was so weak he shouldn't even have been in the army, asked if he could come along. He didn't even have a gun or a knife. He didn't even have a helmet or a cap. He couldn't even walk right—kept bobbing up-and-down, up-and-down, driving everybody crazy, giving their position away. He was pitiful. The Three Musketeers pushed and carried and dragged the college kid all the way back to their own lines, Weary's story went. They saved his God-damned hide for him.

In real life, Weary was retracing his steps, trying to find out what had happened to Billy. He had told the scouts to wait while he went back for the college bastard. He passed under a low branch now. It hit the top of his helmet with a *clonk*. Weary didn't hear it. Somewhere a big dog was barking. Weary didn't hear that, either. His war story was at a very exciting point. An officer was congratulating the Three Musketeers, telling them that he was going to put them in for Bronze Stars.

"Anything else I can do for you boys?" said the officer.

"Yes, sir," said one of the scouts. "We'd like to stick together for the rest of the war, sir. Is there some way you can fix it so nobody will ever break up the Three Musketeers?"

Billy Pilgrim had stopped in the forest. He was leaning against a tree with his eyes closed. His head was tilted back and his nostrils were flaring. He was like a poet in the Parthenon.

This was when Billy first came unstuck in time. His attention began to swing grandly through the full arc of his life, passing into death, which was violet light. There wasn't anybody else there, or any thing. There was just violet light—and a hum.

And then Billy swung into life again, going backwards until he was in pre-birth, which was red light and bubbling sounds. And then he swung into life again and stopped. He was a little boy taking a shower with his hairy father at the Ilium Y.M.C.A. He smelled chlorine from the swimming pool next door, heard the springboard boom.

Little Billy was terrified, because his father had said Billy was going to learn to swim by the method of sink-or-swim. His father was going to throw Billy into the deep end, and Billy was going to damn well swim.

It was like an execution. Billy was numb as his father carried him from the shower room to the pool. His eyes were closed. When he opened his eyes, he was on the bottom of the pool, and there was beautiful music everywhere. He lost consciousness, but the music went on. He dimly sensed that somebody was rescuing him. Billy resented that.

From there he traveled in time to 1965. He was forty-one years old, and he was visiting his decrepit mother at Pine Knoll, an old people's home he had put her in only a month before. She had caught pneumonia, and wasn't expected to live. She did live, though, for years after that.

Her voice was nearly gone, so, in order to hear her, Billy had to put his ear right next to her papery lips. She evidently had something very important to say.

"How . . . ?" she began, and she stopped. She was too tired. She hoped that she wouldn't have to say the rest of the sentence, that Billy would finish it for her.

But Billy had no idea what was on her mind. "How *what*, Mother?" he prompted.

She swallowed hard, shed some tears. Then she gathered energy from all over her ruined body, even from her toes and fingertips. At last she had accumulated enough to whisper this complete sentence:

"How did I get so *old?*"

Billy's antique mother passed out, and Billy was led from the room by a pretty nurse. The body of an old man covered by a sheet was wheeled by just as Billy entered the corridor. The man had been a famous marathon runner in his day. So it goes. This was before Billy had his head broken in an airplane crash, by the way—before he became so vocal about flying saucers and traveling in time.

Billy sat down in a waiting room. He wasn't a widower yet. He sensed something hard under the cushion of his overstuffed chair. He dug it out, discovered that it was a book, *The Execution of Private Slovik,* by William Bradford Huie. It was a true account of the death before an American firing squad of Private Eddie D. Slovik, 36896415, the only American soldier to be shot for cowardice since the Civil War. So it goes.

Billy read the opinion of a staff judge advocate who reviewed Slovik's case, which ended like this: *He has directly challenged the authority of the government, and future discipline depends upon a resolute reply to this challenge. If the death penalty is ever to be imposed for desertion, it should be imposed in this case, not as a punitive measure nor as retribution, but to maintain that discipline upon which alone an army can succeed against the enemy. There was no recommendation for clemency in the case and none is here recommended.* So it goes.

Billy blinked in 1965, traveled in time to 1958. He was at a banquet in honor of a Little League team of which his son Robert was a member. The coach, who had never been married, was speaking. He was all choked up. "Honest to God," he was saying, "I'd consider it an honor just to be *water* boy for these kids."

Billy blinked in 1958, traveled in time to 1961. It was New Year's Eve, and Billy was disgracefully drunk at a party where everybody was in optometry or married to an optometrist.

Billy usually didn't drink much, because the war had ruined his stomach, but he certainly had a snootful now, and he was being unfaithful to his wife Valencia for the first and only time. He had somehow persuaded a woman to come into the laundry room of the house, and then sit up on the gas dryer, which was running.

The woman was very drunk herself, and she helped Billy get her girdle off. "What was it you wanted to talk about?" she said.

"It's all right," said Billy. He honestly thought it was all right. He couldn't remember the name of the woman.

"How come they call you Billy instead of William?"

"Business reasons," said Billy. That was true. His father-in-law, who owned the Ilium School of Optometry, who had set Billy up in practice, was a genius in his field. He told Billy to encourage people to call him Billy—because it would stick in their memories. It would also make him seem slightly magical, since there weren't any other grown Billys around. It also compelled people to think of him as a friend right away.

Somewhere in there was an awful scene, with people expressing disgust for Billy and the woman, and Billy found himself out in his automobile, trying to find the steering wheel.

The main thing now was to find the steering wheel. At first, Billy windmilled his arms, hoping to find it by luck. When that didn't work, he became methodical, working in such a way that the wheel could not possibly escape him. He placed himself hard against the left-hand door, searched every square inch of the area before him. When he failed to find the wheel, he moved over six inches, and searched again. Amazingly, he was eventually hard against the right-hand door, without having found the wheel. He concluded that somebody had stolen it. This angered him as he passed out.

He was in the back seat of his car, which was why he couldn't find the steering wheel.

Now somebody was shaking Billy awake. Billy still felt drunk, was still angered by the stolen steering wheel. He was back in World War Two again, behind the German lines. The person who was shaking him was Roland Weary. Weary had gathered the front of Billy's field jacket into his hands. He banged Billy against a tree, then pulled him away from it, flung him in the direction he was suppose to take under his own power.

Billy stopped, shook his head. "You go on," he said.

"What?"

"You guys go on without me. I'm all right."

"You're what?"

"I'm O.K."

"Jesus—I'd hate to see somebody *sick*," said Weary, through five layers of humid scarf from home. Billy had never seen Weary's face. He had tried to imagine it one time, had imaged a toad in a fishbowl.

Weary kicked and shoved Billy for a quarter of a mile. The scouts were waiting between the banks of a frozen creek. They had heard the dog. They had heard men calling back and forth, too—calling like hunters who had a pretty good idea of where their quarry was.

The banks of the creek were high enough to allow the scouts to stand without being seen. Billy staggered down the bank ridiculously. After him came Weary, clanking and clinking and tinkling and hot.

"Here he is, boys," said Weary. "He don't want to live, but he's gonna live anyway. When he gets out of this, by God, he's gonna owe his life to the Three Musketeers." This was the first the scouts had heard that Weary thought of himself and them as the Three Musketeers.

Billy Pilgrim, there in the creekbed, thought he, Billy Pilgrim, was turning to steam painlessly. If everybody would leave him alone for just a little while, he thought, he wouldn't cause anybody any more trouble. He would turn to steam and float up among the treetops.

Somewhere the big dog barked again. With the help of fear and echoes and winter silences, that dog had a voice like a big bronze gong.

Roland Weary, eighteen years old, insinuated himself between the scouts, draped a heavy arm around the shoulder of each. "So what do the Three Musketeers do now?" he said.

Billy Pilgrim was having a delightful hallucination. He was wearing dry, warm, white sweatsocks, and he was skating on a ballroom floor. Thousands cheered. This wasn't time-travel. It had never happened, never would happen. It was the craziness of a dying young man with his shoes full of snow.

One scout hung his head, let spit fall from his lips. The other did the same. They studied the infinitesimal effects of spit on snow and history. They were small, graceful people. They had been behind German lines before many times—living like woods creatures, living from moment to moment in useful terror, thinking brainlessly with their spinal cords.

Now they twisted out from under Weary's loving arms. They told Weary that he and Billy had better find somebody to surrender to. The scouts weren't going to wait for them any more.

And they ditched Weary and Billy in the creekbed.

Billy Pilgrim went on skating, doing tricks in sweatsocks, tricks that most people would consider impossible—making turns, stopping on a dime and so on. The cheering went on, but its tone was altered as the hallucination gave way to time-travel.

Billy stopped skating, found himself at a lectern in a Chinese restaurant in Ilium, New York, on an early afternoon in the autumn of 1957. He was receiving a standing ovation from the Lions Club. He had just been elected President, and it was necessary that he speak. He was scared stiff, thought a ghastly mistake had been made. All those prosperous, solid men out there would discover now that they had elected a ludicrous waif. They would hear his reedy voice, the one he'd had in the war. He swallowed, knew that all he had for a voice box was a little whistle cut from a willow switch. Worse—he had nothing to say. The crowd quieted down. Everybody was pink and beaming.

Billy opened his mouth, and out came a deep, resonant tone. His voice was a gorgeous instrument. It told jokes which brought down the house. It grew serious, told jokes again, and ended on a note of humility. The explanation of the miracle was this: Billy had taken a course in public speaking.

And then he was back in the bed of the frozen creek again. Roland Weary was about to beat the living shit out of him.

Weary was filled with a tragic wrath. He had been ditched again. He stuffed his pistol into its holster. He slipped his knife into its scabbard. Its triangular blade and blood gutters on all three faces. And then he shook Billy hard, rattled his skeleton, slammed him against a bank.

Weary barked and whimpered through his layers of scarf from home. He spoke unintelligibly of the sacrifices he had made on Billy's behalf. He dilated upon the piety and heroism of "The Three Musketeers," portrayed, in the most glowing and impassioned hues, their virtue and magnanimity, the imperishable honor they acquired for themselves, and the great services they rendered to Christianity.

It was entirely Billy's fault that this fighting organization no longer existed, Weary felt, and Billy was going to pay. Weary socked Billy a good one on the side of his jaw, knocked Billy away from the bank and onto the snow-covered ice of the creek. Billy was down on all fours on the ice, and Weary kicked him in the ribs, rolled him over on his side. Billy tried to form himself into a ball.

"You shouldn't even *be* in the Army," said Weary.

Billy was involuntarily making convulsive sounds that were a lot like laughter. "You think it's funny, huh?" Weary inquired. He walked around to Billy's back. Billy's jacket and shirt and undershirt had been hauled up around his shoulders by the violence, so his back was naked. There, inches from the tips of Weary's combat boots, were the pitiful buttons of Billy's spine.

Weary drew back his right boot, aimed a kick at the spine, at the tube which had so many of Billy's important wires in it. Weary was going to break that tube.

But then Weary saw that he had an audience. Five German soldiers and a police dog on a leash were looking down into the bed of the creek. The soldiers' blue eyes were filled with a bleary civilian curiosity as to why one American would try to murder another one so far from home, and why the victim should laugh.

3

The Germans and the dog were engaged in a military operation which had an amusingly self-explanatory name, a human enterprise which is seldom described in detail, whose name alone, when reported as news or history, gives many war enthusiasts a sort of post-coital satisfaction. It is, in the imagination of combat's fans, the divinely listless loveplay that follows the orgasm of victory. It is called "mopping up."

The dog, who had sounded so ferocious in the winter distances, was a female German shepherd. She was shivering. Her tail was between her legs. She had been borrowed that morning from a farmer. She had never been to war before. She had no idea what game was being played. Her name was Princess.

Two of the Germans were boys in their early teens. Two were ramshackle old men—droolers as toothless as carp. They were irregulars, armed and clothed fragmentarily with junk taken from real soldiers who were newly dead. So it goes. They were farmers from just across the German border, not far away.

Their commander was a middle-aged corporal—red-eyed, scrawny, tough as dried beef, sick of war. He had been wounded four times—and patched up, and sent back to war. He was a very good soldier—about to quit, about to find somebody to surrender to. His bandy legs were thrust into golden cavalry boots which he had taken from a dead Hungarian colonel on the Russian front. So it goes.

Those boots were almost all he owned in this world. They were his home. An anecdote: One time a recruit was watching him bone and wax those golden boots, and he held one up to the recruit and said, "If you look in there deeply enough, you'll see Adam and Eve."

Billy Pilgrim had not heard this anecdote. But, lying on the black ice there, Billy stared into the patina of the corporal's boots, saw Adam and Eve in the golden depths. They were naked. They were so innocent, so vulnerable, so eager to behave decently. Billy Pilgrim loved them.

Next to the golden boots were a pair of feet which were swaddled in rags. They were crisscrossed by canvas straps, were shod with hinged wooden clogs. Billy looked up at the face that went with the clogs. It was the face of a blond angel, of a fifteen-year-old boy.

The boy was as beautiful as Eve.

Billy was helped to his feet by the lovely boy, by the heavenly androgyne. And the others came forward to dust the snow off Billy, and then they searched him for weapons. He didn't have any. The most dangerous thing they found on his person was a two-inch pencil stub.

Three inoffensive *bangs* came from far away. They came from German rifles. The two scouts who had ditched Billy and Weary had just been shot. They had been lying in ambush for Germans. They had been discovered and shot from behind. Now they were dying in the snow, feeling nothing, turning the snow to the color of raspberry sherbet. So it goes. So Roland Weary was the last of the Three Musketeers.

And Weary, bug-eyed with terror, was being disarmed. The corporal gave Weary's pistol to the pretty boy. He marveled at Weary's cruel trench knife, said in German that Weary would no doubt like to use the knife on him, to tear his face off with the spiked knuckles, to stick the blade into his belly or throat. He spoke no English, and Billy and Weary understood no German.

"Nice playthings you have," the corporal told Weary, and he handed the knife to an old man. "Isn't that a pretty thing? Hmmm?"

He tore open Weary's overcoat and blouse. Brass buttons flew like popcorn. The corporal reached into Weary's gaping bosom as though he meant to tear out his pounding heart, but he brought out Weary's bullet-proof Bible instead.

A bullet-proof Bible is a Bible small enough to be slipped into a soldier's breast pocket, over his heart. It is sheathed in steel.

The corporal found the dirty picture of the woman and the pony in Weary's hip pocket. "What a lucky pony, eh?" he said. "Hmmmm? Hmmmm? Don't you wish you were that pony?" He handed the picture to the other old man. "Spoils of war! It's yours, all yours, you lucky lad."

Then he made Weary sit down in the snow and take off his combat boots, which he gave to the beautiful boy. He gave Weary the boy's clogs. So Weary and Billy were both without decent military footwear now, and they had to walk for miles and miles, with Weary's clogs clacking, with Billy bobbing up-and-down, up-and-down, crashing into Weary from time to time.

"Excuse me," Billy would say, or "I beg your pardon."

They were brought at last to a stone cottage at a fork in the road. It was a collecting point for prisoners of war. Billy and Weary were taken inside, where it was warm and smoky. There was a fire sizzling and popping in the fireplace. The fuel was furniture. There were about twenty other Americans in there, sitting on the floor with their backs to the wall, staring into the flames—thinking whatever there was to think, which was zero.

Nobody talked. Nobody had any good war stories to tell.

Billy and Weary found places for themselves, and Billy went to sleep with his head on the shoulder of an unprotesting captain. The captain was a chaplain. He was a rabbi. He had been shot through the hand.

Billy traveled in time, opened his eyes, found himself staring into the glass eyes of a jade green mechanical owl. The owl was hanging upside down from a rod of stainless steel. The owl was Billy's optometer in his office in Ilium. An optometer is an instrument for measuring refractive errors in eyes—in order that corrective lenses may be prescribed.

Billy had fallen asleep while examining a female patient who was in a chair on the other side of the owl. He had fallen asleep at work before. It had been funny at first. Now Billy was starting to get worried about it, about his mind in general. He tried to remember how old he was, couldn't. He tried to remember what year it was. He couldn't remember that, either.

"Doctor—" said the patient tentatively.

"Hm?" he said.

"You're so quiet."

"Sorry."

"You were talking away there—and then you got so quiet."

"Um."

"You see something terrible?"

"Terrible?"

"Some disease in my eyes?"

"No, no," said Billy, wanting to doze again. "Your eyes are fine. You just need glasses for reading." He told her to go across the corridor—to see the wide selection of frames there.

When she was gone, Billy opened the drapes and was no wiser as to what was outside. The view was still blocked by a venetian blind, which he hoisted clatteringly. Bright sunlight came crashing in. There were thousands of parked automobiles out there, twinkling on a vast lake of blacktop. Billy's office was part of a suburban shopping center.

Right outside the window was Billy's own Cadillac El Dorado Coupe de Ville. He read the stickers on the bumper. "Visit Ausable Chasm," said one. "Support Your Police Department," said another. There was a third. "Impeach Earl Warren," it said. The stickers about the police and Earl Warren were gifts from Billy's father-in-law, a member of the John Birch Society. The date on the license plate was 1967, which would make Billy Pilgrim forty-four years old. He asked himself this: "Where have all the years gone?"

Billy turned his attention to his desk. There was an open copy of *The Review of Optometry* there. It was opened to an editorial, which Billy now read, his lips moving slightly.

What happens in 1968 will rule the fate of European optometrists for at least 50 years! Billy read. *With this warning, Jean Thiriart, Secretary of the National Union of Belgium Opticians, is pressing for formation of a "European Optometry Society." The alternatives, he says, will be the obtaining of professional status, or, by 1971, reduction to the role of spectacle-sellers.*

Billy Pilgrim tried hard to care.

A siren went off, scared the hell out of him. He was expecting World War Three at any time. The siren was simply announcing high noon. It was housed in a cupola atop a firehouse across the street from Billy's office.

Billy closed his eyes. When he opened them, he was back in World War Two again. His head was on the wounded rabbi's shoulder. A German was kicking his feet, telling him to wake up, that it was time to move on.

The Americans, with Billy among them, formed a fools' parade on the road outside.

There was a photographer present, a German war correspondent with a Leica. He took pictures of Billy's and Roland Weary's feet. The picture was widely published two days later as heartening evidence of how miserably equipped the American Army often was, despite its reputation for being rich.

The photographer wanted something more lively, though, a picture of an actual capture. So the guards staged one for him. They threw Billy into shrubbery. When Billy came out of the shrubbery, his face wreathed in goofy good will, they menaced him with their machine pistols, as though they were capturing him then.

Billy's smile as he came out of the shrubbery was at least as peculiar as Mona Lisa's, for he was simultaneously on foot in Germany in 1944 and riding his Cadillac in 1967. Germany dropped away, and 1967 became bright and clear, free of interference from any other time. Billy was on his way to a Lions Club luncheon meeting. It was a hot August, but Billy's car was air-conditioned. He was stopped by a signal in the middle of Ilium's black ghetto. The people who lived here hated it so much that they had burned down a lot of it a month before. It was all they had, and they'd wrecked it. The neighborhood reminded Billy of some of the towns he had seen in the war. The curbs and sidewalks were crushed in many places, showing where the National Guard tanks and half-tracks had been.

"Blood brother," said a message written in pink paint on the side of a shattered grocery store.

There was a tap on Billy's car window. A black man was out there. He wanted to talk about something. The light had changed. Billy did the simplest thing. He drove on.

Billy drove through a scene of even greater desolation. It looked like Dresden after it was fire-bombed—like the surface of the moon. The house where Billy had grown up used to be somewhere in what was so empty now. This was urban renewal. A new Ilium Government Center and a Pavilion of the Arts and a Peace Lagoon and high-rise apartment buildings were going up here soon.

That was all right with Billy Pilgrim.

The speaker at the Lions Club meeting was a major in the Marines. He said that Americans had no choice but to keep fighting in Vietnam until they achieved victory or until the Communists realized that they could not force their way of life on weak countries. The major had been there on two separate tours of duty. He told of many terrible and many wonderful things he had seen. He was in favor of increased bombings, of bombing North Vietnam back into the Stone Age, if it refused to see reason.

Billy was not moved to protest the bombing of North Vietnam, did not shudder about the hideous things he himself had seen bombing do. He was simply having lunch with the Lions Club, of which he was past president now.

Billy had a framed prayer on his office wall which expressed his method for keeping going, even though he was unenthusiastic about living. A lot of patients who saw the prayer on Billy's wall told him that it helped *them* to keep going, too. It went like this:

GOD GRANT ME
THE SERENITY TO ACCEPT
THE THINGS I CANNOT CHANGE,
COURAGE
TO CHANGE THE THINGS I CAN,
AND WISDOM ALWAYS
TO TELL THE
DIFFERENCE.

Among the things Billy Pilgrim could not change were the past, the present, and the future.

Now he was being introduced to the Marine major. The person who was performing the introduction was telling the major that Billy was a veteran, and that Billy had a son who was a sergeant in the Green Berets—in Vietnam.

The major told Billy that the Green Berets were doing a great job, and that he should be proud of his son.

"I *am*. I certainly *am*," said Billy Pilgrim.

He went home for a nap after lunch. He was under doctor's orders to take a nap every day. The doctor hoped that this would relieve a complaint that Billy had: Every so often, for no apparent reason, Billy Pilgrim would find himself weeping. Nobody had ever caught Billy doing it. Only the doctor knew. It was an extremely quiet thing Billy did, and not very moist.

Billy owned a lovely Georgian home in Ilium. He was rich as Croesus, something he had never expected to be, not in a million years. He had five other optometrists working for him in the shopping plaza location, and netted over sixty thousand dollars a year. In addition, he owned a fifth of the new Holiday Inn out on Route 54, and half of three Tastee-Freeze stands. Tastee-Freeze was a sort of frozen custard. It gave all the pleasure that ice cream could give, without the stiffness and bitter coldness of ice cream.

Billy's home was empty. His daughter Barbara was about to get married, and she and his wife had gone downtown to pick out patterns for her crystal and silverware. There was a note saying so on the kitchen table. There were no servants. People just weren't interested in careers in domestic service anymore. There wasn't a dog, either.

There used to be a dog named Spot, but he died. So it goes. Billy had liked Spot a lot, and Spot had liked him.

Billy went up the carpeted stairway and into his and his wife's bedroom. The room had flowered wallpaper. There was a double bed with a clock-radio on a table beside it. Also on the table were controls for the electric blanket, and a switch to turn on a gentle vibrator which was bolted to the springs of the box mattress. The trade name of the vibrator was "Magic Fingers." The vibrator was the doctor's idea, too.

Billy took off his tri-focals and his coat and his necktie and his shoes, and he closed the venetian blinds and then the drapes, and he lay down on the outside of the coverlet. But sleep would not come. Tears came instead. They seeped. Billy turned on the Magic Fingers, and he was jiggled as he wept.

The doorchimes rang. Billy got off the bed and looked down through a window at the front doorstep, to see if somebody important had come to call. There was a crippled man down there, as spastic in space as Billy Pilgrim was in time. Convulsions made the man dance flappingly all the time, made him change his expressions, too, as though he was trying to imitate various famous movie stars.

Another cripple was ringing a doorbell across the street. He was on crutches. He had only one leg. He was so jammed between his crutches that his shoulders hid his ears.

Billy knew what the cripples were up to: They were selling subscriptions to magazines that would never come. People subscribed to them because the salesmen were so pitiful. Billy had heard about this racket from a speaker at the Lions Club two weeks before—a man from the Better Business Bureau. The man said that anybody who saw cripples working a neighborhood for magazine subscriptions should call the police.

Billy looked down the street, saw a new Buick Riviera parked about half a block away. There was a man in it, and Billy assumed correctly that he was the man who had hired the cripples to do this thing. Billy went on weeping as he contemplated the cripples and their boss. His doorchimes clanged hellishly.

He closed his eyes, and opened them again. He was still weeping, but he was back in Luxembourg again. He was marching with a lot of other prisoners. It was a winter wind that was bringing tears to his eyes.

Ever since Billy had been thrown into shrubbery for the sake of a picture, he had been seeing Saint Elmo's fire, a sort of electronic radiance around the heads of his companions and captors. It was in the treetops and on the rooftops of Luxembourg, too. It was beautiful.

Billy was marching with his hands on top of his head, and so were all the other Americans. Billy was bobbing up-and-down, up-and-down. Now he crashed into Roland Weary accidentally. "I beg your pardon," he said.

Weary's eyes were tearful also. Weary was crying because of horrible pains in his feet. The hinged clogs were transforming his feet into blood puddings.

At each road intersection Billy's group was joined by more Americans with their hands on top of their haloed heads. Billy had smiles for them all. They were moving like water, downhill all the time, and they flowed at last to a main highway on a valley's floor. Through the valley flowed a Mississippi of humiliated Americans. Tens of thousands of Americans shuffled eastward, their hands clasped on top of their heads. They sighed and groaned.

Billy and his group joined the river of humiliation, and the late afternoon sun came out from the clouds. The Americans didn't have the road to themselves. The westbound lane boiled and boomed with vehicles which were rushing German reserves to the front. The reserves were violent, windburned, bristly men. They had teeth like piano keys.

They were festooned with machine-gun belts, smoked cigars and guzzled booze. They took wolfish bites from sausages, patted their horny palms with potato-masher grenades.

One soldier in black was having a drunk hero's picnic all by himself on top of a tank. He spit on the Americans. The spit hit Roland Weary's shoulder, gave Weary a *fourragère* of snot and blutwurst and tobacco juice and Schnapps.

Billy found the afternoon stingingly exciting. There was so much to see—dragon's teeth, killing machines, corpses with bare feet that were blue and ivory. So it goes.

Bobbing up-and-down, up-and-down, Billy beamed lovingly at a bright lavender farmhouse that had been spattered with machine-gun bullets. Standing in its cockeyed doorway was a German colonel. With him was his unpainted whore.

Billy crashed into Weary's shoulder, and Weary cried out sobbingly. "Walk right! Walk right!"

They were climbing a gentle rise now. When they reached the top, they weren't in Luxembourg any more. They were in Germany.

A motion-picture camera was set up at the border—to record the fabulous victory. Two civilians in bearskin coats were leaning on the camera when Billy and Weary came by. They had run out of film hours ago.

One of them singled out Billy's face for a moment, then focused at infinity again. There was a tiny plume of smoke at infinity. There was a battle there. People were dying there. So it goes.

And the sun went down, and Billy found himself bobbing in place in a railroad yard. There were rows and rows of boxcars waiting. They had brought reserves to the front. Now they were going to take prisoners into Germany's interior.

Flashlight beams danced crazily.

The Germans sorted out the prisoners according to rank. They put sergeants with sergeants, majors with majors, and so on. A squad of full colonels was halted near Billy. One of them had double pneumonia. He had a high fever and vertigo. As the railroad yard dipped and swooped around the colonel, he tried to hold himself steady by staring into Billy's eyes.

The colonel coughed and coughed, and then he said to Billy, "You one of my boys?" This was a man who had lost an entire regiment, about forty-five hundred men—a lot of them children, actually. Billy didn't reply. The question made no sense.

"What was your outfit?" said the colonel. He coughed and coughed. Every time he inhaled his lungs rattled like greasy paper bags.

Billy couldn't remember the outfit he was from.

"You from the Four-fifty-first?"

"Four-fifty-first what?" said Billy.

There was a silence. "Infantry regiment," said the colonel at last.

"Oh," said Billy Pilgrim.

There was another long silence, with the colonel dying and dying, drowning where he stood. And then he cried out wetly, "It's me, boys! It's Wild Bob!" That is what he had always wanted his troops to call him: "Wild Bob."

None of the people who could hear him were actually from his regiment, except for Roland Weary, and Weary wasn't listening. All Weary could think of was the agony in his own feet.

But the colonel imagined that he was addressing his beloved troops for the last time, and he told them that they had nothing to be ashamed of, that there were dead Germans all over the battlefield who wished to God that they had never heard of the Four-fifty-first. He said that after the war he was going to have a regimental reunion in his home town, which was Cody, Wyoming. He was going to barbecue whole steers.

He said all this while staring into Billy's eyes. He made the inside of poor Billy's skull echo with balderdash. "God be with you, boys!" he said, and that echoed and echoed. And then he said, "If you're ever in Cody, Wyoming, just ask for Wild Bob!"

I was there. So was my old war buddy, Bernard V. O'Hare.

Billy Pilgrim was packed into a boxcar with many other privates. He and Roland Weary were separated. Weary was packed into another car in the same train.

There were narrow ventilators at the corners of the car, under the eaves. Billy stood by one of these, and, as the crowd pressed against him, he climbed part way up a diagonal corner brace to make more room. This placed his eyes on a level with the ventilator, so he could see another train about ten yards away.

Germans were writing on the cars with blue chalk—the number of persons in each car, their rank, their nationality, the date on which they had been put aboard. Other Germans were securing the hasps on the car doors with wire and spikes and other trackside trash. Billy could hear somebody writing on his car, too, but he couldn't see who was doing it.

Most of the privates on Billy's car were very young—at the end of childhood. But crammed into the corner with Billy was a former hobo who was forty years old.

"I been hungrier than this," the hobo told Billy. "I been in worse places than this. This ain't so bad."

A man in a boxcar across the way called out through the ventilator that a man had just died in there. So it goes. There were four guards who heard him. They weren't excited by the news.

"Yo, yo," said one, nodding dreamily. "Yo, yo."

And the guards didn't open the car with the dead man in it. They opened the next car instead, and Billy Pilgrim was enchanted by what was in there. It was like heaven. There was candlelight, and there were bunks with quilts and blankets heaped on them. There was a cannonball stove with a steaming coffeepot on top. There was a table with a bottle of wine and a loaf of bread and a sausage on it. There were four bowls of soup.

There were pictures of castles and lakes and pretty girls on the walls. This was the rolling home of the railroad guards, men whose business it was to be forever guarding freight rolling from here to there. The four guards went inside and closed the door.

A little while later they came out smoking cigars, talking contentedly in the mellow lower register of the German language. One of them saw Billy's face at the ventilator. He wagged a finger at him in affectionate warning, telling him to be a good boy.

The Americans across the way told the guards again about the dead man on their car. The guards got a stretcher out of their own cozy car, opened the dead man's car and went inside. The dead man's car wasn't crowded at all. There were just six live colonels in there—and one dead one.

The Germans carried the corpse out. The corpse was Wild Bob. So it goes.

During the night, some of the locomotives began to tootle to one another, and then to move. The locomotive and the last car of each train were marked with a striped banner of orange and black, indicating that the train was not fair game for airplanes—that it was carrying prisoners of war.

The war was nearly over. The locomotives began to move east in late December. The war would end in May. German prisons everywhere were absolutely full, and there was no longer any food for the prisoners to eat, and no longer any fuel to keep them warm. And yet—here came more prisoners.

Billy Pilgrim's train, the longest train of all, did not move for two days.

"This ain't bad," the hobo told Billy on the second day. "This ain't nothing at all."

Billy looked out through the ventilator. The railroad yard was a desert now, except for a hospital train marked with red crosses—on a siding far, far away. Its locomotive whistled. The locomotive of Billy Pilgrim's train whistled back. They were saying, "Hello."

Even though Billy's train wasn't moving, its boxcars were kept locked tight. Nobody was to get off until the final destination. To the guards who walked up and down outside, each car became a single organism which ate and drank and excreted through its ventilators. It talked or sometimes yelled through its ventilators, too. In went water and loaves of blackbread and sausage and cheese, and out came shit and piss and language.

Human beings in there were excreting into steel helmets, which were passed to the people at the ventilators, who dumped them. Billy was a dumper. The human beings also passed canteens, which guards would fill with water. When food came in, the human beings were quiet and trusting and beautiful. They shared.

Human beings in there took turns standing or lying down. The legs of those who stood were like fence posts driven into a warm, squirming, farting, sighing earth. The queer earth was a mosaic of sleepers who nestled like spoons.

Now the train began to creep eastward.

Somewhere in there was Christmas. Billy Pilgrim nestled like a spoon with the hobo on Christmas night, and he fell asleep, and he traveled in time to 1967 again—to the night he was kidnapped by a flying saucer from Tralfamadore.

4

Billy Pilgrim could not sleep on his daughter's wedding night. He was forty-four. The wedding had taken place that afternoon in a gaily striped tent in Billy's backyard. The stripes were orange and black.

Billy and his wife, Valencia, nestled like spoons in their big double bed. They were jiggled by Magic Fingers. Valencia didn't need to be jiggled to sleep. Valencia was snoring like a bandsaw. The poor woman didn't have ovaries or a uterus any more. They had been removed by a surgeon—by one of Billy's partners in the new Holiday Inn.

There was a full moon.

Billy got out of bed in the moonlight. He felt spooky and luminous, felt as though he was wrapped in cool fur that was full of static electricity. He looked down at his bare feet. They were ivory and blue.

Billy now shuffled down his upstairs hallway, knowing he was about to be kidnapped by a flying saucer. The hallway was zebra-striped with darkness and moonlight. The moonlight came into the hallway through doorways of the empty rooms of Billy's two children, children no more. They were gone forever. Billy was guided by dread and the lack of dread. Dread told him when to stop. Lack of it told him when to move again. He stopped.

He went into his daughter's room. Her drawers were dumped. Her closet was empty. Heaped in the middle of the room were all the possessions she could not take on a honeymoon. She had a Princess telephone extension all her own—on her windowsill. Its tiny night light stared at Billy. And then it rang.

Billy answered. There was a drunk on the other end. Billy could almost smell his breath—mustard gas and roses. It was a wrong number. Billy hung up. There was a soft drink bottle on the windowsill. Its label boasted that it contained no nourishment whatsoever.

Billy Pilgrim padded downstairs on his blue and ivory feet. He went into the kitchen, where the moonlight called his attention to a half bottle of champagne on the kitchen table, all that was left from the reception in the tent. Somebody had stoppered it again. "Drink me," it seemed to say.

So Billy uncorked it with his thumbs. It didn't make a pop. The champagne was dead. So it goes.

Billy looked at the clock on the gas stove. He had an hour to kill before the saucer came. He went into the living room, swinging the bottle like a dinner bell, turned on the television. He came slightly unstuck in time, saw the late movie backwards, then forwards again. It was a movie about American bombers in the Second World War and the gallant men who flew them. Seen backwards by Billy, the story went like this:

American planes, full of holes and wounded men and corpses took off backwards from an airfield in England. Over France, a few German fighter planes flew at them backwards, sucked bullets and shell fragments from some of the planes and crewmen. They did the same for wrecked American bombers on the ground and those planes flew up backwards to join the formation.

The formation flew backwards over a German city that was in flames. The bombers opened their bomb bay doors, exerted a miraculous magnetism which shrunk the fires, gathered them into cylindrical steel containers, and lifted the containers into the bellies of the planes. The containers were stored neatly in racks. The Germans below had miraculous devices of their own, which were long steel tubes. They used them to suck more fragments from the crewmen and planes. But there were still a few wounded Americans, though, and some of the bombers were in bad repair. Over France, though, German fighters came up again, made everything and everybody as good as new.

When the bombers got back to their base, the steel cylinders were taken from the racks and shipped back to the United States of America, where factories were operating night and day, dismantling the cylinders, separating the dangerous contents into minerals. Touchingly, it was mainly women who did this work. The minerals were then shipped to specialists in remote areas. It was their business to put them into the ground, to hide them cleverly, so they would never hurt anybody ever again.

The American fliers turned in their uniforms, became high school kids. And Hitler turned into a baby, Billy Pilgrim supposed. That wasn't in the movie. Billy was extrapolating. Everybody turned into a baby, and all humanity, without exception, conspired biologically to produce two perfect people named Adam and Eve, he supposed.

Billy saw the war movies backwards then forwards—and then it was time to go out into his backyard to meet the flying saucer. Out he went, his blue and ivory feet crushing the wet salad of the lawn. He stopped, took a swig of the dead champagne. It was like 7-Up. He would not raise his eyes to the sky, though he knew there was a flying saucer from Tralfamadore up there. He would see it soon enough, inside and out, and he would see, too, where it came from soon enough—soon enough.

Overhead he heard the cry of what might have been a melodious owl, but it wasn't a melodious owl. It was a flying saucer from Tralfamadore, navigating in both space and time, therefore seeming to Billy Pilgrim to have come from nowhere all at once. Somewhere a big dog barked.

The saucer was one hundred feet in diameter, with portholes around its rim. The light from the portholes was a pulsing purple. The only noise it made was the owl song. It came down to hover over Billy, and to enclose him in a cylinder of pulsing purple light. Now there was the sound of a seeming kiss as an airtight hatch in the bottom of the saucer was opened. Down snaked a ladder that was outlined in pretty lights like a Ferris wheel.

Billy's will was paralyzed by a zap gun aimed at him from one of the portholes. It became imperative that he take hold of the bottom rung of the sinuous ladder, which he did. The rung was electrified, so that Billy's hands locked onto it hard. He was hauled into the airlock, and machinery closed the bottom door. Only then did the ladder, wound onto a reel in the airlock, let him go. Only then did Billy's brain start working again.

There were two peepholes inside the airlock—with yellow eyes pressed to them. There was a speaker on the wall. The Tralfamadorians had no voice boxes. They communicated telepathically. They were able to talk to Billy by means of a computer and a sort of electric organ which made every Earthling speech sound.

"Welcome aboard, Mr. Pilgrim," said the loudspeaker. "Any questions?"

Billy licked his lips, thought a while, inquired at last: "Why me?"

"That is a very *Earthling* question to ask, Mr. Pilgrim. Why *you*? Why *us* for that matter? Why *anything*? Because this moment simply *is*. Have you ever seen bugs trapped in amber?"

"Yes." Billy, in fact, had a paperweight in his office which was a blob of polished amber with three ladybugs embedded in it.

"Well, here we are, Mr. Pilgrim, trapped in the amber of this moment. There is no *why*."

They introduced an anesthetic into Billy's atmosphere now, put him to sleep. They carried him to a cabin where he was strapped to a yellow Barca-Lounger which they had stolen from a Sears & Roebuck warehouse. The hold of the saucer was crammed with other stolen merchandise, which would be used to furnish Billy's artificial habitat in a zoo on Tralfamadore.

The terrific acceleration of the saucer as it left Earth twisted Billy's slumbering body, distorted his face, dislodged him in time, sent him back to the war.

When he regained consciousness, he wasn't on the flying saucer. He was in a boxcar crossing Germany again.

Some people were rising from the floor of the car, and others were lying down. Billy planned to lie down, too. It would be lovely to sleep. It was black in the car, and black outside the car, which seemed to be going about two miles an hour. The car never seemed to go any faster than that. It was a long time between clicks, between joints in the track. There would be a click, and then a year would go by, and then there would be another click.

The train often stopped to let really important trains bawl and hurtle by. Another thing it did was stop on sidings near prisons, leaving a few cars there. It was creeping across all of Germany, growing shorter all the time.

And Billy let himself down oh so gradually now, hanging onto the diagonal cross-brace in the corner in order to make himself seem nearly weightless to those he was joining on the floor. He knew it was important that he make himself nearly ghostlike when lying down. He had forgotten why, but a reminder soon came.

"Pilgrim—" said a person he was about to nestle with, "is that *you?*"

Billy didn't say anything, but nestled very politely, closed his eyes.

"God damn it," said the person. "That *is* you, isn't it?" He sat up and explored Billy rudely with his hands. "It's you, all right. Get the hell out of here."

Now Billy sat up, too—wretched, close to tears.

"Get out of here! I want to sleep!"

"Shut up," said somebody else.

"I'll shut up when Pilgrim gets away from here."

So Billy stood up again, clung to the cross-brace. "Where *can* I sleep?" he asked quietly.

"Not with me."

"Not with me, you son of a bitch," said somebody else. "You yell. You kick."

"I do?"

"You're God damn right you do. And whimper."

"I do?"

"Keep the hell away from here, Pilgrim."

And now there was an acrimonious madrigal, with parts sung in all quarters of the car. Nearly everybody, seemingly, had an atrocity story of something Billy Pilgrim had done to him in his sleep. Everybody told Billy Pilgrim to keep the hell away.

So Billy Pilgrim had to sleep standing up, or not sleep at all. And food had stopped coming in through the ventilators, and the days and nights were colder all the time.

On the eighth day, the forty-year-old hobo said to Billy, "This ain't bad. I can be comfortable anywhere."

"You can?" said Billy.

On the ninth day, the hobo died. So it goes. His last words were, "You think this is bad? This ain't bad."

There was something about death and the ninth day. There was a death on the ninth day in the car ahead of Billy's too. Roland Weary died—of gangrene that had started in his mangled feet. So it goes.

Weary, in his nearly continuous delirium, told again and again of the Three Musketeers, acknowledged that he was dying, gave many messages to be delivered to his family in Pittsburgh. Above all, he wanted to be avenged, so he said again and again the name of the person who had killed him. Everyone on the car learned the lesson well.

"Who killed me?" he would ask.

And everybody knew the answer, which was this: "Billy Pilgrim."

Listen—on the tenth night the peg was pulled out of the hasp on Billy's boxcar door, and the door was opened. Billy Pilgrim was lying at an angle on the corner-brace, self-crucified, holding himself there with a blue and ivory claw hooked over the sill of the ventilator. Billy coughed when the door was opened, and when he coughed he shit thin gruel. This was in accordance with the Third Law of Motion according to Sir Isaac Newton. This law tells us that for every action there is a reaction which is equal and opposite in direction.

This can be useful in rocketry.

The train had arrived on a siding by a prison which was originally constructed as an extermination camp for Russian prisoners of war.

The guards peeked inside Billy's car owlishly, cooed calmingly. They had never dealt with Americans before, but they surely understood this general sort of freight. They knew that it was essentially a liquid which could be induced to flow slowly toward cooing and light. It was nighttime.

The only light outside came from a single bulb which hung from a pole—high and far away. All was quiet outside, except for the guards, who cooed like doves. And the liquid began to flow. Gobs of it built up in the doorway, plopped to the ground.

Billy was the next-to-last human being to reach the door. The hobo was last. The hobo could not flow, could not plop. He wasn't liquid any more. He was stone. So it goes.

Billy didn't want to drop from the car to the ground. He sincerely believed that he would shatter like glass. So the guards helped him down, cooing still. They set him down facing the train. It was such a dinky train now.

There was a locomotive, a tender, and three little boxcars. The last boxcar was the railroad guards' heaven on wheels. Again —in that heaven on wheels—the table was set. Dinner was served.

At the base of the pole from which the light bulb hung were three seeming haystacks. The Americans were wheedled and teased over to those three stacks, which weren't hay after all.

They were overcoats taken from prisoners who were dead. So it goes.

It was the guards' firmly expressed wish that every American without an overcoat should take one. The coats were cemented together with ice, so the guards used their bayonets as ice picks, pricking free collars and hems and sleeves and so on, then peeling off coats and handing them out at random. The coats were stiff and dome-shaped, having conformed to their piles.

The coat that Billy Pilgrim got had been crumpled and frozen in such a way, and was so small, that it appeared to be not a coat but a sort of large black, three-cornered hat. There were gummy stains on it, too, like crankcase drainings or old strawberry jam. There seemed to be a dead, furry animal frozen to it. The animal was in fact the coat's fur collar.

Billy glanced dully at the coats of his neighbors. Their coats all had brass buttons or tinsel or piping or numbers or stripes or eagles or moons or stars dangling from them. They were soldiers' coats. Billy was the only one who had a coat from a dead civilian. So it goes.

And Billy and the rest were encouraged to shuffle around their dinky train and into the prison camp. There wasn't anything warm or lively to attract them—merely long, low, narrow sheds by the thousands, with no lights inside.

Somewhere a dog barked. With the help of fear and echoes and winter silences, that dog had a voice like a big bronze gong.

Billy and the rest were wooed through gate after gate, and Billy saw his first Russian. The man was all alone in the night—a ragbag with a round, flat face that glowed like a radium dial.

Billy passed within a yard of him. There was barbed wire between them. The Russian did not wave or speak, but he looked directly into Billy's soul with sweet hopefulness, as though Billy might have good news for him—news he might be too stupid to understand, but good news all the same.

Billy blacked out as he walked through gate after gate. He came to in what he thought might be a building on Tralfamadore. It was shrilly lit and lined with white tiles. It was on Earth, though.

It was a delousing station through which all new prisoners had to pass.

Billy did as he was told, took off his clothes. That was the first thing they told him to do on Tralfamadore, too.

A German measured Billy's upper right arm with his thumb and forefinger, asked a companion what sort of an army would send a weakling like that to the front. They looked at the other American bodies now, pointed out a lot more that were nearly as bad as Billy's.

One of the best bodies belonged to the oldest American by far, a high school teacher from Indianapolis. His name was Edgar Derby. He hadn't been in Billy's boxcar. He'd been in Roland Weary's car, had cradled Weary's head while he died. So it goes. Derby was forty-four years old. He was so old he had a son who was a marine in the Pacific theater of war.

Derby had pulled political wires to get into the army at his age. The subject he had taught in Indianapolis was Contemporary Problems in Western Civilization. He also coached the tennis team, and took very good care of his body.

Derby's son would survive the war. Derby wouldn't. That good body of his would be filled with holes by a firing squad in Dresden in sixty-eight days. So it goes.

The worst American body wasn't Billy's. The worst body belonged to a car thief from Cicero, Illinois. His name was Paul Lazzaro. He was tiny, and not only were his bones and teeth rotten, but his skin was disgusting. Lazzaro was polka-dotted all over with dime-sized scars. He had had many plagues of boils.

Lazzaro, too, had been on Roland Weary's boxcar, and had given his word of honor to Weary that he would find some way to make Billy Pilgrim pay for Weary's death. He was looking around now, wondering which naked human being was Billy.

The naked Americans took their places under many showerheads along a white-tiled wall. There were no faucets they could control. They could only wait for whatever was coming. Their penises were shriveled and their balls were retracted. Reproduction was not the main business of the evening.

An unseen hand turned a master valve. Out of the shower-heads gushed scalding rain. The rain was a blowtorch that did not warm. It jazzed and jangled Billy's skin without thawing the ice in the marrow of his long bones.

The Americans' clothes were meanwhile passing through poison gas. Body lice and bacteria and fleas were dying by the billions. So it goes.

And Billy zoomed back in time to his infancy. He was a baby who had just been bathed by his mother. Now his mother wrapped him in a towel, carried him into a rosy room that was filled with sunshine. She unwrapped him, laid him on the tickling towel, powdered him between his legs, joked with him, patted his little jelly belly. Her palm on his little jelly belly made potching sounds.

Billy gurgled and cooed.

And then Billy was a middle-aged optometrist again, playing hacker's golf this time—on a blazing summer Sunday morning. Billy never went to church any more. He was hacking with three other optometrists. Billy was on the green in seven strokes, and it was his turn to putt.

It was an eight-foot putt and he made it. He bent over to take the ball out of the cup, and the sun went behind a cloud. Billy was momentarily dizzy. When he recovered, he wasn't on the golf course any more. He was strapped to a yellow contour chair in a white chamber aboard a flying saucer, which was bound for Tralfamadore.

"Where am I?" said Billy Pilgrim.

"Trapped in another blob of amber, Mr. Pilgrim. We are where we have to be just now—three hundred million miles from Earth, bound for a time warp which will get us to Tralfamadore in hours rather than centuries."

"How—how did I get here?"

"It would take another Earthling to explain it to you. Earthlings are the great explainers, explaining why this event is structured as it is, telling how other events may be achieved or avoided. I am a Tralfamadorian, seeing all time as you might see a stretch of the Rocky Mountains. All time is all time. It does not change. It does not lend itself to warnings or explanations. It simply is.

Take it moment by moment, and you will find that we are all, as I've said before, bugs in amber."

"You sound to me as though you don't believe in free will," said Billy Pilgrim.

"If I hadn't spent so much time studying Earthlings," said the Tralfamadorian, "I wouldn't have any idea what was meant by 'free will.' I've visited thirty-one inhabited planets in the universe, and I have studied reports on one hundred more. Only on Earth is there any talk of free will."

5

Billy Pilgrim says that the Universe does not look like a lot of bright little dots to the creatures from Tralfamadore. The creatures can see where each star has been and where it is going, so that the heavens are filled with rarefied, luminous spaghetti. And Tralfamadorians don't see human beings as two-legged creatures, either. They see them as great millepedes—"with babies' legs at one end and old people's legs at the other," says Billy Pilgrim.

Billy asked for something to read on the trip to Tralfamadore. His captors had five million Earthling books on microfilm, but no way to project them in Billy's cabin. They had only one actual book in English, which would be placed in a Tralfamadorian museum. It was *Valley of the Dolls*, by Jacqueline Susann.

Billy read it, thought it was pretty good in spots. The people in it certainly had their ups and downs, ups and downs. But Billy didn't want to read about the same ups and downs over and over again. He asked if there wasn't, please, some other reading matter around.

"Only Tralfamadorian novels, which I'm afraid you couldn't begin to understand," said the speaker on the wall.

"Let me look at one anyway."

So they sent him in several. They were little things. A dozen of them might have had the bulk of *Valley of the Dolls*—with all its ups and downs, ups and downs.

Billy couldn't read Tralfamadorian, of course, but he could at least see how the books were laid out—in brief clumps of symbols separated by stars. Billy commented that the clumps might be telegrams.

"Exactly," said the voice.

"They *are* telegrams?"

"There are no telegrams on Tralfamadore. But you're right: each clump of symbols is a brief, urgent message—describing a situation, a scene. We Tralfamadorians read them all at once, not one after the other. There isn't any particular relationship between all the messages, except that the author has chosen them carefully, so that, when seen all at once, they produce an image of life that is beautiful and surprising and deep. There is no beginning, no middle, no end, no suspense, no moral, no causes, no effects. What we love in our books are the depths of many marvelous moments seen all at one time."

Moments after that, the saucer entered a time warp, and Billy was flung back into his childhood. He was twelve years old, quaking as he stood with his mother and father on Bright Angel Point, at the rim of Grand Canyon. The little human family was staring at the floor of the canyon, one mile straight down.

"Well—" said Billy's father, manfully kicking a pebble into space, "there it *is*." They had come to this famous place by automobile. They had had seven blowouts on the way.

"It was worth the trip," said Billy's mother raptly. "Oh, God —was it ever *worth* it."

Billy hated the canyon. He was sure that he was going to fall in. His mother touched him, and he wet his pants.

There were other tourists looking down into the canyon, too, and a ranger was there to answer questions. A Frenchman who had come all the way from France asked the ranger in broken English if many people committed suicide by jumping in.

"Yes, sir," said the ranger. "About three folks a year." So it goes.

And Billy took a very short trip through time, made a peewee jump of only ten days, so he was still twelve, still touring the West with his family. Now they were down in Carlsbad Caverns, and Billy was praying to God to get him out of there before the ceiling fell in.

A ranger was explaining that the Caverns had been discovered by a cowboy who saw a huge cloud of bats come out of a hole in the ground. And then he said that he was going to turn out all the lights, and that it would probably be the first time in the lives of most people there that they had ever been in darkness that was total.

Out went the lights. Billy didn't even know whether he was still alive or not. And then something ghostly floated in air to his left. It had numbers on it. His father had taken out his pocket watch. The watch had a radium dial.

Billy went from total dark to total light, found himself back in the war, back in the delousing station again. The shower was over. An unseen hand had turned the water off.

When Billy got his clothes back, they weren't any cleaner, but all the little animals that had been living in them were dead. So it goes. And his new overcoat was thawed out and limp now. It was much too small for Billy. It had a fur collar and a lining of crimson silk, and had apparently been made for an impresario about as big as an organ-grinder's monkey. It was full of bullet holes.

Billy Pilgrim dressed himself. He put on the little overcoat, too. It split up the back, and, at the shoulders, the sleeves came entirely free. So the coat became a fur-collared vest. It was meant to flare at its owner's waist, but the flaring took place at Billy's armpits. The Germans found him to be one of the most screamingly funny things they had seen in all of World War Two. They laughed and laughed.

And the Germans told everybody else to form in ranks of five, with Billy as their pivot. Then out of doors went the parade, and through gate after gate again. There were more starving Russians with faces like radium dials. The Americans were livelier than before. The jazzing with hot water had cheered them up. And they came to a shed where a corporal with only one arm and one eye wrote the name and serial number of each prisoner in a big, red ledger. Everybody was legally alive now. Before they got their names and numbers in the book, they were missing in action and probably dead.

So it goes.

As the Americans were waiting to move on, an altercation broke out in their rear-most rank. An American had muttered something which a guard did not like. The guard knew English, and he hauled the American out of ranks, knocked him down.

The American was astonished. He stood up shakily, spitting blood. He'd had two teeth knocked out. He had meant no harm by what he'd said, evidently, had no idea that the guard would hear and understand.

"Why me?" he asked the guard.

The guard shoved him back into ranks. "Vy you? Vy anybody?" he said.

When Billy Pilgrim's name was inscribed in the ledger of the prison camp, he was given a number, too, and an iron dogtag in which that number was stamped. A slave laborer from Poland had done the stamping. He was dead now. So it goes.

Billy was told to hang the tag around his neck along with his American dogtags, which he did. The tag was like a salt cracker, perforated down its middle so that a strong man could snap it in two with his bare hands. In case Billy died, which he didn't, half of the tag would mark his body and half would mark his grave.

After poor Edgar Derby, the high school teacher, was shot in Dresden later on, a doctor pronounced him dead and snapped his dogtag in two. So it goes.

Properly enrolled and tagged, the Americans were led through gate after gate again. In two days' time now their families would learn from the International Red Cross that they were alive.

Next to Billy was little Paul Lazzaro, who had promised to avenge Roland Weary. Lazzaro wasn't thinking about vengeance. He was thinking about his terrible bellyache. His stomach had shrunk to the size of a walnut. That dry, shriveled pouch was as sore as a boil.

Next to Lazzaro was poor, doomed old Edgar Derby, with his American and German dogs displayed like a necklace, on the outside of his clothes. He had expected to become a captain, a company commander, because of his wisdom and age. Now here he was on the Czechoslovakian border at midnight.

"Halt," said a guard.

The Americans halted. They stood there quietly in the cold. The sheds they were among were outwardly like thousands of other sheds they had passed. There was this difference, though: the sheds had tin chimneys, and out of the chimneys whirled constellations of sparks.

A guard knocked on a door.

The door was flung open from inside. Light leaped out through the door, escaped from prison at 186,000 miles per second. Out marched fifty middle-aged Englishmen. They were singing "Hail, Hail, the Gang's All Here" from the *Pirates of Penzance*.

These lusty, ruddy vocalists were among the first English-speaking prisoners to be taken in the Second World War. Now they were singing to nearly the last. They had not seen a woman or a child for four years or more. They hadn't seen any birds, either. Not even sparrows would come into the camp.

The Englishmen were officers. Each of them had attempted to escape from another prison at least once. Now they were here, dead-center in a sea of dying Russians.

They could tunnel all they pleased. They would inevitably surface within a rectangle of barbed wire, would find themselves greeted listlessly by dying Russians who spoke no English, who had no food or useful information or escape plans of their own. They could scheme all they pleased to hide aboard a vehicle or steal one, but no vehicle ever came into their compound. They could feign illness, if they liked, but that wouldn't earn them a trip anywhere, either. The only hospital in the camp was a six-bed affair in the British compound itself.

The Englishmen were clean and enthusiastic and decent and strong. They sang boomingly well. They had been singing together every night for years.

The Englishmen had also been lifting weights and chinning themselves for years. Their bellies were like washboards. The muscles of their calves and upper arms were like cannonballs. They were all masters of checkers and chess and bridge and cribbage and dominoes and anagrams and charades and Ping-Pong and billiards, as well.

They were among the wealthiest people in Europe, in terms of food. A clerical error early in the war, when food was still getting through to prisoners, had caused the Red Cross to ship them five hundred parcels every month instead of fifty. The Englishmen had hoarded these so cunningly that now, as the war was ending, they had three tons of sugar, one ton of coffee, eleven hundred pounds of chocolate, seven hundred pounds of tobacco, seventeen hundred pounds of tea, two tons of flour, one ton of canned beef, twelve hundred pounds of canned butter, sixteen hundred pounds of canned cheese, eight hundred pounds of powdered milk, and two tons of orange marmalade.

They kept all this in a room without windows. They had rat-proofed it by lining it with flattened tin cans.

They were adored by the Germans, who thought they were exactly what Englishmen ought to be. They made war look stylish and reasonable, and fun. So the Germans let them have four sheds, though one shed would have held them all. And, in exchange for coffee or chocolate or tobacco, the Germans gave them paint and lumber and nails and cloth for fixing things up.

The Englishmen had known for twelve hours that American guests were on their way. They had never had guests before, and they went to work like darling elves, sweeping, mopping, cooking, baking—making mattresses of straw and burlap bags, setting tables, putting party favors at each place.

Now they were singing their welcome to their guests in the winter night. Their clothes were aromatic with the feast they had been preparing. They were dressed half for battle, half for tennis or croquet. They were so elated by their own hospitality, and by all the goodies waiting inside, that they did not take a good look at their guests while they sang. And they imagined that they were singing to fellow officers fresh from the fray.

They wrestled the Americans toward the shed door affectionately, filling the night with manly blather and brotherly rodomontades. They called them "Yank," told them "Good show," promised them that "Jerry was on the run," and so on.

Billy Pilgrim wondered dimly who Jerry was.

Now he was indoors, next to an iron cookstove that was glowing cherry red. Dozens of teapots were boiling there. Some of them had whistles. And there was a witches' cauldron full of golden soup. The soup was thick. Primeval bubbles surfaced it with lethargical majesty as Billy Pilgrim stared.

There were long tables set for a banquet. At each place was a bowl made from a can that had once contained powdered milk. A smaller can was a cup. A taller, more slender can was a tumbler. Each tumbler was filled with warm milk.

At each place was a safety razor, a washcloth, a package of razorblades, a chocolate bar, two cigars, a bar of soap, ten cigarettes, a book of matches, a pencil, and a candle.

Only the candles and the soap were of German origin. They had a ghostly, opalescent similarity. The British had no way of knowing it, but the candles and the soap were made from the fat of rendered Jews and Gypsies and fairies and communists, and other enemies of the State.

So it goes.

The banquet hall was illuminated by candlelight. There were heaps of fresh-baked white bread on the tables, gobs of butter, pots of marmalade. There were platters of sliced beef from cans. Soup and scrambled eggs and hot marmalade pie were yet to come.

And, at the far end of the shed, Billy saw pink arches with azure draperies hanging between them, and an enormous clock, and two golden thrones, and a bucket and a mop. It was in this setting that the evening's entertainment would take place, a musical version of *Cinderella*, the most popular story ever told.

Billy Pilgrim was on fire, having stood too close to the glowing stove. The hem of his little coat was burning. It was a quiet, patient sort of fire—like the burning of punk.

Billy wondered if there was a telephone somewhere. He wanted to call his mother, to tell her he was alive and well.

There was silence now, as the Englishmen looked in astonishment at the frowsy creatures they had so lustily waltzed inside. One of the Englishmen saw that Billy was on fire. "You're on fire, lad!" he said, and he got Billy away from the stove and beat out the sparks with his hands.

When Billy made no comment on this, the Englishman asked him, "Can you talk? Can you hear?"

Billy nodded.

The Englishman touched him exploratorily here and there, filled with pity. "My God—what have they done to you, lad? This isn't a man. It's a broken kite."

"Are you really an American?" said the Englishman.

"Yes," said Billy.

"And your rank?"

"Private."

"What became of your boots, lad?"

"I don't remember."

"Is that coat a *joke*?"

"Sir?"

"Where did you get such a thing?"

Billy had to think hard about that. "They gave it to me," he said at last.

"Jerry gave it to you?"

"Who?"

"The Germans gave it to you?"

"Yes."

Billy didn't like the questions. They were fatiguing.

"Ohhhh—Yank, Yank, Yank—" said the Englishman, "that coat was an *insult*."

"Sir?"

"It was a deliberate attempt to humiliate you. You mustn't let Jerry do things like that."

Billy Pilgrim swooned.

Billy came to on a chair facing the stage. He had somehow eaten, and now he was watching *Cinderella*. Some part of him had evidently been enjoying the performance for quite a while. Billy was laughing hard.

The women in the play were really men, of course. The clock had just struck midnight, and Cinderella was lamenting:

> "Goodness me, the clock has struck—
> Alackday, and fuck my luck."

Billy found the couplet so comical that he not only laughed—he shrieked. He went on shrieking until he was carried out of the shed and into another, where the hospital was. It was a six-bed hospital. There weren't any other patients in there.

Billy was put to bed and tied down, and given a shot of morphine. Another American volunteered to watch over him. This volunteer was Edgar Derby, the high school teacher who would be shot to death in Dresden. So it goes.

Derby sat on a three-legged stool. He was given a book to read. The book was *The Red Badge of Courage*, by Stephen Crane. Derby had read it before. Now he read it again while Billy Pilgrim entered a morphine paradise.

Under morphine, Billy had a dream of giraffes in a garden. The giraffes were following gravel paths, were pausing to munch sugar pears from treetops. Billy was a giraffe, too. He ate a pear. It was a hard one. It fought back against his grinding teeth. It snapped in juicy protest.

The giraffes accepted Billy as one of their own, as a harmless creature as preposterously specialized as themselves. Two approached him from opposite sides, leaned against him. They had long, muscular upper lips which they could shape like the bells of bugles. They kissed him with these. They were female giraffes—cream and lemon yellow. They had horns like doorknobs. The knobs were covered with velvet.

Why?

Night came to the garden of the giraffes, and Billy Pilgrim slept without dreaming for a while, and then he traveled in time. He woke up with his head under a blanket in a ward for nonviolent mental patients in a veterans' hospital near Lake Placid, New York. It was springtime in 1948, three years after the end of the war.

Billy uncovered his head. The windows of the ward were open. Birds were twittering outside. "Poo-tee-weet?" one asked him. The sun was high. There were twenty-nine other patients assigned to the ward, but they were all outdoors now, enjoying the day. They were free to come and go as they pleased, to go home, even, if they liked—and so was Billy Pilgrim. They had come here voluntarily, alarmed by the outside world.

Billy had committed himself in the middle of his final year at the Ilium School of Optometry. Nobody else suspected that he was going crazy. Everybody else thought he looked fine and was acting fine. Now he was in the hospital. The doctors agreed: He *was* going crazy.

They didn't think it had anything to do with the war. They were sure Billy was going to pieces because his father had thrown him into the deep end of the Y.M.C.A. swimming pool when he was a little boy, and had then taken him to the rim of the Grand Canyon.

The man assigned to the bed next to Billy's was a former infantry captain named Eliot Rosewater. Rosewater was sick and tired of being drunk all the time.

It was Rosewater who introduced Billy to science fiction, and in particular to the writings of Kilgore Trout. Rosewater had a tremendous collection of science-fiction paperbacks under his bed. He had brought them to the hospital in a steamer trunk. Those beloved, frumpish books gave off a smell that permeated the ward—like flannel pajamas that hadn't been changed for a month, or like Irish stew.

Kilgore Trout became Billy's favorite living author, and science fiction became the only sort of tales he could read.

Rosewater was twice as smart as Billy, but he and Billy were dealing with similar crises in similar ways. They had both found life meaningless, partly because of what they had seen in war. Rosewater, for instance, had shot a fourteen-year-old fireman, mistaking him for a German soldier. So it goes. And Billy had seen the greatest massacre in European history, which was the fire-bombing of Dresden. So it goes.

So they were trying to re-invent themselves and their universe. Science fiction was a big help.

Rosewater said an interesting thing to Billy one time about a book that wasn't science fiction. He said that everything there was to know about life was in *The Brothers Karamazov*, by

Feodor Dostoevsky. "But that isn't *enough* any more," said Rosewater.

Another time Billy heard Rosewater say to a psychiatrist, "I think you guys are going to have to come up with a lot of wonderful *new* lies, or people just aren't going to want to go on living."

There was a still life on Billy's bedside table—two pills, an ashtray with three lipstick-stained cigarettes in it, one cigarette still burning, and a glass of water. The water was dead. So it goes. Air was trying to get out of that dead water. Bubbles were clinging to the walls of the glass, too weak to climb out.

The cigarettes belonged to Billy's chain-smoking mother. She had sought the ladies' room, which was off the ward for WACS and WAVES and SPARS and WAFS who had gone bananas. She would be back at any moment now.

Billy covered his head with his blanket again. He always covered his head when his mother came to see him in the mental ward—always got much sicker until she went away. It wasn't that she was ugly, or had bad breath or a bad personality. She was a perfectly nice, standard-issue, brown-haired, white woman with a high-school education.

She upset Billy simply by being his mother. She made him feel embarrassed and ungrateful and weak because she had gone to so much trouble to give him life, and to keep that life going, and Billy didn't really like life at all.

Billy heard Eliot Rosewater come in and lie down. Rosewater's bedsprings talked a lot about that. Rosewater was a big man, but not very powerful. He looked as though he might be made out of nose putty.

And then Billy's mother came back from the ladies' room, sat down on a chair between Billy's and Rosewater's bed. Rosewater greeted her with melodious warmth, asked how she was today. He seemed delighted to hear that she was fine. He was experimenting with being ardently sympathetic with everybody he met. He thought that might make the world a slightly more pleasant place to live in. He called Billy's mother "dear." He was experimenting with calling everybody "dear."

"Some day," she promised Rosewater, "I'm going to come in

here, and Billy is going to uncover his head, and do you know what he's going to say?"

"What's he going to say, dear?"

"He's going to say, 'Hello, Mom,' and he's going to smile. He's going to say, 'Gee, it's good to see you, Mom. How have you been?' "

"Today could be the day."

"Every night I pray."

"That's a *good* thing to do."

"People would be surprised if they knew how much in this world was due to prayers."

"You never said a truer word, dear."

"Does your mother come to see you often?"

"My mother is dead," said Rosewater. So it goes.

"I'm sorry."

"At least she had a happy life as long as it lasted."

"That's a consolation, anyway."

"Yes."

"Billy's father is dead, you know," said Billy's mother. So it goes.

"A boy *needs* a father."

And on and on it went—that duet between the dumb, praying lady and the big, hollow man who was so full of loving echoes.

"He was at the top of his class when this happened," said Billy's mother.

"Maybe he was *working* too hard," said Rosewater. He held a book he wanted to read, but he was much too polite to read and talk, too, easy as it was to give Billy's mother satisfactory answers. The book was *Maniacs in the Fourth Dimension*, by Kilgore Trout. It was about people whose mental diseases couldn't be treated because the causes of the diseases were all in the fourth dimension, and three-dimensional Earthling doctors couldn't see those causes at all, or even imagine them.

One thing Trout said that Rosewater liked very much was that there really *were* vampires and werewolves and goblins and angels and so on, but that they were in the fourth dimension. So was William Blake, Rosewater's favorite poet, according to Trout. So were heaven and hell.

"He's engaged to a very rich girl," said Billy's mother.

"That's good," said Rosewater. "Money can be a great comfort sometimes."

"It really *can*."

"Of course it can."

"It isn't much fun if you have to pinch every penny till it screams."

"It's nice to have a little breathing room."

"Her father owns the optometry school where Billy was going. He also owns six offices around our part of the state. He flies his own plane and has a summer place up on Lake George."

"That's a beautiful lake."

Billy fell asleep under his blanket. When he woke up again, he was tied to the bed in the hospital back in prison. He opened one eye, saw poor old Edgar Derby reading *The Red Badge of Courage* by candlelight.

Billy closed that one eye, saw in his memory of the future poor old Edgar Derby in front of a firing squad in the ruins of Dresden. There were only four men in that squad. Billy had heard that one man in each firing squad was customarily given a rifle loaded with blank cartridge. Billy didn't think there would be a blank cartridge issued in a squad that small, in a war that old.

Now the head Englishman came into the hospital to check on Billy. He was an infantry colonel captured at Dunkirk. It was he who had given Billy morphine. There wasn't a real doctor in the compound, so the doctoring was up to him. "How's the patient?" he asked Derby.

"Dead to the world."

"But not actually dead."

"No."

"How nice—to feel nothing, and still get full credit for being alive."

Derby now came to lugubrious attention.

"No, no—please—as you were. With only two men for each officer, and all the men sick, I think we can do without the usual pageantry between officers and men."

Derby remained standing. "You seem older than the rest," said the colonel.

Derby told him he was forty-five, which was two years older than the colonel. The colonel said that the other Americans had all shaved now, that Billy and Derby were the only two still with beards. And he said, "You know—we've had to imagine the war here, and we have imagined that it was being fought by aging men like ourselves. We had forgotten that wars were fought by babies. When I saw those freshly shaved faces, it was a shock. " 'My God, my God—' I said to myself, 'It's the Children's Crusade.' "

The colonel asked old Derby how he had been captured, and Derby told a tale of being in a clump of trees with about a hundred other frightened soldiers. The battle had been going on for five days. The hundred had been driven into the trees by tanks.

Derby described the incredible artificial weather that Earthlings sometimes create for other Earthlings when they don't want those other Earthlings to inhabit Earth any more. Shells were bursting in the treetops with terrific bangs, he said, showering down knives and needles and razorblades. Little lumps of lead in copper jackets were crisscrossing the woods under the shellbursts, zipping along much faster than sound.

A lot of people were being wounded or killed. So it goes.

Then the shelling stopped, and a hidden German with a loudspeaker told the Americans to put their weapons down and come out of the woods with their hands on the top of their heads, or the shelling would start again. It wouldn't stop until everybody in there was dead.

So the Americans put their weapons down, and they came out of the woods with their hands on top of their heads, because they wanted to go on living, if they possibly could.

Billy traveled in time back to the veterans' hospital again. The blanket was over his head. It was quiet outside the blanket. "Is my mother gone?" said Billy.

"Yes."

Billy peeked out from under his blanket. His fiancée was out there now, sitting on the visitor's chair. Her name was Valencia Merble. Valencia was the daughter of the owner of the Ilium School of Optometry. She was rich. She was as big as a house because she couldn't stop eating. She was eating now. She was eating a Three Musketeers Candy Bar. She was wearing trifocal lenses in harlequin frames, and the frames were trimmed with rhinestones. The glitter of the rhinestones was answered by the glitter of the diamond in her engagement ring. The diamond was insured for eighteen hundred dollars. Billy had found that diamond in Germany. It was booty of war.

Billy didn't want to marry ugly Valencia. She was one of the symptoms of his disease. He knew he was going crazy when he heard himself proposing marriage to her, when he begged her to take the diamond ring and be his companion for life.

Billy said, "Hello," to her, and she asked him if he wanted some candy, and he said, "No, thanks."

She asked him how he was, and he said, "Much better, thanks." She said that everybody at the Optometry School was sorry he was sick and hoped he would be well soon, and Billy said, "When you see 'em, tell 'em, 'Hello.' "

She promised she would.

She asked him if there was anything she could bring him from the outside, and he said, "No. I have just about everything I want."

"What about books?" said Valencia.

"I'm right next to one of the biggest private libraries in the world," said Billy, meaning Eliot Rosewater's collection of science fiction.

Rosewater was on the next bed, reading, and Billy drew him into the conversation, asked him what he was reading this time.

So Rosewater told him. It was *The Gospel from Outer Space*, by Kilgore Trout. It was about a visitor from outer space, shaped very much like a Tralfamadorian, by the way. The visitor from outer space made a serious study of Christianity, to learn, if he could, why Christians found it so easy to be cruel. He concluded that at least part of the trouble was slipshod storytelling in the New Testament. He supposed that the intent of the Gospels was to teach people, among other things, to be merciful, even to the lowest of the low.

But the Gospels actually taught this:

Before you kill somebody, make absolutely sure he isn't well connected. So it goes.

The flaw in the Christ stories, said the visitor from outer space, was that Christ, who didn't look like much, was actually the Son of the Most Powerful Being in the Universe. Readers understood that, so, when they came to the crucifixion, they naturally thought, and Rosewater read out loud again:

Oh, boy—they sure picked the wrong guy to lynch that *time!*

And that thought had a brother: "*There are* right people *to lynch.*" Who? People not well connected. So it goes.

The visitor from outer space made a gift to Earth of a new Gospel. In it, Jesus really *was* a nobody, and a pain in the neck to a lot of people with better connections than he had. He still got to say all the lovely and puzzling things he said in the other Gospels.

So the people amused themselves one day by nailing him to a cross and planting the cross in the ground. There couldn't possibly be any repercussions, the lynchers thought. The reader would have to think that, too, since the new Gospel hammered home again and again what a nobody Jesus was.

And then, just before the nobody died, the heavens opened up, and there was thunder and lightning. The voice of God came crashing down. He told the people that he was adopting the bum as his son, giving him the full powers and privileges of The Son of the Creator of the Universe throughout all eternity. God said this: *From this moment on, He will punish horribly anybody who torments a bum who has no connections!*

Billy's fiancée had finished her Three Musketeers Candy Bar. Now she was eating a Milky Way.

"Forget books," said Rosewater, throwing that particular book under his bed. "The hell with 'em."

"That sounded like an interesting one," said Valencia.

"Jesus—if Kilgore Trout could only *write!*" Rosewater exclaimed. He had a point: Kilgore Trout's unpopularity was deserved. His prose was frightful. Only his ideas were good.

"I don't think Trout has ever been out of the country," Rosewater went on. "My God—he writes about Earthlings all the time, and they're all Americans. Practically nobody on Earth is an American."

"Where does he live?" Valencia asked.

"Nobody knows," Rosewater replied. "I'm the only person who ever heard of him, as far as I can tell. No two books have the same publisher, and every time I write him in care of a publisher, the letter comes back because the publisher has failed."

He changed the subject now, congratulated Valencia on her engagement ring.

"Thank you," she said, and held it out so Rosewater could get a close look. "Billy got that diamond in the war."

"That's the attractive thing about war," said Rosewater. "Absolutely everybody gets a little something."

With regard to the whereabouts of Kilgore Trout: he actually lived in Ilium, Billy's hometown, friendless and despised. Billy would meet him by and by.

"Billy—" said Valencia Merble.

"Hm?"

"You want to talk about our silver pattern?"

"Sure."

"I've got it narrowed down pretty much to either Royal Danish or Rambler Rose."

"Rambler Rose," said Billy.

"It isn't something we should *rush* into," she said. "I mean—whatever we decide on, that's what we're going to have to live with the rest of our lives."

Billy studied the pictures. "Royal Danish," he said at last.

"Colonial Moonlight is nice, too."

"Yes, it is," said Billy Pilgrim.

And Billy traveled in time to the zoo on Tralfamadore. He was forty-four years old, on display under a geodesic dome. He was reclining on the lounge chair which had been his cradle during his trip through space. He was naked. The Tralfamadorians were interested in his body—*all* of it. There were thousands of them outside, holding up their little hands so that their eyes could see him. Billy had been on Tralfamadore for six Earthling months now. He was used to the crowd.

Escape was out of the question. The atmosphere outside the

dome was cyanide, and Earth was 446,120,000,000,000,000 miles away.

Billy was displayed there in the zoo in a simulated Earthling habitat. Most of the furnishings had been stolen from the Sears & Roebuck warehouse in Iowa City, Iowa. There was a color television set and a couch that could be converted into a bed. There were end tables with lamps and ashtrays on them by the couch. There was a home bar and two stools. There was a little pool table. There was wall-to-wall carpeting in federal gold, except in the kitchen and bathroom areas and over the iron manhole cover in the center of the floor. There were magazines arranged in a fan on the coffee table in front of the couch.

There was a stereophonic phonograph. The phonograph worked. The television didn't. There was a picture of one cowboy killing another one pasted to the television tube. So it goes.

There were no walls in the dome, no place for Billy to hide. The mint green bathroom fixtures were right out in the open. Billy got off his lounge chair now, went into the bathroom and took a leak. The crowd went wild.

Billy brushed his teeth on Tralfamadore, put in his partial denture, and went into his kitchen. His bottled-gas range and his refrigerator and his dishwasher were mint green, too. There was a picture painted on the door of the refrigerator. The refrigerator had come that way. It was a picture of a Gay Nineties couple on a bicycle built for two.

Billy looked at that picture now, tried to think something about the couple. Nothing came to him. There didn't seem to be *anything* to think about those two people.

Billy ate a good breakfast from cans. He washed his cup and plate and knife and fork and spoon and saucepan, put them away. Then he did exercises he had learned in the Army—straddle jumps, deep knee bends, sit-ups and push-ups. Most Tralfamadorians had no way of knowing Billy's body and face were not beautiful. They supposed that he was a splendid specimen. This had a pleasant effect on Billy, who began to enjoy his body for the first time.

He showered after his exercises and trimmed his toenails. He shaved, and sprayed deodorant under his arms, while a zoo guide on a raised platform outside explained what Billy was doing—and why. The guide was lecturing telepathically, simply standing there, sending out thought waves to the crowd. On the platform with him was the little keyboard instrument with which he would relay questions to Billy from the crowd.

Now the first question came—from the speaker on the television set: "Are you happy here?"

"About as happy as I was on Earth," said Billy Pilgrim, which was true.

There were five sexes on Tralfamadore, each of them performing a step necessary in the creation of a new individual. They looked identical to Billy—because their sex differences were all in the fourth dimension.

One of the biggest moral bombshells handed to Billy by the Tralfamadorians, incidentally, had to do with sex on Earth. They said their flying-saucer crews had identified no fewer than *seven* sexes on Earth, each essential to reproduction. Again: Billy couldn't possibly imagine what five of those seven sexes had to do with the making of a baby, since they were sexually active only in the fourth dimension.

The Tralfamadorians tried to give Billy clues that would help him imagine sex in the invisible dimension. They told him that there could be no Earthling babies without male homosexuals. There *could* be babies without female homosexuals. There couldn't be babies without women over sixty-five years old. There *could* be babies without men over sixty-five. There couldn't be babies without other babies who had lived an hour or less after birth. And so on.

It was gibberish to Billy.

There was a lot that Billy said that was gibberish to the Tralfamadorians, too. They couldn't imagine what time looked like to him. Billy had given up on explaining that. The guide outside had to explain as best he could.

The guide invited the crowd to imagine that they were looking across a desert at a mountain range on a day that was twinkling bright and clear. They could look at a peak or a bird or a cloud, at a stone right in front of them, or even down into a canyon behind them. But among them was this poor Earthling, and his head was encased in a steel sphere which he could never take off. There was only one eyehole through which he could look, and welded to that eyehole were six feet of pipe.

This was only the beginning of Billy's miseries in the metaphor. He was also strapped to a steel lattice which was bolted to a flatcar on rails, and there was no way he could turn his head or touch the pipe. The far end of the pipe rested on a bi-pod which was also bolted to the flatcar. All Billy could see was the little dot at the end of the pipe. He didn't know he was on a flatcar, didn't even know there was anything peculiar about his situation.

The flatcar sometimes crept, sometimes went extremely fast, often stopped—went uphill, downhill, around curves, along straightaways. Whatever poor Billy saw through the pipe, he had no choice but to say to himself, "That's life."

Billy expected the Tralfamadorians to be baffled and alarmed by all the wars and other forms of murder on Earth. He expected them to fear that the Earthling combination of ferocity and spectacular weaponry might eventually destroy part or maybe all of the innocent Universe. Science fiction had led him to expect that.

But the subject of war never came up until Billy brought it up himself. Somebody in the zoo crowd asked him through the lecturer what the most valuable thing he had learned on Tralfamadore was so far, and Billy replied, "How the inhabitants of a whole planet can live in peace! As you know, I am from a planet that has been engaged in senseless slaughter since the beginning of time. I myself have seen the bodies of schoolgirls who were boiled alive in a water tower by my own countrymen, who were proud of fighting pure evil at the time." This was true. Billy saw the boiled bodies in Dresden. "And I have lit my way in a prison at night with candles from the fat of human beings who were butchered by the brothers and fathers of those schoolgirls who were boiled. Earthlings must be the terrors of the Universe! If other planets aren't now in danger from Earth, they soon will be. So tell me the secret so I can take it back to Earth and save us all: How can a planet live at peace?"

Billy felt that he had spoken soaringly. He was baffled when he saw the Tralfamadorians close their little hands on their eyes. He knew from past experience what this meant: He was being stupid.

"Would—would you mind telling me—" he said to the guide, much deflated, "what was so stupid about that?"

"We know how the Universe ends—" said the guide, "and Earth has nothing to do with it, except that *it* gets wiped out, too."

"How—how *does* the Universe end?" said Billy.

"We blow it up, experimenting with new fuels for our flying saucers. A Tralfamadorian test pilot presses a starter button, and the whole Universe disappears." So it goes.

"If you know this," said Billy, "isn't there some way you can prevent it? Can't you keep the pilot from *pressing* the button?"

"He has *always* pressed it, and he always *will*. We *always* let him and we always *will* let him. The moment is *structured* that way."

"So—" said Billy gropingly, "I suppose that the idea of preventing war on Earth is stupid, too."

"Of course."

"But you *do* have a peaceful planet here."

"Today we do. On other days we have wars as horrible as any you've ever seen or read about. There isn't anything we can do about them, so we simply don't look at them. We ignore them. We spend eternity looking at pleasant moments—like today at the zoo. Isn't this a nice moment?"

"Yes."

"That's one thing Earthlings might learn to do, if they tried hard enough: Ignore the awful times, and concentrate on the good ones."

"Um," said Billy Pilgrim.

Shortly after he went to sleep that night, Billy traveled in time to another moment which was quite nice, his wedding night with the former Valencia Merble. He had been out of the veterans' hospital for six months. He was all well. He had graduated from the Ilium School of Optometry—third in his class of forty-seven.

Now he was in bed with Valencia in a delightful studio apartment which was built on the end of a wharf on Cape Ann, Massachusetts. Across the water were the lights of Gloucester. Billy was on top of Valencia, making love to her. One result of this act would be the birth of Robert Pilgrim, who would become a problem in high school, but who would then straighten out as a member of the famous Green Berets.

Valencia wasn't a time-traveler, but she did have a lively imagination. While Billy was making love to her, she imagined that she was a famous woman in history. She was being Queen Elizabeth the First of England, and Billy was supposedly Christopher Columbus.

Billy made a noise like a small, rusty hinge. He had just emptied his seminal vesicles into Valencia, had contributed his share of the Green Beret. According to the Tralfamadorians, of course, the Green Beret would have seven parents in all.

Now he rolled off his huge wife, whose rapt expression did not change when he departed. He lay with the buttons of his spine along the edge of the mattress, folded his hands behind his head. He was rich now. He had been rewarded for marrying a girl nobody in his right mind would have married. His father-in-law had given him a new Buick Roadmaster, an all-electric home, and had made him manager of his most prosperous office, his Ilium office, where Billy could expect to make at least thirty thousand dollars a year. That was good. His father had been only a barber.

As his mother said, "The Pilgrims are coming up in the world."

The honeymoon was taking place in the bittersweet mysteries of Indian Summer in New England. The lovers' apartment had one romantic wall which was all French doors. They opened onto a balcony and the oily harbor beyond.

A green and orange dragger, black in the night, grumbled and drummed past their balcony, not thirty feet from their wedding bed. It was going to sea with only its running lights on. Its empty holds were resonant, made the song of the engines rich and loud.

The wharf began to sing the same song, and then the honeymooners' headboard sang, too. And it continued to sing long after the dragger was gone.

"Thank you," said Valencia at last. The headboard was singing a mosquito song.

"You're welcome."

"It was nice."

"I'm glad."

Then she began to cry.

"What's the matter?"

"I'm so happy."

"Good."

"I never thought anybody would marry me."

"Um," said Billy Pilgrim.

"I'm going to lose weight for you," she said.

"What?"

"I'm going to go on a diet. I'm going to become beautiful for you."

"I like you just the way you are."

"Do you *really*?"

"Really," said Billy Pilgrim. He had already seen a lot of their marriage, thanks to time-travel, knew that it was going to be at least bearable all the way.

A great motor yacht named the *Scheherezade* now slid past the marriage bed. The song its engines sang was a very low organ note. All her lights were on.

Two beautiful people, a young man and a young woman in evening clothes, were at the rail in the stern, loving each other and their dreams and the wake. They were honeymooning, too. They were Lance Rumfoord, of Newport, Rhode Island, and his bride, the former Cynthia Landry, who had been a childhood sweetheart of John F. Kennedy in Hyannis Port, Massachusetts.

There was a slight coincidence here. Billy Pilgrim would later share a hospital room with Rumfoord's uncle, Professor Bertram Copeland Rumfoord of Harvard, official Historian of the United States Air Force.

When the beautiful people were past, Valencia questioned her funny-looking husband about war. It was a simple-minded thing for a female Earthling to do, to associate sex and glamor with war.

"Do you ever think about the war?" she said, laying a hand on his thigh.

"Sometimes," said Billy Pilgrim.

"I look at you sometimes," said Valencia, "and I get a funny feeling that you're just full of secrets."

"I'm not," said Billy. This was a lie, of course. He hadn't told anybody about all the time-traveling he'd done, about Tralfamadore and so on.

"You must have secrets about the war. Or, not secrets, I guess, but things you don't want to talk about."

"No."

"I'm *proud* you were a soldier. Do you know that?"

"Good."

"Was it awful?"

"Sometimes." A crazy thought now occurred to Billy. The truth of it startled him. It would make a good epitaph for Billy Pilgrim—and for me, too.

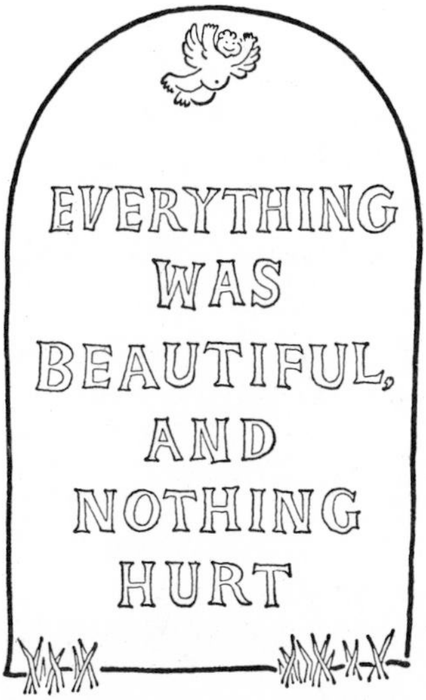

"Would you talk about the war now, if I *wanted* you to?" said Valencia. In a tiny cavity in her great body she was assembling the materials for a Green Beret.

"It would sound like a dream," said Billy. "Other people's dreams aren't very interesting, usually."

"I heard you tell Father one time about a German firing squad." She was referring to the execution of poor old Edgar Derby.

"Um."

"You had to bury him?"

"Yes."

"Did he see you with your shovels before he was shot?"

"Yes."

"Did he *say* anything?"

"No."

"Was he *scared?*"

"They had him doped up. He was sort of glassy-eyed."

"And they pinned a target to him?"

"A piece of paper," said Billy. He got out of bed, said, "Excuse me," went into the darkness of the bathroom to take a leak. He groped for the light, realized as he felt the rough walls that he had traveled back to 1944, to the prison hospital again.

The candle in the hospital had gone out. Poor old Edgar Derby had fallen asleep on the cot next to Billy's. Billy was out of bed, groping along a wall, trying to find a way out because he had to take a leak so badly.

He suddenly found a door, which opened, let him reel out into the prison night. Billy was loony with time-travel and morphine. He delivered himself to a barbed-wire fence which snagged him in a dozen places. Billy tried to back away from it, but the barbs wouldn't let go. So Billy did a silly little dance with the fence, taking a step this way, then that way, then returning to the beginning again.

A Russian, himself out in the night to take a leak, saw Billy dancing—from the other side of the fence. He came over to the curious scarecrow, tried to talk with it gently, asked it what country it was from. The scarecrow paid no attention, went on dancing. So the Russian undid the snags one by one, and the scarecrow danced off into the night again without a word of thanks.

The Russian waved to him, and called after him in Russian, "Good-bye."

Billy took his pecker out, there in the prison night, and peed and peed on the ground. Then he put it away again, more or less, and contemplated a new problem: Where had he come from, and where should he go now?

Somewhere in the night there were cries of grief. With nothing better to do, Billy shuffled in their direction. He wondered what tragedy so many had found to lament out of doors.

Billy was approaching, without knowing it, the back of the latrine. It consisted of a one-rail fence with twelve buckets underneath it. The fence was sheltered on three sides by a screen of scrap lumber and flattened tin cans. The open side faced the black tarpaper wall of the shed where the feast had taken place.

Billy moved along the screen and reached a point where he could see a message freshly painted on the tarpaper wall. The words were written with the same pink paint which had brightened the set for *Cinderella*. Billy's perceptions were so unreliable that he saw the words as hanging in air, painted on a transparent curtain, perhaps. And there were lovely silver dots on the curtain, too. These were really nailheads holding the tarpaper to the shed. Billy could not imagine how the curtain was supported in nothingness, and he supposed that the magic curtain and the theatrical grief were part of some religious ceremony he knew nothing about.

Here is what the message said:

Billy looked inside the latrine. The wailing was coming from in there. The place was crammed with Americans who had taken their pants down. The welcome feast had made them as sick as volcanoes. The buckets were full or had been kicked over.

An American near Billy wailed that he had excreted everything but his brains. Moments later he said, "There they go, there they go." He meant his brains.

That was I. That was me. That was the author of this book.

Billy reeled away from his vision of Hell. He passed three Englishmen who were watching the excrement festival from a distance. They were catatonic with disgust.

"Button your pants!" said one as Billy went by.

So Billy buttoned his pants. He came to the door of the little hospital by accident. He went through the door, and found himself honeymooning again, going from the bathroom back to bed with his bride on Cape Ann.

"I missed you," said Valencia.

"I missed *you*," said Billy Pilgrim.

Billy and Valencia went to sleep nestled like spoons, and Billy traveled in time back to the train ride he had taken in 1944—from maneuvers in South Carolina to his father's funeral in Ilium. He hadn't seen Europe or combat yet. This was still in the days of steam locomotives.

Billy had to change trains a lot. All the trains were slow. The coaches stunk of coal smoke and rationed tobacco and rationed booze and the farts of people eating wartime food. The upholstery of the iron seats was bristly, and Billy couldn't sleep much. He got to sleep soundly when he was only three hours from Ilium, with his legs splayed toward the entrance of the busy dining car.

The porter woke him up when the train reached Ilium. Billy staggered off with his duffel bag, and then he stood on the station platform next to the porter, trying to wake up.

"Have a good nap, did you?" said the porter.

"Yes," said Billy.

"Man," said the porter, "you sure had a hard-on."

At three in the morning on Billy's morphine night in prison, a new patient was carried into the hospital by two lusty Englishmen. He was tiny. He was Paul Lazzaro, the polka-dotted car thief from Cicero, Illinois. He had been caught stealing cigarettes from under the pillow of an Englishman. The Englishman, half asleep, had broken Lazzaro's right arm and knocked him unconscious.

The Englishman who had done this was helping to carry Lazzaro in now. He had fiery red hair and no eyebrows. He had been Cinderella's Blue Fairy Godmother in the play. Now he supported his half of Lazzaro with one hand while he closed the door behind himself with the other. "Doesn't weigh as much as a chicken," he said.

The Englishman with Lazzaro's feet was the colonel who had given Billy his knock-out shot.

The Blue Fairy Godmother was embarrassed, and angry, too. "If I'd known I was fighting a chicken," he said, "I wouldn't have fought so *hard*."

"Um."

The Blue Fairy Godmother spoke frankly about how disgusting all the Americans were. "Weak, smelly, self-pitying—a pack of sniveling, dirty, thieving bastards," he said. "They're worse than the bleeding Russians."

"*Do* seem a scruffy lot," the colonel agreed.

A German major came in now. He considered the Englishmen as close friends. He visited them nearly every day, played games with them, lectured to them on German history, played their piano, gave them lessons in conversational German. He told them often that, if it weren't for their civilized company, he would go mad. His English was splendid.

He was apologetic about the Englishmen's having to put up with the American enlisted men. He promised them that they would not be inconvenienced for more than a day or two, that the Americans would soon be shipped to Dresden as contract labor. He had a monograph with him, published by the German Association of Prison Officials. It was a report on the behavior in Germany of American enlisted men as prisoners of war. It was written by a former American who had risen high in the German Ministry of Propaganda. His name was Howard W. Campbell, Jr.

He would later hang himself while awaiting trial as a war criminal.

So it goes.

While the British colonel set Lazzaro's broken arm and mixed plaster for the cast, the German major translated out loud passages from Howard W. Campbell, Jr.'s monograph. Campbell had been a fairly well-known playwright at one time. His opening line was this one:

America is the wealthiest nation on Earth, but its people are mainly poor, and poor Americans are urged to hate themselves. To quote the American humorist Kin Hubbard, "It ain't no disgrace to be poor, but it might as well be." It is in fact a crime for an American to be poor, even though America is a nation of poor. Every other nation has folk traditions of men who were poor but extremely wise and virtuous, and therefore more estimable than anyone with power and gold. No such tales are told by the American poor. They mock themselves and glorify their betters. The meanest eating or drinking establishment, owned by a man who is himself poor, is very likely to have a sign on its wall asking this cruel question: "If you're so smart, why ain't you rich?" There will also be an American flag no larger than a child's hand —glued to a lollipop stick and flying from the cash register.

The author of the monograph, a native of Schenectady, New York, was said by some to have had the highest I.Q. of all the war criminals who were made to face a death by hanging. So it goes.

Americans, like human beings everywhere, believe many things that are obviously untrue, the monograph went on. *Their most destructive untruth is that it is very easy for any American to make money. They will not acknowledge how in fact hard money is to come by, and, therefore, those who have no money blame and blame and blame themselves. This inward blame has been a treasure for the rich and powerful, who have had to do less for their poor, publicly and privately, than any other ruling class since, say, Napoleonic times.*

Many novelties have come from America. The most startling of these, a thing without precedent, is a mass of undignified poor.

They do not love one another because they do not love themselves. Once this is understood, the disagreeable behavior of American enlisted men in German prisons ceases to be a mystery.

Howard W. Campbell, Jr., now discussed the uniform of the American enlisted in World War Two: *Every other army in history, prosperous or not, has attempted to clothe even its lowliest soldiers so as to make them impressive to themselves and others as stylish experts in drinking and copulation and looting and sudden death. The American Army, however, sends its enlisted men out to fight and die in a modified business suit quite evidently made for another man, a sterilized but unpressed gift from a nose-holding charity which passes out clothing to drunks in the slums.*

When a dashingly-clad officer addresses such a frumpishly dressed bum, he scolds him, as an officer in any army must. But the officer's contempt is not, as in other armies, avuncular theatricality. It is a genuine expression of hatred for the poor, who have no one to blame for their misery but themselves.

A prison administrator dealing with captured American enlisted men for the first time should be warned: Expect no brotherly love, even between brothers. There will be no cohesion between the individuals. Each will be a sulky child who often wishes he were dead.

Campbell told what the German experience with captured American enlisted men had been. They were known everywhere to be the most self-pitying, least fraternal, and dirtiest of all prisoners of war, said Campbell. They were incapable of concerted action on their own behalf. They despised any leader from among their own number, refused to follow or even listen to him, on the grounds that he was no better than they were, that he should stop putting on airs.

And so on. Billy Pilgrim went to sleep, woke up as a widower in his empty home in Ilium. His daughter Barbara was reproaching him for writing ridiculous letters to the newspapers.

"Did you hear what I said?" Barbara inquired. It was 1968 again.

"Of course." He had been dozing.

"If you're going to act like a child, maybe we'll just have to *treat* you like a child."

"That isn't what happens next," said Billy.

"We'll *see* what happens next." Big Barbara now embraced herself. "It's awfully cold in here. Is the heat on?"

"The *heat?*"

"The furnace—the thing in the basement, the thing that makes hot air that comes out of these registers. I don't think it's working."

"Maybe not."

"Aren't you cold?"

"I hadn't noticed."

"Oh, my God, you *are* a child. If we leave you alone here, you'll freeze to death, you'll starve to death." And so on. It was very exciting for her, taking his dignity away in the name of love.

Barbara called the oil-burner man, and she made Billy go to bed, made him promise to stay under the electric blanket until the heat came on. She set the control of the blanket at the highest notch, which soon made Billy's bed hot enough to bake bread in.

When Barbara left, slamming the door behind her, Billy traveled in time to the zoo on Tralfamadore again. A mate had just been brought to him from Earth. She was Montana Wildhack, a motion picture star.

Montana was under heavy sedation. Tralfamadorians wearing gas masks brought her in, put her on Billy's yellow lounge chair; withdrew through his airlock. The vast crowd outside was delighted. All attendance records for the zoo were broken. Everybody on the planet wanted to see the Earthlings mate.

Montana was naked, and so was Billy, of course. He had a tremendous wang, incidentally. You never know who'll get one.

Now she fluttered her eyelids. Her lashes were like buggy whips. "Where *am* I?" she said.

"Everything is all right," said Billy gently. "Please don't be afraid."

Montana had been unconscious during her trip from Earth. The Tralfamadorians hadn't talked to her, hadn't shown themselves to her. The last thing she remembered was sunning herself by a swimming pool in Palm Springs, California. Montana was only twenty years old. Around her neck was a silver chain with a heart-shaped locket hanging from it—between her breasts.

Now she turned her head to see the myriads of Tralfamadorians outside the dome. They were applauding her by opening and closing their little green hands quickly.

Montana screamed and screamed.

All the little green hands closed tight, because Montana's terror was so unpleasant to see. The head zoo keeper ordered a crane operator, who was standing by, to drop a navy blue canopy over the dome, thus simulating Earthling night inside. Real night came to the zoo for only one Earthling hour of every sixty-two.

Billy switched on a floor lamp. The light from the single source threw the baroque detailing of Montana's body into sharp relief. Billy was reminded of fantastic architecture in Dresden, before it was bombed.

In time, Montana came to love and trust Billy Pilgrim. He did not touch her until she made it clear that she wanted him to. After she had been on Tralfamadore for what would have been an Earthling week, she asked him shyly if he wouldn't sleep with her. Which he did. It was heavenly.

And Billy traveled in time from that delightful bed to a bed in 1968. It was his bed in Ilium, and the electric blanket was turned up high. He was drenched in sweat, remembered groggily that his daughter had put him to bed, had told him to stay there until the oil burner was repaired.

Somebody was knocking on his bedroom door.

"Yes?" said Billy.

"Oil-burner man."

"Yes?"

"It's running good now. Heat's coming up."

"Good."

"Mouse ate through a wire from the thermostat."

"I'll be darned."

Billy sniffed. His hot bed smelled like a mushroom cellar. He had had a wet dream about Montana Wildhack.

On the morning after that wet dream, Billy decided to go back to work in his office in the shopping plaza. Business was booming as usual. His assistants were keeping up with it nicely. They were startled to see him. They had been told by his daughter that he might never practice again.

But Billy went into his examining room briskly, asked that the first patient be sent in. So they sent him one—a twelve-year-old boy who was accompanied by his widowed mother. They were strangers, new in town. Billy asked them a little about themselves, learned that the boy's father had been killed in Vietnam—in the famous five-day battle for Hill 875 near Dakto. So it goes.

While he examined the boy's eyes, Billy told him matter-of-factly about his adventures on Tralfamadore, assured the fatherless boy that his father was very much alive still in moments the boy would see again and again.

"Isn't that comforting?" Billy asked.

And somewhere in there, the boy's mother went out and told the receptionist that Billy was evidently going crazy. Billy was taken home. His daughter asked him again, "Father, Father, Father—what *are* we going to *do* with you?"

6

Listen:

Billy Pilgrim says he went to Dresden, Germany, on the day after his morphine night in the British compound in the center of the extermination camp for Russian prisoners of war. Billy woke up at dawn on that day in January. There were no windows in the little hospital, and the ghostly candles had gone out. So the only light came from pin-prick holes in the walls, and from a sketchy rectangle that outlined the imperfectly fitted door. Little Paul Lazzaro, with a broken arm, snored on one bed. Edgar Derby, the high school teacher who would eventually be shot, snored on another.

Billy sat up in bed. He had no idea what year it was or what planet he was on. Whatever the planet's name was, it was cold.

But it wasn't the cold that had awakened Billy. It was animal magnetism which was making him shiver and itch. It gave him profound aches in his musculature, as though he had been exercising hard.

The animal magnetism was coming from behind him. If Billy had had to guess as to the source, he would have said that there was a vampire bat hanging upside down on the wall behind him.

Billy moved down toward the foot of his cot before turning to look at whatever it was. He didn't want the animal to drop into his face and maybe claw his eyes out or bite off his big nose. Then he turned. The source of the magnetism really did resemble a bat. It was Billy's impresario's coat with the fur collar. It was hanging from a nail.

Billy now backed toward it again, looking at it over his shoulder, feeling the magnetism increase. Then he faced it, kneeling on his cot, dared to touch it here and there. He was seeking the exact source of the radiations.

He found two small sources, two lumps an inch apart and hidden in the lining. One was shaped like a pea. The other was shaped like a tiny horseshoe. Billy received a message carried by the radiations. He was told not to find out what the lumps were. He was advised to be content with knowing that they could work miracles for him, provided he did not insist on learning their nature. That was all right with Billy Pilgrim. He was grateful. He was glad.

Billy dozed, awakened in the prison hospital again. The sun was high. Outside were Golgotha sounds of strong men digging holes for upright timbers in hard, hard ground. Englishmen were building themselves a new latrine. They had abandoned their old latrine to the Americans—and their theater, the place where the feast had been held, too.

Six Englishmen staggered through a hospital with a pool table on which several mattresses were piled. They were transferring it to living quarters attached to the hospital. They were followed by an Englishman dragging his mattress and carrying a dartboard.

The man with the dartboard was the Blue Fairy Godmother who had injured little Paul Lazzaro. He stopped by Lazzaro's bed, asked Lazzaro how he was.

Lazzaro told him he was going to have him killed after the war.

"Oh?"

"You made a big mistake," said Lazzaro. "Anybody touches me, he better *kill* me, or I'm gonna have *him* killed."

The Blue Fairy Godmother knew something about killing. He gave Lazzaro a careful smile. "There is still time for *me* to kill *you*," he said, "if you really persuade me that it's the sensible thing to do."

"Why don't you go fuck yourself?"

"Don't think I haven't tried," the Blue Fairy Godmother answered.

The Blue Fairy Godmother left, amused and patronizing. When he was gone, Lazzaro promised Billy and poor old Edgar Derby that he was going to have revenge, and that revenge was sweet.

"It's the sweetest thing there is," said Lazzaro. "People fuck with me," he said, "and Jesus Christ are they ever fucking sorry. I laugh like hell. I don't care if it's a guy or a dame. If the President of the United States fucked around with me, I'd fix him good. You should have seen what I did to a dog one time."

"A dog?" said Billy.

"Son of a bitch bit me. So I got me some steak, and I got me the spring out of a clock. I cut that spring up in little pieces. I put points on the ends of the pieces. They were sharp as razor blades. I stuck 'em into the steak—way inside. And I went past where they had the dog tied up. He wanted to bite me again. I said to him, 'Come on, doggie—let's be friends. Let's not be enemies any more. I'm not mad.' He believed me."

"He *did*?"

"I threw him the steak. He swallowed it down in one big gulp. I waited around for ten minutes." Now Lazzaro's eyes twinkled. "Blood started coming out of his mouth. He started crying, and he rolled on the ground, as though the knives were on the outside of him instead of on the inside of him. Then he tried to bite out his own insides. I laughed, and I said to him, 'You got the right idea now. Tear your own guts out, boy. That's *me* in there with all those knives.'" So it goes.

"Anybody ever asks you what the sweetest thing in life is—" said Lazzaro, "it's revenge."

When Dresden was destroyed later on, incidentally, Lazzaro did not exult. He didn't have anything against the Germans, he said. Also, he said he liked to take his enemies one at a time. He was proud of never having hurt an innocent bystander. "Nobody ever got it from Lazzaro," he said, "who didn't have it coming."

Poor old Edgar Derby, the high school teacher, got into the conversation now. He asked Lazzaro if he planned to feed the Blue Fairy Godmother clock springs and steak.

"Shit," said Lazzaro.

"He's a pretty big man," said Derby, who, of course, was a pretty big man himself.

"Size don't mean a thing."

"You're going to *shoot* him?"

"I'm gonna *have* him shot," said Lazzaro. "He'll get home after the war. He'll be a big hero. The dames'll be climbing all over him. He'll settle down. A couple of years'll go by. And then one day there'll be a knock on his door. He'll answer the door, and there'll be a stranger out there. The stranger'll ask him if he's so-and-so. When he says he is, the stranger'll say, 'Paul Lazzaro sent me.' And he'll pull out a gun and shoot his pecker off. The stranger'll let him think a couple of seconds about who Paul Lazzaro is and what life's gonna be like without a pecker. Then he'll shoot him once in the guts and walk away." So it goes.

Lazzaro said that he could have anybody in the world killed for a thousand dollars plus traveling expenses. He had a list in his head, he said.

Derby asked him who all was on the list, and Lazzaro said, "Just make fucking sure *you* don't get on it. Just don't cross me, that's all." There was a silence, and then he added, "And don't cross my friends."

"You have *friends?*" Derby wanted to know.

"In the *war?*" said Lazzaro. "Yeah—I had a friend in the war. He's dead." So it goes.

"That's too bad."

Lazzaro's eyes were twinkling again. "Yeah. He was my buddy on the boxcar. His name was Roland Weary. He died in my arms." Now he pointed to Billy with his one mobile hand. "He died on account of this silly cocksucker here. So I promised him I'd have this silly cocksucker shot after the war."

Lazzaro erased with his hand anything Billy Pilgrim might be about to say. "Just forget about it, kid," he said. "Enjoy life while you can. Nothing's gonna happen for maybe five, ten, fifteen, twenty years. But lemme give you a piece of advice: Whenever the doorbell rings, have somebody else answer the door."

Billy Pilgrim says now that this really is the way he *is* going to die, too. As a time-traveler, he has seen his own death many times, has described it to a tape recorder. The tape is locked up with his will and some other valuables in his safe-deposit box at the Ilium Merchants National Bank and Trust, he says.

I, Billy Pilgrim, the tape begins, *will die, have died, and always will die on February thirteenth, 1976.*

At the time of his death, he says, he is in Chicago to address a large crowd on the subject of flying saucers and the true nature of time. His home is still in Ilium. He has had to cross three international boundaries in order to reach Chicago. The United States of America has been Balkanized, has been divided into twenty petty nations so that it will never again be a threat to world peace. Chicago has been hydrogen-bombed by angry Chinamen. So it goes. It is all brand new.

Billy is speaking before a capacity audience in a baseball park, which is covered by a geodesic dome. The flag of the country is behind him. It is a Hereford bull on a field of green. Billy predicts his own death within an hour. He laughs about it, invites the crowd to laugh with him. "It is high time I was dead," he says. "Many years ago," he said, "a certain man promised to have me killed. He is an old man now, living not far from here. He has read all the publicity associated with my appearance in your fair city. He is insane. Tonight he will keep his promise."

There are protests from the crowd.

Billy Pilgrim rebukes them. "If you protest, if you think that death is a terrible thing, then you have not understood a word

I've said." Now he closes his speech as he closes every speech—with these words: "Farewell, hello, farewell, hello."

There are police around him as he leaves the stage. They are there to protect him from the crush of popularity. No threats on his life have been made since 1945. The police offer to stay with him. They are floridly willing to stand in a circle around him all night, with their zap guns drawn.

"No, no," says Billy serenely. "It is time for you to go home to your wives and children, and it is time for me to be dead for a little while—and then live again." At that moment, Billy's high forehead is in the cross hairs of a high-powered laser gun. It is aimed at him from the darkened press box. In the next moment, Billy Pilgrim is dead. So it goes.

So Billy experiences death for a while. It is simply violet light and a hum. There isn't anybody else there. Not even Billy Pilgrim is there.

Then he swings back into life again, all the way back to an hour after his life was threatened by Lazzaro—in 1945. He has been told to get out of his hospital bed and dress, that he is well. He and Lazzaro and poor old Edgar Derby are to join their fellows in the theater. There they will choose a leader for themselves by secret ballot in a free election.

Billy and Lazzaro and poor old Edgar Derby crossed the prison yard to the theater now. Billy was carrying his little coat as though it were a lady's muff. It was wrapped around and around his hands. He was the central clown in an unconscious travesty of that famous oil painting, "The Spirit of '76."

Edgar Derby was writing letters home in his head, telling his wife that he was alive and well, that she shouldn't worry, that the war was nearly over, that he would soon be home.

Lazzaro was talking to himself about people he was going to have killed after the war, and rackets he was going to work, and women he was going to make fuck him, whether they wanted to or not. If he had been a dog in a city, a policeman would have shot him and sent his head to a laboratory, to see if he had rabies. So it goes.

As they neared the theater, they came upon an Englishman

who was hacking a groove in the Earth with the heel of his boot. He was marking the boundary between the American and English sections of the compound. Billy and Lazzaro and Derby didn't have to ask what the line meant. It was a familiar symbol from childhood.

The theater was paved with American bodies that nestled like spoons. Most of the Americans were in stupors or asleep. Their guts were fluttering, dry.

"Close the fucking door," somebody said to Billy. "Were you born in a barn?"

Billy closed it, took a hand from his muff, touched a stove. It was as cold as ice. The stage was still set for *Cinderella*. Azure curtains hung from arches which were shocking pink. There were golden thrones and the dummy clock, whose hands were set at midnight. Cinderella's slippers, which were airman's boots painted silver, were capsized side by side under a golden throne.

Billy and poor old Edgar Derby and Lazzaro had been in the hospital when the British passed out blankets and mattresses, so they had none. They had to improvise. The only space open to them was up on the stage, and they went up there, pulled the azure curtains down, made nests.

Billy, curled in his azure nest, found himself staring at Cinderella's silver boots under a throne. And then he remembered that his shoes were ruined, that he *needed* boots. He hated to get out of his nest, but he forced himself to do it. He crawled to the boots on all fours, sat, tried them on.

The boots fit perfectly. Billy Pilgrim was Cinderella, and Cinderella was Billy Pilgrim.

Somewhere in there was a lecture on personal hygiene by the head Englishman, and then a free election. At least half the Americans went on snoozing through it all. The Englishman got up on the stage, and he rapped on the arm of a throne with a swagger stick, called, "Lads, lads, lads—can I have your attention, please?" And so on.

What the Englishman said about survival was this: "If you stop taking pride in your appearance, you will very soon die." He said that he had seen several men die in the following way: "They ceased to stand up straight, then ceased to shave or wash, then ceased to get out of bed, then ceased to talk, then died. There is much to be said for it: it is evidently a very easy and painless way to go." So it goes.

The Englishman said that he, when captured, had made and kept the following vows to himself: To brush his teeth twice a day, to shave once a day, to wash his face and hands before every meal and after going to the latrine, to polish his shoes once a day, to exercise for at least half an hour each morning and then move his bowels, and to look into a mirror frequently, frankly evaluating his appearance, particularly with respect to posture.

Billy Pilgrim heard all this while lying in his nest. He looked not at the Englishman's face but his ankles.

"I *envy* you lads," said the Englishman.

Somebody laughed. Billy wondered what the joke was.

"You lads are leaving this afternoon for Dresden—a beautiful city, I'm told. You won't be cooped up like us. You'll be out where the life is, and the food is certain to be more plentiful than here. If I may inject a personal note: It has been five years now since I have seen a tree or flower or woman or child—or a dog or a cat or a place of entertainment, or a human being doing useful work of any kind.

"You needn't worry about bombs, by the way. Dresden is an open city. It is undefended, and contains no war industries or troop concentrations of any importance."

Somewhere in there, old Edgar Derby was elected head American. The Englishman called for nominations from the floor, and there weren't any. So he nominated Derby, praising him for his maturity and long experience in dealing with people. There were no further nominations, so the nominations were closed.

"All in favor?"

Two or three people said, "Aye."

Then poor old Derby made a speech. He thanked the Englishman for his good advice, said he meant to follow it exactly. He said he was sure that all the other Americans would do the same. He said that his primary responsibility now was to make damn well sure that everybody got home safely.

"Go take a flying fuck at a rolling doughnut," murmured Paul Lazzaro in his azure nest. "Go take a flying fuck at the moon."

The temperature climbed startlingly that day. The noontime was balmy. The Germans brought soup and bread in two-wheeled carts which were pulled by Russians. The Englishman sent over real coffee and sugar and marmalade and cigarettes and cigars, and the doors of the theater were left open, so the warmth could get in.

The Americans began to feel much better. They were able to hold their food. And then it was time to go to Dresden. The Americans marched fairly stylishly out of the British compound. Billy Pilgrim again led the parade. He had silver boots now, and a muff, and a piece of azure curtain which he wore like a toga. Billy still had a beard. So did poor old Edgar Derby, who was beside him. Derby was imagining letters to home, his lips working tremulously:

Dear Margaret—We are leaving for Dresden today. Don't worry. It will never be bombed. It is an open city. There was an election at noon, and guess what? And so on.

They came to the prison railroad yard again. They had arrived on only two cars. They would depart far more comfortably on four. They saw the dead hobo again. He was frozen stiff in the weeds beside the track. He was in a fetal position, trying even in death to nestle like a spoon with others. There were no others now. He was nestling with thin air and cinders. Somebody had taken his boots. His bare feet were blue and ivory. It was all right, somehow, his being dead. So it goes.

The trip to Dresden was a lark. It took only two hours. Shriveled little bellies were full. Sunlight and mild air came in through the ventilators. There were plenty of smokes from the Englishmen.

The Americans arrived in Dresden at five in the afternoon. The boxcar doors were opened, and the doorways framed the loveliest city that most of the Americans had ever seen. The skyline was intricate and voluptuous and enchanted and absurd. It looked like a Sunday school picture of Heaven to Billy Pilgrim.

Somebody behind him in the boxcar said, "Oz." That was I. That was me. The only other city I'd ever seen was Indianapolis, Indiana.

Every other big city in Germany had been bombed and burned ferociously. Dresden had not suffered so much as a cracked windowpane. Sirens went off every day, screamed like hell, and people went down into cellars and listened to radios there. The planes were always bound for someplace else—Leipzig, Chemnitz, Plauen, places like that. So it goes.

Steam radiators still whistled cheerily in Dresden. Streetcars clanged. Telephones rang and were answered. Lights went on and off when switches were clicked. There were theaters and restaurants. There was a zoo. The principal enterprises of the city were medicine and food-processing and the making of cigarettes.

People were going home from work now in the late afternoon. They were tired.

Eight Dresdeners crossed the steel spaghetti of the railroad yard. They were wearing new uniforms. They had been sworn into the army the day before. They were boys and men past middle age, and two veterans who had been shot to pieces in Russia. Their assignment was to guard one hundred American prisoners of war, who would work as contract labor. A grandfather and his grandson were in the squad. The grandfather was an architect.

The eight were grim as they approached the boxcars containing their wards. They knew what sick and foolish soldiers they themselves appeared to be. One of them actually had an artificial leg, and carried not only a loaded rifle but a cane. Still—they were expected to earn obedience and respect from tall, cocky, murderous American infantrymen who had just come from all the killing at the front.

And then they saw bearded Billy Pilgrim in his blue toga and silver shoes, with his hands in a muff. He looked at least sixty years old. Next to Billy was little Paul Lazzaro with a broken arm. He was fizzing with rabies. Next to Lazzaro was the poor old high school teacher, Edgar Derby, mournfully pregnant with patriotism and middle age and imaginary wisdom. And so on.

The eight ridiculous Dresdeners ascertained that these hundred ridiculous creatures really *were* American fighting men fresh from the front. They smiled, and then they laughed. Their terror evaporated. There was nothing to be afraid of. Here were more crippled human beings, more fools like themselves. Here was light opera.

So out of the gate of the railroad yard and into the streets of Dresden marched the light opera. Billy Pilgrim was the star. He led the parade. Thousands of people were on the sidewalks, going home from work. They were watery and putty-colored, having eaten mostly potatoes during the past two years. They had expected no blessings beyond the mildness of the day. Suddenly —here was fun.

Billy did not meet many of the eyes that found him so entertaining. He was enchanted by the architecture of the city. Merry amoretti wove garlands above windows. Roguish fauns and naked nymphs peeked down at Billy from festooned cornices. Stone monkeys frisked among scrolls and seashells and bamboo.

Billy, with his memories of the future, knew that the city would be smashed to smithereens and then burned—in about thirty more days. He knew, too, that most of the people watching him would soon be dead. So it goes.

And Billy worked his hands in his muff as he marched. His fingertips, working there in the hot darkness of the muff, wanted to know what the two lumps in the lining of the little impresario's coat were. The fingertips got inside the lining. They palpated the lumps, the pea-shaped thing and the horseshoe-shaped thing. The parade had to halt by a busy corner. The traffic light was red.

There at the corner, in the front rank of pedestrians, was a surgeon who had been operating all day. He was a civilian, but his posture was military. He had served in two world wars. The sight of Billy offended him, especially after he learned from the guards that Billy was an American. It seemed to him that Billy was in abominable taste, supposed that Billy had gone to a lot of silly trouble to costume himself just so.

The surgeon spoke English, and he said to Billy, "I take it you find war a very comical thing."

Billy looked at him vaguely. Billy had lost track momentarily of where he was or how he had gotten there. He had no idea that people thought he was clowning. It was Fate, of course, which had costumed him—Fate, and a feeble will to survive.

"Did you expect us to *laugh*?" the surgeon asked him.

The surgeon was demanding some sort of satisfaction. Billy was mystified. Billy wanted to be friendly, to help, if he could, but his resources were meager. His fingers now held the two objects from the lining of the coat. Billy decided to show the surgeon what they were.

"You thought we would enjoy being *mocked*?" the surgeon said. "And do you feel *proud* to represent America as you do?"

Billy withdrew a hand from his muff, held it under the surgeon's nose. On his palm rested a two-carat diamond and a partial denture. The denture was an obscene little artifact—silver and pearl and tangerine. Billy smiled.

The parade pranced, staggered and reeled to the gate of the Dresden slaughterhouse, and then it went inside. The slaughterhouse wasn't a busy place any more. Almost all the hooved animals in Germany had been killed and eaten and excreted by human beings, mostly soldiers. So it goes.

The Americans were taken to the fifth building inside the gate. It was a one-story cement-block cube with sliding doors in front and back. It had been built as a shelter for pigs about to be butchered. Now it was going to serve as a home away from home for one hundred American prisoners of war. There were bunks in there, and two potbellied stoves and a water tap. Behind it was a latrine, which was a one-rail fence with buckets under it.

There was a big number over the door of the building. The number was *five*. Before the Americans could go inside, their only English-speaking guard told them to memorize their simple address, in case they got lost in the big city. Their address was this: "Schlachthof-fünf." *Schlachthof* meant *slaughterhouse*. *Fünf* was good old *five*.

7

Billy Pilgrim got onto a chartered airplane in Ilium twenty-five years after that. He knew it was going to crash, but he didn't want to make a fool of himself by saying so. It was supposed to carry Billy and twenty-eight other optometrists to a convention in Montreal.

His wife, Valencia, was outside, and his father-in-law, Lionel Merble, was strapped to the seat beside him.

Lionel Merble was a machine. Tralfamadorians, of course, say that every creature and plant in the Universe is a machine. It amuses them that so many Earthlings are offended by the idea of being machines.

Outside the plane, the machine named Valencia Merble Pilgrim was eating a Peter Paul Mound Bar and waving bye-bye.

The plane took off without incident. The moment was structured that way. There was a barbershop quartet on board. They were optometrists, too. They called themselves "The Febs," which was an acronym for "Four-eyed Bastards."

When the plane was safely aloft, the machine that was Billy's father-in-law asked the quartet to sing his favorite song. They knew what song he meant, and they sang it, and it went like this:

In my prison cell I sit,
With my britches full of shit,
And my balls are bouncing gently on the floor.
And I see the bloody snag
When she bit me in the bag.
Oh, I'll never fuck a Polack any more.

Billy's father-in-law laughed and laughed at that, and he begged the quartet to sing the other Polish song he liked so much. So they sang a song from the Pennsylvania coal mines that began:

Me and Mike, ve vork in mine.
Holy shit, ve have good time.
Vunce a veek ve get our pay.
Holy shit, no vork next day.

Speaking of people from Poland: Billy Pilgrim accidentally saw a Pole hanged in public, about three days after Billy got to Dresden. Billy just happened to be walking to work with some others shortly after sunrise, and they came to a gallows and a small crowd in front of a soccer stadium. The Pole was a farm laborer who was being hanged for having had sexual intercourse with a German woman. So it goes.

Billy, knowing the plane was going to crash pretty soon, closed his eyes, traveled in time back to 1944. He was back in the forest in Luxembourg again—with the Three Musketeers. Roland Weary was shaking him, bonking his head against a tree. "You guys go on without me," said Billy Pilgrim.

The barbershop quartet on the airplane was singing "Wait Till the Sun Shines, Nelly," when the plane smacked into the top of Sugarbush Mountain in Vermont. Everybody was killed but Billy and the copilot. So it goes.

The people who first got to the crash scene were young Austrian ski instructors from the famous ski resort below. They spoke to each other in German as they went from body to body. They wore black wind masks with two holes for their eyes and a red topknot. They looked like golliwogs, like white people pretending to be black for the laughs they could get.

Billy had a fractured skull, but he was still conscious. He didn't know where he was. His lips were working, and one of the golliwogs put his ear close to them to hear what might be his dying words.

Billy thought the golliwog had something to do with World War Two, and he whispered to him his address: "Schlachthof-fünf."

Billy was brought down Sugarbush Mountain on a toboggan. The golliwogs controlled it with ropes and yodeled melodiously for right-of-way. Near the bottom, the trail swooped around the pylons of a chair lift. Billy looked up at all the young people in bright elastic clothing and enormous boots and goggles, bombed out of their skulls with snow, swinging through the sky in yellow chairs. He supposed that they were part of an amazing new phase of World War Two. It was all right with him. Everything was pretty much all right with Billy.

He was taken to a small private hospital. A famous brain surgeon came up from Boston and operated on him for three hours. Billy was unconscious for two days after that, and he dreamed millions of things, some of them true. The true things were time-travel.

One of the true things was his first evening in the slaughterhouse. He and poor old Edgar Derby were pushing an empty two-wheeled cart down a dirt lane between empty pens for animals. They were going to a communal kitchen for supper for all. They were guarded by a sixteen-year-old German named Werner Gluck. The axles of the cart were greased with the fat of dead animals. So it goes.

The sun had just gone down, and its afterglow was back-lighting the city, which formed low cliffs around the bucolic void to the idle stockyards. The city was blacked out because bombers might come, so Billy didn't get to see Dresden do one of the most cheerful things a city is capable of doing when the sun goes down, which is to wink its lights on one by one.

There was a broad river to reflect those lights, which would have made their nighttime winkings very pretty indeed. It was the Elbe.

Werner Gluck, the young guard, was a Dresden boy. He had never been in the slaughterhouse before, so he wasn't sure where the kitchen was. He was tall and weak like Billy, might have been a younger brother of his. They were, in fact, distant cousins, something they never found out. Gluck was armed with an incredibly heavy musket, a single-shot museum piece with an octagonal barrel and a smooth bore. He had fixed his bayonet. It was like a long knitting needle. It had no bloodgutters.

Gluck led the way to a building that he thought might contain the kitchen, and he opened the sliding door in its side. There wasn't a kitchen in there, though. There was a dressing room adjacent to a communal shower, and there was a lot of steam. In the steam were about thirty teen-age girls with no clothes on.

They were German refugees from Breslau, which had been tremendously bombed. They had just arrived in Dresden, too. Dresden was jammed with refugees.

There those girls were with all their private parts bare, for anybody to see. And there in the doorway were Gluck and Derby and Pilgrim—the childish soldier and the poor old high school teacher and the clown in his toga and silver shoes—staring. The girls screamed. They covered themselves with their hands and turned their backs and so on, and made themselves utterly beautiful.

Werner Gluck, who had never seen a naked woman before, closed the door. Billy had never seen one, either. It was nothing new to Derby.

When the three fools found the communal kitchen, whose main job was to make lunch for workers in the slaughterhouse, everybody had gone home but one woman who had been waiting for them impatiently. She was a war widow. So it goes. She had her hat and coat on. She wanted to go home, too, even though there wasn't anybody there. Her white gloves were laid out side by side on the zinc counter top.

She had two big cans of soup for the Americans. It was simmering over low fires on the gas range. She had stacks of loaves of black bread, too.

She asked Gluck if he wasn't awfully young to be in the army. He admitted that he was.

She asked Edgar Derby if he wasn't awfully old to be in the army. He said he was.

She asked Billy Pilgrim what he was supposed to be. Billy said he didn't know. He was just trying to keep warm.

"All the real soldiers are dead," she said. It was true. So it goes.

Another true thing that Billy saw while he was unconscious in Vermont was the work that he and the others had to do in Dresden during the month before the city was destroyed. They washed windows and swept floors and cleaned lavatories and put jars into boxes and sealed cardboard boxes in a factory that made malt syrup. The syrup was enriched with vitamins and minerals.

The syrup was for pregnant women.

The syrup tasted like thin honey laced with hickory smoke, and everybody who worked in the factory secretly spooned it all day long. They weren't pregnant, but they needed vitamins and minerals, too. Billy didn't spoon syrup on his first day at work, but lots of other Americans did.

Billy spooned it on his second day. There were spoons hidden all over the factory, on rafters, in drawers, behind radiators, and so on. They had been hidden in haste by persons who had been spooning syrup, who had heard somebody else coming. Spooning was a crime.

On his second day, Billy was cleaning behind a radiator, and he found a spoon. To his back was a vat of syrup that was cooling. The only other person who could see Billy and his spoon was poor old Edgar Derby, who was washing a window outside. The spoon was a tablespoon. Billy thrust it into the vat, turned it around and around, making a gooey lollipop. He thrust it into his mouth.

A moment went by, and then every cell in Billy's body shook him with ravenous gratitude and applause.

There were diffident raps on the factory window. Derby was out there, having seen all. He wanted some syrup, too.

So Billy made a lollipop for him. He opened the window. He stuck the lollipop into poor old Derby's gaping mouth. A moment passed, and then Derby burst into tears. Billy closed the window and hid the sticky spoon. Somebody was coming.

8

The Americans in the slaughterhouse had a very interesting visitor two days before Dresden was destroyed. He was Howard W. Campbell, Jr., an American who had become a Nazi. Campbell was the one who had written the monograph about the shabby behavior of American prisoners of war. He wasn't doing more research about prisoners now. He had come to the slaughterhouse to recruit men for a German military unit called "The Free American Corps." Campbell was the inventor and commander of the unit, which was supposed to fight only on the Russian front.

Campbell was an ordinary-looking man, but he was extravagantly costumed in a uniform of his own design. He wore a white ten-gallon hat and black cowboy boots decorated with swastikas and stars. He was sheathed in a blue body stocking which had yellow stripes running from his armpits to his ankles. His shoulder patch was a silhouette of Abraham Lincoln's profile on a field of pale green. He had a broad armband which was red, with a blue swastika in a circle of white.

He was explaining this armband now in the cement-block hog barn.

Billy Pilgrim had a boiling case of heartburn, since he had been spooning malt syrup all day long at work. The heartburn brought tears to his eyes, so that his image of Campbell was distorted by jiggling lenses of salt water.

"Blue is for the American sky," Campbell was saying. "White is for the race that pioneered the continent, drained the swamps and cleared the forests and built the roads and bridges. Red is for the blood of American patriots which was shed so gladly in years gone by."

Campbell's audience was sleepy. It had worked hard at the syrup factory, and then it had marched a long way home in the cold. It was skinny and hollow-eyed. Its skins were beginning to blossom with small sores. So were its mouths and throats and intestines. The malt syrup it spooned at the factory contained only a few of the vitamins and minerals every Earthling needs.

Campbell offered the Americans food now, steaks and mashed potatoes and gravy and mince pie, if they would join the Free American Corps. "Once the Russians are defeated," he went on, "you will be repatriated through Switzerland."

There was no response.

"You're going to have to fight the Communists sooner or later," said Campbell. "Why not get it over with now?"

And then it developed that Campbell was not going to go unanswered after all. Poor old Derby, the doomed high school teacher, lumbered to his feet for what was probably the finest moment in his life. There are almost no characters in this story, and almost no dramatic confrontations, because most of the people in it are so sick and so much the listless playthings of enormous forces. One of the main effects of war, after all, is that people are discouraged from being characters. But old Derby was a character now.

His stance was that of a punch-drunk fighter. His head was down. His fists were out front, waiting for information and battle plan. Derby raised his head, called Campbell a snake. He corrected that. He said that snakes couldn't help being snakes, and that Campbell, who *could* help being what he was, was something much lower than a snake or a rat—or even a blood-filled tick.

Campbell smiled.

Derby spoke movingly of the American form of government, with freedom and justice and opportunities and fair play for all. He said there wasn't a man there who wouldn't gladly die for those ideals.

He spoke of the brotherhood between the American and the Russian people, and how those two nations were going to crush the disease of Nazism, which wanted to infect the whole world.

The air-raid sirens of Dresden howled mournfully.

The Americans and their guards and Campbell took shelter in an echoing meat locker which was hollowed in living rock under the slaughterhouse. There was an iron staircase with iron doors at the top and bottom.

Down in the locker were a few cattle and sheep and pigs and horses hanging from iron hooks. So it goes. The locker had empty hooks for thousands more. It was naturally cool. There was no refrigeration. There was candlelight. The locker was whitewashed and smelled of carbolic acid. There were benches along a wall. The Americans went to these, brushing away flakes of whitewash before they sat down.

Howard W. Campbell, Jr., remained standing, like the guards. He talked to the guards in excellent German. He had written many popular German plays and poems in his time, and had married a famous German actress named Resi North. She was dead now, had been killed while entertaining troops in the Crimea. So it goes.

Nothing happened that night. It was the next night that about one hundred and thirty thousand people in Dresden would die.

So it goes. Billy dozed in the meat locker. He found himself engaged again, word for word, gesture for gesture, in the argument with his daughter with which this tale began.

"Father," she said, "What are we going to *do* with you?" And so on. "You know who I could just kill?" she asked.

"*Who* could you kill?" said Billy.

"That Kilgore Trout."

Kilgore Trout was and is a science-fiction writer, of course. Billy has not only read dozens of books by Trout—he has also become Trout's friend, to the extent that anyone can become a friend of Trout, who is a bitter man.

Trout lives in a rented basement in Ilium, about two miles from Billy's nice white home. He himself has no idea how many novels he has written—possibly seventy-five of the things. Not one of them has made money. So Trout keeps body and soul together as a circulation man for the *Ilium Gazette*, manages newspaper delivery boys, bullies and flatters and cheats little kids.

Billy met him for the first time in 1964. Billy drove his Cadillac down a back alley in Ilium, and he found his way blocked by dozens of boys and their bicycles. A meeting was in progress. The boys were harangued by a man in a full beard. He was cowardly and dangerous, and obviously very good at his job. Trout was sixty-two years old back then. He was telling the kids to get off their dead butts and get their daily customers to subscribe to the fucking Sunday edition, too. He said that whoever sold the most Sunday subscriptions during the next two months would get a free trip for himself and his parents to Martha's fucking Vineyard for a week, all expenses paid.

And so on.

One of the newspaper boys was actually a newspaper *girl*. She was electrified.

Trout's paranoid face was terribly familiar to Billy, who had seen it on the jackets of so many books. But, coming upon that face suddenly in a home-town alley, Billy could not guess why the face was familiar. Billy thought maybe he had known this cracked messiah in Dresden somewhere. Trout certainly looked like a prisoner of war.

And then the newspaper girl held up her hand. "Mr. Trout—" she said, "if I win, can I take my sister, too?"

"Hell no," said Kilgore Trout. "You think money grows on *trees?*"

Trout, incidentally, had written a book about a money tree. It had twenty-dollar bills for leaves. Its flowers were government bonds. Its fruit was diamonds. It attracted human beings who killed each other around the roots and made very good fertilizer.

So it goes.

Billy Pilgrim parked his Cadillac in the alley, and waited for the meeting to end. When the meeting broke up, there was still one boy Trout had to deal with. The boy wanted to quit because the work was so hard and the hours were so long and the pay was so small. Trout was concerned, because, if the boy really quit, Trout would have to deliver the boy's route himself, until he could find another sucker.

"What are you?" Trout asked the boy scornfully. "Some kind of gutless wonder?"

This, too, was the title of a book by Trout, *The Gutless Wonder.* It was about a robot who had bad breath, who became popular after his halitosis was cured. But what made the story remarkable, since it was written in 1932, was that it predicted the widespread use of burning jellied gasoline on human beings.

It was dropped on them from airplanes. Robots did the dropping. They had no conscience, and no circuits which would allow them to imagine what was happening to the people on the ground.

Trout's leading robot looked like a human being, and could talk and dance and so on, and go out with girls. And nobody held it against him that he dropped jellied gasoline on people. But they found his halitosis unforgivable. But then he cleared that up, and he was welcomed to the human race.

Trout lost his argument with the boy who wanted to quit. He told the boy about all the millionaires who had carried newspapers as boys, and the boy replied: "Yeah—but I bet they quit after a week, it's *such* a royal screwing."

And the boy left his full newspaper bag at Trout's feet, with the customer book on top. It was up to Trout to deliver these papers. He didn't have a car. He didn't even have a bicycle, and he was scared to death of dogs.

Somewhere a big dog barked.

As Trout lugubriously slung the bag from his shoulder, Billy Pilgrim approached him. "Mr. Trout—?"

"Yes?"

"Are—are you *Kilgore* Trout?"

"Yes." Trout supposed that Billy had some complaint about the way his newspapers were being delivered. He did not think of himself as a writer for the simple reason that the world had never allowed him to think of himself in this way.

"The—the writer?" said Billy.

"The what?"

Billy was certain that he had made a mistake. "There's a writer named Kilgore Trout."

"There *is*?" Trout looked foolish and dazed.

"You never heard of him?"

Trout shook his head. "Nobody—nobody ever did."

Billy helped Trout deliver his papers, driving him from house to house in the Cadillac. Billy was the responsible one, finding the houses, checking them off. Trout's mind was blown. He had never met a fan before, and Billy was such an *avid* fan.

Trout told him that he had never seen a book of his advertised, reviewed, or on sale. "All these years," he said, "I've been opening the window and making love to the world."

"You must surely have gotten letters," said Billy. "I've felt like writing you letters many times."

Trout held up a single finger. "One."

"Was it *enthusiastic*?"

"It was *insane*. The writer said I should be President of the World."

It turned out that the person who had written this letter was Eliot Rosewater, Billy's friend in the veterans' hospital near Lake Placid. Billy told Trout about Rosewater.

"My God—I thought he was about fourteen years old," said Trout.

"A full grown man—a captain in the war."

"He *writes* like a fourteen-year-old," said Kilgore Trout.

Billy invited Trout to his eighteenth wedding anniversary which was only two days hence. Now the party was in progress.

Trout was in Billy's dining room, gobbling canapés. He was talking with a mouthful of Philadelphia cream cheese and salmon roe to an optometrist's wife. Everybody at the party was associated with optometry in some way, except Trout. And he alone was without glasses. He was making a great hit. Everybody was thrilled to have a real author at the party, even though they had never read his books.

Trout was talking to a Maggie White, who had given up being a dental assistant to become a homemaker for an optometrist. She was very pretty. The last book she had read was *Ivanhoe*.

Billy Pilgrim stood nearby, listening. He was palpating something in his pocket. It was a present he was about to give his wife, a white satin box containing a star sapphire cocktail ring. The ring was worth eight hundred dollars.

The adulation that Trout was receiving, mindless and illiterate as it was, affected Trout like marijuana. He was happy and loud and impudent.

"I'm afraid I don't read as much as I *ought* to," said Maggie.

"We're all afraid of something," Trout replied. "I'm afraid of cancer and rats and Doberman pinschers."

"I should know, but I don't, so I have to ask," said Maggie, "what's the most famous thing you ever wrote?"

"It was about a funeral for a great French chef."

"That sounds interesting."

"All the great chefs in the world are there. It's a beautiful ceremony." Trout was making this up as he went along. "Just before the casket is closed, the mourners sprinkle parsley and paprika on the deceased." So it goes.

"Did that really *happen*?" said Maggie White. She was a dull person, but a sensational invitation to make babies. Men looked at her and wanted to fill her up with babies right away. She hadn't had even one baby yet. She used birth control.

"Of course it happened," Trout told her. "If I wrote something that hadn't really happened, and I tried to sell it, I could go to jail. That's *fraud*."

Maggie believed him. "I'd never thought about that before."

"Think about it now."

"It's like advertising. You have to tell the truth in advertising, or you get in trouble."

"Exactly. The same body of law applies."

"Do you think you might put us in a book sometime?"

"I put everything that happens to me in books."

"I guess I better be careful what I say."

"That's right. And I'm not the only one who's listening. God is listening, too. And on Judgment Day he's going to tell you all the things you said and did. If it turns out they're bad things instead of good things, that's too bad for you, because you'll burn forever and ever. The burning never stops hurting."

Poor Maggie turned gray. She believed *that*, too, and was petrified.

Kilgore Trout laughed uproariously. A salmon egg flew out of his mouth and landed in Maggie's cleavage.

Now an optometrist called for attention. He proposed a toast to Billy and Valencia, whose anniversary it was. According to plan, the barbershop quartet of optometrists, "The Febs," sang while people drank and Billy and Valencia put their arms around each other, just glowed. Everybody's eyes were shining. The song was "That Old Gang of Mine."

Gee, that song went, *but I'd give the world to see that old gang of mine.* And so on. A little later it said, *So long forever, old fellows and gals, so long forever old sweethearts and pals—God bless 'em—*And so on.

Unexpectedly, Billy Pilgrim found himself upset by the song and the occasion. He had never had an old gang, old sweethearts and pals, but he missed one anyway, as the quartet made slow, agonized experiments with chords—chords intentionally sour, sourer still, unbearably sour, and then a chord that was suffocatingly sweet, and then some sour ones again. Billy had powerful psychosomatic responses to the changing chords. His mouth filled with the taste of lemonade, and his face became grotesque, as though he really were being stretched on the torture engine called the *rack*.

He looked so peculiar that several people commented on it solicitously when the song was done. They thought he might have been having a heart attack, and Billy seemed to confirm this by going to a chair and sitting down haggardly.

There was silence.

"Oh my God," said Valencia, leaning over him, "Billy—are you all right?"

"Yes."

"You look so awful."

"Really—I'm O.K." And he was, too, except that he could find no explanation for why the song had affected him so grotesquely. He had supposed for years that he had no secrets from himself. Here was proof that he had a great big secret somewhere inside, and he could not imagine what it was.

People drifted away now, seeing the color return to Billy's cheeks, seeing him smile. Valencia stayed with him, and Kilgore Trout, who had been on the fringe of the crowd, came closer, interested, shrewd.

"You looked as though you'd seen a *ghost*," said Valencia.

"No," said Billy. He hadn't seen anything but what was really before him—the faces of the four singers, those four ordinary men, cow-eyed and mindless and anguished as they went from sweetness to sourness to sweetness again.

"Can I make a guess?" said Kilgore Trout. "You saw through a *time window*."

"A what?" said Valencia.

"He suddenly saw the past or the future. Am I right?"

"No," said Billy Pilgrim. He got up, put a hand into his pocket, found the box containing the ring in there. He took out the box, gave it absently to Valencia. He had meant to give it to her at the end of the song, while everybody was watching. Only Kilgore Trout was there to see.

"For me?" said Valencia.

"Yes."

"Oh my God," she said. Then she said it louder, so other people heard. They gathered around, and she opened it, and she almost screamed when she saw the sapphire with a star in it. "Oh, my God," she said. She gave Billy a big kiss. She said, "Thank you, thank you, thank you."

There was a lot of talk about what wonderful jewelry Billy had given to Valencia over the years. "My God—" said Maggie White, "she's already got the biggest diamond I ever saw outside of a movie." She was talking about the diamond Billy had brought back from the war.

The partial denture he had found inside his little impresario's coat, incidentally, was in his cufflinks box in his dresser drawer. Billy had a wonderful collection of cufflinks. It was the custom of the family to give him cufflinks on every Father's Day. He was wearing Father's Day cufflinks now. They had cost over one hundred dollars. They were made out of ancient Roman coins. He had one pair of cufflinks upstairs which were little roulette wheels that really worked. He had another pair which had a real thermometer in one and a real compass in the other.

Billy now moved above the party—outwardly normal. Kilgore Trout was shadowing him, keen to know what Billy had suspected or seen. Most of Trout's novels, after all, dealt with time warps and extrasensory perception and other unexpected things. Trout believed in things like that, was greedy to have their existence proved.

"You ever put a full-length mirror on the floor, and then have a dog stand on it?" Trout asked Billy.

"No."

"The dog will look down, and all of a sudden he'll realize there's nothing under him. He thinks he's standing on thin air. He'll jump a *mile*."

"He *will*?"

"That's how *you* looked—as though you all of a sudden realized you were standing on thin air."

The barbershop quartet sang again. Billy was emotionally racked again. The experience was *definitely* associated with those four men and not what they sang.

Here is what they sang, while Billy was pulled apart inside:

> 'Leven cent cotton, forty cent meat,
> How in the world can a poor man eat?
> Pray for the sunshine, 'cause it will rain.
> Things gettin' worse, drivin' all insane;
> Built a nice barn, painted it brown;
> Lightnin' came along and burnt it down:
> No use talkin', any man's beat,
> With 'leven cent cotton and forty cent meat.
> 'Leven cent cotton, a car-load of tax,
> The load's too heavy for our poor backs . . .

And so on.

Billy fled upstairs in his nice white home.

Trout would have come upstairs with him if Billy hadn't told him not to. Then Billy went into the upstairs bathroom, which was dark. He closed and locked the door. He left it dark, and gradually became aware that he was not alone. His son was in there.

"Dad—?" his son said in the dark. Robert, the future Green Beret, was seventeen then. Billy liked him, but didn't know him very well. Billy couldn't help suspecting that there wasn't much *to* know about Robert.

Billy flicked on the light. Robert was sitting on the toilet with his pajama bottoms around his ankles. He was wearing an electric guitar, slung around his neck on a strap. He had just bought the guitar that day. He couldn't play it yet and, in fact, never learned to play it. It was a nacreous pink.

"Hello, son," said Billy Pilgrim.

Billy went into his bedroom, even though there were guests to be entertained downstairs. He lay down on his bed, turned on the Magic Fingers. The mattress trembled, drove a dog out from under the bed. The dog was Spot. Good old Spot was still alive in those days. Spot lay down again in a corner.

Billy thought hard about the effect the quartet had had on him, and then found an association with an experience he had had long ago. He did not travel in time to the experience. He remembered it shimmeringly—as follows:

He was down in the meat locker on the night that Dresden was destroyed. There were sounds like giant footsteps above. Those were sticks of high-explosive bombs. The giants walked and walked. The meat locker was a very safe shelter. All that happened down there was an occasional shower of calcimine. The Americans and four of their guards and a few dressed carcasses were down there, and nobody else. The rest of the guards had, before the raid began, gone to the comforts of their own homes in Dresden. They were all being killed with their families.

So it goes.

The girls that Billy had seen naked were all being killed, too, in a much shallower shelter in another part of the stockyards.

So it goes.

A guard would go to the head of the stairs every so often to see what it was like outside, then he would come down and whisper to the other guards. There was a fire-storm out there. Dresden was one big flame. The one flame ate everything organic, everything that would burn.

It wasn't safe to come out of the shelter until noon the next day. When the Americans and their guards did come out, the sky was black with smoke. The sun was an angry little pinhead. Dresden was like the moon now, nothing but minerals. The stones were hot. Everybody else in the neighborhood was dead.

So it goes.

The guards drew together instinctively, rolled their eyes. They experimented with one expression and then another, said nothing, though their mouths were often open. They looked like a silent film of a barbershop quartet.

"So long forever," they might have been singing, "old fellows and pals; So long forever, old sweethearts and pals—God bless 'em—"

"Tell me a story," Montana Wildhack said to Billy Pilgrim in the Tralfamadorian zoo one time. They were in bed side by side.

They had privacy. The canopy covered the dome. Montana was six months pregnant now, big and rosy, lazily demanding small favors from Billy from time to time. She couldn't send Billy out for ice cream or strawberries, since the atmosphere outside the dome was cyanide, and the nearest strawberries and ice cream were millions of light years away.

She could send him to the refrigerator, which was decorated with the blank couple on the bicycle built for two—or, as now, she could wheedle, "Tell me a story, Billy boy."

"Dresden was destroyed on the night of February 13, 1945," Billy Pilgrim began. "We came out of our shelter the next day." He told Montana about the four guards who, in their astonishment and grief, resembled a barbershop quartet. He told her about the stockyards with all the fenceposts gone, with roofs and windows gone—told her about seeing little logs lying around. These were people who had been caught in the fire storm. So it goes.

Billy told her what had happened to the buildings that used to form cliffs around the stockyards. They had collapsed. Their wood had been consumed, and their stones had crashed down, had tumbled against one another until they locked at last in low and graceful curves.

"It was like the moon," said Billy Pilgrim.

The guards told the Americans to form in ranks of four, which they did. Then they had them march back to the hog barn which had been their home. Its walls still stood, but its windows and roof were gone, and there was nothing inside but ashes and dollops of melted glass. It was realized then that there was no food or water, and that the survivors, if they were going to continue to survive, were going to have to climb over curve after curve on the face of the moon.

Which they did.

The curves were smooth only when seen from a distance. The people climbing them learned that they were treacherous, jagged things—hot to the touch, often unstable—eager, should certain important rocks be disturbed, to tumble some more, to form lower, more solid curves.

Nobody talked much as the expedition crossed the moon. There was nothing appropriate to say. One thing was clear: Absolutely everybody in the city was supposed to be dead, regardless of what they were, and that anybody that moved in it represented a flaw in the design. There were to be no moon men at all.

American fighter planes came in under the smoke to see if anything was moving. They saw Billy and the rest moving down there. The planes sprayed them with machine-gun bullets, but the bullets missed. Then they saw some other people moving down by the riverside and they shot at them. They hit some of them. So it goes.

The idea was to hasten the end of the war.

Billy's story ended very curiously in a suburb untouched by fire and explosions. The guards and the Americans came at nightfall to an inn which was open for business. There was candlelight. There were fires in three fireplaces downstairs. There were empty tables and chairs waiting for anyone who might come, and empty beds with covers turned down upstairs.

There was a blind innkeeper and his sighted wife, who was the cook, and their two young daughters, who worked as waitresses and maids. This family knew that Dresden was gone. Those with eyes had seen it burn and burn, understood that they were on the edge of a desert now. Still—they had opened for business, had polished the glasses and wound the clocks and stirred the fires, and waited and waited to see who would come.

There was no great flow of refugees from Dresden. The clocks ticked on, the fires crackled, the translucent candles dripped. And then there was a knock on the door, and in came four guards and one hundred American prisoners of war.

The innkeeper asked the guards if they had come from the city.

"Yes."

"Are there more people coming?"

And the guards said that, on the difficult route they had chosen, they had not seen another living soul.

The blind innkeeper said that the Americans could sleep in his stable that night, and he gave them soup and ersatz coffee and a little beer. Then he came out to the stable to listen to them bedding down in the straw.

"Good night, Americans," he said in German. "Sleep well."

9

Here is how Billy Pilgrim lost his wife, Valencia.

He was unconscious in the hospital in Vermont, after the airplane crashed on Sugarbush Mountain, and Valencia, having heard about the crash, was driving from Ilium to the hospital in the family Cadillac El Dorado Coupe de Ville. Valencia was hysterical, because she had been told frankly that Billy might die, or that, if he lived, he might be a vegetable.

Valencia adored Billy. She was crying and yelping so hard as she drove that she missed the correct turnoff from the throughway. She applied her power brakes, and a Mercedes slammed into her from behind. Nobody was hurt, thank God, because both drivers were wearing seat belts. Thank God, thank God. The Mercedes lost only a headlight. But the rear end of the Cadillac was a body-and-fender man's wet dream. The trunk and fenders were collapsed. The gaping trunk looked like the mouth of a village idiot who was explaining that he didn't know anything about anything. The fenders shrugged. The bumper was at a high port arms. "Reagan for President!" a sticker on the bumper said. The back window was veined with cracks. The exhaust system rested on the pavement.

The driver of the Mercedes got out and went to Valencia, to find out if she was all right. She blabbed hysterically about Billy and the airplane crash, and then she put her car in gear and crossed the median divider, leaving her exhaust system behind.

When she arrived at the hospital, people rushed to the windows to see what all the noise was. The Cadillac, with both mufflers gone, sounded like a heavy bomber coming in on a wing and a prayer. Valencia turned off the engine, but then she slumped against the steering wheel, and the horn brayed steadily. A doctor and a nurse ran out to find out what the trouble was. Poor Valencia was unconscious, overcome by carbon monoxide. She was a heavenly azure.

One hour later she was dead. So it goes.

Billy knew nothing about it. He dreamed on, and traveled in time and so forth. The hospital was so crowded that Billy couldn't have a room to himself. He shared a room with a Harvard history professor named Bertram Copeland Rumfoord. Rumfoord didn't have to look at Billy, because Billy was surrounded by white linen screens on rubber wheels. But Rumfoord could hear Billy talking to himself from time to time.

Rumfoord's left leg was in traction. He had broken it while skiing. He was seventy years old, but had the body and spirit of a man half that age. He had been honeymooning with his fifth wife when he broke his leg. Her name was Lily. Lily was twenty-three.

Just about the time poor Valencia was pronounced dead, Lily came into Billy's and Rumfoord's room with an armload of books. Rumfoord had sent her down to Boston to get them. He was working on a one-volume history of the United States Army Air Corps in World War Two. The books were about bombings and sky battles that had happened before Lily was even *born.*

"You guys go on without me." said Billy Pilgrim deliriously, as pretty little Lily came in. She had been an a-go-go girl when Rumfoord saw her and resolved to make her his own. She was a high school dropout. Her I.Q. was 103. "He *scares* me," she whispered to her husband about Billy Pilgrim.

"He bores the *hell* out of *me!*" Rumfoord replied boomingly. "All he does in his sleep is quit and surrender and apologize and ask to be left alone." Rumfoord was a retired brigadier general in the Air Force Reserve, the official Air Force Historian, a full professor, the author of twenty-six books, a multimillionaire since birth, and one of the great competitive sailors of all time. His most popular book was about sex and strenuous athletics for men over sixty-five. Now he quoted Theodore Roosevelt, whom he resembled a lot:

"'I could carve a better man out of a banana.'"

One of the things Rumfoord had told Lily to get in Boston was a copy of President Harry S. Truman's announcement to the world that an atomic bomb had been dropped on Hiroshima. She had a Xerox of it, and Rumfoord asked her if she had read it.

"No." She didn't read well, which was one of the reasons she had dropped out of high school.

Rumfoord ordered her to sit down and read the Truman statement now. He didn't know that she couldn't read much. He knew very little about her, except that she was one more public demonstration that he was a superman.

So Lily sat down and pretended to read the Truman thing, which went like this:

Sixteen hours ago an American airplane dropped one bomb on Hiroshima, an important Japanese Army base. That bomb had more power than 20,000 tons of T. N. T. It had more than two thousand times the blast power of the British "Grand Slam," which is the largest bomb ever yet used in the history of warfare.

The Japanese began the war from the air at Pearl Harbor. They have been repaid many-fold. And the end is not yet. With this bomb we have now added a new and revolutionary increase in destruction to supplement the growing power of our armed forces. In their present form these bombs are now in production, and even more powerful forms are in development.

It is an atomic bomb. It is a harnessing of the basic power of the universe. The force from which the sun draws its power has been loosed against those who brought war to the Far East.

Before 1939, it was the accepted belief of scientists that it was theoretically possible to release atomic energy. But nobody knew any practical method of doing it. By 1942, however, we knew that the Germans were working feverishly to find a way to add atomic energy to all the other engines of war with which they hoped to enslave the world. But they failed. We may be grateful to Providence that the Germans got the V-1's and V-2's late and in limited quantities and even more grateful that they did not get the atomic bomb at all.

The battle of the laboratories held fateful risks for us as well as the battles of the air, land, and sea, and we have now won the battle of the laboratories as we have won the other battles.

We are now prepared to obliterate more rapidly and completely every productive enterprise the Japanese have above ground in any city, said Harry Truman. *We shall destroy their docks, their factories, and their communications. Let there be no mistake; we shall completely destroy Japan's power to make war. It was to spare—*

And so on.

One of the books that Lily had brought Rumfoord was *The Destruction of Dresden*, by an Englishman named David Irving. It was an American edition, published by Holt, Rinehart and Winston in 1964. What Rumfoord wanted from it were portions of the forewords by his friends Ira C. Eaker, Lieutenant General, U.S.A.F., retired, and British Air Marshal Sir Robert Saundby, K.C.B., K.B.E., M.C., D.F.C., A.F.C.

I find it difficult to understand Englishmen or Americans who weep about enemy civilians who were killed but who have not shed a tear for our gallant crews lost in combat with a cruel enemy, wrote his friend General Eaker in part. *I think it would have been well for Mr. Irving to have remembered, when he was drawing the frightful picture of the civilians killed at Dresden, that V-1's and V-2's were at that very time falling on England, killing civilian men, women, and children indiscriminately, as they were designed and launched to do. It might be well to remember Buchenwald and Coventry, too.*

Eaker's foreword ended this way:

I deeply regret that British and U.S. bombers killed 135,000 people in the attack on Dresden, but I remember who started the last war and I regret even more the loss of more than 5,000,000 Allied lives in the necessary effort to completely defeat and utterly destroy nazism.

So it goes.

What Air Marshal Saundby said, among other things, was this:

That the bombing of Dresden was a great tragedy none can deny. That it was really a military necessity few, after reading this book, will believe. It was one of those terrible things that sometimes happen in wartime, brought about by an unfortunate combination of circumstances. Those who approved it were neither wicked nor cruel, though it may well be that they were too remote from the harsh realities of war to understand fully the appalling destructive power of air bombardment in the spring of 1945.

The advocates of nuclear disarmament seem to believe that, if they could achieve their aim, war would become tolerable and decent. They would do well to read this book and ponder the fate of Dresden, where 135,000 people died as the result of an air attack with conventional weapons. On the night of March 9th, 1945, an air attack on Tokyo by American heavy bombers, using incendiary and high explosive bombs, caused the death of 83,793 people. The atom bomb dropped on Hiroshima killed 71,379 people.

So it goes.

"If you're ever in Cody, Wyoming," said Billy Pilgrim behind his white linen screens, "just ask for Wild Bob."

Lily Rumfoord shuddered, went on pretending to read the Harry Truman thing.

Billy's daughter Barbara came in later that day. She was all doped up, had the same glassy-eyed look that poor old Edgar Derby wore just before he was shot in Dresden. Doctors had given her pills so she could continue to function, even though her father was broken and her mother was dead.

So it goes.

She was accompanied by a doctor and a nurse. Her brother Robert was flying home from a battlefield in Vietnam. "Daddy—" she said tentatively. "Daddy—?"

But Billy was ten years away, back in 1958. He was examining the eyes of a young male Mongolian idiot in order to prescribe corrective lenses. The idiot's mother was there, acting as an interpreter.

"How many dots do you see?" Billy Pilgrim asked him.

And then Billy traveled in time to when he was sixteen years old, in the waiting room of a doctor. Billy had an infected thumb. There was only one other patient waiting—an old, old man.

The old man was in agony because of gas. He farted tremendously, and then he belched.

"Excuse me," he said to Billy. Then he did it again. "Oh God—" he said, "I knew it was going to be bad getting old." He shook his head. "I didn't know it was going to be *this* bad."

Billy Pilgrim opened his eyes in the hospital in Vermont, did not know where he was. Watching him was his son Robert. Robert was wearing the uniform of the famous Green Berets. Robert's hair was short, was wheat-colored bristles. Robert was clean and neat. He was decorated with a Purple Heart and a Silver Star and a Bronze Star with two clusters.

This was a boy who had flunked out of high school, who had been an alcoholic at sixteen, who had run with a rotten bunch of kids, who had been arrested for tipping over hundreds of tombstones in a Catholic cemetery one time. He was all straightened out now. His posture was wonderful and his shoes were shined and his trousers were pressed, and he was a leader of men.

"Dad—?"

Billy Pilgrim closed his eyes again.

Billy had to miss his wife's funeral because he was still so sick. He was conscious, though, while Valencia was being put into the ground in Ilium. Billy hadn't said much since regaining consciousness, hadn't responded very elaborately to the news of Valencia's death and Robert's coming home from the war and so on—so it was generally believed that he was a vegetable. There was talk of performing an operation on him later, one which might improve the circulation of blood to his brain.

Actually, Billy's outward listlessness was a screen. The listlessness concealed a mind which was fizzing and flashing thrillingly. It was preparing letters and lectures about the flying saucers, the negligibility of death, and the true nature of time.

Professor Rumfoord said frightful things about Billy within Billy's hearing, confident that Billy no longer had any brain at all. "Why don't they let him *die?*" he asked Lily.

"I don't know," she said.

"That's not a human being anymore. Doctors are for human beings. They should turn him over to a veterinarian or a tree surgeon. *They'd* know what to do. Look at him! That's life, according to the medical profession. Isn't life wonderful?"

"I don't know," said Lily.

Rumfoord talked to Lily about the bombing of Dresden one time, and Billy heard it all. Rumfoord had a problem about Dresden. His one-volume history of the Army Air Force in World War Two was supposed to be a readable condensation of the twenty-seven-volume *Official History of the Army Air Force in World War Two.* The thing was, though, there was almost nothing in the twenty-seven volumes about the Dresden raid, even though it had been such a howling success. The extent of the success had been kept a secret for many years after the war—a secret from the American people. It was no secret from the Germans, of course, or from the Russians, who occupied Dresden after the war, who are in Dresden still.

"Americans have finally heard about Dresden," said Rumfoord, twenty-three years after the raid. "A lot of them know now how much worse it was than Hiroshima. So I've got to put something about it in my book. From the official Air Force standpoint, it'll all be new."

"Why would they keep it a secret so long?" said Lily.

"For fear that a lot of bleeding hearts," said Rumfoord, "might not think it was such a wonderful thing to do."

It was now that Billy Pilgrim spoke up intelligently. "I was there," he said.

It was difficult for Rumfoord to take Billy seriously, since Rumfoord had so long considered Billy a repulsive non-person who would be much better off dead. Now, with Billy speaking clearly and to the point, Rumfoord's ears wanted to treat the words as a foreign language that was not worth learning. "What did he say?" said Rumfoord.

Lily had to serve as an interpreter. "He said he was there," she explained.

"He was where?"
"I don't know," said Lily. "Where were you?" she asked Billy.
"Dresden," said Billy.
"Dresden," Lily told Rumfoord.
"He's simply echoing things we say," said Rumfoord.
"Oh," said Lily.
"He's got echolalia now."
"Oh."

Echolalia is a mental disease which makes people immediately repeat things that well people around them say. But Billy didn't really have it. Rumfoord simply insisted, for his own comfort, that Billy had it. Rumfoord was thinking in a military manner: that an inconvenient person, one whose death he wished for very much, for practical reasons, was suffering from a repulsive disease.

Rumfoord went on insisting for several hours that Billy had echolalia—told nurses and a doctor that Billy had echolalia now. Some experiments were performed on Billy. Doctors and nurses tried to get Billy to echo something, but Billy wouldn't make a sound for them.

"He isn't doing it now," said Rumfoord peevishly. "The minute you go away, he'll start doing it again."

Nobody took Rumfoord's diagnosis seriously. The staff thought Rumfoord was a hateful old man, conceited and cruel. He often said to them, in one way or another, that people who were weak deserved to die. Whereas the staff, of course, was devoted to the idea that weak people should be helped as much as possible, that nobody should die.

There in the hospital, Billy was having an adventure very common among people without power in time of war: He was trying to prove to a willfully deaf and blind enemy that he was interesting to hear and see. He kept silent until the lights went out at night, and then, when there had been a long period of silence containing nothing to echo, he said to Rumfoord, "I was in Dresden when it was bombed. I was a prisoner of war."

Rumfoord sighed impatiently.

"Word of honor," said Billy Pilgrim. "Do you believe me?"

"Must we talk about it now?" said Rumfoord. He had heard. He didn't believe.

"We don't ever have to talk about it," said Billy. "I just want you to know: I was there."

Nothing more was said about Dresden that night, and Billy closed his eyes, traveled in time to a May afternoon, two days after the end of the Second World War in Europe. Billy and five other American prisoners were riding in a coffin-shaped green wagon, which they had found abandoned, complete with two horses, in a suburb of Dresden. Now they were being drawn by the clop-clop-clopping horses down narrow lanes which had been cleared through the moonlike ruins. They were going back to the slaughterhouse for souvenirs of the war. Billy was reminded of the sounds of milkmen's horses early in the morning in Ilium, when he was a boy.

Billy sat in the back of the jiggling coffin. His head was tilted back and his nostrils were flaring. He was happy. He was warm. There was food in the wagon, and wine—and a camera, and a stamp collection, and a stuffed owl, and a mantel clock that ran on changes of barometric pressure. The Americans had gone into empty houses in the suburb where they had been imprisoned, and they had taken these and many other things.

The owners, hearing that the Russians were coming, killing and robbing and raping and burning, had fled.

But the Russians hadn't come yet, even two days after the war. It was peaceful in the ruins. Billy saw only one other person on the way to the slaughterhouse. It was an old man pushing a baby buggy. In the buggy were pots and cups and an umbrella frame, and other things he had found.

Billy stayed in the wagon when it reached the slaughterhouse, sunning himself. The others went looking for souvenirs. Later on in life, the Tralfamadorians would advise Billy to concentrate on the happy moments of his life, and to ignore the unhappy ones—to stare only at pretty things as eternity failed to go by.

If this sort of selectivity had been possible for Billy, he might have chosen as his happiest moment his sun-drenched snooze in the back of the wagon.

Billy Pilgrim was armed as he snoozed. It was the first time he had been armed since basic training. His companions had insisted that he arm himself, since God only knew what sorts of killers might be in burrows on the face of the moon—wild dogs, packs of rats fattened on corpses, escaped maniacs and murderers, soldiers who would never quit killing until they themselves were killed.

Billy had a tremendous cavalry pistol in his belt. It was a relic of World War One. It had a ring in its butt. It was loaded with bullets the size of robins' eggs. Billy had found it in the bedside table in a house. That was one of the things about the end of the war: Absolutely anybody who wanted a weapon could have one. They were lying all around. Billy had a saber, too. It was a Luftwaffe ceremonial saber. Its hilt was stamped with a screaming eagle. The eagle was carrying a swastika and looking down. Billy found it stuck into a telephone pole. He had pulled it out of the pole as the wagon went by.

Now his snoozing became shallower as he heard a man and a woman speaking German in pitying tones. The speakers were commiserating with somebody lyrically. Before Billy opened his eyes, it seemed to him that the tones might have been those used by the friends of Jesus when they took His ruined body down from His cross. So it goes.

Billy opened his eyes. A middle-aged man and wife were crooning to the horses. They were noticing what the Americans had not noticed—that the horses' mouths were bleeding, gashed by the bits, that the horses' hooves were broken, so that every step meant agony, that the horses were insane with thirst. The Americans had treated their form of transportation as though it were no more sensitive than a six-cylinder Chevrolet.

These two horse pitiers moved back along the wagon to where they could gaze in patronizing reproach at Billy—at Billy Pilgrim, who was so long and weak, so ridiculous in his azure toga and silver shoes. They weren't afraid of him. They weren't afraid of anything. They were doctors, both obstetricians. They had been delivering babies until the hospitals were all burned down. Now they were picnicking near where their apartment used to be.

The woman was softly beautiful, translucent from having eaten potatoes for so long. The man wore a business suit, necktie and all. Potatoes had made him gaunt. He was as tall as Billy, wore steel-rimmed tri-focals. This couple, so involved with babies, had never reproduced themselves, though they could have. This was an interesting comment on the whole idea of reproduction.

They had nine languages between them. They tried Polish on Billy Pilgrim first, since he was dressed so clownishly, since the wretched Poles were the involuntary clowns of the Second World War.

Billy asked them in English what it was they wanted, and they at once scolded him in English for the condition of the horses. They made Billy get out of the wagon and come look at the horses. When Billy saw the condition of his means of transportation, he burst into tears. He hadn't cried about anything else in the war.

Later on, as a middle-aged optometrist, he would weep quietly and privately sometimes, but never make loud *boo-hooing* noises.

Which is why the epigraph of this book is the quatrain from the famous Christmas carol. Billy cried very little, though he often saw things worth crying about, and in *that* respect, at least, he resembled the Christ of the carol:

The cattle are lowing,
The Baby awakes.
But the little Lord Jesus
No crying He makes.

Billy traveled in time back to the hospital in Vermont. Breakfast had been eaten and cleared away, and Professor Rumfoord was reluctantly becoming interested in Billy as a human being. Rumfoord questioned Billy gruffly, satisfied himself that Billy really had been in Dresden. He asked Billy what it had been like, and Billy told him about the horses and the couple picnicking on the moon.

The story ended this way: Billy and the doctors unharnessed the horses, but the horses wouldn't go anywhere. Their feet hurt too much. And then Russians came on motorcycles, and they arrested everybody but the horses.

Two days after that, Billy was turned over to the Americans, who shipped him home on a very slow freighter called the *Lucretia A. Mott*. Lucretia A. Mott was a famous American suffragette. She was dead. So it goes.

"It *had* to be done," Rumfoord told Billy, speaking of the destruction of Dresden.

"I know," said Billy.

"That's war."

"I know. I'm not complaining."

"It must have been hell on the ground."

"It was," said Billy Pilgrim.

"Pity the men who had to *do* it."

"I do."

"You must have had mixed feelings, there on the ground."

"It was all right," said Billy. "*Everything* is all right, and everybody has to do exactly what he does. I learned that on Tralfamadore."

Billy Pilgrim's daughter took him home later that day, put him to bed in his house, turned the Magic Fingers on. There was a practical nurse there. Billy wasn't supposed to work or even leave the house for a while, at least. He was under observation.

But Billy sneaked out while the nurse wasn't watching, and he drove to New York City, where he hoped to appear on television. He was going to tell the world about the lessons of Tralfamadore.

Billy Pilgrim checked into the Royalton Hotel on Forty-fourth Street in New York. He by chance was given a room which had once been the home of George Jean Nathan, the critic and editor. Nathan, according to the Earthling concept of time, had died back in 1958. According to the Tralfamadorian concept, of course, Nathan was still alive somewhere and always would be.

The room was small and simple, except that it was on the top floor, and had French doors which opened onto a terrace as large as the room. And beyond the parapet of the terrace was the air space over Forty-fourth Street. Billy now leaned over that parapet, looked down at all the people moving hither and yon. They were jerky little scissors. They were a lot of fun.

It was a chilly night, and Billy came indoors after a while, closed the French doors. Closing those doors reminded him of his honeymoon. There had been French doors on the Cape Ann love nest of his honeymoon, still were, always would be.

Billy turned on his television set, clicking its channel selector around and around. He was looking for programs on which he might be allowed to appear. But it was too early in the evening for programs that allowed people with peculiar opinions to speak out. It was only a little after eight o'clock, so all the shows were about silliness or murder. So it goes.

Billy left his room, went down the slow elevator, walked over to Times Square, looked into the window of a tawdry bookstore. In the window were hundreds of books about fucking and buggery and murder, and a street guide to New York City, and a model of the Statue of Liberty with a thermometer on it. Also in the window, speckled with soot and fly shit, were four paperback novels by Billy's friend, Kilgore Trout.

The news of the day, meanwhile, was being written in a ribbon of lights on a building to Billy's back. The window reflected the news. It was about power and sports and anger and death. So it goes.

Billy went into the bookstore.

A sign in there said that adults only were allowed in the back. There were peep shows in the back that showed movies of young women and men with no clothes on. It cost a quarter to look into a machine for one minute. There were still photographs of naked young people for sale back there, too. You could take those home. The stills were a lot more Tralfamadorian than the movies, since you could look at them whenever you wanted to, and they wouldn't change. Twenty years in the future, those girls would still be young, would still be smiling or smoldering or simply looking stupid, with their legs wide open. Some of them were eating lollipops or bananas. They would still be eating those. And the peckers of the young men would still be semierect, and their muscles would be bulging like cannonballs.

But Billy Pilgrim wasn't beguiled by the back of the store. He was thrilled by the Kilgore Trout novels in the front. The titles were all new to him, or he thought they were. Now he opened one. It seemed all right for him to do that. Everybody else in the store was pawing things. The name of the book was *The Big Board.* He got a few paragraphs into it, and then he realized that he *had* read it before—years ago, in the veterans' hospital. It was about an Earthling man and woman who were kidnapped by extra-terrestrials. They were put on display in a zoo on a planet called Zircon-212.

These fictitious people in the zoo had a big board supposedly showing stock market quotations and commodity prices along one wall of their habitat, and a news ticker, and a telephone that was supposedly connected to a brokerage on Earth. The creatures on Zircon-212 told their captives that they had invested a million dollars for them back on Earth, and that it was up to the captives to manage it so that they would be fabulously wealthy when they were returned to Earth.

The telephone and the big board and the ticker were all fakes, of course. They were simply stimulants to make the Earthlings perform vividly for the crowds at the zoo—to make them jump up and down and cheer, or gloat, or sulk, or tear their hair, to be scared shitless or to feel as contented as babies in their mothers' arms.

The Earthlings did very well on paper. That was part of the rigging, of course. And religion got mixed up in it, too. The news ticker reminded them that the President of the United States had declared National Prayer Week, and that everybody should pray. The Earthlings had had a bad week on the market before that. They had lost a small fortune in olive oil futures. So they gave praying a whirl.

It worked. Olive oil went up.

Another Kilgore Trout book there in the window was about a man who built a time machine so he could go back and see Jesus. It worked, and he saw Jesus when Jesus was only twelve years old. Jesus was learning the carpentry trade from his father.

Two Roman soldiers came into the shop with a mechanical drawing on papyrus of a device they wanted built by sunrise the next morning. It was a cross to be used in the execution of a rabble-rouser.

Jesus and his father built it. They were glad to have the work. And the rabble-rouser was executed on it.

So it goes.

The bookstore was run by seeming quintuplets, by five short, bald men chewing unlit cigars that were sopping wet. They never smiled, and each one had a stool to perch on. They were making money running a paper-and-celluloid whorehouse. They didn't have hard-ons. Neither did Billy Pilgrim. Everybody else did. It was a ridiculous store, all about love and babies.

The clerks occasionally told somebody to buy or get out, not to just look and look and look and paw and paw. Some of the people were looking at each other instead of the merchandise.

A clerk came up to Billy and told him the good stuff was in the back, that the books Billy was reading were window dressing. "That ain't what you want, for Christ's sake," he told Billy. "What you want's in *back*."

So Billy moved a little farther back, but not as far as the part for adults only. He moved because of absentminded politeness, taking a Trout book with him—the one about Jesus and the time machine.

The time-traveler in the book went back to *Bible* times to find out one thing in particular: Whether or not Jesus had really died on the cross, or whether he had been taken down while still alive, whether he had really gone on living. The hero had a stethoscope along.

Billy skipped to the end of the book, where the hero mingled with the people who were taking Jesus down from the cross. The time-traveler was the first one up the ladder, dressed in clothes of the period, and he leaned close to Jesus so people couldn't see him use the stethoscope, and he listened.

There wasn't a sound inside the emaciated chest cavity. The Son of God was dead as a doornail.

So it goes.

The time-traveler, whose name was Lance Corwin, also got to measure the length of Jesus, but not to weigh him. Jesus was five feet and three and a half inches long.

Another clerk came up to Billy and asked him if he was going to buy the book or not, and Billy said that he wanted to buy it, please. He had his back to a rack of paperback books about oral-genital contacts from ancient Egypt to the present and so on, and the clerk supposed Billy was reading one of these. So he was startled when he saw what Billy's book was. He said, "Jesus Christ, where did you find this thing?" and so on, and he had to tell the other clerks about the pervert who wanted to buy the window dressing. The other clerks already knew about Billy. They had been watching him, too.

The cash register where Billy waited for his change was near a bin of old girly magazines. Billy looked at one out of the corner of his eye, and he saw this question on its cover: *What really became of Montana Wildhack?*

So Billy read it. He knew where Montana Wildhack *really* was, of course. She was back on Tralfamadore, taking care of the baby, but the magazine, which was called *Midnight Pussycats*, promised that she was wearing a cement overcoat under thirty fathoms of saltwater in San Pedro Bay.

So it goes.

Billy wanted to laugh. The magazine, which was published for lonesome men to jerk off to, ran the story so it could print pictures taken from blue movies which Montana had made as a teen-ager. Billy did not look closely at these. They were grainy things, soot and chalk. They could have been anybody.

Billy was again directed to the back of the store, and he went this time. A jaded sailor stepped away from a movie machine while the film was still running. Billy looked in, and there was Montana Wildhack alone on a bed, peeling a banana. The picture clicked off. Billy did not want to see what happened next, and a clerk importuned him to come over and see some really hot stuff they kept under the counter for connoisseurs.

Billy was mildly curious as to what could possibly have been kept hidden in such a place. The clerk leered and showed him. It was a photograph of a woman and a Shetland pony. They were attempting to have sexual intercourse between the Doric columns, in front of velvet draperies which were fringed with deedlee-balls.

Billy didn't get onto television in New York that night, but he *did* get onto a radio talk show. There was a radio station right next to Billy's hotel. He saw its call letters over the entrance of an office building, so he went in. He went up to the studio on an automatic elevator, and there were other people up there, waiting to go in. They were literary critics, and they thought Billy was one, too. They were going to discuss whether the novel was dead or not. So it goes.

Billy took his seat with the others around a golden oak table, with a microphone all his own. The master of ceremonies asked him his name and what paper he was from. Billy said he was from the *Ilium Gazette*.

He was nervous and happy. "If you're ever in Cody, Wyoming," he told himself, "just ask for Wild Bob."

Billy put his hand up at the very first part of the program, but he wasn't called on right away. Others got in ahead of him. One of them said that it would be a nice time to bury the novel, now that a Virginian, one hundred years after Appomattox, had written *Uncle Tom's Cabin*. Another one said that people couldn't read well enough anymore to turn print into exciting situations in their skulls, so that authors had to do what Norman Mailer did, which was to perform in public what he had written. The master of ceremonies asked people to say what they thought the function of the novel might be in modern society, and one critic said, "To provide touches of color in rooms with all-white walls." Another one said, "To describe blow-jobs artistically." Another one said, "To teach wives of junior executives what to buy next and how to act in a French restaurant."

And then Billy was allowed to speak. Off he went, in that beautifully trained voice of his, telling about the flying saucers and Montana Wildhack and so on.

He was gently expelled from the studio during a commercial. He went back to his hotel room, put a quarter into the Magic Fingers machine connected to his bed, and he went to sleep. He traveled in time back to Tralfamadore.

"Time-traveling again?" said Montana. It was artificial evening in the dome. She was breast-feeding their child.

"Hmm?" said Billy.

"You've been time-traveling again. I can always tell."

"Um."

"Where did you go this time? It wasn't the war. I can tell that, too."

"New York."

"The Big Apple."

"Hm?"

"That's what they used to call New York."

"Oh."

"You see any plays or movies?"

"No—I walked around Times Square some, bought a book by Kilgore Trout."

"Lucky *you*." She did not share his enthusiasm for Kilgore Trout.

Billy mentioned casually that he had seen part of a blue movie she had made. Her response was no less casual. It was Tralfamadorian and guilt-free:

"Yes—" she said, "and I've heard about you in the war, about what a clown you were. And I've heard about the high-school teacher who was shot. He made a blue movie with a firing squad." She moved the baby from one breast to the other, because the moment was so structured that she *had* to do so.

There was a silence.

"They're playing with the clocks again," said Montana, rising, preparing to put the baby into its crib. She meant that their keepers were making the electric clocks in the dome go fast, then slow, then fast again, and watching the little Earthling family through peepholes.

There was a silver chain around Montana Wildhack's neck. Hanging from it, between her breasts, was a locket containing a photograph of her alcoholic mother—a grainy thing, soot and chalk. It could have been anybody. Engraved on the outside of the locket were these words:

10

Robert Kennedy, whose summer home is eight miles from the home I live in all year round, was shot two nights ago. He died last night. So it goes.

Martin Luther King was shot a month ago. He died, too. So it goes.

And every day my Government gives me a count of corpses created by military science in Vietnam. So it goes.

My father died many years ago now—of natural causes. So it goes. He was a sweet man. He was a gun nut, too. He left me his guns. They rust.

On Tralfamadore, says Billy Pilgrim, there isn't much interest in Jesus Christ. The Earthling figure who is most engaging to the Tralfamadorian mind, he says, is Charles Darwin—who taught that those who die are meant to die, that corpses are improvements. So it goes.

The same general idea appears in *The Big Board* by Kilgore Trout. The flying saucer creatures who capture Trout's hero ask him about Darwin. They also ask him about golf.

If what Billy Pilgrim learned from the Tralfamadorians is true, that we will all live forever, no matter how dead we may sometimes seem to be, I am not overjoyed. Still—if I am going to spend eternity visiting this moment and that, I'm grateful that so many of those moments are nice.

One of the nicest ones in recent times was on my trip back to Dresden with my old war buddy, O'Hare.

We took a Hungarian Airlines plane from East Berlin. The pilot had a handlebar mustache. He looked like Adolph Menjou. He smoked a Cuban cigar while the plane was being fueled. When we took off, there was no talk of fastening seat belts.

When we were up in the air, a young steward served us rye bread and salami and butter and cheese and white wine. The folding tray in front of me would not open out. The steward went into the cockpit for a tool, came back with a beer-can opener. He used it to pry out the tray.

There were only six other passengers. They spoke many languages. They were having nice times, too. East Germany was down below, and the lights were on. I imagined dropping bombs on those lights, those villages and cities and towns.

O'Hare and I had never expected to make any money—and here we were now, extremely well-to-do.

"If you're ever in Cody, Wyoming," I said to him lazily, "just ask for Wild Bob."

O'Hare had a little notebook with him, and printed in the back of it were postal rates and airline distances and the altitudes of famous mountains and other key facts about the world. He was looking up the population of Dresden, which wasn't in the notebook, when he came across this, which he gave me to read:

On an average, 324,000 new babies are born into the world every day. During that same day, 10,000 persons, on an average, will have starved to death or died from malnutrition. So it goes. *In addition, 123,000 persons will die for other reasons.* So it goes. *This leaves a net gain of about 191,000 each day in the world. The Population Reference Bureau predicts that the world's total population will double to 7,000,000,000 before the year 2000.*

"I suppose they will all want dignity," I said.

"I suppose," said O'Hare.

Billy Pilgrim was meanwhile traveling back to Dresden, too, but not in the present. He was going back there in 1945, two days after the city was destroyed. Now Billy and the rest were being marched into the ruins by their guards. I was there. O'Hare was there. We had spent the past two nights in the blind innkeeper's stable. Authorities had found us there. They told us what to do. We were to borrow picks and shovels and crowbars and wheelbarrows from our neighbors. We were to march with these implements to such and such a place in the ruins, ready to go to work.

There were barricades on the main roads leading into the ruins. Germans were stopped there. They were not permitted to explore the moon.

Prisoners of war from many lands came together that morning at such and such a place in Dresden. It had been decreed that here was where the digging for bodies was to begin. So the digging began.

Billy found himself paired as a digger with a Maori, who had been captured at Tobruk. The Maori was chocolate brown. He had whirlpools tattooed on his forehead and his cheeks. Billy and the Maori dug into the inert, unpromising gravel of the moon. The materials were loose, so there were constant little avalanches.

Many holes were dug at once. Nobody knew yet what there was to find. Most holes came to nothing—to pavement, or to boulders so huge they would not move. There was no machinery. Not even horses or mules or oxen could cross the moonscape.

And Billy and the Maori and others helping them with their particular hole came at last to a membrane of timbers laced over rocks which had wedged together to form an accidental dome. They made a hole in the membrane. There was darkness and space under there.

A German soldier with a flashlight went down into the darkness, was gone a long time. When he finally came back, he told a superior on the rim of the hole that there were dozens of bodies down there. They were sitting on benches. They were unmarked.

So it goes.

The superior said that the opening in the membrane should be enlarged, and that a ladder should be put in the hole so that the bodies could be carried out. Thus began the first corpse mine in Dresden.

There were hundreds of corpse mines operating by and by. They didn't smell bad at first, were wax museums. But then the bodies rotted and liquefied, and the stink was like roses and mustard gas.

So it goes.

The Maori Billy had worked with died of the dry heaves, after having been ordered to go down in that stink and work. He tore himself to pieces, throwing up and throwing up.

So it goes.

So a new technique was devised. Bodies weren't brought up any more. They were cremated by soldiers with flamethrowers right where they were. The soldiers stood outside the shelters, simply sent the fire in.

Somewhere in there the poor old high school teacher, Edgar Derby, was caught with a teapot he had taken from the catacombs. He was arrested for plundering. He was tried and shot.

So it goes.

And somewhere in there was springtime. The corpse mines were closed down. The soldiers all left to fight the Russians. In the suburbs, the women and children dug rifle pits. Billy and the rest of his group were locked up in the stable in the suburbs. And then, one morning, they got up to discover that the door was unlocked. World War Two in Europe was over.

Billy and the rest wandered out onto the shady street. The trees were leafing out. There was nothing going on out there, no traffic of any kind. There was only one vehicle, an abandoned wagon drawn by two horses. The wagon was green and coffin-shaped.

Birds were talking

One bird said to Billy Pilgrim, "*Poo-tee-weet?*"

TOPICS FOR PAPERS AND DISCUSSION

1. *Billy Pilgrim as hero or antihero.* Is Billy Pilgrim a believable character? Is he in any sense heroic? Do you find him too outlandish and absurd to be taken seriously? What drives or needs motivate him, or is he merely a "listless plaything of enormous forces"? Does he change in any way as a result of the war? Determine if there is a paradigm for Billy among any of the following: Everyman, Christ, noble fool, innocent initiate, schizophrenic. How much, if anything, do Billy Pilgrim and Kurt Vonnegut have in common? (Refer here not only to the novel, but also to Vonnegut's epigraph on the title page and to his biographical note, p. 715.

2. *The interrelationship of story strands.* Determine if the following four distinct strands of the novel create a unified structure: Vonnegut as author (the autobiographical strand); Billy Pilgrim as citizen (the domestic strand); Tralfamadore (the science-fiction strand); the Dresden fire-bombing (the war strand). Or do these separate strands disrupt the unity? Is the book really "jumbled and jangled," as Vonnegut says? Could any of these strands be removed without doing irreparable harm to the novel?
3. *The function of Tralfamadore and its philosophy.* Consider Tralfamadorian views of time, of free will, of war, of multisexes, of death, of the fourth dimension. What does Billy learn from the Tralfamadorians? Of what use are these philosophical concepts to the reader? How does Tralfamadore provide the reader with new perspectives of earthly events? What is the purpose of these different perspectives? What is your opinion of Tralfamadorian theories?
4. *Time-tripping.* Why has Billy "come unstuck in time"? In fiction, the jumbling of human time is hardly abnormal, but what of Billy's Tralfamadorian adventures? Are we to take this kind of time-travel as reality, as fantasy, as insanity, or a combination of these? Do you believe in a time warp or simultaneous spatial time? Strictly for purposes of the story, decide whether Tralfamadore exists in the universe, or whether it exists only in Billy's head. From the "present" of 1968, sort out various uses of time in the novel: the distant past and the recent past, the near future and the distant future. What is accomplished by all this time-tripping?
5. Slaughterhouse-Five *as "history."* Read David Irving's historical account *The Destruction of Dresden* and compare it with the Dresden sections of the novel. What differences are revealed in the way history and art treat the same event? Enumerate the advantages and disadvantages of the approach used by each author toward "the greatest massacre in European history." Vonnegut has said that his novel could easily have been "2000 pages," but the finished product is less than 200 pages. What was gained or lost by making it short? Do we need to know more specifically about the Dresden fire-bombing than what Vonnegut tells us? Consider understatement as a technique in the novel.
6. *The role of women.* Weigh the relationships of Billy to women, in particular, the two who are closest to him: Valencia and Montana Wildhack. Is he different with each as mate, as lover, as father? Analyze the characterization of these two women. Consider Billy's mother, his daughter Barbara, the drunken woman at the New Year's Eve party, Maggie White, Lily Rumfoord. What attitudes toward them emerge? Also consider the few women mentioned in the opening chapter, and the women in Dresden.

7. *From verbal motif to meaning.* Approximately how many times does the statement "So it goes" appear, and what are its purposes? Is such usage effective or overdone? What about other verbal motifs? Analyze the technique of repetition. What is meant by "if the accident will"? This short novel abounds in leitmotifs woven out of metaphor-image-symbol. Analyze some of them like mustard gas and roses, nestling like spoons, Three Musketeers bars, black and orange as colors, cripples, bugs in amber, blue and ivory feet, the barbershop quartet. Are they all thematically important?
8. *Subtitles as indicators of theme.* What is the significance of "The Children's Crusade"? How is it used in the novel? Is Vonnegut's promise to Mary a sufficient explanation of its significance for the reader? Refer to the conversation between the British colonel and Edgar Derby. What is the meaning of "A Duty-Dance with Death"? In this connection, why does Vonnegut talk about Céline? How do these subtitles function as antiwar statements?
9. *Vonnegut's style.* In the epigraph about himself, Vonnegut refers to his narrative method as "telegraphic schizophrenic." What does he mean? Why does he mention its similarity to the "manner of tales of the planet Tralfamadore"? Compare his novel to the description of Tralfamadorian novels as "brief clumps of symbols." Vonnegut has remarked that each brief section of the novel "should work, roughly as a poem works." Explain what he meant. Is his style productive of dramatic tension? What is the nature of Vonnegut's particular idiom, and why has it become so popular with contemporary Americans, especially young people?
10. *Humor and satire.* In spite of the grimness of basic subject matter like war and death, *Slaughterhouse-Five* is a funny novel. Explore Vonnegut's humor. How does it work? What are the strengths and weaknesses of his satire? He does not seem very solemn about himself, yet he looks upon artists as "agents of change," who should be treasured as "alarm systems." Moreover, his work has been called profoundly moral. How do you reconcile his playful wit with his fundamental seriousness? Also he has remarked that the science-fiction passages are "just like the clowns in Shakespeare," who come on stage to "lighten things up." Evaluate this statement.
11. *Death and rebirth as archetype.* Billy nearly dies as a child (by drowning), as a young soldier (in World War II), as an older man (the plane crash). In each instance he is, as it were, reborn. Dresden is destroyed and reborn over "tons of human bone meal in the ground." Billy looks ahead to his assassination when he will "be dead for a little while—and then live again." How does the archetype of death and rebirth work, and how does it relate to the Tralfamadorian notion of death? Find other archetypes and myths in the novel.

12. *Technology in modern times. Slaughterhouse-Five* is also about machinery, material things, scientific instruments. What are the implications of technology? "Magic Fingers" can soothe human beings; bombs can obliterate them. Is the book opposed to technology? If so, what does it favor? Be sure to consider the significance of optometry. Why is Billy Pilgrim an optometrist, and why does he virtually give up the profession? In relation to technology, what does the novel suggest about "business" and "the work ethic" in America?
13. "*A new Gospel.*" What does Vonnegut say about God's concern with the world? What role does religion play in contemporary life? What technique does Vonnegut use to express his views? Vonnegut has said that he considers Alcoholics Anonymous to be a religion superior to others. What does he mean, and where are evidences of AA as religion in the novel? In what ways is Billy a "pilgrim"? What does the Christmas carol of "the little Lord Jesus" signify? Why are there so many other scattered references to Jesus?
14. *The function of authorial intrusion.* It is not uncommon for an author to be a character in his own fiction. This novel provides a frame for autobiography by the use of a prologue and a partial epilogue. But what about the authorial voice that intrudes into the main portion of the narrative? Do you find it unusual to have the writer stepping in to say "I was there," "That was me," and so on? Trace Vonnegut's appearances within the Billy Pilgrim story. How and why does he make his presence known, and what is accomplished by his intervention?
15. *The use of quotations.* Why does the novel include so many citations, some made up but mostly real? The sources are widely divergent: *The Review of Optometry,* President Truman's atomic-bomb announcement, the Gideon Bible, Howard Campbell's "monograph," *Dresden, History, Stage and Gallery, The Execution of Private Slovik, Extraordinary Popular Delusions and the Madness of Crowds, The Destruction of Dresden,* etc. Why also does the author place so much importance upon relating the plots of Kilgore Trout's science fiction?
16. *Identity crisis and fragmentation.* "Things fall apart; the center cannot hold," Yeats wrote. How have things fallen apart for Billy? Is his problem simply a matter of finding a cohesive identity? Has his difficulty defining "the self" been pervasive and lifelong, or was it caused by either the war or the plane crash? Is it resolved after his experience in the Tralfamadorian geodesic dome? Are Billy's alienation and disorientation intended to reflect contemporary existence? Has the world itself, in Vonnegut's view, become fragmented into multiple states of being and/or nonbeing?
17. *Offbeat effects.* Bombs fly backward into planes; Christ makes a cross as a carpenter; a soldier wears silver boots, a blue toga, and a

muff; a science-fiction writer has written seventy-five books only two people ever heard of; the author calls his own novel "this lousy little book." What are the accomplishments of such eccentric and comic writing? In this connection, how do you explain that Vonnegut "never wrote a story with a villain in it"? Seek out other examples of the offbeat which invert ordinary and traditional ways of looking at things.

18. *"Obscenity," "Immorality," and Censorship.* Recently, *Slaughterhouse-Five* was prohibited from being taught in a small-town high school, and the teacher who assigned it was arrested. Copies of the novel were actually burned. It was said to contain "obscene language" and "filth." It was also thought "to undermine the morals of the students." Is the novel "obscene" or "immoral"? What is your attitude toward censorship in a free society? Who determines what should be read and taught, and how?
19. *Novel as potpourri.* This novel contains many disparate elements that seem to work remarkably well together in the face of incongruousness. Appearing in drawings are a tombstone epitaph, a latrine sign, and a locket inscription. Interspersed are jokes, songs, literary allusions, poems, prayers, limericks, even an untranslated passage of German. A drunk is named Rosewater, the Wearys collect instruments of torture, a muscle-bound Englishman plays the Blue Fairy Godmother. We hear a bird sing *"Poo-tee-weet?"*; we learn the history of a pornographic photo; we see a dream of giraffes in a garden. Can a pastiche of this kind achieve cohesiveness and unity? Try to explain how an apparent hodgepodge becomes a work of art.
20. *Avoiding the pigeonhole.* One critic has referred to the novel as a "meditation on the relationship between history and dreaming." Another critic believes that Vonnegut's writing is less high art than it is "myth and entertainment." While one critic classifies the novel as "a fable," another refers to it as an "anti-novel." It has been called everything from "psychedelic" to "sophomoric," from "a masterpiece" to "an apocalypse." One latter-day Francis Bacon speaks of it as "a club sandwich." Try to explain these assessments, if you can. Why do you suppose critics disagree in their attempts to "place" this novel?

The Ballad of the Sad Café

CARSON McCULLERS

The town itself is dreary; not much is there except the cotton mill, the two-room houses where the workers live, a few peach trees, a church with two colored windows, and a miserable main street only a hundred yards long. On Saturdays the tenants from the near-by farms come in for a day of talk and trade. Otherwise the town is lonesome, sad, and like a place that is far off and estranged from all other places in the world. The nearest train stop is Society City, and the Greyhound and White Bus Lines use the Forks Falls Road which is three miles away. The winters here are short and raw, the summers white with glare and fiery hot.

If you walk along the main street on an August afternoon there is nothing whatsoever to do. The largest building, in the very center of the town, is boarded up completely and leans so far to the right that it seems bound to collapse at any minute. The house is very old. There is about it a curious, cracked look that is very puzzling until you suddenly realize that at one time, and long ago, the right side of the front porch had been painted, and part of the wall—but the painting was left unfinished and one portion of the house is darker and dingier than the other. The building looks completely deserted. Nevertheless, on the second floor there is one window which is not boarded; sometimes in the late afternoon when the heat is at its worst a hand will slowly open the shutter and a face will look down on the town. It is a face like the terrible dim faces known in dreams—sexless and white, with two gray crossed eyes which are turned inward so sharply that they seem to be exchanging with each other one long and secret gaze of grief. The face lingers at the window for an hour or so, then the shutters are closed once more, and as likely as not there will not be another soul to be seen along the main street. These August afternoons—when your snift is finished there is absolutely nothing to do; you might as well walk down to the Forks Falls Road and listen to the chain gang.

However, here in this very town there was once a café. And this old boarded-up house was unlike any other place for many miles around. There were tables with cloths and paper napkins, colored streamers from the electric fans, great gatherings on Saturday nights. The owner of the place was Miss Amelia Evans. But the person most responsible for the success and gaiety of the place was a hunchback called Cousin Lymon. One other person had a part in the story of this café—he was the former husband of Miss Amelia, a terrible character who returned to the town after a long term in the penitentiary, caused ruin, and then went on his way again. The café has long since been closed, but it is still remembered.

The place was not always a café. Miss Amelia inherited the building from her father, and it was a store that carried mostly feed, guano, and staples such as meal and snuff. Miss Amelia was rich. In addition to the store she operated a still three miles back in the swamp, and ran out the best liquor in the county. She was a dark, tall woman with bones and muscles like a man. Her hair was cut short and brushed back from the forehead, and there was about her sunburned face a tense, haggard quality. She might have been a handsome woman if, even then, she was not slightly cross-eyed. There were those who would have courted her, but Miss Amelia cared nothing for the love of men and was a solitary person. Her marriage had been unlike any other marriage ever contracted in this county—it was a strange and dangerous marriage, lasting only for ten days, that left the whole town wondering and shocked. Except for this queer marriage, Miss Amelia had lived her life alone. Often she spent whole nights back in her shed in the swamp, dressed in overalls and gum boots, silently guarding the low fire of the still.

With all things which could be made by the hands Miss Amelia prospered. She sold chitterlins and sausage in the town near-by. On fine autumn days, she ground sorghum, and the syrup from her vats was dark golden and delicately flavored. She built the brick privy behind her store in only two weeks and was skilled in carpentering. It was only with people that Miss Amelia was not at ease. People, unless they are nilly-willy or very sick, cannot be taken into the hands and changed overnight to something more worthwhile and profitable. So that the only use that Miss Amelia had for other people was to make money out of them. And in this she succeeded. Mortgages on crops and property, a sawmill, money in the bank—she was the richest woman for miles around. She would have been rich as a congressman if it were not for her one great failing, and that was her passion for lawsuits and the courts. She would involve herself in long and bitter litigation over just a trifle. It was said that if Miss Amelia so much as stumbled over a rock in the road she would glance around instinctively as though looking for something to sue about it. Aside from these lawsuits she lived a steady life and every day was very much like the day that had gone before. With the exception of her ten-day marriage, nothing happened to change this until the spring of the year that Miss Amelia was thirty years old.

It was toward midnight on a soft quiet evening in April. The sky was the color of a blue swamp iris, the moon clear and bright. The crops that spring promised well and in the past weeks the mill had run a night shift. Down by the creek the square brick factory was yellow with light, and there was the faint, steady hum of the looms. It was such a night when it is good to hear from faraway, across the dark fields, the slow song of a Negro on his way to make love. Or when it is pleasant to sit quietly and pick a guitar, or simply to rest alone and think of nothing at all. The street that evening was deserted, but Miss Amelia's store was lighted and on the porch outside there were five people. One of these was Stumpy MacPhail, a foreman with a red face and dainty, purplish hands. On the top step were two boys in overalls, the Rainey twins—both of them lanky and slow, with white hair and sleepy green eyes. The other man was Henry Macy, a shy and timid person with gentle manners and nervous ways, who sat on the edge of the bottom step. Miss Amelia herself stood leaning against the side of the open door, her feet crossed in their big swamp boots, patiently untying knots in a rope she had come across. They had not talked for a long time.

One of the twins, who had been looking down the empty road, was the first to speak. 'I see something coming,' he said.

'A calf got loose,' said his brother.

The approaching figure was still too distant to be clearly seen. The moon made dim, twisted shadows of the blossoming peach trees along the side of the road. In the air the odor of blossoms and sweet spring grass mingled with the warm, sour smell of the near-by lagoon.

'No. It's somebody's youngun,' said Stumpy MacPhail.

Miss Amelia watched the road in silence. She had put down her rope and was fingering the straps of her overalls with her brown bony hand. She scowled, and a dark lock of hair fell down on her forehead. While they were waiting there, a dog from one of the houses down the road began a wild, hoarse howl that continued until a voice called out and hushed him. It was not until the figure was quite close, within the range of the yellow light from the porch, that they saw clearly what had come.

The man was a stranger, and it is rare that a stranger enters the town on foot at that hour. Besides, the man was a hunchback. He was scarcely more than four feet tall and he wore a ragged, dusty coat that reached only to his knees. His crooked little legs seemed too thin to carry the weight of his great warped chest and the hump that sat on his shoulders. He had a very large head, with deep-set blue eyes and a sharp little mouth. His face was both soft and sassy—at the moment his pale skin was yellowed by dust and there were lavendar shadows beneath his eyes. He carried a lopsided old suitcase which was tied with a rope.

'Evening,' said the hunchback, and he was out of breath.

Miss Amelia and the men on the porch neither answered his greeting nor spoke. They only looked at him.

'I am hunting for Miss Amelia Evans.'

Miss Amelia pushed back her hair from her forehead and raised her chin. 'How come?'

'Because I am kin to her,' the hunchback said.

The twins and Stumpy MacPhail looked up at Miss Amelia.

'That's me,' she said. 'How do you mean "kin"?'

'Because——' the hunchback began. He looked uneasy, almost as though he was about to cry. He rested the suitcase on the bottom step, but did not take his hand from the handle. 'My mother was Fanny Jesup and she come from Cheehaw. She left Cheehaw some thirty years ago when she married her first husband. I remember hearing her tell how she had a half-sister named Martha. And back in Cheehaw today they tell me that was your mother.'

Miss Amelia listened with her head turned slightly aside. She ate her Sunday dinners by herself; her place was never crowded with a flock of relatives, and she claimed kin with no one. She had had a great-aunt who owned the livery stable in Cheehaw, but that aunt was now dead. Aside from her there was only one double first cousin who lived in a town twenty miles away, but this cousin and Miss Amelia did not get on so well, and when they chanced to pass each other they spat on the side of the road. Other people had tried very hard, from time to time, to work out some kind of far-fetched connection with Miss Amelia, but with absolutely no success.

The hunchback went into a long rigmarole, mentioning names and places that were unknown to the listeners on the porch and seemed to have nothing to do with the subject. 'So Fanny and Martha Jesup were half-sisters. And I am the son of Fanny's third husband. So that would make you and I——' He bent down and began to unfasten his suitcase. His hands were like dirty sparrow claws and they were trembling. The bag was full of all manner of junk—ragged clothes and odd rubbish that looked like parts out of a sewing machine, or something just as worthless. The hunchback scrambled among these belongings and brought out an old photograph. 'This is a picture of my mother and her half-sister.'

Miss Amelia did not speak. She was moving her jaw slowly from side to side, and you could tell from her face what she was thinking about. Stumpy MacPhail took the photograph and held it out toward the light. It was a picture of two pale, withered-up little children of about two and three years of age. The faces were tiny white blurs, and it might have been an old picture in anyone's album.

Stumpy MacPhail handed it back with no comment. 'Where you come from?' he asked.

The hunchback's voice was uncertain. 'I was traveling.'

Still Miss Amelia did not speak. She just stood leaning against the side of the door, and looked down at the hunchback. Henry Macy winked nervously and rubbed his hands together. Then quietly he left the bottom step and disappeared. He is a good soul, and the hunchback's situation had touched his heart. Therefore he did not want to wait and watch Miss Amelia chase this newcomer off her property and run him out of town. The hunchback stood with his bag open on the bottom step; he sniffled his nose, and his mouth quivered. Perhaps he began to feel his dismal predicament. Maybe he realized what a miserable thing it was to be a stranger in the town with a suitcase full of junk, and claiming kin with Miss Amelia. At any rate he sat down on the steps and suddenly began to cry.

It was not a common thing to have an unknown hunchback walk to the store at midnight and then sit down and cry. Miss Amelia rubbed back her hair from her forehead and the men looked at each other uncomfortably. All around the town was very quiet.

At last one of the twins said: 'I'll be damned if he ain't a regular Morris Finestein.'

Everyone nodded and agreed, for that is an expression having a certain special meaning. But the hunchback cried louder because he could not know what they were talking about. Morris Finestein was a person who had lived in the town years before. He was only a quick, skipping little Jew who cried if you called him Christ-killer, and ate light bread and canned salmon every day. A calamity had come over him and he had moved away to Society City. But since then if a man were prissy in any way, or if a man ever wept, he was known as a Morris Finestein.

'Well, he is afflicted,' said Stumpy MacPhail. 'There is some cause.'

Miss Amelia crossed the porch with two slow, gangling strides. She went down the steps and stood looking thoughtfully at the stranger. Gingerly, with one long brown forefinger, she touched the hump on his back. The hunchback still wept, but he was quieter now. The night was silent and the moon still shone with a soft, clear light—it was getting colder. Then Miss Amelia did a rare thing; she pulled out a bottle from her hip pocket and after polishing off the top with the palm of her hand she handed it to the hunchback to drink. Miss Amelia could seldom be persuaded to sell her liquor on credit, and for her to give so much as a drop away free was almost unknown.

'Drink,' she said. 'It will liven your gizzard.'

The hunchback stopped crying, neatly licked the tears from around his mouth, and did as he was told. When he was finished, Miss Amelia took a slow swallow, warmed and washed her mouth with it, and spat. Then she also drank. The twins and the foreman had their own bottle they had paid for.

'It is smooth liquor,'' Stumpy MacPhail said. 'Miss Amelia, I have never known you to fail.'

The whisky they drank that evening (two big bottles of it) is important. Otherwise, it would be hard to account for what followed. Perhaps without it there would never have been a café. For the liquor of Miss Amelia has a special quality of its own. It is clean and sharp on the tongue, but once down a man it glows inside him for a long time afterward. And that is not all. It is known that if a message is written with lemon juice on a clean sheet of paper there will be no sign of it. But if the paper is held for a moment to the fire then the letters turn brown and the meaning becomes clear. Imagine that the whisky is the fire and that the message is that which is known only in the soul of a man—then the worth of Miss Amelia's liquor can be understood. Things that have gone unnoticed, thoughts that have been harbored far back in the dark mind, are suddenly recognized and comprehended. A spinner who has thought only of the loom, the dinner pail, the bed, and then the loom again—this spinner might drink some on a Sunday and come across a marsh lily. And in his palm he might hold this flower, examining the golden dainty cup, and in him suddenly might come a sweetness keen as pain. A weaver might look up suddenly and see for the first time the cold, weird radiance of midnight January sky, and a deep fright at his own smallness stop his heart. Such things as these, then, happen when a man has drunk Miss Amelia's liquor. He may suffer, or he may be spent with joy—but the experience has shown the truth; he has warmed his soul and seen the message hidden there.

They drank until it was past midnight, and the moon was clouded over so that the night was cold and dark. The hunchback still sat on the bottom steps, bent over miserably with his forehead resting on his knee. Miss Amelia stood with her hands in her pockets, one foot resting on the second step of the stairs. She had been silent for a long time. Her face had the expression often seen in slightly cross-eyed persons who are thinking deeply, a look that appears to be both very wise and very crazy. At last she said: 'I don't know your name.'

'I'm Lymon Willis,' said the hunchback.

'Well, come on in,' she said. 'Some supper was left in the stove and you can eat.'

Only a few times in her life had Miss Amelia invited anyone to eat with her, unless she were planning to trick them in some way, or make money out of them. So the men on the porch felt there was something wrong. Later, they said among themselves that she must have been drinking back in the swamp the better part of the afternoon. At any rate she left the porch, and Stumpy MacPhail and the twins went on off home. She bolted the front door and looked all around to see that her goods were in order. Then she went to the kitchen, which was at the back of the store. The hunchback followed her, dragging his suitcase, sniffing and wiping his nose on the sleeve of his dirty coat.

'Sit down,' said Miss Amelia. 'I'll just warm up what's here.'

It was a good meal they had together on that night. Miss Amelia was rich and she did not grudge herself food. There was fried chicken (the breast of which the hunchback took on his own plate), mashed rootabeggars, collard greens, and hot, pale golden, sweet potatoes. Miss Amelia ate slowly and with the relish of a farm hand. She sat with both elbows on the table, bent over the plate, her knees spread wide apart and her feet braced on the rungs of the chair. As for the hunchback, he gulped down his supper as though he had not smelled food in months. During the meal one tear crept down his dingy cheek—but it was just a little leftover tear and meant nothing at all. The lamp on the table was well-trimmed, burning blue at the edges of the wick, and casting a cheerful light in the kitchen. When Miss Amelia had eaten her supper she wiped her plate carefully with a slice of light bread, and then poured her own clear, sweet syrup over the bread. The hunchback did likewise—except that he was more finicky and asked for a new plate. Having finished, Miss Amelia tilted back her chair, tightened her fist, and felt the hard, supple muscles of her right arm beneath the clean, blue cloth of her shirtsleeves —an unconscious habit with her, at the close of a meal. Then she took the lamp from the table and jerked her head toward the staircase as an invitation for the hunchback to follow after her.

Above the store there were the three rooms where Miss Amelia had lived during all her life—two bedrooms with a large parlor in between. Few people had even seen these rooms, but it was generally known that they were well-furnished and extremely clean. And now Miss Amelia was taking up with her a dirty little hunchbacked stranger, come from God knows where. Miss Amelia walked slowly, two steps at a time, holding the lamp high. The hunchback hovered so close behind her that the swinging light made on the staircase wall one great, twisted shadow of the two of them. Soon the premises above the store were dark as the rest of the town.

The next morning was serene, with a sunrise of warm purple mixed with rose. In the fields around the town the furrows were newly plowed, and very early the tenants were at work setting out the young, deep green tobacco plants. The wild crows flew down close to the fields, making swift blue shadows on the earth. In town the people set out early with their dinner pails, and the windows of the mill were blinding gold in the sun. The air was fresh and the peach trees light as March clouds with their blossoms.

Miss Amelia came down at about dawn, as usual. She washed her head at the pump and very shortly set about her business. Later in the morning she saddled her mule and went to see about her property, planted with cotton, up near the Forks Falls Road. By noon, of course, everybody had heard about the hunchback who had come to the store in the middle of the night. But no one as yet had seen him. The day soon grew hot and the sky was a rich, midday blue. Still no one had laid an eye on this strange guest. A few people remembered that Miss Amelia's mother had had a half-sister—but there was some difference of opinion as to whether she had died or had run off with a tobacco stringer. As for the hunchback's claim, everyone thought it was a trumped-up business. And the town, knowing Miss Amelia, decided that surely she had put him out of the house after feeding him. But toward evening, when the sky had whitened, and the shift was done, a woman claimed to have seen a crooked face at the window of one of the rooms up over the store. Miss Amelia herself said nothing. She clerked in the store for a while, argued for an hour with a farmer over a plow shaft, mended some chicken wire, locked up near sundown, and went to her rooms. The town was left puzzled and talkative.

The next day Miss Amelia did not open the store, but stayed locked up inside her premises and saw no one. Now this was the day that the rumor started—the rumor so terrible that the town and all the country about were stunned by it. The rumor was started by a weaver called Merlie Ryan. He is a man of not much account—sallow, shambling, and with no teeth in his head. He has the three-day malaria, which means that every third day the fever comes on him. So on two days he is dull and cross, but on the third day he livens up and sometimes has an idea or two, most of which are foolish. It was while Merlie Ryan was in his fever that he turned suddenly and said:

'I know what Miss Amelia done. She murdered that man for something in that suitcase.'

He said this in a calm voice, as a statement of fact. And within an hour the news had swept through the town. It was a fierce and sickly tale the town built up that day. In it were all the things which cause the heart to shiver—a hunchback, a midnight burial in the swamp, the dragging of Miss Amelia through the streets of the town on the way to prison, the squabbles over what would happen to her property—all told in hushed voices and repeated with some fresh and weird detail. It rained and women forgot to bring in the washing from the lines. One or two mortals, who were in debt to Miss Amelia, even put on Sunday clothes as though it were a holiday. People clustered together on the main street, talking and watching the store.

It would be untrue to say that all the town took part in this evil festival. There were a few sensible men who reasoned that Miss Amelia, being rich, would not go out of her way to murder a vagabond for a few trifles of junk. In the town there were even three good people, and they did not want this crime, not even for the sake of the interest and the great commotion it would entail; it gave them no pleasure to think of Miss Amelia holding to the bars of the penitentiary and being electrocuted in Atlanta. These good people judged Miss Amelia in a different way from what the others judged her. When a person is as contrary in every single respect as she was and when the sins of a person have amounted to such a point that they can hardly be remembered all at once—then this person plainly requires a special judgment. They remembered that Miss Amelia had been born dark and somewhat queer of face, raised motherless by her father who was a solitary man, that early in youth she had grown to be six feet two inches tall which in itself is not natural for a woman, and that her ways and habits of life were too peculiar ever to reason about. Above all, they remembered her puzzling marriage, which was the most unreasonable scandal ever to happen in this town.

So these good people felt toward her something near to pity. And when she was out on her wild business, such as rushing in a house to drag forth a sewing machine in payment for a debt, or getting herself worked up over some matter concerning the law—they had toward her a feeling which was a mixture of exasperation, a ridiculous little inside tickle, and a deep, unnamable sadness. But enough of the good people, for there were only three of them; the rest of the town was making a holiday of this fancied crime the whole of the afternoon.

Miss Amelia herself, for some strange reason, seemed unaware of all this. She spent most of her day upstairs. When down in the store, she prowled around peacefully, her hands deep in the pockets of her overalls and head bent so low that her chin was tucked inside the collar of her shirt. There was no bloodstain on her anywhere. Often she stopped and just stood somberly looking down at the cracks in the floor, twisting a lock of her short-cropped hair, and whispering something to herself. But most of the day was spent upstairs.

Dark came on. The rain that afternoon had chilled the air, so that the evening was bleak and gloomy as in wintertime. There were no stars in the sky, and a light, icy drizzle had set in. The lamps in the houses made mournful, wavering flickers when watched from the street. A wind had come up, not from the swamp side of the town but from the cold black pinewoods to the north.

The clocks in the town struck eight. Still nothing had happened. The bleak night, after the gruesome talk of the day, put a fear in some people, and they stayed home close to the fire. Others were gathered in groups together. Some eight or ten men had convened on the porch of Miss Amelia's store. They were silent and were indeed just waiting about. They themselves did not know what they were waiting for, but it was this: in times of tension, when some great action is impending, men gather and wait in this way. And after a time there will come a moment when all together they will act in unison, not from thought or from the will of any one man, but as though their instincts had merged together so that the decision belongs to no single one of them, but to the group as a whole. At such a time, no individual hesitates. And whether the matter will be settled peaceably, or whether the joint action will result in ransacking, violence, and crime, depends on destiny. So the men waited soberly on the porch of Miss Amelia's store, not one of them realizing what they would do, but knowing inwardly that they must wait, and that the time had almost come.

Now the door to the store was open. Inside it was bright and natural-looking. To the left was the counter where slabs of white meat, rock candy, and tobacco were kept. Behind this were shelves of salted white meat and meal. The right side of the store was mostly filled with farm implements and such. At the back of the store, to the left, was the door leading up the stairs, and it was open. And at the far right of the store there was another door which led to a little room that Miss Amelia called her office. This door was also open. And at eight o'clock that evening Miss Amelia could be seen there sitting before her rolltop desk, figuring with a fountain pen and some pieces of paper.

The office was cheerfully lighted, and Miss Amelia did not seem to notice the delegation on the porch. Everything around her was in great order, as usual. This office was a room well-known, in a dreadful way, throughout the country. It was there Miss Amelia transacted all business. On the desk was a carefully covered typewriter which she knew how to run, but used only for the most important documents. In the drawers were literally thousands of papers, all filed according to the alphabet. This office was also the place where Miss Amelia received sick people, for she enjoyed doctoring and did a great deal of it. Two whole shelves were crowded with bottles and various paraphernalia. Against the wall was a bench where the patients sat. She could sew up a wound with a burnt needle so that it would not turn green. For burns she had a cool, sweet syrup. For unlocated sickness there were any number of different medicines which she had brewed herself from unknown recipes. They wrenched loose the bowels very well, but they could not be given to small children, as they caused bad convulsions; for them she had an entirely separate draught, gentler and sweet-flavored. Yes, all in all, she was considered a good doctor. Her hands, though very large and bony, had a light touch about them. She possessed great imagination and used hundreds of different cures. In the face of the most dangerous and extraordinary treatment she did not hesitate, and no disease was so terrible but what she would undertake to cure it. In this there was one exception. If a patient came with a female complaint she could do nothing. Indeed at the mere mention of the words her face would slowly darken with shame, and she would stand there craning her neck against the collar of her shirt, or rubbing her swamp boots together, for all the world like a great, shamed, dumb-tongued child. But in other matters people trusted her. She charged no fees whatsoever and always had a raft of patients.

On this evening, Miss Amelia wrote with her fountain pen a good deal. But even so she could not be forever unaware of the group waiting out there on the dark porch, and watching her. From time to time she looked up and regarded them steadily. But she did not holler out to them to demand why they were loafing around her property like a sorry bunch of gabbies. Her face was proud and stern, as it always was when she sat at the desk of her office. After a time their peering in like that seemed to annoy her. She wiped her cheek with a red handkerchief, got up, and closed the office door.

Now to the group on the porch this gesture acted as a signal. The time had come. They had stood for a long while with the night raw and gloomy in the street behind them. They had waited long and just at that moment the instinct to act came on them.

All at once, as though moved by one will, they walked into the store. At that moment the eight men looked very much alike—all wearing blue overalls, most of them with whitish hair, all pale of face, and all with a set, dreaming look in the eye. What they would have done next no one knows. But at that instant there was a noise at the head of the staircase. The men looked up and then stood dumb with shock. It was the hunchback, whom they had already murdered in their minds. Also, the creature was not at all as had been pictured to them—not a pitiful and dirty little chatterer, alone and beggared in this world. Indeed, he was like nothing any man among them had ever beheld until that time. The room was still as death.

The hunchback came down slowly with the proudness of one who owns every plank of the floor beneath his feet. In the past days he had greatly changed. For one thing he was clean beyond words. He still wore his little coat, but it was brushed off and neatly mended. Beneath this was a fresh red and black checkered shirt belonging to Miss Amelia. He did not wear trousers such as ordinary men are meant to wear, but a pair of tight-fitting little knee-length breeches. On his skinny legs he wore black stockings, and his shoes were of a special kind, being queerly shaped, laced up over the ankles, and newly cleaned and polished with wax. Around his neck, so that his large, pale ears were almost completely covered, he wore a shawl of lime-green wool, the fringes of which almost touched the floor.

The hunchback walked down the store with his stiff little strut and then stood in the center of the group that had come inside. They cleared a space about him and stood looking with hands loose at their sides and eyes wide open. The hunchback himself got his bearings in an odd manner. He regarded each person steadily at his own eye-level, which was about belt line for an ordinary man. Then with shrewd deliberation he examined each man's lower regions—from the waist to the sole of the shoe. When he had satisfied himself he closed his eyes for a moment and shook his head, as though in his opinion what he had seen did not amount to much. Then with assurance, only to confirm himself, he tilted back his head and took in the halo of faces around him with one long, circling stare. There was a half-filled sack of guano on the left side of the store, and when he had found his bearings in this way, the hunchback sat down upon it. Cozily settled, with his little legs crossed, he took from his coat pocket a certain object.

Now it took some moments for the men in the store to regain their ease. Merlie Ryan, he of the three-day fever who had started the rumor that day, was the first to speak. He looked at the object which the hunchback was fondling, and said in a hushed voice:

'What is it you have there?'

Each man knew well what it was the hunchback was handling. For it was the snuffbox which had belonged to Miss Amelia's father. The snuffbox was of blue enamel with a dainty embellishment of wrought gold on the lid. The group knew it well and marveled. They glanced warily at the closed office door, and heard the low sound of Miss Amelia whistling to herself.

'Yes, what is it, Peanut?'

The hunchback looked up quickly and sharpened his mouth to speak. 'Why, this is a lay-low to catch meddlers.'

The hunchback reached in the box with his scrambly little fingers and ate something, but he offered no one around him a taste. It was not even proper snuff which he was taking, but a mixture of sugar and cocoa. This he took, though, as snuff, pocketing a little wad of it beneath his lower lip and licking down neatly into this with a flick of his tongue which made a frequent grimace come over his face.

'The very teeth in my head have always tasted sour to me,' he said in explanation. 'That is the reason why I take this kind of sweet snuff.'

The group still clustered around, feeling somewhat gawky and bewildered. This sensation never quite wore off, but it was soon tempered by another feeling—an air of intimacy in the room and a vague festivity. Now the names of the men of the group there on that evening were as follows: Hasty Malone, Robert Calvert Hale, Merlie Ryan, Reverend T. M. Willin, Rosser Cline, Rip Wellborn, Henry Ford Crimp, and Horace Wells. Except for Reverend Willin, they are all alike in many ways as has been said—all having taken pleasure from something or other, all having wept and suffered in some way, most of them tractable unless exasperated. Each of them worked in the mill, and lived with others in a two- or three-room house for which the rent was ten dollars or twelve dollars a month. All had been paid that afternoon, for it was Saturday. So, for the present, think of them as a whole.

The hunchback, however, was already sorting them out in his mind. Once comfortably settled he began to chat with everyone, asking questions such as if a man was married, how old he was, how much his wages came to in an average week, et cetera—picking his way along to inquiries which were downright intimate. Soon the group was joined by others in the town, Henry Macy, idlers who had sensed something extraordinary, women come to fetch their men who lingered on, and even one loose, towhead child who tiptoed into the store, stole a box of animal crackers, and made off very quietly. So the premises of Miss Amelia were soon crowded, and she herself had not yet opened her office door.

There is a type of person who has a quality about him that sets him apart from other and more ordinary human beings. Such a person has an instinct which is usually found only in small children, an instinct to establish immediate and vital contact between himself and all things in the world. Certainly the hunchback was of this type. He had only been in the store half an hour before an immediate contact had been established between him and each other individual. It was as though he had lived in the town for years, was a well-known character, and had been sitting and talking there on that guano sack for countless evenings. This, together with the fact that it was Saturday night, could account for the air of freedom and illicit gladness in the store. There was a tension, also, partly because of the oddity of the situation and because Miss Amelia was still closed off in her office and had not yet made her appearance.

She came out that evening at ten o'clock. And those who were expecting some drama at her entrance were disappointed. She opened the door and walked in with her slow, gangling swagger. There was a streak of ink on one side of her nose, and she had knotted the red handkerchief about her neck. She seemed to notice nothing unusual. Her gray, crossed eyes glanced over to the place where the hunchback was sitting, and for a moment lingered there. The rest of the crowd in her store she regarded with only a peaceable surprise.

'Does anyone want waiting on?' she asked quietly.

There were a number of customers, because it was Saturday night, and they all wanted liquor. Now Miss Amelia had dug up an aged barrel only three days past and had siphoned it into bottles back by the still. This night she took the money from the customers and counted it beneath the bright light. Such was the ordinary procedure. But after this what happened was not ordinary. Always before, it was necessary to go around to the dark back yard, and there she would hand out your bottle through the kitchen door. There was no feeling of joy in the transaction. After getting his liquor the customer walked off into the night. Or, if his wife would not have it in the home, he was allowed to come back around to the front porch of the store and guzzle there or in the street. Now, both the porch and the street before it were the property of Miss Amelia, and no mistake about it—but she did not regard them as her premises; the premises began at the front door and took in the entire inside of the building. There she had never allowed liquor to be opened or drunk by anyone but herself. Now for the first time she broke this rule. She went to the kitchen, with the hunchback close at her heels, and she brought back the bottles into the warm, bright store. More than that she furnished some glasses and opened two boxes of crackers so that they were there hospitably in a platter on the counter and anyone who wished could take one free.

She spoke to no one but the hunchback, and she only asked him in a somewhat harsh and husky voice: 'Cousin Lymon, will you have yours straight, or warmed in a pan with water on the stove?'

'If you please, Amelia,' the hunchback said. (And since what time had anyone presumed to address Miss Amelia by her bare name, without a title of respect?—Certainly not her bridegroom and her husband of ten days. In fact, not since the death of her father, who for some reason had always called her Little, had anyone dared to address her in such a familiar way.) 'If you please, I'll have it warmed.'

Now, this was the beginning of the café. It was as simple as that. Recall that the night was gloomy as in wintertime, and to have sat around the property outside would have made a sorry celebration. But inside there was company and a genial warmth. Someone had rattled up the stove in the rear, and those who bought bottles shared their liquor with friends. Several women were there and they had twists of licorice, a Nehi, or even a swallow of the whisky. The hunchback was still a novelty and his presence amused everyone. The bench in the office was brought in, together with several extra chairs. Other people leaned against the counter or made themselves comfortable on barrels and sacks. Nor did the opening of liquor on the premises cause any rambunctiousness, indecent giggles, or misbehavior whatsoever. On the contrary the company was polite even to the point of a certain timidness. For people in this town were then unused to gathering together for the sake of pleasure. They met to work in the mill. Or on Sunday there would be an all-day camp meeting —and though that is a pleasure, the intention of the whole affair is to sharpen your view of Hell and put into you a keen fear of the Lord Almighty. But the spirit of a café is altogether different. Even the richest, greediest old rascal will behave himself, insulting no one in a proper café. And poor people look about them gratefully and pinch up the salt in a dainty and modest manner. For the atmosphere of a proper café implies these qualities: fellowship, the satisfactions of the belly, and a certain gaiety and grace of behavior. This had never been told to the gathering in Miss Amelia's store that night. But they knew it of themselves, although never, of course, until that time had there been a café in the town.

Now, the cause of all this, Miss Amelia, stood most of the evening in the doorway leading to the kitchen. Outwardly she did not seem changed at all. But there were many who noticed her face. She watched all that went on, but most of the time her eyes were fastened lonesomely on the hunchback. He strutted about the store, eating from his snuffbox, and being at once sour and agreeable. Where Miss Amelia stood, the light from the chinks of the stove cast a glow, so that her brown, long face was somewhat brightened. She seemed to be looking inward. There was in her expression pain, perplexity, and uncertain joy. Her lips were not so firmly set as usual, and she swallowed often. Her skin had paled and her large empty hands were sweating. Her look that night, then, was the lonesome look of the lover.

This opening of the café came to an end at midnight. Everyone said good-bye to everyone else in a friendly fashion. Miss Amelia shut the front door of her premises, but forgot to bolt it. Soon everything—the main street with its three stores, the mill, the houses—all the town, in fact—was dark and silent. And so ended three days and nights in which had come an arrival of a stranger, an unholy holiday, and the start of the café.

Now time must pass. For the next four years are much alike. There are great changes, but these changes are brought about bit by bit, in simple steps which in themselves do not appear to be important. The hunchback continued to live with Miss Amelia. The café expanded in a gradual way. Miss Amelia began to sell her liquor by the drink, and some tables were brought into the store. There were customers every evening, and on Saturday a great crowd. Miss Amelia began to serve fried catfish suppers at fifteen cents a plate. The hunchback cajoled her into buying a fine mechanical piano. Within two years the place was a store no longer, but had been converted into a proper café, open every evening from six until twelve o'clock.

Each night the hunchback came down the stairs with the air of one who has a grand opinion of himself. He always smelled slightly of turnip greens, as Miss Amelia rubbed him night and morning with pot liquor to give him strength. She spoiled him to a point beyond reason, but nothing seemed to strengthen him; food only made his hump and his head grow larger while the rest of him remained weakly and deformed. Miss Amelia was the same in appearance. During the week she still wore swamp boots and overalls, but on Sunday she put on a dark red dress that hung on her in a most peculiar fashion. Her manners, however, and her way of life were greatly changed. She still loved a fierce lawsuit, but she was not so quick to cheat her fellow man and to exact cruel payments. Because the hunchback was so extremely sociable, she even went about a little—to revivals, to funerals, and so forth. Her doctoring was as successful as ever, her liquor even finer than before, if that were possible. The café itself proved profitable and was the only place of pleasure for many miles around.

So for the moment regard these years from random and disjointed views. See the hunchback marching in Miss Amelia's footsteps when on a red winter morning they set out for the pinewoods to hunt. See them working on her properties—with Cousin Lymon standing by and doing absolutely nothing, but quick to point out any laziness among the hands. On autumn afternoons they sat on the back steps chopping sugar cane. The glaring summer days they spent back in the swamp where the water cypress is a deep black green, where beneath the tangled swamp trees there is a drowsy gloom. When the path leads through a bog or a stretch of blackened water see Miss Amelia bend down to let Cousin Lymon scramble on her back—and see her wading forward with the hunchback settled on her shoulders, clinging to her ears or to her broad forehead. Occasionally Miss Amelia cranked up the Ford which she had bought and treated Cousin Lymon to a picture-show in Cheehaw, or to some distant fair or cockfight; the hunchback took a passionate delight in spectacles. Of course, they were in their café every morning, they would often sit for hours together by the fireplace in the parlor upstairs. For the hunchback was sickly at night and dreaded to lie looking into the dark. He had a deep fear of death. And Miss Amelia would not leave him by himself to suffer with this fright. It may even be reasoned that the growth of the café came about mainly on this account; it was a thing that brought him company and pleasure and that helped him through the night. So compose from such flashes an image of these years as a whole. And for a moment let it rest.

Now some explanation is due for all this behavior. The time has come to speak about love. For Miss Amelia loved Cousin Lymon. So much was clear to everyone. They lived in the same house together and were never seen apart. Therefore, according to Mrs. MacPhail, a warty-nosed old busybody who is continually moving her sticks of furniture from one part of the front room to another; according to her and to certain others, these two were living in sin. If they were related, they were only a cross between first and second cousins, and even that could in no way be proved. Now, of course, Miss Amelia was a powerful blunderbuss of a person, more than six feet tall—and Cousin Lymon a weakly little hunchback reaching only to her waist. But so much the better for Mrs. Stumpy MacPhail and her cronies, for they and their kind glory in conjunctions which are ill-matched and pitiful. So let them be. The good people thought that if those two had found some satisfaction of the flesh between themselves, then it was a matter concerning them and God alone. All sensible people agreed in their opinion about this conjecture—and their answer was a plain, flat *no*. What sort of thing, then, was this love?

First of all, love is a joint experience between two persons—but the fact that it is a joint experience does not mean that it is a similar experience to the two people involved. There are the lover and the beloved, but these two come from different countries. Often the beloved is only a stimulus for all the stored-up love which has lain quiet within the lover for a long time hitherto. And somehow every lover knows this. He feels in his soul that his love is a solitary thing. He comes to know a new, strange loneliness and it is this knowledge which makes him suffer. So there is only one thing for the lover to do. He must house his love within himself as best he can; he must create for himself a whole new inward world—a world intense and strange, complete in himself. Let it be added here that this lover about whom we speak need not necessarily be a young man saving for a wedding ring—this lover can be man, woman, child, or indeed any human creature on this earth.

Now, the beloved can also be of any description. The most outlandish people can be the stimulus for love. A man may be a doddering great-grandfather and still love only a strange girl he saw in the streets of Cheehaw one afternoon two decades past. The preacher may love a fallen woman. The beloved may be treacherous, greasy-headed, and given to evil habits. Yes, and the lover may see this as clearly as anyone else—but that does not affect the evolution of his love one whit. A most mediocre person can be the object of a love which is wild, extravagant, and beautiful as the poison lilies of the swamp. A good man may be the stimulus for a love both violent and debased, or a jabbering madman may bring about in the soul of someone a tender and simple idyll. Therefore, the value and quality of any love is determined solely by the lover himself.

It is for this reason that most of us would rather love than be loved. Almost everyone wants to be the lover. And the curt truth is that, in a deep secret way, the state of being beloved is intolerable to many. The beloved fears and hates the lover, and with the best of reasons. For the lover is forever trying to strip bare his beloved. The lover craves any possible relation with the beloved, even if this experience can cause him only pain.

It has been mentioned before that Miss Amelia was once married. And this curious episode might as well be accounted for at this point. Remember that it all happened long ago, and that it was Miss Amelia's only personal contact, before the hunchback came to her, with this phenomenon—love.

The town then was the same as it is now, except there were two stores instead of three and the peach trees along the street were more crooked and smaller than they are now. Miss Amelia was nineteen years old at the time, and her father had been dead many months. There was in the town at that time a loom-fixer named Marvin Macy. He was the brother of Henry Macy, although to know them you would never guess that those two could be kin. For Marvin Macy was the handsomest man in this region—being six feet one inch tall, hard-muscled, and with slow gray eyes and curly hair. He was well off, made good wages, and had a gold watch which opened in the back to a picture of a waterfall. From the outward and worldly point of view Marvin Macy was a fortunate fellow; he needed to bow and scrape to no one and always got just what he wanted. But from a more serious and thoughtful viewpoint Marvin Macy was not a person to be envied, for he was an evil character. His reputation was as bad, if not worse, than that of any young man in the county. For years, when he was a boy, he had carried about with him the dried and salted ear of a man he had killed in a razor fight. He had chopped off the tails of squirrels in the pinewoods just to please his fancy, and in his left hip pocket he carried forbidden marijuana weed to tempt those who were discouraged and drawn toward death. Yet in spite of his well-known reputation he was the beloved of many females in this region—and there were at the time several young girls who were clean-haired and soft-eyed, with tender sweet little buttocks and charming ways. These gentle young girls he degraded and shamed. Then finally, at the age of twenty-two, this Marvin Macy chose Miss Amelia. That solitary, gangling, queer-eyed girl was the one he longed for. Nor did he want her because of her money, but solely out of love.

And love changed Marvin Macy. Before the time when he loved Miss Amelia it could be questioned if such a person had within him a heart and soul. Yet there is some explanation for the ugliness of his character, for Marvin Macy had had a hard beginning in this world. He was one of seven unwanted children whose parents could hardly be called parents at all; these parents were wild younguns who liked to fish and roam around the swamp. Their own children, and there was a new one almost every year, were only a nuisance to them. At night when they came home from the mill they would look at the children as though they did not know wherever they had come from. If the children cried they were beaten, and the first thing they learned in this world was to seek the darkest corner of the room and try to hide themselves as best they could. They were as thin as little whitehaired ghosts, and they did not speak, not even to each other. Finally, they were abandoned by their parents altogether and left to the mercies of the town. It was a hard winter, with the mill closed down almost three months, and much misery everywhere. But this is not a town to let white orphans perish in the road before your eyes. So here is what came about: the eldest child, who was eight years old, walked into Cheehaw and disappeared—perhaps he took a freight train somewhere and went out into the world, nobody knows. Three other children were boarded out amongst the town, being sent around from one kitchen to another, and as they were delicate they died before Easter time. The last two children were Marvin Macy and Henry Macy, and they were taken into a home. There was a good woman in the town named Mrs. Mary Hale, and she took Marvin Macy and Henry Macy and loved them as her own. They were raised in her household and treated well.

But the hearts of small children are delicate organs. A cruel beginning in this world can twist them into curious shapes. The heart of a hurt child can shrink so that forever afterward it is hard and pitted as the seed of a peach. Or again, the heart of such a child may fester and swell until it is a misery to carry within the body, easily chafed and hurt by the most ordinary things.

This last is what happened to Henry Macy, who so opposite to his brother, is the kindest and gentlest man in town. He lends his wages to those who are unfortunate, and in the old days he used to care for the children whose parents were at the café on Saturday night. But he is a shy man, and he has the look of one who has a swollen heart and suffers. Marvin Macy, however, grew to be bold and fearless and cruel. His heart turned tough as the horns of Satan, and until the time when he loved Miss Amelia he brought to his brother and the good woman who raised him nothing but shame and trouble.

But love reversed the character of Marvin Macy. For two years he loved Miss Amelia, but he did not declare himself. He would stand near the door of her premises, his cap in his hand, his eyes meek and longing and misty gray. He reformed himself completely. He was good to his brother and foster mother, and he saved his wages and learned thrift. Moreover, he reached out toward God. No longer did he lie around on the floor of the front porch all day Sunday, singing and playing his guitar; he attended church services and was present at all religious meetings. He learned good manners: he trained himself to rise and give his chair to a lady, and he quit swearing and fighting and using holy names in vain. So for two years he passed through this transformation and improved his character in every way. Then at the end of the two years he went one evening to Miss Amelia, carrying a bunch of swamp flowers, a sack of chitterlins, and a silver ring—that night Marvin Macy declared himself.

And Miss Amelia married him. Later everyone wondered why. Some said it was because she wanted to get herself some wedding presents. Others believed it came about through the nagging of Miss Amelia's great-aunt in Cheehaw, who was a terrible old woman. Anyway, she strode with great steps down the aisle of the church wearing her dead mother's bridal gown, which was of yellow satin and at least twelve inches too short for her. It was a winter afternoon and the clear sun shone through the ruby windows of the church and put a curious glow on the pair before the altar. As the marriage lines were read Miss Amelia kept making an odd gesture—she would rub the palm of her right hand down the side of her satin wedding gown. She was reaching for the pocket of her overalls, and being unable to find it her face became impatient, bored, and exasperated. At last when the lines were spoken and the marriage prayer was done Miss Amelia hurried out of the church, not taking the arm of her husband, but walking at least two paces ahead of him.

The church is no distance from the store so the bride and groom walked home. It is said that on the way Miss Amelia began to talk about some deal she had worked up with a farmer over a load of kindling wood. In fact, she treated her groom in exactly the same manner she would have used with some customer who had come into the store to buy a pint from her. But so far all had gone decently enough; the town was gratified, as people had seen what this love had done to Marvin Macy and hoped that it might also reform his bride. At least, they counted on the marriage to tone down Miss Amelia's temper, to put a bit of bride-fat on her, and to change her at last into a calculable woman.

They were wrong. The young boys who watched through the window on that night said that this is what actually happened: The bride and groom ate a grand supper prepared by Jeff, the old Negro who cooked for Miss Amelia. The bride took second servings of everything, but the groom picked with his food. Then the bride went about her ordinary business—reading the newspaper, finishing an inventory of the stock in the store, and so forth. The groom hung about in the doorway with a loose, foolish, blissful face and was not noticed. At eleven o'clock the bride took a lamp and went upstairs. The groom followed close behind her. So far all had gone decently enough, but what followed after was unholy.

Within half an hour Miss Amelia had stomped down the stairs in breeches and a khaki jacket. Her face had darkened so that it looked quite black. She slammed the kitchen door and gave it an ugly kick. Then she controlled herself. She poked up the fire, sat down, and put her feet up on the kitchen stove. She read the Farmer's Almanac, drank coffee, and had a smoke with her father's pipe. Her face was hard, stern, and had now whitened to its natural color. Sometimes she paused to jot down some information from the Almanac on a piece of paper. Toward dawn she went into her office and uncovered her typewriter, which she had recently bought and was only just learning how to run.

That was the way in which she spent the whole of her wedding night. At daylight she went out to her yard as though nothing whatsoever had occurred and did some carpentering on a rabbit hutch which she had begun the week before and intended to sell somewhere.

A groom is in a sorry fix when he is unable to bring his well-beloved bride to bed with him, and when the whole town knows it. Marvin Macy came down that day still in his wedding finery, and with a sick face. God knows how he had spent the night. He moped about the yard, watching Miss Amelia, but keeping some distance away from her. Then toward noon an idea came to him and he went off in the direction of Society City. He returned with presents—an opal ring, a pink enamel doreen of the sort which was then in fashion, a silver bracelet with two hearts on it, and a box of candy which had cost two dollars and a half. Miss Amelia looked over these fine gifts and opened the box of candy, for she was hungry. The rest of the presents she judged shrewdly for a moment to sum up their value—then she put them in the counter out for sale. The night was spent in much the same manner as the preceding one—except that Miss Amelia brought her feather mattress to make a pallet by the kitchen stove, and she slept fairly well.

Things went on like this for three days. Miss Amelia went about her business as usual, and took great interest in some rumor that a bridge was to be built some ten miles down the road. Marvin Macy still followed her about around the premises, and it was plain from his face how he suffered. Then on the fourth day he did an extremely simple-minded thing: he went to Cheehaw and came back with a lawyer. Then in Miss Amelia's office he signed over to her the whole of his wordly goods, which was ten acres of timberland which he had bought with the money he had saved. She studied the paper sternly to make sure there was no possibility of a trick and filed it soberly in the drawer of her desk. That afternoon Marvin Macy took a quart bottle of whisky and went with it alone out in the swamp while the sun was still shining. Toward evening he came in drunk, went up to Miss Amelia with wet wide eyes, and put his hand on her shoulder. He was trying to tell her something, but before he could open his mouth she had swung once with her fist and hit his face so hard that he was thrown back against the wall and one of his front teeth was broken.

The rest of this affair can only be mentioned in bare outline. After this first blow Miss Amelia hit him whenever he came within arm's reach of her, and whenever he was drunk. At last she turned him off the premises altogether, and he was forced to suffer publicly. During the day he hung around just outside the boundary line of Miss Amelia's property and sometimes with a drawn crazy look he would fetch his rifle and sit there cleaning it, peering at Miss Amelia steadily. If she was afraid she did not show it, but her face was sterner than ever, and often she spat on the ground. His last foolish effort was to climb in the window of her store one night and to sit there in the dark, for no purpose whatsoever, until she came down the stairs next morning. For this Miss Amelia set off immediately to the courthouse in Cheehaw with some notion that she could get him locked in the penitentiary for trespassing. Marvin Macy left the town that day, and no one saw him go, or knew just where he went. On leaving he put a long curious letter, partly written in pencil and partly with ink, beneath Miss Amelia's door. It was a wild love letter—but in it were also included threats, and he swore that in his life he would get even with her. His marriage had lasted for ten days. And the town felt the special satisfaction that people feel when someone has been thoroughly done in by some scandalous and terrible means.

Miss Amelia was left with everything that Marvin Macy had ever owned—his timberwood, his gold watch, every one of his possessions. But she seemed to attach little value to them and that spring she cut up his Klansman's robe to cover her tobacco plants. So all that he had ever done was to make her richer and to bring her love. But, strange to say, she never spoke of him but with a terrible and spiteful bitterness. She never once referred to him by name but always mentioned him scornfully as 'that loom-fixer I was married to.'

And later, when horrifying rumors concerning Marvin Macy reached the town, Miss Amelia was very pleased. For the true character of Marvin Macy finally revealed itself, once he had freed himself of his love. He became a criminal whose picture and whose name were in all the papers in the state. He robbed three filling stations and held up the A & P store of Society City with a sawed-off gun. He was suspected of the murder of Slit-Eye Sam who was a noted highjacker. All these crimes were connected with the name of Marvin Macy, so that his evil became famous through many counties. Then finally the law captured him, drunk, on the floor of a tourist cabin, his guitar by his side, and fifty-seven dollars in his right shoe. He was tried, sentenced, and sent off to the penitentiary near Atlanta. Miss Amelia was deeply gratified.

Well, all this happened a long time ago, and it is the story of Miss Amelia's marriage. The town laughed a long time over this grotesque affair. But though the outward facts of this love are indeed sad and ridiculous, it must be remembered that the real story was that which took place in the soul of the lover himself. So who but God can be the final judge of this or any other love? On the very first night of the café there were several who suddenly thought of this broken bridegroom, locked in the gloomy penitentiary, many miles away. And in the years that followed, Marvin Macy was not altogether forgotten in this town. His name was never mentioned in the presence of Miss Amelia or the hunchback. But the memory of his passion and his crimes, and the thought of him trapped in his cell in the penitentiary, was like a troubling undertone beneath the happy love of Miss Amelia and the gaiety of the café. So do not forget this Marvin Macy, as he is to act a terrible part in the story which is yet to come.

During the four years in which the store became a café the rooms upstairs were not changed. This part of the premises remained exactly as it had been all of Miss Amelia's life, as it was in the time of her father, and most likely his father before him. The three rooms, it is already known, were immaculately clean. The smallest object had its exact place, and everything was wiped and dusted by Jeff, the servant of Miss Amelia, each morning. The front room belonged to Cousin Lymon—it was the room where Marvin Macy had stayed during the few nights he was allowed on the premises, and before that it was the bedroom of Miss Amelia's father. The room was furnished with a large chiffo-robe, a bureau covered with a stiff white linen cloth crocheted at the edges, and a marble-topped table. The bed was immense, an old fourposter made of carved, dark rosewood. On it were two feather mattresses, bolsters, and a number of handmade comforts. The bed was so high that beneath it were two wooden steps—no occupant had ever used these steps before, but Cousin Lymon drew them out each night and walked up in state. Beside the steps, but pushed modestly out of view, there was a china chamber-pot painted with pink roses. No rug covered the dark, polished floor and the curtains were of some white stuff, also crocheted at the edges.

On the other side of the parlor was Miss Amelia's bedroom, and it was smaller and very simple. The bed was narrow and made of pine. There was a bureau for her breeches, shirts, and Sunday dress, and she had hammered two nails in the closet wall on which to hang her swamp boots. There were no curtains, rugs, or ornaments of any kind.

The large middle room, the parlor, was elaborate. The rose-wood sofa, upholstered in threadbare green silk, was before the fireplace. Marble-topped tables, two Singer sewing machines, a big vase of pampas grass—everything was rich and grand. The most important piece of furniture in the parlor was a big, glass-doored cabinet in which was kept a number of treasures and curios. Miss Amelia had added two objects to this collection—one was a large acorn from a water oak, the other a little velvet box holding two small, grayish stones. Sometimes when she had nothing much to do, Miss Amelia would take out this velvet box and stand by the window with the stones in the palm of her hand, looking down at them with a mixture of fascination, dubious respect, and fear. They were the kidney stones of Miss Amelia herself, and had been taken from her by the doctor in Cheehaw some years ago. It had been a terrible experience, from the first minute to the last, and all she had got out of it were those two little stones; she was bound to set great store by them, or else admit to a mighty sorry bargain. So she kept them and in the second year of Cousin Lymon's stay with her she had them set as ornaments in a watch chain which she gave to him. The other object she had added to the collection, the large acorn, was precious to her—but when she looked at it her face was always saddened and perplexed.

'Amelia, what does it signify?' Cousin Lymon asked her.

'Why, it's just an acorn,' she answered. 'Just an acorn I picked up on the afternoon Big Papa died.'

'How do you mean?' Cousin Lymon insisted.

'I mean it's just an acorn I spied on the ground that day. I picked it up and put it in my pocket. But I don't know why.'

'What a peculiar reason to keep it,' Cousin Lymon said.

The talks of Miss Amelia and Cousin Lymon in the rooms upstairs, usually in the first few hours of the morning when the hunchback could not sleep, were many. As a rule, Miss Amelia was a silent woman, not letting her tongue run wild on any subject that happened to pop into her head. There were certain topics of conversation, however, in which she took pleasure. All these subjects had one point in common—they were interminable. She liked to contemplate problems which could be worked over for decades and still remain insoluble. Cousin Lymon, on the other hand, enjoyed talking on any subject whatsoever, as he was a great chatterer. Their approach to any conversation was altogether different. Miss Amelia always kept to the broad, rambling generalities of the matter, going on endlessly in a low, thoughtful voice and getting nowhere—while Cousin Lymon would interrupt her suddenly to pick up, magpie fashion, some detail which, even if unimportant, was at least concrete and bearing on some practical facet close at hand. Some of the favorite subjects of Miss Amelia were: the stars, the reason why Negroes are black, the best treatment for cancer, and so forth. Her father was also an interminable subject which was dear to her.

'Why, Law,' she would say to Lymon. 'Those days I slept. I'd go to bed just as the lamp was turned on and sleep—why, I'd sleep like I was drowned in warm axle grease. Then come daybreak Big Papa would walk in and put his hand down on my shoulder. "Get stirring, Little," he would say. Then later he would holler up the stairs from the kitchen when the stove was hot. "Fried grits," he would holler. "White meat and gravy. Ham and eggs.'' And I'd run down the stairs and dress by the hot stove while he was out washing at the pump. Then off we'd go to the still or maybe——'

'The grits we had this morning was poor,' Cousin Lymon said. 'Fried too quick so that the inside never heated.'

'And when Big Papa would run off the liquor in those days——' The conversation would go on endlessly, with Miss Amelia's long legs stretched out before the hearth; for winter or summer there was always a fire in the grate, as Lymon was cold-natured. He sat in a low chair across from her, his feet not quite touching the floor and his torso usually well-wrapped in a blanket or the green wool shawl. Miss Amelia never mentioned her father to anyone else except Cousin Lymon.

That was one of the ways in which she showed her love for him. He had her confidence in the most delicate and vital matters. He alone knew where she kept the chart that showed where certain barrels of whisky were buried on a piece of property near by. He alone had access to her bank-book and the key to the cabinet of curios. He took money from the cash register, whole handfuls of it, and appreciated the loud jingle it made inside his pockets. He owned almost everything on the premises, for when he was cross Miss Amelia would prowl about and find him some present —so that now there was hardly anything left close at hand to give him. The only part of her life that she did not want Cousin Lymon to share with her was the memory of her ten-day marriage. Marvin Macy was the one subject that was never, at any time, discussed between the two of them.

So let the slow years pass and come to a Saturday evening six years after the time when Cousin Lymon came first to the town. It was August and the sky had burned above the town like a sheet of flame all day. Now the green twilight was near and there was a feeling of repose. The street was coated an inch deep with dry golden dust and the little children ran about half-naked, sneezed often, sweated, and were fretful. The mill had closed down at noon. People in the houses along the main street sat resting on their steps and the women had palmetto fans. At Miss Amelia's there was a sign at the front of the premises saying CAFÉ. The back porch was cool with latticed shadows and there Cousin Lymon sat turning the ice-cream freezer—often he unpacked the salt and ice and removed the dasher to lick a bit and see how the work was coming on. Jeff cooked in the kitchen. Early that morning Miss Amelia had put a notice on the wall of the front porch reading: Chicken Dinner—Twenty Cents Tonite. The café was already open and Miss Amelia had just finished a period of work in her office. All the eight tables were occupied and from the mechanical piano came a jingling tune.

In a corner near the door and sitting at a table with a child, was Henry Macy. He was drinking a glass of liquor, which was unusual for him, as liquor went easily to his head and made him cry or sing. His face was very pale and his left eye worked constantly in a nervous tic, as it was apt to do when he was agitated. He had come into the café sidewise and silent, and when he was greeted he did not speak. The child next to him belonged to Horace Wells, and he had been left at Miss Amelia's that morning to be doctored.

Miss Amelia came out from her office in good spirits. She attended to a few details in the kitchen and entered the café with the pope's nose of a hen between her fingers, as that was her favorite piece. She looked about the room, saw that in general all was well, and went over to the corner table by Henry Macy. She turned the chair around and sat straddling the back, as she only wanted to pass the time of day and was not yet ready for her supper. There was a bottle of Kroup Kure in the hip pocket of her overalls—a medicine made from whisky, rock candy, and a secret ingredient. Miss Amelia uncorked the bottle and put it to the mouth of the child. Then she turned to Henry Macy and, seeing the nervous winking of his left eye, she asked:

'What ails you?'

Henry Macy seemed on the point of saying something difficult, but, after a long look into the eyes of Miss Amelia, he swallowed and did not speak.

So Miss Amelia returned to her patient. Only the child's head showed above the table top. His face was very red, with the eyelids half-closed and the mouth partly open. He had a large, hard, swollen boil on his thigh, and had been brought to Miss Amelia so that it could be opened. But Miss Amelia used a special method with children; she did not like to see them hurt, struggling, and terrified. So she had kept the child around the premises all day, giving him licorice and frequent doses of the Kroup Kure, and toward evening she tied a napkin around his neck and let him eat his fill of the dinner. Now as he sat at the table his head wobbled slowly from side to side and sometimes as he breathed there came from him a little worn-out grunt.

There was a stir in the café and Miss Amelia looked around quickly. Cousin Lymon had come in. The hunchback strutted into the café as he did every night, and when he reached the exact center of the room he stopped short and looked shrewdly around him, summing up the people and making a quick pattern of the emotional material at hand that night. The hunchback was a great mischief-maker. He enjoyed any kind of to-do, and without saying a word he could set the people at each other in a way that was miraculous. It was due to him that the Rainey twins had quarreled over a jackknife two years past, and had not spoken one word to each other since. He was present at the big fight between Rip Wellborn and Robert Calvert Hale, and every other fight for that matter since he had come into the town. He nosed around everywhere, knew the intimate business of everybody, and trespassed every waking hour. Yet, queerly enough, in spite of this it was the hunchback who was most responsible for the great popularity of the café. Things were never so gay as when he was around. When he walked into the room there was always a quick feeling of tension, because with this busybody about there was never any telling what might descend on you, or what might suddenly be brought to happen in the room. People are never so free with themselves and so recklessly glad as when there is some possibility of commotion or calamity ahead. So when the hunchback marched into the café everyone looked around at him and there was a quick outburst of talking and a drawing of corks.

Lymon waved his hand to Stumpy MacPhail who was sitting with Merlie Ryan and Henry Ford Crimp. 'I walked to Rotten Lake today to fish,' he said. 'And on the way I stepped over what appeared at first to be a big fallen tree. But then as I stepped over I felt something stir and I taken this second look and there

I was straddling this here alligator long as from the front door to the kitchen and thicker than a hog.'

The hunchback chattered on. Everyone looked at him from time to time, and some kept track of his chattering and others did not. There were times when every word he said was nothing but lying and bragging. Nothing he said tonight was true. He had lain in bed with a summer quinsy all day long, and had only got up in the late afternoon in order to turn the ice-cream freezer. Everybody knew this, yet he stood there in the middle of the café and held forth with such lies and boasting that it was enough to shrivel the ears.

Miss Amelia watched him with her hands in her pockets and her head turned to one side. There was a softness about her gray, queer eyes and she was smiling gently to herself. Occasionally she glanced from the hunchback to the other people in the café—and then her look was proud, and there was in it the hint of a threat, as though daring anyone to try to hold him to account for all his foolery. Jeff was bringing in the suppers, already served on the plates, and the new electric fans in the café made a pleasant stir of coolness in the air.

'The little youngun is asleep,' said Henry Macy finally.

Miss Amelia looked down at the patient beside her, and composed her face for the matter in hand. The child's chin was resting on the table edge and a trickle of spit or Kroup Kure had bubbled from the corner of his mouth. His eyes were quite closed, and a little family of gnats had clustered peacefully in the corners. Miss Amelia put her hand on his head and shook it roughly, but the patient did not awake. So Miss Amelia lifted the child from the table, being careful not to touch the sore part of his leg, and went into the office. Henry Macy followed after her and they closed the office door.

Cousin Lymon was bored that evening. There was not much going on, and in spite of the heat the customers in the café were good-humored. Henry Ford Crimp and Horace Wells sat at the middle table with their arms around each other, sniggering over some long joke—but when he approached them he could make nothing of it as he had missed the beginning of the story. The moonlight brightened the dusty road, and the dwarfed peach trees were black and motionless: there was no breeze. The drowsy buzz of swamp mosquitoes was like an echo of the silent night. The town seemed dark, except far down the road to the right there was the flicker of a lamp. Somewhere in the darkness a woman sang in a high wild voice and the tune had no start and no finish and was made up of only three notes which went on and on and on. The hunchback stood leaning against the banister of the porch, looking down the empty road as though hoping that someone would come along.

There were footsteps behind him, then a voice: 'Cousin Lymon, your dinner is set out upon the table.'

'My appetite is poor tonight,' said the hunchback, who had been eating sweet snuff all the day. 'There is a sourness in my mouth.'

'Just a pick,' said Miss Amelia. 'The breast, the liver, and the heart.'

Together they went back into the bright café, and sat down with Henry Macy. Their table was the largest one in the café, and on it there was a bouquet of swamp lilies in a Coca Cola bottle. Miss Amelia had finished with her patient and was satisfied with herself. From behind the closed office door there had come only a few sleepy whimpers, and before the patient could wake up and become terrified it was all over. The child was now slung across the shoulder of his father, sleeping deeply, his little arms dangling loose along his father's back, and his puffed-up face very red—they were leaving the café to go home.

Henry Macy was still silent. He ate carefully, making no noise when he swallowed, and was not a third as greedy as Cousin Lymon who had claimed to have no appetite and was now putting down helping after helping of the dinner. Occasionally Henry Macy looked across at Miss Amelia and again held his peace.

It was a typical Saturday night. An old couple who had come in from the country hesitated for a moment at the doorway, holding each other's hand, and finally decided to come inside. They had lived together so long, this old country couple, that they looked as similar as twins. They were brown, shriveled, and like two little walking peanuts. They left early, and by midnight most of the other customers were gone. Rosser Cline and Merlie Ryan still played checkers, and Stumpy MacPhail sat with a liquor bottle on his table (his wife would not allow it in the home) and carried on peaceable conversations with himself. Henry Macy had not yet gone away, and this was unusual, as he almost always went to bed soon after nightfall. Miss Amelia yawned sleepily, but Lymon was restless and she did not suggest that they close up for the night.

Finally, at one o'clock, Henry Macy looked up at the corner of the ceiling and said quietly to Miss Amelia: 'I got a letter today.'

Miss Amelia was not one to be impressed by this, because all sorts of business letters and catalogues came addressed to her.

'I got a letter from my brother,' said Henry Macy.

The hunchback, who had been goose-stepping about the café with his hands clasped behind his head, stopped suddenly. He was quick to sense any change in the atmosphere of a gathering. He glanced at each face in the room and waited.

Miss Amelia scowled and hardened her right fist. 'You are welcome to it,' she said.

'He is on parole. He is out of the penitentiary.'

The face of Miss Amelia was very dark, and she shivered although the night was warm. Stumpy MacPhail and Merlie Ryan pushed aside their checker game. The café was very quiet.

'Who?' asked Cousin Lymon. His large, pale ears seemed to grow on his head and stiffen. 'What?'

Miss Amelia slapped her hands palm down on the table. 'Because Marvin Macy is a——' But her voice hoarsened and after a few moments she only said: 'He belongs to be in that penitentiary the balance of his life.'

'What did he do?' asked Cousin Lymon.

There was a long pause, as no one knew exactly how to answer this. 'He robbed three filling stations,' said Stumpy MacPhail. But his words did not sound complete and there was a feeling of sins left unmentioned.

The hunchback was impatient. He could not bear to be left out of anything, even a great misery. The name Marvin Macy was unknown to him, but it tantalized him as did any mention of subjects which others knew about and of which he was ignorant—such as any reference to the old sawmill that had been torn down before he came, or a chance word about poor Morris Finestein, or the recollection of any event that had occurred before his time. Aside from this inborn curiosity, the hunchback took a great interest in robbers and crimes of all varieties. As he strutted around the table he was muttering the words 'released on parole' and 'penitentiary' to himself. But although he questioned insistently, he was unable to find anything, as nobody would dare to talk about Marvin Macy before Miss Amelia in the café.

'The letter did not say very much,' said Henry Macy. 'He did not say where he was going.'

'Humph!' said Miss Amelia, and her face was still hardened and very dark. 'He will never set his split hoof on my premises.'

She pushed back her chair from the table, and made ready to close the café. Thinking about Marvin Macy may have set her to brooding, for she hauled the cash register back to the kitchen and put it in a private place. Henry Macy went off down the dark road. But Henry Ford Crimp and Merlie Ryan lingered for a time on the front porch. Later Merlie Ryan was to make certain claims, to swear that on that night he had a vision of what was to come. But the town paid no attention, for that was just the sort of thing that Merlie Ryan would claim. Miss Amelia and Cousin Lymon talked for a time in the parlor. And when at last the hunchback thought that he could sleep she arranged the mosquito netting over his bed and waited until he had finished with his prayers. Then she put on her long nightgown, smoked two pipes, and only after a long time went to sleep.

That autumn was a happy time. The crops around the countryside were good, and over at the Forks Falls market the price of tobacco held firm that year. After the long hot summer the first cool days had a clean bright sweetness. Goldenrod grew along the dusty roads, and the sugar cane was ripe and purple. The bus came each day from Cheehaw to carry off a few of the younger children to the consolidated school to get an education. Boys hunted foxes in the pinewoods, winter quilts were aired out on the wash lines, and sweet potatoes bedded in the ground with straw against the colder months to come. In the evening, delicate shreds of smoke rose from the chimneys, and the moon was round and orange in the autumn sky. There is no stillness like the quiet of the first cold nights in the fall. Sometimes, late in the night when there was no wind, there could be heard in the town the thin wild whistle of the train that goes through Society City on its way far off to the North.

For Miss Amelia Evans this was a time of great activity. She was at work from dawn until sundown. She made a new and bigger condenser for her still, and in one week ran off enough liquor to souse the whole county. Her old mule was dizzy from grinding so much sorghum, and she scalded her Mason jars and put away pear preserves. She was looking forward greatly to the first frost, because she had traded for three tremendous hogs, and intended to make much barbecue, chitterlins, and sausage.

During these weeks there was a quality about Miss Amelia that many people noticed. She laughed often, with a deep ringing laugh, and her whistling had a sassy, tuneful trickery. She was forever trying out her strength, lifting up heavy objects, or poking her tough biceps with her finger. One day she sat down to her typewriter and wrote a story—a story in which there were foreigners, trap doors, and millions of dollars. Cousin Lymon was with her always, traipsing along behind her coat-tails, and when she watched him her face had a bright, soft look, and when she spoke his name there lingered in her voice the undertone of love.

The first cold spell came at last. When Miss Amelia awoke one morning there were frost flowers on the windowpanes, and rime had silvered the patches of grass in the yard. Miss Amelia built a roaring fire in the kitchen stove, then went out of doors to judge the day. The air was cold and sharp, the sky pale green and cloudless. Very shortly people began to come in from the country to find out what Miss Amelia thought of the weather; she decided to kill the biggest hog, and word got round the countryside. The hog was slaughtered and a low oak fire started in the barbecue pit. There was the warm smell of pig blood and smoke in the back yard, the stamp of footsteps, the ring of voices in the winter air. Miss Amelia walked around giving orders and soon most of the work was done.

She had some particular business to do in Cheehaw that day, so after making sure that all was going well, she cranked up her car and got ready to leave. She asked Cousin Lymon to come with her, in fact, she asked him seven times, but he was loath to leave the commotion and wanted to remain. This seemed to trouble Miss Amelia, as she always liked to have him near to her, and was prone to be terribly homesick when she had to go any distance away. But after asking him seven times, she did not urge him any further. Before leaving she found a stick and drew a heavy line all around the barbecue pit, about two feet back from the edge, and told him not to trespass beyond that boundary. She left after dinner and intended to be back before dark.

Now, it is not so rare to have a truck or an automobile pass along the road and through the town on the way from Cheehaw to somewhere else. Every year the tax collector comes to argue with rich people such as Miss Amelia. And if somebody in the town, such as Merlie Ryan, takes a notion that he can connive to get a car on credit, or to pay down three dollars and have a fine electric icebox such as they advertise in the store windows of Cheehaw, then a city man will come out asking meddlesome questions, finding out all his troubles, and ruining his chances of buying anything on the installment plan. Sometimes, especially since they are working on the Forks Falls highway, the cars hauling the chain gang come through the town. And frequently people in automobiles get lost and stop to inquire how they can find the right road again. So, late that afternoon it was nothing unusual to have a truck pass the mill and stop in the middle of the road near the café of Miss Amelia. A man jumped down from the back of the truck, and the truck went on its way.

The man stood in the middle of the road and looked about him. He was a tall man, with brown curly hair, and slow-moving, deep-blue eyes. His lips were red and he smiled the lazy, half-mouthed smile of the braggart. The man wore a red shirt, and a wide belt of tooled leather; he carried a tin suitcase and a guitar. The first person in the town to see this newcomer was Cousin Lymon, who had heard the shifting of gears and come around to investigate. The hunchback stuck his head around the corner of the porch, but did not step out altogether into full view. He and the man stared at each other, and it was not the look of two strangers meeting for the first time and swiftly summing up each other. It was a peculiar stare they exchanged between them, like the look of two criminals who recognize each other. Then the man in the red shirt shrugged his left shoulder and turned away. The face of the hunchback was very pale as he watched the man go down the road, and after a few moments he began to follow along carefully, keeping many paces away.

It was immediately known throughout the town that Marvin Macy had come back again. First, he went to the mill, propped his elbows lazily on a window sill and looked inside. He liked to watch others hard at work, as do all born loafers. The mill was thrown into a sort of numb confusion. The dyers left the hot vats, the spinners and weavers forgot about their machines, and even Stumpy MacPhail, who was foreman, did not know exactly what to do. Marvin Macy still smiled his wet half-mouthed smiles, and when he saw his brother, his bragging expression did not change. After looking over the mill Marvin Macy went down the road to the house where he had been raised, and left his suitcase and guitar on the front porch. Then he walked around the mill-pond, looked over the church, the three stores, and the rest of the town. The hunchback trudged along quietly at some distance behind him, his hands in his pockets, and his little face still very pale.

It had grown late. The red winter sun was setting, and to the west the sky was deep gold and crimson. Ragged chimney swifts flew to their nests; lamps were lighted. Now and then there was the smell of smoke, and the warm rich odor of the barbecue slowly cooking in the pit behind the café. After making the rounds of the town Marvin Macy stopped before Miss Amelia's premises and read the sign above the porch. Then, not hesitating to trespass, he walked through the side yard. The mill whistle blew a thin, lonesome blast, and the day's shift was done. Soon there were others in Miss Amelia's back yard beside Marvin Macy—Henry Ford Crimp, Merlie Ryan, Stumpy MacPhail, and any number of children and people who stood around the edges of the property and looked on. Very little was said. Marvin Macy stood by himself on one side of the pit, and the rest of the people clustered together on the other side. Cousin Lymon stood somewhat apart from everyone, and he did not take his eyes from the face of Marvin Macy.

'Did you have a good time in the penitentiary?' asked Merlie Ryan, with a silly giggle.

Marvin Macy did not answer. He took from his hip pocket a

large knife, opened it slowly, and honed the blade on the seat of his pants. Merlie Ryan grew suddenly very quiet and went to stand directly behind the broad back of Stumpy MacPhail.

Miss Amelia did not come home until almost dark. They heard the rattle of her automobile while she was still a long distance away, then the slam of the door and a bumping noise as though she were hauling something up the front steps of her premises. The sun had already set, and in the air there was the blue smoky glow of early winter evenings. Miss Amelia came down the back steps slowly, and the group in her yard waited very quietly. Few people in this world could stand up to Miss Amelia, and against Marvin Macy she had this special and bitter hate. Everyone waited to see her burst into a terrible holler, snatch up some dangerous object, and chase him altogether out of town. At first she did not see Marvin Macy, and her face had the relieved and dreamy expression that was natural to her when she reached home after having gone some distance away.

Miss Amelia must have seen Marvin Macy and Cousin Lymon at the same instant. She looked from one to the other, but it was not the wastrel from the penitentiary on whom she finally fixed her gaze of sick amazement. She, and everyone else, was looking at Cousin Lymon, and he was a sight to see.

The hunchback stood at the end of the pit, his pale face lighted by the soft glow from the smoldering oak fire. Cousin Lymon had a very peculiar accomplishment, which he used whenever he wished to ingratiate himself with someone. He would stand very still, and with just a little concentration, he could wiggle his large pale ears with marvelous quickness and ease. This trick he always used when he wanted to get something special out of Miss Amelia, and to her it was irresistible. Now as he stood there the hunchback's ears were wiggling furiously on his head, but it was not Miss Amelia at whom he was looking this time. The hunchback was smiling at Marvin Macy with an entreaty that was near to desperation. At first Marvin Macy paid no attention to him, and when he did finally glance at the hunchback it was without any appreciation whatsoever.

'What ails this Brokeback?' he asked with a rough jerk of his thumb.

No one answered. And Cousin Lymon, seeing that his accomplishment was getting him nowhere, added new efforts of persuasion. He fluttered his eyelids, so that they were like pale, trapped moths in his sockets. He scraped his feet around on the ground, waved his hands about, and finally began doing a little trotlike dance. In the last gloomy light of the winter afternoon he resembled the child of a swamphaunt.

Marvin Macy, alone of all the people in the yard, was unimpressed.

'Is the runt throwing a fit?' he asked, and when no one answered he stepped forward and gave Cousin Lymon a cuff on the side of his head. The hunchback staggered, then fell back on the ground. He sat where he had fallen, still looking up at Marvin Macy, and with great effort his ears managed one last forlorn little flap.

Now everyone turned to Miss Amelia to see what she would do. In all these years no one had so much as touched a hair of Cousin Lymon's head, although many had had the itch to do so. If anyone even spoke crossly to the hunchback, Miss Amelia would cut off this rash mortal's credit and find ways of making things go hard for him a long time afterward. So now if Miss Amelia had split open Marvin Macy's head with the ax on the back porch no one would have been surprised. But she did nothing of the kind.

There were times when Miss Amelia seemed to go into a sort of trance. And the cause of these trances was usually known and understood. For Miss Amelia was a fine doctor, and did not grind up swamp roots and other untried ingredients and give them to the first patient who came along; whenever she invented a new medicine she always tried it out first on herself. She would swallow an enormous dose and spend the following day walking thoughtfully back and forth from the café to the brick privy. Often, when there was a sudden keen gripe, she would stand quite still, her queer eyes staring down at the ground and her fists clenched; she was trying to decide which organ was being worked upon, and what misery the new medicine might be most likely to cure.

And now as she watched the hunchback and Marvin Macy, her face wore this same expression, tense with reckoning some inward pain, although she had taken no new medicine that day.

'That will learn you, Brokeback,' said Marvin Macy.

Henry Macy pushed back his limp whitish hair from his forehead and coughed nervously. Stumpy MacPhail and Merlie Ryan shuffled their feet, and the children and black people on the outskirts of the property made not a sound. Marvin Macy folded the knife he had been honing, and after looking about him fearlessly he swaggered out of the yard. The embers in the pit were turning to gray feathery ashes and it was now quite dark.

That was the way Marvin Macy came back from the penitentiary. Not a living soul in all the town was glad to see him. Even Mrs. Mary Hale, who was a good woman and had raised him with love and care—at the first sight of him even this old foster mother dropped the skillet she was holding and burst into tears. But nothing could faze that Marvin Macy. He sat on the back steps of the Hale house, lazily picking his guitar, and when the supper was ready, he pushed the children of the household out of the way and served himself a big meal, although there had been barely enough hoecakes and white meat to go round. After eating he settled himself in the best and warmest sleeping place in the front room and was untroubled by dreams.

Miss Amelia did not open the café that night. She locked the doors and all the windows very carefully, nothing was seen of her and Cousin Lymon, and a lamp burned in her room all the night long.

Marvin Macy brought with him bad fortune, right from the first, as could be expected. The next day the weather turned suddenly, and it became hot. Even in the early morning there was a sticky sultriness in the atmosphere, the wind carried the rotten smell of the swamp, and delicate shrill mosquitoes webbed the green millpond. It was unseasonable, worse than August, and much damage was done. For nearly everyone in the county who owned a hog had copied Miss Amelia and slaughtered the day before. And what sausage could keep in such weather as this? After a few days there was everywhere the smell of slowly spoiling meat, and an atmosphere of dreary waste. Worse yet, a family reunion near the Forks Falls highway ate pork roast and died, every one of them. It was plain that their hog had been infected—and who could tell whether the rest of the meat was safe or not? People were torn between the longing for the good taste of pork, and the fear of death. It was a time of waste and confusion.

The cause of all this, Marvin Macy, had no shame in him. He was seen everywhere. During work hours he loafed about the mill, looking in at the windows, and on Sundays he dressed in his red shirt and paraded up and down the road with his guitar. He was still handsome—with his brown hair, his red lips, and his broad strong shoulders; but the evil in him was now too famous for his good looks to get him anywhere. And this evil was not measured only by the actual sins he had committed. True, he had robbed those filling stations. And before that he had ruined the tenderest girls in the county, and laughed about it. Any number of wicked things could be listed against him, but quite apart from these crimes there was about him a secret meanness that clung to him almost like a smell. Another thing—he never sweated, not even in August, and that surely is a sign worth pondering over.

Now it seemed to the town that he was more dangerous than he had ever been before, as in the penitentiary in Atlanta he must have learned the method of laying charms. Otherwise how could his effect on Cousin Lymon be explained? For since first setting eyes on Marvin Macy the hunchback was possessed by an unnatural spirit. Every minute he wanted to be following along behind this jailbird, and he was full of silly schemes to attract attention to himself. Still Marvin Macy either treated him hatefully or failed to notice him at all. Sometimes the hunchback would give up, perch himself on the banister of the front porch much as a sick bird huddles on a telephone wire, and grieve publicly.

'But why?' Miss Amelia would ask, staring at him with her crossed, gray eyes, and her fists closed tight.

'Oh, Marvin Macy,' groaned the hunchback, and the sound of the name was enough to upset the rhythm of his sobs so that he hiccuped. 'He has been to Atlanta.'

Miss Amelia would shake her head and her face was dark and hardened. To begin with she had no patience with any traveling;

those who had made the trip to Atlanta or traveled fifty miles from home to see the ocean—those restless people she despised. 'Going to Atlanta does no credit to him.'

'He has been to the penitentiary,' said the hunchback, miserable with longing.

How are you going to argue against such envies as these? In her perplexity Miss Amelia did not herself sound any too sure of what she was saying. 'Been to the penitentiary, Cousin Lymon? Why, a trip like that is no travel to brag about.'

During these weeks Miss Amelia was closely watched by everyone. She went about absent-mindedly, her face remote as though she had lapsed into one of her gripe trances. For some reason, after the day of Marvin Macy's arrival, she put aside her overalls and wore always the red dress she had before this time reserved for Sundays, funerals, and sessions of the court. Then as the weeks passed she began to take some steps to clear up the situation. But her efforts were hard to understand. If it hurt her to see Cousin Lymon follow Marvin Macy about the town, why did she not make the issues clear once and for all, and tell the hunchback that if he had dealings with Marvin Macy she would turn him off the premises? That would have been simple, and Cousin Lymon would have had to submit to her, or else face the sorry business of finding himself loose in the world. But Miss Amelia seemed to have lost her will; for the first time in her life she hesitated as to just what course to pursue. And, like most people in such a position of uncertainty, she did the worst thing possible—she began following several courses at once, all of them contrary to each other.

The café was opened every night as usual, and, strangely enough, when Marvin Macy came swaggering through the door, with the hunchback at his heels, she did not turn him out. She even gave him free drinks and smiled at him in a wild, crooked way. At the same time she set a terrible trap for him out in the swamp that surely would have killed him if he had got caught. She let Cousin Lymon invite him to Sunday dinner, and then tried to trip him up as he went down the steps. She began a great campaign of pleasure for Cousin Lymon—making exhausting trips to various spectacles being held in distant places, driving the automobile thirty miles to a Chautauqua, taking him to Forks

Falls to watch a parade. All in all it was a distracting time for Miss Amelia. In the opinion of most people she was well on her way in the climb up fools' hill, and everyone waited to see how it would all turn out.

The weather turned cold again, the winter was upon the town, and night came before the last shift in the mill was done. Children kept on all their garments when they slept, and women raised the backs of their skirts to toast themselves dreamily at the fire. After it rained, the mud in the road made hard frozen ruts, there were faint flickers of lamplight from the windows of the houses, the peach trees were scrawny and bare. In the dark, silent nights of winter-time the café was the warm center point of the town, the lights shining so brightly that they could be seen a quarter of a mile away. The great iron stove at the back of the room roared, crackled, and turned red. Miss Amelia had made red curtains for the windows, and from a salesman who passed through the town she bought a great bunch of paper roses that looked very real.

But it was not only the warmth, the decorations, and the brightness, that made the café what it was. There is a deeper reason why the café was so precious to this town. And this deeper reason has to do with a certain pride that had not hitherto been known in these parts. To understand this new pride the cheapness of human life must be kept in mind. There were always plenty of people clustered around a mill—but it was seldom that every family had enough meal, garments, and fat back to go the rounds. Life could become one long dim scramble just to get the things needed to keep alive. And the confusing point is this: All useful things have a price, and are bought only with money, as that is the way the world is run. You know without having to reason about it the price of a bale of cotton, or a quart of molasses. But no value has been put on human life; it is given to us free and taken without being paid for. What is it worth? If you look around, at times the value may seem to be little or nothing at all. Often after you have sweated and tried and things are not better for you, there comes a feeling deep down in the soul that you are not worth much.

But the new pride that the café brought to this town had an effect on almost everyone, even the children. For in order to come to the café you did not have to buy the dinner, or a portion of liquor. There were cold bottled drinks for a nickel. And if you could not even afford that, Miss Amelia had a drink called Cherry Juice which sold for a penny a glass, and was pink-colored and very sweet. Almost everyone, with the exception of Reverend T. M. Willin, came to the café at least once during the week. Children love to sleep in houses other than their own, and to eat at a neighbor's table; on such occasions they behave themselves decently and are proud. The people in the town were likewise proud when sitting at the tables in the café. They washed before coming to Miss Amelia's, and scraped their feet very politely on the threshold as they entered the café. There, for a few hours at least, the deep bitter knowing that you are not worth much in this world could be laid low.

The café was a special benefit to bachelors, unfortunate people, and consumptives. And here it may be mentioned that there was some reason to suspect that Cousin Lymon was consumptive. The brightness of his gray eyes, his insistence, his talkativeness, and his cough—these were all signs. Besides, there is generally supposed to be some connection between a hunched spine and consumption. But whenever this subject had been mentioned to Miss Amelia she had become furious; she denied these symptoms with bitter vehemence, but on the sly she treated Cousin Lymon with hot chest plasters, Kroup Kure, and such. Now this winter the hunchback's cough was worse, and sometimes even on cold days he would break out in a heavy sweat. But this did not prevent him from following along after Marvin Macy.

Early every morning he left the premises and went to the back door of Mrs. Hale's house, and waited and waited—as Marvin Macy was a lazy sleeper. He would stand there and call out softly. His voice was just like the voices of children who squat patiently over those tiny little holes in the ground where doodlebugs are thought to live, poking the hole with a broom straw, and calling plaintively: 'Doodlebug, Doodlebug—fly away home. Mrs. Doodlebug, Mrs. Doodlebug. Come out, come out. Your house is on fire and all your children are burning up.' In just such a voice—at once sad, luring, and resigned—would the hunchback call Marvin Macy's name each morning. Then when Marvin Macy came out for the day, he would trail him about the town, and sometimes they would be gone for hours together out in the swamp.

And Miss Amelia continued to do the worst thing possible: that is, to try to follow several courses at once. When Cousin Lymon left the house she did not call him back, but only stood in the middle of the road and watched lonesomely until he was out of sight. Nearly every day Marvin Macy turned up with Cousin Lymon at dinnertime, and ate at her table. Miss Amelia opened the pear preserves, and the table was well-set with ham or chicken, great bowls of hominy grits, and winter peas. It is true that on one occasion Miss Amelia tried to poison Marvin Macy—but there was a mistake, the plates were confused, and it was she herself who got the poisoned dish. This she quickly realized by the slight bitterness of the food, and that day she ate no dinner. She sat tilted back in her chair, feeling her muscle, and looking at Marvin Macy.

Every night Marvin Macy came to the café and settled himself at the best and largest table, the one in the center of the room. Cousin Lymon brought him liquor, for which he did not pay a cent. Marvin Macy brushed the hunchback aside as if he were a swamp mosquito, and not only did he show no gratitude for these favors, but if the hunchback got in his way he would cuff him with the back of his hand, or say: 'Out of my way, Brokeback—I'll snatch you bald-headed.' When this happened Miss Amelia would come out from behind her counter and approach Marvin Macy very slowly, her fists clenched, her peculiar red dress hanging awkwardly around her bony knees. Marvin Macy would also clench his fists and they would walk slowly and meaningfully around each other. But, although everyone watched breathlessly, nothing ever came of it. The time for the fight was not yet ready.

There is one particular reason why this winter is remembered and still talked about. A great thing happened. People woke up on the second of January and found the whole world about them altogether changed. Little ignorant children looked out of the windows, and they were so puzzled that they began to cry. Old people harked back and could remember nothing in these parts to equal the phenomenon. For in the night it had snowed. In the dark hours after midnight the dim flakes started falling softly on the town. By dawn the ground was covered, and the strange snow banked the ruby windows of the church, and whitened the roofs of the houses. The snow gave the town a drawn, bleak look. The two-room houses near the mill were dirty, crooked, and seemed about to collapse, and somehow everything was dark and shrunken. But the snow itself—there was a beauty about it few people around here had ever known before. The snow was not white, as Northerners had pictured it to be; in the snow there were soft colors of blue and silver, the sky was a gentle shining gray. And the dreamy quietness of falling snow—when had the town been so silent?

People reacted to the snowfall in various ways. Miss Amelia, on looking out of her window, thoughtfully wiggled the toes of her bare foot, gathered close to her neck the collar of her nightgown. She stood there for some time, then commenced to draw the shutters and lock every window on the premises. She closed the place completely, lighted the lamps, and sat solemnly over her bowl of grits. The reason for this was not that Miss Amelia feared the snowfall. It was simply that she was unable to form an immediate opinion of this new event, and unless she knew exactly and definitely what she thought of a matter (which was nearly always the case) she preferred to ignore it. Snow had never fallen in this county in her lifetime, and she had never thought about it one way or the other. But if she admitted this snowfall she would have to come to some decision, and in those days there was enough distraction in her life as it was already. So she poked about the gloomy, lamplighted house and pretended that nothing had happened. Cousin Lymon, on the contrary, chased around in the wildest excitement, and when Miss Amelia turned her back to dish him some breakfast he slipped out of the door.

Marvin Macy laid claim to the snowfall. He said that he knew snow, had seen it in Atlanta, and from the way he walked about the town that day it was as though he owned every flake. He sneered at the little children who crept timidly out of the houses and scooped up handfuls of snow to taste. Reverend Willin hurried down the road with a furious face, as he was thinking deeply and trying to weave the snow into his Sunday sermon. Most people were humble and glad about this marvel; they spoke in hushed voices and said 'thank you' and 'please' more than was necessary. A few weak characters, of course, were demoralized and got drunk —but they were not numerous. To everyone this was an occasion and many counted their money and planned to go to the café that night.

Cousin Lymon followed Marvin Macy about all day, seconding his claim to the snow. He marveled that snow did not fall as does rain, and stared up at the dreamy, gently falling flakes until he stumbled from dizziness. And the pride he took on himself, basking in the glory of Marvin Macy—it was such that many people could not resist calling out to him: '"Oho," said the fly on the chariot wheel. "What a dust we do raise."'

Miss Amelia did not intend to serve a dinner. But when, at six o'clock, there was the sound of footsteps on the porch she opened the front door cautiously. It was Henry Ford Crimp, and though there was no food, she let him sit at a table and served him a drink. Others came. The evening was blue, bitter, and though the snow fell no longer there was a wind from the pine trees that swept up delicate flurries from the ground. Cousin Lymon did not come until after dark, with him Marvin Macy, and he carried his tin suitcase and his guitar.

'So you mean to travel?' said Miss Amelia quickly.

Marvin Macy warmed himself at the stove. Then he settled down at his table and carefully sharpened a little stick. He picked his teeth, frequently taking the stick out of his mouth to look at the end and wipe it on the sleeve of his coat. He did not bother to answer.

The hunchback looked at Miss Amelia, who was behind the counter. His face was not in the least beseeching; he seemed quite sure of himself. He folded his hands behind his back and perked up his ears confidently. His cheeks were red, his eyes shining, and his clothes were soggy wet. 'Marvin Macy is going to visit a spell with us,' he said.

Miss Amelia made no protest. She only came out from behind the counter and hovered over the stove, as though the news had made her suddenly cold. She did not warm her backside modestly, lifting her skirt only an inch or so, as do most women when in public. There was not a grain of modesty about Miss Amelia, and she frequently seemed to forget altogether that there were men in the room. Now as she stood warming herself, her red dress was pulled up quite high in the back so that a piece of her strong, hairy thigh could be seen by anyone who cared to look at it. Her head was turned to one side, and she had begun talking with herself, nodding and wrinkling her forehead, and there was the tone of accusation and reproach in her voice although the words were not plain. Meanwhile, the hunchback and Marvin Macy had gone upstairs—up to the parlor with the pampas grass and the two sewing machines, to the private rooms where Miss Amelia had lived the whole of her life. Down in the café you could hear them bumping around, unpacking Marvin Macy, and getting him settled.

That is the way Marvin Macy crowded into Miss Amelia's home. At first Cousin Lymon, who had given Marvin Macy his own room, slept on the sofa in the parlor. But the snowfall had a bad effect on him; he caught a cold that turned into a winter quinsy, so Miss Amelia gave up her bed to him. The sofa in the parlor was much too short for her, her feet lapped over the edges, and often she rolled off onto the floor. Perhaps it was this lack of sleep that clouded her wits; everything she tried to do against Marvin Macy rebounded on herself. She got caught in her own tricks, and found herself in many pitiful positions. But still she did not put Marvin Macy off the premises, as she was afraid that she would be left alone. Once you have lived with another, it is a great torture to have to live alone. The silence of a firelit room when suddenly the clock stops ticking, the nervous shadows in an empty house—it is better to take in your mortal enemy than face the terror of living alone.

The snow did not last. The sun came out and within two days the town was just as it had always been before. Miss Amelia did not open her house until every flake had melted. Then she had a big house cleaning and aired everything out in the sun. But before that, the very first thing she did on going out again into her yard, was to tie a rope to the largest branch of the chinaberry tree. At the end of the rope she tied a crocus sack tightly stuffed with sand. This was the punching bag she made for herself and from that day on she would box with it out in her yard every morning. Already she was a fine fighter—a little heavy on her feet, but knowing all manner of mean holds and squeezes to make up for this.

Miss Amelia, as has been mentioned, measured six feet two inches in height. Marvin Macy was one inch shorter. In weight they were about even—both of them weighing close to a hundred and sixty pounds. Marvin Macy had the advantage in slyness of movement, and in toughness of chest. In fact from the outward point of view the odds were altogether in his favor. Yet almost everybody in the town was betting on Miss Amelia; scarcely a person would put up money on Marvin Macy. The town remembered the great fight between Miss Amelia and a Fork Falls lawyer who had tried to cheat her. He had been a huge strapping fellow, but he was left three-quarters dead when she had finished with him. And it was not only her talent as a boxer that had impressed everyone—she could demoralize her enemy by making terrifying faces and fierce noises, so that even the spectators were sometimes cowed. She was brave, she practiced faithfully with her punching bag, and in this case she was clearly in the right. So people had confidence in her, and they waited. Of course there was no set date for this fight. There were just the signs that were too plain to be overlooked.

During these times the hunchback strutted around with a pleased little pinched-up face. In many delicate and clever ways he stirred up trouble between them. He was constantly plucking at Marvin Macy's trouser leg to draw attention to himself. Sometimes he followed in Miss Amelia's footsteps—but these days it was only in order to imitate her awkward long-legged walk; he crossed his eyes and aped her gestures in a way that made her appear to be a freak. There was something so terrible about this that even the silliest customers of the café, such as Merlie Ryan, did not laugh. Only Marvin Macy drew up the left corner of his mouth and chuckled. Miss Amelia, when this happened, would be divided between two emotions. She would look at the hunchback with a lost, dismal reproach—then turn toward Marvin Macy with her teeth clamped.

'Bust a gut!' she would say bitterly.

And Marvin Macy, most likely, would pick up the guitar from the floor beside his chair. His voice was wet and slimy, as he always had too much spit in his mouth. And the tunes he sang glided slowly from his throat like eels. His strong fingers picked the strings with dainty skill, and everything he sang both lured and exasperated. This was usually more than Miss Amelia could stand.

'Bust a gut!' she would repeat, in a shout.

But always Marvin Macy had the answer ready for her. He would cover the strings to silence the quivering left-over tones, and reply with slow, sure insolence.

'Everything you holler at me bounces back on yourself. Yah! Yah!'

Miss Amelia would have to stand there helpless, as no one has ever invented a way out of this trap. She could not shout out abuse that would bounce back on herself. He had the best of her, there was nothing she could do.

So things went on like this. What happened between the three of them during the nights in the rooms upstairs nobody knows. But the café became more and more crowded every night. A new table had to be brought in. Even the Hermit, the crazy man named Rainer Smith, who took to the swamp years ago, heard something of the situation and came one night to look in at the window and brood over the gathering in the bright café. And the climax each evening was the time when Miss Amelia and Marvin Macy doubled their fists, squared up, and glared at each other. Usually this did not happen after any especial argument, but it seemed to come about mysteriously, by means of some instinct on the part of both of them. At these times the café would become so quiet that you could hear the bouquet of paper roses rustling in the draft. And each night they held this fighting stance a little longer than the night before.

The fight took place on Ground Hog Day, which is the second of February. The weather was favorable, being neither rainy nor sunny, and with a neutral temperature. There were several signs that this was the appointed day, and by ten o'clock the news spread all over the county. Early in the morning Miss Amelia went out and cut down her punching bag. Marvin Macy sat on the back step with a tin can of hog fat between his knees and carefully greased his arms and his legs. A hawk with a bloody breast flew over the town and circled twice around the property of Miss Amelia. The tables in the café were moved out to the back porch, so that the whole big room was cleared for the fight. There was every sign. Both Miss Amelia and Marvin Macy ate four helpings of half-raw roast for dinner, and then lay down in the afternoon to store up strength. Marvin Macy rested in the big room upstairs, while Miss Amelia stretched herself out on the bench in her office. It was plain from her white stiff face what a torment it was for her to be lying still and doing nothing, but she lay there quiet as a corpse with her eyes closed and her hands crossed on her chest.

Cousin Lymon had a restless day, and his little face was drawn and tightened with excitement. He put himself up a lunch, and set out to find the ground hog—within an hour he returned, the lunch eaten, and said that the ground hog had seen his shadow and there was to be bad weather ahead. Then, as Miss Amelia and Marvin Macy were both resting to gather strength, and he was left to himself, it occurred to him that he might as well paint the front porch. The house had not been painted for years—in fact, God knows if it had ever been painted at all. Cousin Lymon scrambled around, and soon he had painted half the floor of the porch a gay bright green. It was a loblolly job, and he smeared himself all over. Typically enough he did not even finish the floor, but changed over to the walls, painting as high as he could reach and then standing on a crate to get up a foot higher. When the paint ran out, the right side of the floor was bright green and there was a jagged portion of wall that had been painted. Cousin Lymon left it at that.

There was something childish about his satisfaction with his painting. And in this respect a curious fact should be mentioned. No one in the town, not even Miss Amelia, had any idea how old the hunchback was. Some maintained that when he came to town he was about twelve years old, still a child—others were certain that he was well past forty. His eyes were blue and steady as a child's but there were lavender crêpy shadows beneath these blue eyes that hinted of age. It was impossible to guess his age by his hunched queer body. And even his teeth gave no clue—they were all still in his head (two were broken from cracking a pecan), but he had stained them with so much sweet snuff that it was impossible to decide whether they were old teeth or young teeth. When questioned directly about his age the hunchback professed to know absolutely nothing—he had no idea how long he had been on the earth, whether for ten years or a hundred! So his age remained a puzzle.

Cousin Lymon finished his painting at five-thirty o'clock in the afternoon. The day had turned colder and there was a wet taste in the air. The wind came up from the pinewoods, rattling windows, blowing an old newspaper down the road until at last it caught upon a thorn tree. People began to come in from the country; packed automobiles that bristled with the poked-out heads of children, wagons drawn by old mules who seemed to smile in a weary, sour way and plodded along with their tired eyes half-closed. Three young boys came from Society City. All three of them wore yellow rayon shirts and caps put on backward—they were as much alike as triplets, and could always be seen at cock fights and camp meetings. At six o'clock the mill whistle sounded the end of the day's shift and the crowd was complete. Naturally, among the newcomers there were some riffraff, unknown characters, and so forth—but even so the gathering was quiet. A hush was on the town and the faces of people were strange in the fading light. Darkness hovered softly; for a moment the sky was a pale clear yellow against which the gables of the church stood out in dark and bare outline, then the sky died slowly and the darkness gathered into night.

Seven is a popular number, and especially it was a favorite with Miss Amelia. Seven swallows of water for hiccups, seven runs around the millpond for cricks in the neck, seven doses of Amelia Miracle Mover as a worm cure—her treatment nearly always hinged on this number. It is a number of mingled possibilities, and all who love mystery and charms set store by it. So the fight was to take place at seven o'clock. This was known to everyone, not by announcement or words, but understood in the unquestioning way that rain is understood, or an evil odor from the swamp. So before seven o'clock everyone gathered gravely around the property of Miss Amelia. The cleverest got into the café itself and stood lining the walls of the room. Others crowded onto the front porch, or took a stand in the yard.

Miss Amelia and Marvin Macy had not yet shown themselves. Miss Amelia, after resting all afternoon on the office bench, had gone upstairs. On the other hand Cousin Lymon was at your elbow every minute, threading his way through the crowd, snapping his fingers nervously, and batting his eyes. At one minute to seven o'clock he squirmed his way into the café and climbed up on the counter. All was very quiet.

It must have been arranged in some manner beforehand. For just at the stroke of seven Miss Amelia showed herself at the head of the stairs. At the same instant Marvin Macy appeared in front of the café and the crowd made way for him silently. They walked toward each other with no haste, their fists already gripped, and their eyes like the eyes of dreamers. Miss Amelia had changed her red dress for her old overalls, and they were rolled up to the knees. She was barefooted and she had an iron strengthband around her right wrist. Marvin Macy had also rolled his trouser legs—he was naked to the waist and heavily greased; he wore the heavy shoes that had been issued him when he left the penitentiary. Stumpy MacPhail stepped forward from the crowd and slapped their hip pockets with the palm of his right hand to make sure there would be no sudden knives. Then they were alone in the cleared center of the bright café.

There was no signal, but they both struck out simultaneously. Both blows landed on the chin, so that the heads of Miss Amelia and Marvin Macy bobbed back and they were left a little groggy. For a few seconds after the first blows they merely shuffled their feet around on the bare floor, experimenting with various positions, and making mock fists. Then, like wildcats, they were suddenly on each other. There was the sounds of knocks, panting, and thumpings on the floor. They were so fast that it was hard to take in what was going on—but once Miss Amelia was hurled backward so that she staggered and almost fell, and another time Marvin Macy caught a knock on the shoulder that spun him around like a top. So the fight went on in this wild violent way with no sign of weakening on either side.

During a struggle like this, when the enemies are as quick and strong as these two, it is worth-while to turn from the confusion of the fight itself and observe the spectators. The people had flattened back as close as possible against the walls. Stumpy MacPhail was in a corner, crouched over and with his fists tight in sympathy, making strange noises. Poor Merlie Ryan had his mouth so wide open that a fly buzzed into it, and was swallowed before Merlie realized what had happened. And Cousin Lymon —he was worth watching. The hunchback still stood on the counter, so that he was raised up above everyone else in the café. He had his hands on his hips, his big head thrust forward, and his little legs bent so that the knees jutted outward. The excitement had made him break out in a rash, and his pale mouth shivered.

Perhaps it was half an hour before the course of the fight shifted. Hundreds of blows had been exchanged, and there was still a deadlock. Then suddenly Marvin Macy managed to catch hold of Miss Amelia's left arm and pinion it behind her back. She struggled and got a grasp around his waist; the real fight was now begun. Wrestling is the natural way of fighting in this county —as boxing is too quick and requires much thinking and concentration. And now that Miss Amelia and Marvin were locked in a hold together the crowd came out of its daze and pressed in closer. For a while the fighters grappled muscle to muscle, their hipbones braced against each other. Backward and forward, from side to side, they swayed in this way. Marvin Macy still had not sweated, but Miss Amelia's overalls were drenched and so much sweat had trickled down her legs that she left wet foot-prints on the floor. Now the test had come, and in these moments of terrible effort, it was Miss Amelia who was the stronger. Marvin Macy was greased and slippery, tricky to grasp, but she was stronger. Gradually she bent him over backward, and inch by inch she forced him to the floor. It was a terrible thing to watch and their deep hoarse breaths were the only sound in the café. At last she had him down, and straddled; her strong big hands were on his throat.

But at that instant, just as the fight was won, a cry sounded in the café that caused a shrill bright shiver to run down the spine. And what took place has been a mystery ever since. The whole town was there to testify what happened, but there were those who doubted their own eyesight. For the counter on which Cousin Lymon stood was at least twelve feet from the fighters in the center of the café. Yet at the instant Miss Amelia grasped the throat of Marvin Macy the hunchback sprang forward and sailed through the air as though he had grown hawk wings. He landed on the broad strong back of Miss Amelia and clutched at her neck with his clawed little fingers.

The rest is confusion. Miss Amelia was beaten before the crowd could come to their senses. Because of the hunchback the fight was won by Marvin Macy, and at the end Miss Amelia lay sprawled on the floor, her arms flung outward and motionless. Marvin Macy stood over her, his face somewhat popeyed, but smiling his old half-mouthed smile. And the hunchback, he had suddenly disappeared. Perhaps he was frightened about what he had done, or maybe he was so delighted that he wanted to glory with himself alone—at any rate he slipped out of the café and crawled under the back steps. Someone poured water on Miss Amelia, and after a time she got up slowly and dragged herself into her office. Through the open door the crowd could see her sitting at her desk, her head in the crook of her arm, and she was sobbing with the last of her grating, winded breath. Once she gathered her right fist together and knocked it three times on the top of her office desk, then her hand opened feebly and lay palm upward and still. Stumpy MacPhail stepped forward and closed the door.

The crowd was quiet, and one by one the people left the café. Mules were waked up and untied, automobiles cranked, and the three boys from Society City roamed off down the road on foot. This was not a fight to hash over and talk about afterward; people went home and pulled the covers up over their heads. The town was dark, except for the premises of Miss Amelia, but every room was lighted there the whole night long.

Marvin Macy and the hunchback must have left the town an hour or so before daylight. And before they went away this is what they did:

They unlocked the private cabinet of curios and took everything in it.

They broke the mechanical piano.

They carved terrible words on the café tables.

They found the watch that opened in the back to show a picture of a waterfall and took that also.

They poured a gallon of sorghum syrup all over the kitchen floor and smashed the jars of preserves.

They went out in the swamp and completely wrecked the still, ruining the big new condenser and the cooler, and setting fire to the shack itself.

They fixed a dish of Miss Amelia's favorite food, grits with sausage, seasoned it with enough poison to kill off the county, and placed this dish temptingly on the café counter.

They did everything ruinous they could think of without actually breaking into the office where Miss Amelia stayed the night. Then they went off together, the two of them.

That was how Miss Amelia was left alone in the town. The people would have helped her if they had known how, as people in this town will as often as not be kindly if they have a chance. Several housewives nosed around with brooms and offered to clear up the wreck. But Miss Amelia only looked at them with lost crossed eyes and shook her head. Stumpy MacPhail came in on the third day to buy a plug of Queenie tobacco, and Miss Amelia said the price was one dollar. Everything in the café had suddenly risen in price to be worth one dollar. And what sort of a café is that? Also, she changed very queerly as a doctor. In all the years before she had been much more popular than the Cheehaw doctor. She had never monkeyed with a patient's soul, taking away from him such real necessities as liquor, tobacco, and so forth. Once in a great while she might carefully warn a patient never to eat fried watermelon or some such dish it had never occurred to a person to want in the first place. Now all this wise doctoring was over. She told one-half of her patients that they were going to die outright, and to the remaining half she recommended cures so far-fetched and agonizing that no one in his right mind would consider them for a moment.

Miss Amelia let her hair grow ragged, and it was turning gray. Her face lengthened, and the great muscles of her body shrank until she was thin as old maids are thin when they go crazy. And those gray eyes—slowly day by day they were more crossed, and it was as though they sought each other out to exchange a little glance of grief and lonely recognition. She was not pleasant to listen to; her tongue had sharpened terribly.

When anyone mentioned the hunchback she would say only this: 'Ho! if I could lay hand to him I would rip out his gizzard and throw it to the cat!' But it was not so much the words that were terrible, but the voice in which they were said. Her voice had lost its old vigor; there was none of the ring of vengeance it used to have when she would mention 'that loom-fixer I was married to,' or some other enemy. Her voice was broken, soft, and sad as the wheezy whine of the church pump-organ.

For three years she sat out on the front steps every night, alone and silent, looking down the road and waiting. But the hunchback never returned. There were rumors that Marvin Macy used him to climb into windows and steal, and other rumors that Marvin Macy had sold him into a side show. But both these reports were traced back to Merlie Ryan. Nothing true was ever heard of him. It was in the fourth year that Miss Amelia hired a Cheehaw carpenter and had him board up the premises, and there in those closed rooms she has remained ever since.

Yes, the town is dreary. On August afternoons the road is empty, white with dust, and the sky above is bright as glass. Nothing moves—there are no children's voices, only the hum of the mill. The peach trees seem to grow more crooked every summer, and the leaves are dull gray and of a sickly delicacy. The house of Miss Amelia leans so much to the right that it is now only a question of time when it will collapse completely, and people are careful not to walk around the yard. There is no good liquor to be bought in the town; the nearest still is eight miles away, and the liquor is such that those who drink it grow warts on their livers the size of goobers, and dream themselves into a dangerous inward world. There is absolutely nothing to do in the town. Walk around the millpond, stand kicking at a rotten stump, figure out what you can do with the old wagon wheel by the side of the road near the church. The soul rots with boredom. You might as well go down to the Forks Falls highway and listen to the chain gang.

THE TWELVE MORTAL MEN

The Forks Falls highway is three miles from the town, and it is here the chain gang has been working. The road is of macadam, and the county decided to patch up the rough places and widen it at a certain dangerous place. The gang is made up of twelve men, all wearing black and white striped prison suits, and chained at the ankles. There is a guard, with a gun, his eyes drawn to red slits by the glare. The gang works all the day long, arriving huddled in the prison cart soon after daybreak, and being driven off again in the gray August twilight. All day there is the sound of the picks striking into the clay earth, hard sunlight, the smell of sweat. And every day there is music. One dark voice will start a phrase, half-sung, and like a question. And after a moment another voice will join in, soon the whole gang will be singing. The voices are dark in the golden glare, the music intricately blended, both somber and joyful. The music will swell until at last it seems that the sound does not come from the twelve men on the gang, but from the earth itself, or the wide sky. It is music that causes the heart to broaden and the listener to grow cold with ecstasy and fright. Then slowly the music will sink down until at last there remains one lonely voice, then a great hoarse breath, the sun, the sound of the picks in the silence.

And what kind of gang is this that can make such music? Just twelve mortal men, seven of them black and five of them white boys from this county. Just twelve mortal men who are together.

TOPICS FOR PAPERS AND DISCUSSION

1. *The love theme.* Reread the passage on pp. 168–169 beginning "First of all, love is a joint experience between two persons." Is McCullers' concept of love entirely clear? What does love include and apparently exclude? Define what she means by the term as it is worked out with her three principal characters. Attempt to apply her concept to other relationships among the good people and the bad. If it is applied to all relationships in her story, what modifications in it would be needed? Does the end of the novel necessitate an enlargement of her discussion of love?
2. *Creation and destruction.* Amelia and all the other characters prosper in some way under certain conditions. What are they? And what is the creative form of this prosperity? Yet decay and disintegration threaten. How is this counterforce rendered in terms of setting, the

characters, and their ethical behavior? What is the significance of the change in Amelia's eyes? Why do the eyes of Marvin and Lymon change color? Explain how alienation and isolation join decay and disintegration as themes. Are they, in turn, related to the theme of love?

3. *The theme of betrayal.* Through what strengths and weaknesses does Amelia betray herself? In what sense does she betray the town? How do the inhabitants betray her out of ritual necessity? In this respect, examine the events after the fight. Scrutinize the townspeople and cite examples of their self-betrayal. Discuss the reasons for Marvin's return and his subsequent actions. How does Lymon function in rendering this theme?
4. *The problem of communication.* The principal characters and the citizens are remarkably silent, yet they communicate without words. How? Examine compulsions, actions, gestures, glances, as well as traditions and ritualizations. When the people do speak with each other, what is the quality of their language? Examine Amelia's response to Marvin's playing and singing. What connection is there between the themes of love and communication? Does love make communication any easier? How is the chain gang involved in the communication theme?
5. The Ballad of the Sad Cafe *as social novel.* What features make the novel a candidate for a sociological interpretation? Consider the time and place, the class structure, and town government. Ascertain what the people do for recreation, where the children receive their education, what the homes are like. Is the cotton industry depicted as a particularly ennobling institution? How open to exploitation are the workers? Determine to what extent social conditions are the cause of the grotesqueries of characters. Does Amelia represent capitalism in any way? How much of a case can be made for a sociological reading exclusive of any other, without destroying the rather special qualities of McCullers' work?
6. *Creation of characters.* The author seldom enters the thoughts of her characters; therefore we are denied direct access to their feelings, ideas, ruminations, and the like, which might better help us understand their motivations. Furthermore, most of the characters are one-dimensional; only the three principals are presented with any fullness. How does the very flatness of the characters point to thematics? How does McCullers create an ambience of authenticity of character in regard to Amelia, Lymon, and Marvin?
7. *Grotesquerie.* One critic called the characters "metaphors and grotesques." What is meant by that phrase, and how does the grotesque serve as metaphor? Assess the devices employed by the author to make the characters grotesque. Does the entire community share this characteristic in some manner, whether physical or psychological? If we are to comment on grotesquerie, what is the basis of our

judgment? How does it compare with the basis of the community's judgment? What artistic effects are achieved and what ends are served by grotesquerie? Finally, can you define the particular quality of McCullers' writing that prevents her characters from becoming freaks?

8. *The character of Amelia.* In what ways did Amelia's motherless childhood with her father affect her relationship with men? Is there any connection between his calling her "Little" and her psychological development? Explain the significance of her finding and keeping an acorn on the afternoon "Big Papa" died. What are the psychological overtones of the relationship between "Little" and "dwarf"? Psychologically, what is meant by the fact that she inherited the store from her father, but that Lymon provoked her to establish the café? How is her emotional life related to her fantastic wedding and its aftermath? Why doesn't she throw Marvin out of the café when he returns? Examine her many roles and the varied facets of her personality.
9. *Importance of minor characters.* How do Henry Macy, Merlie Ryan, Mary Hale, Stumpy MacPhail, and his wife define the town's relationship to Amelia? Point out ways these minor characters are used to fill out, give depth to, and play variations on the main ideas of the novel. Consider the chain reaction when they suspect her of murder. Examine also their condition in the town, at work, and at home, and their natural gravitation to the café when it is established. Do they fulfill a realistic function within an authentic atmosphere of place, time, and social conditions? How, indeed, are they helpful in creating a texture in which such extraordinary events may believably take place?
10. *Characters as archetypes.* In Carl Jung's *Man and His Symbols,* read "Approaching the Unconscious" and "The Process of Individuation," which are helpful in understanding the characters in the novel as psychological, mythological, and archetypal entities. Then determine what sense is to be made of Marvin Macy as Amelia's "animus" (her psychological masculine counterpart)? How does he demonstrate the positive and negative nature of this archetypal figure? What caused the triumph of the negative aspect, and who is responsible? Relate these findings to McCullers' doctrine of love. Show how the trickster Lymon is also Amelia's "shadow" (her repressed, antisocial impulses) in disguise. Why do the "animus" and the "shadow" have a natural affinity for each other, and what is their combined effect on Amelia's ego?
11. *Conflicts between "private need and communal fulfillment."* Why do the townspeople regard Amelia in a special light? How does tradition influence their judgments of her behavior? In what way is she affected by their needs and beliefs? How do personal actions like healing, making whiskey, running a café and store relate

to community needs? Ascertain the forgotten ritual-need that lies behind their suspecting her of murder, seeking out her presence, buying her goods, and even on occasion boxing and wrestling with her. What is the meaning of their hesitation at the moment when she has beaten Marvin, and Lymon throws himself on her from the counter? Why does the town "cave in" when she shuts herself away?

12. *The fight scene.* Analyze the fight carefully for mythological and legendary overtones. First, trace preparations for it. How are the town and Society City at least symbolically involved? What is to be made of the hour the contest starts? Why is the crowd in such a daze, yet why do some of the townspeople reenact the fight in pantomime? Why is the description of the actual blows minimized? What is the connection between the bloody hawk, which appears at the beginning of the scene, and Lymon, who flies "as though he had grown hawk wings"? Why is the event ritualistically closed by one of the crowd? Explain how the word "mystery" is used. Examine the scenic structure; what in it enlarges or universalizes the context?
13. *The novel and the ballad form.* Look up the typical features of folk and literary ballads. Compare them with the novel. Point out how the characteristics of the ballad help one understand the unique qualities of McCullers' story. Is her presentation of character, action, and idea similar to that of the ballad? Where and in what manner does she deviate from the subject matter of the ballad, and to what ends? How is her handling of time, place, and scene balladlike?
14. *Alienation and isolation.* Given the title of the novel, why is the town so isolated from the rest of the world? Why is Amelia set apart from the other characters? How does individual loneliness relate to McCullers' vision of the world? Explain why nothing much is made of loneliness except in the cases of Marvin, Lymon, and perhaps Amelia. What is the effect of love (and McCullers' love doctrine) on alienation and loneliness? In what manner are alienation and loneliness overcome or at least ameliorated by the individual and then by the community?
15. *The store-café.* Psychiatrists have suggested that buildings are symbols of human personality. Analyze the physical world around Amelia. What is the meaning of the store as a symbol of her personality before the advent of Lymon? As it changes over the years from store into café, what needs of the community does it fulfill, beyond "a special benefit to bachelors, unfortunate people, and consumptives"? There is of course an equivalent psychological transformation in Amelia. What are the changes, and what causes them? Next consider the office and the three rooms on the second floor. Why does the latter part of the building remain unchanged? Why is Lymon prompted to paint part of the front porch on the day of the fight? What does the final view of "the house of Miss Amelia" suggest about her and the town's personality?

16. *Supportive symbolism.* In the novel, colors are carefully controlled for their symbolic effectiveness. Discuss the use of red and blue, with special emphasis on the latter. How is number symbolism used? What significant aspects of character do descriptions of clothing and changes of clothing reveal or disguise? For instance, why should Amelia change to a red dress when Marvin arrives? Determine the symbolic functions of food, whiskey, and medicine. Explain why Lymon should inherit Big Papa's snuffbox and receive a gift of Amelia's kidney stones? Discuss the simplicity or complexity of other symbols such as the hawk, the white dust that settles on the town, the large bouquet of paper roses, and Marvin Macy's guitar.
17. *Descriptions of weather and functions of landscape.* The author deftly handles her descriptions of weather conditions in order to create a tone, atmosphere, or mood appropriate to subsequent events. Examine the novel for instances where weather conditions serve as a backdrop for upcoming events. How does weather occur in a perceivable rhythm of increased or decreased normality and mystery? Account for the bluish snow in regard to Ground Hog Day and subsequent events. What is the function of the careful description of the town at the beginning and at the end? How is the swamp significant? Could the town, swamp, and outside world represent separate areas of the psyche of the community? Explain your answer.
18. *Style.* "The style . . . transforms this eccentric tale into something as universal as the old ballads about love and dread, madness and revenge." Comment on this critical assessment. Analyze sentence structure, diction, the rhythmic repetition of certain words and phrases, the deliberate striving after poetic effects, the establishment of dense atmospheres to evoke mood, authorial intrusions, portentous phraseology, and deliberate mystery. Is the style appropriate to the themes? Explain how it universalizes the novel.
19. *Myth, literature, and the individual.* In *Rites and Symbols of Initiation,* Mircia Eliade has observed that myth, ritual, and "initiatory scenarios . . . are the expression of a psycho-drama that answers a deep need in the human being. Everyone wants to experience certain perilous situations, to confront exceptional ordeals, to make his way into the Other World—and he experiences all this, on the level of his imaginative life, by reading fairy tales and by dreaming." With *The Ballad of the Sad Café* in mind, respond to the validity of these statements. Does the appeal of the novel spring from the reader's subsconscious needs? Are myth and ritual therapeutic in literature? Comment on the following: "readers are enthralled as much as the town witnessing the mysterious unfolding of Amelia's fate."
20. *"Twelve Mortal Men."* The final section concerning the chain gang appears to be gratuitous. Nevertheless, it can be related to the

principal action. How? Is the entire section a kind of metaphor for the rest of the novel? Does the episode afford some sense of hopeful resolution? Examine the idea of men, both black and white, as metaphorical prisoners suffering existential guilt. What is the meaning of man chained to man here and elsewhere? How is this section related to the fate of the café, Amelia, and the town? Why are Marvin and Lymon described as exchanging "the look of two criminals who recognize each other"? Explain why the chain-gang music comes from three different places. What is the music's relationship to the mechanical piano broken by Marvin and Lymon? In what way might the final episode fulfill or modify the doctrine of love?

Goodbye, Columbus

PHILIP ROTH

"The heart is half a prophet."
Yiddish proverb

The first time I saw Brenda she asked me to hold her glasses. Then she stepped out to the edge of the diving board and looked foggily into the pool; it could have been drained, myopic Brenda would never have known it. She dove beautifully, and a moment later she was swimming back to the side of the pool, her head of short-clipped auburn hair held up, straight ahead of her, as though it were a rose on a long stem. She glided to the edge and then was beside me. "Thank you," she said, her eyes watery though not from the water. She extended a hand for her glasses but did not put them on until she turned and headed away. I watched her move off. Her hands suddenly appeared behind her. She caught the bottom of her suit between thumb and index finger and flicked what flesh had been showing back where it belonged. My blood jumped.

That night, before dinner, I called her.

"Who are you calling?" my Aunt Gladys asked.

"Some girl I met today."

"Doris introduced you?"

"Doris wouldn't introduce me to the guy who drains the pool, Aunt Gladys."

"Don't criticize all the time. A cousin's a cousin. How did you meet her?"

"I didn't really meet her. I saw her."

"Who is she?"

"Her last name is Patimkin."

"Patimkin I don't know," Aunt Gladys said, as if she knew anybody who belonged to the Green Lane Country Club. "You're going to call her you don't know her?"

"Yes," I explained. "I'll introduce myself."

"Casanova," she said, and went back to preparing my uncle's dinner. None of us ate together: my Aunt Gladys ate at five o'clock, my cousin Susan at five-thirty, me at six, and my uncle at six-thirty. There is nothing to explain this beyond the fact that my aunt is crazy.

"Where's the suburban phone book?" I asked after pulling out all the books tucked under the telephone table.

"What?"

"The suburban phone book. I want to call Short Hills."

"That skinny book? What, I gotta clutter my house with that, I never use it?"

"Where is it?"

"Under the dresser where the leg came off."

"For God's sake," I said.

"Call information better. You'll go yanking around there, you'll mess up my drawers. Don't bother me, you see your uncle'll be home soon. I haven't even fed *you* yet."

"Aunt Gladys, suppose tonight we all eat together. It's hot, it'll be easier for you."

"Sure, I should serve four different meals at once. You eat pot roast, Susan with the cottage cheese, Max has steak. Friday night is his steak night, I wouldn't deny him. And I'm having a little cold chicken. I should jump up and down twenty different times? What am I, a workhorse?"

"Why don't we all have steak, or cold chicken—"

"Twenty years I'm running a house. Go call your girl friend."

But when I called, Brenda Patimkin wasn't home. She's having dinner at the club, a woman's voice told me. Will she be home after (my voice was two octaves higher than a choirboy's)? I don't know, the voice said, she may go driving golf balls. Who is this? I mumbled some words—nobody she wouldn't know I'll call back no message thank you sorry to bother . . . I hung up somewhere along in there. Then my aunt called me and I steeled myself for dinner.

She pushed the black whirring fan up to *High* and that way it managed to stir the cord that hung from the kitchen light.

"What kind of soda you want? I got ginger ale, plain seltzer, black raspberry, and a bottle cream soda I could open up."

"None, thank you."

"You want water?"

"I don't drink with my meals. Aunt Gladys, I've told you that every day for a year already—"

"Max could drink a whole case with his chopped liver only. He works hard all day. If you worked hard you'd drink more."

At the stove she heaped up a plate with pot roast, gravy, boiled potatoes, and peas and carrots. She put it in front of me and I could feel the heat of the food in my face. Then she cut two pieces of rye bread and put that next to me, on the table.

I forked a potato in half and ate it, while Aunt Gladys, who had seated herself across from me, watched. "You don't want bread," she said, "I wouldn't cut it it should go stale."

"I *want* bread," I said.

"You don't like with seeds, do you?"

I tore a piece of bread in half and ate it.

"How's the meat?" she said.

"Okay. Good."

"You'll fill yourself with potatoes and bread, the meat you'll leave over I'll have to throw it out."

Suddenly she leaped up from the chair. "Salt!" When she returned to the table she plunked a salt shaker down in front of me—pepper wasn't served in her home: she'd heard on Galen Drake that it was not absorbed by the body, and it was disturbing to Aunt Gladys to think that anything she served might pass through a gullet, stomach, and bowel just for the pleasure of the trip.

"You're going to pick the peas out is all? You tell me that, I wouldn't buy with the carrots."

"I love carrots," I said, "I love them." And to prove it, I dumped half of them down my throat and the other half onto my trousers.

"Pig," she said.

Though I am very fond of desserts, especially fruit, I chose not to have any. I wanted, this hot night, to avoid the conversation that revolved around my choosing fresh fruit over canned fruit, or canned fruit over fresh fruit; whichever I preferred, Aunt Gladys always had an abundance of the other jamming her refrigerator like stolen diamonds. "He wants canned peaches, I have a refrigerator full of grapes I have to get rid of . . ." Life was a throwing off for poor Aunt Gladys, her greatest joys were taking out the garbage, emptying her pantry, and making threadbare bundles for what she still referred to as the Poor Jews in Palestine. I only hope she dies with an empty refrigerator, otherwise she'll ruin eternity for everyone else, what with her Velveeta turning green, and her navel oranges growing fuzzy jackets down below.

My Uncle Max came home and while I dialed Brenda's number once again, I could hear soda bottles being popped open in the kitchen. The voice that answered this time was high, curt, and tired. "Hullo."

I launched into my speech. "Hello-Brenda-Brenda-you-don't-know-me-that-is-you-don't-know-my-name-but-I-held-your-glasses-for-you-this-afternoon-at-the-club . . . You-asked-me-to-I'm-not-a-member-my-cousin-Doris-is-Doris-Klugman-I-asked-who-you-were . . ." I breathed, gave her a chance to speak, and then went ahead and answered the silence on the other end. "Doris? She's the one who's always reading *War and Peace*. That's how I know it's the summer, when Doris is reading *War and Peace*." Brenda didn't laugh; right from the start she was a practical girl.

"What's your name?" she said.

"Neil Klugman. I held your glasses at the board, remember?"

She answered me with a question of her own, one, I'm sure, that is an embarrassment to both the homely and the fair. "What do you look like?"

"I'm . . . dark."

"Are you a Negro?"

"No," I said.

"What *do* you look like?"

"May I come see you tonight and show you?"

"That's nice," she laughed. "I'm playing tennis tonight."

"I thought you were driving golf balls."

"I drove them already."

"How about after tennis?"

"I'll be sweaty after," Brenda said.

It was not to warn me to clothespin my nose and run in the opposite direction; it was a fact, it apparently didn't bother Brenda, but she wanted it recorded.

"I don't mind," I said, and hoped by my tone to earn a niche somewhere between the squeamish and the grubby. "Can I pick you up?"

She did not answer a minute; I heard her muttering, "Doris Klugman, Doris Klugman . . ." Then she said, "Yes, Briarpath Hills, eight-fifteen."

"I'll be driving a—" I hung back with the year, "a tan Plymouth. So you'll know me. How will I know you?" I said with a sly, awful laugh.

"I'll be sweating," she said and hung up.

Once I'd driven out of Newark, past Irvington and the packed-in tangle of railroad crossings, switchmen shacks, lumberyards, Dairy Queens, and used-car lots, the night grew cooler. It was, in fact, as though the hundred and eighty feet that the suburbs rose in altitude above Newark brought one closer to heaven, for the sun itself became bigger, lower, and rounder, and soon I was driving past long lawns which seemed to be twirling water on themselves, and past houses where no one sat on stoops, where lights were on but no windows open, for those inside, refusing to share the very texture of life with those of us outside, regulated with a dial the amounts of moisture that were allowed access to their skin. It was only eight o'clock, and I did not want to be early, so I drove up and down the streets whose names were those of eastern colleges, as though the township, years ago, when things were named, had planned the destinies of the sons of its citizens. I thought of my Aunt Gladys and Uncle Max sharing a Mounds bar in the cindery darkness of their alley, on beach chairs, each cool breeze sweet to them as the promise of afterlife, and after a while I rolled onto the gravel roads of the small park where Brenda was playing tennis. Inside my glove compartment it was as though the map of *The City Streets of Newark* had metamorphosed into crickets, for those mile-long tarry streets did not exist for me any longer, and the night noises sounded loud as the blood whacking at my temples.

I parked the car under the black-green canopy of three oaks, and walked towards the sound of the tennis balls. I heard an exasperated voice say, "Deuce *again.*" It was Brenda and she sounded as though she was sweating considerably. I crackled slowly up the gravel and heard Brenda once more. "My ad," and then just as I rounded the path, catching a cuff full of burrs, I heard, "Game!" Her racket went spinning up in the air and she caught it neatly as I came into sight.

"Hello," I called.

"Hello, Neil. One more game," she called. Brenda's words seemed to infuriate her opponent, a pretty brown-haired girl, not quite so tall as Brenda, who stopped searching for the ball that had been driven past her, and gave both Brenda and myself a dirty look. In a moment I learned the reason why: Brenda was ahead five games to four, and her cocksureness about there being just one game remaining aroused enough anger in her opponent for the two of us to share.

As it happened, Brenda finally won, though it took more games than she'd expected. The other girl, whose name sounded like Simp, seemed happy to end it at six all, but Brenda, shifting, running, up on her toes, would not stop, and finally all I could see moving in the darkness were her glasses, a glint of them, the clasp of her belt, her socks, her sneakers, and, on occasion, the ball. The darker it got the more savagely did Brenda rush the net, which seemed curious, for I had noticed that earlier, in the light, she had stayed back, and even when she had had to rush, after smashing back a lob, she didn't look entirely happy about being so close to her opponent's racket. Her passion for winning a point seemed outmatched by an even stronger passion for maintaining her beauty as it was. I suspected that the red print of a tennis ball on her cheek would pain her more than losing all the points in the world. Darkness pushed her in, however, and she stroked harder, and at last Simp seemed to be running on her ankles. When it was all over, Simp refused my offer of a ride home and indicated with a quality of speech borrowed from some old Katherine Hepburn movie that she could manage for herself; apparently her manor lay no further than the nearest briar patch. She did not like me and I her, though I worried it, I'm sure, more than she did.

"Who is *she*?"

"Laura Simpson Stolowitch."

"Why don't you call her Stolo?" I asked.

"Simp is her Bennington name. The ass."

"Is that where you go to school?" I asked.

She was pushing her shirt up against her skin to dry the perspiration. "No. I go to school in Boston."

I disliked her for the answer. Whenever anyone asks me where I went to school I come right out with it: Newark Colleges of Rutgers University. I may say it a bit too ringingly, too fast, too up-in-the-air, but I say it. For an instant Brenda reminded me of the pug-nosed little bastards from Montclair who come down to the library during vacations, and while I stamp out their books, they stand around tugging their elephantine scarves until they hang to their ankles, hinting all the while at "Boston" and "New Haven."

"Boston University?" I asked, looking off at the trees.

"Radcliffe."

We were still standing on the court, bounded on all sides by white lines. Around the bushes back of the court, fire-flies were cutting figure eights in the thorny-smelling air and then, as the night suddenly came all the way in, the leaves on the trees shone for an instant, as though they'd just been rained upon. Brenda walked off the court, with me a step behind her. Now I had grown accustomed to the dark, and as she ceased being merely a voice and turned into a sight again, some of my anger at her "Boston" remark floated off and I let myself appreciate her. Her hands did not twitch at her bottom, but the form revealed itself, covered or not, under the closeness of her khaki Bermudas. There were two wet triangles on the back of her tiny-collared white polo shirt, right where her wings would have been if she'd had a pair. She wore, to complete the picture, a tartan belt, white socks, and white tennis sneakers.

As she walked she zipped the cover on her racket.

"Are you anxious to get home?" I said.

"No."

"Let's sit here. It's pleasant."

"Okay."

We sat down on a bank of grass slanted enough for us to lean back without really leaning; from the angle it seemed as though we were preparing to watch some celestial event, the christening of a new star, the inflation to full size of a half-ballooned moon. Brenda zipped and unzipped the cover while she spoke; for the first time she seemed edgy. Her edginess coaxed mine back, and so we were ready now for what, magically, it seemed we might be able to get by without: a meeting.

"What does your cousin Doris look like?" she asked.

"She's dark—"

"Is she—"

"No," I said. "She has freckles and dark hair and she's very tall."

"Where does she go to school?"

"Northampton."

She did not answer and I don't know how much of what I meant she had understood.

"I guess I don't know her," she said after a moment. "Is she a new member?"

"I think so. They moved to Livingston only a couple of years ago."

"Oh."

No new star appeared, at least for the next five minutes.

"Did you remember me from holding your glasses?" I said.

"Now I do," she said. "Do you live in Livingston too?"

"No. Newark."

"We lived in Newark when I was a baby," she offered.

"Would you like to go home?" I was suddenly angry.

"No. Let's walk though."

Brenda kicked a stone and walked a step ahead of me.

"Why is it you rush the net only after dark?" I said.

She turned to me and smiled. "You noticed? Old Simp the Simpleton doesn't."

"Why do you?"

"I don't like to be up too close, unless I'm sure she won't return it."

"Why?"

"My nose."

"What?"

"I'm afraid of my nose. I had it bobbed."

"What?"

"I had my nose fixed."

"What was the matter with it?"

"It was bumpy."

"A lot?"

"No," she said, "I was pretty. Now I'm prettier. My brother's having his fixed in the fall."

"Does he want to be prettier?"

She didn't answer and walked ahead of me again.

"I don't mean to sound facetious. I mean why's he doing it?"

"He *wants* to . . . unless he becomes a gym teacher . . . but he won't," she said. "We all look like my father."

"Is he having his fixed?"

"Why are you so nasty?"

"I'm not. I'm sorry." My next question was prompted by a desire to sound interested and thereby regain civility; it didn't quite come out as I'd expected—I said it too loud. "How much does it cost?"

Brenda waited a moment but then she answered. "A thousand dollars. Unless you go to a butcher."

"Let me see if you got your money's worth."

She turned again; she stood next to a bench and put the racket down on it. "If I let you kiss me would you stop being nasty?"

We had to take about two too many steps to keep the approach from being awkward, but we pursued the impulse and kissed. I felt her hand on the back of my neck and so I tugged her towards me, too violently perhaps, and slid my own hands across the side of her body and around to her back. I felt the wet spots on her shoulder blades, and beneath them, I'm sure of it, a faint fluttering, as though something stirred so deep in her breasts, so far back it could make itself felt through her shirt. It was like the fluttering of wings, tiny wings no bigger than her breasts. The smallness of the wings did not bother me—it would not take an eagle to carry me up those lousy hundred and eighty feet that make summer nights so much cooler in Short Hills than they are in Newark.

2

The next day I held Brenda's glasses for her once again, this time not as momentary servant but as afternoon guest; or perhaps as both, which still was an improvement. She wore a black tank suit and went barefooted, and among the other women, with their Cuban heels and boned-up breasts, their knuckle-sized rings, their straw hats, which resembled immense wicker pizza plates and had been purchased, as I heard one deeply tanned woman rasp, "from the cutest little *shvartze* when we docked at Barbados," Brenda among them was elegantly simple, like a sailor's dream of a Polynesian maiden, albeit one with prescription sun glasses and the last name of Patimkin. She brought a little slurp of water with her when she crawled back towards the pool's edge, and at the edge she grabbed up with her hands and held my ankles, tightly and wet.

"Come in," she said up to me, squinting. "We'll play."

"Your glasses," I said.

"Oh break the goddam things. I hate them."

"Why don't you have your eyes fixed?"

"There you go again."

"I'm sorry," I said. "I'll give them to Doris."

Doris, in the surprise of the summer, had gotten past Prince Andrey's departure from his wife, and now sat brooding, not, it turned out, over the lonely fate of poor Princess Liza, but at the skin which she had lately discovered to be peeling off her shoulders.

"Would you watch Brenda's glasses?" I said.

"Yes." She fluffed little scales of translucent flesh into the air. "Damn it."

I handed her the glasses.

"Well, for God's sake," she said, "I'm not going to hold them. Put them down. *I'm* not her slave."

"You're a pain in the ass, you know that, Doris?" Sitting there, she looked a little like Laura Simpson Stolowitch, who was, in fact, walking somewhere off at the far end of the pool, avoiding Brenda and me because (I liked to think) of the defeat Brenda had handed her the night before; or maybe (I didn't like to think) because of the strangeness of my presence. Regardless, Doris had to bear the weight of my indictment of both Simp and herself.

"Thank you," she said. "After I invite you up for the day."

"That was yesterday."

"What about last year?"

"That's right, your mother told you last year too—invite Esther's boy so when he writes his parents they won't complain we don't look after him. Every summer I get my day."

"You should have gone with them. That's not our fault. You're not our charge," and when she said it, I could just tell it was something she'd heard at home, or received in a letter one Monday mail, after she'd returned to Northampton from Stowe, or Dartmouth, or perhaps from that weekend when she'd taken a shower with her boyfriend in Lowell House.

"Tell your father not to worry. Uncle Aaron, the sport. I'll take care of myself," and I ran on back to the pool, ran into a dive, in fact, and come up like a dolphin beside Brenda, whose legs I slid upon with my own.

"How's Doris?" she said.

"Peeling," I said. "She's going to have her skin fixed."

"*Stop* it," she said, and dove down beneath us till I felt her clamping her hands on the soles of my feet. I pulled back and then down too, and then, at the bottom, no more than six inches above the wiggling black lines that divided the pool into lanes for races, we bubbled a kiss into each other's lips. She was smiling there, at *me*, down at the bottom of the swimming pool of the Green Lane Country Club. Way above us, legs shimmied in the water and a pair of fins skimmed greenly by: my cousin Doris could peel away to nothing for all I cared, my Aunt Gladys have twenty feedings every night, my father and mother could roast away their asthma down in the furnace of Arizona, those penniless deserters—I didn't care for anything but Brenda. I went to pull her towards me just as she started fluttering up; my hand hooked on to the front of her suit and the cloth pulled away from her. Her breasts swam towards me like two pink-nosed fish and she let me hold them. Then, in a moment, it was the sun who kissed us both, and we were out of the water, too pleased with each other to smile. Brenda shook the wetness of her hair onto my face and with the drops that touched me I felt she had made a promise to me about the summer, and, I hoped, beyond.

"Do you want your sun glasses?"

"You're close enough to see," she said. We were under a big blue umbrella, side-by-side on two chaise longues, whose plastic covers sizzled against our suits and flesh; I turned my head to look at Brenda and smelled that pleasant little burning odor in the skin of my shoulders. I turned back up to the sun, as did she, and as we talked, and it grew hotter and brighter, the colors splintered under my closed eyelids.

"This is all very fast," she said.

"Nothing's happened," I said softly.

"No. I guess not. I sort of feel something has."

"In eighteen hours?"

"Yes. I feel . . . pursued," she said after a moment.

"*You* invited *me*, Brenda."

"Why do you always sound a little nasty to me?"

"Did I sound nasty? I don't mean to. Truly."

"You do! *You* invited *me*, Brenda. So what?" she said. "That isn't what I mean anyway."

"I'm sorry."

"Stop apologizing. You're so automatic about it, you don't even mean it."

"Now you're being nasty to me," I said.

"No. Just stating the facts. Let's not argue. I like you." She turned her head and looked as though she too paused a second to smell the summer on her own flesh. "I like the way you look." She saved it from embarrassing me with that factual tone of hers.

"Why?" I said.

"Where did you get those fine shoulders? Do you play something?"

"No," I said. "I just grew up and they came with me."

"I like your body. It's fine."

"I'm glad," I said.

"You like mine, don't you?"

"No," I said.

"Then it's denied you," she said.

I brushed her hair flat against her ear with the back of my hand and then we were silent a while.

"Brenda," I said, "you haven't asked me anything about me."

"How you feel? Do you want me to ask you how you feel?"

"Yes," I said, accepting the back door she gave me, though probably not for the same reasons she had offered it.

"How *do* you feel?"

"I want to swim."

"Okay," she said.

We spent the rest of the afternoon in the water. There were eight of those long lines painted down the length of the pool and by the end of the day I think we had parked for a while in every lane, close enough to the dark stripes to reach out and touch them. We came back to the chairs now and then and sang hesitant, clever, nervous, gentle dithyrambs about how we were beginning to feel towards one another. Actually we did not have the feelings we said we had until we spoke them—at least I didn't; to phrase them was to invent them and own them. We whipped our strangeness and newness into a froth that resembled love, and we dared not play too long with it, talk too much of it, or it would flatten and fizzle away. So we moved back and forth from chairs to water, from talk to silence, and considering my unshakable edginess with Brenda, and the high walls of ego that rose, buttresses and all, between her and her knowledge of herself, we managed pretty well.

At about four o'clock, at the bottom of the pool, Brenda suddenly wrenched away from me and shot up to the surface. I shot up after her.

"What's the matter?" I said.

First she whipped the hair off her forehead. Then she pointed a hand down towards the base of the pool. "My brother," she said, coughing some water free inside her.

And suddenly, like a crew-cut Proteus rising from the sea, Ron Patimkin emerged from the lower depths we'd just inhabited and his immensity was before us.

"Hey, Bren," he said, and pushed a palm flat into the water so that a small hurricane beat up against Brenda and me.

"What are you so happy about?" she said.

"The Yankees took two."

"Are we going to have Mickey Mantle for dinner?" she said. "When the Yankees win," she said to me, treading so easily she seemed to have turned the chlorine to marble beneath her, "we set an extra place for Mickey Mantle."

"You want to race?" Ron asked.

"No, Ronald. Go race alone."

Nobody had as yet said a word about me. I treaded unobtrusively as I could, as a third party, unintroduced, will step back and say nothing, awaiting the amenities. I was tired, however, from the afternoon's sport, and wished to hell brother and sister would not tease and chat much longer. Fortunately Brenda introduced me. "Ronald, this is Neil Klugman. This is my brother, Ronald Patimkin."

Of all things there in the fifteen feet water, Ron reached out his hand to shake. I returned the shake, not quite as monumentally as he apparently expected; my chin slipped an inch into the water and all at once I was exhausted.

"Want to race?" Ron asked me good-naturedly.

"Go ahead, Neil, race with him. I want to call home and tell them you're coming to dinner."

"Am I? I'll have to call my aunt. You didn't say anything. My clothes—"

"We dine *au naturel.*"

"What?" Ronald said.

"Swim, baby," Brenda said to him and it ached me some when she kissed him on the face.

I begged out of the race, saying I had to make a phone call myself, and once upon the tiled blue border of the pool, looked back to see Ron taking the length in sleek, immense strokes. He gave one the feeling that after swimming the length of the pool a half dozen times he would have earned the right to drink its contents; I imagined he had, like my Uncle Max, a colossal thirst and a gigantic bladder.

Aunt Gladys did not seem relieved when I told her she'd have only three feedings to prepare that night. "Fancy-shmancy" was all she said to me on the phone.

We did not eat in the kitchen; rather, the six of us—Brenda, myself, Ron, Mr. and Mrs. Patimkin, and Brenda's little sister, Julie—sat around the dining room table, while the maid, Carlota, a Navaho-faced Negro who had little holes in her ears but no earrings, served us the meal. I was seated next to Brenda, who was dressed in what was *au naturel* for her: Bermudas, the close ones, white polo shirt, tennis sneakers and white socks. Across from me was Julie, ten, round-faced, bright, who before dinner, while the other little girls on the street had been playing with jacks and boys and each other, had been on the back lawn putting golf balls with her father. Mr. Patimkin reminded me of my father, except that when he spoke he did not surround each syllable with a wheeze. He was tall, strong, ungrammatical, and a ferocious eater. When he attacked his salad—after drenching it in bottled French dressing—the veins swelled under the heavy skin of his forearm. He ate three helpings of salad, Ron had four, Brenda and Julie had two, and only Mrs. Patimkin and I had one each. I did not like Mrs. Patimkin, though she was certainly the handsomest of all of us at the table. She was disastrously polite to me, and with her purple eyes, her dark hair, and large, persuasive frame, she gave me the feeling of some captive beauty, some wild princess, who has been tamed and made the servant to the king's daughter—who was Brenda.

Outside, through the wide picture window, I could see the back lawn with its twin oak trees. I say oaks, though fancifully, one might call them sporting-goods trees. Beneath their branches, like fruit dropped from their limbs, were two irons, a golf ball, a tennis can, a baseball bat, basketball, a first-baseman's glove, and what was apparently a riding crop. Further back, near the scrubs that bounded the Patimkin property and in front of the small basketball court, a square red blanket, with a white O stitched in the center, looked to be on fire against the green grass. A breeze must have blown outside, for the net on the basket moved; inside we ate in the steady coolness of air by Westinghouse. It was a pleasure, except that eating among those Brobdingnags, I felt for quite a while as though four inches had been clipped from my shoulders, three inches from my height, and for good measure, someone had removed my ribs and my chest had settled meekly in towards my back.

There was not much dinner conversation; eating was heavy and methodical and serious, and it would be just as well to record all that was said in one swoop, rather than indicate the sentences lost in the passing of food, the words gurgled into mouthfuls, the syntax chopped and forgotten in heapings, spillings, and gorgings.

To Ron: When's Harriet calling?

Ron: Five o'clock.

Julie: It *was* five o'clock.

Ron: Their time.

Julie: Why is it that it's earlier in Milwaukee? Suppose you took a plane back and forth all day. You'd never get older.

Brenda: That's right, sweetheart.

Mrs. P.: What do you give the child misinformation for? Is that why she goes to school?

Brenda: I don't know why she goes to school.

Mr. P. (lovingly): College girl.

Ron: Where's Carlota? Carlota!

Mrs. P.: Carlota, give Ronald more.

Carlota (calling): More what?

Ron: Everything.

Mr. P.: Me too.

Mrs. P.: They'll have to *roll* you on the links.

Mr. P. (pulling his shirt up and slapping his black, curved belly): What are you talking about? Look at that?

Ron (yanking his T-shirt up): Look at *this*.

Brenda [to me]: Would you care to bare your middle?

Me [the choir boy again]: No.

Mrs. P.: That's right, Neil.

Me: Yes. Thank you.

Carlota (over my shoulder, like an unsummoned spirit): Would you like more?

Me: No.

Mr. P.: He eats like a bird.

Julie: Certain birds eat a lot.

Brenda: Which ones?

Mrs. P.: Let's not talk about animals at the dinner table. Brenda, why do you encourage her?

Ron: Where's Carlota, I gotta play tonight.

Mr. P.: Tape your wrist, don't forget.

Mrs. P.: Where do you live, Bill?

Brenda: Neil.

Mrs. P.: Didn't I say Neil?

Julie: You said "Where do you live, *Bill?*"

Mrs. P.: I must have been thinking of something else.

Ron: I hate tape. How the hell can I play in tape?
Julie: Don't curse.
Mrs. P.: That's right.
Mr. P.: What is Mantle batting now?
Julie: Three twenty-eight.
Ron: Three twenty-five.
Julie: Eight!
Ron: Five, jerk! He got three for four in the second game.
Julie: Four for four.
Ron: That was an error, Minoso should have had it.
Julie: I didn't think so.
Brenda (to me): See?
Mrs. P.: See what?
Brenda: I was talking to Bill.
Julie: Neil.
Mr. P.: Shut up and eat.
Mrs. P.: A little less talking, young lady.
Julie: I didn't say anything.
Brenda: She was talking to me, sweetie.
Mr. P.: What's this *she* business. Is that how you call your mother? What's dessert?

The phone rings, and though we are awaiting dessert, the meal seems at a formal end, for Ron breaks for his room, Julie shouts "Harriet!" and Mr. Patimkin is not wholly successful in stifling a belch, though the failure even more than the effort ingratiates him to me. Mrs. Patimkin is directing Carlota not to mix the milk silverware and the meat silverware again, and Carlota is eating a peach while she listens; under the table I feel Brenda's fingers tease my calf. I am full.

We sat under the biggest of the oak trees while out on the basketball court Mr. Patimkin played five and two with Julie. In the driveway Ron was racing the motor of the Volkswagen. "Will somebody *please* move the Chrysler out from behind me?" he called angrily. "I'm late as it is."

"Excuse me," Brenda said, getting up.

"I think I'm behind the Chrysler," I said.

"Let's go," she said.

We backed the cars out so that Ron could hasten on to his game. Then we reparked them and went back to watching Mr. Patimkin and Julie.

"I like your sister," I said.

"So do I," she said. "I wonder what she'll turn out to be."

"Like you," I said.

"I don't know," she said. "Better probably." And then she added, "or maybe worse. How can you tell? My father's nice to her, but I'll give her another three years with my mother . . . Bill," she said, musingly.

"I didn't mind that," I said. "She's very beautiful, your mother."

"I can't even think of her as my mother. She hates me. Other girls, when they pack in September, at least their mothers help them. Not mine. She'll be busy sharpening pencils for Julie's pencil box while I'm carrying my trunk around upstairs. And it's so obvious why. It's practically a case study."

"Why?"

"She's jealous. It's so corny I'm ashamed to say it. Do you know my mother had the best back-hand in New Jersey? Really, she was the best tennis player in the state, man or woman. You ought to see the pictures of her when she was a girl. She was so healthy-looking. But not chubby or anything. She was soulful, truly. I love her in those pictures. Sometimes I say to her how beautiful the pictures are. I even asked to have one blown up so I could have it at school. 'We have other things to do with our money, young lady, than spend it on old photographs.' Money! My father's up to here with it, but whenever I buy a coat you should hear her. 'You don't have to go to Bonwit's, young lady, Ohrbach's has the strongest fabrics of any of them.' Who *wants* a strong fabric! Finally I get what I want, but not till she's had a chance to aggravate me. Money is a waste for her. She doesn't even know how to enjoy it. She still thinks we live in Newark."

"But you get what you want," I said.

"Yes. Him," and she pointed out to Mr. Patimkin who had just swished his third straight set shot through the basket to the disgruntlement, apparently, of Julie, who stamped so hard at the ground that she raised a little dust storm around her perfect young legs.

"He's not too smart but he's sweet at least. He doesn't treat my brother the way she treats me. Thank God, for that. Oh, I'm tired of talking about them. Since my freshman year I think every conversation I've ever had has always wound up about my parents and how awful it is. It's universal. The only trouble is they don't know it."

From the way Julie and Mr. Patimkin were laughing now, out on the court, no problem could ever have seemed less universal; but, of course, it was universal for Brenda, more than that, cosmic—it made every cashmere sweater a battle with her mother, and her life, which, I was certain, consisted to a large part of cornering the market on fabrics that felt soft to the skin, took on the quality of a Hundred Years' War . . .

I did not intend to allow myself such unfaithful thoughts, to line up with Mrs. Patimkin while I sat beside Brenda, but I could not shake from my elephant's brain that she-still-thinks-we-live-in-Newark remark. I did not speak, however, fearful that my tone would shatter our post-dinner ease and intimacy. It had been so simple to be intimate with water pounding and securing all our pores, and later, with the sun heating them and drugging our senses, but now, in the shade and the open, cool and clothed on her own grounds, I did not want to voice a word that would lift the cover and reveal that hideous emotion I always felt for her, and is the underside of love. It will not always *stay* the underside—but I am skipping ahead.

Suddenly, little Julie was upon us. "Want to play?" she said to me. "Daddy's tired."

"C'mon," Mr. Patimkin called. "Finish for me."

I hesitated—I hadn't held a basketball since high school—but Julie was dragging at my hand, and Brenda said, "Go ahead."

Mr. Patimkin tossed the ball towards me while I wasn't looking and it bounced off my chest, leaving a round dust spot, like the shadow of a moon, on my shirt. I laughed, insanely.

"Can't you catch?" Julie said.

Like her sister, she seemed to have a knack for asking practical, infuriating questions.

"Yes."

"Your turn," she said. "Daddy's behind forty-seven to thirty-nine. Two hundred wins."

For an instant, as I placed my toes in the little groove that over the years had been nicked into a foul line, I had one of those instantaneous waking dreams that plague me from time to time, and send, my friends tell me, deadly cataracts over my eyes: the sun had sunk, crickets had come and gone, the leaves had blackened, and still Julie and I stood alone on the lawn, tossing the ball at the basket; "Five hundred wins," she called, and then when she beat me to five hundred she called, "Now *you* have to reach it," and I did, and the night lengthened, and she called, "*Eight* hundred wins," and we played on and then it was eleven hundred that won and we played on and it never was morning.

"Shoot," Mr. Patimkin said. "You're me."

That puzzled me, but I took my set shot and, of course, missed. With the Lord's blessing and a soft breeze, I made the lay-up.

"You have forty-one. I go," Julie said.

Mr. Patimkin sat on the grass at the far end of the court. He took his shirt off, and in his undershirt, and his whole day's growth of beard, looked like a trucker. Brenda's old nose fitted him well. There was a bump in it, all right; up at the bridge it seemed as though a small eight-sided diamond had been squeezed in under the skin. I knew Mr. Patimkin would never bother to have that stone cut from his face, and yet, with joy and pride, no doubt, had paid to have Brenda's diamond removed and dropped down some toilet in Fifth Avenue Hospital.

Julie missed her set shot, and I admit to a slight, gay, flutter of heart.

"Put a little spin on it," Mr. Patimkin told her.

"Can I take it again?" Julie asked me.

"Yes." What with paternal directions from the sidelines and my own grudging graciousness on the court, there did not seem much of a chance for me to catch up. And I wanted to, suddenly, I wanted to win, to run little Julie into the ground. Brenda was back on one elbow, under the tree, chewing on a leaf, watching. And up in the house, at the kitchen window, I could see that the curtain had swished back—the sun too low now to glare off electrical appliances—and Mrs. Patimkin was looking steadily out at the game. And then Carlota appeared on the back steps, eating a peach and holding a pail of garbage in her free hand. She stopped to watch too.

It was my turn again. I missed the set shot and laughingly turned to Julie and said, "Can I take it again?"

"No!"

So I learned how the game was played. Over the years Mr. Patimkin had taught his daughters that free throws were theirs for the asking; he could afford to. However, with the strange eyes of Short Hills upon me, matrons, servants, and providers, I somehow felt I couldn't. But I had to and I did.

"Thanks a lot, Neil," Julie said when the game was ended—at 100—and the crickets had come.

"You're welcome."

Under the trees, Brenda smiled. "Did you let her win?"

"I think so," I said. "I'm not sure."

There was something in my voice that prompted Brenda to say, comfortingly, "Even Ron lets her win."

"It's all nice for Julie," I said.

3

The next morning I found a parking space on Washington Street directly across from the library. Since I was twenty minutes early I decided to stroll in the park rather than cross over to work; I didn't particularly care to join my colleagues, who I knew would be sipping early morning coffee in the binding room, smelling still of all the orange crush they'd drunk that weekend at Asbury Park. I sat on a bench and looked out towards Broad Street and the morning traffic. The Lackawanna commuter trains were rumbling in a few blocks to the north and I could hear them, I thought—the sunny green cars, old and clean, with windows that opened all the way. Some mornings, with time to kill before work, I would walk down to the tracks and watch the open windows roll in, on their sills the elbows of tropical suits and the edges of briefcases, the properties of businessmen arriving in town from Maplewood, the Oranges, and the suburbs beyond.

The park, bordered by Washington Street on the west and Broad on the east, was empty and shady and smelled of trees, night, and dog leavings; and there was a faint damp smell too, indicating that the huge rhino of a water cleaner had passed by already, soaking and whisking the downtown streets. Down Washington Street, behind me, was the Newark Museum—I could see it without even looking: two oriental vases in front like spittoons for a rajah, and next to it the little annex to which we had traveled on special buses as schoolchildren. The annex was a brick building, old and vine-covered, and always reminded me of New Jersey's link with the beginning of the country, with George Washington, who had trained his scrappy army—a little bronze tablet informed us children—in the very park where I now sat. At the far end of the park, beyond the Museum, was the bank building where I had gone to college. It had been converted some years before into an extension of Rutgers University; in fact, in what once had been the bank president's waiting room I had taken a course called Contemporary Moral Issues. Though it was summer now, and I was out of college three years, it was not hard for me to remember the other students, my friends, who had worked evenings in Bamberger's and Kresge's and had used the commissions they'd earned pushing ladies' out-of-season shoes to pay their laboratory fees. And then I looked out to Broad Street again. Jammed between a grimy-windowed bookstore and a cheesy luncheonette was the marquee of a tiny art theater—how many years had passed since I'd stood beneath that marquee, lying about the year of my birth so as to see Hedy Lamarr swim naked in *Ecstasy;* and then, having slipped the ticket taker an extra quarter, what disappointment I had felt at the frugality of her Slavic charm . . . Sitting there in the park, I felt a deep knowledge of Newark, an attachment so rooted that it could not help but branch out into affection.

Suddenly it was nine o'clock and everything was scurrying. Wobbly-heeled girls revolved through the doors of the telephone building across the way, traffic honked desperately, policeman barked, whistled, and waved motorists to and fro. Over at St. Vincent's Church the huge dark portals swung back and those bleary-eyes that had risen early for Mass now blinked at the light. Then the worshipers had stepped off the church steps and were racing down the streets towards desks, filing cabinets, secretaries, bosses, and—if the Lord had seen fit to remove a mite of harshness from their lives—to the comfort of air-conditioners pumping at their windows. I got up and crossed over to the library, wondering if Brenda was awake yet.

The pale cement lions stood unconvincing guard on the library steps, suffering their usual combination of elephantiasis and arteriosclerosis, and I was prepared to pay them as little attention as I had for the past eight months were it not for a small colored boy who stood in front of one of them. The lion had lost all of its toes the summer before to a safari of juvenile delinquents, and now a new tormentor stood before him, sagging a little in his knees, and growling. He would growl, low and long, drop back, wait, then growl again. Then he would straighten up, and, shaking his head, he would say to the lion, "Man, you's a coward . . ." Then, once again, he'd growl.

The day began the same as any other. From behind the desk on the main floor, I watched the hot high-breasted teen-age girls walk twitchingly up the wide flight of marble stairs that led to the main reading room. The stairs were an imitation of a staircase somewhere in Versailles, though in their toreador pants and sweaters these young daughters of Italian leatherworkers, Polish brewery hands, and Jewish furriers were hardly duchesses. They were not Brenda either, and any lust that sparked inside me through the dreary day was academic and time-passing. I looked at my watch occasionally, thought of Brenda, and waited for lunch and then for after lunch, when I would take over the Information Desk upstairs and John McKee, who was only twenty-one but wore elastic bands around his sleeves, would march starchily down the stairs to work assiduously at stamping books in and out. John McRubberbands was in his last year at Newark State Teachers College where he was studying at the Dewey Decimal System in preparation for his lifework. The library was not going to be my lifework, I knew it. Yet, there had been some talk—from Mr. Scapello, an old eunuch who had learned somehow to disguise his voice as a man's—that when I returned from my summer vacation I would be put in charge of the Reference Room, a position that had been empty ever since that morning when Martha Winney had fallen off a high stool in the Encyclopedia Room and shattered all those frail bones that come together to form what in a woman half her age we would call the hips.

I had strange fellows at the library and, in truth, there were many hours when I never quite knew how I'd gotten there or why I stayed. But I did stay and after a while waited patiently for that day when I would go into the men's room on the main floor for a cigarette and, studying myself as I expelled smoke into the mirror, would see that at some moment during the morning I had gone pale, and that under my skin, as under McKee's and Scapello's and Miss Winney's, there was a thin cushion of air separating the blood from the flesh. Someone had pumped it there while I was stamping out a book, and so life from now on would be not a throwing off, as it was for Aunt Gladys, and not a gathering in, as it was for Brenda, but a bouncing off, a numbness. I began to fear this, and yet, in my muscleless devotion to my work, seemed edging towards it, silently, as Miss Winney used to edge up to the *Britannica*. Her stool was empty now and awaited me.

Just before lunch the lion tamer came wide-eyed into the library. He stood still for a moment, only his fingers moving, as though he were counting the number of marble stairs before him. Then he walked creepily about on the marble floor, snickering at the clink of his taps and the way his little noise swelled up to the vaulted ceiling. Otto, the guard at the door, told him to make less noise with his shoes, but that did not seem to bother the little boy. He clacked on his tiptoes, high, secretively, delighted at the opportunity Otto had given him to practice this posture. He tiptoed up to me.

"Hey," he said, "where's the heart section?"

"The what?" I said.

"The heart section. Ain't you got no heart section?"

He had the thickest sort of southern Negro dialect and the only word that came clear to me was the one that sounded like heart.

"How do you spell it?" I said.

"*Heart*. Man, pictures. Drawing books. Where you got them?"

"You mean art books? Reproductions?"

He took my polysyllabic word for it. "Yea, they's them."

"In a couple places," I told him. "Which artist are you interested in?"

The boy's eyes narrowed so that his whole face seemed black. He started backing away, as he had from the lion. "All of them . . ." he mumbled.

"That's okay," I said. "You go look at whichever ones you want. The next flight up. Follow the arrow to where it says Stack Three. You remember that? Stack Three. Ask somebody upstairs."

He did not move; he seemed to be taking my curiosity about his taste as a kind of poll-tax investigation. "Go ahead," I said, slashing my face with a smile, "right up there . . ."

And like a shot he was scuffling and tapping up towards the heart section.

After lunch I came back to the in-and-out desk and there was John McKee, waiting, in his pale blue slacks, his black shoes, his barber-cloth shirt with the elastic bands, and a great knit tie, green, wrapped into a Windsor knot, that was huge and jumped when he talked. His breath smelled of hair oil and his hair of breath and when he spoke, spittle cobwebbed the corners of his mouth. I did not like him and at times had the urge to yank back on his armbands and slingshoot him out past Otto and the lions into the street.

"Has a little Negro boy passed the desk? With a thick accent? He's been hiding in the art books all morning. You know what those boys *do* in there."

"I saw him come in, John."

"So did I. Has he gone *out* though."

"I haven't noticed. I guess so."

"Those are *very* expensive books."

"Don't be so nervous, John. People are supposed to touch them."

"There is touching," John said sententiously, "and there is touching. Someone should check on him. I was afraid to leave the desk here. You know the way they treat the housing projects we give them."

"*You* give them?"

"The city. Have you seen what they do at Seth Boyden? They threw *beer* bottles, those big ones, on the *lawn*. They're taking over the city."

"Just the Negro sections."

"It's easy to laugh, you don't live near them. I'm going to call

Mr. Scapello's office to check the Art Section. Where did he ever find out about art?"

"You'll give Mr. Scapello an ulcer, so soon after his egg-and-pepper sandwich. I'll check, I have to go upstairs anyway."

"You know what they do in there," John warned me.

"Don't worry, Johnny, *they're* the ones who'll get warts on their dirty little hands."

"Ha ha. Those books happen to cost—"

So that Mr. Scapello would not descend upon the boy with his chalky fingers, I walked up the three flights to Stack Three, past the receiving room where rheumy-eyed Jimmy Boylen, our fifty-one-year-old boy, unloaded books from a cart; past the reading room, where bums off Mulberry Street slept over *Popular Mechanics;* past the smoking corridor where damp-browed summer students from the law school relaxed, some smoking, others trying to rub the colored dye from their tort texts off their fingertips; and finally, past the periodical room, where a few ancient ladies who'd been motored down from Upper Montclair now huddled in their chairs, pince-nezing over yellowed, fraying society pages in old old copies of the Newark *News.* Up on Stack Three I found the boy. He was seated on the glass-brick floor holding an open book in his lap, a book, in fact, that was bigger than his lap and had to be propped up by his knees. By the light of the window behind him I could see the hundreds of spaces between the hundreds of tiny black corkscrews that were his hair. He was very black and shiny, and the flesh of his lips did not so much appear to be a different color as it looked to be unfinished and awaiting another coat. The lips were parted, the eyes wide, and even the ears seemed to have a heightened receptivity. He looked ecstatic—until he saw me, that is. For all he knew I was John McKee.

"That's okay," I said before he could even move, "I'm just passing through. You read."

"Ain't nothing *to* read. They's pictures."

"Fine." I fished around the lowest shelves a moment, playing at work.

"Hey, mister," the boy said after a minute, "where is this?"

"Where is what?"

"Where is these pictures? These people, man, they sure does

look cool. They ain't no yelling or shouting here, you could just see it."

He lifted the book so I could see. It was an expensive large-sized edition of Gauguin reproductions. The page he had been looking at showed an $8\frac{1}{2} \times 11$ print, in color, of three native women standing knee-high in a rose-colored stream. It *was* a silent picture, he was right.

"That's Tahiti. That's an island in the Pacific Ocean."

"That ain't no place you could go, is it? Like a ree-*sort*?"

"You could go there, I suppose. It's very far. People live there . . ."

"Hey, *look*, look here at this one." He flipped back to a page where a young brown-skinned maid was leaning forward on her knees, as though to dry her hair. "Man," the boy said, "that's the fuckin life." The euphoria of his diction would have earned him eternal banishment from the Newark Public Library and its branches had John or Mr. Scapello—or, God forbid, the hospitalized Miss Winney—come to investigate.

"Who took these pictures?" he asked me.

"Gauguin. He didn't take them, he painted them. Paul Gauguin. He was a Frenchman."

"Is he a white man or a colored man?"

"He's white."

"Man," the boy smiled, chuckled almost, "I knew that. He don't *take* pictures like no colored men would. He's a good picture taker . . . *Look, look,* look here at this one. Ain't that the fuckin *life*?"

I agreed it was and left.

Later I sent Jimmy Boylen hopping down the stairs to tell McKee that everything was all right. The rest of the day was uneventful. I sat at the Information Desk thinking about Brenda and reminding myself that that evening I would have to get gas before I started up to Short Hills, which I could see now, in my mind's eye, at dusk, rose-colored, like a Gauguin stream.

When I pulled up to the Patimkin house that night, everybody but Julie was waiting for me on the front porch: Mr. and Mrs.,

Ron, and Brenda, wearing a dress. I had not seen her in a dress before and for an instant she did not look like the same girl. But that was only half the surprise. So many of those Lincolnesque college girls turn out to be limbed for shorts alone. Not Brenda. She looked, in a dress, as though she'd gone through life so attired, as though she'd never worn shorts, or bathing suits, or pajamas, or anything but that pale linen dress. I walked rather bouncingly up the lawn, past the huge weeping willow, towards the waiting Patimkins, wishing all the while that I'd had my car washed. Before I'd even reached them, Ron stepped forward and shook my hand, vigorously, as though he hadn't seen me since the Diaspora. Mrs. Patimkin smiled and Mr. Patimkin grunted something and continued twitching his wrists before him, then raising an imaginary golf club and driving a ghost of a golf ball up and away towards the Orange Mountains, that are called Orange, I'm convinced, because in that various suburban light that's the *only* color they do not come dressed in.

"We'll be right back," Brenda said to me. "You have to sit with Julie. Carlota's off."

"Okay," I said.

"We're taking Ron to the airport."

"Okay."

"Julie doesn't want to go. She says Ron pushed her in the pool this afternoon. We've been waiting for you, so we don't miss Ron's plane. Okay?"

"*Okay.*"

Mr. and Mrs. Patimkin and Ron moved off, and I flashed Brenda just the hint of a glare. She reached out and took my hand a moment.

"How do you like me?" she said.

"You're great to baby-sit for. Am I allowed all the milk and cake I want?"

"Don't be angry, baby. We'll be right back." Then she waited a moment, and when I failed to deflate the pout from my mouth, she gave *me* a glare, no hints about it. "I *meant* how do you like me in a dress!" Then she ran off towards the Chrysler, trotting in her high heels like a colt.

When I walked into the house, I slammed the screen door behind me.

"Close the other door too," a little voice shouted. "The air-conditioning."

I closed the other door, obediently.

"Neil?" Julie called.

"Yes."

"Hi. Want to play five and two?"

"No."

"Why not?"

I did not answer.

"I'm in the television room," she called.

"Good."

"Are you supposed to stay with me?"

"Yes."

She appeared unexpectedly through the dining room. "Want to read a book report I wrote?"

"Not now."

"What do you want to do?" she said.

"Nothing, honey. Why don't you watch TV?"

"All right," she said disgustedly, and kicked her way back to the television room.

For a while I remained in the hall, bitten with the urge to slide quietly out of the house, into my car, and back to Newark, where I might even sit in the alley and break candy with my own. I felt like Carlota; no, not even as comfortable as that. At last I left the hall and began to stroll in and out of rooms on the first floor. Next to the living room was the study, a small knotty-pine room jammed with cater-cornered leather chairs and a complete set of *Information Please Almanacs*. On the wall hung three colored photo-paintings; they were the kind which, regardless of the subjects, be they vital or infirm, old or youthful, are characterized by bud-cheeks, wet lips, pearly teeth, and shiny, metallized hair. The subjects in this case were Ron, Brenda, and Julie at about ages fourteen, thirteen, and two. Brenda had long auburn hair, her diamond-studded nose, and no glasses; all combined to make her look a regal thirteen-year-old who'd just gotten smoke in her eyes. Ron was rounder and his hairline was lower, but that love of spherical objects and lined courts twinkled in his boyish eyes. Poor little Julie was lost in the photo-painter's Platonic idea of childhood; her tiny humanity was smothered somewhere back of gobs of pink and white.

There were other pictures about, smaller ones, taken with a Brownie Reflex before photo-paintings had become fashionable. There was a tiny picture of Brenda on a horse; another of Ron in bar mitzvah suit, *yamalkah,* and *tallas;* and two pictures framed together—one of a beautiful, faded woman, who must have been, from the eyes, Mrs. Patimkin's mother, and the other of Mrs. Patimkin herself, her hair in a halo, her eyes joyous and not those of a slowly aging mother with a quick and lovely daughter.

I walked through the archway into the dining room and stood a moment looking out at the sporting goods tree. From the television room that winged off the dining room, I could hear Julie listening to *This Is Your Life.* The kitchen, which winged off the other side, was empty, and apparently, with Carlota off, the Patimkins had had dinner at the club. Mr. and Mrs. Patimkin's bedroom was in the middle of the house, down the hall, next to Julie's, and for a moment I wanted to see what size bed those giants slept in—I imagined it wide and deep as a swimming pool—but I postponed my investigation while Julie was in the house, and instead opened the door in the kitchen that led down to the basement.

The basement had a different kind of coolness from the house, and it had a smell, which was something the upstairs was totally without. It felt cavernous down there, but in a comforting way, like the simulated caves children make for themselves on rainy days, in hall closets, under blankets, or in between the legs of dining room tables. I flipped on the light at the foot of the stairs and was not surprised at the pine paneling, the bamboo furniture, the ping-pong table, and the mirrored bar that was stocked with every kind and size of glass, ice bucket, decanter, mixer, swizzle stick, shot glass, pretzel bowl—all the bacchanalian paraphernalia, plentiful, orderly, and untouched, as it can be only in the bar of a wealthy man who never entertains drinking people, who himself does not drink, who, in fact, gets a fishy look from his wife when every several months he takes a shot of schnapps before dinner. I went behind the bar where there was an aluminum sink that had not seen a dirty glass, I'm sure, since Ron's bar mitzvah party, and would not see another, probably, until one of the Patimkin children was married or engaged. I would have poured myself a drink—just as a wicked wage for being forced into servantry—but I was uneasy about breaking the label on a bottle of whiskey. You had to break a label to get a drink. On the shelf back of the bar were two dozen bottles—twenty-three to be exact—of Jack Daniels, each with a little booklet tied to its collared neck informing patrons how patrician of them it was to drink the stuff. And over the Jack Daniels were more photos: there was a blown-up newspaper photo of Ron palming a basketball in one hand like a raisin; under the picture it said, "*Center*, Ronald Patimkin, Millburn High School, 6′4″, 217 pounds." And there was another picture of Brenda on a horse, and next to that, a velvet mounting board with ribbons and medals clipped to it: Essex County Horse Show 1949, Union County Horse Show 1950, Garden State Fair 1952, Morristown Horse Show 1953, and so on—all for Brenda, for jumping and running or galloping or whatever else young girls receive ribbons for. In the entire house I hadn't seen one picture of Mr. Patimkin.

The rest of the basement, back of the wide pine-paneled room, was gray cement walls and linoleum floor and contained innumerable electrical appliances, including a freezer big enough to house a family of Eskimos. Beside the freezer, incongruously, was a tall old refrigerator; its ancient presence was a reminder to me of the Patimkin roots in Newark. This same refrigerator had once stood in the kitchen of an apartment in some four-family house, probably in the same neighborhood where I had lived all my life, first with my parents and then, when the two of them went wheezing off to Arizona, with my aunt and uncle. After Pearl Harbor the refrigerator had made the move up to Short Hills; Patimkin Kitchen and Bathroom Sinks had gone to war: no new barracks was complete until it had a squad of Patimkin sinks lined up in its latrine.

I opened the door of the old refrigerator; it was not empty. No longer did it hold butter, eggs, herring in cream sauce, ginger ale, tuna fish salad, an occasional corsage—rather it was heaped with fruit, shelves swelled with it, every color, every texture, and hidden within, every kind of pit. There were greengage plums, black plums, red plums, apricots, nectarines, peaches, long horns of grapes, black, yellow, red, and cherries, cherries flowing out of boxes and staining everything scarlet. And there were melons—cantaloupes and honeydews—and on the top shelf, half of a huge watermelon, a thin sheet of wax paper clinging to its bare red face like a wet lip. Oh Patimkin! Fruit grew in their refrigerator and sporting goods dropped from their trees!

I grabbed a handful of cherries and then a nectarine, and I bit right down to its pit.

"You better wash that or you'll get diarrhea."

Julie was standing behind me in the pine-paneled room. She was wearing *her* Bermudas and *her* white polo shirt which was unlike Brenda's only in that it had a little dietary history of its own.

"What?" I said.

"They're not washed yet," Julie said, and in such a way that it seemed to place the refrigerator itself out-of-bounds, if only for me.

"That's all right," I said, and devoured the nectarine and put the pit in my pocket and stepped out of the refrigerator room, all in one second. I still didn't know what to do with the cherries. "I was just looking around," I said.

Julie didn't answer.

"Where's Ron going?" I asked, dropping the cherries into my pocket, among my keys and change.

"Milwaukee."

"For long?"

"To see Harriet. They're in love."

We looked at each other for longer than I could bear. "Harriet?" I asked.

"Yes."

Julie was looking at me as though she were trying to look behind me, and then I realized that I was standing with my hands out of sight. I brought them around to the front, and, I swear it, she did peek to see if they were empty.

We confronted one another again; she seemed to have a threat in her face.

Then she spoke. "Want to play ping-pong?"

"God, yes," I said, and made for the table with two long, bounding steps. "You can serve."

Julie smiled and we began to play.

I have no excuses to offer for what happened next. I began to win and I liked it.

"Can I take that one over?" Julie said. "I hurt my finger yesterday and it just hurt when I served."

"No."

I continued to win.

"That wasn't fair, Neil. My shoelace came untied. Can I take it—"

"No."

We played, I ferociously.

"Neil, you leaned over the table. That's illegal—"

"I didn't lean and it's not illegal."

I felt the cherries hopping among my nickels and pennies.

"Neil, you gypped me out of a point. You have nineteen and I have eleven—"

"Twenty and *ten*," I said. "Serve!"

She did and I smashed my return past her—it zoomed off the table and skittered into the refrigerator room.

"You're a cheater!" she screamed at me. "You cheat!" Her jaw was trembling as though she carried a weight on top of her pretty head. "*I hate* you!" And she threw her racket across the room and it clanged off the bar, just as, outside, I heard the Chrysler crushing gravel in the driveway.

"The game isn't over," I said to her.

"You cheat! And you were stealing fruit!" she said, and ran away before I had my chance to win.

Later that night, Brenda and I made love, our first time. We were sitting on the sofa in the television room and for some ten minutes had not spoken a word to each other. Julie had long since gone to a weepy bed, and though no one had said anything to me about her crying, I did not know if the child had mentioned my fistful of cherries, which, some time before, I had flushed down the toilet.

The television set was on and though the sound was off and the house quiet, the gray pictures still wiggled at the far end of the room. Brenda was quiet and her dress circled her legs, which were tucked back beneath her. We sat there for some while and did not speak. Then she went into the kitchen and when she came back she said that it sounded as though everyone was asleep. We sat a while longer, watching the soundless bodies on the screen eating a silent dinner in someone's silent restaurant. When I began to unbutton her dress she resisted me, and I like to think it was because she knew how lovely she looked in it. But she looked lovely, my Brenda, anyway, and we folded it carefully and held each other close and soon there we were, Brenda falling, slowly but with a smile, and me rising.

How can I describe loving Brenda? It was so sweet, as though I'd finally scored that twenty-first point.

When I got home I dialed Brenda's number, but not before my aunt heard and rose from her bed.

"Who are you calling at this hour? The doctor?"

"No."

"What kind phone calls, one o'clock at night?"

"Shhh!" I said.

"He tells *me* shhh. Phone calls one o'clock at night, we haven't got a big enough bill," and then she dragged herself back into the bed, where with a martyr's heart and bleary eyes she had resisted the downward tug of sleep until she'd heard my key in the door.

Brenda answered the phone.

"Neil?" she said.

"Yes," I whispered. "You didn't get out of bed, did you?"

"No," she said, "the phone is next to the bed."

"Good. How is it in bed?"

"Good. Are you in bed?"

"Yes," I lied, and tried to right myself by dragging the phone by its cord as close as I could to my bedroom.

"I'm in bed with you," she said.

"That's right," I said, "and I'm with you."

"I have the shades down, so it's dark and I don't see you."

"I don't see you either."

"That was so nice, Neil."

"Yes. Go to sleep, sweet, I'm here," and we hung up without goodbyes. In the morning, as planned, I called again, but I could hardly hear Brenda or myself for that matter, for Aunt Gladys and Uncle Max were going on a Workmen's Circle picnic in the afternoon, and there was some trouble about grape juice that had dripped all night from a jug in the refrigerator and by morning had leaked out onto the floor. Brenda was still in bed and so could play our game with some success, but I had to pull down all the shades of my senses to imagine myself beside her. I could only pray our nights and mornings would come, and soon enough they did.

4

Over the next week and a half there seemed to be only two people in my life: Brenda and the little colored kid who liked Gauguin. Every morning before the library opened, the boy was waiting; sometimes he seated himself on the lion's back, sometimes under his belly, sometimes he just stood around throwing pebbles at his mane. Then he would come inside, tap around the main floor until Otto stared him up on tiptoes, and finally headed up the long marble stairs that led to Tahiti. He did not always stay to lunch time, but one very hot day he was there when I arrived in the morning and went through the door behind me when I left at night. The next morning, it was, that he did not show up, and as though in his place, a very old man appeared, white, smelling of Life Savers, his nose and jowls showing erupted veins beneath them. "Could you tell me where I'd find the art section?"

"Stack Three," I said.

In a few minutes, he returned with a big brown-covered book in his hand. He placed it on my desk, withdrew his card from a long moneyless billfold and waited for me to stamp out the book.

"Do you want to take this book *out*?" I said.

He smiled.

I took his card and jammed the metal edge into the machine; but I did not stamp down. "Just a minute," I said. I took a clipboard from under the desk and flipped through a few pages, upon which were games of battleship and tick-tack-toe that I'd been playing through the week with myself. "I'm afraid there's a hold on this book."

"A what?"

"A hold. Someone's called up and asked that we hold it for them. Can I take your name and address and drop a card when it's free . . ."

And so I was able, not without flushing once or twice, to get the book back in the stacks. When the colored kid showed up later in the day, it was just where he'd left it the afternoon before.

As for Brenda, I saw her every evening and when there was not a night game that kept Mr. Patimkin awake and in the TV room, or a Hadassah card party that sent Mrs. Patimkin out of the house and brought her in at unpredictable hours, we made love before the silent screen. One muggy, low-skied night Brenda took me swimming at the club. We were the only ones in the pool, and all the chairs, the cabañas, the lights, the diving boards, the very water seemed to exist only for our pleasure. She wore a blue suit that looked purple in the lights and down beneath the water it flashed sometimes green, sometimes black. Late in the evening a breeze came up off the golf course and we wrapped ourselves in one huge towel, pulled two chaise longues together, and despite the bartender, who was doing considerable pacing back and forth by the bar window, which overlooked the pool, we rested side by side on the chairs. Finally the bar light itself flipped off, and then, in a snap, the lights around the pool went down and out. My heart must have beat faster, or something, for Brenda seemed to guess my sudden doubt—*we should go,* I thought.

She said: "That's okay."

It was very dark, the sky was low and starless, and it took a while for me to see, once again, the diving board a shade lighter than the night, and to distinguish the water from the chairs that surrounded the far side of the pool.

I pushed the straps of her bathing suit down but she said no and rolled an inch away from me, and for the first time in the two weeks I'd known her she asked me a question about me.

"Where are your parents?" she said.

"Tucson," I said. "Why?"

"My mother asked me."

I could see the life guard's chair now, white almost.

"Why are you still here? Why aren't you with them?" she asked.

"I'm not a child any more, Brenda," I said, more sharply than I'd intended. "I just can't go wherever my parents are."

"But then why do you stay with your aunt and uncle?"

"They're not my parents."

"They're better?"

"No. Worse. I don't *know* why I stay with them."

"Why?" she said.

"Why don't I know?"

"Why do you stay? You do know, don't you?"

"My job, I suppose. It's convenient from there, and it's cheap, and it pleases my parents. My aunt's all right really . . . Do I really have to explain to your mother why I live where I do?"

"It's not for my mother. I want to know. I wondered why you weren't with your parents, that's all."

"Are you cold?" I asked.

"No."

"Do you want to go home?"

"No, not unless you do. Don't you feel well, Neil?"

"I feel all right," and to let her know that I was still me, I held her to me, though that moment I was without desire.

"Neil?"

"What?"

"What about the library?"

"Who wants to know that?"

"My father," she laughed.

"And you?"

She did not answer a moment. "And me," she said finally.

"Well, what about it? Do I like it? It's okay. I sold shoes once and like the library better. After the Army they tried me for a couple months at Uncle Aaron's real estate company—Doris' father—and I like the library better than that . . ."

"How did you get a job *there*?"

"I worked there for a little while when I was in college, then when I quit Uncle Aaron's, oh, I don't know . . ."

"What did you take in college?"

"At Newark Colleges of Rutgers University I majored in philosophy. I am twenty-three years old. I—"

"Why do you sound nasty again?"

"Do I?"

"Yes."

I didn't say I was sorry.

"Are you planning on making a career of the library?"

"Bren, I'm not planning anything. I haven't planned a thing in three years. At least for the year I've been out of the Army. In the Army I used to plan to go away weekends. I'm—I'm not a planner." After all the truth I'd suddenly given her, I shouldn't have ruined it for myself with that final lie. I added, "I'm a liver."

"I'm a pancreas," she said.

"I'm a—"

And she kissed the absurd game away; she wanted to be serious.

"Do you love me, Neil?"

I did not answer.

"I'll sleep with you whether you do or not, so tell me the truth."

"That was pretty crude."

"Don't be prissy," she said.

"No, I mean a crude thing to say about me."

"I don't understand," she said, and she didn't, and that she didn't pained me; I allowed myself the minor subterfuge, however, of forgiving Brenda her obtuseness. "Do you?" she said.

"No."

"I want you to."

"What about the library?"

"What about it?" she said.

Was it obtuseness again? I thought not—and it wasn't, for Brenda said, "When you love me, there'll be nothing to worry about."

"Then of course I'll love you." I smiled.

"I know you will," she said. "Why don't you go in the water, and I'll wait for you and close my eyes, and when you come back you'll surprise me with the wet. Go ahead."

"You like games, don't you?"

"Go ahead. I'll close my eyes."

I walked down to the edge of the pool and dove in. The water felt colder than it had earlier, and when I broke through and was headed blindly down I felt a touch of panic. At the top again, I started to swim the length of the pool and then turned at the end and started back, but suddenly I was sure that when I left the water Brenda would be gone. I'd be alone in this damn place. I started for the side and pulled myself up and ran to the chairs and Brenda was there and I kissed her.

"God," she shivered, "you didn't stay long."

"I know."

"My turn," she said, and then she was up and a second later I heard a little crack of water and then nothing. Nothing for quite a while.

"Bren," I called softly, "are you all right?" but no one answered.

I found her glasses on the chair beside me and held them in my hands. "Brenda?"

Nothing.

"Brenda?"

"No fair calling," she said and gave me her drenched self. "Your turn," she said.

This time I stayed below the water for a long while and when I surfaced again my lungs were ready to pop. I threw my head back for air and above me saw the sky, low like a hand pushing down, and I began to swim as though to move out from under its pressure. I wanted to get back to Brenda, for I worried once again—and there was no evidence, was there?—that if I stayed away too long she would not be there when I returned. I wished that I had carried her glasses away with me, so she would have to wait for me to lead her back home. I was having crazy thoughts, I knew, and yet they did not seem uncalled for in the darkness and strangeness of that place. Oh how I wanted to call out to her from the pool, but I knew she would not answer and I forced myself to swim the length a third time, and then a fourth, but midway through the fifth I felt a weird fright again, had momentary thoughts of my own extinction, and that time when I came back I held her tighter than either of us expected.

"Let go, let go," she laughed, "my turn—"

"But Brenda—"

But Brenda was gone and this time it seemed as though she'd never come back. I settled back and waited for the sun to dawn over the ninth hole, prayed it would if only for the comfort of its light, and when Brenda finally returned to me I would not let her go, and her cold wetness crept into me somehow and made me shiver. "That's it, Brenda. Please, no more games," I said and then when I spoke again I held her so tightly I almost dug my body into hers, "I love you," I said, "I do."

So the summer went on. I saw Brenda every evening: we went swimming, we went for walks, we went for rides, up through the mountains so far and so long that by the time we started back the fog had begun to emerge from the trees and push out into the road, and I would tighten my hands on the wheel and Brenda would put on her glasses and watch the white line for me. And we would eat—a few nights after my discovery of the fruit refrigerator Brenda led me to it herself. We would fill huge soup bowls with cherries, and in serving dishes for roast beef we would heap slices of watermelon. Then we would go up and out the back doorway of the basement and onto the back lawn and sit under the sporting-goods tree, the light from the TV room the only brightness we had out there. All we would hear for a while were just the two of us spitting pits. "I wish they would take root overnight and in the morning there'd just be watermelons and cherries."

"If they took root in this yard, sweetie, they'd grow refrigerators and Westinghouse Preferred. I'm not being nasty," I'd add quickly, and Brenda would laugh, and say she felt like a greengage plum, and I would disappear down into the basement and the cherry bowl would now be a greengage plum bowl, and then a nectarine bowl, and then a peach bowl, until, I have to admit it, I cracked my frail bowel, and would have to spend the following night, sadly, on the wagon. And then too we went out for corned beef sandwiches, pizza, beer and shrimp, ice cream sodas, and hamburgers. We went to the Lions Club Fair one night and Brenda won a Lions Club ashtray by shooting three baskets in a row. And when Ron came home from Milwaukee we went from time to time to see him play basketball in the semi-pro summer league, and it was those evenings that I felt a stranger with Brenda, for she knew all the players' names, and though for the most part they were gawky-limbed and dull, there was one named Luther

Ferrari who was neither, and whom Brenda had dated for a whole year in high school. He was Ron's closest friend and I remembered his name from the Newark *News:* he was one of the great Ferrari brothers, All State all of them in at least two sports. It was Ferrari who called Brenda Buck, a nickname which apparently went back to her ribbon-winning days. Like Ron, Ferrari was exceedingly polite, as though it was some affliction of those over six feet three; he was gentlemanly towards me and gentle towards Brenda, and after a while I balked when the suggestion was made that we go to see Ron play. And then one night we discovered that at eleven o'clock the cashier of the Hilltop Theatre went home and the manager disappeared into his office, and so that summer we saw the last quarter of at least fifteen movies, and then when we were driving home—driving Brenda home, that is —we would try to reconstruct the beginnings of the films. Our favorite last quarter of a movie was *Ma and Pa Kettle in the City,* our favorite fruit, greengage plums, and our favorite, our only, people, each other. Of course we ran into others from time to time, some of Brenda's friends, and occasionally, one or two of mine. One night in August we even went to a bar out on Route 6 with Laura Simpson Stolowitch and her fiancé, but it was a dreary evening. Brenda and I seemed untrained in talking to others, and so we danced a great deal, which we realized was one thing we'd never done before. Laura's boyfriend drank stingers pompously and Simp—Brenda wanted me to call her Stolo but I didn't—Simp drank a tepid combination of something like ginger ale and soda. Whenever we returned to the table, Simp would be talking about "the dance" and her fiancé about "the film," until finally Brenda asked him "Which film?" and then we danced till closing time. And when we went back to Brenda's we filled a bowl with cherries which we carried into the TV room and ate sloppily for a while; and later, on the sofa, we loved each other and when I moved from the darkened room to the bathroom I could always feel cherry pits against my bare soles. At home, undressing for the second time that night, I would find red marks on the undersides of my feet.

And how did her parents take all of this? Mrs. Patimkin continued to smile at me and Mr. Patimkin continued to think I ate like a bird. When invited to dinner I would, for his benefit, eat twice what I wanted, but the truth seemed to be that after he'd characterized my appetite that first time, he never really bothered to look again. I might have eaten ten times my normal amount, have finally killed myself with food, he would still have considered me not a man but a sparrow. No one seemed distressed by my presence, though Julie had cooled considerably; consequently, when Brenda suggested to her father that at the end of August I spend a week of my vacation at the Patimkin house, he pondered a moment, decided on the five iron, made his approach shot, and said yes. And when she passed on to her mother the decision of Patimkin Sink, there wasn't much Mrs. Patimkin could do. So, through Brenda's craftiness, I was invited.

On that Friday morning that was to be my last day of work, my Aunt Gladys saw me packing my bag and she asked where I was going. I told her. She did not answer and I thought I saw awe in those red-rimmed hysterical eyes—I had come a long way since that day she'd said to me on the phone, "Fancy-shmancy."

"How long you going, I should know how to shop I wouldn't buy too much. You'll leave me with a refrigerator full of milk it'll go bad it'll stink up the refrigerator—"

"A week," I said.

"A *week*?" she said. "They got room for a week?"

"Aunt Gladys, they don't live over the store."

"I lived over a store I wasn't ashamed. Thank God we always had a roof. We never went begging in the streets," she told me as I packed the Bermudas I'd just bought, "and your cousin Susan we'll put through college, Uncle Max should live and be well. We didn't send her away to camp for August, she doesn't have shoes when she wants them, sweaters she doesn't have a drawerful—"

"I didn't say anything, Aunt Gladys."

"You don't get enough to eat here? You leave over sometimes I show your Uncle Max your plate it's a shame. A child in Europe could make a four-course meal from what you leave over."

"Aunt Gladys." I went over to her. "I get everything I want here. I'm just taking a vacation. Don't I deserve a vacation?"

She held herself to me and I could feel her trembling. "I told your mother I would take care of her Neil she shouldn't worry. And now you go running—'

I put my arms around her and kissed her on the top of her head. "C'mon," I said, "you're being silly. I'm not running away. I'm just going away for a week, on a vacation."

"You'll leave their telephone number God forbid you should get sick."

"Okay."

"Millburn they live?"

"Short Hills. I'll leave the number."

"Since when do Jewish people live in Short Hills? They couldn't be real Jews believe me."

"They're real Jews," I said.

"I'll see it I'll believe it." She wiped her eyes with the corner of her apron, just as I was zipping up the sides of the suitcase. "Don't close the bag yet. I'll make a little package with some fruit in it, you'll take with you."

"Okay, Aunt Gladys," and on the way to work that morning I ate the orange and the two peaches that she'd put in a bag for me.

A few hours later Mr. Scapello informed me that when I returned from my vacation after Labor Day, I would be hoisted up onto Martha Winney's stool. He himself, he said, had made the same move some twelve years ago, and so it appeared that if I could manage to maintain my balance I might someday be Mr. Scapello. I would also get an eight-dollar increase in salary which was five dollars more than the increase Mr. Scapello had received years before. He shook my hand and then started back up the long flight of marble stairs, his behind barging against his suit jacket like a hoop. No sooner had he left my side than I smelled spearmint and looked up to see the old man with veiny nose and jowls.

"Hello, young man," he said pleasantly. "Is the book back?"

"What book?"

"The Gauguin. I was shopping and I thought I'd stop by to ask. I haven't gotten the card yet. It's two weeks already."

"No," I said, and as I spoke I saw that Mr. Scapello had stopped midway up the stairs and turned as though he'd forgotten to tell me something. "Look," I said to the old man, "it should be back any day." I said it with a finality that bordered on rudeness, and

I alarmed myself, for suddenly I saw what would happen: the old man making a fuss, Mr. Scapello gliding down the stairs, Mr. Scapello scampering up to the stacks, Scapello scandalized, Scapello profuse, Scapello presiding at the ascension of John McKee to Miss Winney's stool. I turned to the old man, "Why don't you leave your phone number and I'll try to get a hold of it this afternoon—" but my attempt at concern and courtesy came too late, and the man growled some words about public servants, a letter to the Mayor, snotty kids, and left the library, thank God, only a second before Mr. Scapello returned to my desk to remind me that everyone was chipping in for a present for Miss Winney and that if I liked I should leave a half dollar on his desk during the day.

After lunch the colored kid came in. When he headed past the desk for the stairs, I called over to him. "Come here," I said. "Where are you going?"

"The heart section."

"What book are you reading?"

"That Mr. Go-again's book. Look, man, I ain't doing nothing wrong. I didn't do *no* writing in *any*thing. You could search me—"

"I know you didn't. Listen, if you like that book so much why don't you please take it home? Do you have a library card?"

"No sir, I didn't take *nothing.*"

"No, a library card is what we give to you so you can take books home. Then you won't have to come down here every day. Do you go to school?"

"Yes, sir. Miller Street School. But this here's summertime. It's okay I'm not in school. I ain't *supposed* to be in school."

"I know. As long as you go to school you can *have* a library card. You could take the book home."

"What you keep telling me take that book home for? At home somebody dee-*stroy* it."

"You could hide it someplace, in a desk—"

"Man," he said, squinting at me, "why don't you want me to come round here?"

"I didn't say you shouldn't."

"I *likes* to come here. I likes them stairs."

"I like them too," I said. "But the trouble is that someday somebody's going to take that book out."

He smiled. "Don't you worry," he said to me. "Ain't nobody done that yet," and he tapped off to the stairs and Stack Three.

Did I perspire that day! It was the coolest of the summer, but when I left work in the evening my shirt was sticking to my back. In the car I opened my bag, and while the rush-hour traffic flowed down Washington Street, I huddled in the back and changed into a clean shirt so that when I reached Short Hills I'd look as though I was deserving of an interlude in the suburbs. But driving up Central Avenue I could not keep my mind on my vacation, or for that matter on my driving: to the distress of pedestrians and motorists, I ground gears, overshot cross-walks, hesitated at green and red lights alike. I kept thinking that while I was on vacation that jowly bastard would return to the library, that the colored kid's book would disappear, that my new job would be taken away from me, that, in fact my old job—but then why should I worry about all that: the library wasn't going to be *my* life.

5

"Ron's getting married!" Julie screamed at me when I came through the door. "Ron's getting married!"

"Now?" I said.

"Labor Day! He's marrying Harriet, he's marrying Harriet." She began to sing it like a jump-rope song, nasal and rhythmic. "I'm going to be a sister-in-law!"

"Hi," Brenda said, "I'm going to be a sister-in-law."

"So I hear. When did it happen?"

"This afternoon he told us. They spoke long distance for forty minutes last night. She's flying here next week, and there's going to be a *huge* wedding. My parents are flittering all over the place. They've got to arrange everything in about a day or two. And my father's taking Ron in the business—but he's going to have to start at two hundred a week and then work himself up. That'll take till October."

"I thought he was going to be a gym teacher."

"He was. But now he has responsibilities . . ."

And at dinner Ron expanded on the subject of responsibilities and the future.

"We're going to have a boy," he said, to his mother's delight, "and when he's about six months old I'm going to sit him down with a basketball in front of him, and a football, and a baseball, and then whichever one he reaches for, that's the one we're going to concentrate on."

"Suppose he doesn't reach for any of them," Brenda said.

"Don't be funny, young lady," Mrs. Patimkin said.

"I'm going to be an aunt," Julie sang, and she stuck her tongue out at Brenda.

"When is Harriet coming?" Mr. Patimkin breathed through a mouthful of potatoes.

"A week from yesterday."

"Can she sleep in my room?" Julie cried. "*Can* she?"

"No, the guest room—" Mrs. Patimkin began, but then she remembered me—with a crushing side glance from those purple eyes, and said, "Of course."

Well, I did eat like a bird. After dinner my bag was carried—by me—up to the guest room which was across from Ron's room and right down the hall from Brenda. Brenda came along to show me the way.

"Let me see your bed, Bren."

"Later," she said.

"Can we? Up here?"

"I think so," she said. "Ron sleeps like a log."

"Can I stay the night?"

"I don't know."

"I could get up early and come back in here. We'll set the alarm."

"It'll wake everybody up."

"I'll remember to get up. I can do it."

"I better not stay up here with you too long," she said. "My mother'll have a fit. I think she's nervous about your being here."

"So am I. I hardly know them. Do you think I should really stay a whole week?"

"A whole week? Once Harriet gets here it'll be so chaotic you can probably stay two months."

"You think so?"

"Yes."

"Do you want me to?"

"Yes," she said, and went down the stairs so as to ease her mother's conscience.

I unpacked my bag and dropped my clothes into a drawer that was empty except for a packet of dress shields and a high school yearbook. In the middle of my unpacking, Ron came clunking up the stairs.

"Hi," he called into my room.

"Congratulations," I called back. I should have realized that any word of ceremony would provoke a handshake from Ron; he interrupted whatever it was he was about to do in his room, and came into mine.

"Thanks." He pumped me. "Thanks."

Then he sat down on my bed and watched me as I finished unpacking. I have one shirt with a Brooks Brothers label and I let it linger on the bed a while; the Arrows I heaped in the drawer. Ron sat there rubbing his forearm and grinning. After a while I was thoroughly unsettled by the silence.

"Well," I said, "that's something."

He agreed, to *what* I don't know.

"How does it feel?" I asked, after another longer silence.

"Better. Ferrari smacked it under the boards."

"Oh. Good," I said. "How does getting married feel?"

"Ah, okay, I guess."

I leaned against the bureau and counted stitches in the carpet.

Ron finally risked a journey into language. "Do you know anything about music?" he asked.

"Something, yes."

"You can listen to my phonograph if you want."

"Thanks, Ron. I didn't know you were interested in music."

"Sure. I got all the Andre Kostelanetz records ever made. You like Mantovani? I got all of him too. I like semiclassical a lot. You can hear my Columbus record if you want . . ." he dwindled off. Finally he shook my hand and left.

Downstairs I could hear Julie singing. "I'm going to be an a-a-aunt," and Mrs. Patimkin saying to her, "No, honey, you're going to be a sister-in-law. Sing that, sweetheart," but Julie continued to sing, "I'm going to be an a-a-aunt," and then I heard Brenda's voice joining hers, singing, "We're going to be an a-a-aunt," and then Julie joined that, and finally Mrs. Patimkin called to Mr. Patimkin, "Will you make her stop encouraging her . . ." and soon the duet ended.

And then I heard Mrs. Patimkin again. I couldn't make out the words but Brenda answered her. Their voices grew louder; finally I could hear perfectly. "I need a houseful of company at a time like this?" It was Mrs. Patimkin. "I asked you, Mother." "You asked your father. I'm the one you should have asked first. He doesn't know how much extra work this is for me . . ." "My God, Mother, you'd think we didn't have Carlota and Jenny." "Carlota and Jenny can't do everything. This is not the Salvation Army!" "What the hell does that mean?" "Watch your tongue, young lady. That may be very well for your college friends." "Oh, *stop* it, Mother!" "Don't raise your voice to me. When's the last time you lifted a finger to help around here?" "I'm not a slave . . . I'm a daughter." "You ought to learn what a day's work means." "Why?" Brenda said. "*Why?*" "Because you're lazy," Mrs. Patimkin answered, "and you think the world owes you a living." "Whoever said *that?*" "You ought to earn some money and buy your own clothes." "Why? Good God, Mother, Daddy could live off the stocks alone, for God's sake. What are you complaining about?" "When's the last time you washed the dishes!" "Jesus Christ!" Brenda flared, "Carlota washes the dishes!" "Don't Jesus Christ me!" "Oh, Mother!" and Brenda was crying. "Why the hell are you like this!" "That's it," Mrs. Patimkin said "cry in front of your company . . ." "My *company* . . ." Brenda wept, "why don't you go yell at him too . . . why is everyone so nasty to me . . ."

From across the hall I heard Andre Kostelanetz let several thousand singing violins loose on "Night and Day." Ron's door was open and I saw he was stretched out, colossal, on his bed; he was singing along with the record. The words belonged to "Night and Day," but I didn't recognize Ron's tune. In a minute he picked up the phone and asked the operator for a Milwaukee number. While she connected him, he rolled over and turned up the volume on the record player, so that it would carry the nine hundred miles west.

I heard Julie downstairs. "Ha ha, Brenda's crying, ha ha, Brenda's crying."

And then Brenda was running up the stairs. "Your day'll come, you little bastard!" she called.

"*Brenda!*" Mrs. Patimkin called.

"*Mommy!*" Julie cried. "Brenda cursed at me!"

"What's going *on* here!" Mr. Patimkin shouted.

"You call *me*, Mrs. P?" Carlota shouted.

And Ron, in the other room, said, "Hello, Har, I told them . . ."

I sat down on my Brooks Brothers shirt and pronounced my own name out loud.

"Goddam her!" Brenda said to me as she paced up and down my room.

"Bren, do you think I should go—"

"Shhh . . ." She went to the door of my room and listened. "They're going visiting, thank God."

"Brenda—"

"Shhh . . . They've gone."

"Julie too?"

"Yes," she said. "Is Ron in his room? His door is closed."

"He went out."

"You can't hear anybody move around here. They all creep around in *sneakers*. Oh Neil."

"Bren, I asked you, maybe I should just stay through tomorrow and then go."

"Oh, it isn't you she's angry about."

"I'm not helping any."

"It's Ron, really. That he's getting married just has her flipped. And me. Now with that goody-good Harriet around she'll just forget I ever exist."

"Isn't that okay with you?"

She walked off to the window and looked outside. It was dark and cool; the trees rustled and flapped as though they were sheets that had been hung out to dry. Everything outside hinted at September, and for the first time I realized how close we were to Brenda's departure for school.

"Is it, Bren?" but she was not listening to me.

She walked across the room to a door at the far end of the room. She opened it.

"I thought that was a closet," I said.

"Come here."

She held the door back and we leaned into the darkness and could hear the strange wind hissing in the eaves of the house.

"What's in here?" I said.

"Money."

Brenda went into the room. When the puny sixty-watt bulb was twisted on, I saw that the place was full of old furniture—two wing chairs with hair-oil lines at the back, a sofa with a paunch in its middle, a bridge table, two bridge chairs with their stuffing showing, a mirror whose backing had peeled off, shadeless lamps, lampless shades, a coffee table with a cracked glass top, and a pile of rolled up shades.

"What is this?" I said.

"A storeroom. Our old furniture."

"How old?"

"From Newark," she said. "Come here." She was on her hands and knees in front of the sofa and was holding up its paunch to peek beneath.

"Brenda, what the hell are we doing here? You're getting filthy."

"It's not here."

"*What?*"

"The money. I told you."

I sat down on a wing chair, raising some dust. It had begun to rain outside, and we could smell the fall dampness coming through the vent that was outlined at the far end of the storeroom. Brenda got up from the floor and sat down on the sofa. Her knees and Bermudas were dirty and when she pushed her hair back she dirtied her forehead. There among the disarrangement and dirt I had the strange experience of seeing us, *both* of us, placed among disarrangement and dirt: we looked like a young couple who had just moved into a new apartment; we had suddenly taken stock of our furniture, finances, and future, and all we could feel any pleasure about was the clean smell of outside, which reminded us we were alive, but which, in a pinch, would not feed us.

"What money?" I said again.

"The hundred-dollar bills. From when I was a little girl . . ." and she breathed deeply. "When I was little and we'd just moved from Newark, my father took me up here one day. He took me into this room and told me that if anything should ever happen to him, he wanted me to know where there was some money that I should have. He said it wasn't for anybody else but me, and that I should never tell anyone about it, not even Ron. Or my mother."

"How much was it?"

"Three hundred-dollar bills. I'd never seen them before. I was nine, around Julie's age. I don't think we'd been living here a month. I remember I used to come up here about once a week, when no one was home but Carlota, and crawl under the sofa and make sure it was still here. And it always was. He never mentioned it once again. Never."

"Where is it? Maybe someone stole it."

"I don't know, Neil. I suppose he took it back."

"When it was gone," I said, "my God, didn't you tell him? Maybe Carlota—"

"I never knew it was gone, until just now. I guess I stopped looking at one time or another . . . And then I forgot about it. Or just didn't think about it. I mean I always had enough, I didn't need this. I guess one day *he* figured I wouldn't need it."

Brenda paced up to the narrow, dust-covered window and drew her initials on it.

"Why did you want it now?" I said.

"I don't know . . ." she said and went over and twisted the bulb off.

I didn't move from the chair and Brenda, in her tight shorts and shirt, seemed naked standing there a few feet away. Then I saw her shoulders shaking. "I wanted to find it and tear it up in little pieces and put the goddam pieces in her purse! If it was there, I swear it, I would have done it."

"I wouldn't have let you, Bren."

"Wouldn't you have?"

"No."

"Make love to me, Neil. Right now."

"Where?"

"Do it! *Here*. On this cruddy cruddy cruddy sofa."

And I obeyed her.

The next morning Brenda made breakfast for the two of us. Ron had gone off to his first day of work—I'd heard him singing in the shower only an hour after I'd returned to my own room; in fact, I had still been awake when the Chrysler had pulled out of the garage, carrying boss and son down to the Patimkin works in Newark. Mrs. Patimkin wasn't home either; she had taken her car and had gone off to the Temple to talk to Rabbi Kranitz about the wedding. Julie was on the back lawn playing at helping Carlota hang the clothes.

"You know what I want to do this morning?" Brenda said. We were eating a grapefruit, sharing it rather sloppily, for Brenda couldn't find a paring knife, and so we'd decided to peel it down like an orange and eat the segments separately.

"What?" I said.

"Run," she said. "Do you ever run?"

"You mean on a track? God, yes. In high school we had to run a mile every month. So we wouldn't be Momma's boys. I think the bigger your lungs get the more you're supposed to hate your mother."

"I want to run," she said, "and I want you to run. Okay?"

"Oh, Brenda . . ."

But an hour later, after a breakfast that consisted of another grapefruit, which apparently is all a runner is supposed to eat in the morning, we had driven the Volkswagen over to the high school, behind which was a quarter-mile track. Some kids were playing with a dog out in the grassy center of the track, and at the far end, near the woods, a figure in white shorts with slits in the side, and no shirt, was twirling, twirling, and then flinging a shot put as far as he could. After it left his hand he did a little eagle-eyed tap dance while he watched it arch and bend and land in the distance.

"You know," Brenda said, "you look like me. Except bigger."

We were dressed similarly, sneakers, sweat socks, khaki Bermudas, and sweat shirts, but I had the feeling that Brenda was not talking about the accidents of our dress—if they were accidents. She meant, I was sure, that I was somehow beginning to look the way she wanted me to. Like herself.

"Let's see who's faster," she said, and then we started along the track. Within the first eighth of a mile the three little boys and their dog were following us. As we passed the corner where the shot putter was, he waved at us; Brenda called "Hi!" and I smiled, which, as you may or may not know, makes one engaged in serious running feel inordinately silly. At the quarter mile the kids dropped off and retired to the grass, the dog turned and started the other way, and I had a tiny knife in my side. Still I was abreast of Brenda, who as we started on the second lap, called "Hi!" once again to the lucky shot putter, who was reclining on the grass now, watching us, and rubbing his shot like a crystal ball. Ah, I thought, there's the sport.

"How about us throwing the shot put?" I panted.

"After," she said, and I saw beads of sweat clinging to the last strands of hair that shagged off her ear. When we approached the half mile Brenda suddenly swerved off the track onto the grass and tumbled down; her departure surprised me and I was still running.

"Hey, Bob Mathias," she called, "let's lie in the sun . . ."

But I acted as though I didn't hear her and though my heart pounded in my throat and my mouth was dry as a drought, I made my legs move, and swore I would not stop until I'd finished one more lap. As I passed the shot putter for the third time, I called "Hi!"

She was excited when I finally pulled up alongside of her. "You're good," she said. My hands were on my hips and I was looking at the ground and sucking air—rather, air was sucking me, I didn't have much to say about it.

"Uh-huh," I breathed.

"Let's do this every morning," she said. "We'll get up and have two grapefruit, and then you'll come out here and run. I'll time you. In two weeks you'll break four minutes, won't you, sweetie? I'll get Ron's stop watch." She was so excited—she'd slid over on the grass and was pushing my socks up against my wet ankles and calves. She bit my kneecap.

"Okay," I said.

"Then we'll go back and have a real breakfast."

"Okay."

"You drive back," she said, and suddenly she was up and running ahead of me, and then we were headed back in the car.

And the next morning, my mouth still edgy from the grapefruit segments, we were at the track. We had Ron's stop watch and a towel for me, for when I was finished.

"My legs are a little sore," I said.

"Do some exercises," Brenda said. "I'll do them with you." She heaped the towel on the grass and together we did deep knee bends, and sit-ups, and push-ups, and some high-knee raising in place. I felt overwhelmingly happy.

"I'm just going to run a half today, Bren. We'll see what I do . . ." and I heard Brenda click the watch, and then when I was on the far side of the track, the clouds trailing above me like my own white, fleecy tail, I saw that Brenda was on the ground, hugging her knees, and alternately checking the watch and looking out at me. We were the only ones there, and it all reminded me of one of those scenes in race-horse movies, where an old trainer like Walter Brennan and a young handsome man clock the beautiful girl's horse in the early Kentucky morning, to see if it really is the fastest two-year-old alive. There were differences all right—one being simply that at the quarter mile Brenda shouted out to me, "A minute and fourteen seconds," but it was pleasant and exciting and clean and when I was finished Brenda was standing up and waiting for me. Instead of a tape to break I had Brenda's sweet flesh to meet, and I did, and it was the first time she said that she loved me.

We ran—I ran—every morning, and by the end of the week I was running a 7:02 mile, and always at the end there was the little click of the watch and Brenda's arms.

At night, I would read in my pajamas, while Brenda, in her room, read, and we would wait for Ron to go to sleep. Some nights we had to wait longer than others, and I would hear the leaves swishing outside, for it had grown cooler at the end of August, and the air-conditioning was turned off at night and we were all allowed to open our windows. Finally Ron would be ready for bed. He would stomp around his room and then he would come to the door in his shorts and T-shirt and go into the bathroom where he would urinate loudly and brush his teeth.

After he brushed his teeth I would go in to brush mine. We would pass in the hall and I would give him a hearty and sincere "Good-night." Once in the bathroom, I would spend a moment admiring my tan in the mirror; behind me I could see Ron's jock straps hanging out to dry on the Hot and Cold knobs of the shower. Nobody ever questioned their tastefulness as adornment, and after a few nights I didn't even notice them.

While Ron brushed his teeth and I waited in my bed for my turn, I could hear the record player going in his room. Generally, after coming in from basketball, he would call Harriet—who was now only a few days away from us—and then would lock himself up with *Sports Illustrated* and Mantovani; however, when he emerged from his room for his evening toilet, it was not a Mantovani record I would hear playing, but something else, apparently what he'd once referred to as his Columbus record. I *imagined* that was what I heard, for I could not tell much from the last moments of sound. All I heard were bells moaning evenly and soft patriotic music behind them, and riding over it all, a deep kind of Edward R. Murrow gloomy voice: "*And so goodbye, Columbus*," the voice intoned, "*. . . goodbye, Columbus . . . goodbye . . .*" Then there would be silence and Ron would be back in his room; the light would switch off and in only a few minutes I would hear him rumbling down into that exhilarating, restorative, vitamin-packed sleep that I imagined athletes to enjoy.

One morning near sneaking-away time I had a dream and when I awakened from it, there was just enough dawn coming into the room for me to see the color of Brenda's hair. I touched her in her sleep, for the dream had unsettled me: it had taken place on a ship, an old sailing ship like those you see in pirate movies. With me on the ship was the little colored kid from the library—I was the captain and he my mate, and we were the only crew members. For a while it was a pleasant dream; we were anchored in the harbor of an island in the Pacific and it was very sunny. Up on the beach there were beautiful bare-skinned Negresses, and none of them moved; but suddenly *we* were moving, our ship, out of the harbor, and the Negresses moved slowly down to the shore and began to throw leis at us and say "Goodbye, Columbus . . . goodbye, Columbus . . . goodbye . . ." and though we did not want to go, the little boy and I, the boat was moving and there was nothing we could do about it, and he shouted at me that it was my fault and I shouted it was his for not having a library card, but we were wasting our breath, for we were further and further from the island, and soon the natives were nothing at all. Space was all out of proportion in the dream, and things were sized and squared in no way I'd ever seen before, and I think it was that more than anything else that steered me into consciousness. I did not want to leave Brenda's side that morning, and for a while I played with the little point at the nape of her neck, where she'd had her hair cut. I stayed longer than I should have, and when finally I returned to my room I almost ran into Ron who was preparing for his day at Patimkin Kitchen and Bathroom Sinks.

6

That morning was supposed to have been my last at the Patimkin house; however, when I began to throw my things into my bag late in the day, Brenda told me I could unpack—somehow she'd managed to inveigle another week out of her parents, and I would be able to stay right through till Labor Day, when Ron would be married; then, the following morning Brenda would be off to school and I would go back to work. So we would be with each other until the summer's last moment.

This should have made me overjoyed, but as Brenda trotted back down the stairs to accompany her family to the airport—where they were to pick up Harriet—I was not joyful but disturbed as I had been more and more with the thought that when Brenda went back to Radcliffe, that would be the end for me. I was convinced that even Miss Winney's stool was not high enough for me to see clear up to Boston. Nevertheless, I tossed my clothing back into the drawer and was able, finally, to tell myself that there'd been no hints of ending our affair from Brenda, and any suspicions I had, any uneasiness, was spawned in my own uncertain heart. Then I went into Ron's room to call my aunt.

"Hello?" she said.

"Aunt Gladys," I said, "how are you?"

"You're sick."

"No, I'm having a fine time. I wanted to call you, I'm going to stay another week."

"Why?"

"I told you. I'm having a good time. Mrs. Patimkin asked me to stay until Labor Day."

"You've got clean underwear?"

"I'm washing it at night. I'm okay, Aunt Gladys."

"By hand you can't get it clean."

"It's clean enough. Look, Aunt Gladys, I'm having a wonderful time."

"*Shmutz* he lives in and I shouldn't worry."

"How's Uncle Max?" I asked.

"What should he be? Uncle Max is Uncle Max. You, I don't like the way your voice sounds."

"Why? Do I sound like I've got on dirty underwear?"

"Smart guy. Someday you'll learn."

"What?"

"What do you mean *what*? You'll find out. You'll stay there too long you'll be too good for us."

"Never, sweetheart," I said.

"I'll see it I'll believe it."

"Is it cool in Newark, Aunt Gladys?"

"It's snowing," she said.

"Hasn't it been cool all week?"

"You sit around all day it's cool. For me it's not February, believe me."

"Okay, Aunt Gladys. Say hello to everybody."

"You got a letter from your mother."

"Good. I'll read it when I get home."

"You couldn't take a ride down you'll read it?"

"It'll wait. I'll drop them a note. Be a good girl," I said.

"What about your socks?"

"I go barefoot. Goodbye, honey." And I hung up.

Down in the kitchen Carlota was getting dinner ready. I was always amazed at how Carlota's work never seemed to get in the way of her life. She made household chores seem like illustrative gestures of whatever it was she was singing, even, if as now, it was "I Get a Kick out of You." She moved from the oven to the automatic dishwasher—she pushed buttons, turned dials, peeked in the glass-doored oven, and from time to time picked a big black grape out of a bunch that lay on the sink. She chewed and chewed, humming all the time, and then, with a deliberated casualness, shot the skin and the pit directly into the garbage disposal unit. I said hello to her as I went out the back door, and though she did not return the greeting, I felt a kinship with one who, like me, had been partially wooed and won on Patimkin fruit.

Out on the lawn I shot baskets for a while; then I picked up an iron and drove a cotton golf ball limply up into the sunlight; then I kicked a soccer ball towards the oak tree; then I tried shooting foul shots again. Nothing diverted me—I felt open-stomached, as though I hadn't eaten for months, and though I went back inside and came out with my own handful of grapes, the feeling continued, and I knew it had nothing to do with my caloric intake; it was only a rumor of the hollowness that would come when Brenda was away. The fact of her departure had, of course, been on my mind for a while, but overnight it had taken on a darker hue. Curiously, the darkness seemed to have something to do with Harriet, Ron's intended, and I thought for a time that it was simply the reality of Harriet's arrival that had dramatized the passing of time: we had been talking about it and now suddenly it was here—just as Brenda's departure would be here before we knew it.

But it was more than that: the union of Harriet and Ron reminded me that separation need not be a permanent state. People could marry each other, even if they were young! And yet Brenda and I had never mentioned marriage, except perhaps for that night at the pool when she'd said, "When you love me, everything will be all right." Well, I loved her, and she me, and things didn't seem all right at all. Or was I inventing troubles again? I supposed I should really have thought my lot improved considerably; yet, there on the lawn, the August sky seemed too beautiful and temporary to bear, and I wanted Brenda to marry me. Marriage, though, was not what I proposed to her when she drove the car up the driveway, alone, some fifteen minutes later. That proposal would have taken a kind of courage that I did not think I had. I did not feel myself prepared for any answer but "Hallelujah!" Any other kind of yes wouldn't have satisfied me, and any kind of no, even one masked behind the words, "Let's wait, sweetheart," would have been my end. So I imagine that's why I proposed the surrogate, which turned out finally to be far more daring than I knew it to be at the time.

"Harriet's plane is late, so I drove home," Brenda called.

"Where's everyone else?"

"They're going to wait for her and have dinner at the airport. I have to tell Carlota," and she went inside.

In a few minutes she appeared on the porch. She wore a yellow dress that cut a wide-bottomed U across her shoulders and neck, and showed where the tanned flesh began above her breasts. On the lawn she stepped out of her heels and walked barefoot over to where I was sitting under the oak tree.

"Women who wear high heels all the time get tipped ovaries," she said.

"Who told you that?"

"I don't remember. I like to think everything's ship-shape in there."

"Brenda, I want to ask you something . . ."

She yanked the blanket with the big O on it over to us and sat down.

"What?" she said.

"I know this is out of the blue, though really it's not . . . I want you to buy a diaphragm. To go to a doctor and get one."

She smiled. "Don't worry, sweetie, we're careful. Everything is okay."

"But that's the safest."

"We're safe. It'd be a waste."

"Why take chances?"

"But we *aren't*. How many things do you need."

"Honey, it isn't bulk I'm interested in. It's not even safety," I added.

"You just want me to own one, is that it? Like a walking stick, or a pith helmet—"

"Brenda, I want you to own one for . . . for the sake of pleasure."

"Pleasure? Whose? The doctor's?"

"Mine," I said.

She did not answer me, but rubbed her fingers along the ridge of her collarbone to wipe away the tiny globes of perspiration that had suddenly formed there.

"No, Neil, it's silly."

"Why?"

"Why? It just is."

"You know why it's silly, Brenda—because *I* asked you to do it?"

"That's sillier."

"If you asked *me* to buy a diaphragm we'd have to go straight to the Yellow Pages and find a gynecologist open on Saturday afternoon."

"I would never ask you to do that, baby."

"It's the truth," I said, though I was smiling. "It's the truth."

"It's not," she said, and got up and walked over to the basketball court, where she walked on the white lines that Mr. Patimkin had laid the day before.

"Come back here," I said.

"Neil, it's silly and I don't want to talk about it."

"Why are you being so selfish?"

"Selfish? You're the one who's being selfish. It's your pleasure . . ."

"That's right. My pleasure. Why not!"

"Don't raise your voice. Carlota."

"Then get the hell over here," I said.

She walked over to me, leaving white footprints on the grass. "I didn't think you were such a creature of the flesh," she said.

"Didn't you?" I said. "I'll tell you something that you ought to know. It's not even the pleasures of the flesh I'm talking about."

"Then frankly, I don't know *what* you're talking about. Why you're even bothering. Isn't what we use sufficient?"

"I'm bothering just because I want you to go to a doctor and get a diaphragm. That's all. No explanation. Just do it. Do it because I asked you to."

"You're not being reasonable—"

"Goddamit, Brenda!"

"Goddamit yourself!" she said and went up into the house.

I closed my eyes and leaned back and in fifteen minutes, or maybe less, I heard somebody stroking at the cotton golf ball.

She had changed into shorts and a blouse and was still barefoot.

We didn't speak with each other, but I watched her bring the club back of her ear, and then swing through, her chin tilted up with the line of flight a regular golf ball would have taken.

"That's five hundred yards," I said.

She didn't answer but walked after the cotton ball and then readied for another swing.

"Brenda. Please come here."

She walked over, dragging the club over the grass.

"What?"

"I don't want to argue with you."

"Nor I with you," she said. "It was the first time."

"Was it such an awful thing for me to ask?"

She nodded.

"Bren, I know it was probably a surprise. It was for me. But we're not children."

"Neil, I just don't want to. It's not because you asked me to, either. I don't know where you get that from. That's not it."

"Then why is it?"

"Oh everything. I just don't feel *old* enough for all that equipment."

"What does age have to do with it?"

"I don't mean age. I just mean—well, *me*. I mean it's so conscious a thing to do."

"Of course it's conscious. That's exactly it. Don't you see? It would change us."

"It would change me."

"Us. Together."

"Neil, how do you think I'd feel lying to some doctor."

"You can go to Margaret Sanger, in New York. They don't ask any questions."

"You've done this before?"

"No," I said. "I just know. I read Mary McCarthy."

"That's exactly right. That's just what I'd feel like, somebody out of *her*."

"Don't be dramatic," I said.

"You're the one who's being dramatic. You think there would be something affairish about it, then. Last summer I went with this whore who I sent out to buy—"

"Oh, Brenda, you're a selfish egotistical bitch! You're the one who's thinking about 'last summer,' about an end for us. In fact, that's the whole thing, isn't it—"

"That's right, I'm a bitch. I want this to end. That's why I ask you to stay another week, that's why I let you sleep with me in my own house. What's the *matter* with you! Why don't you and my mother take turns—one day she can plague me, the next you—"

"Stop it!"

"Go to hell, all of you!" Brenda said, and now she was crying and I knew when she ran off I would not see her, as I didn't, for the rest of the afternoon.

Harriet Ehrlich impressed me as a young lady singularly unconscious of a motive in others or herself. All was surfaces, and she seemed a perfect match for Ron, and too for the Patimkins. Mrs. Patimkin, in fact, did just as Brenda prophesied: Harriet appeared, and Brenda's mother lifted one wing and pulled the girl in towards the warm underpart of her body, where Brenda herself would have liked to nestle. Harriet was built like Brenda, although a little chestier, and she nodded her head insistently whenever anyone spoke. Sometimes she would even say the last few words of your sentence with you, though that was infrequent; for the most part she nodded and kept her hands folded. All evening, as the Patimkins planned where the newlyweds should live, what furniture they should buy, how soon they should have a baby—all through this I kept thinking that Harriet was wearing white gloves, but she wasn't.

Brenda and I did not exchange a word or a glance; we sat, listening, Brenda somewhat more impatient than me. Near the end Harriet began calling Mrs. Patimkin "Mother," and once, "Mother Patimkin," and that was when Brenda went to sleep. I stayed behind, mesmerized almost by the dissection, analysis, reconsideration, and finally, the embracing of the trivial. At last Mr. and Mrs. Patimkin tumbled off to bed, and Julie, who had fallen asleep on her chair, was carried into her room by Ron. That left us two non-Patimkins together.

"Ron tells me you have a very interesting job."

"I work in the library."

"I've always liked reading."

"That'll be nice, married to Ron."

"Ron likes music."

"Yes," I said. What had I *said?*

"You must get first crack at the best-sellers," she said.

"Sometimes." I said.

"Well," she said, flapping her hands on her knees, "I'm sure we'll all have a good time together. Ron and I hope you and Brenda will double with us soon."

"Not tonight." I smiled. "Soon. Will you excuse me?"

"Good night. I like Brenda very much."

"Thank you," I said as I started up the stairs.

I knocked gently on Brenda's door.

"I'm sleeping."

"Can I come in?" I asked.

Her door opened an inch and she said, "Ron will be up soon."

"We'll leave the door open. I only want to talk."

She let me in and I sat in the chair that faced the bed.

"How do you like your sister-in-law?"

"I've met her before."

"Brenda, you don't have to sound so damn terse."

She didn't answer and I just sat there yanking the string on the shade up and down.

"Are you still angry?" I asked at last.

"Yes."

"Don't be," I said. "You can forget about my suggestion. It's not worth it if this is what's going to happen."

"What did you expect to happen?"

"Nothing. I didn't think it would be so horrendous."

"That's because you can't understand my side."

"Perhaps."

"No perhaps about it."

"*Okay*," I said. "I just wish you'd realize what it is you're getting angry about. It's not my suggestion, Brenda."

"No? What is it?"

"It's me."

"Oh don't start that again, will you? I can't win, no matter what I say."

"Yes, you can," I said. "You have."

I walked out of her room, closing the door behind me for the night.

When I got downstairs the following morning there was a great deal of activity. In the living room I heard Mrs. Patimkin reading a list to Harriet while Julie ran in and out of rooms in search of a skate key. Carlota was vacuuming the carpet; every appliance in the kitchen was bubbling, twisting, and shaking. Brenda greeted me with a perfectly pleasant smile and in the dining room, where I walked to look out at the back lawn and the weather, she kissed me on the shoulder.

"Hello," she said.

"Hello."

"I have to go with Harriet this morning," Brenda told me. "So we can't run. Unless you want to go alone."

"No. I'll read or something. Where are you going?"

"We're going to New York. Shopping. She's going to buy a wedding dress. For after the wedding. To go away in."

"What are *you* going to buy?"

"A dress to be maid of honor in. If I go with Harriet then I can go to Bergdorf's without all that Ohrbach's business with my mother."

"Get me something, will you?" I said.

"Oh, Neil, are you going to bring that up again!"

"I was only *fooling*. I wasn't even thinking about that."

"Then why did you say it?"

"Oh Jesus!" I said, and went outside and drove my car down into Millburn Center where I had some eggs and coffee.

When I came back, Brenda was gone, and there were only Carlota, Mrs. Patimkin, and myself in the house. I tried to stay out of whichever rooms they were in, but finally Mrs. Patimkin and I wound up sitting opposite each other in the TV room. She was checking off names on a long sheet of paper she held; next to her, on the table, were two thin phone books which she consulted from time to time.

"No rest for the weary," she said to me.

I smiled hugely, embracing the proverb as though Mrs. Patimkin had just then coined it. "Yes. Of course," I said. "Would you like some help? Maybe I could help you check something."

"Oh, no," she said with a little head-shaking dismissal, "it's for Hadassah."

"Oh," I said.

I sat and watched her until she asked, "Is your mother in Hadassah?"

"I don't know if she is now. She was in Newark."

"Was she an active member?"

"I guess so, she was always planting trees in Israel for someone."

"Really?" Mrs. Patimkin said. "What's her name?"

"Esther Klugman. She's in Arizona now. Do they have Hadassah there?"

"Wherever there are Jewish women."

"Then I guess she is. She's with my father. They went there for their asthma. I'm staying with my aunt in Newark. She's not in Hadassah. My Aunt Sylvia is, though. Do you know her, Aaron Klugman and Sylvia? They belong to your club. They have a daughter, my cousin Doris—" I couldn't stop myself "—They live in Livingston. Maybe it isn't Hadassah my Aunt Sylvia belongs to. I think it's some TB organization. Or cancer. Muscular dystrophy, maybe. I know she's interested in *some* disease."

"That's very nice," Mrs. Patimkin said.

"Oh yes."

"They do very good work."

"I know."

Mrs. Patimkin, I thought, had begun to warm to me; she let the purple eyes stop peering and just look out at the world for a while without judging. "Are you interested in B'nai Brith?" she asked me. "Ron is joining, you know, as soon as he gets married."

"I think I'll wait till then," I said.

Petulantly, Mrs. Patimkin went back to her lists, and I realized it had been foolish of me to risk lightheartedness with her about Jewish affairs. "You're active in the Temple, aren't you?" I asked with all the interest I could muster.

"Yes," she said.

"What Temple do *you* belong to?" she asked in a moment.

"We used to belong to Hudson Street Synagogue. Since my parents left, I haven't had much contact."

I didn't know whether Mrs. Patimkin caught a false tone in my voice. Personally I thought I had managed my rueful confession pretty well, especially when I recalled the decade of paganism prior to my parents' departure. Regardless, Mrs. Patimkin asked immediately—and strategically it seemed—"We're all going to Temple Friday night. Why don't you come with us? I mean, are you orthodox or conservative?"

I considered. "Well, I haven't gone in a long time . . . I sort of switch . . ." I smiled. "I'm just Jewish," I said well-meaningly, but that too sent Mrs. Patimkin back to her Hadassah work. Desperately I tried to think of something that would convince her I wasn't an infidel. Finally I asked: "Do you know Martin Buber's work?"

"Buber . . . Buber," she said, looking at her Hadassah list. "Is he orthodox or conservative?" she asked.

". . . He's a philosopher."

"Is he *reformed*?" she asked, piqued either at my evasiveness or at the possibility that Buber attended Friday night services without a hat, and Mrs. Buber had only one set of dishes in her kitchen.

"Orthodox," I said faintly.

"That's very nice," she said.

"Yes."

"Isn't Hudson Street Synagogue orthodox?" she asked.

"I don't know."

"I thought you belonged."

"I was bar-mitzvahed there."

"And you don't know that it's orthodox?"

"Yes. I do. It is."

"Then *you* must be."

"Oh, yes, I am," I said. "What are you?" I popped, flushing.

"Orthodox. My husband is conservative," which meant, I took it, that he didn't care. "Brenda is nothing, as you probably know."

"Oh?" I said. "No, I didn't know that."

"She was the best Hebrew student I've ever seen," Mrs. Patimkin said, "but then, of course, she got too big for her britches."

Mrs. Patimkin looked at me, and I wondered whether courtesy demanded that I agree. "Oh, I don't know," I said at last, "I'd say

Brenda is conservative. Maybe a little reformed . . ."

The phone rang, rescuing me, and I spoke a silent orthodox prayer to the Lord.

"Hello," Mrs. Patimkin said. ". . . no . . . I can *not*, I have all the Hadassah calls to make . . ."

I acted as though I were listening to the birds outside, though the closed windows let no natural noises in.

"Have Ronald drive them up . . . But we can't wait, not if we want it on time . . ."

Mrs. Patimkin glanced up at me; then she put one hand over the mouthpiece. "Would you ride down to Newark for me?"

I stood. "Yes. Surely."

"Dear?" she said back into the phone, "Neil will come for it . . . No, *Neil*, Brenda's friend . . . Yes . . . Goodbye.

"Mr. Patimkin has some silver patterns I have to see. Would you drive down to his place and pick them up?"

"Of course."

"Do you know where the shop is?"

"Yes."

"Here," she said, handing a key ring to me, "take the Volkswagen."

"My car is right outside."

"Take these," she said.

Patimkin Kitchen and Bathroom Sinks was in the heart of the Negro section of Newark. Years ago, at the time of the great immigration, it had been the Jewish section, and still one could see the little fish stores, the kosher delicatessens, the Turkish baths, where my grandparents had shopped and bathed at the beginning of the century. Even the smells had lingered: whitefish, corned beef, sour tomatoes—but now, on top of these, was the grander greasier smell of auto wrecking shops, the sour stink of a brewery, the burning odor from a leather factory; and on the streets, instead of Yiddish, one heard the shouts of Negro children playing at Willie Mays with a broom handle and half a rubber ball. The neighborhood had changed: the old Jews like my grandparents had struggled and died, and their offspring had struggled and prospered, and moved further and further west, towards the edge of Newark, then out of it, and up the slope of the Orange Mountains, until they had reached the crest and started down the other side, pouring into Gentile territory as the Scotch-Irish had poured through the Cumberland Gap. Now, in fact, the Negroes were making the same migration, following the steps of the Jews, and those who remained in the Third Ward lived the most squalid of lives and dreamed in their fetid mattresses of the piny smell of Georgia nights.

I wondered, for an instant only, if I would see the colored kid from the library on the streets here. I didn't, of course, though I was sure he lived in one of the scabby, peeling buildings out of which dogs, children, and aproned women moved continually. On the top floors, windows were open, and the very old, who could no longer creak down the long stairs to the street, sat where they had been put, in the screenless windows, their elbows resting on fluffless pillows, and their heads tipping forward on their necks, watching the push of the young and the pregnant and the unemployed. Who would come after the Negroes? Who was left? No one, I thought, and someday these streets, where my grandmother drank hot tea from an old *jahrzeit* glass, would be empty and we would all of us have moved to the crest of the Orange Mountains, and wouldn't the dead stop kicking at the slats in their coffins then?

I pulled the Volkswagen up in front of a huge garage door that said across the front of it:

PATIMKIN KITCHEN AND BATHROOM SINKS
"Any Size—Any Shape"

Inside I could see a glass-enclosed office; it was in the center of an immense warehouse. Two trucks were being loaded in the rear, and Mr. Patimkin, when I saw him, had a cigar in his mouth and was shouting at someone. It was Ron, who was wearing a white T-shirt that said Ohio State Athletic Association across the front. Though he was taller than Mr. Patimkin, and almost as stout, his hands hung weakly at his sides like a small boy's; Mr. Patimkin's cigar locomoted in his mouth. Six Negroes were loading one of the trucks feverishly, tossing—my stomach dropped—sink bowls at one another.

Ron left Mr. Patimkin's side and went back to directing the men. He thrashed his arms about a good deal, and though on the whole he seemed rather confused, he didn't appear to be at all concerned about anybody dropping a sink. Suddenly I could see myself directing the Negroes—I would have an ulcer in an hour. I could almost hear the enamel surfaces shattering on the floor. And I could hear myself: "Watch it, you guys. Be careful, will you? *Whoops!* Oh, please be—*watch* it! Watch! Oh!" Suppose Mr. Patimkin should come up to me and say, "Okay, boy, you want to marry my daughter, let's see what you can do." Well, he would see: in a moment that floor would be a shattered mosaic, a crunchy path of enamel. "Klugman, what kind of worker are you? You work like you eat!" "That's right, that's right, I'm a sparrow, let me go." "Don't you even know how to load and unload?" "Mr. Patimkin, even breathing gives me trouble, sleep tires me out, let me go, let me go . . ."

Mr. Patimkin was headed back to the fish bowl to answer a ringing phone, and I wrenched myself free of my reverie and headed towards the office too. When I entered, Mr. Patimkin looked up from the phone with his eyes; the sticky cigar was in his free hand—he moved it at me, a greeting. From outside I heard Ron call in a high voice, "You can't all go to lunch at the same time. We haven't got all day!"

"Sit down," Mr. Patimkin shot at me, though when he went back to his conversation I saw there was only one chair in the office, his. People did not sit at Patimkin Sink—here you earned your money the hard way, standing up. I busied myself looking at the several calendars that hung from filing cabinets; they showed illustrations of women so dreamy, so fantastically thighed and uddered, that one could not think of them as pornographic. The artist who had drawn the calendar girls for "Lewis Construction Company," and "Earl's Truck and Auto Repair," and "Grossman and Son, Paper Box" had been painting some third sex I had never seen.

"Sure, sure, sure," Mr. Patimkin said into the phone. "Tomorrow, don't tell me tomorrow. Tomorrow the world could blow up."

At the other end someone spoke. Who was it? Lewis from the construction company? Earl from truck repair?

"I'm running a business, Grossman, not a charity."

So it was Grossman being browbeaten at the other end.

"Shit on that," Mr. Patimkin said. "You're not the only one in town, my good friend," and he winked at me.

Ah-ha, a conspiracy against Grossman. Me and Mr. Patimkin. I smiled as collusively as I knew how.

"All right then, we're here till five . . . No later."

He wrote something on a piece of paper. It was only a big X.

"My kid'll be here," he said. "Yea, he's in the business."

Whatever Grossman said on the other end, it made Mr. Patimkin laugh. Mr. Patimkin hung up without a goodbye.

He looked out the back to see how Ron was doing. "Four years in college he can't unload a truck."

I didn't know what to say but finally chose the truth. "I guess I couldn't either."

"You could learn. What am I, a genius? I learned. Hard work never killed anybody."

To that I agreed.

Mr. Patimkin looked at his cigar. "A man works hard he's got something. You don't get anywhere sitting on your behind, you know . . . The biggest men in the country worked hard, believe me. Even Rockefeller. Success don't come easy . . ." He did not say this so much as he mused it out while he surveyed his dominion. He was not a man enamored of words, and I had the feeling that what had tempted him into this barrage of universals was probably the combination of Ron's performance and my presence—me, the outsider who might one day be an insider. But did Mr. Patimkin ever consider that possibility? I did not know; I only knew that these few words he did speak could hardly transmit all the satisfaction and surprise he felt about the life he had managed to build for himself and his family.

He looked out at Ron again. "Look at him, if he played basketball like that they'd throw him the hell off the court." But he was smiling when he said it.

He walked over to the door. "Ronald, let them go to lunch."

Ron shouted back, "I thought I'd let some go now, and some later."

"Why?"

"Then somebody'll always be—"

"No fancy deals here," Mr. Patimkin shouted. "We all go to lunch at once."

Ron turned back. "All right, boys, lunch!"

His father smiled at me. "Smart boy? Huh?" He tapped his head. "That took brains, huh? He ain't got the stomach for business. He's an idealist," and then I think Mr. Patimkin suddenly realized who *I* was, and eagerly corrected himself so as not to offend. "That's all right, you know, if you're a schoolteacher, or like you, you know, a student or something like that. Here you need a little of the *gonif* in you. You know what that means? *Gonif?*"

"Thief," I said.

"You know more than my own kids. They're *goyim,* my kids, that's how much they understand." He watched the Negro loading gang walk past the office and shouted out to them, "You guys know how long an hour is? All right, you'll be back in an hour!"

Ron came into the office and of course shook my hand.

"Do you have that stuff for Mrs. Patimkin?" I asked.

"Ronald, get him the silver patterns." Ron turned away and Mr. Patimkin said, "When I got married we had forks and knives from the five and ten. This kid needs gold to eat off," but there was no anger; far from it.

I drove to the mountains in my own car that afternoon, and stood for a while at the wire fence watching the deer lightly prance, coyly feed, under the protection of signs that read DO NOT FEED THE DEER, *By Order of South Mountain Reservation.* Alongside me at the fence were dozens of kids; they giggled and screamed when the deer licked the popcorn from their hands, and then were sad when their own excitement sent the young loping away towards the far end of the field where their tawny-skinned mothers stood regally watching the traffic curl up the mountain road. Young white-skinned mothers, hardly older than I, and in many instances younger, chatted in their convertibles behind me, and looked down from time to time to see what their children were about. I had seen them before, when Brenda and I had gone out for a bite in the afternoon, or had driven up here for lunch: in clotches of three and four they sat in the rustic hamburger joints that dotted the Reservation area while their children gobbled hamburgers and malteds and were given dimes to feed the jukebox. Though none of the little ones were old enough to read the song titles, almost all of them could holler out the words, and they did, while the mothers, a few of whom I recognized as high school mates of mine, compared suntans, supermarkets, and vacations. They looked immortal sitting there. Their hair would always stay the color they desired, their clothes the right texture and shade; in their homes they would have simple Swedish modern when that was fashionable, and if huge, ugly baroque ever came back, out would go the long, midget-legged marble coffee table and in would come Louis Quatorze. These were the goddesses, and if I were Paris I could not have been able to choose among them, so microscopic were the differences. Their fates had collapsed them into one. Only Brenda shone. Money and comfort would not erase her singleness—they hadn't yet, or had they? What was I loving, I wondered, and since I am not one to stick scalpels into myself, I wiggled my hand in the fence and allowed a tiny-nosed buck to lick my thoughts away.

When I returned to the Patimkin house, Brenda was in the living room looking more beautiful than I had ever seen her. She was modeling her new dress for Harriet and her mother. Even Mrs. Patimkin seemed softened by the sight of her; it looked as though some sedative had been injected into her, and so relaxed the Brenda-hating muscles around her eyes and mouth.

Brenda, without glasses, modeled in place; when she looked at me it was a kind of groggy, half-waking look I got, and though others might have interpreted it as sleepiness it sounded in my veins as lust. Mrs. Patimkin told her finally that she'd bought a very nice dress and I told her she looked lovely and Harriet told her she was very beautiful and that *she* ought to be the bride, and then there was an uncomfortable silence while all of us wondered who ought to be the groom.

Then when Mrs. Patimkin had led Harriet out to the kitchen, Brenda came up to me and said, "I *ought* to be the bride."

"You ought, sweetheart." I kissed her, and suddenly she was crying.

"What is it, honey?" I said.

"Let's go outside."

On the lawn, Brenda was no longer crying but her voice sounded very tired.

"Neil, I called Margaret Sanger Clinic," she said. "When I was in New York."

I didn't answer.

"Neil, they *did* ask if I was married. God, the woman sounded like my mother . . ."

"What did you say?"

"I said *no*."

"What did she say?"

"I don't know. I hung up." She walked away and around the oak tree. When she appeared again she'd stepped out of her shoes and held one hand on the tree, as though it were a Maypole she were circling.

"You can call them back," I said.

She shook her head. "No, I can't. I don't even know why I called in the first place. We were shopping and I just walked away, looked up the number, and called."

"Then you can go to a doctor."

She shook again.

"Look, Bren," I said, rushing to her, "we'll go together, to a doctor. In New York—"

"I don't want to go to some dirty little office—"

"We won't. We'll go to the most posh gynecologist in New York. One who gets *Harper's Bazaar* for the reception room. How does that sound?"

She bit her lower lip.

"You'll come with me?" she asked.

"I'll come with you."

"To the office?"

"Sweetie, your husband wouldn't come to the office."

"No?"

"He'd be working."

"But you're not," she said.

"I'm on vacation," I said, but I had answered the wrong question. "Bren, I'll wait and when you're all done we'll buy a drink. We'll go out to dinner."

"Neil, I shouldn't have called Margaret Sanger—it's not right."

"It is, Brenda. It's the most right thing we can do." She walked away and I was exhausted from pleading. Somehow I felt I could have convinced her had I been a bit more crafty; and yet I did not want it to be craftiness that changed her mind. I was silent when she came back, and perhaps it was just that, my *not* saying anything, that prompted her finally to say, "I'll ask Mother Patimkin if she wants us to take Harriet too . . ."

7

I shall never forget the heat and mugginess of that afternoon we drove into New York. It was four days after the day she'd called Margaret Sanger—she put it off and put it off, but finally on Friday, three days before Ron's wedding and four before her departure, we were heading through the Lincoln Tunnel, which seemed longer and fumier than ever, like Hell with tiled walls. Finally we were in New York and smothered again by the thick day. I pulled around the policeman who directed traffic in his shirt sleeves and up onto the Port Authority roof to park the car.

"Do you have cab fare?" I said.

"Aren't you going to come with me?"

"I thought I'd wait in the bar. Here, downstairs."

"You can wait in Central Park. His office is right across the street."

"Bren, what's the diff—" But when I saw the look that invaded her eyes I gave up the air-conditioned bar to accompany her across the city. There was a sudden shower while our cab went crosstown, and when the rain stopped the streets were sticky and shiny, and below the pavement was the rumble of the subways, and in all it was like entering the ear of a lion.

The doctor's office was in the Squibb Building, which is across from Bergdorf Goodman's and so was a perfect place for Brenda to add to her wardrobe. For some reason we had never once considered her going to a doctor in Newark, perhaps because it was too close to home and might allow for possibilities of discovery. When Brenda got to the revolving door she looked back at me;

her eyes were very watery, even with her glasses, and I did not say a word, afraid what a word, any word, might do. I kissed her hair and motioned that I would be across the street by the Plaza fountain, and then I watched her revolve through the doors. Out on the street the traffic moved slowly as though the humidity were a wall holding everything back. Even the fountain seemed to be bubbling boiling water on the people who sat at its edge, and in an instant I decided against crossing the street, and turned south on Fifth and began to walk the steaming pavement towards St. Patrick's. On the north steps a crowd was gathered; everyone was watching a model being photographed. She was wearing a lemon-colored dress and had her feet pointed like a ballerina, and as I passed into the church I heard some lady say, "If I ate cottage cheese *ten* times a day, I couldn't be that skinny."

It wasn't much cooler inside the church, though the stillness and the flicker of the candles made me think it was. I took a seat at the rear and while I couldn't bring myself to kneel, I did lean forward onto the back of the bench before me, and held my hands together and closed my eyes. I wondered if I looked like a Catholic, and in my wonderment I began to make a little speech to myself. Can I call the self-conscious words I spoke prayer? At any rate, I called my audience God. God, I said, I am twenty-three years old. I want to make the best of things. Now the doctor is about to wed Brenda to me, and I am not entirely certain this is all for the best. What is it I love, Lord? Why have I chosen? Who is Brenda? The race is to the swift. Should I have stopped to think?

I was getting no answers, but I went on. If we meet You at all, God, it's that we're carnal, and acquisitive, and thereby partake of You. I am carnal, and I know You approve, I just know it. But how carnal can I get? I am acquisitive. Where do I turn now in my acquisitiveness? Where do we meet? Which prize is You?

It was an ingenious meditation, and suddenly I felt ashamed. I got up and walked outside, and the noise of Fifth Avenue met me with an answer:

Which prize do you think, *schmuck?* Gold dinnerware, sporting-goods trees, nectarines, garbage disposals, bumpless noses, Patimkin Sink, Bonwit Teller—

But damn it, God, that *is* You!

And God only laughed, that clown.

On the steps around the fountain I sat in a small arc of a rainbow that the sun had shot through the spray of the water. And then I saw Brenda coming out of the Squibb Building. She carried nothing with her, like a woman who's only been window shopping, and for a moment I was glad that in the end she had disobeyed my desire.

As she crossed the street, though, that little levity passed, and then I was myself again.

She walked up before me and looked down at where I sat; when she inhaled she filled her entire body, and then let her breath out with a "Whew!"

"Where is it?" I said.

My answer, at first, was merely that victorious look of hers, the one she'd given Simp the night she'd beaten her, the one I'd gotten the morning I finished the third lap alone. At last she said, "I'm wearing it."

"Oh, Bren."

"He said shall I wrap it or will you take it with you?"

"Oh Brenda, I love you."

We slept together that night, and so nervous were we about our new toy that we performed like kindergartners, or (in the language of that country) like a lousy double-play combination. And then the next day we hardly saw one another at all, for with the last-minute wedding preparations came scurrying, telegramming, shouting, crying, rushing—in short, lunacy. Even the meals lost their Patimkin fullness, and were tortured out of Kraft cheese, stale onion rolls, dry salami, a little chopped liver, and fruit cocktail. It was hectic all weekend, and I tried as best I could to keep clear of the storm, at whose eye, Ron, clumsy and smiling, and Harriet, flittering and courteous, were being pulled closer and closer together. By Sunday night fatigue had arrested hysteria and all of the Patimkins, Brenda included, had gone off to an early sleep. When Ron went into the bathroom to brush his teeth I decided to go in and brush mine. While I stood over the sink he checked his supports for dampness; then he hung them on the shower knobs and asked me if I would like to listen to his records for a while. It was not out of boredom and loneliness that I accepted; rather a brief spark of lockerroom comradery had been struck there among the soap and the water and the tile, and I thought that perhaps Ron's invitation was prompted by a desire to spend his last moments as a Single Man with another Single Man. If I was right, then it was the first real attestation he'd given to my masculinity. How could I refuse?

I sat on the unused twin bed.

"You want to hear Mantovani?"

"Sure," I said.

"Who do you like better, him or Kostelanetz?"

"It's a toss-up."

Ron went to his cabinet. "Hey, how about the Columbus record? Brenda ever play it for you?"

"No. I don't think so."

He extracted a record from its case, and like a giant with a sea shell, placed it gingerly on the phonograph. Then he smiled at me and leaned back onto his bed. His arms were behind his head and his eyes fixed on the ceiling. "They give this to all the seniors. With the yearbook—" but he hushed as soon as the sound began. I watched Ron and listened to the record.

At first there was just a roll of drums, then silence, then another drum roll—and then softly, a marching song, the melody of which was very familiar. When the song ended, I heard the bells, soft, loud, then soft again. And finally there came a Voice, bowel-deep and historic, the kind one associates with documentaries about the rise of Fascism.

"The year, 1956. The season, fall. The place, Ohio State University . . ."

Blitzkrieg! Judgment Day! The Lord had lowered his baton, and the Ohio State Glee Club were lining out the Alma Mater as if their souls depended on it. After one desperate chorus, they fell, still screaming, into bottomless oblivion, and the Voice resumed:

"The leaves had begun to turn and redden on the trees. Smoky fires line Fraternity Row, as pledges rake the leaves and turn them to a misty haze. Old faces greet new ones, new faces meet old, and another year has begun . . ."

Music. Glee Club in great comeback. Then the Voice: "The place, the banks of the Olentangy. The event, Homecoming Game, 1956. The opponent, the ever dangerous Illini . . ."

Roar of crowd. New voice—Bill Stern: "Illini over the ball. The snap. Linday fading to pass, he finds a receiver, he passes long *long* down field—and IT'S INTERCEPTED BY NUMBER 43, HERB CLARK OF OHIO STATE! Clark evades one tackler, he evades another as he comes up to midfield. Now he's picking up blockers, he's down to the 45, the 40, the 35—"

And as Bill Stern egged on Clark, and Clark, Bill Stern, Ron, on his bed, with just a little body-english, eased Herb Clark over the goal.

"And it's the Buckeyes ahead now, 21 to 19. *What a game!*"

The Voice of History baritoned in again: "But the season was up and down, and by the time the first snow had covered the turf, it was the sound of dribbling and the cry *Up and In!* that echoed through the fieldhouse . . ."

Ron closed his eyes.

"The Minnesota game," a new, high voice announced, "and for some of our seniors, their last game for the red and white . . . The players are ready to come out on the floor and into the spotlight. There'll be a big hand of appreciation from this capacity crowd for some of the boys who won't be back next year. Here comes Larry Gardner, big Number 7, out onto the floor, Big Larry from Akron, Ohio . . ."

"Larry—" announced the P.A. system; "Larry," the crowd roared back.

"And here comes Ron Patimkin dribbling out. Ron, Number 11, from Short Hills, New Jersey. Big Ron's last game, and it'll be some time before Buckeye fans forget him . . ."

Big Ron tightened on his bed as the loudspeaker called his name; his ovation must have set the nets to trembling. Then the rest of the players were announced, and then basketball season was over, and it was Religious Emphasis Week, the Senior Prom (Billy May blaring at the gymnasium roof), Fraternity Skit Night, E. E. Cummings reading to students (verse, silence, applause); and then, finally, commencement:

"The campus is hushed this day of days. For several thousand young men and women it is a joyous yet a solemn occasion. And for their parents a day of laughter and a day of tears. It is a bright green day, it is June the seventh of the year one thousand nine hundred and fifty-seven and for these young Americans the most stirring day of their lives. For many this will be their last glimpse of the campus, of Columbus, for many many years. Life calls us, and anxiously if not nervously we walk out into the world and away from the pleasures of these ivied walls. But not from its memories. They will be the concomitant, if not the fundament, of our lives. We shall choose husbands and wives, we shall choose jobs and homes, we shall sire children and grandchildren, but we will not forget you, Ohio State. In the years ahead we will carry with us always memories of thee, Ohio State . . ."

Slowly, softly, the OSU band begins the Alma Mater, and then the bells chime that last hour. Soft, very soft, for it is spring.

There was goose flesh on Ron's veiny arms as the Voice continued. "We offer ourselves to you then, world, and come at you in search of Life. And to you, Ohio State, to you Columbus, we say thank you, thank you and goodbye. We will miss you, in the fall, in the winter, in the spring, but some day we shall return. Till then, goodbye, Ohio State, goodbye, red and white, goodbye, Columbus . . . goodbye, Columbus . . . goodbye . . ."

Ron's eyes were closed. The band was upending its last truckload of nostalgia, and I tiptoed from the room, in step with the 2163 members of the Class of '57.

I closed my door, but then opened it and looked back at Ron: he was still humming on his bed. Thee! I thought, my brother-in-law!

The wedding.

Let me begin with the relatives.

There was Mrs. Patimkin's side of the family: her sister Molly, a tiny buxom hen whose ankles swelled and ringed her shoes, and who would remember Ron's wedding if for no other reason than she'd martyred her feet in three-inch heels, and Molly's husband, the butter and egg man, Harry Grossbart, who had earned his fortune with barley and corn in the days of Prohibition. Now he was active in the Temple and whenever he saw Brenda he swatted her on the can; it was a kind of physical bootlegging that passed, I guess, for familial affection. Then there was Mrs. Patimkin's brother, Marty Kreiger, the Kosher Hot-Dog King, an immense man, as many stomachs as he had chins, and already, at fifty-five, with as many heart attacks as chins and stomachs combined. He had just come back from a health cure in the Catskills, where he said he'd eaten nothing but All-Bran and had won $1500 at gin rummy. When the photographer came by to take pictures, Marty put his hand on his wife's pancake breasts and said, "Hey, how about a picture of this!" His wife, Sylvia, was a frail, spindly woman with bones like a bird's. She had cried throughout the ceremony, and sobbed openly, in fact, when the rabbi had pronounced Ron and Harriet "man and wife in the eyes of God and the State of New Jersey." Later, at dinner, she had hardened enough to slap her husband's hand as it reached out for a cigar. However, when he reached across to hold her breast she just looked aghast and said nothing.

Also there were Mrs. Patimkin's twin sisters, Rose and Pearl, who both had white hair, the color of Lincoln convertibles, and nasal voices, and husbands who followed after them but talked only to each other, as though, in fact, sister had married sister, and husband had married husband. The husbands, named Earl Klein and Manny Kartzman, sat next to each other during the ceremony, then at dinner, and once, in fact, while the band was playing between courses, they rose, Klein and Kartzman, as though to dance, but instead walked to the far end of the hall where together they paced off the width of the floor. Earl, I learned later, was in the carpet business, and apparently he was trying to figure how much money he would make if the Hotel Pierre favored him with a sale.

On Mr. Patimkin's side there was only Leo, his half-brother. Leo was married to a woman named Bea whom nobody seemed to talk to. Bea kept hopping up and down during the meal and running over to the kiddie table to see if her little girl, Sharon, was being taken care of. "I told her not to take the kid. Get a babysitter, I said." Leo told me this while Brenda danced with Ron's best man, Ferrari. "She says what are we, millionaires? No, for Christ sake, but my brother's kids gets married, I can have a little celebration. No, we gotta *shlep* the kid with us. Aah, it gives her something to do! . . ." He looked around the hall. Up on the stage

Harry Winters (né Weinberg) was leading his band in a medley from *My Fair Lady;* on the floor, all ages, all sizes, all shapes were dancing. Mr. Patimkin was dancing with Julie, whose dress had slipped down from her shoulders to reveal her soft small back, and long neck, like Brenda's. He danced in little squares and was making considerable effort not to step on Julie's toes. Harriet, who was, as everyone said, a beautiful bride, was dancing with her father. Ron danced with Harriet's mother, Brenda with Ferrari, and I had sat down for a while in the empty chair beside Leo so as not to get maneuvered into dancing with Mrs. Patimkin, which seemed to be the direction towards which things were moving.

"You're Brenda's boy friend? Huh?" Leo said.

I nodded—earlier in the evening I'd stopped giving blushing explanations. "You gotta deal there, boy," Leo said, "you don't louse it up."

"She's very beautiful," I said.

Leo poured himself a glass of champagne, and then waited as though he expected a head to form on it; when one didn't he filled the glass to the brim.

"Beautiful, not beautiful, what's the difference. I'm a practical man. I'm on the bottom, so I gotta be. You're Aly Khan you worry about marrying movie stars. I wasn't born yesterday . . . You know how old I was when I got married? Thirty-five years old. I don't know what the hell kind of hurry I was in." He drained his glass and refilled it. "I'll tell you something, one good thing happened to me in my whole life. Two maybe. Before I came back from overseas I got a letter from my wife—she wasn't my wife then. My mother-in-law found an apartment for us in Queens. Sixty-two fifty a month it cost. That's the last good thing that happened."

"What was the first?"

"What first?"

"You said *two* things," I said.

"I don't remember. I say two because my wife tells me I'm sarcastic and a cynic. That way maybe she won't think I'm such a wise guy."

I saw Brenda and Ferrari separate, and so excused myself and started for Brenda, but just then Mr. Patimkin separated from

Julie and it looked as though the two men were going to switch partners. Instead the four of them stood on the dance floor and when I reached them they were laughing and Julie was saying, "What's so funny!" Ferrari said "Hi" to me and whisked Julie away, which sent her into peals of laughter.

Mr. Patimkin had one hand on Brenda's back and suddenly the other one was on mine. "You kids having a good time?" he said.

We were sort of swaying, the three of us, to "Get Me to the Church on Time."

Brenda kissed her father. "Yes," she said. "I'm so drunk my head doesn't even need my neck."

"It's a fine wedding, Mr. Patimkin."

"You want anything just ask me . . ." he said, a little drunken himself. "You're two good kids . . . How do you like that brother of yours getting married? . . . Huh? . . . Is that a girl or is that a girl?"

Brenda smiled, and though she apparently thought her father had spoken of her, I was sure he'd been referring to Harriet.

"You like weddings, Daddy?" Brenda said.

"I like my kids' weddings . . ." He slapped me on the back. "You two kids, you want anything? Go have a good time. Remember," he said to Brenda, "you're my honey . . ." Then he looked at me. "Whatever my Buck wants is good enough for me. There's no business too big it can't use another head."

I smiled though not directly at him, and beyond I could see Leo sopping up champagne and watching the three of us; when he caught my eye he made a sign with his hand, a circle with his thumb and forefinger, indicating, "That a boy, that a boy!"

After Mr. Patimkin departed, Brenda and I danced closely, and we only sat down when the waiters began to circulate with the main course. The head table was noisy, particularly at our end where the men were almost all teammates of Ron's, in one sport or another; they ate a fantastic number of rolls. Tank Feldman, Ron's roommate, who had flown in from Toledo, kept sending the waiter back for rolls, for celery, for olives, and always to the squealing delight of Gloria Feldman, his wife, a nervous, undernourished girl who continually looked down the front of her gown as though there was some sort of construction project going on under her clothes. Gloria and Tank, in fact, seemed to be self-appointed precinct captains at our end. They proposed toasts, burst into wild song, and continually referred to Brenda and me as "love birds." Brenda smiled at this with her eyeteeth and I brought up a cheery look from some fraudulent auricle of my heart.

And the night continued: we ate, we drank, we danced—Rose and Pearl did the Charleston with one another (while their husbands examined woodwork and chandeliers), and then I did the Charleston with none other than Gloria Feldman, who made coy, hideous faces at me all the time we danced. Near the end of the evening, Brenda, who'd been drinking champagne like her Uncle Leo, did a Rita Hayworth tango with herself, and Julie fell asleep on some ferns she'd whisked off the head table and made into a mattress at the far end of the hall. I felt a numbness creep into my hard palate, and by three o'clock people were dancing in their coats, shoeless ladies were wrapping hunks of wedding cake in napkins for their children's lunch, and finally Gloria Feldman made her way over to our end of the table and said, freshly, "Well, our little Radcliffe smarty, what have *you* been doing all summer?"

"Growing a penis."

Gloria smiled and left as quickly as she'd come, and Brenda without another word headed shakily away for the ladies' room and the rewards of overindulgence. No sooner had she left than Leo was beside me, a glass in one hand, a new bottle of champagne in the other.

"No sign of the bride and groom?" he said, leering. He'd lost most of his consonants by this time and was doing the best he could with long, wet vowels. "Well, you're next, kid, I see it in the cards . . . You're nobody's sucker . . ." And he stabbed me in the side with the top of the bottle, spilling champagne onto the side of my rented tux. He straightened up, poured more onto his hand and glass, but then suddenly he stopped. He was looking into the lights which were hidden beneath a long bank of flowers that adorned the front of the table. He shook the bottle in his hand as though to make it fizz. "The son of a bitch who invented the fluorescent bulb should drop dead!" He set the bottle down and drank.

Up on the stage Harry Winters brought his musicians to a halt. The drummer stood up, stretched, and they all began to open up cases and put their instruments away. On the floor, relatives, friends, associates, were holding each other around the waists and the shoulders, and small children huddled around their parents' legs. A couple of kids ran in and out of the crowd, screaming at tag, until one was grabbed by an adult and slapped soundly on the behind. He began to cry, and couple by couple the floor emptied. Our table was a tangle of squashed everything; napkins, fruits, flowers; there were empty whisky bottles, droopy ferns, and dishes puddled with unfinished cherry jubilee, gone sticky with the hours. At the end of the table Mr. Patimkin was sitting next to his wife, holding her hand. Opposite them, on two bridge chairs that had been pulled up, sat Mr. and Mrs. Ehrlich. They spoke quietly and evenly, as though they had known each other for years and years. Everything had slowed down now, and from time to time people would come up to the Patimkins and Ehrlichs, wish them *mazel tov*, and then drag themselves and their families out into the September night, which was cool and windy, someone said, and reminded me that soon would come winter and snow.

"They never wear out, those things, you know that." Leo was pointing to the fluorescent lights that shone through the flowers. "They last for years. They could make a car like that if they wanted, that could never wear out. It would run on water in the summer and snow in the winter. But they wouldn't do it, the big boys . . . Look at me," Leo said, splashing his suit front with champagne, "I sell a good bulb. You can't get the kind of bulb I sell in the drugstores. It's a quality bulb. But I'm the little guy. I don't even own a car. His brother, and I don't even own an automobile. I take a train wherever I go. I'm the only guy I know who wears out three pairs of rubbers every winter. Most guys get new ones when they lose the old ones. I wear them out, like shoes. Look," he said, leaning into me, "I could sell a crappy bulb, it wouldn't break my heart. But it's not good business."

The Ehrlichs and Patimkins scraped back their chairs and headed away, all except Mr. Patimkin who came down the table towards Leo and me.

He slapped Leo on the back. "Well, how you doing, *shtarke?*"

"All right, Ben. All right . . ."

"You have a good time?"

"You had a nice affair, Ben, it must've cost a pretty penny, believe me . . ."

Mr. Patimkin laughed. "When I make out my income tax I go to see Leo. He knows just how much money I spent . . . You need a ride home?" he asked me.

"No, thanks. I'm waiting for Brenda. We have my car."

"Good night," Mr. Patimkin said.

I watched him step down off the platform that held the head table, and then start towards the exit. Now the only people in the hall—the shambles of a hall—were myself, Leo, and his wife and child who slept, both of them, with their heads pillowed on a crumpled tablecloth at a table down on the floor before us. Brenda still wasn't around.

"When you got it," Leo said, rubbing his fingers together, "you can afford to talk like a big shot. Who needs a guy like me any more. Salesmen, you spit on them. You can go to the supermarket and buy anything. Where my wife shops you can buy sheets and pillowcases. Imagine, a grocery store! Me, I sell to gas stations, factories, small businesses, all up and down the east coast. Sure, you can sell a guy in a gas station a crappy bulb that'll burn out in a week. For inside the pumps I'm talking, it takes a certain kind of bulb. A utility bulb. All right, so you sell him a crappy bulb, and then a week later he puts in a new one, and while he's screwing it in he still remembers your name. Not me. I sell a quality bulb. It lasts a month, five weeks, before it even flickers, then it gives you another couple days, dim maybe, but so you shouldn't go blind. It hangs on, it's a quality bulb. Before it even burns out you notice it's getting darker, so you put a new one in. What people don't like is when one minute it's sunlight and the next dark. Let it glimmer a few days and they don't feel so bad. Nobody ever throws out my bulb—they figure they'll save them, can always use them in a pinch. Sometimes I say to a guy, you ever throw out a bulb you bought from Leo Patimkin? You gotta use psychology. That's why I'm sending my kid to college. You don't know a little psychology these days, you're licked . . ."

He lifted an arm and pointed out to his wife; then he slumped down in his seat. "Aaach!" he said, and drank off half a glass of champagne. "I'll tell you, I go as far as New London, Connecticut. That's as far as I'll go, and when I come home at night I stop first for a couple drinks. Martinis. Two I have, sometimes three. That seems fair, don't it? But to her a little sip or a bathtubful, it smells the same. She says it's bad for the kid if I come home smelling. The kid's a baby, for God's sake, she thinks that's the way I'm *supposed* to smell. A forty-eight-year-old man with a three-year-old kid! She'll give me a thrombosis that kid. My wife, she wants me to come home early and play with the kid before she goes to bed. Come home, she says, and *I'll* make you a drink. Hah! I spend all day sniffing gas, leaning under hoods with grimy *poilishehs* in New London, trying to force a lousy bulb into a socket—I'll screw it in myself, I tell them—and she thinks I want to come home and drink a martini from a jelly glass! How long are you going to stay in bars, she says. Till a Jewish girl is Miss Rheingold!

"Look," he went on after another drink, "I love my kid like Ben loves his Brenda. It's not that I don't want to play with her. But if I play with the kid and then at night get into bed with my wife, then she can't expect fancy things from me. It's one or the other. I'm no movie star."

Leo looked at his empty glass and put it on the table; he tilted the bottle up and drank the champagne like soda water. "How much do you think I make a week?" he said.

"I don't know."

"Take a guess."

"A hundred dollars."

"Sure, and tomorrow they're gonna let the lions out of the cage in Central Park. What do you think I make?"

"I can't tell."

"A cabdriver makes more than me. That's a fact. My wife's brother is a cabdriver, *he* lives in Kew Gardens. And he don't take no crap, no sir, not those cabbies. Last week it was raining one night and I said the hell with it, I'm taking a cab. I'd been all day in Newton, Mass. I don't usually go so far, but on the train in the morning I said to myself, stay on, go further, it'll be a change. And I know all the time I'm kidding myself. I wouldn't even make up the extra fare it cost me. But I stay on. And at night I still had a couple boxes with me, so when the guy pulls up at Grand Central there's like a genie inside me says get in. I even threw the bulbs in, not even caring if they broke. And this cabbie says, Whatya want to do, buddy, rip the leather? Those are brand new seats I got. No, I said. Jesus Christ, he says, some goddam people. I get in and give him a Queens address which ought to shut him up, but no, all the way up the Drive he was Jesus Christ-ing me. It's hot in the cab, so I open a window and *then* he turns around and says, Whatya want to do, give me a cold in the neck? I just got over a goddam cold . . ." Leo looked at me, bleary-eyed. "This city is crazy! If I had a little money I'd get out of here in a minute. I'd go to California. They don't need bulbs out there it's so light. I went to New Guinea during the war from San Francisco. *There*," he burst, "there is the other good thing that happened to me, that night in San Francisco with this Hannah Schreiber. That's the both of them, you asked me I'm telling you—the apartment my mother-in-law got us, and this Hannah Schreiber. One night was all. I went to a B'nai Brith dance for servicemen in the basement of some big temple, and I met her. I wasn't married then, so don't make faces."

"I'm not."

"She had a nice little room by herself. She was going to school to be a teacher. Already I knew something was up because she let me feel inside her slip in the cab. Listen to me, I sound like I'm always in cabs. Maybe two other times in my life. To tell the truth I don't even enjoy it. All the time I'm riding I'm watching the meter. Even the pleasures I can't enjoy!"

"What about Hannah Schreiber?"

He smiled, flashing some gold in his mouth. "How do you like that name? She was only a girl, but she had an old lady's name. In the room she says to me she believes in oral love. I can still hear her: Leo Patimkin, I believe in oral love. I don't know what the hell she means. I figure she was one of those Christian Scientists or some cult or something. So I said, But what about for soldiers, guys going overseas who may get killed, God forbid." He shrugged his shoulders. "The smartest guy in the world I wasn't. But that's twenty years almost, I was still wet behind the ears. I'll tell you, every once in a while my wife—you know, she does for me what Hannah Schreiber did. I don't like to force her, she works hard. That to her is like a cab to me. I wouldn't force her. I can remember every time, I'll bet. Once after a Seder, my mother was still living, she should rest in peace. My wife was up to here with Mogen David. In fact, *twice* after Seders. Aachhh! Everything good in my life I can count on my fingers! God forbid some one should leave me a million dollars, I wouldn't even have to take off my shoes. I got a whole other hand yet."

He pointed to the fluorescent bulbs with the nearly empty champagne bottle. "You call that a light? That's a light to *read* by? It's purple, for God's sake! Half the blind men in the world ruined themselves by those damn things. You know who's behind them? The optometrists! I'll tell you, if I could get a couple hundred for all my stock and the territory, I'd sell tomorrow. That's right, Leo A. Patimkin, one semester accounting, City College nights, will sell equipment, territory, good name. I'll buy two inches in the *Times*. The territory is from here to everywhere. I go where I want, my own boss, no one tells me what to do. You know the Bible? 'Let there be light—and there's Leo Patimkin!' That's my trademark, I'll sell that too. I tell them that slogan, the *poilishehs*, they think I'm making it up. What good is it to be smart unless you're in on the ground floor! I got more brains in my pinky than Ben got in his whole *head*. Why is it he's on top and I'm on the bottom! *Why!* Believe me, if you're born lucky, you're lucky!" And then he exploded into silence.

I had the feeling that he was going to cry, so I leaned over and whispered to him, "You better go home." He agreed, but I had to raise him out of his seat and steer him by one arm down to his wife and child. The little girl could not be awakened, and Leo and Bea asked me to watch her while they went out into the lobby to get their coats. When they returned, Leo seemed to have dragged himself back to the level of human communication. He shook my hand with real feeling. I was very touched.

"You'll go far," he said to me. "You're a smart boy, you'll play it safe. Don't louse things up."

"I won't."

"Next time we see you it'll be *your* wedding," and he winked at me. Bea stood alongside, muttering goodbye all the while he spoke. He shook my hand again and then picked the child out of her seat, and they turned towards the door. From the back, round-shouldered, burdened, child-carrying, they looked like people fleeing a captured city.

Brenda, I discovered, was asleep on a couch in the lobby. It was almost four o'clock and the two of us and the desk clerk were the only ones in the hotel lobby. At first I did not waken Brenda, for she was pale and wilted and I knew she had been sick. I sat beside her, smoothing her hair back off her ears. How would I ever come to know her, I wondered, for as she slept I felt I knew no more of her than what I could see in a photograph. I stirred her gently and in a half-sleep she walked beside me out to the car.

It was almost dawn when we came out of the Jersey side of the Lincoln Tunnel. I switched down to my parking lights, and drove on to the Turnpike, and there out before me I could see the swampy meadows that spread for miles and miles, watery, blotchy, smelly, like an oversight of God. I thought of that other oversight, Leo Patimkin, half-brother to Ben. In a few hours he would be on a train heading north, and as he passed Scarsdale and White Plains, he would belch and taste champagne and let the flavor linger in his mouth. Alongside him on the seat, like another passenger, would be cartons of bulbs. He would get off at New London, or maybe, inspired by the sight of his half-brother, he would stay on again, hoping for some new luck further north. For the world was Leo's territory, every city, every swamp, every road and highway. He could go on to Newfoundland if he wanted, Hudson Bay, and on up to Thule, and then slide down the other side of the globe and rap on frosted windows on the Russian steppes, if he wanted. But he wouldn't. Leo was forty-eight years old and he had learned. He pursued discomfort and sorrow, all right, but if you had a heartful by the time you reached New London, what new awfulness could you look forward to in Vladivostok?

The next day the wind was blowing the fall in and the branches of the weeping willow were fingering at the Patimkin front lawn. I drove Brenda to the train at noon, and she left me.

8

Autumn came quickly. It was cold and in Jersey the leaves turned and fell overnight. The following Saturday I took a ride up to see the deer, and did not even get out of the car, for it was too brisk to be standing at the wire fence, and so I watched the animals walk and run in the dimness of the late afternoon, and after a while everything, even the objects of nature, the trees, the clouds, the grass, the weeds, reminded me of Brenda, and I drove back down to Newark. Already we had sent our first letters and I had called her late one night, but in the mail and on the phone we had some difficulty discovering one another; we had not the style yet. That night I tried her again, and someone on her floor said she was out and would not be in till late.

Upon my return to the library I was questioned by Mr. Scapello about the Gauguin book. The jowly gentleman *had* sent a nasty letter about my discourtesy, and I was only able to extricate myself by offering a confused story in an indignant tone. In fact, I even managed to turn it around so that Mr. Scapello was apologizing to me as he led me up to my new post, there among the encyclopedias, the bibliographies, the indexes and guides. My bullying surprised me, and I wondered if some of it had not been learned from Mr. Patimkin that morning I'd heard him giving Grossman an earful on the phone. Perhaps I was more of a businessman than I thought. Maybe I could learn to become a Patimkin with ease . . .

Days passed slowly; I never did see the colored kid again, and when, one noon, I looked in the stacks, Gauguin was gone, apparently charged out finally by the jowly man. I wondered what it had been like that day the colored kid had discovered the book was gone. Had he cried? For some reason I imagined that he had blamed it on me, but then I realized that I was confusing the dream I'd had with reality. Chances were he had discovered someone else, Van Gogh, Vermeer . . . But no, they were not his kind of artists. What had probably happened was that he'd given up on the library and gone back to playing Willie Mays in the streets. He was better off, I thought. No sense carrying dreams of Tahiti in your head, if you can't afford the fare.

Let's see, what else did I do? I ate, I slept, I went to the movies, I sent broken-spined books to the bindery—I did everything I'd ever done before, but now each activity was surrounded by a fence, existed alone, and my life consisted of jumping from one fence to the next. There was no flow, for that had been Brenda.

And then Brenda wrote saying that she could be coming in for the Jewish holidays which were only a week away. I was so overjoyed I wanted to call Mr. and Mrs. Patimkin, just to tell them of my pleasure. However, when I got to the phone and had actually dialed the first two letters, I knew that at the other end there would be silence; if there was anything said, it would only be Mrs. Patimkin asking, "What is it you want?" Mr. Patimkin had probably forgotten my name.

That night, after dinner, I gave Aunt Gladys a kiss and told her she shouldn't work so hard.

"In less than a week it's Rosh Hashana and he thinks I should take a vacation. Ten people I'm having. What do you think, a chicken cleans itself? Thank God, the holidays come once a year, I'd be an old woman before my time."

But then it was only nine people Aunt Gladys was having, for only two days after her letter Brenda called.

"Oy Gut!" Aunt Gladys called. "Long *distance!*"

"Hello?" I said.

"Hello, sweetie?"

"Yes." I said.

"What *is* it?" Aunt Gladys tugged at my shirt. "What is it?"

"It's for me."

"Who?" Aunt Gladys said, pointing into the receiver.

"Brenda," I said.

"Yes?" Brenda said.

"Brenda?" Aunt Gladys said. "What does she call long distance, I almost had a heart attack."

"Because she's in Boston," I said. "Please, Aunt Gladys . . ."

And Aunt Gladys walked off, mumbling, "These kids . . ."

"Hello," I said again into the phone.

"Neil, how are you?"

"I love you."

"Neil, I have bad news. I can't come in this week."

"But, honey, it's the Jewish holidays."

"Sweet*heart*," she laughed.

"Can't you say that, for an excuse?"

"I have a test Saturday, and a paper, and you know if I went home I wouldn't get anything done . . ."

"You would."

"Neil, I just *can't*. My Mother'd make me go to Temple, and I wouldn't even have enough time to see *you*."

"Oh God, Brenda."

"Sweetie?"

"Yes?"

"Can't you come up here?" she asked.

"I'm working."

"The Jewish holidays," she said.

"Honey, I can't. Last year I didn't take them off, I can't all—"

"You can say you had a conversion."

"Besides, my aunt's having all the family for dinner, and you know what with my parents—"

"Come up, Neil."

"I can't just take two days off, Bren. I just got promoted and a raise—"

"The hell with the raise."

"Baby, it's my job."

"Forever?" she said.

"No."

"Then come. I've got a hotel room."

"For me?"

"For us."

"Can you do that?"

"No and yes. People do it."

"Brenda, you tempt me."

"Be tempted."

"I could take a train Wednesday right from work."

"You could stay till Sunday night."

"Bren, I can't. I still have to be back to work on Saturday."

"Don't you ever get a day *off*?" she said.

"Tuesdays," I said glumly.

"God."

"And Sunday," I added.

Brenda said something but I did not hear her, for Aunt Gladys called, "You talk all day long distance?"

"Quiet!" I shouted back to her.

"Neil, will you?"

"Damn it, yes," I said.

"Are you angry?"

"I don't think so. I'm going to come up."

"Till Sunday."

"We'll see."

"Don't feel upset, Neil. You sound upset. It is the Jewish holidays. I mean you *should* be off."

"That's right," I said. "I'm an orthodox Jew, for God's sake, I ought to take advantage of it."

"That's right," she said.

"Is there a train around six?"

"Every hour, I think."

"Then I'll be on the one that leaves at six."

"I'll be at the station," she said. "How will I know you?"

"I'll be disguised as an orthodox Jew."

"Me too," she said.

"Good night, love," I said.

Aunt Gladys cried when I told her I was going away for Rosh Hashana.

"And I was preparing a big meal," she said.

"You can still prepare it."

"What will I tell your mother?"

"I'll tell her, Aunt Gladys. Please. You have no right to get upset . . ."

"Someday you'll have a family you'll know what it's like."

"I have a family now."

"What's a matter," she said, blowing her nose, "That girl couldn't come home to see her family it's the holidays?"

"She's in school, she just can't—"

"If she loved her family she'd find time. We don't live six hundred years."

"She does love her family."

"Then one day a year you could break your heart and pay a visit."

"Aunt Gladys, you don't understand."

"Sure," she said, "when I'm twenty-three years old I'll understand everything."

I went to kiss her and she said, "Go away from me, go run to Boston . . ."

The next morning I discovered that Mr. Scapello didn't want me to leave on Rosh Hashana either, but I unnerved him, I think, by hinting that his coldness about my taking the two days off might just be so much veiled anti-Semitism, so on the whole he was easier to manage. At lunch time I took a walk down to Penn Station and picked up a train schedule to Boston. That was my bedtime reading for the next three nights.

She did not look like Brenda, at least for the first minute. And probably to her I did not look like me. But we kissed and held each other, and it was strange to feel the thickness of our coats between us.

"I'm letting my hair grow," she said in the cab, and that in fact was all she said. Not until I helped her out of the cab did I notice the thin gold band shining on her left hand.

She hung back, strolling casually about the lobby while I signed the register "Mr. and Mrs. Neil Klugman," and then in the room we kissed again.

"Your heart's pounding," I said to her.

"I know," she said.

"Are you nervous?"

"No."

"Have you done this before?" I said.

"I read Mary McCarthy."

She took off her coat and instead of putting it in the closet, she tossed it across the chair. I sat down on the bed; she didn't.

"What's the matter?"

Brenda took a deep breath and walked over to the window, and I thought that perhaps it would be best for me to ask nothing—

for us to get used to each other's presence in quiet. I hung her coat and mine in the empty closet, and left the suitcases—mine and hers—standing by the bed.

Brenda was kneeling backwards in the chair, looking out the window as though out the window was where she'd rather be. I came up behind her and put my hands around her body and held her breasts, and when I felt the cool draft that swept under the sill, I realized how long it had been since that first warm night when I had put my arms around her and felt the tiny wings beating in her back. And then I realized why I'd really come to Boston—it had been long enough. It was time to stop kidding about marriage.

"Is something the matter?" I said.

"Yes."

It wasn't the answer I'd expected; I wanted no answer really, only to soothe her nervousness with my concern.

But I asked, "What is it? Why didn't you mention it on the phone?"

"It only happened today."

"School?"

"Home. They found out about us."

I turned her face up to mine. "That's okay. I told my aunt I was coming here too. What's the difference?"

"About the summer. About our sleeping together."

"Oh?"

"Yes."

". . . Ron?"

"No."

"That night, you mean, did Julie—"

"No," she said, "it wasn't *anybody*."

"I don't get it."

Brenda got up and walked over to the bed where she sat down on the edge. I sat in the chair.

"My mother found the thing."

"The diaphragm?"

She nodded.

"When?" I asked.

"The other day, I guess." She walked to the bureau and opened her purse. "Here, you can read them in the order I got them."

She tossed an envelope at me; it was dirty-edged and crumpled, as though it had been in and out of her pockets a good many times. "I got this one this morning," she said. "Special delivery."

I took out the letter and read:

PATIMKIN KITCHEN AND BATHROOM SINKS

"Any Size—Any Shape"

Dear Brenda—

Don't pay any Attention to your Mother's Letter when you get it. I love you honey if you want a coat I'll buy You a coat. You could always have anything you wanted. We have every faith in you so you won't be too upset by what your mother says in her Letter. Of course she is a little hystericall because of the shock and she has been Working so hard for Hadassah. She is a Woman and it is hard for her to understand some of the Shocks in life. Of course I can't say We weren't all surprised because from the beginning I was nice to him and Thought he would appreciate the nice vacation we supplied for him. Some People never turn out the way you hope and pray but I am willing to forgive and call Buy Gones, Buy Gones, You have always up till now been a good Buck and got good scholastic Grades and Ron has always been what we wanted a Good Boy, most important, and a Nice boy. This late in my life believe me I am not going to start hating my own flesh and blood. As for your mistake it takes Two to make a mistake and now that you will be away at school and from him and what you got involved in you will probably do all right I have every faith you will. You have to have faith in your children like in a Business or any serious undertaking and there is nothing that is so bad that we can't forgive especially when Our own flesh and blood is involved. We have a nice close nitt family and why not???? Have a nice Holiday and in Temple I will say a Prayer for you as I do every year. On Monday I want you to go into Boston and buy a coat. Whatever you need because I know how Cold it gets up where you are . . . Give my regards to Linda and remember to bring her home with you on Thanksgiving like last year. You two had such a nice time. I have always never said bad things about any of your friends or Rons and that this should happen is only the exception that proves the rule. Have a Happy Holiday.

Your Father

And then it was signed "Ben Patimkin", but that was crossed out and written beneath "Your Father" were again, like an echo, the words, "Your Father."

"Who's Linda?" I asked.

"My roommate, last year." She tossed another envelope to me. "Here. I got this one in the afternoon. Air Mail."

The letter was from Brenda's mother. I started to read it and then put it down a moment. "You got this *after?*"

"Yes," she said. "When I got his I didn't know what was happening. Read hers."

I began again.

Dear Brenda:

I don't even know how to begin. I have been crying all morning and have had to skip my board meeting this afternoon because my eyes are so red. I never thought this would happen to a daughter of mine. I wonder if you know what I mean, if it is at least on your conscience, so I won't have to degrade either of us with a description. All I can say is that this morning when I was cleaning out the drawers and putting away your summer clothing I came upon something in your bottom drawer, *under* some sweaters which you probably remember leaving there. I cried the minute I saw it and I haven't stopped crying yet. Your father called a while ago and now he is driving home because he heard how upset I was on the phone.

I don't know what we ever did that you should reward us this way. We gave you a nice home and all the love and respect a child needs. I always was proud when you were a little girl that you could take care of yourself so well. You took care of Julie so beautifully it was a treat to see, when you were only fourteen years old. But you drifted away from your family, even though we sent you to the best schools and gave you the best money could buy. Why you should reward us this way is a question I'll carry with me to the grave.

About your friend I have no words. He is his parents' responsibility and I cannot imagine what kind of home life he had that he could act that way. Certainly that was a fine way to repay us for the hospitality we were nice enough to show to him, a perfect stranger. That the two of you should be carrying on like that in our very house I will never in my life be able to understand. Times certainly have changed since I was a girl that this kind of thing could go on. I keep asking myself if at least you didn't think of us while you were doing that. If not for me, how could you do this to your father? God forbid Julie should ever learn of this.

God only knows what you have been doing all these years we put our trust in you.

You have broken your parents' hearts and you should know that. This is some thank you for all we gave you.

Mother

She only signed "Mother" once, and that was in an extraordinarily miniscule hand, like a whisper.

"Brenda," I said.

"What?"

"Are you starting to cry?"

"No. I cried already."

"Don't start again."

"I'm trying not to, for God's sake."

"Okay . . . Brenda, can I ask you one question?"

"What?"

"Why did you leave it home?"

"Because I didn't plan on using it here, that's why."

"Suppose I'd come up. I mean I have come up, what about that?"

"I thought I'd come down first."

"So then couldn't you have carried it down then? Like a toothbrush?"

"Are you trying to be funny?"

"No. I'm just asking you why you left it home."

"I told you," Brenda said. "I thought I'd come home."

"But, Brenda, that doesn't make any sense. Suppose you did come home, and then you came back again. Wouldn't you have taken it with you then?"

"I don't *know*."

"Don't get angry," I said.

"You're the one who's angry."

"I'm upset, I'm not angry."

"I'm upset then too."

I did not answer but walked to the window and looked out. The stars and moon were out, silver and hard, and from the window I could see over to the Harvard campus where lights burned and then seemed to flicker when the trees blew across them.

"Brenda . . ."

"What?"

"Knowing how your mother feels about you, wasn't it silly to leave it home? Risky?"

"What does how she feels about me have to do with it?"

"You can't trust her."

"Why can't I?"

"Don't you see. You *can't*."

"Neil, she was only cleaning out the drawers."

"Didn't you know she would?"

"She never did before. Or maybe she did. Neil, I couldn't think of everything. We slept together night after night and nobody heard or noticed—"

"Brenda, why the hell are you willfully confusing things?"

"I'm not!"

"Okay," I said softly. "All right."

"It's you who's confusing things," Brenda said. "You act as though I wanted her to find it."

I didn't answer.

"Do you believe *that*?" she said, after neither of us had spoken for a full minute.

"I don't know."

"Oh, Neil, you're *crazy*."

"What was crazier than leaving that damn thing around?"

"It was an oversight."

"Now it's an oversight, before it was deliberate."

"It was an oversight about the drawer. It wasn't an oversight about leaving it," she said.

"Brenda, sweetheart, wouldn't the safest, smartest, easiest, simplest thing have been to have taken it with you? Wouldn't it?"

"It didn't make any difference either way."

"Brenda, this is the most frustrating argument of my life!"

"You keep making it seem as though I *wanted* her to find it. Do you think I need this? Do you? I can't even go home any more."

"Is that so?"

"Yes!"

"No," I said. "You can go home—your father will be waiting with two coats and a half-dozen dresses."

"What about my mother?"

"It'll be the same with her."

"Don't be absurd. How can I face them!"

"Why can't you face them? Did you do anything wrong?"

"Neil, look at the reality of the thing, will you?"

"*Did* you do anything wrong?"

"Neil, *they* think it's wrong. They're my parents."

"But do you think it's wrong—"

"That doesn't *matter*."

"It does to me, Brenda . . ."

"Neil, why are *you* confusing things? You keep accusing me of things."

"Damn it, Brenda, you're guilty of some things."

"*What?*"

"Of leaving that damn diaphragm there. How can you call it an oversight!"

"Oh, Neil, don't start any of that psychoanalytic crap!"

"Then why else did you do it? You wanted her to find it!"

"Why?"

"I don't know, Brenda, *why?*"

"Oh!" she said, and she picked up the pillow and threw it back on to the bed.

"What happens now, Bren?" I said.

"What does that mean?"

"Just that. What happens now?"

She rolled over on to the bed and buried her head in it.

"Don't start crying," I said.

"I'm *not*."

I was still holding the letters and took Mr. Patimkin's from its envelope.

"Why does your father capitalize all these letters?"

She didn't answer.

"'As for your mistake,'" I read aloud to Brenda, "'it takes Two to make a mistake and now that you will be away at school and from him and what you got involved in you will probably do all right I have every faith you will. Your Father. Your Father.'"

She turned and looked at me; but silently.

"'I have always never said bad things about any of your friends or Rons and that this should happen is only the exception that proves the rule. Have a Happy Holiday.'" I stopped; in Brenda's face there was positively no threat of tears; she looked, suddenly, solid and decisive. "Well, what are you going to do?" I asked.

"Nothing."

"Who are you going to bring home Thanksgiving—Linda?" I said, "or me?"

"Who *can* I bring home, Neil?"

"I don't know, who can you?"

"Can I bring you home?"

"I don't know," I said, "can you?"

"Stop repeating the question!"

"I sure as hell can't give you the answer."

"Neil, be realistic. After this, can I bring you home? Can you see us all sitting around the table?"

"I can't if you can't, and I can if you can."

"Are you going to speak Zen, for God's sake!"

"Brenda, the choices aren't mine. You can bring Linda or me. You can go home or not go home. That's another choice. Then you don't even have to worry about choosing between me and Linda."

"Neil, you don't understand. They're still my parents. They did send me to the best schools, didn't they? They have given me everything I've wanted, haven't they?"

"Yes."

"Then how can I not go home? I *have* to go home."

"Why?"

"You don't understand. Your parents don't bother you any more. You're lucky."

"Oh, sure. I live with my crazy aunt, that's a real bargain."

"Families are different. You don't understand."

"Goddamit, I understand more than you think. I understand why the hell you left that thing lying around. Don't you? Can't you put two and two together?"

"Neil, what are you talking about! You're the one who doesn't understand. You're the one who from the very beginning was accusing me of things? Remember? Isn't it so? Why don't you have your eyes fixed? Why don't you have this fixed, that fixed? As if it were my fault that I *could* have them fixed. You kept acting as if I was going to run away from you every minute. And now you're doing it again, telling me I planted that thing on purpose."

"I loved you, Brenda, so I cared."

"I loved *you*. That's why I got that damn thing in the first place."

And then we heard the tense in which we'd spoken and we settled back into ourselves and silence.

A few minutes later I picked up my bag and put on my coat. I think Brenda was crying too when I went out the door.

Instead of grabbing a cab immediately, I walked down the street and out towards the Harvard Yard which I had never seen before. I entered one of the gates and then headed out along a path, under the tired autumn foliage and the dark sky. I wanted to be alone, in the dark; not because I wanted to think about anything, but rather because, for just a while, I wanted to think about nothing. I walked clear across the Yard and up a little hill and then I was standing in front of the Lamont Library, which, Brenda had once told me, had Patimkin Sinks in its rest rooms. From the light of the lamp on the path behind me I could see my reflection in the glass front of the building. Inside, it was dark and there were no students to be seen, no librarians. Suddenly, I wanted to set down my suitcase and pick up a rock and heave it right through the glass, but of course I didn't. I simply looked at myself in the mirror the light made of the window. I was only that substance, I thought, those limbs, that face that I saw in front of me. I looked, but the outside of me gave up little information about the inside of me. I wished I could scoot around to the other side of the window, faster than light or sound or Herb Clark on Homecoming Day, to get behind that image and catch whatever it was that looked through those eyes. What was it inside me that had turned pursuit and clutching into love, and then turned it inside out again? What was it that had turned winning into losing, and losing —who knows—into winning? I was sure I had loved Brenda, though standing there, I knew I couldn't any longer. And I knew it would be a long while before I made love to anyone the way I had made love to her. With anyone else, could I summon up such a passion? Whatever spawned my love for her, had that spawned such lust too? If she had only been slightly *not* Brenda . . . but then would I have loved her? I looked hard at the image of me, at that darkening of the glass, and then my gaze pushed through it, over the cool floor, to a broken wall of books, imperfectly shelved.

I did not look very much longer, but took a train that got me into Newark just as the sun was rising on the first day of the Jewish New Year. I was back in plenty of time for work.

TOPICS FOR PAPERS AND DISCUSSION

1. *The novel as social commentary.* From an insular love story oriented toward Jewish life, this novel expands outward to examine contemporary American society. What does it reveal of lower-class and upper-middle-class American Jewish life, and how does it radiate to our society in general? Explain the ways the novel reflects national absorption with any of the following: social status, financial gain, material acquisitions, suburbia, eating, mechanical conveniences, personal comfort, physical beauty and stylish apparel, work, education, sex, sports, and leisure time.
2. *The ambiguities of Neil Klugman.* What is Neil's background? He is an intelligent and sensitive narrator-participant, yet his character presents puzzling contradictions. Explain how he can be alternately genuine and hypocritical, firm and malleable, wise and foolish, mean and considerate, passive and competitive, arrogant and humble, dependent and independent. If Neil is unsettled, why is he also deeply attached to Newark? Why does he remain working at the library when he dislikes it? At the end he feels simultaneous gain and loss. Why? Is he left finally in a state of limbo?

3. *Interrelationships in the Patimkin family.* "The family is at the core of the Jewish social character," Frederick J. Hoffman has observed. Are the Patimkins exemplary? Mr. Patimkin writes, "We have a nice close nitt family. . . ." Is it closely knit? Judge whether the Patimkins are allies or foes, unified or disconnected. Analyze the letters from the mother and father to Brenda. Consider the Patimkin marriage, the parental and sibling relationships, and the Patimkin relatives. Compare Neil's family, only one of whom, Aunt Gladys, actually appears.
4. *Physical settings.* Analyze the use of these major locations: (1) the home of Aunt Gladys in Newark, (2) the Patimkin residence in the suburb of Short Hills, (3) the Newark Public Library, (4) the Pierre Hotel ballroom in Manhattan. Locate other settings and comment upon their thematic and symbolic function, particularly the Patimkin business in Newark and the Lamont Library at Harvard. What is the significance of the upward movement from Newark to Short Hills to the deer reserve in "the mountains"? How does the visitors' area of the reserve function symbolically as a summit?
5. *Ethnic grouping.* In what ways are ethnic groups separated in the novel? How are they mixed? Does the novel make implicit distinctions among Jews who have maintained their religious and cultural traditions and those who have become virtually gentile? Establish gradations in the attitudes of whites toward blacks, ranging from animosity to kinship. Explain why the city of Newark is especially apt as a central locale for the novel. Also, why is it important that the library be a place open to all social classes and nationalities?
6. *The diaphragm perplex.* As a major symbol, what are the varied meanings of the diaphragm? How does it define the Neil-Brenda relationship? How does it function as objective correlative? Why does Neil insist that Brenda get a diaphragm, and why does she angrily refuse, then later relent? What is your interpretation of Brenda's act of leaving the diaphragm at home? Deliberate these possibilities: (1) she was forgetful and the result accidental; (2) she was provident, but failed to anticipate the consequences; (3) it was an intentional, ruthless act to achieve a premeditated end. Which is most likely?
7. *Resonance of symbolism.* Explain how these objects connected with the Patimkins have symbolic meaning: the bounteous fruit, sports equipment, the old refrigerator, the old furniture stored in the attic, Brenda's glasses, Ron's Ohio State blanket, the "Goodbye, Columbus" record. Consider the following at the library: the lions, the stairs, the paintings of Gauguin. How is the wedding feast symbolic? Explain how sports and physical actions like running and swimming work symbolically. What do names mean, for example, Klugman? How are the seasons of summer and fall symbolic? Analyze the symbols to be found in the novel's first paragraph and last paragraph.

8. *The Roth brand of humor.* How is humor used? Make distinctions among satire, irony, and sarcasm. Who is being mocked by Roth, by Neil, by Brenda? In what ways does Roth reveal phony standards? Analyze the following examples of humor: Neil's answer about Doris: "Peeling . . . . She's going to have her skin fixed"; Neil's description of the "Goodbye, Columbus" record; his observation of the Patimkin library: "a complete set of *Information Please Almanacs*"; Brenda's answer to Gloria about what she has been doing all summer: "Growing a penis."
9. *The dialectic pattern of themes.* The novel contains numerous thematic polarities, which may be placed under three general headings: (1) *the social,* such as Jewishness and the loss or avoidance of Jewishness, social climbing and resistance to social climbing, wealth and poverty, outsiders and insiders; (2) *the psychological,* such as reality and illusion, the past and present, intellect and emotion, physical and aesthetic life, materialism and spirituality; and (3) *the romantic,* such as quest and seduction, the battle of the sexes, fulfillment and destruction. Analyze any of these dualities.
10. *"And God only laughed, that clown."* Is religion made notable by its virtual absence in the lives of the major characters? Analyze Neil's "self-conscious words" to God in the cathedral in Manhattan. Why does he conclude that God is "gold dinnerware, sporting-goods trees, nectarines, garbage disposals, bumpless noses, Patimkin Sink, Bonwit Teller"? Review the conversation between Neil and Mrs. Patimkin during "her Hadassah work." What does it reveal? Why is she concerned over whether one is Orthodox, Conservative, or Reformed? How is Rosh Hashana made symbolically important?
11. *The American success myth.* Ben Patimkin is surprised "about the life he had managed to build for himself and his family." He admits that "success don't come easy." What is to account for his rise to wealth from impoverished beginnings? What are his attitudes toward work? Where does he place his values? What do you find missing from them? Analyze Ben's positive qualities and his weaknesses. Is "success myth" the wrong term to use? Consider his half-brother Leo's statement about Ben: "Why is it he's on top and I'm on the bottom!" Set up an equation between two Patimkin families (Ben's and Leo's) and two Klugman families (Uncle Aaron's and Uncle Max's).
12. *Techniques of "the double."* Analyze use of prototypes, replicas, and reflectors. How and to what ends are they used? The major "double" relationship obviously consists of Neil and the black boy who visits the library. Trace parallels between them. How do they both relate to "Tahiti"? Why is Neil so protective of the boy? Analyze the meaning of Brenda's remark to Neil: "You know, you look like me. Except bigger." Compare Ben and Ron, Brenda and Julie, Brenda

and her mother, the Kleins and the Kartzmans at the wedding party.

13. *Social mobility and immobility.* Reread the memorable paragraph on pages 292–293 beginning "Patimkin Kitchen and Bathroom Sinks was in the heart of the Negro section of Newark." Brenda says that her mother "still thinks we live in Newark." And Aunt Gladys asks, "Since when do Jewish people live in Short Hills"? Relate these and other pertinent passages to (in Irving Howe's words) "the moral and psychic consequences of the great transformation in American Jewish life." For all its depiction of the flux in urban and suburban areas, the novel also reveals social immobility. Where? Concentrate on specific evidence of movement and stasis in the novel.
14. *"Let there be light—and there's Leo Patimkin!"* Although he appears only in the wedding scene, Ben's half-brother is important. Why? A sad comic schlimazel, he is also a hero of sorts. How is he heroic? Carefully analyze his long, nearly nonstop speech. What does it reveal about him and his values? How is he different from the other Patimkins? Weigh his statement: "I got more brains in my pinky than Ben got in his whole *head.*"
15. *The thematic meaning of athletics and competitiveness.* The Patimkins reflect America's passion for sports and physical fitness. Furthermore, they would seem to consecrate the adage, "A family that plays together stays together." But what does competition do to them? Why are athletics so important to Ron, to Brenda, and even to little Julie? How does Neil fare as an athlete? Why does Brenda ask him to run, and why does she try to overpower him in the swimming "game"? Review Brenda's tennis match with Laura Simpson Stolowitch for what it reveals about the theme. Also consider the elder Patimkins' motives in letting Julie win at basketball and other games, and Neil's pleasure in beating her at Ping-Pong.
16. *Significance of the title.* "Goodbye, Columbus" recurs like a melancholy refrain through the course of the novel and is multi-edged in meaning. What is its direct application to Ron? What is the significance of the Ohio State record? How does the title apply indirectly but in a very important way to Neil himself, especially to his dream about the ship and the black boy, his mate? In what ways does the title perhaps comment upon America as a country?
17. *The engagement and marriage of Ron and Harriet.* Why are they so well suited for one another? Provide specific evidence for their "perfect match." Why does the marriage occur on the East Coast, rather than in Milwaukee? Why does everything have to be arranged "in about a day or two"? Is this pair made so innocuous and banal and are they treated so satirically that any serious consideration of them becomes pointless?
18. *Bren-Buck-Brenda.* Which is the "real" one? Why is she in need of familial and monetary security? Analyze her behavior during the

"hidden money" incident in the attic. Why does she use Neil as a weapon against her way of life, and paradoxically want to mold him in its image? Why can't she get along with her mother? Analyze her abrasive egotism, her avoidance of Jewishness and its traditions, her fierce competitiveness, her shortsightedness. Contrast her perceptiveness and her obtuseness, her masculinity and her femininity. At what level is her emotional maturity? Conjecture what becomes of her.

19. *The Brenda-Neil relationship.* How does this novel escape from being a cliché of "love affair of society girl and boy from across the tracks"? How are the two alike and different? For all their apparent sexual compatibility, are there signs of a love-hate relationship? Explain. Brenda says, "When you love me there'll be nothing to worry about." What does her statement mean? Compare their ideas, their values, their actions. How is Neil made to seem servile, and how does he dominate? Apply the thematic polarity of "initiation and withdrawal" to both of them. Would they have ever married? Analyze the hotel room scene in which each affirms certain ties.
20. *"The American dream" and reality.* How is Neil's development as a character reflected in his awareness of this disparity? Does Brenda ever reflect any awareness of it? Does her loyalty to her family relate to the dream or to reality? How has Neil's "reality" been changed by his experience with the "dream" world of the elite suburb? Does he rise or fall? What is revealed about the attitudes of the black boy and Leo toward the American dream? Finally, in a larger sense, how does the novel reflect the dream and the reality of our nation?

Noon Wine

KATHERINE ANNE PORTER

Time: 1896-1905
Place: Small South Texas Farm

The two grubby small boys with tow-colored hair who were digging among the ragweed in the front yard sat back on their heels and said, "Hello," when the tall bony man with straw-colored hair turned in at their gate. He did not pause at the gate; it had swung back, conveniently half open, long ago, and was now sunk so firmly on its broken hinges no one thought of trying to close it. He did not even glance at the small boys, much less give them good-day. He just clumped down his big square dusty shoes one after the other steadily, like a man following a plow, as if he knew the place well and knew where he was going and what he would find there. Rounding the right-hand corner of the house under the row of chinaberry trees, he walked up to the side porch where Mr. Thompson was pushing a big swing churn back and forth.

Mr. Thompson was a tough weather-beaten man with stiff black hair and a week's growth of black whiskers. He was a noisy proud man who held his neck so straight his whole face stood level with his Adam's apple, and the whiskers continued down his neck and disappeared into a black thatch under his open collar. The churn rumbled and swished like the belly of a trotting horse, and Mr. Thompson seemed somehow to be driving a horse with one hand, reining it in and urging it forward; and every now and then he turned halfway around and squirted a tremendous spit of tobacco juice out over the steps. The door stones were brown and gleaming with fresh tobacco juice. Mr. Thompson had been churning quite a while and he was tired of it. He was just fetching a mouthful of juice to squirt again when the stranger came around the corner and stopped. Mr. Thompson saw a narrow-chested man with blue eyes so pale they were almost white, looking and not looking at him from a long gaunt face, under white eyebrows. Mr. Thompson judged him to be another of these Irishmen, by his long upper lip.

"Howdy do, sir," said Mr. Thompson politely, swinging his churn.

"I need work," said the man, clearly enough but with some kind of foreign accent Mr. Thompson couldn't place. It wasn't Cajun and it wasn't Nigger and it wasn't Dutch, so it had him stumped. "You need a man here?"

Mr. Thompson gave the churn a great shove and it swung back and forth several times on its own momentum. He sat on the steps, shot his quid into the grass, and said, "Set down. Maybe we can make a deal. I been kinda lookin' round for somebody. I had two niggers but they got into a cutting scrape up the creek last week, one of 'em dead now and the other in the hoosegow at Cold Springs. Neither one of 'em worth killing, come right down to it. So it looks like I'd better get somebody. Where'd you work last?"

"North Dakota," said the man, folding himself down on the other end of the steps, but not as if he were tired. He folded up and settled down as if it would be a long time before he got up again. He never had looked at Mr. Thompson, but there wasn't anything sneaking in his eye, either. He didn't seem to be looking anywhere else. His eyes sat in his head and let things pass by them. They didn't seem to be expecting to see anything worth looking at. Mr. Thompson waited a long time for the man to say something more, but he had gone into a brown study.

"North Dakota," said Mr. Thompson, trying to remember where that was. "That's a right smart distance off, seems to me."

"I can do everything on farm," said the man; "cheap. I need work."

Mr. Thompson settled himself to get down to business. "My name's Thompson, Mr. Royal Earle Thompson," he said.

"I'm Mr. Helton," said the man, "Mr. Olaf Helton." He did not move.

"Well, now," said Mr. Thompson in his most carrying voice, "I guess we'd better talk turkey."

When Mr. Thompson expected to drive a bargain he always grew very hearty and jovial. There was nothing wrong with him except that he hated like the devil to pay wages. He said so himself. "You furnish grub and a shack," he said, "and then you got to pay 'em besides. It ain't right. Besides the wear and tear on your implements," he said, "they just let everything go to rack and ruin." So he began to laugh and shout his way through the deal.

"Now, what I want to know is, how much you fixing to gouge outa me?" he brayed, slapping his knee. After he had kept it up as long as he could, he quieted down, feeling a little sheepish, and cut himself a chew. Mr. Helton was staring out somewhere between the barn and the orchard, and seemed to be sleeping with his eyes open.

"I'm good worker," said Mr. Helton as from the tomb. "I get dollar a day."

Mr. Thompson was so shocked he forgot to start laughing again at the top of his voice until it was nearly too late to do any good. "Haw, haw," he bawled. "Why, for a dollar a day I'd hire out myself. What kinda work is it where they pay you a dollar a day?"

"Wheatfields, North Dakota," said Mr. Helton, not even smiling.

Mr. Thompson stopped laughing. "Well, this ain't any wheatfield by a long shot. This is more of a dairy farm," he said, feeling apologetic. "My wife, she was set on a dairy, she seemed to like working around with cows and calves, so I humored her. But it was a mistake," he said. "I got nearly everything to do, anyhow. My wife ain't very strong. She's sick today, that's a fact. She's been porely for the last few days. We plant a little feed, and a corn patch, and there's the orchard, and a few pigs and chickens, but our main hold is the cows. Now just speakin' as one man to another, there ain't any money in it. Now I can't give you no dollar a day because ackshally I don't make that much out of it. No, sir, we get along on a lot less than a dollar a day, I'd say, if we figger up everything in the long run. Now, I paid seven dollars a month to the two niggers, three-fifty each, and grub, but what I say is, one middlin'-good white man ekals a whole passel of niggers any day in the week, so I'll give you seven dollars and you eat at the table with us, and you'll be treated like a white man, as the feller says—"

"That's all right," said Mr. Helton. "I take it."

"Well, now I guess we'll call it a deal, hey?" Mr. Thompson jumped up as if he had remembered important business. "Now, you just take hold of that churn and give it a few swings, will you, while I ride to town on a coupla little errands. I ain't been able to leave the place all week. I guess you know what to do with butter after you get it, don't you?"

"I know," said Mr. Helton without turning his head. "I know butter business." He had a strange drawling voice, and even when he spoke only two words his voice waved slowly up and down and the emphasis was in the wrong place. Mr. Thompson wondered what kind of foreigner Mr. Helton could be.

"Now just where did you say you worked last?" he asked, as if he expected Mr. Helton to contradict himself.

"North Dakota," said Mr. Helton.

"Well, one place is good as another once you get used to it," said Mr. Thompson, amply. "You're a forriner, ain't you?"

"I'm a Swede," said Mr. Helton, beginning to swing the churn.

Mr. Thompson let forth a booming laugh, as if this was the best joke on somebody he'd ever heard. "Well, I'll be damned," he said at the top of his voice. "A Swede: well, now, I'm afraid you'll get pretty lonesome around here. I never seen any Swedes in this neck of the woods."

"That's all right," said Mr. Helton. He went on swinging the churn as if he had been working on the place for years.

"In fact, I might as well tell you, you're practically the first Swede I ever laid eyes on."

"That's all right," said Mr. Helton.

Mr. Thompson went into the front room where Mrs. Thompson was lying down, with the green shades drawn. She had a bowl of water by her on the table and a wet cloth over her eyes. She took the cloth off at the sound of Mr. Thompson's boots and said, "What's all the noise out there? Who is it?"

"Got a feller out there says he's a Swede, Ellie," said Mr. Thompson; "says he knows how to make butter."

"I hope it turns out to be the truth," said Mrs. Thompson. "Looks like my head never will get any better."

"Don't you worry," said Mr. Thompson. "You fret too much. Now I'm gointa ride into town and get a little order of groceries."

"Don't you linger, now, Mr. Thompson," said Mrs. Thompson. "Don't go to the hotel." She meant the saloon; the proprietor also had rooms for rent upstairs.

"Just a coupla little toddies," said Mr. Thompson, laughing loudly, "never hurt anybody."

"I never took a dram in my life," said Mrs. Thompson, "and what's more I never will."

"I wasn't talking about the womenfolks," said Mr. Thompson.

The sound of the swinging churn rocked Mrs. Thompson first into a gentle doze, then a deep drowse from which she waked suddenly knowing that the swinging had stopped a good while ago. She sat up shading her weak eyes from the flat strips of late summer sunlight between the sill and the lowered shades. There she was, thank God, still alive, with supper to cook but no churning on hand, and her head still bewildered, but easy. Slowly she realized she had been hearing a new sound even in her sleep. Somebody was playing a tune on the harmonica, not merely shrilling up and down making a sickening noise, but really playing a pretty tune, merry and sad.

She went out through the kitchen, stepped off the porch, and stood facing the east, shading her eyes. When her vision cleared and settled, she saw a long, pale-haired man in blue jeans sitting in the doorway of the hired man's shack, tilted back in a kitchen chair, blowing away at the harmonica with his eyes shut. Mrs. Thompson's heart fluttered and sank. Heavens, he looked lazy and worthless, he did, now. First a lot of no-count fiddling darkies and then a no-count white man. It was just like Mr. Thompson to take on that kind. She did wish he would be more considerate, and take a little trouble with his business. She wanted to believe in her husband, and there were too many times when she couldn't. She wanted to believe that tomorrow, or at least the day after, life, such a battle at best, was going to be better.

She walked past the shack without glancing aside, stepping carefully, bent at the waist because of the nagging pain in her side, and went to the springhouse, trying to harden her mind to speak very plainly to that new hired man if he had not done his work.

The milk house was only another shack of weather-beaten boards nailed together hastily years before because they needed a milk house; it was meant to be temporary, and it was; already shapeless, leaning this way and that over a perpetual cool trickle of water that fell from a little grot, almost choked with pallid ferns. No one else in the whole countryside had such a spring on his land. Mr. and Mrs. Thompson felt they had a fortune in that spring, if ever they got around to doing anything with it.

Rickety wooden shelves clung at hazard in the square around the small pool where the larger pails of milk and butter stood, fresh and sweet in the cold water. One hand supporting her flat, pained side, the other shading her eyes, Mrs. Thompson leaned over and peered into the pails. The cream had been skimmed and set aside, there was a rich roll of butter, the wooden molds and shallow pans had been scrubbed and scalded for the first time in who knows when, the barrel was full of buttermilk ready for the pigs and the weanling calves, the hard packed-dirt floor had been swept smooth. Mrs. Thompson straightened up again, smiling tenderly. She had been ready to scold him, a poor man who needed a job, who had just come there and who might not have been expected to do things properly at first. There was nothing she could do to make up for the injustice she had done him in her thoughts but to tell him how she appreciated his good clean work, finished already, in no time at all. She ventured near the door of the shack with her careful steps; Mr. Helton opened his eyes, stopped playing, and brought his chair down straight, but did not look at her, or get up. She was a little frail woman with long thick brown hair in a braid, a suffering patient mouth and diseased eyes which cried easily. She wove her fingers into an eyeshade, thumbs on temples, and, winking her tearful lids, said with a polite little manner, "Howdy do, sir. I'm Miz Thompson, and I wanted to tell you I think you did real well in the milk house. It's always been a hard place to keep."

He said, "That's all right," in a slow voice, without moving.

Mrs. Thompson waited a moment. "That's a pretty tune you're playing. Most folks don't seem to get much music out of a harmonica."

Mr. Helton sat humped over, long legs sprawling, his spine in a bow, running his thumb over the square mouth-stops; except for his moving hand he might have been asleep. The harmonica was a big shiny new one, and Mrs. Thompson, her gaze wandering about, counted five others, all good and expensive, standing in a row on the shelf beside his cot. "He must carry them around in his jumper pocket," she thought, and noted there was not a sign of any other possession lying about. "I see you're mighty fond of music," she said. "We used to have an old accordion, and Mr. Thompson could play it right smart, but the little boys broke it up."

Mr. Helton stood up rather suddenly, the chair clattered under him, his knees straightened though his shoulders did not, and he looked at the floor as if he were listening carefully. "You know how little boys are," said Mrs. Thompson. "You'd better set them harmonicas on a high shelf or they'll be after them. They're great hands for getting into things. I try to learn 'em, but it don't do much good."

Mr. Helton, in one wide gesture of his long arms, swept his harmonicas up against his chest, and from there transferred them in a row to the ledge where the roof joined to the wall. He pushed them back almost out of sight.

"That'll do, maybe," said Mrs. Thompson. "Now I wonder," she said, turning and closing her eyes helplessly against the stronger western light, "I wonder what became of them little tads. I can't keep up with them." She had a way of speaking about her children as if they were rather troublesome nephews on a prolonged visit.

"Down by the creek," said Mr. Helton, in his hollow voice. Mrs. Thompson, pausing confusedly, decided he had answered her question. He stood in silent patience, not exactly waiting for her to go, perhaps, but pretty plainly not waiting for anything else. Mrs. Thompson was perfectly accustomed to all kinds of men full of all kinds of cranky ways. The point was, to find out just how Mr. Helton's crankiness was different from any other man's, and then get used to it, and let him feel at home. Her father had been cranky, her brothers and uncles had all been set in their ways and none of them alike; and every hired man she'd ever seen had quirks and crotchets of his own. Now here was Mr.

Helton, who was a Swede, who wouldn't talk, and who played the harmonica besides.

"They'll be needing something to eat," said Mrs. Thompson in a vague friendly way, "pretty soon. Now I wonder what I ought to be thinking about for supper? Now what do you like to eat, Mr. Helton? We always have plenty of good butter and milk and cream, that's a blessing. Mr. Thompson says we ought to sell all of it, but I say my family comes first." Her little face went all out of shape in a pained blind smile.

"I eat anything," said Mr. Helton, his words wandering up and down.

He *can't* talk, for one thing, thought Mrs. Thompson, it's a shame to keep at him when he don't know the language good. She took a slow step away from the shack, looking back over her shoulder. "We usually have cornbread except on Sundays," she told him. "I suppose in your part of the country you don't get much good cornbread."

Not a word from Mr. Helton. She saw from her eye-corner that he had sat down again, looking at his harmonica, chair tilted. She hoped he would remember it was getting near milking time. As she moved away, he started playing again, the same tune.

Milking time came and went. Mrs. Thompson saw Mr. Helton going back and forth between the cow barn and the milk house. He swung along in an easy lope, shoulders bent, head hanging, the big buckets balancing like a pair of scales at the ends of his bony arms. Mr. Thompson rode in from town sitting straighter than usual, chin in, a towsack full of supplies swung behind the saddle. After a trip to the barn, he came into the kitchen full of good will, and gave Mrs. Thompson a hearty smack on the cheek after dusting her face off with his tough whiskers. He had been to the hotel, that was plain. "Took a look around the premises, Ellie," he shouted. "That Swede sure is grinding out the labor. But he is the closest mouthed feller I ever met up with in all my days. Looks like he's scared he'll crack his jaw if he opens his front teeth."

Mrs. Thompson was stirring up a big bowl of buttermilk cornbread. "You smell like a toper, Mr. Thompson," she said with perfect dignity. "I wish you'd get one of the little boys to bring me in an extra load of firewood. I'm thinking about baking a batch of cookies tomorrow."

Mr. Thompson, all at once smelling the liquor on his own breath, sneaked out, justly rebuked, and brought in the firewood himself. Arthur and Herbert, grubby from thatched head to toes, from skin to shirt, came stamping in yelling for supper. "Go wash your faces and comb your hair," said Mrs. Thompson, automatically. They retired to the porch. Each one put his hand under the pump and wet his forelock, combed it down with his fingers, and returned at once to the kitchen, where all the fair prospects of life were centered. Mrs. Thompson set an extra plate and commanded Arthur, the eldest, eight years old, to call Mr. Helton for supper.

Arthur, without moving from the spot, bawled like a bull calf, "Saaaaaay, Helllllton, suuuuuupper's ready!" and added in a lower voice, "You big Swede!"

"Listen to me," said Mrs. Thompson, "that's no way to act. Now you go out there and ask him decent, or I'll get your daddy to give you a good licking."

Mr. Helton loomed, long and gloomy, in the doorway. "Sit right there," boomed Mr. Thompson, waving his arm. Mr. Helton swung his square shoes across the kitchen in two steps, slumped onto the bench and sat. Mr. Thompson occupied his chair at the head of the table, the two boys scrambled into place opposite Mr. Helton, and Mrs. Thompson sat at the end nearest the stove. Mrs. Thompson clasped her hands, bowed her head and said aloud hastily, "Lord, for all these and Thy other blessings we thank Thee in Jesus' name, amen," trying to finish before Herbert's rusty little paw reached the nearest dish. Otherwise she would be duty-bound to send him away from the table, and growing children need their meals. Mr. Thompson and Arthur always waited, but Herbert, aged six, was too young to take training yet.

Mr. and Mrs. Thompson tried to engage Mr. Helton in conversation, but it was a failure. They tried first the weather, and then the crops, and then the cows, but Mr. Helton simply did not reply. Mr. Thompson then told something funny he had seen in town. It was about some of the other old grangers at the hotel, friends of his, giving beer to a goat, and the goat's subsequent behavior.

Mr. Helton did not seem to hear. Mrs. Thompson laughed dutifully, but she didn't think it was very funny. She had heard it often before, though Mr. Thompson, each time he told it, pretended it had happened that self-same day. It must have happened years ago if it ever happened at all, and it had never been a story that Mrs. Thompson thought suitable for mixed company. The whole thing came of Mr. Thompson's weakness for a dram too much now and then, though he voted for local option at every election. She passed the food to Mr. Helton, who took a helping of everything, but not much, not enough to keep him up to his full powers if he expected to go on working the way he had started.

At last, he took a fair-sized piece of cornbread, wiped his plate up as clean as if it had been licked by a hound dog, stuffed his mouth full, and, still chewing, slid off the bench and started for the door.

"Good night, Mr. Helton," said Mrs. Thompson, and the other Thompsons took it up in a scattered chorus. "Good night, Mr. Helton!"

"Good night," said Mr. Helton's wavering voice grudgingly from the darkness.

"Gude not," said Arthur, imitating Mr. Helton.

"Gude not," said Herbert, the copy-cat.

"You don't do it right," said Arthur. "Now listen to me. Guuuuuude naht," and he ran a hollow scale in a luxury of successful impersonation. Herbert almost went into a fit with joy.

"Now you *stop* that," said Mrs. Thompson. "He can't help the way he talks. You ought to be ashamed of yourselves, both of you, making fun of a poor stranger like that. How'd you like to be a stranger in a strange land?"

"I'd like it," said Arthur. "I think it would be fun."

"They're both regular heathens, Ellie," said Mr. Thompson. "Just plain ignoramuses." He turned the face of awful fatherhood upon his young. "You're both going to get sent to school next year, and that'll knock some sense into you."

"I'm going to git sent to the 'formatory when I'm old enough," piped up Herbert. "That's where I'm goin'."

"Oh, you are, are you?" asked Mr. Thompson. "Who says so?"

"The Sunday School Supintendant," said Herbert, a bright boy showing off.

"You see?" said Mr. Thompson, staring at his wife. "What did I tell you?" He became a hurricane of wrath. "Get to bed, you two," he roared until his Adam's apple shuddered. "Get now before I take the hide off you!" They got, and shortly from their attic bedroom the sounds of scuffling and snorting and giggling and growling filled the house and shook the kitchen ceiling.

Mrs. Thompson held her head and said in a small uncertain voice, "It's no use picking on them when they're so young and tender. I can't stand it."

"My goodness, Ellie," said Mr. Thompson, "we've got to raise 'em. We can't just let 'em grow up hog wild."

She went on in another tone. "That Mr. Helton seems all right, even if he can't be made to talk. Wonder how he comes to be so far from home."

"Like I said, he isn't no whamper-jaw," said Mr. Thompson, "but he sure knows how to lay out the work. I guess that's the main thing around here. Country's full of fellers trampin' round looking for work."

Mrs. Thompson was gathering up the dishes. She now gathered up Mr. Thompson's plate from under his chin. "To tell you the honest truth," she remarked, "I think it's a mighty good change to have a man round the place who knows how to work and keep his mouth shut. Means he'll keep out of our business. Not that we've got anything to hide, but it's convenient."

"That's a fact," said Mr. Thompson. "Haw, haw," he shouted suddenly. "Means you can do all the talking, huh?"

"The only thing," went on Mrs. Thompson, "is this: he don't eat hearty enough to suit me. I like to see a man set down and relish a good meal. My granma used to say it was no use putting dependence on a man who won't set down and make out his dinner. I hope it won't be that way this time."

"Tell you the truth, Ellie," said Mr. Thompson, picking his teeth with a fork and leaning back in the best of good humors, "I always thought your granma was a ter'ble ole fool. She'd just say the first thing that popped into her head and call it God's wisdom."

"My granma wasn't anybody's fool. Nine times out of ten she knew what she was talking about. I always say, the first thing you think is the best thing you can say."

"Well," said Mr. Thompson, going into another shout, "you're so reefined about that goat story, you just try speaking out in mixed comp'ny sometime! You just try it. S'pose you happened to be thinking about a hen and a rooster, hey? I reckon you'd shock the Babtist preacher!" He gave her a good pinch on her thin little rump. "No more meat on you than a rabbit," he said, fondly. "Now I like 'em cornfed."

Mrs. Thompson looked at him open-eyed and blushed. She could see better by lamplight. "Why, Mr. Thompson, sometimes I think you're the evilest-minded man that ever lived." She took a handful of hair on the crown of his head and gave it a good, slow pull. "That's to show you how it feels, pinching so hard when you're supposed to be playing," she said, gently.

In spite of his situation in life, Mr. Thompson had never been able to outgrow his deep conviction that running a dairy and chasing after chickens was woman's work. He was fond of saying that he could plow a furrow, cut sorghum, shuck corn, handle a team, build a corn crib, as well as any man. Buying and selling, too, were man's work. Twice a week he drove the spring wagon to market with the fresh butter, a few eggs, fruits in their proper season, sold them, pocketed the change, and spent it as seemed best, being careful not to dig into Mrs. Thompson's pin money.

But from the first the cows worried him, coming up regularly twice a day to be milked, standing there reproaching him with their smug female faces. Calves worried him, fighting the rope and strangling themselves until their eyes bulged, trying to get at the teat. Wrestling with a calf unmanned him, like having to change a baby's diaper. Milk worried him, coming bitter sometimes, drying up, turning sour. Hens worried him, cackling, clucking, hatching out when you least expected it and leading their broods into the barnyard where the horses could step on them; dying of roup and wryneck and getting plagues of chicken lice; laying eggs all over God's creation so that half of them were spoiled before a man could find them, in spite of a rack of nests Mrs. Thompson had set out for them in the feed room. Hens were a blasted nuisance.

Slopping hogs was hired man's work, in Mr. Thompson's opinion. Killing hogs was a job for the boss, but scraping them and cutting them up was for the hired man again; and again woman's proper work was dressing meat, smoking, pickling, and making lard and sausage. All his carefully limited fields of activity were related somehow to Mr. Thompson's feeling for the appearance of things, his own appearance in the sight of God and man. "It don't *look* right," was his final reason for not doing anything he did not wish to do.

It was his dignity and his reputation that he cared about, and there were only a few kinds of work manly enough for Mr. Thompson to undertake with his own hands. Mrs. Thompson, to whom so many forms of work would have been becoming, had simply gone down on him early. He saw, after a while, how short-sighted it had been of him to expect much from Mrs. Thompson; he had fallen in love with her delicate waist and lace-trimmed petticoats and big blue eyes, and, though all those charms had disappeared, she had in the meantime become Ellie to him, not at all the same person as Miss Ellen Bridges, popular Sunday School teacher in the Mountain City First Baptist Church, but his dear wife, Ellie, who was not strong. Deprived as he was, however, of the main support in life which a man might expect in marriage, he had almost without knowing it resigned himself to failure. Head erect, a prompt payer of taxes, yearly subscriber to the preacher's salary, land owner and father of a family, employer, a hearty good fellow among men, Mr. Thompson knew, without putting it into words, that he had been going steadily down hill. God amighty, it did look like somebody around the place might take a rake in hand now and then and clear up the clutter around the barn and the kitchen steps. The wagon shed was so full of broken-down machinery and ragged harness and old wagon wheels and battered milk pails and rotting lumber you could hardly drive in there any more. Not a soul on the place would raise a hand to it, and as for him, he had all he could do with his regular work. He would sometimes in the slack season sit for hours worrying about it, squirting tobacco on the ragweeds growing in a thicket against the wood pile, wondering what a fellow could do, handicapped as he was. He looked forward to the boys growing up soon; he was going to put them through the mill just as his own father had done with him when he was a boy; they were going to learn how to take hold and run the place right. He wasn't going to overdo it, but those two boys were going to earn their salt, or he'd know why. Great big lubbers sitting around whittling! Mr. Thompson sometimes grew quite enraged with them, when imagining their possible future, big lubbers sitting around whittling or thinking about fishing trips. Well, he'd put a stop to that, mighty damn quick.

As the seasons passed, and Mr. Helton took hold more and more, Mr. Thompson began to relax in his mind a little. There seemed to be nothing the fellow couldn't do, all in the day's work and as a matter of course. He got up at five o'clock in the morning, boiled his own coffee and fried his own bacon and was out in the cow lot before Mr. Thompson had even begun to yawn, stretch, groan, roar and thump around looking for his jeans. He milked the cows, kept the milk house, and churned the butter; rounded the hens up and somehow persuaded them to lay in the nests, not under the house and behind the haystacks; he fed them regularly and they hatched out until you couldn't set a foot down for them. Little by little the piles of trash around the barns and house disappeared. He carried buttermilk and corn to the hogs, and curried cockleburs out of the horses' manes. He was gentle with the calves, if a little grim with the cows and hens; judging by his conduct, Mr. Helton had never heard of the difference between man's and woman's work on a farm.

In the second year, he showed Mr. Thompson the picture of a cheese press in a mail order catalogue, and said, "This is a good thing. You buy this, I make cheese." The press was bought and Mr. Helton did make cheese, and it was sold, along with the increased butter and the crates of eggs. Sometimes Mr. Thompson felt a little contemptuous of Mr. Helton's ways. It did seem kind of picayune for a man to go around picking up half a dozen ears of corn that had fallen off the wagon on the way from the field, gathering up fallen fruit to feed to the pigs, storing up old nails and stray parts of machinery, spending good time stamping a fancy pattern on the butter before it went to market. Mr. Thompson, sitting up high on the spring-wagon seat, with the decorated butter in a five-gallon lard can wrapped in wet towsack, driving to town, chirruping to the horses and snapping the reins over their backs, sometimes thought that Mr. Helton was a pretty meeching sort of fellow; but he never gave way to these feelings, he knew a good thing when he had it. It was a fact the hogs were in better shape and sold for more money. It was a fact that Mr. Thompson stopped buying feed, Mr. Helton managed the crops so well. When beef- and hog-slaughtering time came, Mr. Helton knew how to save the scraps that Mr. Thompson had thrown away, and wasn't above scraping guts and filling them with sausages that he made by his own methods. In all, Mr. Thompson had no grounds for complaint. In the third year, he raised Mr. Helton's wages though Mr. Helton had not asked for a raise. The fourth year, when Mr. Thompson was not only out of debt but had a little cash in the bank, he raised Mr. Helton's wages again, two dollars and a half a month each time.

"The man's worth it, Ellie," said Mr. Thompson, in a glow of self-justification for his extravagance. "He's made this place pay, and I want him to know I appreciate it."

Mr. Helton's silence, the pallor of his eyebrows and hair, his long, glum jaw and eyes that refused to see anything, even the work under his hands, had grown perfectly familiar to the Thompsons. At first, Mrs. Thompson complained a little. "It's like sitting down at the table with a disembodied spirit," she said. "You'd think he'd find something to say, sooner or later."

"Let him alone," said Mr. Thompson. "When he gets ready to talk, he'll talk."

The years passed, and Mr. Helton never got ready to talk. After his work was finished for the day, he would come up from the barn or the milk house or the chicken house, swinging his lantern, his big shoes clumping like pony hoofs on the hard path. They, sitting in the kitchen in the winter, or on the back porch in summer, would hear him drag out his wooden chair, hear the creak of it tilted back, and then for a little while he would play his single tune on one or another of his harmonicas. The harmonicas were in different keys, some lower and sweeter than the others, but the same changeless tune went on, a strange tune, with sudden turns in it, night after night, and sometimes even in the afternoons when Mr. Helton sat down to catch his breath. At first the Thompsons liked it very much, and always stopped to listen. Later there came a time when they were fairly sick of it, and began to wish to each other that he would learn a new one. At last they did not hear it any more, it was as natural as the sound of the wind rising in the evenings, or the cows lowing, or their own voices.

Mrs. Thompson pondered now and then over Mr. Helton's soul. He didn't seem to be a church-goer, and worked straight through Sunday as if it were any common day of the week. "I think we ought to invite him to go to hear Dr. Martin," she told Mr. Thompson. "It isn't very Christian of us not to ask him. He's not a forward kind of man. He'd wait to be asked."

"Let him alone," said Mr. Thompson. "The way I look at it, his religion is every man's own business. Besides, he ain't got any Sunday clothes. He wouldn't want to go to church in them jeans and jumpers of his. I don't know what he does with his money. He certainly don't spend it foolishly."

Still, once the notion got into her head, Mrs. Thompson could not rest until she invited Mr. Helton to go to church with the family next Sunday. He was pitching hay into neat little piles in the field back of the orchard. Mrs. Thompson put on smoked glasses and a sunbonnet and walked all the way down there to speak to him. He stopped and leaned on his pitchfork, listening, and for a moment Mrs. Thompson was almost frightened at his face. The pale eyes seemed to glare past her, the eyebrows frowned, the long jaw hardened. "I got work," he said bluntly, and lifting his pitchfork he turned from her and began to toss the hay. Mrs. Thompson, her feelings hurt, walked back thinking that by now she should be used to Mr. Helton's ways, but it did seem like a man, even a foreigner, could be just a little polite when you gave him a Christian invitation. "He's not polite, that's the only thing I've got against him," she said to Mr. Thompson. "He just can't seem to behave like other people. You'd think he had a grudge against the world," she said. "I sometimes don't know what to make of it."

In the second year something had happened that made Mrs. Thompson uneasy, the kind of thing she could not put into words, hardly into thoughts, and if she had tried to explain to Mr. Thompson it would have sounded worse than it was, or not bad enough. It was that kind of queer thing that seems to be giving a warning, and yet, nearly always nothing comes of it. It was on a hot, still spring day, and Mrs. Thompson had been down to the garden patch to pull some new carrots and green onions and string beans for dinner. As she worked, sunbonnet low over her eyes, putting each kind of vegetable in a pile by itself in her basket, she noticed how neatly Mr. Helton weeded, and how rich the soil was. He had spread it all over with manure from the barns, and worked it in, in the fall, and the vegetables were coming up fine and full. She walked back under the nubbly little fig trees where the unpruned branches leaned almost to the ground, and the thick leaves made a cool screen. Mrs. Thompson was always looking for shade to save her eyes. So she, looking idly about, saw through the screen a sight that struck her as very strange. If it had been a noisy spectacle, it would have been quite natural. It was the silence that struck her. Mr. Helton was shaking Arthur by the shoulders, ferociously, his face most terribly fixed and pale. Arthur's head snapped back and forth and he had not stiffened in resistance, as he did when Mrs. Thompson tried to shake him. His eyes were rather frightened, but surprised, too, probably more surprised than anything else. Herbert stood by meekly, watching. Mr. Helton dropped Arthur, and seized Herbert, and shook him with the same methodical ferocity, the same face of hatred. Herbert's mouth crumpled as if he would cry, but he made no sound. Mr. Helton let him go, turned and strode into the shack, and the little boys ran, as if for their lives, without a word. They disappeared around the corner to the front of the house.

Mrs. Thompson took time to set her basket on the kitchen table, to push her sunbonnet back on her head and draw it forward again, to look in the stove and make certain the fire was going, before she followed the boys. They were sitting huddled together under a clump of chinaberry trees in plain sight of her bedroom window, as if it were a safe place they had discovered.

"What are you doing?" asked Mrs. Thompson.

They looked hang-dog from under their foreheads and Arthur mumbled, "Nothin'."

"Nothing *now*, you mean," said Mrs. Thompson, severely. "Well, I have plenty for you to do. Come right in here this minute and help me fix vegetables. This minute."

They scrambled up very eagerly and followed her close. Mrs. Thompson tried to imagine what they had been up to; she did not like the notion of Mr. Helton taking it on himself to correct her little boys, but she was afraid to ask them for reasons. They might tell her a lie, and she would have to overtake them in it, and whip them. Or she would have to pretend to believe them, and they would get in the habit of lying. Or they might tell her the truth, and it would be something she would have to whip them for. The very thought of it gave her a headache. She supposed she might ask Mr. Helton, but it was not her place to ask. She would wait and tell Mr. Thompson, and let him get at the bottom of it. While her mind ran on, she kept the little boys hopping. "Cut those carrot tops closer, Herbert, you're just being careless. Arthur, stop breaking up the beans so little. They're little enough already. Herbert, you go get an armload of wood. Arthur, you take these onions and wash them under the pump. Herbert, as soon as you're done here, you get a broom and sweep out this kitchen. Arthur, you get a shovel and take up the ashes. Stop picking your nose, Herbert. How often must I tell you? Arthur, you go look in the top drawer of my bureau, left-hand side, and bring me the vaseline for Herbert's nose. Herbert, come here to me. . . ."

They galloped through their chores, their animal spirits rose with activity, and shortly they were out in the front yard again, engaged in a wrestling match. They sprawled and fought, scrambled, clutched, rose and fell shouting, as aimlessly, noisily, monotonously as two puppies. They imitated various animals, not a human sound from them, and their dirty faces were streaked with sweat. Mrs. Thompson, sitting at her window, watched them with baffled pride and tenderness, they were so sturdy and healthy and growing so fast; but uneasily, too, with her pained little smile and the tears rolling from her eyelids that clinched themselves against the sunlight. They were so idle and careless, as if they had no future in this world, and no immortal souls to save, and oh, what had they been up to that Mr. Helton had shaken them, with his face positively dangerous?

In the evening before supper, without a word to Mr. Thompson of the curious fear the sight had caused her she told him that Mr. Helton had shaken the little boys for some reason. He stepped out to the shack and spoke to Mr. Helton. In five minutes he was back, glaring at his young. "He says them brats been fooling with his harmonicas, Ellie, blowing in them and getting them all dirty and full of spit and they don't play good."

"Did he say all that?" asked Mrs. Thompson. "It doesn't seem possible."

"Well, that's what he meant, anyhow," said Mr. Thompson. "He didn't say it just that way. But he acted pretty worked up about it."

"That's a shame," said Mrs. Thompson, "a perfect shame. Now we've got to do something so they'll remember they mustn't go into Mr. Helton's things."

"I'll tan their hides for them," said Mr. Thompson. "I'll take a calf rope to them if they don't look out."

"Maybe you'd better leave the whipping to me," said Mrs. Thompson. "You haven't got a light enough hand for children."

"That's just what's the matter with them now," shouted Mr. Thompson, "rotten spoiled and they'll wind up in the penitentiary. You don't half whip 'em. Just little love taps. My pa used to knock me down with a stick of stove wood or anything else that came handy."

"Well, that's not saying it's right," said Mrs. Thompson. "I don't hold with that way of raising children. It makes them run away from home. I've seen too much of it."

"I'll break every bone in 'em," said Mr. Thompson, simmering down, "if they don't mind you better and stop being so bull-headed."

"Leave the table and wash your face and hands," Mrs. Thompson commanded the boys, suddenly. They slunk out and dabbled at the pump and slunk in again, trying to make themselves small. They had learned long ago that their mother always made them wash when there was trouble ahead. They looked at their plates. Mr. Thompson opened up on them.

"Well, now, what you got to say for yourselves about going into Mr. Helton's shack and ruining his harmonicas?"

The two little boys wilted, their faces drooped into the grieved hopeless lines of children's faces when they are brought to the terrible bar of blind adult justice; their eyes telegraphed each other in panic, "Now we're really going to catch a licking"; in despair, they dropped their buttered cornbread on their plates, their hands lagged on the edge of the table.

"I ought to break your ribs," said Mr. Thompson, "and I'm a good mind to do it."

"Yes, sir," whispered Arthur, faintly.

"Yes, sir," said Herbert, his lip trembling.

"Now, papa," said Mrs. Thompson in a warning tone. The children did not glance at her. They had no faith in her good will. She had betrayed them in the first place. There was no trusting her. Now she might save them and she might not. No use depending on her.

"Well, you ought to get a good thrashing. You deserve it, don't you, Arthur?"

Arthur hung his head. "Yes, sir."

"And the next time I catch either of you hanging around Mr. Helton's shack, I'm going to take the hide off *both* of you, you hear me, Herbert?"

Herbert mumbled and choked, scattering his cornbread. "Yes, sir."

"Well, now sit up and eat your supper and not another word out of you," said Mr. Thompson, beginning on his own food. The little boys perked up somewhat and started chewing, but every time they looked around they met their parents' eyes, regarding them steadily. There was no telling when they would think of something new. The boys ate warily, trying not to be seen or heard, the cornbread sticking, the buttermilk gurgling, as it went down their gullets.

"And something else, Mr. Thompson," said Mrs. Thompson after a pause. "Tell Mr. Helton he's to come straight to us when they bother him, and not to trouble shaking them himself. Tell him we'll look after that."

"They're so mean," answered Mr. Thompson, staring at them. "It's a wonder he don't just kill 'em off and be done with it." But there was something in the tone that told Arthur and Herbert that nothing more worth worrying about was going to happen this time. Heaving deep sighs, they sat up, reaching for the food nearest them.

"Listen," said Mrs. Thompson, suddenly. The little boys stopped eating. "Mr. Helton hasn't come for his supper. Arthur, go and tell Mr. Helton he's late for supper. Tell him nice, now."

Arthur, miserably depressed, slid out of his place and made for the door, without a word.

There were no miracles of fortune to be brought to pass on a small dairy farm. The Thompsons did not grow rich, but they kept out of the poor house, as Mr. Thompson was fond of saying, meaning he had got a little foothold in spite of Ellie's poor health, and unexpected weather, and strange declines in market prices, and his own mysterious handicaps which weighed him down. Mr. Helton was the hope and the prop of the family, and all the Thompsons became fond of him, or at any rate they ceased to regard him as in any way peculiar, and looked upon him, from a distance they did not know how to bridge, as a good man and a good friend. Mr. Helton went his way, worked, played his tune. Nine years passed. The boys grew up and learned to work. They could not remember the time when Ole Helton hadn't been there: a grouchy cuss, Brother Bones; Mr. Helton, the dairymaid; that Big Swede. If he had heard them, he might have been annoyed at some of the names they called him. But he did not hear them, and besides they meant no harm—or at least such harm as existed was all there, in the names; the boys referred to their father as the Old Man, or the Old Geezer, but not to his face. They lived through by main strength all the grimy, secret, oblique phases of growing up and got past the crisis safely if anyone does. Their parents could see they were good solid boys with hearts of gold in spite of their rough ways. Mr. Thompson was relieved to find that, without knowing how he had done it, he had succeeded in raising a set of boys who were not trifling whittlers. They were such good boys Mr. Thompson began to believe they were born that way, and that he had never spoken a harsh word to them in their lives, much less thrashed them. Herbert and Arthur never disputed his word.

Mr. Helton, his hair wet with sweat, plastered to his dripping forehead, his jumper streaked dark and light blue and clinging to his ribs, was chopping a little firewood. He chopped slowly, struck the ax into the end of the chopping log, and piled the wood up neatly. He then disappeared round the house into his shack, which shared with the wood pile a good shade from a row of mulberry trees. Mr. Thompson was lolling in a swing chair on the front porch, a place he had never liked. The chair was new, and Mrs. Thompson had wanted it on the front porch, though the side porch was the place for it, being cooler; and Mr. Thompson wanted to sit in the chair, so there he was. As soon as the new wore off of it, and Ellie's pride in it was exhausted, he would move it round to the side porch. Meantime the August heat was almost unbearable, the air so thick you could poke a hole in it. The dust was inches thick on everything, though Mr. Helton sprinkled the whole yard regularly every night. He even shot the hose upward and washed the tree tops and the roof of the house. They had laid waterpipes to the kitchen and an outside faucet. Mr. Thompson must have dozed, for he opened his eyes and shut his mouth just in time to save his face before a stranger who had driven up to the front gate. Mr. Thompson stood up, put on his hat, pulled up his jeans, and watched while the stranger tied his team, attached to a light spring wagon, to the hitching post. Mr. Thompson recognized the team and wagon. They were from a livery stable in Buda. While the stranger was opening the gate, a strong gate that Mr. Helton had built and set firmly on its hinges several years back, Mr. Thompson strolled down the path to greet him and find out what in God's world a man's business might be that would bring him out at this time of day, in all this dust and welter.

He wasn't exactly a fat man. He was more like a man who had been fat recently. His skin was baggy and his clothes were too big for him, and he somehow looked like a man who should be fat, ordinarily, but who might have just got over a spell of sickness. Mr. Thompson didn't take to his looks at all, he couldn't say why.

The stranger took off his hat. He said in a loud hearty voice, "Is this Mr. Thompson, Mr. Royal Earle Thompson?"

"That's my name," said Mr. Thompson, almost quietly, he was so taken aback by the free manner of the stranger.

"My name is Hatch," said the stranger, "Mr. Homer T. Hatch, and I've come to see you about buying a horse."

"I reckon you've been misdirected," said Mr. Thompson. "I haven't got a horse for sale. Usually if I've got anything like that to sell," he said, "I tell the neighbors and tack up a little sign on the gate."

The fat man opened his mouth and roared with joy, showing rabbit teeth brown as shoeleather. Mr. Thompson saw nothing to laugh at, for once. The stranger shouted, "That's just an old joke of mine." He caught one of his hands in the other and shook hands with himself heartily. "I always say something like that when I'm calling on a stranger, because I've noticed that when a feller says he's come to buy something nobody takes him for a suspicious character. You see? Haw, haw, haw."

His joviality made Mr. Thompson nervous, because the expression in the man's eyes didn't match the sounds he was making. "Haw, haw," laughed Mr. Thompson obligingly, still not seeing the joke. "Well, that's all wasted on me because I never take any man for a suspicious character 'til he shows hisself to be one. Says or does something," he explained. "Until that happens, one man's as good as another, so far's *I'm* concerned."

"Well," said the stranger, suddenly very sober and sensible, "I ain't come neither to buy nor sell. Fact is, I want to see you about something that's of interest to us both. Yes, sir, I'd like to have a little talk with you, and it won't cost you a cent."

"I guess that's fair enough," said Mr. Thompson, reluctantly. "Come on around the house where there's a little shade."

They went round and seated themselves on two stumps under a chinaberry tree.

"Yes, sir, Homer T. Hatch is my name and America is my nation," said the stranger. "I reckon you must know the name? I used to have a cousin named Jameson Hatch lived up the country a ways."

"Don't think I know the name," said Mr. Thompson. "There's some Hatchers settled somewhere around Mountain City."

"Don't know the old Hatch family," cried the man in deep concern. He seemed to be pitying Mr. Thompson's ignorance. "Why, we came over from Georgia fifty years ago. Been here long yourself?"

"Just all my whole life," said Mr. Thompson, beginning to feel peevish. "And my pa and my grampap before me. Yes, sir, we've been right here all along. Anybody wants to find a Thompson knows where to look for him. My grampap immigrated in 1836."

"From Ireland, I reckon?" said the stranger.

"From Pennsylvania," said Mr. Thompson. "Now what makes you think we came from Ireland?"

The stranger opened his mouth and began to shout with merriment, and he shook hands with himself as if he hadn't met himself for a long time. "Well, what I always says is, a feller's got to come from *somewhere*, ain't he?"

While they were talking, Mr. Thompson kept glancing at the face near him. He certainly did remind Mr. Thompson of somebody, or maybe he really had seen the man himself somewhere. He couldn't just place the features. Mr. Thompson finally decided it was just that all rabbit-teethed men looked alike.

"That's right," acknowledged Mr. Thompson, rather sourly, "but what I always say is, Thompsons have been settled here for so long it don't make much difference any more *where* they come from. Now a course, this is the slack season, and we're all just laying round a little, but nevertheless we've all got our chores to do, and I don't want to hurry you, and so if you've come to see me on business maybe we'd better get down to it."

"As I said, it's not in a way, and again in a way it is," said the fat man. "Now I'm looking for a man named Helton, Mr. Olaf Eric Helton, from North Dakota, and I was told up around the country a ways that I might find him here, and I wouldn't mind having a little talk with him. No, siree, I sure wouldn't mind, if it's all the same to you."

"I never knew his middle name," said Mr. Thompson, "but Mr. Helton is right here, and been here now for going on nine years. He's a mighty steady man, and you can tell anybody I said so."

"I'm glad to hear that," said Mr. Homer T. Hatch. "I like to hear of a feller mending his ways and settling down. Now when I knew Mr. Helton he was pretty wild, yes, sir, wild is what he was, he didn't know his own mind at all. Well, now, it's going to be a great pleasure to me to meet up with an old friend and find him all settled down and doing well by hisself."

"We've all got to be young once," said Mr. Thompson. "It's like the measles, it breaks out all over you, and you're a nuisance to yourself and everybody else, but it don't last, and it usually don't leave no ill effects." He was so pleased with this notion he forgot and broke into a guffaw. The stranger folded his arms over his stomach and went into a kind of fit, roaring until he had tears in his eyes. Mr. Thompson stopped shouting and eyed the stranger uneasily. Now he liked a good laugh as well as any man, but there ought to be a little moderation. Now this feller laughed like a perfect lunatic, that was a fact. And he wasn't laughing because he really thought things were funny, either. He was laughing for reasons of his own. Mr. Thompson fell into a moody silence, and waited until Mr. Hatch settled down a little.

Mr. Hatch got out a very dirty blue cotton bandanna and wiped his eyes. "That joke just about caught me where I live," he said, almost apologetically. "Now I wish I could think up things as funny as that to say. It's a gift. It's . . ."

"If you want to speak to Mr. Helton, I'll go and round him up," said Mr. Thompson, making motions as if he might get up. "He may be in the milk house and he may be setting in his shack this time of day." It was drawing towards five o'clock. "It's right around the corner," he said.

"Oh, well, there ain't no special hurry," said Mr. Hatch. "I've been wanting to speak to him for a good long spell now and I guess a few minutes more won't make no difference. I just more wanted to locate him, like. That's all."

Mr. Thompson stopped beginning to stand up, and unbuttoned one more button of his shirt, and said, "Well, he's here, and he's this kind of man, that if he had any business with you he'd like to get it over. He don't dawdle, that's one thing you can say for him."

Mr. Hatch appeared to sulk a little at these words. He wiped his face with the bandanna and opened his mouth to speak, when round the house there came the music of Mr. Helton's harmonica. Mr. Thompson raised a finger. "There he is," said Mr. Thompson. "Now's your time."

Mr. Hatch cocked an ear towards the east side of the house and listened for a few seconds, a very strange expression on his face.

"I know that tune like I know the palm of my own hand," said Mr. Thompson, "but I never heard Mr. Helton say what it was."

"That's a kind of Scandahoovian song," said Mr. Hatch. "Where I come from they sing it a lot. In North Dakota, they sing it. It says something about starting out in the morning feeling so good you can't hardly stand it, so you drink up all your likker before noon. All the likker, y' understand, that you was saving for the noon lay-off. The words ain't much, but it's a pretty tune. It's a kind of drinking song." He sat there drooping a little, and Mr. Thompson didn't like his expression. It was a satisfied expression, but it was more like the cat that et the canary.

"So far as I know," said Mr. Thompson, "he ain't touched a drop since he's been on the place, and that's nine years this coming September. Yes, sir, nine years, so far as I know, he ain't wetted his whistle once. And that's more than I can say for myself," he said, meekly proud.

"Yes, that's a drinking song," said Mr. Hatch. "I used to play 'Little Brown Jug' on the fiddle when I was younger than I am now," he went on, "but this Helton, he just keeps it up. He just sits and plays it by himself."

"He's been playing it off and on for nine years right here on the place," said Mr. Thompson, feeling a little proprietary.

"And he was certainly singing it as well, fifteen years before that, in North Dakota," said Mr. Hatch. "He used to sit up in a straitjacket, practically, when he was in the asylum—"

"What's that you say?" said Mr. Thompson. "What's that?"

"Shucks, I didn't mean to tell you," said Mr. Hatch, a faint leer of regret in his drooping eyelids. "Shucks, that just slipped out. Funny, now I'd made up my mind I wouldn' say a word, because it would just make a lot of excitement, and what I say is, if a man has lived harmless and quiet for nine years it don't matter if he *is* loony, does it? So long's he keeps quiet and don't do nobody harm."

"You mean they had him in a straitjacket?" asked Mr. Thompson, uneasily. "In a lunatic asylum?"

"They sure did," said Mr. Hatch. "That's right where they had him, from time to time."

"They put my Aunt Ida in one of them things in the State asylum," said Mr. Thompson. "She got vi'lent, and they put her in one of these jackets with long sleeves and tied her to an iron ring in the wall, and Aunt Ida got so wild she broke a blood vessel and when they went to look after her she was dead. I'd think one of them things was dangerous."

"Mr. Helton used to sing his drinking song when he was in a

straitjacket," said Mr. Hatch. "Nothing ever bothered him, except if you tried to make him talk. That bothered him, and he'd get vi'lent, like your Aunt Ida. He'd get vi'lent and then they'd put him in the jacket and go off and leave him, and he'd lay there perfickly contented, so far's you could see, singing his song. Then one night he just disappeared. Left, you might say, just went, and nobody ever saw hide or hair of him again. And then I come along and find him here," said Mr. Hatch, "all settled down and playing the same song."

"He never acted crazy to me," said Mr. Thompson. "He always acted like a sensible man, to me. He never got married, for one thing, and he works like a horse, and I bet he's got the first cent I paid him when he landed here, and he don't drink, and he never says a word, much less swear, and he don't waste time runnin' around Saturday nights, and if he's crazy," said Mr. Thompson, "why, I think I'll go crazy myself for a change."

"Haw, ha," said Mr. Hatch, "heh, he, that's good! Ha, ha, ha, I hadn't thought of it jes like that. Yeah, that's right! Let's all go crazy and get rid of our wives and save our money, hey?" He smiled unpleasantly, showing his little rabbit teeth.

Mr. Thompson felt he was being misunderstood. He turned around and motioned toward the open window back of the honeysuckle trellis. "Let's move off down here a little," he said. "I oughta thought of that before." His visitor bothered Mr. Thompson. He had a way of taking the words out of Mr. Thompson's mouth, turning them around and mixing them up until Mr. Thompson didn't know himself what he had said. "My wife's not very strong," said Mr. Thompson. "She's been kind of invalid now goin' on fourteen years. It's mighty tough on a poor man, havin' sickness in the family. She had four operations," he said proudly, "one right after the other, but they didn't do any good. For five years handrunnin', I just turned every nickel I made over to the doctors. Upshot is, she's a mighty delicate woman."

"My old woman," said Mr. Homer T. Hatch, "had a back like a mule, yes, sir. That woman could have moved the barn with her bare hands if she'd ever took the notion. I used to say, it was a good thing she didn't know her own stren'th. She's dead now, though. That kind wear out quicker than the puny ones. I never had much use for a woman always complainin'. I'd get rid of her mighty quick, yes, sir, mighty quick. It's just as you say: a dead loss, keepin' one of 'em up."

This was not at all what Mr. Thompson had heard himself say; he had been trying to explain that a wife as expensive as his was a credit to a man. "She's a mighty reasonable woman," said Mr. Thompson, feeling baffled, "but I wouldn't answer for what she'd say or do if she found out we'd had a lunatic on the place all this time." They had moved away from the window; Mr. Thompson took Mr. Hatch the front way, because if he went the back way they would have to pass Mr. Helton's shack. For some reason he didn't want the stranger to see or talk to Mr. Helton. It was strange but that was the way Mr. Thompson felt.

Mr. Thompson sat down again, on the chopping log, offering his guest another tree stump. "Now, I mighta got upset myself at such a thing, once," said Mr. Thompson, "but now I *deefy* anything to get me lathered up." He cut himself an enormous plug of tobacco with his horn-handled pocketknife, and offered it to Mr. Hatch, who then produced his own plug and, opening a huge bowie knife with a long blade sharply whetted, cut off a large wad and put it in his mouth. They then compared plugs and both of them were astonished to see how different men's ideas of good chewing tobacco were.

"Now, for instance," said Mr. Hatch, "mine is lighter colored. That's because, for one thing, there ain't any sweetenin' in this plug. I like it dry, natural leaf, medium strong."

"A little sweetenin' don't do no harm so far as I'm concerned," said Mr. Thompson, "but it's got to be mighty little. But with me, now, I want a strong leaf, I want it heavy-cured, as the feller says. There's a man near here, named Williams, Mr. John Morgan Williams, who chews a plug—well, sir, it's black as your hat and soft as melted tar. It fairly drips with molasses, jus' plain molasses, and it chews like licorice. Now, I don't call that a good chew."

"One man's meat," said Mr. Hatch, "is another man's poison. Now, such a chew would simply gag me. I couldn't begin to put it in my mouth."

"Well," said Mr. Thompson, a tinge of apology in his voice, "I jus' barely tasted it myself, you might say. Just took a little piece in my mouth and spit it out again."

"I'm dead sure I couldn't even get that far," said Mr. Hatch.

"I like a dry natural chew without any artificial flavorin' of any kind."

Mr. Thompson began to feel that Mr. Hatch was trying to make out he had the best judgment in tobacco, and was going to keep up the argument until he proved it. He began to feel seriously annoyed with the fat man. After all, who was he and where did he come from? Who was he to go around telling other people what kind of tobacco to chew?

"Artificial flavorin'," Mr. Hatch went on, doggedly, "is jes put in to cover up a cheap leaf and make a man think he's gettin' somethin' more than he *is* gettin'. Even a little sweetenin' is a sign of a cheap leaf, you can mark my words."

"I've always paid a fair price for my plug," said Mr. Thompson, stiffly. "I'm not a rich man and I don't go round settin' myself up for one, but I'll say this, when it comes to such things as tobacco, I buy the best on the market."

"Sweetenin', even a little," began Mr. Hatch, shifting his plug and squirting tobacco juice at a dry-looking little rose bush that was having a hard enough time as it was, standing all day in the blazing sun, its roots clenched in the baked earth, "is the sign of—"

"About this Mr. Helton, now," said Mr. Thompson, determinedly, "I don't see no reason to hold it against a man because he went loony once or twice in his lifetime and so I don't expect to take no steps about it. Not a step. I've got nothin' against the man, he's always treated me fair. They's things and people," he went on, "'nough to drive any man loony. The wonder to me is, more men don't wind up in straitjackets, the way things are going these days and times."

"That's right," said Mr. Hatch, promptly, entirely too promptly, as if he were turning Mr. Thompson's meaning back on him. "You took the words right out of my mouth. There ain't every man in a straitjacket that ought to be there. Ha, ha, you're right all right. You got the idea."

Mr. Thompson sat silent and chewed steadily and stared at a spot on the ground about six feet away and felt a slow muffled resentment climbing from somewhere deep down in him, climbing and spreading all through him. What was this fellow driving at? What was he trying to say? It wasn't so much his words, but his looks and his way of talking: that droopy look in the eye, that tone of voice, as if he was trying to mortify Mr. Thompson about something. Mr. Thompson didn't like it, but he couldn't get hold of it either. He wanted to turn around and shove the fellow off the stump, but it wouldn't look reasonable. Suppose something happened to the fellow when he fell off the stump, just for instance, if he fell on the ax and cut himself, and then someone should ask Mr. Thompson why he shoved him, and what could a man say? It would look mighty funny, it would sound mighty strange to say, Well him and me fell out over a plug of tobacco. He might just shove him anyhow and then tell people he was a fat man not used to the heat and while he was talking he got dizzy and fell off by himself, or something like that, and it wouldn't be the truth either, because it wasn't the heat and it wasn't the tobacco. Mr. Thompson made up his mind to get the fellow off the place pretty quick, without seeming to be anxious, and watch him sharp till he was out of sight. It doesn't pay to be friendly with strangers from another part of the country. They're always up to something, or they'd stay at home where they belong.

"And they's some people," said Mr. Hatch, "would jus' as soon have a loonatic around their house as not, they can't see no difference between them and anybody else. I always say, if that's the way a man feels, don't care who he associates with, why, why, that's his business, not mine. I don't wanta have a thing to do with it. Now back home in North Dakota, we don't feel that way. I'd like to a seen anybody hiring a loonatic there, aspecially after what he done."

"I didn't understand your home was North Dakota," said Mr. Thompson. "I thought you said Georgia."

"I've got a married sister in North Dakota," said Mr. Hatch, "married a Swede, but a white man if ever I saw one. So I say *we* because we got into a little business together out that way. And it seems like home, kind of."

"What did he do?" asked Mr. Thompson, feeling very uneasy again.

"Oh, nothin' to speak of," said Mr. Hatch, jovially, "jus' went loony one day in the hayfield and shoved a pitchfork right square through his brother, when they was makin' hay. They was goin' to execute him, but they found out he had went crazy with the heat, as the feller says, and so they put him in the asylum. That's all he done. Nothin' to get lathered up about, ha, ha, ha!" he said, and taking out his sharp knife he began to slice off a chew as carefully as if he were cutting cake.

"Well," said Mr. Thompson, "I don't deny that's news. Yes, sir, news. But I still say somethin' must have drove him to it. Some men make you feel like giving 'em a good killing just by lookin' at you. His brother may a been a mean ornery cuss."

"Brother was going to get married," said Mr. Hatch; "used to go courtin' his girl nights. Borrowed Mr. Helton's harmonica to give her a serenade one evenin', and lost it. Brand new harmonica."

"He thinks a heap of his harmonicas," said Mr. Thompson. "Only money he ever spends, now and then he buys hisself a new one. Must have a dozen in that shack, all kinds and sizes."

"Brother wouldn't buy him a new one," said Mr. Hatch, "so Mr. Helton just ups, as I says, and runs his pitchfork through his brother. Now you know he musta been crazy to get all worked up over a little thing like that."

"Sounds like it," said Mr. Thompson, reluctant to agree in anything with this intrusive and disagreeable fellow. He kept thinking he couldn't remember when he had taken such a dislike to a man on first sight.

"Seems to me you'd get pretty sick of hearin' the same tune year in, year out," said Mr. Hatch.

"Well, sometimes I think it wouldn't do no harm if he learned a new one," said Mr. Thompson, "but he don't, so there's nothin' to be done about it. It's a pretty good tune, though."

"One of the Scandahoovians told me what it meant, that's how I come to know," said Mr. Hatch. "Especially that part about getting so gay you jus' go ahead and drink up all the likker you got on hand before noon. It seems like up in them Swede countries a man carries a bottle of wine around with him as a matter of course, at least that's the way I understood it. Those fellers will tell you anything, though—" He broke off and spat.

The idea of drinking any kind of liquor in this heat made Mr. Thompson dizzy. The idea of anybody feeling good on a day like this, for instance, made him tired. He felt he was really suffering from the heat. The fat man looked as if he had grown to the stump;

he slumped there in his damp, dark clothes too big for him, his belly slack in his pants, his wide black felt hat pushed off his narrow forehead red with prickly heat. A bottle of good cold beer, now, would be a help, thought Mr. Thompson, remembering the four bottles sitting deep in the pool at the springhouse, and his dry tongue squirmed in his mouth. He wasn't going to offer this man anything, though, not even a drop of water. He wasn't even going to chew any more tobacco with him. He shot out his quid suddenly, and wiped his mouth on the back of his hand, and studied the head near him attentively. The man was no good, and he was there for no good, but what was he up to? Mr. Thompson made up his mind he'd give him a little more time to get his business, whatever it was, with Mr. Helton over, and then if he didn't get off the place he'd kick him off.

Mr. Hatch, as if he suspected Mr. Thompson's thoughts, turned his eyes, wicked and pig-like, on Mr. Thompson. "Fact is," he said, as if he had made up his mind about something, "I might need your help in the little matter I've got on hand, but it won't cost you any trouble. Now, this Mr. Helton here, like I tell you, he's a dangerous escaped loonatic, you might say. Now fact is, in the last twelve years or so I musta rounded up twenty-odd escaped loonatics, besides a couple of escaped convicts that I just run into by accident, like. I don't make a business of it, but if there's a reward, and there usually is a reward, of course, I get it. It amounts to a tidy little sum in the long run, but that ain't the main question. Fact is, I'm for law and order, I don't like to see lawbreakers and loonatics at large. It ain't the place for them. Now I reckon you're bound to agree with me on that, aren't you?"

Mr. Thompson said, "Well, circumstances alters cases, as the feller says. Now, what I know of Mr. Helton, he ain't dangerous, as I told you." Something serious was going to happen, Mr. Thompson could see that. He stopped thinking about it. He'd just let this fellow shoot off his head and then see what could be done about it. Without thinking he got out his knife and plug and started to cut a chew, then remembered himself and put them back in his pocket.

"The law," said Mr. Hatch, "is solidly behind me. Now this Mr. Helton, he's been one of my toughest cases. He's kept my record from being practically one hundred per cent. I knew him before he went loony, and I know the fam'ly, so I undertook to help out rounding him up. Well, sir, he was gone slick as a whistle, for all we knew the man was as good as dead long while ago. Now we never might have caught up with him, but do you know what he did? Well, sir, about two weeks ago his old mother gets a letter from him, and in that letter, what do you reckon she found? Well, it was a check on that little bank in town for eight hundred and fifty dollars, just like that; the letter wasn't nothing much, just said he was sending her a few little savings, she might need something, but there it was, name, postmark, date, everything. The old woman practically lost her mind with joy. She's gettin' childish, and it looked like she kinda forgot that her only living son killed his brother and went loony. Mr. Helton said he was getting along all right, and for her not to tell nobody. Well, natchally, she couldn't keep it to herself, with that check to cash and everything. So that's how I come to know." His feelings got the better of him. "You coulda knocked me down with a feather." He shook hands with himself and rocked, wagging his head, going "Heh, heh," in his throat. Mr. Thompson felt the corners of his mouth turning down. Why, the dirty low-down hound, sneaking around spying into other people's business like that. Collecting blood money, that's what it was! Let him talk!

"Yea, well, that musta been a surprise all right," he said, trying to hold his voice even. "I'd say a surprise."

"Well, siree," said Mr. Hatch, "the more I got to thinking about it, the more I just come to the conclusion that I'd better look into the matter a little, and so I talked to the old woman. She's pretty decrepit, now, half blind and all, but she was all for taking the first train out and going to see her son. I put it up to her square—how she was too feeble for the trip, and all. So, just as a favor to her, I told her for my expenses I'd come down and see Mr. Helton and bring her back all the news about him. She gave me a new shirt she made herself by hand, and a big Swedish kind of cake to bring to him, but I musta mislaid them along the road somewhere. It don't reely matter, though, he prob'ly ain't in any state of mind to appreciate 'em."

Mr. Thompson sat up and turning round on the log looked at Mr. Hatch and asked as quietly as he could, "And now what are you aiming to do? That's the question."

Mr. Hatch slouched up to his feet and shook himself. "Well, I come all prepared for a little scuffle," he said. "I got the handcuffs," he said, "but I don't want no violence if I can help it. I didn't want to say nothing around the countryside, making an uproar. I figured the two of us could overpower him." He reached into his big inside pocket and pulled them out. Handcuffs, for God's sake, thought Mr. Thompson. Coming round on a peaceable afternoon worrying a man, and making trouble, and fishing handcuffs out of his pocket on a decent family homestead, as if it was all in the day's work.

Mr. Thompson, his head buzzing, got up too. "Well," he said, roundly, "I want to tell you I think you've got a mighty sorry job on hand, you sure must be hard up for something to do, and now I want to give you a good piece of advice. You just drop the idea that you're going to come here and make trouble for Mr. Helton, and the quicker you drive that hired rig away from my front gate the better I'll be satisfied."

Mr. Hatch put one handcuff in his outside pocket, the other dangling down. He pulled his hat down over his eyes, and reminded Mr. Thompson of a sheriff, somehow. He didn't seem in the least nervous, and didn't take up Mr. Thompson's words. He said, "Now listen just a minute, it ain't reasonable to suppose that a man like yourself is going to stand in the way of getting an escaped loonatic back to the asylum where he belongs. Now I know it's enough to throw you off, coming sudden like this, but fact is I counted on your being a respectable man and helping me out to see that justice is done. Now a course, if you won't help, I'll have to look around for help somewheres else. It won't look very good to your neighbors that you was harbring an escaped loonatic who killed his own brother, and then you refused to give him up. It will look mighty funny."

Mr. Thompson knew almost before he heard the words that it would look funny. It would put him in a mighty awkward position. He said, "But I've been trying to tell you all along that the man ain't loony now. He's been perfectly harmless for nine years. He's—he's—"

Mr. Thompson couldn't think how to describe how it was with Mr. Helton. "Why, he's been like one of the family," he said, "the best standby a man ever had." Mr. Thompson tried to see his way out. It was a fact Mr. Helton might go loony again any minute, and now this fellow talking around the country would put Mr. Thompson in a fix. It was a terrible position. He couldn't think of any way out. "You're crazy," Mr. Thompson roared suddenly, "you're the crazy one around here, you're crazier than he ever was! You get off this place or I'll handcuff you and turn you over to the law. You're trespassing," shouted Mr. Thompson. "Get out of here before I knock you down!"

He took a step towards the fat man, who backed off, shrinking, "Try it, try it, go ahead!" and then something happened that Mr. Thompson tried hard afterwards to piece together in his mind, and in fact it never did come straight. He saw the fat man with his long bowie knife in his hand, he saw Mr. Helton come round the corner on the run, his long jaw dropped, his arms swinging, his eyes wild. Mr. Helton came in between them, fists doubled up, then stopped short, glaring at the fat man, his big frame seemed to collapse, he trembled like a shied horse; and then the fat man drove at him, knife in one hand, handcuffs in the other. Mr. Thompson saw it coming, he saw the blade going into Mr. Helton's stomach, he knew he had the ax out of the log in his own hands, felt his arms go up over his head and bring the ax down on Mr. Hatch's head as if he were stunning a beef.

Mrs. Thompson had been listening uneasily for some time to the voices going on, one of them strange to her, but she was too tired at first to get up and come out to see what was going on. The confused shouting that rose so suddenly brought her up to her feet and out across the front porch without her slippers, hair half-braided. Shading her eyes, she saw first Mr. Helton, running all stooped over through the orchard, running like a man with dogs after him; and Mr. Thompson supporting himself on the ax handle was leaning over shaking by the shoulder a man Mrs. Thompson had never seen, who lay doubled up with the top of his head smashed and the blood running away in a greasy-looking puddle. Mr. Thompson without taking his hand from the man's shoulder, said in a thick voice, "He killed Mr. Helton, he killed him, I saw him do it. I had to knock him out," he called loudly, "but he won't come to."

Mrs. Thompson said in a faint scream, "Why, yonder goes Mr. Helton," and she pointed. Mr. Thompson pulled himself up and looked where she pointed. Mrs. Thompson sat down slowly against the side of the house and began to slide forward on her face; she felt as if she were drowning, she couldn't rise to the top somehow, and her only thought was she was glad the boys were not there, they were out, fishing at Halifax, oh, God, she was glad the boys were not there.

Mr. and Mrs. Thompson drove up to their barn about sunset. Mr. Thompson handed the reins to his wife, got out to open the big door, and Mrs. Thompson guided old Jim in under the roof. The buggy was gray with dust and age, Mrs. Thompson's face was gray with dust and weariness, and Mr. Thompson's face, as he stood at the horse's head and began unhitching, was gray except for the dark blue of his freshly shaven jaws and chin, gray and blue and caved in, but patient, like a dead man's face.

Mrs. Thompson stepped down to the hard packed manure of the barn floor, and shook out her light flower-sprigged dress. She wore her smoked glasses, and her wide shady leghorn hat with the wreath of exhausted pink and blue forget-me-nots hid her forehead, fixed in a knot of distress.

The horse hung his head, raised a huge sigh and flexed his stiffened legs. Mr. Thompson's words came up muffled and hollow. "Poor ole Jim," he said, clearing his throat, "he looks pretty sunk in the ribs. I guess he's had a hard week." He lifted the harness up in one piece, slid it off and Jim walked out of the shafts halting a little. "Well, this is the last time," Mr. Thompson said, still talking to Jim. "Now you can get a good rest."

Mrs. Thompson closed her eyes behind her smoked glasses. The last time, and high time, and they should never have gone at all. She did not need her glasses any more, now the good darkness was coming down again, but her eyes ran full of tears steadily, though she was not crying, and she felt better with the glasses, safer, hidden away behind them. She took out her handkerchief with her hands shaking as they had been shaking ever since *that day*, and blew her nose. She said, "I see the boys have lighted the lamps. I hope they've started the stove going."

She stepped along the rough path holding her thin dress and starched petticoats around her, feeling her way between the sharp small stones, leaving the barn because she could hardly bear to be near Mr. Thompson, advancing slowly towards the house because she dreaded going there. Life was all one dread, the faces of her neighbors, of her boys, of her husband, the face of the whole world, the shape of her own house in the darkness, the very smell of the grass and the trees were horrible to her. There was no place to go, only one thing to do, bear it somehow—but how? She asked herself that question often. How was she going to keep on living now? Why had she lived at all? She wished now she had died one of those times when she had been so sick, instead of living on for this.

The boys were in the kitchen; Herbert was looking at the funny pictures from last Sunday's newspapers, the Katzenjammer Kids and Happy Hooligan. His chin was in his hands and his elbows on the table, and he was really reading and looking at the pictures, but his face was unhappy. Arthur was building the fire, adding kindling a stick at a time, watching it catch and blaze. His face was heavier and darker than Herbert's, but he was a little sullen by nature; Mrs. Thompson thought, he takes things harder, too. Arthur said, "Hello, Momma," and went on with his work. Herbert swept the papers together and moved over on the bench. They were big boys—fifteen and seventeen, and Arthur as tall as his father. Mrs. Thompson sat down beside Herbert, taking off her hat. She said, "I guess you're hungry. We were late today. We went the Log Hollow road, it's rougher than ever." Her pale mouth drooped with a sad fold on either side.

"I guess you saw the Mannings, then," said Herbert.

"Yes, and the Fergusons, and the Allbrights, and that new family McClellan."

"Anybody say anything?" asked Herbert.

"Nothing much, you know how it's been all along, some of them keeps saying, yes, they know it was a clear case and a fair trial and they say how glad they are your papa came out so well, and all that, some of 'em do, anyhow, but it looks like they don't really take sides with him. I'm about wore out," she said, the tears rolling again from under her dark glasses. "I don't know what good it does, but your papa can't seem to rest unless he's telling how it happened. I don't know."

"I don't think it does any good, not a speck," said Arthur, moving away from the stove. "It just keeps the whole question stirred up in people's minds. Everybody will go round telling what he heard, and the whole thing is going to get worse mixed up than ever. It just makes matters worse. I wish you could get Papa to stop driving round the country talking like that."

"Your papa knows best," said Mrs. Thompson. "You oughtn't to criticize him. He's got enough to put up with without that."

Arthur said nothing, his jaw stubborn. Mr. Thompson came in, his eyes hollowed out and dead-looking, his thick hands gray white and seamed from washing them clean every day before he started out to see the neighbors to tell them his side of the story. He was wearing his Sunday clothes, a thick pepper-and-salt-colored suit with a black string tie.

Mrs. Thompson stood up, her head swimming. "Now you-all get out of the kitchen, it's too hot in here and I need room. I'll get us a little bite of supper, if you'll just get out and give me some room."

They went as if they were glad to go, the boys outside, Mr. Thompson into his bedroom. She heard him groaning to himself as he took off his shoes, and heard the bed creak as he lay down. Mrs. Thompson opened the icebox and felt the sweet coldness flow out if it; she had never expected to have an icebox, much less did she hope to afford to keep it filled with ice. It still seemed like a miracle, after two or three years. There was the food, cold and clean, all ready to be warmed over. She would never have had that icebox if Mr. Helton hadn't happened along one day, just by the strangest luck; so saving, and so managing, so good, thought Mrs. Thompson, her heart swelling until she feared she would faint again, standing there with the door open and leaning her head upon it. She simply could not bear to remember Mr. Helton, with his long sad face and silent ways, who had always been so quiet and harmless, who had worked so hard and helped Mr. Thompson so much, running through the hot fields and woods, being hunted like a mad dog, everybody turning out with ropes and guns and sticks to catch and tie him. Oh, God, said Mrs. Thompson in a long dry moan, kneeling before the icebox and fumbling inside for the dishes, even if they did pile mattresses all over the jail floor and against the walls, and five men there to hold him to keep him from hurting himself any more, he was already hurt too badly, he couldn't have lived anyway. Mr. Barbee, the sheriff, told her about it. He said, well, they didn't aim to harm him but they had to catch him, he was crazy as a loon; he picked up rocks and tried to brain every man that got near him. He had two harmonicas in his jumper pocket, said the sheriff, but they fell out in the scuffle, and Mr. Helton tried to pick 'em up again, and that's when they finally got him. "They *had* to be rough, Miz Thompson, he fought like a wildcat." Yes, thought Mrs. Thompson again with the same bitterness, of course, they had to be rough. They always have to be rough. Mr. Thompson can't argue with a man and get him off the place peaceably; no, she thought, standing up and shutting the icebox, he has to kill somebody, he has to be a murderer and ruin his boys' lives and cause Mr. Helton to be killed like a mad dog.

Her thoughts stopped with a little soundless explosion, cleared and began again. The rest of Mr. Helton's harmonicas were still in the shack, his tune ran in Mrs. Thompson's head at certain times of the day. She missed it in the evenings. It seemed so strange she had never known the name of that song, nor what it meant, until after Mr. Helton was gone. Mrs. Thompson, trembling in the knees, took a drink of water at the sink and poured the red beans into the baking dish, and began to roll the pieces of chicken in flour to fry them. There was a time, she said to herself, when I thought I had neighbors and friends, there was a time when we could hold up our heads, there was a time when my husband hadn't killed a man and I could tell the truth to anybody about anything.

Mr. Thompson, turning on his bed, figured that he had done all he could, he'd just try to let the matter rest from now on. His lawyer, Mr. Burleigh, had told him right at the beginning, "Now you keep calm and collected. You've got a fine case, even if you haven't got witnesses. Your wife must sit in court, she'll be a powerful argument with the jury. You just plead not guilty and I'll do the rest. The trial is going to be a mere formality, you haven't got a thing to worry about. You'll be clean out of this before you know it." And to make talk Mr. Burleigh had got to telling about all the men he knew around the country who for one reason or another had been forced to kill somebody, always in self-defense, and there just wasn't anything to it at all. He even told about how his own father in the old days had shot and killed a man just for setting foot inside his gate when he told him not to. "Sure, I shot the scoundrel," said Mr. Burleigh's father, "in self-defense; I *told* him I'd shoot him if he set his foot in my yard, and he did, and I did." There had been bad blood between them for years, Mr. Burleigh said, and his father had waited a long time to catch the other fellow in the wrong, and when he did he certainly made the most of his opportunity.

"But Mr. Hatch, as I told you," Mr. Thompson had said, "made a pass at Mr. Helton with his bowie knife. That's why I took a hand."

"All the better," said Mr. Burleigh. "That stranger hadn't any right coming to your house on such an errand. Why, hell," said Mr. Burleigh, "that wasn't even manslaughter you committed. So now you just hold your horses and keep your shirt on. And don't say one word without I tell you."

Wasn't even manslaughter. Mr. Thompson had to cover Mr. Hatch with a piece of wagon canvas and ride to town to tell the sheriff. It had been hard on Ellie. When they got back, the sheriff and the coroner and two deputies, they found her sitting beside the road, on a low bridge over a gulley, about half a mile from the place. He had taken her up behind his saddle and got her back to the house. He had already told the sheriff that his wife had witnessed the whole business, and now he had time, getting her to her room and in bed, to tell her what to say if they asked anything. He had left out the part about Mr. Helton being crazy all along, but it came out at the trial. By Mr. Burleigh's advice Mr. Thompson had pretended to be perfectly ignorant; Mr. Hatch hadn't said a word about that. Mr. Thompson pretended to believe that Mr. Hatch had just come looking for Mr. Helton to settle old scores, and the two members of Mr. Hatch's family who had come down to try to get Mr. Thompson convicted didn't get anywhere, at all. It hadn't been much of a trial, Mr. Burleigh saw to that. He had charged a reasonable fee, and Mr. Thompson had paid him and felt grateful, but after it was over Mr. Burleigh didn't seem pleased to see him when he got to dropping into the office to talk it over, telling him things that had slipped his mind at first: trying to explain what an ornery low hound Mr. Hatch had been, anyhow. Mr. Burleigh seemed to have lost his interest; he looked sour and upset when he saw Mr. Thompson at the door. Mr. Thompson kept saying to himself that he'd got off, all right, just as Mr. Burleigh had predicted, but, but—and it was right there that Mr. Thompson's mind stuck, squirming like an angleworm on a fishhook: he had killed Mr. Hatch, and he was a murderer. That was the truth about himself that Mr. Thompson couldn't grasp, even when he said the word to himself. Why, he had not even once *thought* of killing anybody, much less Mr. Hatch, and if Mr. Helton hadn't come out so unexpectedly, hearing the row, why, then—but then, Mr. Helton had come on the run that way to help him. What he couldn't understand was what happened next. He had seen Mr. Hatch go after Mr. Helton with the knife, he had seen the point, blade up, go into Mr. Helton's stomach and slice up like you slice a hog, but when they finally caught Mr. Helton there wasn't a knife scratch on him. Mr. Thompson knew he had the ax in his own hands and felt himself lifting it, but he couldn't remember hitting Mr. Hatch. He couldn't remember it. He couldn't. He remembered only that he had been determined to stop Mr. Hatch from cutting Mr. Helton. If he was given a chance he could explain the whole matter. At the trial they hadn't let him talk. They just asked questions and he answered yes or no, and they never did get to the core of the matter. Since the trial, now, every day for a week he had washed and shaved and put on his best clothes and had taken Ellie with him to tell every neighbor he had that he never killed Mr. Hatch on purpose, and what good did it do? Nobody believed him. Even when he turned to Ellie and said, "You was there, you saw it, didn't you?" and Ellie spoke up, saying, "Yes, that's the truth. Mr. Thompson was trying to save Mr. Helton's life," and he added, "If you don't believe me, you can believe my wife. She won't lie," Mr. Thompson saw something in all their faces that disheartened him, made him feel empty and tired out. They didn't believe he was not a murderer.

Even Ellie never said anything to comfort him. He hoped she would say finally, "I remember now, Mr. Thompson, I really did come round the corner in time to see everything. It's not a lie, Mr. Thompson. Don't you worry." But as they drove together in silence, with the days still hot and dry, shortening for fall, day after day, the buggy jolting in the ruts, she said nothing; they grew to dread the sight of another house, and the people in it: all houses looked alike now, and the people—old neighbors or new—had the same expression when Mr. Thompson told them why he had come and began his story. Their eyes looked as if someone had pinched the eyeball at the back; they shriveled and the light went out of them. Some of them sat with fixed tight smiles trying to be friendly. "Yes, Mr. Thompson, we know how you must feel. It must be terrible for you, Mrs. Thompson. Yes, you know, I've about come to the point where I believe in such a thing as killing in self-defense. Why, certainly, we believe you, Mr. Thompson, why shouldn't we believe you? Didn't you have a perfectly fair and above-board trial? Well, now, natchally, Mr. Thompson, we think you done right."

Mr. Thompson was satisfied they didn't think so. Sometimes the air around him was so thick with their blame he fought and pushed with his fists, and the sweat broke out all over him, he shouted his story in a dust-choked voice, he would fairly bellow at last: "My wife, here, you know her, she was there, she saw and heard it all, if you don't believe me, ask her, she won't lie!" and Mrs. Thompson, with her hands knotted together, aching, her chin trembling, would never fail to say: "Yes, that's right, that's the truth—"

The last straw had been laid on today, Mr. Thompson decided. Tom Allbright, an old beau of Ellie's, why, he had squired Ellie around a whole summer, had come out to meet them when they drove up, and standing there bareheaded had stopped them from getting out. He had looked past them with an embarrassed frown on his face, telling them his wife's sister was there with a raft of young ones, and the house was pretty full and everything upset, or he'd ask them to come in. "We've been thinking of trying to get up to your place one of these days," said Mr. Allbright, moving away trying to look busy, "we've been mighty occupied up here of late." So they had to say, "Well, we just happened to be driving this way," and go on. "The Allbrights," said Mrs. Thompson, "always was fair-weather friends." "They look out for number one, that's a fact," said Mr. Thompson. But it was cold comfort to them both.

Finally Mrs. Thompson had given up. "Let's go home," she said. "Old Jim's tired and thirsty, and we've gone far enough."

Mr. Thompson said, "Well, while we're out this way, we might as well stop at the McClellans'." They drove in, and asked a little cotton-haired boy if his mamma and papa were at home. Mr. Thompson wanted to see them. The little boy stood gazing with his mouth open, then galloped into the house shouting, "Mommer, Popper, come out hyah. That man that kilt Mr. Hatch has come ter see yer!"

The man came out in his sock feet, with one gallus up, the other broken and dangling, and said, "Light down, Mr. Thompson, and come in. The ole woman's washing, but she'll git here." Mrs. Thompson, feeling her way, stepped down and sat in a broken rocking-chair on the porch that sagged under her feet. The woman of the house, barefooted, in a calico wrapper, sat on the edge of the porch, her fat sallow face full of curiosity. Mr. Thompson began, "Well, as I reckon you happen to know, I've had some strange troubles lately, and, as the feller says, it's not the kind of trouble that happens to a man every day in the year, and there's some things I don't want no misunderstanding about in the neighbors' minds, so—" He halted and stumbled forward, and the two listening faces took on a mean look, a greedy, despising look, a look that said plain as day, "My, you must be a purty sorry feller to come round worrying about what *we* think, *we* know you wouldn't be here if you had anybody else to turn to—my, I wouldn't lower myself that much, myself." Mr. Thompson was ashamed of himself, he was suddenly in a rage, he'd like to knock their dirty skunk heads together, the low-down white trash—but he held himself down and went on to the end. "My wife will tell you," he said, and this was the hardest place, because Ellie always without moving a muscle seemed to stiffen as if somebody had threatened to hit her; "ask my wife, she won't lie."

"It's true, I saw it—"

"Well, now," said the man, drily, scratching his ribs inside his shirt, "that sholy is too bad. Well, now, I kaint see what we've got to do with all this here, however. I kaint see no good reason for us to git mixed up in these murder matters, I shore kaint. Whichever way you look at it, it ain't none of my business. However, it's mighty nice of you-all to come around and give us the straight of it, fur we've heerd some mighty queer yarns about it, mighty queer, I golly you couldn't hardly make head ner tail of it."

"Evvybody goin' round shootin' they heads off," said the woman. "Now we don't hold with killin'; the Bible says—"

"Shet yer trap," said the man, "and keep it shet 'r I'll shet it fer yer. Now it shore looks like to me—"

"We mustn't linger," said Mrs. Thompson, unclasping her hands. "We've lingered too long now. It's getting late, and we've far to go." Mr. Thompson took the hint and followed her. The man and the woman lolled against their rickety porch poles and watched them go.

Now lying on his bed, Mr. Thompson knew the end had come. Now, this minute, lying in the bed where he had slept with Ellie for eighteen years; under this roof where he had laid the shingles when he was waiting to get married; there as he was with his whiskers already sprouting since his shave that morning; with his fingers feeling his bony chin, Mr. Thompson felt he was a dead man. He was dead to his other life, he had got to the end of something without knowing why, and he had to make a fresh start, he did not know how. Something different was going to begin, he didn't know what. It was in some way not his business. He didn't feel he was going to have much to do with it. He got up, aching, hollow, and went out to the kitchen where Mrs. Thompson was just taking up the supper.

"Call the boys," said Mrs. Thompson. They had been down to the barn, and Arthur put out the lantern before hanging it on a nail near the door. Mr. Thompson didn't like their silence. They had hardly said a word about anything to him since that day. They seemed to avoid him, they ran the place together as if he wasn't there, and attended to everything without asking him for any advice. "What you boys been up to?" he asked, trying to be hearty. "Finishing your chores?"

"No, sir," said Arthur, "there ain't much to do. Just greasing some axles." Herbert said nothing. Mrs. Thompson bowed her head: "For these and all Thy blessings. . . . Amen," she whispered weakly, and the Thompsons sat there with their eyes down and their faces sorrowful, as if they were at a funeral.

Every time he shut his eyes, trying to sleep, Mr. Thompson's mind started up and began to run like a rabbit. It jumped from one thing to another, trying to pick up a trail here or there that would straighten out what had happened that day he killed Mr. Hatch. Try as he might, Mr. Thompson's mind would not go anywhere that it had not already been, he could not see anything but what he had seen once, and he knew that was not right. If he had not seen straight that first time, then everything about his killing Mr. Hatch was wrong from start to finish, and there was nothing more to be done about it, he might just as well give up. It still seemed to him that he had done, maybe not the right thing, but the only thing he could do, that day, but had he? *Did he have to kill Mr. Hatch?* He had never seen a man he hated more, the minute he laid eyes on him. He knew in his bones the fellow was there for trouble. What seemed so funny now was this: Why hadn't he just told Mr. Hatch to get out before he ever even got in?

Mrs. Thompson, her arms crossed on her breast, was lying beside him, perfectly still, but she seemed awake, somehow. "Asleep, Ellie?"

After all, he might have got rid of him peaceably, or maybe he might have had to overpower him and put those handcuffs on him and turn him over to the sheriff for disturbing the peace. The most they could have done was to lock Mr. Hatch up while he cooled off for a few days, or fine him a little something. He would try to think of things he might have said to Mr. Hatch. Why, let's see, I could just have said, Now look here, Mr. Hatch, I want to talk to you as man to man. But his brain would go empty. What could he have said or done? But if he *could* have done anything else almost except kill Mr. Hatch, then nothing would have happened to Mr. Helton. Mr. Thompson hardly ever thought of Mr. Helton. His mind just skipped over him and went on. If he stopped to think about Mr. Helton he'd never in God's world get anywhere. He tried to imagine how it might all have been, this very night even, if Mr. Helton were still safe and sound out in his shack playing his tune about feeling so good in the morning, drinking up all the wine so you'd feel even better; and Mr. Hatch safe in jail somewhere, mad as hops, maybe, but out of harm's way and ready to listen to reason and to repent of his meanness, the dirty, yellow-livered hound coming around persecuting an innocent man and ruining a whole family that never harmed him! Mr. Thompson felt the veins of his forehead start up, his fists clutched as if they seized an ax handle, the sweat broke out on him, he bounded up from the bed with a yell smothered in his throat, and Ellie started up after him, crying out, "Oh, oh, don't! Don't! Don't!" as if she were having a nightmare. He stood shaking until his bones rattled in him, crying hoarsely, "Light the lamp, light the lamp, Ellie."

Instead, Mrs. Thompson gave a shrill weak scream, almost the same scream he had heard on that day she came around the house when he was standing there with the ax in his hand. He could not see her in the dark, but she was on the bed, rolling violently. He felt for her in horror, and his groping hands found her arms, up, and her own hands pulling her hair straight out from her head, her neck strained back, and the tight screams strangling her. He shouted out for Arthur, for Herbert. "Your mother!" he bawled, his voice cracking. As he held Mrs. Thompson's arms, the boys came tumbling in, Arthur with the lamp above his head. By this light Mr. Thompson saw Mrs. Thompson's eyes, wide open, staring dreadfully at him, the tears pouring. She sat up at sight of the boys, and held out one arm towards them, the hand wagging in a crazy circle, then dropped on her back again, and suddenly went limp. Arthur set the lamp on the table and turned on Mr. Thompson. "She's scared," he said, "she's scared to death." His face was in a knot of rage, his fists were doubled up, he faced his father as if he meant to strike him. Mr. Thompson's jaw fell, he was so surprised he stepped back from the bed. Herbert went to the other side. They stood on each side of Mrs. Thompson and watched Mr. Thompson as if he were a dangerous wild beast. "What did you do to her?" shouted Arthur, in a grown man's voice. "You touch her again and I'll blow your heart out!" Herbert was pale and his cheek twitched, but he was on Arthur's side; he would do what he could to help Arthur.

Mr. Thompson had no fight left in him. His knees bent as he stood, his chest collapsed. "Why, Arthur," he said, his words crumbling and his breath coming short. "She's fainted again. Get the ammonia." Arthur did not move. Herbert brought the bottle, and handed it, shrinking, to his father.

Mr. Thompson held it under Mrs. Thompson's nose. He poured a little in the palm of his hand and rubbed it on her forehead. She gasped and opened her eyes and turned her head away from him. Herbert began a doleful hopeless sniffling. "Mamma," he kept saying, "Mamma, don't die."

"I'm all right," Mrs. Thompson said. "Now don't you worry around. Now Herbert, you mustn't do that. I'm all right." She closed her eyes. Mr. Thompson began pulling on his best pants; he put on his socks and shoes. The boys sat on each side of the bed, watching Mrs. Thompson's face. Mr. Thompson put on his shirt and coat. He said, "I reckon I'll ride over and get the doctor. Don't look like all this fainting is a good sign. Now you just keep watch until I get back." They listened, but said nothing. He said, "Don't you get any notions in your head. I never did your mother any harm in my life, on purpose." He went out, and, looking back, saw Herbert staring at him from under his brows, like a stranger. "You'll know how to look after her," said Mr. Thompson.

Mr. Thompson went through the kitchen. There he lighted the lantern, took a thin pad of scratch paper and a stub pencil from the shelf where the boys kept their schoolbooks. He swung the lantern on his arm and reached into the cupboard where he kept the guns. The shotgun was there to his hand, primed and ready, a man never knows when he may need a shotgun. He went out of the house without looking around, or looking back when he had left it, passed his barn without seeing it, and struck out to the farthest end of his fields, which ran for half a mile to the east. So many blows had been struck at Mr. Thompson and from so many directions he couldn't stop any more to find out where he was hit. He walked on, over plowed ground and over meadow, going through barbed wire fences cautiously, putting his gun through first; he could almost see in the dark, now his eyes were used to it. Finally he came to the last fence; here he sat down, back against a post, lantern at his side, and, with the pad on his knee, moistened the stub pencil and began to write:

"Before Almighty God, the great judge of all before who I am about to appear, I do hereby solemnly swear that I did not take the life of Mr. Homer T. Hatch on purpose. It was done in defense of Mr. Helton. I did not aim to hit him with the ax but only to keep him off Mr. Helton. He aimed a blow at Mr. Helton who was not looking for it. It was my belief at the time that Mr. Hatch would of taken the life of Mr. Helton if I did not interfere. I have told all this to the judge and the jury and they let me off but nobody believes it. This is the only way I can prove I am not a cold blooded murderer like everybody seems to think. If I had been in Mr. Helton's place he would of done the same for me. I still think I done the only thing there was to do. My wife—"

Mr. Thompson stopped here to think a while. He wet the pencil point with the tip of his tongue and marked out the last two words. He sat a while blacking out the words until he had made a neat oblong patch where they had been, and started again:

"It was Mr. Homer T. Hatch who came to do wrong to a harmless man. He caused all this trouble and he deserved to die but I am sorry it was me who had to kill him."

He licked the point of his pencil again, and signed his full name carefully, folded the paper and put it in his outside pocket. Taking off his right shoe and sock, he set the butt of the shotgun along the ground with the twin barrels pointed towards his head. It was very awkward. He thought about this a little, leaning his head against the gun mouth. He was trembling and his head was drumming until he was deaf and blind, but he lay down flat on the earth on his side, drew the barrel under his chin and fumbled for the trigger with his great toe. That way he could work it.

TOPICS FOR PAPERS AND DISCUSSION

1. *Creating one's own fate.* If Mr. Thompson has created his own fate, how has he done so? Take into account his attitude toward work, his expectations for and use of Ellie, his peculiar method of disciplining his sons, and his overt and covert attitudes toward everyone, especially Helton and Hatch. Examine Porter's ironic use of Thompson's trips to town and elsewhere, and her repetitive comments about his character as manifest in his appearance and bearing. Consider incidental character traits such as Thompson's joking when seriousness is called for, his typical response in crises, and his moral, ethical, and religious attitudes.
2. *Motifs that point to the themes.* In literature, repetitions of motifs usually point to central ideas. Consider these, for instance, in trying to arrive at a statement of theme: "stranger," "stranger in a strange land," and "proud, stiff-necked man" (which may be biblical allusions); various kinds of restrictive choices, judgments, and

actions; joking (including the reference to comic strips); repetitive music; diseased sight. How do the phrases and words "god's world," "stumped," "blink," "blasted"-"shoot"-"gun"-"killing," "stiff," and "that's all right" function?

3. *The relationship of structure to theme.* Each of the four sections that come before and after the very short central passage (p. 354) is devoted to what separate aspects of the Thompsons' lives? What is the general theme of the fifth, pivotal section? Since it is central, what does it suggest about the inevitability of the last half of the action when balanced against the first half? Consider the relationship to the novel's time span, noted at the beginning (p. 334). How do you account for reversals, contrasts, parallelism (exact or antithetical) of events, actions, and settings?
4. *The thematic significance of journeys.* In fiction, traveling often signifies discovery, longing, initiation, and the changing of one's spiritual, ethical, or social condition; it can even be a way of revealing the meaning of existence. In addition, encounters along the way often uncover and test previously unseen facets of character. Explore the significance of the journeys in the novel: Mr. Thompson's initial trip to town; his trip to market; his taking Hatch around the house to the stumps; his journey to get the sheriff; his multiple journeys to visit his neighbors, especially the McClellans, after he has been cleared of the murder charge; his final journey with the gun. What is the significance to Thompson of Hatch's and Helton's various journeys?
5. *Some paired characters that point to the theme.* Attempt to deduce the meaning of these pairings: Thompson and Helton; Thompson and Hatch; Helton and Hatch; Thompson and his sons (as boys and as young men); Thompson and McClellan; Thompson and Burleigh's father; Thompson and the posse; Thompson and his wife; and finally Thompson and the various men he visits on his final series of journeys.
6. *Incipient and actual violence.* What does violence in all its manifestations signify thematically? What are meant by Thompson's method of handling the churn, his attitude toward his recently departed farmhands, his scoldings of Arthur and Herbert? What does the phrase "a man's work" signify? How are Ellie, Old Mr. Burleigh, and the neighbor men related to the theme of violence? Why are Hatch, Thompson, and Helton linked so closely in the murder scene? Explain Ellie's fear of her husband, Arthur's challenge to his father, and Thompson's final act of violence. How does all the submerged and overt violence summarize and give point to Thompson's suicide?
7. *Irony as a controlling device.* In the last four sections of the novel, the reader must reevaluate the tone of the first four in view of the repetition of much of the earlier material, often in somewhat changed

form. Explain how Porter controls our interpretations of the Thompsons and their fate in the first half. Concentrating solely on the first four sections, consider such elements as character, action, scene, motif, and symbol. For instance, Royal Earle is a relatively "good" man, but is he? Ellie has weak eyes, but what does she really not see? In some ways, Arthur, Herbert, Burleigh, Helton, and the neighbors are unlike Thompson, but how are they exactly like him?

8. *The "inexplicable" tragedy.* The Thompson family finds itself involved in and living a "tragedy," in the extended sense of that word. The nature of their tragic circumstances is apparently inexplicable to them, and certainly to Royal Earle. How and where does the author slowly and relentlessly show this tragic development from the apparently innocent decisions, attitudes, and actions of the characters and the community at large? Are the characters mere victims of chance and circumstance, society and place? Or are they to be understood as victims of themselves? Explain your choices.
9. *Affective scenes.* A number of scenes demand complex responses from the reader, for they lose much of their power and meaning if seen from only one vantage. Determine what multiple, if often apparently ambiguous, significances the following scenes convey: the pinching scene; the scene following Helton's shaking of Arthur and Herbert; the murder scene (consider that it is also humorous); the confrontation between Arthur and his father over Ellie after the McClellan visit; and the final scene. In analyzing these, consider your immediate feelings for the scene first; then, upon reflection and in light of Porter's consistently ironic treatment of the situation and characters, decide upon other possible vantages.
10. *The complex relationship of Ellie and Earle Thompson.* Why is their relationship not clear-cut and obvious? How are their conflicts revealed by the author's use of their sons? What scenes uncover unexpected depths and nuances hardly suspected, nuances which "humanize" even the stiff, proud, and self-satisfied Royal Earle Thompson and his "little woman" Ellie? How do they fail each other? Are failures naturally to be expected in any human relationship? Point out instances of rationalizations in their relationship. How, indeed, is Ellie partially responsible for Earle's attitudes? What are the stages of her growing awareness of Royal Earle's true nature? Include the final bedroom scene with all its terror and its comedy. What is her reaction at that point to her beloved husband? Why should such "good" people come to such an end? What in their relationship pointed to the inevitability of murder, rejection, and suicide?
11. *Point of view.* What advantages do you see in the point of view Porter uses to relate the experience of Thompson? Is the point of view consistently held? When it shifts, if it does, what purpose is served?

What would be lost or gained if another point of view were used? For instance, why not see the entire experience from a first-person narrative point of view (Arthur's or Herbert's), which would have the virtue of dramatic immediacy? What knowledge about character or the immediate world is conveyed by using precisely the point of view chosen?

12. *The symbolic use of names.* It can be said with a good deal of certainty that Porter has given her characters symbolic or allegorical names. Determine what these names tell us about the characters themselves and about their relationships to one another and to the theme: Royal Earle Thompson, Olaf Eric Helton, Homer T. Hatch, the Hatchers of Mountain City, Ellie Bridges Thompson of Mountain City, Crazy Aunt Ida, Herbert and Arthur Thompson, Lawyer Burleigh, and the final visitation group: Manning, Ferguson, Allbright, and McClellan.
13. *Naturalism and symbolism.* Check an encyclopedia of literary terms for the definition of *naturalism*. How closely does *Noon Wine* follow the general principles given for the term? How are they helpful in deriving the intentions of the novel? In what ways does the story deviate from the principles? Are these deviations enriching? In what manner are they merely erratic or especially meaningful? Also show how the novel's rich and pervasive symbolism is compatible with its naturalistic qualities, and how the two elements actually enhance and support each other.
14. *Time, place, social conditions.* The headnote to the novel suggests that these three factors are important in judging the story, but how is this true? Would the novel's experiences and characters ring true if it were set in contemporary rural Texas, rural California, or Oregon? What might need to be changed, if anything, and why? Entertain the idea that the central experience and ideas are so universal that they transcend time, place, and even specific social conditions. Describe as fully as you can the social atmosphere of the novel. Be sure to consider the town and neighbors whom we do not see but of whom we hear a great deal.
15. *Myth and archetype.* Comment on the use (whether metaphorical, psychological, or historical) of some of the following fragments of myth and archetype: the wasteland which becomes a demiparadise; the idea of a land of milk and honey ("that's a blessing," says Ellie); the fallen Adam ("Well, I'll be damned," says Royal Earle) and Eve expelled from Eden; their two sons; the shunned and ostracized sinner; the Ancient Mariner; the magic stranger, whether Dionysus, Hercules, or Moses; opposition to the weak, sick, or maimed king, leader, or father; ritual murder and suicide; opposition to gross, legal self-righteousness. Consider also such archetypal symbolism as light and darkness, noise and music, sight and blindness, normality and madness.

16. *"Things" that represent ideas.* Examine the ideas expressed by the following pairs of things in the novel: the choked and then free-flowing spring; the harmonica and other musical instruments; the trashy and ordered yard; the unhinged and hinged gate; sweet and plain chewing tobacco; eyes with and without glasses; handcuffs and straitjackets; the churn and the axe; hens and pigs; Earle's "loud mouth" and the gun barrel under his chin; Hatch's dirty blue bandanna and Ellie's blue eyes; "Likker" and the Scandahoovian song, "Noon Wine."
17. *Microcosm and macrocosm through close analysis.* Section four (pp. 345–354) serves a special purpose as an epitomization of Thompson, past, present, and future. Examine it carefully. How does Porter make it serve as a microcosm for the larger world and for the events in which it is embedded? Why is a time shift used here, and what is gained? What "philosophy" does Thompson live by? How does it pay off? What is his relationship to Ellie, Helton, and his sons? How are these issues reflected later when larger, more important things are at stake? Explain the rhythmic building of the idea of violence in this section and its relationship to section nine (pp. 377–381).
18. *Thesis, antithesis, synthesis.* Images, metaphors, symbols, actions, characters, and settings in the novel can be examined by applying the pattern of thesis, antithesis, and possibly synthesis to them. Choose one or several of the images, actions, characters, etc., and demonstrate the structuring of the ideas or themes of the novel through the use of this paradigm. For example, if we examine characters and what they signify, thesis includes Thompson, Hatch, and McClellan; antithesis includes Ellie, Helton, and his mother; synthesis includes Arthur, Herbert, and Allbright.
19. *Dramatic scenes and general summary scenes.* What is there about the dramatic scenes that renders them more important than the scenes of general summary? Discuss the following: Mr. and Mrs. Thompson's first meetings with Helton, the dinner and chastisement scene after Helton shakes Arthur and Herbert, the meeting of Thompson and Hatch, the Thompson-McClellan encounter, etc. What is accomplished by shifting to Thompson's thoughts exclusively in the following instances: his judgment of Helton and his methods of work, his recounting the story of the trial and its aftermath to himself, and his final scene? What is gained by the various shifts to Ellie's thoughts?
20. *Wordplay and clichés.* Comment on as many instances of wordplay as you can locate. What does the technique reveal about the characters, their principles, and their world? Consider such examples as swing, stump, saving and losing face, hatch, thatch, jovial, Scandahoovian (etc.), shucks, Ellen-McClellan, shooting off one's mouth, Bridges-bridge, Swede-sweet, slaughtering, crazy, lath-

ered up, cutting, funny, and many others. What does wordplay suggest about tone and about the way Porter views her characters? Contrast wordplay with the multiple clichés sewn through Thompson and Hatch's conversation.

Seize the Day

SAUL BELLOW

1

When it came to concealing his troubles, Tommy Wilhelm was not less capable than the next fellow. So at least he thought, and there was a certain amount of evidence to back him up. He had once been an actor—no, not quite, an extra—and he knew what acting should be. Also, he was smoking a cigar, and when a man is smoking a cigar, wearing a hat, he has an advantage; it is harder to find out how he feels. He came from the twenty-third floor down to the lobby on the mezzanine to collect his mail before breakfast, and he believed—he hoped—that he looked passably well: doing all right. It was a matter of sheer hope, because there was not much that he could add to his present effort. On the fourteenth floor he looked for his father to enter the elevator; they often met at this hour, on the way to breakfast. If he worried about his appearance it was mainly for his old father's sake. But there was no stop on the fourteenth, and the elevator sank and sank. Then the smooth door opened and the great dark red uneven carpet that covered the lobby billowed toward Wilhelm's feet. In the foreground the lobby was dark, sleepy. French drapes like sails kept out the sun, but three high, narrow windows were open, and in the blue air Wilhelm saw a pigeon about to light on the great chain that supported the marquee of the movie house directly underneath the lobby. For one moment he heard the wings beating strongly.

Most of the guests at the Hotel Gloriana were past the age of retirement. Along Broadway in the Seventies, Eighties, and Nineties, a great part of New York's vast population of old men and women lives. Unless the weather is too cold or wet they fill the benches about the tiny railed parks and along the subway gratings from Verdi Square to Columbia University, they crowd the shops and cafeterias, the dime stores, the tea-rooms, the bakeries, the beauty parlors, the reading rooms and club rooms. Among these old people at the Gloriana, Wilhelm felt out of place. He was comparatively young, in his middle forties, large and blond, with big shoulders; his back was heavy and strong, if already a little stooped or thickened. After breakfast the old guests sat down on the green leather armchairs and sofas in the lobby and began to gossip and look into the papers; they had nothing to do but wait out the day. But Wilhelm was used to an active life and liked to go out energetically in the morning. And for several months, because he had no position, he had kept up his morale by rising early; he was shaved and in the lobby by eight o'clock. He bought the paper and some cigars and drank a Coca-Cola or two before he went in to breakfast with his father. After breakfast—out, out, out to attend to business. The getting out had in itself become the chief business. But he had realized that he could not keep this up much longer, and today he was afraid. He was aware that his routine was about to break up and he sensed that a huge trouble long presaged but till now formless was due. Before evening, he'd know.

Nevertheless he followed his daily course and crossed the lobby.

Rubin, the man at the newsstand, had poor eyes. They may not have been actually weak but they were poor in expression, with lacy lids that furled down at the corners. He dressed well. It didn't seem necessary—he was behind the counter most of the time—but he dressed very well. He had on a rich brown suit; the cuffs embarrassed the hairs on his small hands. He wore a Countess Mara painted necktie. As Wilhelm approached, Rubin did not see him; he was looking out dreamily at the Hotel Ansonia, which was visible from his corner, several blocks away. The Ansonia, the neighborhood's great landmark, was built by Stanford White. It looks like a baroque palace from Prague or

Munich enlarged a hundred times, with towers, domes, huge swells and bubbles of metal gone green from exposure, iron fretwork and festoons. Black television antennae are densely planted on its round summits. Under the changes of weather it may look like marble or like sea water, black as slate in the fog, white as tufa in sunlight. This morning it looked like the image of itself reflected in deep water, white and cumulous above, with cavernous distortions underneath. Together, the two men gazed at it.

Then Rubin said, "Your dad is in to breakfast already, the old gentleman."

"Oh, yes? Ahead of me today?"

"That's a real knocked-out shirt you got on," said Rubin. "Where's it from, Saks?"

"No, it's a Jack Fagman—Chicago."

Even when his spirits were low, Wilhelm could still wrinkle his forehead in a pleasing way. Some of the slow, silent movements of his face were very attractive. He went back a step, as if to stand away from himself and get a better look at his shirt. His glance was comic, a comment upon his untidiness. He liked to wear good clothes, but once he had put it on each article appeared to go its own way. Wilhelm, laughing, panted a little; his teeth were small; his cheeks when he laughed and puffed grew round, and he looked much younger than his years. In the old days when he was a college freshman and wore a raccoon coat and a beanie on his large blond head his father used to say that, big as he was, he could charm a bird out of a tree. Wilhelm had great charm still.

"I like this dove-gray color," he said in his sociable, good-natured way. "It isn't washable. You have to send it to the cleaner. It never smells as good as washed. But it's a nice shirt. It cost sixteen, eighteen bucks."

This shirt had not been bought by Wilhelm; it was a present from his boss—his former boss, with whom he had had a falling out. But there was no reason why he should tell Rubin the history of it. Although perhaps Rubin knew—Rubin was the kind of man who knew, and knew and knew. Wilhelm also knew many things about Rubin, for that matter, about Rubin's wife and Rubin's business, Rubin's health. None of these could be mentioned, and the great weight of the unspoken left them little to talk about.

"Well, y'lookin' pretty sharp today," Rubin said.

And Wilhelm said gladly, "Am I? Do you really think so?" He could not believe it. He saw his reflection in the glass cupboard full of cigar boxes, among the grand seals and paper damask and the gold-embossed portraits of famous men, García, Edward the Seventh, Cyrus the Great. You had to allow for the darkness and deformations of the glass, but he thought he didn't look too good. A wide wrinkle like a comprehensive bracket sign was written upon his forehead, the point between his brows, and there were patches of brown on his dark blond skin. He began to be half amused at the shadow of his own marveling, troubled, desirous eyes, and his nostrils and his lips. Fair-haired hippopotamus!—that was how he looked to himself. He saw a big round face, a wide, flourishing red mouth, stump teeth. And the hat, too; and the cigar, too. I should have done hard labor all my life, he reflected. Hard honest labor that tires you out and makes you sleep. I'd have worked off my energy and felt better. Instead, I had to distinguish myself—yet.

He had put forth plenty of effort, but that was not the same as working hard, was it? And if as a young man he had got off to a bad start it was due to this very same face. Early in the nineteen-thirties, because of his striking looks, he had been very briefly considered star material, and he had gone to Hollywood. There for seven years, stubbornly, he had tried to become a screen artist. Long before that time his ambition or delusion had ended, but through pride and perhaps also through laziness he had remained in California. At last he turned to other things, but those seven years of persistence and defeat had unfitted him somehow for trades and businesses, and then it was too late to go into one of the professions. He had been slow to mature, and he had lost ground, and so he hadn't been able to get rid of his energy and he was convinced that this energy itself had done him the greatest harm.

"I didn't see you at the gin game last night," said Rubin.

"I had to miss it. How did it go?"

For the last few weeks Wilhelm had played gin almost nightly, but yesterday he had felt that he couldn't afford to lose any more. He had never won. Not once. And while the losses were small they weren't gains, were they? They were losses. He was tired of losing, and tired also of the company, and so he had gone by himself to the movies.

"Oh," said Rubin, "it went okay. Carl made a chump of himself yelling at the guys. This time Doctor Tamkin didn't let him get away with it. He told him the psychological reason why."

"What was the reason?"

Rubin said, "I can't quote him. Who could? You know the way Tamkin talks. Don't ask me. Do you want the *Trib*? Aren't you going to look at the closing quotations?"

"It won't help much to look. I know what they were yesterday at three," said Wilhelm. "But I suppose I better had get the paper." It seemed necessary for him to lift one shoulder in order to put his hand into his jacket pocket. There, among little packets of pills and crushed cigarette butts and strings of cellophane, the red tapes of packages which he sometimes used as dental floss, he recalled that he had dropped some pennies.

"That doesn't sound so good," said Rubin. He meant to be conversationally playful, but his voice had no tone and his eyes, slack and lid-blinded, turned elsewhere. He didn't want to hear. It was all the same to him. Maybe he already knew, being the sort of man who knew and knew.

No, it wasn't good. Wilhelm held three orders of lard in the commodities market. He and Dr. Tamkin had bought this lard together four days ago at 12.96, and the price at once began to fall and was still falling. In the mail this morning there was sure to be a call for additional margin payment. One came every day.

The psychologist, Dr. Tamkin, had got him into this. Tamkin lived at the Gloriana and attended the card game. He had explained to Wilhelm that you could speculate in commodities at one of the uptown branches of a good Wall Street house without making the full deposit of margin legally required. It was up to the branch manager. If he knew you—and all the branch managers knew Tamkin—he would allow you to make short-term purchases. You needed only to open a small account.

"The whole secret of this type of speculation," Tamkin had told him, "is in the alertness. You have to act fast—buy it and sell it; sell it and buy it again. But quick! Get to the window and have them wire Chicago at just the right second. Strike and strike again! Then get out the same day. In no time at all you turn over fifteen, twenty thousand dollars' worth of soy beans, coffee, corn, hides, wheat, cotton." Obviously the doctor understood the market well. Otherwise he could not make it sound so simple. "People lose because they are greedy and can't get out when it starts to go up. They gamble, but I do it scientifically. This is not guesswork. You must take a few points and get out. Why, ye gods!" said Dr. Tamkin with his bulging eyes, his bald head, and his drooping lip. "Have you stopped to think how much dough people are making in the market?"

Wilhelm with a quick shift from gloomy attention to the panting laugh which entirely changed his face had said, "Ho, have I ever! What do you think? Who doesn't know it's way beyond nineteen-twenty-eight—twenty-nine and still on the rise? Who hasn't read the Fulbright investigation? There's money everywhere. Everyone is shoveling it in. Money is—is—"

"And can you rest—can you sit still while this is going on?" said Dr. Tamkin. "I confess to you I can't. I think about people, just because they have a few bucks to invest, making fortunes. They have no sense, they have no talent, they just have the extra dough and it makes them more dough. I get so worked up and tormented and restless, so restless! I haven't even been able to practice my profession. With all this money around you don't want to be a fool while everyone else is making. I know guys who make five, ten thousand a week just by fooling around. I know a guy at the Hotel Pierre. There's nothing to him, but he has a whole case of Mumm's champagne at lunch. I know another guy on Central Park South— But what's the use of talking. They make millions. They have smart lawyers who get them out of taxes by a thousand schemes."

"Whereas I got taken," said Wilhelm. "My wife refused to sign a joint return. One fairly good year and I got into the thirty-two-per-cent bracket and was stripped bare. What of all my bad years?"

"It's a businessmen's government," said Dr. Tamkin. "You can be sure that these men making five thousand a week—"

"I don't need that sort of money," Wilhelm had said. "But oh! if I could only work out a little steady income from this. Not much. I don't ask much. But how badly I need—! I'd be so grateful if you'd show me how to work it."

"Sure I will. *I* do it regularly. I'll bring you my receipts if you like. And do you want to know something? I approve of your attitude very much. You want to avoid catching the money fever. This type of activity is filled with hostile feeling and lust. You should see what it does to some of these fellows. They go on the market with murder in their hearts."

"What's that I once heard a guy say?" Wilhelm remarked. "A man is only as good as what he loves."

"That's it—just it," Tamkin said. "You don't have to go about it their way. There's also a calm and rational, a psychological approach."

Wilhelm's father, old Dr. Adler, lived in an entirely different world from his son, but he had warned him once against Dr. Tamkin. Rather casually—he was a very bland old man—he said, "Wilky, perhaps you listen too much to this Tamkin. He's interesting to talk to. I don't doubt it. I think he's pretty common but he's a persuasive man. However, I don't know how reliable he may be."

It made Wilhelm profoundly bitter that his father should speak to him with such detachment about his welfare. Dr. Adler liked to appear affable. Affable! His own son, his one and only son, could not speak his mind or ease his heart to him. I wouldn't turn to Tamkin, he thought, if I could turn to him. At least Tamkin sympathizes with me and tries to give me a hand, whereas Dad doesn't want to be disturbed.

Old Dr. Adler had retired from practice; he had a considerable fortune and could easily have helped his son. Recently Wilhelm had told him, "Father—it so happens that I'm in a bad way now. I hate to have to say it. You realize that I'd rather have good news to bring you. But it's true. And since it's true, Dad— What else am I supposed to say? It's true."

Another father might have appreciated how difficult this confession was—so much bad luck, weariness, weakness, and failure. Wilhelm had tried to copy the old man's tone and made himself sound gentlemanly, low-voiced, tasteful. He didn't allow his voice to tremble; he made no stupid gesture. But the doctor had no answer. He only nodded. You might have told him that Seattle was near Puget Sound, or that the Giants and Dodgers were playing a night game, so little was he moved from his expression of healthy, handsome, good-humored old age. He behaved toward his son as he had formerly done toward his patients, and it was a great grief to Wilhelm; it was almost too much to bear. Couldn't he see—couldn't he feel? Had he lost his family sense?

Greatly hurt, Wilhelm struggled however to be fair. Old people are bound to change, he said. They have hard things to think about. They must prepare for where they are going. They can't live by the old schedule any longer and all their perspectives change, and other people become alike, kin and acquaintances. Dad is no longer the same person, Wilhelm reflected. He was thirty-two when I was born, and now he's going on eighty. Furthermore, it's time I stopped feeling like a kid toward him, a small son.

The handsome old doctor stood well above the other old people in the hotel. He was idolized by everyone. This was what people said: "That's old Professor Adler, who used to teach internal medicine. He was a diagnostician, one of the best in New York, and had a tremendous practice. Isn't he a wonderful-looking old guy? It's a pleasure to see such a fine old scientist, clean and immaculate. He stands straight and understands every single thing you say. He still has all his buttons. You can discuss any subject with him." The clerks, the elevator operators, the telephone girls and waitresses and chambermaids, the management flattered and pampered him. That was what he wanted. He had always been a vain man. To see how his father loved himself sometimes made Wilhelm madly indignant.

He folded over the *Tribune* with its heavy, black, crashing sensational print and read without recognizing any of the words, for his mind was still on his father's vanity. The doctor had created his own praise. People were primed and did not know it. And what did he need praise for? In a hotel where everyone was busy and contacts were so brief and had such small weight, how could it satisfy him? He could be in people's thoughts here and there for a moment; in and then out. He could never matter much to them. Wilhelm let out a long, hard breath and raised the brows of his round and somewhat circular eyes. He stared beyond the thick borders of the paper.

. . . love that well which thou must leave ere long.

Involuntary memory brought him this line. At first he thought it referred to his father, but then he understood that it was for himself, rather. *He* should love that well. "This thou perceivest, which makes *thy* love more strong." Under Dr. Tamkin's influence Wilhelm had recently begun to remember the poems he used to read. Dr. Tamkin knew, or said he knew, the great English poets and once in a while he mentioned a poem of his own. It was a long time since anyone had spoken to Wilhelm about this sort of thing. He didn't like to think about his college days, but if there was one course that now made sense it was Literature I. The textbook was Lieder and Lovett's *British Poetry and Prose*, a black heavy book with thin pages. Did I read that? he asked himself. Yes, he had read it and there was one accomplishment at least he could recall with pleasure. He had read "Yet once more, O ye laurels." How pure this was to say! It was beautiful.

Sunk though he be beneath the wat'ry floor . . .

Such things had always swayed him, and now the power of such words was far, far greater.

Wilhelm respected the truth, but he could lie and one of the things he lied often about was his education. He said he was an alumnus of Penn State; in fact he had left school before his sophomore year was finished. His sister Catherine had a B.S. degree. Wilhelm's late mother was a graduate of Bryn Mawr. He was the only member of the family who had no education. This was another sore point. His father was ashamed of him.

But he had heard the old man bragging to another old man, saying, "My son is a sales executive. He didn't have the patience to finish school. But he does all right for himself. His income is up in the five figures somewhere."

"What—thirty, forty thousand?" said his stooped old friend.

"Well, he needs at least that much for his style of life. Yes, he needs that."

Despite his troubles, Wilhelm almost laughed. Why, that boasting old hypocrite. He knew the sales executive was no more. For many weeks there had been no executive, no sales, no income. But how we love looking fine in the eyes of the world—how beautiful are the old when they are doing a snow job! It's Dad, thought Wilhelm, who is the salesman. He's selling me. *He* should have gone on the road.

But what of the truth? Ah, the truth was that there were problems, and of these problems his father wanted no part. His father was ashamed of him. The truth, Wilhelm thought, was very awkward. He pressed his lips together, and his tongue went soft; it pained him far at the back, in the cords and throat, and a knot of ill formed in his chest. Dad never was a pal to me when I was young, he reflected. He was at the office or the hospital, or lecturing. He expected me to look out for myself and never gave me much thought. Now he looks down on me. And maybe in some respects he's right.

No wonder Wilhelm delayed the moment when he would have to go into the dining room. He had moved to the end of Rubin's counter. He had opened the *Tribune;* the fresh pages drooped from his hands; the cigar was smoked out and the hat did not defend him. He was wrong to suppose that he was more capable than the next fellow when it came to concealing his troubles. They were clearly written out upon his face. He wasn't even aware of it.

There was the matter of the different names, which, in the hotel, came up frequently. "Are you Doctor Adler's son?" "Yes, but my name is Tommy Wilhelm." And the doctor would say, "My son and I use different monickers. I uphold tradition. He's for the new." The Tommy was Wilhelm's own invention. He adopted it when he went to Hollywood, and dropped the Adler. Hollywood was his own idea, too. He used to pretend that it had all been the doing of a certain talent scout named Maurice Venice. But the scout had never made him a definite offer of a studio connection. He had approached him, but the results of the screen tests had not been good. After the test Wilhelm took the initiative and pressed Maurice Venice until he got him to say, "Well, I suppose you might make it out there." On the strength of this Wilhelm had left college and had gone to California.

Someone had said, and Wilhelm agreed with the saying, that in Los Angeles all the loose objects in the country were collected, as if America had been tilted and everything that wasn't tightly screwed down had slid into Southern California. He himself had been one of these loose objects. Sometimes he told people, "I was too mature for college. I was a big boy, you see. Well, I thought, when do you start to become a man?" After he had driven a painted flivver and had worn a yellow slicker with slogans on it, and played illegal poker, and gone out on Coke dates, he had *had* college. He wanted to try something new and quarreled with his parents about his career. And then a letter came from Maurice Venice.

The story of the scout was long and intricate and there were several versions of it. The truth about it was never told. Wilhelm had lied first boastfully and then out of charity to himself. But his memory was good, he could still separate what he had invented from the actual happenings, and this morning he found it necessary as he stood by Rubin's showcase with his *Tribune* to recall the crazy course of the true events.

I didn't seem even to realize that there was a depression. How could I have been such a jerk as not to prepare for anything and just go on luck and inspiration? With round gray eyes expanded and his large shapely lips closed in severity toward himself he forced open all that had been hidden. Dad I couldn't affect one way or another. Mama was the one who tried to stop me, and we carried on and yelled and pleaded. The more I lied the louder I raised my voice, and charged—like a hippopotamus. Poor Mother! How I disappointed her. Rubin heard Wilhelm give a broken sigh as he stood with the forgotten *Tribune* crushed under his arm.

When Wilhelm was aware that Rubin watched him, loitering and idle, apparently not knowing what to do with himself this morning, he turned to the Coca-Cola machine. He swallowed hard at the Coke bottle and coughed over it, but he ignored his coughing, for he was still thinking, his eyes upcast and his lips closed behind his hand. By a peculiar twist of habit he wore his coat collar turned up always, as though there were a wind. It never lay flat. But on his broad back, stooped with its own weight, its strength warped almost into deformity, the collar of his sports coat appeared anyway to be no wider than a ribbon.

He was listening to the sound of his own voice as he explained, twenty-five years ago in the living room on West End Avenue, "But Mother, if I don't pan out as an actor I can still go back to school."

But she was afraid he was going to destroy himself. She said, "Wilky, Dad could make it easy for you if you wanted to go into medicine." To remember this stifled him.

"I can't bear hospitals. Besides, I might make a mistake and hurt someone or even kill a patient. I couldn't stand that. Besides, I haven't got that sort of brains."

Then his mother had made the mistake of mentioning her nephew Artie, Wilhelm's cousin, who was an honor student at Columbia in math and languages. That dark little gloomy Artie with his disgusting narrow face, and his moles and self-sniffing ways and his unclean table manners, the boring habit he had of conjugating verbs when you went for a walk with him. "Roumanian is an easy language. You just add a *tl* to everything." He was now a professor, this same Artie with whom Wilhelm had played near the soldiers' and sailors' monument on Riverside Drive. Not that to be a professor was in itself so great. How could anyone bear to know so many languages? And Artie also had to remain Artie, which was a bad deal. But perhaps success had changed him. Now that he had a place in the world perhaps he was better. Did Artie love his languages, and live for them, or was he also, in his heart, cynical? So many people nowadays were. No one seemed satisfied, and Wilhelm was especially horrified by the cynicism of successful people. Cynicism was bread and meat to everyone. And irony, too. Maybe it couldn't be helped. It was probably even necessary. Wilhelm, however, feared it intensely. Whenever at the end of the day he was unusually fatigued he attributed it to cynicism. Too much of the world's business done. Too much falsity. He had various words to express the effect this had on him. Chicken! Unclean! Congestion! he exclaimed in his heart. Rat race! Phony! Murder! Play the Game! Buggers!

At first the letter from the talent scout was nothing but a flattering sort of joke. Wilhelm's picture in the college paper when he was running for class treasurer was seen by Maurice Venice, who wrote to him about a screen test. Wilhelm at once took the train to New York. He found the scout to be huge and oxlike, so stout that his arms seemed caught from beneath in a grip of flesh and fat; it looked as though it must be positively painful. He had little hair. Yet he enjoyed a healthy complexion. His breath was noisy and his voice rather difficult and husky because of the fat in his throat. He had on a double-breasted suit of the type then known as the pillbox; it was chalk-striped, pink on blue; the trousers hugged his ankles.

They met and shook hands and sat down. Together these two big men dwarfed the tiny Broadway office and made the furnishings look like toys. Wilhelm had the color of a Golden Grimes apple when he was well, and then his thick blond hair had been vigorous and his wide shoulders unwarped; he was leaner in the jaws, his eyes fresher and wider; his legs were then still awkward but he was impressively handsome. And he was about to make his first great mistake. Like, he sometimes thought, I was going to pick up a weapon and strike myself a blow with it.

Looming over the desk in the small office darkened by overbuilt midtown—sheer walls, gray spaces, dry lagoons of tar and pebbles—Maurice Venice proceeded to establish his credentials. He said, "My letter was on the regular stationery, but maybe you want to check on me?"

"Who, *me*?" said Wilhelm. "Why?"

"There's guys who think I'm in a racket and make a charge for the test. I don't ask a cent. I'm no agent. There ain't no commission."

"I never even thought of it," said Wilhelm. Was there perhaps something fishy about this Maurice Venice? He protested too much.

In his husky, fat-weakened voice he finally challenged Wilhelm, "If you're not sure, you can call the distributor and find out who I am, Maurice Venice."

Wilhelm wondered at him. "Why shouldn't I be sure? Of course I am."

"Because I can see the way you size me up, and because this is a dinky office. Like you don't believe me. Go ahead. Call. I won't care if you're cautious. I mean it. There's quite a few people who doubt me at first. They can't really believe that fame and fortune are going to hit 'em."

"But I tell you I do believe you," Wilhelm had said, and bent inward to accommodate the pressure of his warm, panting laugh. It was purely nervous. His neck was ruddy and neatly shaved about the ears—he was fresh from the barbershop; his face anxiously glowed with his desire to make a pleasing impression. It was all wasted on Venice, who was just as concerned about the impression *he* was making.

"If you're surprised, I'll just show you what I mean," Venice had said. "It was about fifteen months ago right in this identical same office when I saw a beautiful thing in the paper. It wasn't even a photo but a drawing, a brassière ad, but I knew right away that this was star material. I called up the paper to ask who the girl was, they gave me the name of the advertising agency; I phoned the agency and they gave me the name of the artist; I got hold of the artist and he gave me the number of the model agency. Finally, finally I got her number and phoned her and said, 'This is Maurice Venice, scout for Kaskaskia Films.' So right away she says, 'Yah, so's your old lady.' Well, when I saw I wasn't getting nowhere with her I said to her, 'Well, miss. I don't blame you. You're a very beautiful thing and must have a dozen admirers after you all the time, boy friends who like to call and pull your leg and give a tease. But as I happen to be a very busy fellow and don't have the time to horse around or argue, I tell you what to do. Here's my number, and here's the number of the Kaskaskia Distributors, Inc. Ask them who am I, Maurice Venice. The scout.' She did it. A little while later she phoned me back, all apologies and excuses, but I didn't want to embarrass her and get off on the wrong foot with an artist. I know better than to do that. So I told her it was a natural precaution, never mind. I wanted to run a screen test right away. Because I seldom am wrong about talent. If I see it, it's there. Get that, please. And do you know who that little girl is today?"

"No," Wilhelm said eagerly. "Who is she?"

Venice said impressively, "'Nita Christenberry."

Wilhelm sat utterly blank. This was failure. He didn't know the name, and Venice was waiting for his response and would be angry.

And in fact Venice had been offended. He said, "What's the matter with you! Don't you read a magazine? She's a starlet."

"I'm sorry," Wilhelm answered. "I'm at school and don't have time to keep up. If I don't know her, it doesn't mean a thing. She made a big hit, I'll bet."

"You can say that again. Here's a photo of her." He handed

Wilhelm some pictures. She was a bathing beauty—short, the usual breasts, hips, and smooth thighs. Yes, quite good, as Wilhelm recalled. She stood on high heels and wore a Spanish comb and mantilla. In her hand was a fan.

He had said, "She looks awfully peppy."

"Isn't she a divine girl? And what personality! Not just another broad in the show business, believe me." He had a surprise for Wilhelm. "I have found happiness with her," he said.

"You have?" said Wilhelm, slow to understand.

"Yes, boy, we're engaged."

Wilhelm saw another photograph, taken on the beach. Venice was dressed in a terry-cloth beach outfit, and he and the girl, cheek to cheek, were looking into the camera. Below, in white ink, was written "Love at Malibu Colony."

"I'm sure you'll be very happy. I wish you—"

"I *know*," said Venice firmly, "I'm going to be happy. When I saw that drawing, the breath of fate breathed on me. I felt it over my entire body."

"Say, it strikes a bell suddenly," Wilhelm had said. "Aren't you related to Martial Venice the producer?"

Venice was either a nephew of the producer or the son of a first cousin. Decidedly he had not made good. It was easy enough for Wilhelm to see this now. The office was so poor, and Venice bragged so nervously and identified himself so scrupulously—the poor guy. He was the obscure failure of an aggressive and powerful clan. As such he had the greatest sympathy from Wilhelm.

Venice had said, "Now I suppose you want to know where you come in. I seen your school paper, by accident. You take quite a remarkable picture."

"It can't be so much," said Wilhelm, more panting than laughing.

"You don't want to tell me my business," Venice said. "Leave it to me. I studied up on this."

"I never imagined— Well, what kind of roles do you think I'd fit?"

"All this time that we've been talking, I've been watching. Don't think I haven't. You remind me of someone. Let's see who it can be—one of the great old-timers. Is it Milton Sills? No, that's not the one. Conway Tearle, Jack Mulhall? George Bancroft? No, his face was ruggeder. One thing I can tell you, though, a George Raft type you're not—those tough, smooth, black little characters."

"No, I wouldn't seem to be."

"No, you're not that flyweight type, with the fists, from a nightclub, and the glamorous sideburns, doing the tango or the bolero. Not Edward G. Robinson, either—I'm thinking aloud. Or the Cagney fly-in-your-face role, a cabbie, with that mouth and those punches."

"I realize that."

"Not suave like William Powell, or a lyric juvenile like Buddy Rogers. I suppose you don't play the sax? No. But—"

"But what?"

"I have you placed as the type that loses the girl to the George Raft type or the William Powell type. You are steady, faithful, you get stood up. The older women would know better. The mothers are on your side. With what they been through, if it was up to them, they'd take you in a minute. You're very sympathetic, even the young girls feel that. You'd make a good provider. But they go more for the other types. It's as clear as anything."

This was not how Wilhelm saw himself. And as he surveyed the old ground he recognized now that he had been not only confused but hurt. Why, he thought, he cast me even then for a loser.

Wilhelm had said, with half a mind to be defiant, "Is that your opinion?"

It never occurred to Venice that a man might object to stardom in such a role. "Here is your chance," he said. "Now you're just in college. What are you studying?" He snapped his fingers. "Stuff." Wilhelm himself felt this way about it. "You may plug along fifty years before you get anywheres. This way, in one jump, the world knows who you are. You become a name like Roosevelt, Swanson. From east to west, out to China, into South America. This is no bunk. You become a lover to the whole world. The world wants it, needs it. One fellow smiles, a billion people also smile. One fellow cries, the other billion sob with him. Listen, bud—" Venice had pulled himself together to make an effort. On his imagination there was some great weight which he could not discharge. He wanted Wilhelm, too, to feel it. He twisted his large, clean, well-meaning, rather foolish features as though he were their unwilling captive, and said in his choked, fat-obstructed voice, "Listen, everywhere there are people trying hard, miserable, in trouble, downcast, tired, trying and trying. They need a break, right? A break through, a help, luck or sympathy."

"That certainly is the truth," said Wilhelm. He had seized the feeling and he waited for Venice to go on. But Venice had no more to say; he had concluded. He gave Wilhelm several pages of blue hectographed script, stapled together, and told him to prepare for the screen test. "Study your lines in front of a mirror," he said. "Let yourself go. The part should take ahold of you. Don't be afraid to make faces and be emotional. Shoot the works. Because when you start to act you're no more an ordinary person, and those things don't apply to you. You don't behave the same way as the average."

And so Wilhelm had never returned to Penn State. His roommate sent his things to New York for him, and the school authorities had to write to Dr. Adler to find out what had happened.

Still, for three months Wilhelm delayed his trip to California. He wanted to start out with the blessings of his family, but they were never given. He quarreled with his parents and his sister. And then, when he was best aware of the risks and knew a hundred reasons against going and had made himself sick with fear, he left home. This was typical of Wilhelm. After much thought and hesitation and debate he invariably took the course he had rejected innumerable times. Ten such decisions made up the history of his life. He had decided that it would be a bad mistake to go to Hollywood, and then he went. He had made up his mind not to marry his wife, but ran off and got married. He had resolved not to invest money with Tamkin, and then had given him a check.

But Wilhelm had been eager for life to start. College was merely another delay. Venice had approached him and said that the world had named Wilhelm to shine before it. He was to be freed from the anxious and narrow life of the average. Moreover, Venice had claimed that he never made a mistake. His instinct for talent was infallible, he said.

But when Venice saw the results of the screen test he did a

quick about-face. In those days Wilhelm had had a speech difficulty. It was not a true stammer, it was a thickness of speech which the sound track exaggerated. The film showed that he had many peculiarities, otherwise unnoticeable. When he shrugged, his hands drew up within his sleeves. The vault of his chest was huge, but he really didn't look strong under the lights. Though he called himself a hippopotamus, he more nearly resembled a bear. His walk was bearlike, quick and rather soft, toes turned inward, as though his shoes were an impediment. About one thing Venice had been right. Wilhelm was photogenic, and his wavy blond hair (now graying) came out well, but after the test Venice refused to encourage him. He tried to get rid of him. He couldn't afford to take a chance on him, he had made too many mistakes already and lived in fear of his powerful relatives.

Wilhelm had told his parents, "Venice says I owe it to myself to go." How ashamed he was now of this lie! He had begged Venice not to give him up. He had said, "Can't you help me out? It would kill me to go back to school now."

Then when he reached the Coast he learned that a recommendation from Maurice Venice was the kiss of death. Venice needed help and charity more than he, Wilhelm, ever had. A few years later when Wilhelm was down on his luck and working as an orderly in a Los Angeles hospital, he saw Venice's picture in the papers. He was under indictment for pandering. Closely following the trial, Wilhelm found out that Venice had indeed been employed by Kaskaskia Films but that he had evidently made use of the connection to organize a ring of call girls. Then what did he want with me? Wilhelm had cried to himself. He was unwilling to believe anything very bad about Venice. Perhaps he was foolish and unlucky, a fall guy, a dupe, a sucker. You didn't give a man fifteen years in prison for that. Wilhelm often thought that he might write him a letter to say how sorry he was. He remembered the breath of fate and Venice's certainty that he would be happy. 'Nita Christenberry was sentenced to three years. Wilhelm recognized her although she had changed her name.

By that time Wilhelm too had taken his new name. In California he became Tommy Wilhelm. Dr. Adler would not accept the change. Today he still called his son Wilky, as he had done for more than forty years. Well, now, Wilhelm was thinking, the paper crowded in disarray under his arm, there's really very little that a man can change at will. He can't change his lungs, or nerves, or constitution or temperament. They're not under his control. When he's young and strong and impulsive and dissatisfied with the way things are he wants to rearrange them to assert his freedom. He can't overthrow the government or be differently born; he only has a little scope and maybe a foreboding, too, that essentially you can't change. Nevertheless, he makes a gesture and becomes Tommy Wilhelm. Wilhelm had always had a great longing to be Tommy. He had never, however, succeeded in feeling like Tommy, and in his soul had always remained Wilky. When he was drunk he reproached himself horribly as Wilky. "You fool, you clunk, you Wilky!" he called himself. He thought that it was a good thing perhaps that he had not become a success as Tommy since that would not have been a genuine success. Wilhelm would have feared that not he but Tommy had brought it off, cheating Wilky of his birthright. Yes, it had been a stupid thing to do, but it was his imperfect judgment at the age of twenty which should be blamed. He had cast off his father's name, and with it his father's opinion of him. It was, he knew it was, his bid for liberty, Adler being in his mind the title of the species, Tommy the freedom of the person. But Wilky was his inescapable self.

In middle age you no longer thought such thoughts about free choice. Then it came over you that from one grandfather you had inherited such and such a head of hair which looked like honey when it whitens or sugars in the jar; from another, broad thick shoulders; an oddity of speech from one uncle, and small teeth from another, and the gray eyes with darkness diffused even into the whites, and a wide-lipped mouth like a statue from Peru. Wandering races have such looks, the bones of one tribe, the skin of another. From his mother he had gotten sensitive feelings, a soft heart, a brooding nature, a tendency to be confused under pressure.

The changed name was a mistake, and he would admit it as freely as you liked. But this mistake couldn't be undone now, so why must his father continually remind him how he had sinned? It was too late. He would have to go back to the pathetic day when the sin was committed. And where was that day? Past and dead. Whose humiliating memories were these? His and not his father's. What had he to think back on that he could call good? Very, very little. You had to forgive. First, to forgive yourself, and then general forgiveness. Didn't he suffer from his mistakes far more than his father could?

"Oh, God," Wilhelm prayed. "Let me out of my trouble. Let me out of my thoughts, and let me do something better with myself. For all the time I have wasted I am very sorry. Let me out of this clutch and into a different life. For I am all balled up. Have mercy."

2

The mail.

The clerk who gave it to him did not care what sort of appearance he made this morning. He only glanced at him from under his brows, upward, as the letters changed hands. Why should the hotel people waste courtesies on him? They had his number. The clerk knew that he was handing him, along with the letters, a bill for his rent. Wilhelm assumed a look that removed him from all such things. But it was bad. To pay the bill he would have to withdraw money from his brokerage account, and the account was being watched because of the drop in lard. According to the *Tribune's* figures lard was still twenty points below last year's level. There were government price supports. Wilhelm didn't know how these worked but he understood that the farmer was protected and that the SEC kept an eye on the market and therefore he believed that lard would rise again and he wasn't greatly worried as yet. But in the meantime his father might have offered to pick up his hotel tab. Why didn't he? What a selfish old man he was! He saw his son's hardships; he could so easily help him. How little it would mean to him, and how much to Wilhelm! Where was the old man's heart? Maybe, thought Wilhelm, I was sentimental in the past and exaggerated his kindliness—warm family life. It may never have been there.

Not long ago his father had said to him in his usual affable, pleasant way, "Well, Wilky, here we are under the same roof again, after all these years."

Wilhelm was glad for an instant. At last they would talk over old times. But he was also on guard against insinuations. Wasn't his father saying, "Why are you here in a hotel with me and not at home in Brooklyn with your wife and two boys? You're neither a widower nor a bachelor. You have brought me all your confusions. What do you expect me to do with them?"

So Wilhelm studied the remark for a bit, then said, "The roof is twenty-six stories up. But how many years has it been?"

"That's what I was asking you."

"Gosh, Dad, I'm not sure. Wasn't it the year Mother died? What year was that?"

He asked this question with an innocent frown on his Golden Grimes, dark blond face. *What year was it!* As though he didn't know the year, the month, the day, the very hour of his mother's death.

"Wasn't it nineteen-thirty-one?" said Dr. Adler.

"Oh, was it?" said Wilhelm. And in hiding the sadness and the overwhelming irony of the question he gave a nervous shiver and wagged his head and felt the ends of his collar rapidly.

"Do you know?" his father said. "You must realize, an old fellow's memory becomes unreliable. It was in winter, that I'm sure of. Nineteen-thirty-two?"

Yes, it was age. Don't make an issue of it, Wilhelm advised himself. If you were to ask the old doctor in what year he had interned, he'd tell you correctly. All the same, don't make an issue. Don't quarrel with your own father. Have pity on an old man's failings.

"I believe the year was closer to nineteen-thirty-four, Dad," he said.

But Dr. Adler was thinking, Why the devil can't he stand still when we're talking? He's either hoisting his pants up and down by the pockets or jittering with his feet. A regular mountain of tics, he's getting to be. Wilhelm had a habit of moving his feet back and forth as though, hurrying into a house, he had to clean his shoes first on the doormat.

Then Wilhelm had said, "Yes, that was the beginning of the end, wasn't it, Father?"

Wilhelm often astonished Dr. Adler. Beginning of the end? What could he mean—what was he fishing for? Whose end? The end of family life? The old man was puzzled but he would not give Wilhelm an opening to introduce his complaints. He had learned that it was better not to take up Wilhelm's strange challenges. So he merely agreed pleasantly, for he was a master of social behavior, and said, "It was an awful misfortune for us all."

He thought, What business has he to complain to *me* of his mother's death?

Face to face they had stood, each declaring himself silently after his own way. It was: it was not, the beginning of the end—*some* end.

Unaware of anything odd in his doing it, for he did it all the time, Wilhelm had pinched out the coal of his cigarette and dropped the butt in his pocket, where there were many more. And as he gazed at his father the little finger of his right hand began to twitch and tremble; of that he was unconscious, too.

And yet Wilhelm believed that when he put his mind to it he could have perfect and even distinguished manners, outdoing his father. Despite the slight thickness in his speech—it amounted almost to a stammer when he started the same phrase over several times in his effort to eliminate the thick sound—he could be fluent. Otherwise he would never have made a good salesman. He claimed also that he was a good listener. When he listened he made a tight mouth and rolled his eyes thoughtfully. He would soon tire and begin to utter short, loud, impatient breaths, and he would say, "Oh yes . . . yes . . . yes. I couldn't agree more." When he was forced to differ he would declare, "Well, I'm not sure. I don't really see it that way. I'm of two minds about it." He would never willingly hurt any man's feelings.

But in conversation with his father he was apt to lose control of himself. After any talk with Dr. Adler, Wilhelm generally felt dissatisfied, and his dissatisfaction reached its greatest intensity when they discussed family matters. Ostensibly he had been trying to help the old man to remember a date, but in reality he meant to tell him, "You were set free when Ma died. You wanted to forget her. You'd like to get rid of Catherine, too. Me, too. You're not kidding anyone"—Wilhelm striving to put this across, and the old man not having it. In the end he was left struggling, while his father seemed unmoved.

And then once more Wilhelm had said to himself, "But man! you're not a kid. Even then you weren't a kid!" He looked down over the front of his big, indecently big, spoiled body. He was beginning to lose his shape, his gut was fat, and he looked like a hippopotamus. His younger son called him "a hummuspotamus"; that was little Paul. And here he was still struggling with his old dad, filled with ancient grievances. Instead of saying, "Good-by, youth! Oh, good-by those marvelous, foolish wasted days. What a big clunk I was—I *am*."

Wilhelm was still paying heavily for his mistakes. His wife Margaret would not give him a divorce, and he had to support her and the two children. She would regularly agree to divorce him, and then think things over again and set new and more difficult conditions. No court would have awarded her the amounts he paid. One of today's letters, as he had expected, was from her. For the first time he had sent her a postdated check, and she protested. She also enclosed bills for the boys' educational insurance policies, due next week. Wilhelm's mother-in-law had taken out these policies in Beverly Hills, and since her death two years ago he had to pay the premiums. Why couldn't she have minded her own business! They were his kids, and he took care of them and always would. He had planned to set up a trust fund. But that was on his former expectations. Now he had to rethink the future, because of the money problem. Meanwhile, here were the bills to be paid. When he saw the two sums punched out so neatly on the cards he cursed the company and its IBM equipment. His heart and his head were congested with anger. Everyone was supposed to have money. It was nothing to the company. It published pictures of funerals in the magazines and frightened the suckers, and then punched out little holes, and the customers would lie awake to think out ways to raise the dough. They'd be ashamed not to have it. They couldn't let a great company down, either, and they got the scratch. In the old days a man was put in prison for debt, but there were subtler things now. They made it a shame not to have money and set everybody to work.

Well, and what else had Margaret sent him? He tore the envelope open with his thumb, swearing that he would send any other bills back to her. There was, luckily, nothing more. He put the hole-punched cards in his pocket. Didn't Margaret know that he was nearly at the end of his rope? Of course. Her instinct told her that this was her opportunity, and she was giving him the works.

He went into the dining room, which was under Austro-Hungarian management at the Hotel Gloriana. It was run like a European establishment. The pastries were excellent, especially the strudel. He often had apple strudel and coffee in the afternoon.

As soon as he entered he saw his father's small head in the sunny bay at the farther end, and heard his precise voice. It was with an odd sort of perilous expression that Wilhelm crossed the dining room.

Dr. Adler liked to sit in a corner that looked across Broadway down to the Hudson and New Jersey. On the other side of the street was a supermodern cafeteria with gold and purple mosaic columns. On the second floor a private-eye school, a dental laboratory, a reducing parlor, a veteran's club, and a Hebrew school shared the space. The old man was sprinkling sugar on his strawberries. Small hoops of brilliance were cast by the water glasses on the white tablecloth, despite a faint murkiness in the sunshine. It was early summer, and the long window was turned inward; a moth was on the pane; the putty was broken and the white enamel on the frames was streaming with wrinkles.

"Ha, Wilky," said the old man to his tardy son. "You haven't met our neighbor Mr. Perls, have you? From the fifteenth floor."

"How d'do," Wilhelm said. He did not welcome this stranger; he began at once to find fault with him. Mr. Perls carried a heavy cane with a crutch tip. Dyed hair, a skinny forehead—these were not reasons for bias. Nor was it Mr. Perls's fault that Dr. Adler was using him, not wishing to have breakfast with his son alone. But a gruffer voice within Wilhelm spoke, asking, "Who is this damn frazzle-faced herring with his dyed hair and his fish teeth and this drippy mustache? Another one of Dad's German friends. Where does he collect all these guys? What is the stuff on his teeth? I never saw such pointed crowns. Are they stainless steel, or a kind of silver? How can a human face get into this condition. Uch!" Staring with his widely spaced gray eyes, Wilhelm sat, his broad back stooped under the sports jacket. He clasped his hands on the table with an implication of suppliance. Then he began to relent a little toward Mr. Perls, beginning at the teeth. Each of those crowns represented a tooth ground to the quick, and estimating a man's grief with his teeth as two per cent of the total, and adding to that his flight from Germany and the probable origin of his wincing wrinkles, not to be confused with the wrinkles of his smile, it came to a sizable load.

"Mr. Perls was a hosiery wholesaler," said Dr. Adler.

"Is this the son you told me was in the selling line?" said Mr. Perls.

Dr. Adler replied, "I have only this one son. One daughter. She was a medical technician before she got married—anesthetist. At one time she had an important position in Mount Sinai."

He couldn't mention his children without boasting. In Wilhelm's opinion, there was little to boast of. Catherine, like Wilhelm, was big and fair-haired. She had married a court reporter who had a pretty hard time of it. She had taken a professional name, too—Philippa. At forty she was still ambitious to become a painter. Wilhelm didn't venture to criticize her work. It didn't do much to him, he said, but then he was no critic. Anyway, he and his sister were generally on the outs and he didn't often see her paintings. She worked very hard, but there were fifty thousand people in New York with paints and brushes, each practically a law unto himself. It was the Tower of Babel in paint. He didn't want to go far into this. Things were chaotic all over.

Dr. Adler thought that Wilhelm looked particularly untidy this morning—unrested, too, his eyes red-rimmed from excessive smoking. He was breathing through his mouth and he was evidently much distracted and rolled his red-shot eyes barbarously. As usual, his coat collar was turned up as though he had had to go out in the rain. When he went to business he pulled himself together a little; otherwise he let himself go and looked like hell.

"What's the matter, Wilky, didn't you sleep last night?"

"Not very much."

"You take too many pills of every kind—first stimulants and then depressants, anodynes followed by analeptics, until the poor organism doesn't know what's happened. Then the luminal won't put people to sleep, and the Pervitin or Benzedrine won't wake them. God knows! These things get to be as serious as poisons, and yet everyone puts all their faith in them."

"No, Dad, it's not the pills. It's that I'm not used to New York any more. For a native, that's very peculiar, isn't it? It was never so noisy at night as now, and every little thing is a strain. Like the alternate parking. You have to run out at eight to move your car. And where can you put it? If you forget for a minute they tow you away. Then some fool puts advertising leaflets under your windshield wiper and you have heart failure a block away because you think you've got a ticket. When you do get stung with a ticket, you can't argue. You haven't got a chance in court and the city wants the revenue."

"But in your line you have to have a car, eh?" said Mr. Perls.

"Lord knows why any lunatic would want one in the city who didn't need it for his livelihood."

Wilhelm's old Pontiac was parked in the street. Formerly, when on an expense account, he had always put it up in a garage. Now he was afraid to move the car from Riverside Drive lest he lose his space, and he used it only on Saturdays when the Dodgers were playing in Ebbets Field and he took his boys to the game. Last Saturday, when the Dodgers were out of town, he had gone out to visit his mother's grave.

Dr. Adler had refused to go along. He couldn't bear his son's driving. Forgetfully, Wilhelm traveled for miles in second gear; he was seldom in the right lane and he neither gave signals nor watched for lights. The upholstery of his Pontiac was filthy with grease and ashes. One cigarette burned in the ashtray, another in his hand, a third on the floor with maps and other waste paper and Coca-Cola bottles. He dreamed at the wheel or argued and gestured, and therefore the old doctor would not ride with him.

Then Wilhelm had come back from the cemetery angry because the stone bench between his mother's and his grandmother's graves had been overturned and broken by vandals. "Those damn teen-age hoodlums get worse and worse," he said. "Why, they must have used a sledge-hammer to break the seat smack in half like that. If I could catch one of them!" He wanted the doctor to pay for a new seat, but his father was cool to the idea. He said he was going to have himself cremated.

Mr. Perls said, "I don't blame you if you get no sleep up where you are." His voice was tuned somewhat sharp, as though he were slightly deaf. "Don't you have Parigi the singing teacher there? God, they have some queer elements in this hotel. On which floor is that Estonian woman with all her cats and dogs? They should have made her leave long ago."

"They've moved her down to twelve," said Dr. Adler.

Wilhelm ordered a large Coca-Cola with his breakfast. Working in secret at the small envelopes in his pocket, he found two pills by touch. Much fingering had worn and weakened the paper. Under cover of a napkin he swallowed a Phenaphen sedative and a Unicap, but the doctor was sharp-eyed and said, "Wilky, what are you taking now?"

"Just my vitamin pills." He put his cigar butt in an ashtray on the table behind him, for his father did not like the odor. Then he drank his Coca-Cola.

"That's what you drink for breakfast, and not orange juice?" said Mr. Perls. He seemed to sense that he would not lose Dr. Adler's favor by taking an ironic tone with his son.

"The caffeine stimulates brain activity," said the old doctor. "It does all kinds of things to the respiratory center."

"It's just a habit of the road, that's all," Wilhelm said. "If you drive around long enough it turns your brains, your stomach, and everything else."

His father explained, "Wilky used to be with the Rojax Corporation. He was their northeastern sales representative for a good many years but recently ended the connection."

"Yes," said Wilhelm, "I was with them from the end of the war." He sipped the Coca-Cola and chewed the ice, glancing at one and the other with his attitude of large, shaky, patient dignity. The waitress set two boiled eggs before him.

"What kind of line does this Rojax company manufacture?" said Mr. Perls.

"Kiddies' furniture. Little chairs, rockers, tables, Jungle-Gyms, slides, swings, seesaws."

Wilhelm let his father do the explaining. Large and stiff-backed, he tried to sit patiently, but his feet were abnormally restless. All right! His father had to impress Mr. Perls? He would go along once more, and play his part. Fine! He would play along and help his father maintain his style. Style was the main consideration. That was just fine!

"I was with the Rojax Corporation for almost ten years," he said. "We parted ways because they wanted me to share my territory. They took a son-in-law into the business—a new fellow. It was his idea."

To himself, Wilhelm said, Now God alone can tell why I have to lay my whole life bare to this blasted herring here. I'm sure nobody else does it. Other people keep their business to themselves. Not me.

He continued, "But the rationalization was that it was too big a territory for one man. I had a monopoly. That wasn't so. The real reason was that they had gotten to the place where they would have to make me an officer of the corporation. Vice presidency. I was in line for it, but instead this son-in-law got in, and—"

Dr. Adler thought Wilhelm was discussing his grievances much too openly and said, "My son's income was up in the five figures."

As soon as money was mentioned, Mr. Perls's voice grew eagerly sharper. "Yes? What, the thirty-two-per-cent bracket? Higher even, I guess?" He asked for a hint, and he named the figures not idly but with a sort of hugging relish. Uch! How they love money, thought Wilhelm. They adore money! Holy money! Beautiful money! It was getting so that people were feeble-minded about everything except money. While if you didn't have it you were a dummy, a dummy! You had to excuse yourself from the face of the earth. Chicken! that's what it was. The world's business. If only he could find a way out of it.

Such thinking brought on the usual congestion. It would grow into a fit of passion if he allowed it to continue. Therefore he stopped talking and began to eat.

Before he struck the egg with his spoon he dried the moisture with his napkin. Then he battered it (in his father's opinion) more than was necessary. A faint grime was left by his fingers on the white of the egg after he had picked away the shell. Dr. Adler saw it with silent repugnance. What a Wilky he had given to the world! Why, he didn't even wash his hands in the morning. He used an electric razor so that he didn't have to touch water. The doctor couldn't bear Wilky's dirty habits. Only once—and never again, he swore—had he visited his room. Wilhelm, in pajamas and stockings had sat on his bed, drinking gin from a coffee mug and rooting for the Dodgers on television. "That's two and two on you, Duke. Come on—hit it, now." He came down on the mattress—bam! The bed looked kicked to pieces. Then he drank the gin as though it were tea, and urged his team on with his fist. The smell of dirty clothes was outrageous. By the bedside lay a quart bottle and foolish magazines and mystery stories for the hours of insomnia. Wilhelm lived in worse filth than a savage. When the Doctor spoke to him about this he answered, "Well, I have no wife to look after my things." And who—*who!*—had done the leaving? Not Margaret. The Doctor was certain that she wanted him back.

Wilhelm drank his coffee with a trembling hand. In his full face his abused bloodshot gray eyes, moved back and forth. Jerkily he set his cup back and put half the length of a cigarette into his mouth; he seemed to hold it with his teeth, as though it were a cigar.

"I can't let them get away with it," he said. "It's also a question of morale."

His father corrected him. "Don't you mean a moral question, Wilky?"

"I mean that, too. I have to do something to protect myself. I was promised executive standing." Correction before a stranger mortified him, and his dark blond face changed color, more pale, and then more dark. He went on talking to Perls but his eyes spied on his father. "I was the one who opened the territory for them. I could go back for one of their competitors and take away their customers. *My* customers. Morale enters into it because they've tried to take away my confidence."

"Would you offer a different line to the same people?" Mr. Perls wondered.

"Why not? I know what's wrong with the Rojax product."

"Nonsense," said his father. "Just nonsense and kid's talk, Wilky. You're only looking for trouble and embarrassment that way. What would you gain by such a silly feud? You have to think about making a living and meeting your obligations."

Hot and bitter, Wilhelm said with pride, while his feet moved angrily under the table, "I don't have to be told about my obligations. I've been meeting them for years. In more than twenty years I've never had a penny of help from anybody. I preferred to dig a ditch on the WPA but never asked anyone to meet my obligations for me."

"Wilky has had all kinds of experiences," said Dr. Adler.

The old doctor's face had a wholesome reddish and almost translucent color, like a ripe apricot. The wrinkles beside his ears were deep because the skin conformed so tightly to his bones. With all his might, he was a healthy and fine small old man. He wore a white vest of a light check pattern. His hearing-aid doodad was in the pocket. An unusual shirt of red and black stripes covered his chest. He bought his clothes in a college shop farther uptown. Wilhelm thought he had no business to get himself up like a jockey, out of respect for his profession.

"Well," said Mr. Perls. "I can understand how you feel. You want to fight it out. By a certain time of life, to have to start all over again can't be a pleasure, though a good man can always do it. But anyway you want to keep on with a business you know already, and not have to meet a whole lot of new contacts."

Wilhelm again thought, Why does it have to be me and my life that's discussed, and not him and his life? He would never allow it. But I am an idiot. I have no reserve. To me it can be done. I talk. I must ask for it. Everybody wants to have intimate conversations, but the smart fellows don't give out, only the fools. The smart fellows talk intimately about the fools, and examine them all over and give them advice. Why do I allow it? The hint about his age had hurt him. No, you can't admit it's as good as ever, he conceded. Things do give out.

"In the meanwhile," Dr. Adler said, "Wilky is taking it easy and considering various propositions. Isn't that so?"

"More or less," said Wilhelm. He suffered his father to increase Mr. Perls's respect for him. The WPA ditch had brought the family into contempt. He was a little tired. The spirit, the peculiar burden of his existence lay upon him like an accretion, a load, a hump. In any moment of quiet, when sheer fatigue prevented him from struggling, he was apt to feel this mysterious weight, this growth or collection of nameless things which it was the business of his life to carry about. That must be what a man was for. This large, odd, excited, fleshy, blond, abrupt personality named Wilhelm, or Tommy, was here, present, in the present—Dr. Tamkin had been putting into his mind many suggestions about the present moment, the here and now—this Wilky, or Tommy Wilhelm, forty-four years old, father of two sons, at present living in the Hotel Gloriana, was assigned to be the carrier of a load which was his own self, his characteristic self. There was no figure or estimate for the value of this load. But it is probably exaggerated by the subject, T. W. Who is a visionary sort of animal. Who has to believe that he can know why he exists. Though he has never seriously tried to find out why.

Mr. Perls said, "If he wants time to think things over and have a rest, why doesn't he run down to Florida for a while? Off season it's cheap and quiet. Fairyland. The mangoes are just coming in. I got two acres down there. You'd think you were in India."

Mr. Perls utterly astonished Wilhelm when he spoke of fairyland with a foreign accent. Mangoes—India? What did he mean, India?

"Once upon a time," said Wilhelm, "I did some public-relations work for a big hotel down in Cuba. If I could get them a notice in Leonard Lyons or one of the other columns it might be good for another holiday there, gratis. I haven't had a vacation for a long time, and I could stand a rest after going so hard. You know that's true, Father." He meant that his father knew how deep the crisis was becoming; how badly he was strapped for money; and that he could not rest but would be crushed if he stumbled; and that his obligations would destroy him. He couldn't falter. He thought, The money! When I had it, I flowed money. They bled it away from me. I hemorrhaged money. But now it's almost all gone, and where am I supposed to turn for more?

He said, "As a matter of fact, Father, I am tired as hell."

But Mr. Perls began to smile and said, "I understand from Doctor Tamkin that you're going into some kind of investment with him, partners."

"You know, he's a very ingenious fellow," said Dr. Adler. "I really enjoy hearing him go on. I wonder if he really is a medical doctor."

"Isn't he?" said Perls. "Everybody thinks he is. He talks about his patients. Doesn't he write prescriptions?"

"I don't really know what he does," said Dr. Adler. "He's a cunning man."

"He's a psychologist, I understand," said Wilhelm.

"I don't know what sort of psychologist or psychiatrist he may be," said his father. "He's a little vague. It's growing into a major industry, and a very expensive one. Fellows have to hold down very big jobs in order to pay those fees. Anyway, this Tamkin is clever. He never said he practiced here, but I believe he was a doctor in California. They don't seem to have much legislation out there to cover these things, and I hear a thousand dollars will get you a degree from a Los Angeles correspondence school. He gives the impression of knowing something about chemistry, and things like hypnotism. I wouldn't trust him, though."

"And why wouldn't you?" Wilhelm demanded.

"Because he's probably a liar. Do you believe he invented all the things he claims?"

Mr. Perls was grinning.

"He was written up in *Fortune*," said Wilhelm. "Yes, in *Fortune* magazine. He showed me the article. I've seen his clippings."

"That doesn't make him legitimate," said Dr. Adler. "It might have been another Tamkin. Make no mistake, he's an operator. Perhaps even crazy."

"Crazy, you say?"

Mr. Perls put in, "He could be both sane and crazy. In these days nobody can tell for sure which is which."

"An electrical device for truck drivers to wear in their caps," said Dr. Adler, describing one of Tamkin's proposed inventions. "To wake them with a shock when they begin to be drowsy at the wheel. It's triggered by the change in blood-pressure when they start to doze."

"It doesn't sound like such an impossible thing to me," said Wilhelm.

Mr. Perls said, "To me he described an underwater suit so a man could walk on the bed of the Hudson in case of an atomic attack. He said he could walk to Albany in it."

"Ha, ha, ha, ha, ha!" cried Dr. Adler in his old man's voice. "Tamkin's Folly. You could go on a camping trip under Niagara Falls."

"This is just his kind of fantasy," said Wilhelm. "It doesn't mean a thing. Inventors are supposed to be like that. I get funny ideas myself. Everybody wants to make something. Any American does."

But his father ignored this and said to Perls, "What other inventions did he describe?"

While the frazzle-faced Mr. Perls and his father in the unseemly, monkey-striped shirt were laughing, Wilhelm could not restrain himself and joined in with his own panting laugh. But he was in despair. They were laughing at the man to whom he had given a power of attorney over his last seven hundred dollars to speculate for him in the commodities market. They had bought all that lard. It had to rise today. By ten o'clock, or half-past ten, trading would be active, and he would see.

3

Between white tablecloths and glassware and glancing silverware, through overfull light, the long figure of Mr. Perls went away into the darkness of the lobby. He thrust with his cane, and dragged a large built-up shoe which Wilhelm had not included in his estimate of troubles. Dr. Adler wanted to talk about him. "There's a poor man," he said, "with a bone condition which is gradually breaking him up."

"One of those progressive diseases?" said Wilhelm.

"Very bad. I've learned," the doctor told him, "to keep my sympathy for the real ailments. This Perls is more to be pitied than any man I know."

Wilhelm understood he was being put on notice and did not express his opinion. He ate and ate. He did not hurry but kept putting food on his plate until he had gone through the muffins and his father's strawberries, and then some pieces of bacon that were left; he had several cups of coffee, and when he was finished he sat gigantically in a state of arrest and didn't seem to know what he should do next.

For a while father and son were uncommonly still. Wilhelm's preparations to please Dr. Adler had failed completely, for the old man kept thinking, You'd never guess he had a clean upbringing, and, What a dirty devil this son of mine is. Why can't he try to sweeten his appearance a little? Why does he want to drag himself like this? And he makes himself look so idealistic.

Wilhelm sat, mountainous. He was not really so slovenly as his father found him to be. In some aspects he even had a certain delicacy. His mouth, though broad, had a fine outline, and his brow and his gradually incurved nose, dignity, and in his blond hair there was white but there were also shades of gold and chestnut. When he was with the Rojax Corporation Wilhelm had kept a small apartment in Roxbury, two rooms in a large house with a small porch and garden, and on mornings of leisure, in late spring weather like this, he used to sit expanded in a wicker chair with the sunlight pouring through the weave, and sunlight through the slug-eaten holes of the young hollyhocks and as deeply as the grass allowed into small flowers. This peace (he forgot that that time had had its troubles, too), this peace was gone. It must not have belonged to him, really, for to be here in New York with his old father was more genuinely like his life. He was well aware that he didn't stand a chance of getting sympathy from his father, who said he kept his for real ailments. Moreover, he advised himself repeatedly not to discuss his vexatious problems with him, for his father, with some justice, wanted to be left in peace. Wilhelm also knew that when he began to talk about these things he made himself feel worse, he became congested with them and worked himself into a clutch. Therefore he warned himself, Lay off, pal. It'll only be an aggravation. From a deeper source, however, came other promptings. If he didn't keep his troubles before him he risked losing them altogether, and he knew by experience that this was worse. And furthermore, he could not succeed in excusing his father on the ground of old age. No. No, he could not. I am his son, he thought. He is my father. He is as much father as I am son—old or not. Affirming this, though in complete silence, he sat, and, sitting, he kept his father at the table with him.

"Wilky," said the old man, "have you gone down to the baths here yet?"

"No, Dad, not yet."

"Well, you know the Gloriana has one of the finest pools in New York. Eighty feet, blue tile. It's a beauty."

Wilhelm had seen it. On the way to the gin game you passed the stairway to the pool. He did not care for the odor of the wall-locked and chlorinated water.

"You ought to investigate the Russian and Turkish baths, and the sunlamps and massage. I don't hold with sunlamps. But the massage does a world of good, and there's nothing better than hydrotherapy when you come right down to it. Simple water has a calming effect and would do you more good than all the barbiturates and alcohol in the world."

Wilhelm reflected that this advice was as far as his father's help and sympathy would extend.

"I thought," he said, "that the water cure was for lunatics."

The doctor received this as one of his son's jokes and said with a smile, "Well, it won't turn a sane man into a lunatic. It does a great deal for me. I couldn't live without my massages and steam."

"You're probably right. I ought to try it one of these days. Yesterday, late in the afternoon, my head was about to bust and I just had to have a little air, so I walked around the reservoir, and I sat down for a while in a playground. It rests me to watch the kids play potsy and skiprope."

The doctor said with approval, "Well, now that's more like the idea."

"It's the end of the lilacs," said Wilhelm. "When they burn it's the beginning of summer. At least, in the city. Around the time of year when the candy stores take down the windows and start to sell sodas on the sidewalk. But even though I was raised here, Dad, I can't take city life any more, and I miss the country. There's too much push here for me. It works me up too much. I take things too hard. I wonder why you never retired to a quieter place."

The doctor opened his small hand on the table in a gesture so old and so typical that Wilhelm felt it like an actual touch upon the foundations of his life. "I am a city boy myself, you must remember," Dr. Adler explained. "But if you find the city so hard on you, you ought to get out."

"I'll do that," said Wilhelm, "as soon as I can make the right connection. Meanwhile—"

His father interrupted, "Meanwhile I suggest you cut down on drugs."

"You exaggerate that, Dad. I don't really—I give myself a little boost against—" He almost pronounced the word "misery" but he kept his resolution not to complain.

The doctor, however, fell into the error of pushing his advice too hard. It was all he had to give his son and he gave it once more. "Water and exercise," he said.

He wants a young, smart, successful son, thought Wilhelm, and he said, "Oh, Father, it's nice of you to give me this medical advice, but steam isn't going to cure what ails me."

The doctor measurably drew back, warned by the sudden weak strain of Wilhelm's voice and all that the droop of his face, the swell of his belly against the restraint of his belt intimated.

"Some new business?" he asked unwillingly.

Wilhelm made a great preliminary summary which involved the whole of his body. He drew and held a long breath, and his color changed and his eyes swam. "New?" he said.

"You make too much of your problems," said the doctor. "They ought not to be turned into a career. Concentrate on real troubles—fatal sickness, accidents." The old man's whole manner said, Wilky, don't start this on me. I have a right to be spared.

Wilhelm himself prayed for restraint; he knew this weakness of his and fought it. He knew, also, his father's character. And he began mildly, "As far as the fatal part of it goes, everyone on this side of the grave is the same distance from death. No, I guess my trouble is not exactly new. I've got to pay premiums on two policies for the boys. Margaret sent them to me. She unloads everything on me. Her mother left her an income. She won't even file a joint tax return. I get stuck. Etcetera. But you've heard the whole story before."

"I certainly have," said the old man. "And I've told you to stop giving her so much money."

Wilhelm worked his lips in silence before he could speak. The congestion was growing. "Oh, but my kids, Father. My kids. I love them. I don't want them to lack anything."

The doctor said with a half-deaf benevolence, "Well, naturally. And she, I'll bet, is the beneficiary of that policy."

"Let her be. I'd sooner die myself before I collected a cent of such money."

"Ah yes." The old man sighed. He did not like the mention of death. "Did I tell you that your sister Catherine—Philippa—is after me again."

"What for?"

"She wants to rent a gallery for an exhibition."

Stiffly fair-minded, Wilhelm said, "Well, of course that's up to you, Father."

The round-headed old man with his fine, feather-white, ferny hair said, "No, Wilky. There's not a thing on those canvases. I don't believe it; it's a case of the emperor's clothes. I may be old enough for my second childhood, but at least the first is well behind me. I was glad enough to buy crayons for her when she was four. But now she's a woman of forty and too old to be encouraged in her delusions. She's no painter."

"I wouldn't go so far as to call her a born artist," said Wilhelm, "but you can't blame her for trying something worth while."

"Let her husband pamper her."

Wilhelm had done his best to be just to his sister, and he had sincerely meant to spare his father, but the old man's tight, benevolent deafness had its usual effect on him. He said, "When it comes to women and money, I'm completely in the dark. What makes Margaret act like this?"

"She's showing you that you can't make it without her," said the doctor. "She aims to bring you back by financial force."

"But if she ruins me, Dad, how can she expect me to come back? No, I have a sense of honor. What you don't see is that she's trying to put an end to me."

His father stared. To him this was absurd. And Wilhelm thought, Once a guy starts to slip, he figures he might as well be a clunk. A real big clunk. He even takes pride in it. But there's nothing to be proud of—hey, boy? Nothing. I don't blame Dad for his attitude. And it's no cause for pride.

"I don't understand that. But if you feel like this why don't you settle with her once and for all?"

"What do you mean, Dad?" said Wilhelm, surprised. "I thought I told you. Do you think I'm not willing to settle? Four years ago when we broke up I gave her everything—goods, furniture, savings. I tried to show good will, but I didn't get anywhere. Why when I wanted Scissors, the dog, because the animal and I were so attached to each other—it was bad enough to leave the kids—she absolutely refused me. Not that she cared a damn about the animal. I don't think you've seen him. He's an Australian sheep dog. They usually have one blank or whitish eye which gives a misleading look, but they're the gentlest dogs and have unusual delicacy about eating or talking. Let me at least have the companionship of this animal. Never." Wilhelm was greatly moved. He wiped his face at all corners with his napkin. Dr. Adler felt that his son was indulging himself too much in his emotions.

"Whenever she can hit me, she hits, and she seems to live for that alone. And she demands more and more, and still more. Two years ago she wanted to go back to college and get another degree. It increased my burden but I thought it would be wiser in the end if she got a better job through it. But still she takes as much from me as before. Next thing she'll want to be a Doctor of Philosophy. She says the women in her family live long, and I'll have to pay and pay for the rest of my life."

The doctor said impatiently, "Well, these are details, not principles. Just details which you can leave out. The dog! You're mixing up all kinds of irrelevant things. Go to a good lawyer."

"But I've already told you, Dad. I got a lawyer, and she got one, too, and both of them talk and send me bills, and I eat my heart out. Oh, Dad, Dad, what a hole I'm in!" said Wilhelm in utter misery. "The lawyers—see?—draw up an agreement, and she says okay on Monday and wants more money on Tuesday. And it begins again."

"I always thought she was a strange kind of woman," said Dr. Adler. He felt that by disliking Margaret from the first and disapproving of the marriage he had done all that he could be expected to do.

"Strange, Father? I'll show you what she's like." Wilhelm took hold of his broad throat with brown-stained fingers and bitten nails and began to choke himself.

"What are you doing?" cried the old man.

"I'm showing you what she does to me."

"Stop that—stop it!" the old man said and tapped the table commandingly.

"Well, Dad, she hates me. I feel that she's strangling me. I can't catch my breath. She just has fixed herself on me to kill me. She can do it at long distance. One of these days I'll be struck down by suffocation or apoplexy because of her. I just can't catch my breath."

"Take your hands off your throat, you foolish man," said his father. "Stop this bunk. Don't expect me to believe in all kinds of voodoo."

"If that's what you want to call it, all right." His face flamed and paled and swelled and his breath was laborious.

"But I'm telling you that from the time I met her I've been a slave. The Emancipation Proclamation was only for colored people. A husband like me is a slave, with an iron collar. The churches go up to Albany and supervise the law. They won't have divorces. The court says, 'You want to be free. Then you have to work twice as hard—twice, at least! Work! you bum.' So then guys kill each other for the buck, and they may be free of a wife who hates them but they are sold to the company. The company knows a guy has got to have his salary, and takes full advantage of him. Don't talk to me about being free. A rich man may be free on an income of a million net. A poor man may be free because nobody cares what he does. But a fellow in my position has to sweat it out until he drops dead."

His father replied to this, "Wilky, it's entirely your own fault. You don't have to allow it."

Stopped in his eloquence, Wilhelm could not speak for a while. Dumb and incompetent, he struggled for breath and frowned with effort into his father's face.

"I don't understand your problems," said the old man. "I never had any like them."

By now Wilhelm had lost his head and he waved his hands and said over and over, "Oh, Dad, don't give me that stuff, don't give me that. Please don't give me that sort of thing."

"It's true," said his father. "I come from a different world. Your mother and I led an entirely different life."

"Oh, how can you compare Mother," Wilhelm said. "Mother was a help to you. Did she harm you ever?"

"There's no need to carry on like an opera, Wilky," said the doctor. "This is only your side of things."

"What? It's the truth," said Wilhelm.

The old man could not be persuaded and shook his round head and drew his vest down over the gilded shirt, and leaned back with a completeness of style that made this look, to anyone out of hearing, like an ordinary conversation between a middle-aged man and his respected father. Wilhelm towered and swayed, big and sloven, with his gray eyes red-shot and his honey-colored hair twisted in flaming shapes upward. Injustice made him angry, made him beg. But he wanted an understanding with his father, and he tried to capitulate to him. He said, "You can't compare Mother and Margaret, and neither can you and I be compared, because you, Dad, were a success. And a success—is a success. I never made a success."

The doctor's old face lost all of its composure and became hard and angry. His small breast rose sharply under the red and black shirt and he said, "Yes. Because of hard work. I was not self-indulgent, not lazy. My old man sold dry goods in Williamsburg. We were nothing, do you understand? I knew I couldn't afford to waste my chances."

"I wouldn't admit for one minute that I was lazy," said Wilhelm. "If anything, I tried too hard. I admit I made many mistakes. Like I thought I shouldn't do things you had done already. Study chemistry. You had done it already. It was in the family."

His father continued, "I didn't run around with fifty women, either. I was not a Hollywood star. I didn't have time to go to Cuba for a vacation. I stayed at home and took care of my children."

Oh, thought Wilhelm, eyes turning upward. Why did I come here in the first place, to live near him? New York is like a gas. The colors are running. My head feels so tight, I don't know what I'm doing. He thinks I want to take away his money or that I envy him. He doesn't see what I want.

"Dad," Wilhelm said aloud, "you're being very unfair. It's true the movies was a false step. But I love my boys. I didn't abandon them. I left Margaret because I had to."

"Why did you have to?"

"Well—" said Wilhelm, struggling to condense his many reasons into a few plain words. "I had to—I had to."

With sudden and surprising bluntness his father said, "Did you have bed-trouble with her? Then you should have stuck it out. Sooner or later everyone has it. Normal people stay with it. It passes. But you wouldn't, so now you pay for your stupid romantic notions. Have I made my view clear?"

It was very clear. Wilhelm seemed to hear it repeated from various sides and inclined his head different ways, and listened and thought. Finally he said, "I guess that's the medical standpoint. You may be right. I just couldn't live with Margaret. I wanted to stick it out, but I was getting very sick. She was one way and I was another. She wouldn't be like me, so I tried to be like her, and I couldn't do it."

"Are you sure she didn't tell *you* to go?" the doctor said.

"I wish she had. I'd be in a better position now. No, it was me. I didn't want to leave, but I couldn't stay. Somebody had to take the initiative. I did. Now I'm the fall guy too."

Pushing aside in advance all the objections that his son would make, the doctor said, "Why did you lose your job with Rojax?"

"I didn't, I've told you."

"You're lying. You wouldn't have ended the connection. You need the money too badly. But you must have got into trouble." The small old man spoke concisely and with great strength. "Since you have to talk and can't let it alone, tell the truth. Was there a scandal—a woman?"

Wilhelm fiercely defended himself. "No, Dad, there wasn't any woman. I told you how it was."

"Maybe it was a man, then," the old man said wickedly.

Shocked, Wilhelm stared at him with burning pallor and dry lips. His skin looked a little yellow. "I don't think you know what you're talking about," he answered after a moment. "You shouldn't let your imagination run so free. Since you're been living here on Broadway you must think you understand life, up to date. You ought to know your own son a little better. Let's drop that, now."

"All right, Wilky, I'll withdraw it. But something must have happened in Roxbury nevertheless. You'll never go back. You're just talking wildly about representing a rival company. You won't. You've done something to spoil your reputation, I think. But you've got girl friends who are expecting you back, isn't that so?"

"I take a lady out now and then while on the road," said Wilhelm. "I'm not a monk."

"No one special? Are you sure you haven't gotten into complications?"

He had tried to unburden himself and instead, Wilhelm thought, he had to undergo an inquisition to prove himself worthy of a sympathetic word. Because his father believed that he did all kinds of gross things.

"There is a woman in Roxbury that I went with. We fell in love and wanted to marry, but she got tired of waiting for my divorce. Margaret figured that. On top of which the girl was a Catholic and I had to go with her to the priest and make an explanation."

Neither did this last confession touch Dr. Adler's sympathies or sway his calm old head or affect the color of his complexion.

"No, no, no, no; all wrong," he said.

Again Wilhelm cautioned himself. Remember his age. He is no longer the same person. He can't bear trouble. I'm so choked up and congested anyway I can't see straight. Will I ever get out of the woods, and recover my balance? You're never the same afterward. Trouble rusts out the system.

"You really *want* a divorce?" said the old man.

"For the price I pay I should be getting something."

"In that case," Dr. Adler said, "it seems to me no normal person would stand for such treatment from a woman."

"Ah, Father, Father!" said Wilhelm. "It's always the same thing with you. Look how you lead me on. You always start out to help me with my problems, and be sympathetic and so forth. It gets my hopes up and I begin to be grateful. But before we're through I'm a hundred times more depressed than before. Why is that? You have no sympathy. You want to shift all the blame on to me. Maybe you're wise to do it." Wilhelm was beginning to lose himself. "All you seem to think about is your death. Well, I'm sorry. But I'm going to die too. And I'm your son. It isn't my fault in the first place. There ought to be a right way to do this, and be fair to each other. But what I want to know is, why do you start up with me if you're not going to help me? What do you want to know about my problems for, Father? So you can lay the whole responsibility on me—so that you won't have to help me? D'you want me to comfort you for having such a son?" Wilhelm had a great knot of wrong tied tight within his chest, and tears approached his eyes but he didn't let them out. He looked shabby enough as it was. His voice was thick and hazy, and he was stammering and could not bring his awful feelings forth.

"You have some purpose of your own," said the doctor, "in acting so unreasonable. What do you want from me? What do you expect?"

"What do I expect?" said Wilhelm. He felt as though he were unable to recover something. Like a ball in the surf, washed beyond reach, his self-control was going out. "I expect *help!*" The words escaped him in a loud, wild, frantic cry and startled the old man, and two or three breakfasters within hearing glanced their way. Wilhelm's hair, the color of whitened honey, rose dense and tall with the expansion of his face, and he said, "When I suffer—you aren't even sorry. That's because you have no affection for me, and you don't want any part of me."

"Why must I like the way you behave? No, I don't like it," said Dr. Adler.

"All right. You want me to change myself. But suppose I could do it—what would I become? What could I? Let's suppose that all my life I have had the wrong ideas about myself and wasn't what I thought I was. And wasn't even careful to take a few precautions, as most people do—like a woodchuck has a few exits to his tunnel. But what shall I do now? More than half my life is over. More than half. And now you tell me I'm not even normal."

The old man too had lost his calm. "You cry about being helped," he said. "When you thought you had to go into the service I sent a check to Margaret every month. As a family man you could have had an exemption. But no! The war couldn't be fought without you and you had to get yourself drafted and be an office-boy in the Pacific theater. Any clerk could have done what you did. You could find nothing better to become than a GI."

Wilhelm was going to reply, and half raised his bearish figure from the chair, his fingers spread and whitened by their grip on the table, but the old man would not let him begin. He said, "I see other elderly people here with children who aren't much good, and they keep backing them and holding them up at a great sacrifice. But I'm not going to make that mistake. It doesn't enter your mind that when I die—a year, two years from now—you'll still be here. I do think of it."

He had intended to say that he had a right to be left in peace. Instead he gave Wilhelm the impression that he meant it was not fair for the better man of the two, and the more useful, the more admired, to leave the world first. Perhaps he meant that, too—a little; but he would not under other circumstances have come out with it so flatly.

"Father," said Wilhelm with an unusual openness of appeal. "Don't you think I know how you feel? I have pity. I want you to live on and on. If you outlive me, that's perfectly okay by me." As his father did not answer this avowal and turned away his glance, Wilhelm suddenly burst out, "No, but you hate me. And if I had money you wouldn't. By God, you have to admit it. The money makes the difference. Then we would be a fine father and son, if I was a credit to you—so you could boast and brag about me all over the hotel. But I'm not the right type of son. I'm too old, I'm too old and too unlucky."

His father said, "I can't give you any money. There would be no end to it if I started. You and your sister would take every last buck from me. I'm still alive, not dead. I am still here. Life isn't over yet. I am as much alive as you or anyone. And I want nobody on my back. Get off! And I give you the same advice, Wilky. Carry nobody on your back."

"Just keep your money," said Wilhelm miserably. "Keep it and enjoy it yourself. That's the ticket!"

4

Ass! Idiot! Wild Boar! Dumb mule! Slave! Lousy, wallowing hippopotamus! Wilhelm called himself as his bending legs carried him from the dining room. His pride! His inflamed feelings! His begging and feebleness! And trading insults with his old father—and spreading confusion over everything. Oh, how poor, contemptible, and ridiculous he was! When he remembered how he had said, with great reproof, "You ought to know your own son"—why, how corny and abominable it was.

He could not get out of the sharply brilliant dining room fast enough. He was horribly worked up; his neck and shoulders, his entire chest ached as though they had been tightly tied with ropes. He smelled the salt odor of tears in his nose.

But at the same time, since there were depths in Wilhelm not unsuspected by himself, he received a suggestion from some remote element in his thoughts that the business of life, the real business—to carry his peculiar burden, to feel shame and impotence, to taste these quelled tears—the only important business, the highest business was being done. Maybe the making of mistakes expressed the very purpose of his life and the essence of his being here. Maybe he was supposed to make them and suffer from them on this earth. And though he had raised himself above Mr. Perls and his father because they adored money, still they were called to act energetically and this was better than to yell and cry, pray and beg, poke and blunder and go by fits and starts and fall upon the thorns of life. And finally sink beneath that watery floor—would that be tough luck, or would it be good riddance?

But he raged once more against his father. Other people with money, while they're still alive, want to see it do some good. Granted, he shouldn't support me. But have I ever asked him to do that? Have I ever asked for dough at all, either for Margaret or for the kids or for myself? It isn't the money, but only the assistance; not even assistance, but just the feeling. But he may be trying to teach me that a grown man should be cured of such feeling. Feeling got me in dutch at Rojax. I had the *feeling* that I belonged to the firm, and my *feelings* were hurt when they put Gerber in over me. Dad thinks I'm too simple. But I'm not so simple as he thinks. What about his feelings? He doesn't forget death for one single second, and that's what makes him like this. And not only is death on his mind but through money he forces me to think about it, too. It gives him power over me. He forces me that way, he himself, and then he's sore. If he was poor, I could care for him and show it. The way I *could* care, too, if I only had a chance. He'd see how much love and respect I had in me. It would make him a different man, too. He'd put his hands on me and give me his blessing.

Someone in a gray straw hat with a wide cocoa-colored band spoke to Wilhelm in the lobby. The light was dusky, splotched with red underfoot; green, the leather furniture; yellow, the indirect lighting.

"Hey, Tommy. Say, there."

"Excuse me," said Wilhelm, trying to reach a house phone. But this was Dr. Tamkin, whom he was just about to call.

"You have a very obsessional look on your face," said Dr. Tamkin.

Wilhelm thought, Here he is, Here he is. If I could only figure this guy out.

"Oh," he said to Tamkin. "Have I got such a look? Well, whatever it is, you name it and I'm sure to have it."

The sight of Dr. Tamkin brought his quarrel with his father to a close. He found himself flowing into another channel.

"What are we doing?" he said. "What's going to happen to lard today?"

"Don't worry yourself about that. All we have to do is hold on to it and it's sure to go up. But what's made you so hot under the collar, Wilhelm?"

"Oh, one of those family situations." This was the moment to take a new look at Tamkin, and he viewed him closely but gained nothing by the new effort. It was conceivable that Tamkin was everything that he claimed to be, and all the gossip false. But was he a scientific man, or not? If he was not, this might be a case for the district attorney's office to investigate. Was he a liar? That was a delicate question. Even a liar might be trustworthy in some ways. Could he trust Tamkin—could he? He feverishly, fruitlessly sought an answer.

But the time for this question was past, and he had to trust him now. After a long struggle to come to a decision, he had given him the money. Practical judgment was in abeyance. He had worn himself out, and the decision was no decision. How had this happened? But how had his Hollywood career begun? It was not because of Maurice Venice, who turned out to be a pimp. It was because Wilhelm himself was ripe for the mistake. His marriage, too, had been like that. Through such decisions somehow his life had taken form. And so, from the moment when he tasted the peculiar flavor of fatality in Dr. Tamkin, he could no longer keep back the money.

Five days ago Tamkin had said, "Meet me tomorrow, and we'll go to the market." Wilhelm, therefore, had had to go. At eleven o'clock they had walked to the brokerage office. On the way, Tamkin broke the news to Wilhelm that though this was an equal partnership he couldn't put up his half of the money just yet; it was tied up for a week or so in one of his patents. Today he would be two hundred dollars short; next week, he'd make it up. But neither of them needed an income from the market, of course. This was only a sporting proposition anyhow, Tamkin said. Wilhelm had to answer, "Of course." It was too late to withdraw. What else could he do? Then came the formal part of the transaction, and it was frightening. The very shade of green of Tamkin's check looked wrong; it was a false, disheartening color. His handwriting was peculiar, even monstrous; the e's were like i's, the t's and l's the same, and the h's like wasps' bellies. He wrote like a fourth-grader. Scientists, however, dealt mostly in symbols; they printed. This was Wilhelm's explanation.

Dr. Tamkin had given him his check for three hundred dollars. Wilhelm, in a blinded and convulsed aberration, pressed and pressed to try to kill the trembling of his hand as he wrote out his check for a thousand. He set his lips tight, crouched with his huge back over the table, and wrote with crumbling, terrified fingers, knowing that if Tamkin's check bounced his own would not be honored either. His sole cleverness was to set the date ahead by one day to give the green check time to clear.

Next he had signed a power of attorney, allowing Tamkin to speculate with his money, and this was an even more frightening document. Tamkin had never said a word about it, but here they were and it had to be done.

After delivering his signatures, the only precaution Wilhelm took was to come back to the manager of the brokerage office and ask him privately, "Uh, about Doctor Tamkin. We were in here a few minutes ago, remember?"

That day had been a weeping, smoky one and Wilhelm had

gotten away from Tamkin on the pretext of having to run to the post office. Tamkin had gone to lunch alone, and here was Wilhelm, back again, breathless, his hat dripping, needlessly asking the manager if he remembered.

"Yes, sir, I know," the manager had said. He was a cold, mild, lean German who dressed correctly and around his neck wore a pair of opera glasses with which he read the board. He was an extremely correct person except that he never shaved in the morning, not caring, probably, how he looked to the fumblers and the old people and the operators and the gamblers and the idlers of Broadway uptown. The market closed at three. Maybe, Wilhelm guessed, he had a thick beard and took a lady out to dinner later and wanted to look fresh-shaven.

"Just a question," said Wilhelm. "A few minutes ago I signed a power of attorney so Doctor Tamkin could invest for me. You gave me the blanks."

"Yes, sir, I remember."

"Now this is what I want to know," Wilhelm had said. "I'm no lawyer and I only gave the paper a glance. Does this give Doctor Tamkin power of attorney over any other assets of mine—money, or property?"

The rain had dribbled from Wilhelm's deformed, transparent raincoat; the buttons of his shirt, which always seemed tiny, were partly broken, in pearly quarters of the moon, and some of the dark, thick golden hairs that grew on his belly stood out. It was the manager's business to conceal his opinion of him; he was shrewd, gray, correct (although unshaven) and had little to say except on matters that came to his desk. He must have recognized in Wilhelm a man who reflected long and then made the decision he had rejected twenty separate times. Silvery, cool, level, long-profiled, experienced, indifferent, observant, with unshaven refinement, he scarcely looked at Wilhelm, who trembled with fearful awkwardness. The manager's face, low-colored, long-nostriled, acted as a unit of perception; his eyes merely did their reduced share. Here was a man, like Rubin, who knew and knew and knew. He, a foreigner, knew; Wilhelm, in the city of his birth, was ignorant.

The manager had said, "No, sir, it does not give him."

"Only over the funds I deposited with you?"

"Yes, that is right, sir."

"Thank you, that's what I wanted to find out," Wilhelm had said, grateful.

The answer comforted him. However, the question had no value. None at all. For Wilhelm had no other assets. He had given Tamkin his last money. There wasn't enough of it to cover his obligations anyway, and Wilhelm had reckoned that he might as well go bankrupt now as next month. "Either broke or rich," was how he had figured, and that formula had encouraged him to make the gamble. Well, not rich; he did not expect that, but perhaps Tamkin might really show him how to earn what he needed in the market. By now, however, he had forgotten his own reckoning and was aware only that he stood to lose his seven hundred dollars to the last cent.

Dr. Tamkin took the attitude that they were a pair of gentlemen experimenting with lard and grain futures. The money, a few hundred dollars, meant nothing much to either of them. He said to Wilhelm, "Watch. You'll get a big kick out of this and wonder why more people don't go into it. You think the Wall Street guys are so smart—geniuses? That's because most of us are psychologically afraid to think about the details. Tell me this. When you're on the road, and you don't understand what goes on under the hood of your car, you'll worry what'll happen if something goes wrong with the engine. Am I wrong?" No, he was right. "Well," said Dr. Tamkin with an expression of quiet triumph about his mouth, almost the suggestion of a jeer. "It's the same psychological principle, Wilhelm. They are rich because you don't understand what goes on. But it's no mystery, and by putting in a little money and applying certain principles of observation, you begin to grasp it. It can't be studied in the abstract. You have to take a specimen risk so that you feel the process, the money-flow, the whole complex. To know how it feels to be a seaweed you have to get in the water. In a very short time we'll take out a hundred-per-cent profit." Thus Wilhelm had had to pretend at the outset that his interest in the market was theoretical.

"Well," said Tamkin when he met him now in the lobby, "what's the problem, what is this family situation? Tell me."

He put himself forward as the keen mental scientist. Whenever this happened Wilhelm didn't know what to reply. No matter what he said or did it seemed that Dr. Tamkin saw through him.

"I had some words with my dad."

Dr. Tamkin found nothing extraordinary in this. "It's the eternal same story," he said. "The elemental conflict of parent and child. It won't end, ever. Even with a fine old gentleman like your dad."

"I don't suppose it will. I've never been able to get anywhere with him. He objects to my feelings. He thinks they're sordid. I upset him and he gets mad at me. But maybe all old men are alike."

"Sons, too. Take it from one of them," said Dr. Tamkin. "All the same, you should be proud of such a fine old patriarch of a father. It should give you hope. The longer he lives, the longer your life-expectancy becomes."

Wilhelm answered, brooding, "I guess so. But I think I inherit more from my mother's side, and she died in her fifties."

"A problem arose between a young fellow I'm treating and his dad—I just had a consultation," said Dr. Tamkin as he removed his dark gray hat.

"So early in the morning?" said Wilhelm with suspicion.

"Over the telephone, of course."

What a creature Tamkin was when he took off his hat! The indirect light showed the many complexities of his bald skull, his gull's nose, his rather handsome eyebrows, his vain mustache, his deceiver's brown eyes. His figure was stocky, rigid, short in the neck, so that the large ball of the occiput touched his collar. His bones were peculiarly formed, as though twisted twice where the ordinary human bone was turned only once, and his shoulders rose in two pagoda-like points. At midbody he was thick. He stood pigeon-toed, a sign perhaps that he was devious or had much to hide. The skin of his hands was aging, and his nails were moonless, concave, clawlike, and they appeared loose. His eyes were as brown as beaver fur and full of strange lines. The two large brown naked balls looked thoughtful—but were they? And honest—but was Dr. Tamkin honest? There was a hypnotic power in his eyes, but this was not always of the same strength, nor was Wilhelm convinced that it was completely natural. He felt that

Tamkin tried to make his eyes deliberately conspicuous, with studied art, and that he brought forth his hypnotic effect by an exertion. Occasionally it failed or drooped, and when this happened the sense of his face passed downward to his heavy (possibly foolish?) red underlip.

Wilhelm wanted to talk about the lard holdings, but Dr. Tamkin said, "This father-and-son case of mine would be instructive to you. It's a different psychological type completely than your dad. This man's father thinks that he isn't his son."

"Why not?"

"Because he has found out something about the mother carrying on with a friend of the family for twenty-five years."

"Well, what do you know!" said Wilhelm. His silent thought was, Pure bull. Nothing but bull!

"You must note how interesting the woman is, too. She has two husbands. Whose are the kids? The fellow detected her and she gave a signed confession that two of the four children were not the father's."

"It's amazing," said Wilhelm, but he said it in a rather distant way. He was always hearing such stories from Dr. Tamkin. If you were to believe Tamkin, most of the world was like this. Everybody in the hotel had a mental disorder, a secret history, a concealed disease. The wife of Rubin at the newsstand was supposed to be kept by Carl, the yelling, loud-mouthed gin-rummy player. The wife of Frank in the barbershop had disappeared with a GI while he was waiting for her to disembark at the French Lines pier. Everyone was like the faces on a playing card, upside down either way. Every public figure had a character-neurosis. Maddest of all were the businessmen, the heartless, flaunting, boisterous business class who ruled this country with their hard manners and their bold lies and their absurd words that nobody could believe. They were crazier than anyone. They spread the plague. Wilhelm, thinking of the Rojax Corporation, was inclined to agree that many businessmen were insane. And he supposed that Tamkin, for all his peculiarities, spoke a kind of truth and did some people a sort of good. It confirmed Wilhelm's suspicions to hear that there was a plague, and he said, "I couldn't agree with you more. They trade on anything, they steal everything, they're cynical right to the bones."

"You have to realize," said Tamkin, speaking of his patient, or his client, "that the mother's confession isn't good. It's a confession of duress. I try to tell the young fellow he shouldn't worry about a phony confession. But what does it help him if I am rational with him?"

"No?" said Wilhelm, intensely nervous. "I think we ought to go over to the market. It'll be opening pretty soon."

"Oh, come on," said Tamkin. "It isn't even nine o'clock, and there isn't much trading the first hour anyway. Things don't get hot in Chicago until half-past ten, and they're an hour behind us, don't forget. Anyway, I say lard will go up, and it will. Take my word. I've made a study of the guilt-aggression cycle which is behind it. I ought to know *something* about that. Straighten your collar."

"But meantime," said Wilhelm, "we have taken a licking this week. Are you sure your insight is at its best? Maybe when it isn't we should lay off and wait."

"Don't you realize," Dr. Tamkin told him, "you can't march in a straight line to the victory? You fluctuate toward it. From Euclid to Newton there was straight lines. The modern age analyzes the wavers. On my own accounts, I took a licking in hides and coffee. But I have confidence. I'm sure I'll out-guess them." He gave Wilhelm a narrow smile, friendly, calming, shrewd, and wizard-like, patronizing, secret, potent. He saw his fears and smiled at them. "It's something," he remarked, "to see how the competition-factor will manifest itself in different individuals."

"So? Let's go over."

"But I haven't had my breakfast yet."

"I've had mine."

"Come, have a cup of coffee."

"I wouldn't want to meet my dad." Looking through the glass doors, Wilhelm saw that his father had left by the other exit. Wilhelm thought, He didn't want to run into me, either. He said to Dr. Tamkin, "Okay, I'll sit with you, but let's hurry it up because I'd like to get to the market while there's still a place to sit. Everybody and his uncle gets in ahead of you."

"I want to tell you about this boy and his dad. It's highly absorbing. The father was a nudist. Everybody went naked in the house. Maybe the woman found men *with* clothes attractive. Her husband didn't believe in cutting his hair, either. He practiced dentistry. In his office he wore riding pants and a pair of boots, and he wore a green eyeshade."

"Oh, come off it," said Wilhelm.

"This is a true case history."

Without warning, Wilhelm began to laugh. He himself had had no premonition of his change of humor. His face became warm and pleasant, and he forgot his father, his anxieties; he panted bearlike, happily, through his teeth. "This sounds like a horse-dentist. He wouldn't have to put on pants to treat a horse. Now what else are you going to tell me? Did the wife play the mandolin? Does the boy join the cavalry? Oh, Tamkin, you really are a killer-diller."

"Oh, you think I'm trying to amuse you," said Tamkin. "That's because you aren't familiar with my outlook. I deal in facts. Facts always are sensational. I'll say that a second time. Facts *always!* are sensational."

Wilhelm was reluctant to part with his good mood. The doctor had little sense of humor. He was looking at him earnestly.

"I'd bet you any amount of money," said Tamkin, "that the facts about you are sensational."

"Oh—ha, ha! You want them? You can sell them to a true confession magazine."

"People forget how sensational the things are that they do. They don't see it on themselves. It blends into the background of their daily life."

Wilhelm smiled. "Are you sure this boy tells you the truth?"

"Yes, because I've known the whole family for years."

"And you do psychological work with your own friends? I didn't know that was allowed."

"Well, I'm a radical in the profession. I have to do good wherever I can."

Wilhelm's face became ponderous again and pale. His whitened gold hair lay heavy on his head, and he clasped uneasy fingers on the table. Sensational, but oddly enough, dull, too. Now how do you figure that out? It blends with the background. Funny but unfunny. True but false. Casual but laborious, Tamkin was. Wilhelm was most suspicious of him when he took his driest tone.

"With me," said Dr. Tamkin, "I am at my most efficient when

I don't need the fee. When I only love. Without a financial reward. I remove myself from the social influence. Especially money. The spiritual compensation is what I look for. Bringing people into the here-and-now. The real universe. That's the present moment. The past is no good to us. The future is full of anxiety. Only the present is real—the here-and-now. Seize the day."

"Well," said Wilhelm, his earnestness returning. "I know you are a very unusual man. I like what you say about here-and-now. Are all the people who come to see you personal friends and patients too? Like that tall handsome girl, the one who always wears those beautiful broomstick skirts and belts?"

"She was an epileptic, and a most bad and serious pathology, too. I'm curing her successfully. She hasn't had a seizure in six months, and she used to have one every week."

"And that young cameraman, the one who showed us those movies from the jungles of Brazil, isn't he related to her?"

"Her brother. He's under my care, too. He has some terrible tendencies, which are to be expected when you have an epileptic sibling. I came into their lives when they needed help desperately, and took hold of them. A certain man forty years older than she had her in his control and used to give her fits by suggestion whenever she tried to leave him. If you only knew one per cent of what goes on in the city of New York! You see, I understand what it is when the lonely person begins to feel like an animal. When the night comes and he feels like howling from his window like a wolf. I'm taking complete care of that young fellow and his sister. I have to steady him down or he'll go from Brazil to Australia the next day. The way I keep him in the here-and-now is by teaching him Greek."

This was a complete surprise! "What, do you know Greek?"

"A friend of mine taught me when I was in Cairo. I studied Aristotle with him to keep from being idle."

Wilhelm tried to take in these new claims and examine them. Howling from the window like a wolf when night comes sounded genuine to him. That was something really to think about. But the Greek! He realized that Tamkin was watching to see how he took it. More elements were continually being added. A few days ago Tamkin had hinted that he had once been in the underworld, one of the Detroit Purple Gang. He was once head of a mental clinic in Toledo. He had worked with a Polish inventor on an unsinkable ship. He was a technical consultant in the field of television. In the life of a man of genius, all of these things might happen. But had they happened to Tamkin? Was he a genius? He often said that he had attended some of the Egyptian royal family as a psychiatrist. "But everybody is alike, common or aristocrat," he told Wilhelm. "The aristocrat knows less about life."

An Egyptian princess whom he had treated in California, for horrible disorders he had described to Wilhelm, retained him to come back to the old country with her, and there he had had many of her friends and relatives under his care. They turned over a villa on the Nile to him. "For ethical reasons, I can't tell you many of the details about them," he said—but Wilhelm had already heard all these details, and strange and shocking they were, if true. *If* true—he could not be free from doubt. For instance, the general who had to wear ladies' silk stockings and stand otherwise naked before the mirror—and all the rest. Listening to the doctor when he was so strangely factual, Wilhelm had to translate his words into his own language, and he could not translate fast enough or find terms to fit what he heard.

"Those Egyptian big shots invested in the market, too, for the heck of it. What did they need extra money for? By association, I almost became a millionaire myself, and if I had played it smart there's no telling what might have happened. I could have been the ambassador." The American? The Egyptian ambassador? "A friend of mine tipped me off on the cotton. I made a heavy purchase of it. I didn't have that kind of money, but everybody there knew me. It never entered their minds that a person of their social circle didn't have dough. The sale was made on the phone. Then, while the cotton shipment was at sea, the price tripled. When the stuff suddenly became so valuable all hell broke loose on the world cotton market, they looked to see who was the owner of this big shipment. Me! They investigated my credit and found out I was a mere doctor, and they canceled. This was illegal. I sued them. But as I didn't have the money to fight them I sold the suit to a Wall Street lawyer for twenty thousand dollars. He fought it and was winning. They settled with him out of court for more than a million. But on the way back from Cairo, flying, there was a crash. All on board died. I have this guilt on my conscience, of being the murderer of that lawyer. Although he was a crook."

Wilhelm thought, I must be a real jerk to sit and listen to such impossible stories. I guess I am a sucker for people who talk about the deeper things of life, even the way he does.

"We scientific men speak of irrational guilt, Wilhelm," said Dr. Tamkin, as if Wilhelm were a pupil in his class. "But in such a situation, because of the money, I wished him harm. I realize it. This isn't the time to describe all the details, but the money made me guilty. Money and Murder both begin with M. Machinery. Mischief."

Wilhelm, his mind thinking for him at random, said, "What about Mercy? Milk-of-human-kindness?"

"One fact should be clear to you by now. Money-making is aggression. That's the whole thing. The functionalistic explanation is the only one. People come to the market to kill. They say, 'I'm going to make a killing.' It's not accidental. Only they haven't got the genuine courage to kill, and they erect a symbol of it. The money. They make a killing by a fantasy. Now, counting and number is always a sadistic activity. Like hitting. In the Bible, the Jews wouldn't allow you to count them. They knew it was sadistic."

"I don't understand what you mean," said Wilhelm. A strange uneasiness tore at him. The day was growing too warm and his head felt dim. "What makes them want to kill?"

"By and by, you'll get the drift," Dr. Tamkin assured him. His amazing eyes had some of the rich dryness of a brown fur. Innumerable crystalline hairs or spicules of light glittered in their bold surfaces. "You can't understand without first spending years on the study of the ultimates of human and animal behavior, the deep chemical, organismic, and spiritual secrets of life. I am a psychological poet."

"If you're this kind of poet," said Wilhelm, whose fingers in his pocket were feeling in the little envelopes for the Phenaphen capsules, "what are you doing on the market?"

"That's a good question. Maybe I am better at speculation because I don't care. Basically, I don't wish hard enough for money, and therefore I come with a cool head to it."

Wilhelm thought, Oh, sure! That's an answer, is it? I bet that if I took a strong attitude he'd back down on everything. He'd grovel in front of me. The way he looks at me on the sly, to see if I'm being taken in! He swallowed his Phenaphen pill with a long gulp of water. The rims of his eyes grew red as it went down. And then he felt calmer.

"Let me see if I can give you an answer that will satisfy you," said Dr. Tamkin. His flapjacks were set before him. He spread the butter on them, poured on brown maple syrup, quartered them, and began to eat with hard, active, muscular jaws which sometimes gave a creak at the hinges. He pressed the handle of his knife against his chest and said, "In here, the human bosom—mine, yours, everybody's—there isn't just one soul. There's a lot of souls. But there are two main ones, the real soul and a pretender soul. Now! Every man realizes that he has to love something or somebody. He feels that he must go outward. 'If thou canst not love, what art thou?' Are you with me?"

"Yes, Doc, I think so," said Wilhelm listening—a little skeptically but nonetheless hard.

"'What art thou?' Nothing. That's the answer. Nothing. In the heart of hearts—Nothing! So of course you can't stand that and want to be Something, and you try. But instead of being this Something, the man puts it over on everybody instead. You can't be that strict to yourself. You love a *little*. Like you have a dog" *(Scissors!)* "or give some money to a charity drive. Now that isn't love, is it? What is it? Egotism, pure and simple. It's a way to love the pretender soul. Vanity. Only vanity, is what it is. And social control. The interest of the pretender soul is the same as the interest of the social life, the society mechanism. This is the main tragedy of human life. Oh, it is terrible! Terrible! You are not free. Your own betrayer is inside of you and sells you out. You have to obey him like a slave. He makes you work like a horse. And for what? For who?"

"Yes, for what?" The doctor's words caught Wilhelm's heart. "I couldn't agree more," he said. "When do we get free?"

"The purpose is to keep the whole thing going. The true soul is the one that pays the price. It suffers and gets sick, and it realizes that the pretender can't be loved. Because the pretender is a lie. The true soul loves the truth. And when the true soul feels like this, it wants to kill the pretender. The love has turned into hate. Then you become dangerous. A killer. You have to kill the deceiver."

"Does this happen to everybody?"

The doctor answered simply, "Yes, to everybody. Of course, for simplification purposes, I have spoken of the soul; it isn't a scientific term, but it helps you to understand it. Whenever the slayer slays, he wants to slay the soul in him which has gypped and deceived him. Who is his enemy? Him. And his lover? Also. Therefore, all suicide is murder, and all murder is suicide. It's the one and identical phenomenon. Biologically, the pretender soul takes away the energy of the true soul and makes it feeble, like a parasite. It happens unconsciously, unawaringly, in the depths of the organism. Ever take up parasitology?"

"No, it's my dad who's the doctor."

"You should read a book about it."

Wilhelm said, "But this means that the world is full of murderers. So it's not the world. It's a kind of hell."

"Sure," the doctor said. "At least a kind of purgatory. You walk on the bodies. They are all around. I can hear them cry *de profundis* and wring their hands. I hear them, poor human beasts. I can't help hearing. And my eyes are open to it. I have to cry, too. This is the human tragedy-comedy."

Wilhelm tried to capture his vision. And again the doctor looked untrustworthy to him, and he doubted him. "Well," he said, "there are also kind, ordinary, helpful people. They're— out in the country. All over. What kind of morbid stuff do you read, anyway?" The doctor's room was full of books.

"I read the best of literature, science and philosophy," Dr. Tamkin said. Wilhelm had observed that in his room even the TV aerial was set upon a pile of volumes. "Korzybski, Aristotle, Freud, W. H. Sheldon, and all the great poets. You answer me like a layman. You haven't applied your mind strictly to this."

"Very interesting," said Wilhelm. He was aware that he hadn't applied his mind strictly to anything. "You don't have to think I'm a dummy, though. I have ideas, too." A glance at the clock told him that the market would soon open. They could spare a few minutes yet. There were still more things he wanted to hear from Tamkin. He realized that Tamkin spoke faultily, but then scientific men were not always strictly literate. It was the description of the two souls that had awed him. In Tommy he saw the pretender. And even Wilky might not be himself. Might the name of his true soul be the one by which his old grandfather had called him—Velvel? The name of a soul, however, must be only that—soul. What did it look like? Does my soul look like me? Is there a soul that looks like Dad? Like Tamkin? Where does the true soul get its strength? Why does it have to love truth? Wilhelm was tormented, but tried to be oblivious to his torment. Secretly, he prayed the doctor would give him some useful advice and transform his life. "Yes, I understand you," he said. "It isn't lost on me."

"I never said you weren't intelligent, but only you just haven't made a study of it all. As a matter of fact you're a profound personality with very profound creative capacities but also disturbances. I've been concerned with you, and for some time I've been treating you."

"Without my knowing it? I haven't felt you doing anything. What do you mean? I don't think I like being treated without my knowledge. I'm of two minds. What's the matter, don't you think I'm normal?" And he really was divided in mind. That the doctor cared about him pleased him. This was what he craved, that someone should care about him, wish him well. Kindness, mercy, he wanted. But—and here he retracted his heavy shoulders in his peculiar way, drawing his hands up into his sleeves; his feet moved uneasily under the table—but he was worried, too, and even somewhat indignant. For what right had Tamkin to meddle without being asked? What kind of privileged life did this man lead? He took other people's money and speculated with it. Everybody came under his care. No one could have secrets from him.

The doctor looked at him with his deadly brown, heavy, impenetrable eyes, his naked shining head, his red hanging underlip, and said, "You have lots of guilt in you."

Wilhelm helplessly admitted, as he felt the heat rise to his wide face, "Yes, I think so too. But personally," he added, "I don't feel like a murderer. I always try to lay off. It's the others who get me. You know—make me feel oppressed. And if you don't mind, and it's all the same to you, I would rather know it when you start to treat me. And now, Tamkin, for Christ's sake, they're putting out the lunch menus already. Will you sign the check, and let's go!"

Tamkin did as he asked, and they rose. They were passing the bookkeeper's desk when he took out a substantial bundle of onionskin papers and said, "These are receipts of the transactions. Duplicates. You'd better keep them as the account is in your name and you'll need them for income taxes. And here is a copy of a poem I wrote yesterday."

"I have to leave something at the desk for my father," Wilhelm said, and he put his hotel bill in an envelope with a note. *Dear Dad, Please carry me this month, Yours, W.* He watched the clerk with his sullen pug's profile and his stiff-necked look push the envelope into his father's box.

"May I ask you really why you and your dad had words?" said Dr. Tamkin, who had hung back, waiting.

"It was about my future," said Wilhelm. He hurried down the stairs with swift steps, like a tower in motion, his hands in his trousers pockets. He was ashamed to discuss the matter. "He says there's a reason why I can't go back to my old territory, and there is. I told everybody I was going to be an officer of the corporation. And I was supposed to. It was promised. But then they welshed because of the son-in-law. I bragged and made myself look big."

"If you was humble enough, you could go back. But it doesn't make much difference. We'll make you a good living on the market."

They came into the sunshine of upper Broadway, not clear but throbbing through the dust and fumes, a false air of gas visible at eye-level as it spurted from the bursting buses. From old habit, Wilhelm turned up the collar of his jacket.

"Just a technical question," Wilhelm said. "What happens if your losses are bigger than your deposit?"

"Don't worry. They have ultra-modern electronic bookkeeping machinery, and it won't let you get in debt. It puts you out automatically. But I want you to read this poem. You haven't read it yet."

Light as a locust, a helicopter bringing mail from Newark Airport to La Guardia sprang over the city in a long leap.

The paper Wilhelm unfolded had ruled borders in red ink. He read:

Mechanism vs Functionalism
Ism vs Hism

If thee thyself couldst only see
Thy greatness that is and yet to be,
Thou would feel joy-beauty-what ecstasy.
They are at thy feet, earth-moon-sea, the trinity.

Why-forth then dost thou tarry
And partake thee only of the crust
And skim the earth's surface narry
When all creations art thy just?

Seek ye then that which art not there
In thine own glory let thyself rest.
Witness. Thy power is not bare.
Thou art King. Thou art at thy best.

Look then right before thee.
Open thine eyes and see.
At the foot of Mt. Serenity
Is thy cradle to eternity.

Utterly confused, Wilhelm said to himself explosively, What kind of mishmash, claptrap is this! What does he want from me? Damn him to hell, he might as well hit me on the head, and lay me out, kill me. What does he give me this for? What's the purpose? Is it a deliberate test? Does he want to mix me up? He's already got me mixed up completely. I was never good at riddles. Kiss those seven hundred bucks good-by, and call it one more mistake in a long line of mistakes— Oh, Mama, what a line! He stood near the shining window of a fancy fruit store, holding Tamkin's paper, rather dazed, as though a charge of photographer's flash powder had gone up in his eyes.

But he's waiting for my reaction. I have to say something to him about his poem. It really is no joke. What will I tell him? Who is this King? The poem is written *to* someone. But who? I can't even bring myself to talk. I feel too choked and strangled. With all the books he reads, how come the guy is so illiterate? And why do people just naturally assume that you'll know what they're talking about? No, I don't know, and nobody knows. The planets don't, the stars don't, infinite space doesn't. It doesn't square with Planck's Constant or anything else. So what's the good of it? Where's the need of it? What does he mean here by Mount Serenity? Could it be a figure of speech for Mount Everest? As he says people are all committing suicide, maybe those guys who climbed Everest were only trying to kill themselves, and if we want peace we should stay at the foot of the mountain. In the here-and-now. But it's also here-and-now on the slope, and on the top, where they climbed to seize the day. Surface narry is something he can't mean, I don't believe. I'm about to start foaming at the mouth. "Thy cradle . . . *Who* is resting in his cradle—in his glory? My thoughts are at an end. I feel the wall. No more. So ——k it all! The money and everything. Take it away! When I have the money they eat me alive, like those piranha fish in the movie about the Brazilian jungle. It was hideous when they ate up that Brahma bull in the river. He turned pale, just like clay, and in five minutes nothing was left except the skeleton still in one piece, floating away. When I haven't got it any more, at least they'll let me alone.

"Well, what do you think of this?" said Dr. Tamkin. He gave a special sort of wise smile, as though Wilhelm must now see what kind of man he was dealing with.

"Nice. Very nice. Have you been writing long?"

"I've been developing this line of thought for years and years. You follow it all the way?"

"I'm trying to figure out who this Thou is."

"Thou? Thou is you."

"Me! Why? This applies to *me*?"

"Why shouldn't it apply to you. You were in my mind when I composed it. Of course, the hero of the poem is sick humanity. If it would open its eyes it would be great."

"Yes, but how do I get into this?"

"The main idea of the poem is *con*struct or *de*struct. There is no ground in between. Mechanism is *de*struct. Money of course is *de*struct. When the last grave is dug, the gravedigger will have to be paid. If you could have confidence in nature you would not have to fear. It would keep you up. Creative is nature. Rapid. Lavish. Inspirational. It shapes leaves. It rolls the waters of the earth. Man is the chief of this. All creations are his just inheritance. You don't know what you've got within you. A person either creates or he destroys. There is no neutrality . . ."

"I realize you were no beginner," said Wilhelm with propriety. "I have only one criticism to make. I think 'why-forth' is wrong. You should write 'Wherefore then dost thou . . .'" And he reflected, So? I took a gamble. It'll have to be a miracle, though, to save me. My money will be gone, then it won't be able to destruct me. He can't just take and lose it, though. He's in it, too. I think he's in a bad way himself. He must be. I'm sure because, come to think of it, he sweated blood when he signed that check. But what have I let myself in for? The waters of the earth are going to roll over me.

5

Patiently, in the window of the fruit store, a man with a scoop spread crushed ice between his rows of vegetables. There were also Persian melons, lilacs, tulips with radiant black at the middle. The many street noises came back after a little while from the caves of the sky. Crossing the tide of Broadway traffic, Wilhelm was saying to himself, The reason Tamkin lectures me is that somebody has lectured him, and the reason for the poem is that he wants to give me good advice. Everybody seems to know something. Even fellows like Tamkin. Many people know what to do, but how many can do it?

He believed that he must, that he could and would recover the good things, the happy things, the easy tranquil things of life. He had made mistakes, but he could overlook these. He had been a fool, but that could be forgiven. The time wasted—must be relinquished. What else could one do about it? Things were too complex, but they might be reduced to simplicity again. Recovery was possible. First he had to get out of the city. No, first he had to pull out his money. . . .

From the carnival of the street—pushcarts, accordion and fiddle, shoeshine, begging, the dust going round like a woman on stilts—they entered the narrow crowded theater of the brokerage office. From front to back it was filled with the Broadway crowd. But how was lard doing this morning? From the rear of the hall Wilhelm tried to read the tiny figures. The German manager was looking through his binoculars. Tamkin placed himself on Wilhelm's left and covered his conspicuous bald head. "The guy'll ask me about the margin," he muttered. They passed, however, unobserved. "Look, the lard has held its place," he said.

Tamkin's eyes must be very sharp to read the figures over so many heads and at this distance—another respect in which he was unusual.

The room was always crowded. Everyone talked. Only at the front could you hear the flutter of the wheels within the board. Teletyped news items crossed the illuminated screen above.

"Lard. Now what about rye?" said Tamkin, rising on his toes. Here he was a different man, active and impatient. He parted people who stood in his way. His face turned resolute, and on either side of his mouth odd bulges formed under his mustache. Already he was pointing out to Wilhelm the appearance of a new pattern on the board. "There's something up today," he said.

"Then why'd you take so long with breakfast?" said Wilhelm.

There were no reserved seats in the room, only customary ones. Tamkin always sat in the second row, on the commodities side of the aisle. Some of his acquaintances kept their hats on the chairs for him.

"Thanks. Thanks," said Tamkin, and he told Wilhelm, "I fixed it up yesterday."

"That was a smart thought," said Wilhelm. They sat down.

With folded hands, by the wall, sat an old Chinese businessman in a seersucker coat. Smooth and fat, he wore a white Vandyke. One day Wilhelm had seen him on Riverside Drive pushing two little girls along in a baby carriage—his grandchildren. Then there were two women in their fifties, supposed to be sisters, shrewd and able money-makers, according to Tamkin. They had never a word to say to Wilhelm. But they would chat with Tamkin. Tamkin talked to everyone.

Wilhelm sat between Mr. Rowland, who was elderly, and Mr. Rappaport, who was very old. Yesterday Rowland had told him that in the year 1908, when he was a junior at Harvard, his mother had given him twenty shares of steel for his birthday, and then he had started to read the financial news and had never practiced law but instead followed the market for the rest of his life. Now he speculated only in soy beans, of which he had made a specialty. By his conservative method, said Tamkin, he cleared two hundred a week. Small potatoes, but then he was a bachelor, retired, and didn't need money.

"Without dependents," said Tamkin. "He doesn't have the problems that you and I do."

Did Tamkin have dependents? He had everything that it was possible for a man to have—science, Greek, chemistry, poetry, and now dependents too. That beautiful girl with epilepsy, perhaps. He often said that she was a pure, marvelous, spiritual child who had no knowledge of the world. He protected her, and, if he was not lying, adored her. And if you encouraged Tamkin by believing him, or even if you refrained from questioning him, his hints became more daring. Sometimes he said that he paid for her music lessons. Sometimes he seemed to have footed the bill for the brother's camera expedition to Brazil. And he spoke of paying for the support of the orphaned child of a dead sweetheart. These hints, made dully as asides, grew by repetition into sensational claims.

"For myself, I don't need much," said Tamkin. "But a man can't live for himself and I need the money for certain important things. What do you figure you have to have, to get by?"

"Not less than fifteen grand, after taxes. That's for my wife and the two boys."

"Isn't there anybody else?" said Tamkin with a shrewdness almost cruel. But his look grew more sympathetic as Wilhelm stumbled, not willing to recall another grief.

"Well—there was. But it wasn't a money matter."

"I should hope!" said Tamkin. "If love is love, it's free. Fifteen grand, though, isn't too much for a man of your intelligence to ask out of life. Fools, hard-hearted criminals, and murderers have millions to squander. They burn up the world—oil, coal, wood, metal, and soil, and suck even the air and the sky. They consume, and they give back no benefit. A man like you, humble for life, who wants to feel and live, has trouble—not wanting," said Tamkin in his parenthetical fashion, "to exchange an ounce of soul for a pound of social power—he'll never make it without help in a world like this. But don't you worry." Wilhelm grasped at this assurance. "Just you never mind. We'll go easily beyond your figure."

Dr. Tamkin gave Wilhelm comfort. He often said that he had made as much as a thousand a week in commodities. Wilhelm had examined the receipts, but until this moment it had never occurred to him that there must be debit slips too; he had been shown only the credits.

"But fifteen grand is not an ambitious figure," Tamkin was telling him. "For that you don't have to wear yourself out on the road, dealing with narrow-minded people. A lot of them don't like Jews, either, I suppose?"

"I can't afford to notice. I'm lucky when I have my occupation. Tamkin, do you mean you can save our money?"

"Oh, did I forget to mention what I did before closing yesterday? You see, I closed out one of the lard contracts and bought a hedge of December rye. The rye is up three points already and takes some of the sting out. But lard will go up, too."

"Where? God, yes, you're right," said Wilhelm, eager, and got to his feet to look. New hope freshened his heart. "Why didn't you tell me before?"

And Tamkin, smiling like a benevolent magician, said, "You must learn to have trust. The slump in lard can't last. And just take a look at eggs. Didn't I predict they couldn't go any lower? They're rising and rising. If we had taken eggs we'd be far ahead."

"Then why didn't we take them?"

"We were just about to. I had a buying order in at .24, but the tide turned at .26¼ and we barely missed. Never mind. Lard will go back to last year's levels."

Maybe. But when? Wilhelm could not allow his hopes to grow too strong. However, for a little while he could breathe more easily. Late-morning trading was getting active. The shining numbers whirred on the board, which sounded like a huge cage of artificial birds. Lard fluctuated between two points, but rye slowly climbed.

He closed his strained, greatly earnest eyes briefly and nodded his Buddha's head, too large to suffer such uncertainties. For several moments of peace he was removed to his small yard in Roxbury.

He breathed in the sugar of the pure morning.

He heard the long phrases of the birds.

No enemy wanted his life.

Wilhelm thought, I will get out of here. I don't belong in New York any more. And he sighed like a sleeper.

Tamkin said, "Excuse me," and left his seat. He could not sit still in the room but passed back and forth between the stocks and commodities sections. He knew dozens of people and was continually engaging in discussions. Was he giving advice, gathering information, or giving it, or practicing—whatever mysterious profession he practiced? Hypnotism? Perhaps he could put people in a trance while he talked to them. What a rare, peculiar bird he was, with those pointed shoulders, that bare head, his loose nails, almost claws, and those brown, soft, deadly, heavy eyes.

He spoke of things that mattered, and as very few people did this he could take you by surprise, excite you, move you. Maybe he wished to do good, maybe give himself a lift to a higher level, maybe believe his own prophecies, maybe touch his own heart. Who could tell? He had picked up a lot of strange ideas; Wilhelm could only suspect, he could not say with certainty, that Tamkin hadn't made them his own.

Now Tamkin and he were equal partners, but Tamkin had put up only three hundred dollars. Suppose he did this not only once but five times; then an investment of fifteen hundred dollars gave him five thousand to speculate with. If he had power of attorney in every case, he could shift the money from one account to another. No, the German probably kept an eye on him. Nevertheless it was possible. Calculations like this made Wilhelm feel ill. Obviously Tamkin was a plunger. But how did he get by? He must be in his fifties. How did he support himself? Five years in Egypt; Hollywood before that; Michigan; Ohio; Chicago. A man of fifty has supported himself for at least thirty years. You could be sure that Tamkin had never worked in a factory or in an office. How did he make it? His taste in clothes was horrible, but he didn't buy cheap things. He wore corduory or velvet shirts from Clyde's, painted neckties, striped socks. There was a slightly acid or pasty smell about his person; for a doctor, he didn't bathe much. Also, Dr. Tamkin had a good room at the Gloriana and had had it for about a year. But so was Wilhelm himself a guest, with an unpaid bill at present in his father's box. Did the beautiful girl with the skirts and belts pay him? Was he defrauding his so-called patients? So many questions impossible to answer could not be asked about an honest man. Nor perhaps about a sane man. Was Tamkin a lunatic, then? That sick Mr. Perls at breakfast had said that there was no easy way to tell the sane from the mad, and he was right about that in any big city and especially in New York—the end of the world, with its complexity and machinery, bricks and tubes, wires and stones, holes and heights. And was everybody crazy here? What sort of people did you see? Every other man spoke a language entirely his own, which he had figured out by private thinking; he had his own ideas and peculiar ways. If you wanted to talk about a glass of water, you had to start back with God creating the heavens and earth; the apple; Abraham; Moses and Jesus; Rome; the Middle Ages; gun-powder; the Revolution; back to Newton; up to Einstein; then war and Lenin and Hitler. After reviewing this and getting it all straight again you could proceed to talk about a glass of water. "I'm fainting, please get me a little water." You were lucky even then to make yourself understood. And this happened over and over and over with everyone you met. You had to translate and translate, explain and explain, back and forth, and it was the punishment of hell itself not to understand or be understood, not to know the crazy from the sane, the wise from the fools, the young from the old or the sick from the well. The fathers were no fathers and the sons no sons. You had to talk with yourself in the daytime and reason with yourself at night. Who else was there to talk to in a city like New York?

A queer look came over Wilhelm's face with its eyes turned up and his silent mouth with its high upper lip. He went several degrees further—when you are like this, dreaming that everybody is outcast, you realize that this must be one of the small matters. There is a larger body, and from this you cannot be separated.

The glass of water fades out. You do not go from simple *a* and simple *b* to the great x and *y*, nor does it matter whether you agree about the glass but, far beneath such details, what Tamkin would call the real soul says plain and understandable things to everyone. There sons and fathers are themselves, and a glass of water is only an ornament; it makes a hoop of brightness on the cloth; it is an angel's mouth. There truth for everybody may be found, and confusion is only—only temporary, thought Wilhelm.

The idea of this larger body had been planted in him a few days ago beneath Times Square, when he had gone downtown to pick up tickets for the baseball game on Saturday (a doubleheader at the Polo Grounds). He was going through an underground corridor, a place he had always hated and hated more than ever now. On the walls between the advertisements were words in chalk: "Sin No More," and "Do Not Eat the Pig," he had particularly noticed. And in the dark tunnel, in the haste, heat, and darkness which disfigure and make freaks and fragments of nose and eyes and teeth, all of a sudden, unsought, a general love for all these imperfect and lurid-looking people burst out in Wilhelm's breast. He loved them. One and all, he passionately loved them. They were his brothers and his sisters. He was imperfect and disfigured himself, but what difference did that make if he was united with them by this blaze of love? And as he walked he began to say, "Oh my brothers—my brothers and my sisters," blessing them all as well as himself.

So what did it matter how many languages there were, or how hard it was to describe a glass of water? Or matter that a few minutes later he didn't feel anything like a brother toward the man who sold him the tickets?

On that very same afternoon he didn't hold so high an opinion of this same onrush of loving kindness. What did it come to? As they had the capacity and must use it once in a while, people were bound to have such involuntary feelings. It was only another one of those subway things. Like having a hard-on at random. But today, his day of reckoning, he consulted his memory again and thought, I must go back to that. That's the right clue and may do me the most good. Something very big. Truth, like.

The old fellow on the right, Mr. Rappaport, was nearly blind and kept asking Wilhelm, "What's the new figure on November wheat? Give me July soy beans too." When you told him he didn't say thank you. He said, "Okay," instead, or, "Check," and turned away until he needed you again. He was very old, older even than Dr. Adler, and if you believed Tamkin he had once been the Rockefeller of the chicken business and had retired with a large fortune.

Wilhelm had a queer feeling about the chicken industry, that it was sinister. On the road, he frequently passed chicken farms. Those big, rambling, wooden buildings out in the neglected fields; they were like prisons. The lights burned all night in them to cheat the poor hens into laying. Then the slaughter. Pile all the coops of the slaughtered on end, and in one week they'd go higher than Mount Everest or Mount Serenity. The blood filling the Gulf of Mexico. The chicken shit, acid, burning the earth.

How old—old this Mr. Rappaport was! Purple stains were buried in the flesh of his nose, and the cartilage of his ear was twisted like a cabbage heart. Beyond remedy by glasses, his eyes were smoky and faded.

"Read me that soy-bean figure now, boy," he said, and Wilhelm did. He thought perhaps the old man might give him a tip, or some useful advice or information about Tamkin. But no. He only wrote memoranda on a pad, and put the pad in his pocket. He let no one see what he had written. And Wilhelm thought this was the way a man who had grown rich by the murder of millions of animals, little chickens, would act. If there was a life to come he might have to answer for the killing of all those chickens. What if they all were waiting? But if there was a life to come, everybody would have to answer. But if there was a life to come, the chickens themselves would be all right.

Well! What stupid ideas he was having this morning. Phooey!

Finally old Rappaport did address a few remarks to Wilhelm. He asked him whether he had reserved his seat in the synagogue for Yom Kippur.

"No," said Wilhelm.

"Well, you better hurry up if you expect to say *Yiskor* for your parents. I never miss."

And Wilhelm thought, Yes, I suppose I should say a prayer for Mother once in a while. His mother had belonged to the Reform congregation. His father had no religion. At the cemetery

Wilhelm had paid a man to say a prayer for her. He was among the tombs and he wanted to be tipped for the *El molai rachamin*. "Thou God of Mercy," Wilhelm thought that meant. *B'gan Aden* —"in Paradise." Singing, they drew it out. *B'gan Ay-den*. The broken bench beside the grave made him wish to do something. Wilhelm often prayed in his own manner. He did not go to the synagogue but he would occasionally perform certain devotions, according to his feelings. Now he reflected, In Dad's eyes I am the wrong kind of Jew. He doesn't like the way I act. Only he is the right kind of Jew. Whatever you are, it always turns out to be the wrong kind.

Mr. Rappaport grumbled and whiffed at his long cigar, and the board, like a swarm of electrical bees, whirred.

"Since you were in the chicken business, I thought you'd speculate in eggs, Mr. Rappaport." Wilhelm, with his warm, panting laugh, sought to charm the old man.

"Oh, Yeah. Loyalty, hey?" said old Rappaport. "I should stick to them. I spent a lot of time amongst chickens. I got to be an expert chicken-sexer. When the chick hatches you have to tell the boys from the girls. It's not easy. You need long, long experience. What do you think, it's a joke? A whole industry depends on it. Yes, now and then I buy a contract eggs. What have you got today?"

Wilhelm said anxiously, "Lard. Rye."

"Buy? Sell?"

"Bought."

"Uh," said the old man. Wilhelm could not determine what he meant by this. But of course you couldn't expect him to make himself any clearer. It was not in the code to give information to anyone. Sick with desire, Wilhelm waited for Mr. Rappaport to make an exception in his case. Just this once! Because it was critical. Silently, by a sort of telepathic concentration, he begged the old man to speak the single word that would save him, give him the merest sign. "Oh, please—please help," he nearly said. If Rappaport would close one eye, or lay his head to one side, or raise his finger and point to a column in the paper or to a figure on his pad. A hint! A hint!

A long perfect ash formed on the end of the cigar, the white ghost of the leaf with all its veins and its fainter pungency. It was ignored, in its beauty, by the old man. For it was beautiful. Wilhelm he ignored as well.

Then Tamkin said to him, "Wilhelm, look at the jump our rye just took."

December rye climbed three points as they tensely watched; the tumblers raced and the machine's lights buzzed.

"A point and a half more, and we can cover the lard losses," said Tamkin. He showed him his calculations on the margin of the *Times*.

"I think you should put in the selling order now. Let's get out with a small loss."

"Get out now? Nothing doing."

"Why not? Why should we wait?"

"Because," said Tamkin with a smiling, almost openly scoffing look, "you've got to keep your nerve when the market starts to go places. Now's when you can make something."

"I'd get out while the getting's good."

"No, you shouldn't lose your head like this. It's obvious to me what the mechanism is, back in the Chicago market. There's a short supply of December rye. Look, it's just gone up another quarter. We should ride it."

"I'm losing my taste for the gamble," said Wilhelm. "You can't feel safe when it goes up so fast. It's liable to come down just as quick."

Dryly, as though he were dealing with a child, Tamkin told him in a tone of tiring patience, "Now listen, Tommy. I have it diagnosed right. If you wish I should sell I can give the sell order. But this is the difference between healthiness and pathology. One is objective, doesn't change his mind every minute, enjoys the risk element. But that's not the neurotic character. The neurotic character—"

"Damn it, Tamkin!" said Wilhelm roughly. "Cut that out. I don't like it. Leave my character out of consideration. Don't pull any more of that stuff on me. I tell you I don't like it."

Tamkin therefore went no further; he backed down. "I meant," he said, softer, "that as a salesman you are basically an artist type. The seller is in the visionary sphere of the business function. And then you're an actor, too."

"No matter what type I am—" An angry and yet weak sweetness rose into Wilhelm's throat. He coughed as though he had the flu. It was twenty years since he had appeared on the screen as an extra. He blew the bagpipes in a film called *Annie Laurie.* Annie had come to warn the young Laird; he would not believe her and called the bagpipers to drown her out. He made fun of her while she wrung her hands. Wilhelm, in a kilt, barelegged, blew and blew and blew and not a sound came out. Of course all the music was recorded. He fell sick with the flu after that and still suffered sometimes from chest weakness.

"Something stuck in your throat?" said Tamkin. "I think maybe you are too disturbed to think clearly. You should try some of my 'here-and-now' mental exercises. It stops you from thinking so much about the future and the past and cuts down confusion."

"Yes, yes, yes, yes," said Wilhelm, his eyes fixed on December rye.

"Nature only knows one thing, and that's the present. Present, present, eternal present, like a big, huge, giant wave—colossal, bright and beautiful, full of life and death, climbing into the sky, standing in the seas. You must go along with the actual, the Here-and-Now, the glory—"

. . . chest weakness, Wilhelm's recollection went on. Margaret nursed him. They had had two rooms of furniture, which was later seized. She sat on the bed and read to him. He made her read for days, and she read stories, poetry, everything in the house. He felt dizzy, stifled when he tried to smoke. They had him wear a flannel vest.

> Come then, Sorrow!
> Sweetest Sorrow!
> Like an own babe I nurse thee on my breast!

Why did he remember that? Why?

"You have to pick out something that's in the actual, immediate present moment," said Tamkin. "And say to yourself here-and-now, here-and-now, here-and-now. 'Where am I?' 'Here.' 'When is it?' 'Now.' Take an object or a person. Anybody. 'Here and now I see a person.' 'Here and now I see a man.' 'Here and now I see a man sitting on a chair.' Take me, for instance. Don't let your mind wander. 'Here and now I see a man in a brown suit. Here and now I see a corduroy shirt.' You have to narrow it down, one item at a time, and not let your imagination shoot ahead. Be in the present. Grasp the hour, the moment, the instant."

Is he trying to hypnotize or con me? Wilhelm wondered. To take my mind off selling? But even if I'm back at seven hundred bucks, then where am I?

As if in prayer, his lids coming down with raised veins, frayed out, on his significant eyes, Tamkin said, "'Here and now I see a button. Here and now I see the thread that sews the button. Here and now I see the green thread.'" Inch by inch he contemplated himself in order to show Wilhelm how calm it would make him. But Wilhelm was hearing Margaret's voice as she read, somewhat unwillingly,

> Come then, Sorrow!
>
> . . . .
>
> I thought to leave thee,
> And deceive thee,
> But now of all the world I love thee best.

Then Mr. Rappaport's old hand pressed his thigh, and he said, "What's my wheat? Those damn guys are blocking the way. I can't see."

6

Rye was still ahead when they went out to lunch, and lard was holding its own.

They ate in the cafeteria with the gilded front. There was the same art inside as outside. The food looked sumptuous. Whole fishes were framed like pictures with carrots, and the salads were like terraced landscapes or like Mexican pyramids; slices of lemon and onion and radishes were like sun and moon and stars; the cream pies were about a foot thick and the cakes swollen as if sleepers had baked them in their dreams.

"What'll you have?" said Tamkin.

"Not much. I ate a big breakfast. I'll find a table. Bring me some yogurt and crackers and a cup of tea. I don't want to spend much time over lunch."

Tamkin said, "You've got to eat."

Finding an empty place at this hour was not easy. The old people idled and gossiped over their coffee. The elderly ladies were rouged and mascaraed and hennaed and used blue hair rinse and eye shadow and wore costume jewelry, and many of them were proud and stared at you with expressions that did not belong to their age. Were there no longer any respectable old ladies who knitted and cooked and looked after their grandchildren? Wilhelm's grandmother had dressed him in a sailor suit and danced him on her knee, blew on the porridge for him and said, "Admiral, you must eat." But what was the use of remembering this so late in the day?

He managed to find a table, and Dr. Tamkin came along with a tray piled with plates and cups. He had Yankee pot roast, purple cabbage, potatoes, a big slice of watermelon, and two cups of coffee. Wilhelm could not even swallow his yogurt. His chest pained him still.

At once Tamkin involved him in a lengthy discussion. Did he do it to stall Wilhelm and prevent him from selling out the rye—or to recover the ground lost when he had made Wilhelm angry by hints about the neurotic character? Or did he have no purpose except to talk?

"I think you worry a lot too much about what your wife and your father will say. Do they matter so much?"

Wilhelm replied, "A person can become tired of looking himself over and trying to fix himself up. You can spend the entire second half of your life recovering from the mistakes of the first half."

"I believe your dad told me he had some money to leave you."

"He probably does have something."

"A lot?"

"Who can tell," said Wilhelm guardedly.

"You ought to think over what you'll do with it."

"I may be too feeble to do anything by the time I get it. If I get anything."

"A thing like this you ought to plan out carefully. Invest it properly." He began to unfold schemes whereby you bought bonds, and used the bonds as security to buy something else and thereby earned twelve per cent safely on your money. Wilhelm failed to follow the details. Tamkin said, "If he made you a gift now, you wouldn't have to pay the inheritance taxes."

Bitterly, Wilhelm told him, "My father's death blots out all other considerations from his mind. He forces me to think about it, too. Then he hates me because he succeeds. When I get desperate—of course I think about money. But I don't want anything to happen to him. I certainly don't want him to die." Tamkin's brown eyes glittered shrewdly at him. "You don't believe it. Maybe it's not psychological. But on my word of honor. A joke is a joke, but I don't want to joke about stuff like this. When he dies, I'll be robbed, like. I'll have no more father."

"You love your old man?"

Wilhelm grasped at this. "Of course, of course I love him. My father. My mother—" As he said this there was a great pull at the very center of his soul. When a fish strikes the line you feel the live force in your hand. A mysterious being beneath the water, driven by hunger, has taken the hook and rushes away and fights, writhing. Wilhelm never identified what struck within him. It did not reveal itself. It got away.

And Tamkin, the confuser of the imagination, began to tell, or to fabricate, the strange history of *his* father. "He was a great singer," he said. "He left us five kids because he fell in love with an opera soprano. I never held it against him, but admired the way he followed the life-principle. I wanted to do the same. Because of unhappiness, at a certain age, the brain starts to die back." (True, true! thought Wilhelm) "Twenty years later I was doing experiments in Eastman Kodak, Rochester, and I found the old fellow. He had five more children." (False, false!) "He wept; he was ashamed. I had nothing against him. I naturally felt strange."

"My dad is something of a stranger to me, too," said Wilhelm, and he began to muse. Where is the familiar person he used to be? Or I used to be? Catherine—she won't even talk to me any more, my own sister. It may not be so much my trouble that Papa turns his back on as my confusion. It's too much. The ruins of life, and on top of that confusion—chaos and old night. Is it an easier farewell for Dad if we don't part friends? He should maybe do it angrily— "Blast you with my curse!" And why, Wilhelm further asked, should he or anybody else pity me; or why should I be pitied sooner than another fellow? It is my childish mind that thinks people are ready to give it just because you need it.

Then Wilhelm began to think about his own two sons and to wonder how he appeared to them, and what they would think of him. Right now he had an advantage through baseball. When he went to fetch them, to go to Ebbets Field, though, he was not himself. He put on a front but he felt as if he had swallowed a fistful of sand. The strange, familiar house, horribly awkward; the dog, Scissors, rolled over on his back and barked and whined. Wilhelm acted as if there were nothing irregular, but a weary heaviness came over him. On the way to Flatbush he would think up anecdotes about old Pigtown and Charlie Ebbets for the boys and reminiscences of the old stars, but it was very heavy going. They did not know how much he cared for them. No. It hurt him greatly and he blamed Margaret for turning them against him. She wanted to ruin him, while she wore the mask of kindness. Up in Roxbury he had to go and explain to the priest, who was not sympathetic. They don't care about individuals, their rules come first. Olive said she would marry him outside the Church when he was divorced. But Margaret would not let go. Olive's father was a pretty decent old guy, an osteopath, and he understood what it was all about. Finally he said, "See here, I have to advise Olive. She is asking me. I am mostly a freethinker myself, but the girl has to live in this town." And by now, Wilhelm and Olive had had a great many troubles and she was beginning to dread his days in Roxbury, she said. He trembled at offending this small, pretty, dark girl whom he adored. When she would get up late on Sunday morning she would wake him almost in tears at being late for Mass. He would try to help her hitch her garters and smooth out her slip and dress and even put on her hat with shaky hands; then he would rush her to church and drive in second gear in his forgetful way, trying to apologize and to calm her. She got out a block from church to avoid gossip. Even so she loved him, and she would have married him if he had obtained the divorce. But Margaret must have sensed this. Margaret would tell him he did not really want a divorce; he was afraid of it. He cried, "Take everything I've got, Margaret. Let me go to Reno. Don't you want to marry again?" No. She went out with other men, but took his money. She lived in order to punish him.

Dr. Tamkin told Wilhelm, "Your dad is jealous of you."

Wilhelm smiled. "Of *me*? That's rich."

"Sure. People are always jealous of a man who leaves his wife."

"Oh," said Wilhelm scornfully. "When it comes to wives he wouldn't have to envy me."

"Yes, and your wife envies you, too. She thinks, He's free and goes with young women. Is she getting old?"

"Not exactly old," said Wilhelm, whom the mention of his wife made sad. Twenty years ago, in a neat blue wool suit, in a soft hat made of the same cloth—he could plainly see her. He stooped his yellow head and looked under the hat at her clear, simple face, her living eyes moving, her straight small nose, her jaw beautifully, painfully clear in its form. It was a cool day, but he smelled the odor of pines in the sun, in the granite canyon. Just south of Santa Barbara, this was.

"She's forty-some years old," he said.

"I was married to a lush," said Tamkin. "A painful alcoholic. I couldn't take her out to dinner because she'd say she was going to the ladies' toilet and disappear into the bar. I'd ask the bartenders they shouldn't serve her. But I loved her deeply. She was the most spiritual woman of my entire experience."

"Where is she now?"

"Drowned," said Tamkin. "At Provincetown, Cape Cod. It must have been a suicide. She was that way—suicidal. I tried everything in my power to cure her. Because," said Tamkin, "my real calling is to be a healer. I get wounded. I suffer from it. I would like to escape from the sicknesses of others, but I can't. I am only on loan to myself, so to speak. I belong to humanity."

Liar! Wilhelm inwardly called him. Nasty lies. He invented a woman and killed her off and then called himself a healer, and made himself so earnest he looked like a bad-natured sheep. He's a puffed-up little bogus and humbug with smelly feet. A doctor! A doctor would wash himself. He believes he's making a terrific impression, and he practically invites you to take off your hat when he talks about himself; and he thinks he has an imagination, but he hasn't, neither is he smart.

Then what am I doing with him here, and why did I give him the seven hundred dollars? thought Wilhelm.

Oh, this was a day of reckoning. It was a day, he thought, on which, willing or not, he would take a good close look at the truth. He breathed hard and his misshapen hat came low upon his congested dark blond face. A rude look. Tamkin was a charlatan, and furthermore he was desperate. And furthermore, Wilhelm had always known this about him. But he appeared to have worked it out at the back of his mind that Tamkin for thirty or forty years had gotten through many a tight place, that he would get through this crisis too and bring him, Wilhelm, to safety also. And Wilhelm realized that he was on Tamkin's back. It made him feel that he had virtually left the ground and was riding upon the other man. He was in the air. It was for Tamkin to take the steps.

The doctor, if he was a doctor, did not look anxious. But then his face did not have much variety. Talking always about spontaneous emotion and open receptors and free impulses, he was about as expressive as a pincushion. When his hypnotic spell failed, his big underlip made him look weak-minded. Fear stared from his eyes, sometimes, so humble as to make you sorry for him. Once or twice Wilhelm had seen that look. Like a dog, he thought. Perhaps he didn't look it now, but he was very nervous. Wilhelm knew, but he could not afford to recognize this too openly. The doctor needed a little room, a little time. He should not be pressed now. So Tamkin went on, telling his tales.

Wilhelm said to himself, I am on his back—his back. I gambled seven hundred bucks, so I must take this ride. I have to go along with him. It's too late. I can't get off.

"You know," Tamkin said, "that blind old man Rappaport—he's pretty close to totally blind—is one of the most interesting personalities around here. If you could only get him to tell his true story. It's fascinating. This is what he told me. You often hear about bigamists with a secret life. But this old man never hid anything from anybody. He's a regular patriarch. Now, I'll tell you what he did. He had two whole families, separate and apart, one in Williamsburg and the other in the Bronx. The two wives knew about each other. The wife in the Bronx was younger; she's close to seventy now. When he got sore at one wife he went to live with the other one. Meanwhile he ran his chicken business in New Jersey. By one wife he had four kids, and by the other six. They're all grown, but they never have met their half-brothers and sisters and don't want to. The whole bunch of them are listed in the telephone book."

"I can't believe it," said Wilhelm.

"He told me this himself. And do you know what else? While he had his eyesight he used to read a lot, but the only books he would read were by Theodore Roosevelt. He had a set in each of the places where he lived, and he brought his kids up on those books."

"Please," said Wilhelm, "don't feed me any more of this stuff, will you? Kindly do not—"

"In telling you this," said Tamkin with one of his hypnotic subtleties, "I do have a motive. I want you to see how some people free themselves from morbid guilt feelings and follow their instincts. Innately, the female knows how to cripple by sickening a man with guilt. It is a very special destruct, and she sends her curse to make a fellow impotent. As if she says, 'Unless I allow it, you will never more be a man.' But men like my old dad or Mr. Rappaport answer, 'Woman, what art thou to me?' You can't do that yet. You're a halfway case. You want to follow your instinct, but you're too worried still. For instance, about your kids—"

"Now look here," said Wilhelm, stamping his feet. "One thing! Don't bring up my boys. Just lay off."

"I was only going to say that they are better off than with conflicts in the home."

"I'm deprived of my children." Wilhelm bit his lip. It was too late to turn away. The anguish struck him. "I pay and pay. I never see them. They grow up without me. She makes them like herself. She'll bring them up to be my enemies. Please let's not talk about this."

But Tamkin said, "Why do you let her make you suffer so? It

defeats the original object in leaving her. Don't play her game. Now, Wilhelm, I'm trying to do you some good. I want to tell you, don't marry suffering. Some people do. They get married to it, and sleep and eat together, just as husband and wife. If they go with joy they think it's adultery."

When Wilhelm heard this he had, in spite of himself, to admit that there was a great deal in Tamkin's words. Yes, thought Wilhelm, suffering is the only kind of life they are sure they can have, and if they quit suffering they're afraid they'll have nothing. He knows it. This time the faker knows what he's talking about.

Looking at Tamkin he believed he saw all this confessed from his usually barren face. Yes, yes, he too. One hundred falsehoods, but at last one truth. Howling like a wolf from the city window. No one can bear it any more. Everyone is so full of it that at last everybody must proclaim it. It! It!

Then suddenly Wilhelm rose and said, "That's enough of this. Tamkin, let's go back to the market."

"I haven't finished my melon."

"Never mind that. You've had enough to eat. I want to go back."

Dr. Tamkin slid the two checks across the table. "Who paid yesterday? It's your turn, I think."

It was not until they were leaving the cafeteria that Wilhelm remembered definitely that he had paid yesterday too. But it wasn't worth arguing about.

Tamkin kept repeating as they walked down the street that there were many who were dedicated to suffering. But he told Wilhelm, "I'm optimistic in your case, and I have seen a world of maladjustment. There's hope for you. You don't really want to destroy yourself. You're trying hard to keep your feelings open, Wilhelm. I can see it. Seven per cent of this country is committing suicide by alcohol. Another three, maybe, narcotics. Another sixty just fading away into dust by boredom. Twenty more who have sold their souls to the Devil. Then there's a small percentage of those who want to live. That's the only significant thing in the whole world of today. Those are the only two classes of people there are. Some want to live, but the great majority don't." This fantastic Tamkin began to surpass himself. "They don't. Or else, why these wars? I'll tell you more," he said. "The love of the dying amounts to one thing; they want you to die with them. It's because they love you. Make no mistake."

True, true! thought Wilhelm, profoundly moved by these revelations. How does he know these things? How can he be such a jerk, and even perhaps an operator, a swindler, and understand so well what gives? I believe what he says. It simplifies much—everything. People are dropping like flies. I am trying to stay alive and work too hard at it. That's what's turning my brains. This working hard defeats its own end. At what point should I start over? Let me go back a ways and try once more.

Only a few hundred yards separated the cafeteria from the broker's, and within that short space Wilhelm turned again, in measurable degrees, from these wide considerations to the problems of the moment. The closer he approached to the market, the more Wilhelm had to think about money.

They passed the newsreel theater where the ragged shoeshine kids called after them. The same old bearded man with his bandaged beggar face and his tiny ragged feet and the old press clipping on his fiddle case to prove he had once been a concert violinist, pointed his bow at Wilhelm, saying, "You!" Wilhelm went by with worried eyes, bent on crossing Seventy-second Street. In full tumult the great afternoon current raced for Columbus Circle, where the mouth of midtown stood open and the skyscrapers gave back the yellow fire of the sun.

As they approached the polished stone front of the new office building, Dr. Tamkin said, "Well, isn't that old Rappaport by the door? I think he should carry a white cane, but he will never admit there's a single thing the matter with his eyes."

Mr. Rappaport did not stand well; his knees were sunk, while his pelvis only half filled his trousers. His suspenders held them, gaping.

He stopped Wilhelm with an extended hand, having somehow recognized him. In his deep voice he commanded him, "Take me to the cigar store."

"You want me—? Tamkin!" Wilhelm whispered, "You take him."

Tamkin shook his head. "He wants you. Don't refuse the old gentleman." Significantly he said in a lower voice. "This minute is another instance of the 'here-and-now.' You have to live in this very minute, and you don't want to. A man asks you for help. Don't think of the market. It won't run away. Show your respect to the old boy. Go ahead. That may be more valuable."

"Take me," said the old chicken merchant again.

Greatly annoyed, Wilhelm wrinkled his face at Tamkin. He took the old man's big but light elbow at the bone. "Well, let's step on it," he said. "Or wait—I want to have a look at the board first to see how we're doing."

But Tamkin had already started Mr. Rappaport forward. He was walking, and he scolded Wilhelm, saying, "Don't leave me standing in the middle of the sidewalk. I'm afraid to get knocked over."

"Let's get a move on. Come." Wilhelm urged him as Tamkin went into the broker's.

The traffic seemed to come down Broadway out of the sky, where the hot spokes of the sun rolled from the south. Hot, stony odors rose from the subway grating in the street.

"These teen-age hoodlums worry me. I'm ascared of these Puerto Rican kids, and these young characters who take dope," said Mr. Rappaport. "They go around all hopped up."

"Hoodlums?" said Wilhelm. "I went to the cemetery and my mother's stone bench was split. I could have broken somebody's neck for that. Which store do you go to?"

"Across Broadway. That La Magnita sign next door to the Automat."

"What's the matter with this store here on this side?"

"They don't carry my brand, that's what's the matter."

Wilhelm cursed, but checked the words.

"What are you talking?"

"Those damn taxis," said Wilhelm. "They want to run everybody down."

They entered the cool, odorous shop. Mr. Rappaport put away his large cigars with great care in various pockets while Wilhelm muttered, "Come on, you old creeper. What a poky old character! The whole world waits on him." Rappaport did not offer Wilhelm a cigar, but, holding one up, he asked, "What do you say at the size of these, huh? They're Churchill-type cigars."

He barely crawls along, thought Wilhelm. His pants are dropping off because he hasn't got enough flesh for them to stick to. He's almost blind, and covered with spots, but this old man still makes money in the market. Is loaded with dough, probably. And I bet he doesn't give his children any. Some of them must be in their fifties. This is what keeps middle-aged men as children. He's master over the dough. Think—just think! Who controls everything? Old men of this type. Without needs. They don't need therefore they have. I need, therefore I don't have. That would be too easy.

"I'm older even than Churchill," said Rappaport.

Now he wanted to talk! But if you asked him a question in the market, he couldn't be bothered to answer.

"I bet you are," said Wilhelm. "Come, let's get going."

"I was a fighter, too, like Churchill," said the old man. "When we licked Spain I went into the Navy. Yes, I was a gob that time. What did I have to lose? Nothing. After the battle of San Juan Hill, Teddy Roosevelt kicked me off the beach."

"Come, watch the curb," said Wilhelm.

"I was curious and wanted to see what went on. I didn't have no business there, but I took a boat and rowed myself to the beach. Two of our guys was dead, layin' under the American flag to keep the flies off. So I says to the guy on duty, there, who was the sentry, 'Let's have a look at these guys. I want to see what went on here,' and he says, 'Naw,' but I talked him into it. So he took off the flag and there were these two tall guys, both gentlemen, lying in their boots. They was very tall. The two of them had long mustaches. They were high-society boys. I think one of them was called Fish, from up the Hudson, a big-shot family. When I looked up, there was Teddy Roosevelt, with his hat off, and he was looking at these fellows, the only ones who got killed there. Then he says to me, 'What's the Navy want here? Have you got orders?' 'No, sir,' I says to him. 'Well, get the hell off the beach, then.'"

Old Rappaport was very proud of this memory. "Everything he said had such snap, such class. Man! I love that Teddy Roosevelt," he said, "I love him!"

Ah, what people are! He is almost not with us, and his life is nearly gone, but T. R. once yelled at him, so he loves him. I guess it is love, too. Wilhelm smiled. So maybe the rest of Tamkin's story was true, about the ten children and the wives and the telephone directory.

He said, "Come on, come on, Mr. Rappaport," and hurried the old man back by the large hollow elbow; he gripped it through the thin cotton cloth. Re-entering the brokerage office where under the lights the tumblers were speeding with the clack of drumsticks upon wooden blocks, more than ever resembling a Chinese theater, Wilhelm strained his eyes to see the board.

The lard figures were unfamiliar. That amount couldn't be lard! They must have put the figures in the wrong slot. He traced the line back to the margin. It was down to .19, and had dropped twenty points since noon. And what about the contract of rye? It had sunk back to its earlier position, and they had lost their chance to sell.

Old Mr. Rappaport said to Wilhelm, "Read me my wheat figure."

"Oh, leave me alone for a minute," he said, and positively hid his face from the old man behind one hand. He looked for Tamkin, Tamkin's bald head, or Tamkin with his gray straw and the cocoa-colored band. He couldn't see him. Where was he? The seats next to Rowland were taken by strangers. He thrust himself over the one on the aisle, Mr. Rappaport's former place, and pushed at the back of the chair until the new occupant, a red-headed man with a thin, determined face, leaned forward to get out of his way but would not surrender the seat. "Where's Tamkin?" Wilhelm asked Rowland.

"Gee, I don't know. Is anything wrong?"

"You must have seen him. He came in a while back."

"No, but I didn't."

Wilhelm fumbled out a pencil from the top pocket of his coat and began to make calculations. His very fingers were numb, and in his agitation he was afraid he made mistakes with the decimal points and went over the subtraction and multiplication like a schoolboy at an exam. His heart, accustomed to many sorts of crisis, was now in a new panic. And, as he had dreaded, he was wiped out. It was unnecessary to ask the German manager. He could see for himself that the electronic bookkeeping device must have closed him out. The manager probably had known that Tamkin wasn't to be trusted, and on that first day he might have warned him. But you couldn't expect him to interfere.

"You get hit?" said Mr. Rowland.

And Wilhelm, quite coolly, said, "Oh, it could have been worse, I guess." He put the piece of paper into his pocket with its cigarette butts and packets of pills. The lie helped him out—although, for a moment, he was afraid he would cry. But he hardened himself. The hardening effort made a violent, vertical pain go through his chest, like that caused by a pocket of air under the collar bones. To the old chicken millionaire, who by this time had become acquainted with the drop in rye and lard, he also denied that anything serious had happened. "It's just one of those temporary slumps. Nothing to be scared about," he said, and remained in possession of himself. His need to cry, like someone in a crowd, pushed and jostled and abused him from behind, and Wilhelm did not dare turn. He said to himself, I will not cry in front of these people. I'll be damned if I'll break down in front of them like a kid, even though I never expect to see them again. No! No! And yet his unshed tears rose and rose and he looked like a man about to drown. But when they talked to him, he answered very distinctly. He tried to speak proudly.

". . . going away?" he heard Rowland ask.

"What?"

"I thought you might be going away too. Tamkin said he was going to Maine this summer for his vacation."

"Oh, going away?"

Wilhelm broke off and went to look for Tamkin in the men's toilet. Across the corridor was the room where the machinery of the board was housed. It hummed and whirred like mechanical birds, and the tubes glittered in the dark. A couple of businessmen with cigarettes in their fingers were having a conversation in the lavatory. At the top of the closet door sat a gray straw hat with a cocoa-colored band. "Tamkin," said Wilhelm. He tried to identify the feet below the door. "Are you in there, Doctor Tamkin?" he said with stifled anger. "Answer me. It's Wilhelm."

The hat was taken down, the latch lifted, and a stranger came out who looked at him with annoyance.

"You waiting?" said one of the businessmen. He was warning Wilhelm that he was out of turn.

"Me? Not me," said Wilhelm. "I'm looking for a fellow."

Bitterly angry, he said to himself that Tamkin would pay him the two hundred dollars at least, his share of the original deposit. "And before he takes the train to Maine, too. Before he spends a penny on vacation—that liar! We went into this as equal partners."

7

I was the man beneath; Tamkin was on my back, and I thought I was on his. He made me carry him, too, besides Margaret. Like this they ride on me with hoofs and claws. Tear me to pieces, stamp on me and break my bones.

Once more the hoary old fiddler pointed his bow at Wilhelm as he hurried by. Wilhelm rejected his begging and denied the omen. He dodged heavily through traffic and with his quick, small steps ran up the lower stairway of the Gloriana Hotel with its dark-tinted mirrors, kind to people's defects. From the lobby he phoned Tamkin's room, and when no one answered he took the elevator up. A rouged woman in her fifties with a mink stole led three tiny dogs on a leash, high-strung creatures with prominent black eyes, like dwarf deer, and legs like twigs. This was the eccentric Estonian lady who had been moved with her pets to the twelfth floor.

She identified Wilhelm. "You are Doctor Adler's son," she said.

Formally, he nodded.

"I am a dear friend of your father."

He stood in the corner and would not meet her glance, and she thought he was snubbing her and made a mental note to speak of it to the doctor.

The linen-wagon stood at Tamkin's door, and the chambermaid's key with its big brass tongue was in the lock.

"Has Doctor Tamkin been here?" he asked her.

"No, I haven't seen him."

Wilhelm came in, however, to look around. He examined the photos on the desk, trying to connect the faces with the strange people in Tamkin's stories. Big, heavy volumes were stacked under the double-pronged TV aerial. *Science and Sanity,* he read, and there were several books of poetry. The *Wall Street Journal* hung in separate sheets from the bed-table under the weight of the silver water jug. A bathrobe with lightning streaks of red and white was laid across the foot of the bed with a pair of expensive batik pajamas. It was a box of a room, but from the windows you saw the river as far uptown as the bridge, as far downtown as Hoboken. What lay between was deep, azure, dirty, complex, crystal, rusty, with the red bones of new apartments rising on the bluffs of New Jersey, and huge liners in their berths, the tugs with matted beards of cordage. Even the brackish tidal river smell rose this high, like the smell of mop water. From every side he heard pianos, and the voices of men and women singing scales and opera, all mixed, and the sounds of pigeons on the ledges.

Again Wilhelm took the phone. "Can you locate Doctor Tamkin in the lobby for me?" he asked. And when the operator reported that she could not, Wilhelm gave the number of his father's room, but Dr. Adler was not in either. "Well, please give me the masseur. I say the massage room. Don't you understand me? The men's health club. Yes, Max Schilper's—how am I supposed to know the name of it?"

There a strange voice said, "Toktor Adler?" It was the old Czech prizefighter with the deformed nose and ears who was attendant down there and gave out soap, sheets, and sandals. He went away. A hollow endless silence followed. Wilhelm flickered the receiver with his nails, whistled into it, but could not summon either the attendant or the operator.

The maid saw him examining the bottles of pills on Tamkin's table and seemed suspicious of him. He was running low on Phenaphen pills and was looking for something else. But he swallowed one of his own tablets and went out and rang again for the elevator. He went down to the health club. Through the steamy windows, when he emerged, he saw the reflection of the swimming pool swirling green at the bottom of the lowest stair-way. He went through the locker-room curtains. Two men wrapped in towels were playing Ping-pong. They were awkward and the ball bounded high. The Negro in the toilet was shining shoes. He did not know Dr. Adler by name, and Wilhelm descended to the massage room. On the tables naked men were lying. It was not a brightly lighted place, and it was very hot, and under the white faint moons of the ceiling shone pale skins. Calendar pictures of pretty girls dressed in tiny fringes were pinned on the wall. On the first table, eyes deeply shut in heavy silent luxury lay a man with a full square beard and short legs, stocky and black-haired. He might have been an orthodox Russian. Wrapped in a sheet, waiting, the man beside him was newly shaved and red from the steambath. He had a big happy face and was dreaming. And after him was an athlete, strikingly muscled, powerful and young, with a strong white curve to his genital and a half-angry smile on his mouth. Dr. Adler was on the fourth table, and Wilhelm stood over his father's pale, slight body. His ribs were narrow and small, his belly round, white, and high. It had its own being, like something separate. His thighs were weak, the muscles of his arms had fallen, his throat was creased.

The masseur in his undershirt bent and whispered in his ear, "It's your son," and Dr. Adler opened his eyes into Wilhelm's face. At once he saw the trouble in it, and by an instantaneous reflex he removed himself from the danger of contagion, and he said serenely, "Well, have you taken my advice, Wilky?"

"Oh, Dad," said Wilhelm.

"To take a swim and get a massage?"

"Did you get my note?" said Wilhelm.

"Yes, but I'm afraid you'll have to ask somebody else, because I can't. I had no idea you were so low on funds. How did you let it happen? Didn't you lay anything aside?"

"Oh, please, Dad," said Wilhelm, almost bringing his hands together in a clasp.

"I'm sorry," said the doctor. "I really am. But I have set up a rule. I've thought about it, I believe it is a good rule, and I don't want to change it. You haven't acted wisely. What's the matter?"

"Everything. Just everything. What isn't? I did have a little, but I haven't been very smart."

"You took some gamble? You lost it? Was it Tamkin? I told you, Wilky, not to build on that Tamkin. Did you? I suspect—"

"Yes, Dad, I'm afraid I trusted him."

Dr. Adler surrendered his arm to the masseur, who was using wintergreen oil.

"Trusted! And got taken?"

"I'm afraid I kind of—" Wilhelm glanced at the masseur but he was absorbed in his work. He probably did not listen to conversations. "I did. I might as well say it. I should have listened to you."

"Well, I won't remind you how often I warned you. It must be very painful."

"Yes, Father, it is."

"I don't know how many times you have to be burned in order to learn something. The same mistakes, over and over."

"I couldn't agree with you more," said Wilhelm with a face of despair. "You're so right, Father. It's the same mistakes, and I get burned again and again. I can't seem to—I'm stupid, Dad, I just can't breathe. My chest is all up—I feel choked. I just simply can't catch my breath."

He stared at his father's nakedness. Presently he became aware that Dr. Adler was making an effort to keep his temper. He was on the verge of an explosion. Wilhelm hung his face and said, "Nobody likes bad luck, eh Dad?"

"So! It's bad luck, now. A minute ago it was stupidity."

"It is stupidity—it's some of both. It's true that I can't learn. But I—"

"I don't want to listen to the details," said his father. "And I want you to understand that I'm too old to take on new burdens. I'm just too old to do it. And people who will just wait for help—must *wait* for help. They have got to stop waiting."

"It isn't all a question of money—there are other things a father can give to a son." He lifted up his gray eyes and his nostrils grew wide with a look of suffering appeal that stirred his father even more deeply against him.

He warningly said to him, "Look out, Wilky, you're tiring my patience very much."

"I try not to. But one word from you, just a word, would go a long way. I've never asked you for very much. But you are not a kind man, Father. You don't give the little bit I beg you for."

He recognized that his father was now furiously angry. Dr. Adler started to say something, and then raised himself and gathered the sheet over him as he did so. His mouth opened, wide, dark, twisted, and he said to Wilhelm, "You want to make yourself into my cross. But I am not going to pick up a cross. I'll see you dead, Wilky, by Christ, before I let you do that to me."

"Father, listen! Listen!"

"Go away from me now. It's torture for me to look at you, you slob!" cried Dr. Adler.

Wilhelm's blood rose up madly, in anger equal to his father's, but then it sank down and left him helplessly captive to misery. He said stiffly, and with a strange sort of formality, "Okay, Dad. That'll be enough. That's about all we should say." And he stalked out heavily by the door adjacent to the swimming pool and the steam room, and labored up two long flights from the basement. Once more he took the elevator to the lobby on the mezzanine.

He inquired at the desk for Dr. Tamkin.

The clerk said, "No, I haven't seen him. But I think there's something in the box for you."

"Me? Give it here," said Wilhelm and opened a telephone message from his wife. It read, "Please phone Mrs. Wilhelm on return. Urgent."

Whenever he received an urgent message from his wife he was always thrown into a great fear for the children. He ran to the phone booth, spilled out the change from his pockets onto the little curved steel shelf under the telephone, and dialed the Digby number.

"Yes?" said his wife. Scissors barked in the parlor.

"Margaret?"

"Yes, hello." They never exchanged any other greeting. She instantly knew his voice.

"The boys all right?"

"They're out on their bicycles. Why shouldn't they be all right? Scissors, quiet!"

"Your message scared me," he said. "I wish you wouldn't make 'urgent' so common."

"I had something to tell you."

Her familiar unbending voice awakened in him a kind of hungry longing, not for Margaret but for the peace he had once known.

"You sent me a postdated check," she said. "I can't allow that. It's already five days past the first. You dated your check for the twelfth."

"Well, I have no money. I haven't got it. You can't send me to prison for that. I'll be lucky if I can raise it by the twelfth."

She answered, "You better get it, Tommy."

"Yes? What for?" he said. "Tell me. For the sake of what? To tell lies about me to everyone? You—"

She cut him off. "You know what for. I've got the boys to bring up."

Wilhelm in the narrow booth broke into a heavy sweat. He dropped his head and shrugged while with his fingers he arranged nickels, dimes, and quarters in rows. "I'm doing my best," he said. "I've had some bad luck. As a matter of fact, it's been so bad that I don't know where I am. I couldn't tell you what day of the week this is. I can't think straight. I'd better not even try. This has been one of those days, Margaret. May I never live to go through another like it. I mean that with all my heart. So I'm not going to try to do any thinking today. Tomorrow I'm going to see some guys. One is a sales manager. The other is in television. But not to act," he hastily added. "On the business end."

"That's just some more of your talk, Tommy," she said. "You ought to patch things up with Rojax Corporation. They'd take you back. You've got to stop thinking like a youngster."

"What do you mean?"

"Well," she said, measured and unbending, remorselessly unbending, "you still think like a youngster. But you can't do that any more. Every other day you want to make a new start. But in eighteen years you'll be eligible for retirement. Nobody wants to hire a new man of your age."

"I know. But listen, you don't have to sound so hard. I can't get on my knees to them. And really you don't have to sound so hard. I haven't done you so much harm."

"Tommy, I have to chase you and ask you for money that you owe us, and I hate it."

She hated also to be told that her voice was hard.

"I'm making an effort to control myself," she told him.

He could picture her, her graying bangs cut with strict fixity above her pretty, decisive face. She prided herself on being fair-minded. We could not bear, he thought, to know what we do. Even though blood is spilled. Even though the breath of life is taken from someone's nostrils. This is the way of the weak; quiet and fair. And then smash! They smash!

"Rojax take me back? I'd have to crawl back. They don't need me. After so many years I should have got stock in the firm. How can I support the three of you, and live myself, on half the territory? And why should I even try when you won't lift a finger to help? I sent you back to school, didn't I? At that time you said—"

His voice was rising. She did not like that and intercepted him. "You misunderstood me," she said.

"You must realize you're killing me. You can't be as blind as all that. Thou shalt not kill! Don't you remember that?"

She said, "You're just raving now. When you calm down it'll be different. I have great confidence in your earning ability."

"Margaret, you don't grasp the situation. You'll have to get a job."

"Absolutely not. I'm not going to have two young children running loose."

"They're not babies," Wilhelm said. "Tommy is fourteen. Paulie is going to be ten."

"Look," Margaret said in her deliberate manner. "We can't continue this conversation if you're going to yell so, Tommy. They're at a dangerous age. There are teen-aged gangs—the parents working, or the families broken up."

Once again she was reminding him that it was he who had left her. She had the bringing up of the children as her burden, while he must expect to pay the price of his freedom.

Freedom! he thought with consuming bitterness. Ashes in his mouth, not freedom. Give me my children. For they are mine too.

Can you be the woman I lived with? he started to say. Have you forgotten that we slept so long together? Must you now deal with me like this, and have no mercy?

He would be better off with Margaret again than he was today. This was what she wanted to make him feel, and she drove it home. "Are you in misery?" she was saying. "But you have deserved it." And he could not return to her any more than he could beg Rojax to take him back. If it cost him his life, he could not. Margaret had ruined him with Olive. She hit him and hit him, beat him, battered him, wanted to beat the very life out of him.

"Margaret, I want you please to reconsider about work. You have that degree now. Why did I pay your tuition?"

"Because it seemed practical. But it isn't. Growing boys need parental authority and a home."

He begged her, "Margaret, go easy on me. You ought to. I'm at the end of my rope and feel that I'm suffocating. You don't want to be responsible for a person's destruction. You've got to let up. I feel I'm about to burst." His face had expanded. He struck a blow upon the tin and wood and nails of the wall of the booth. "You've got to let me breathe. If I should keel over, what then? And it's something I can never understand about you. How you can treat someone like this whom you lived with so long. Who gave you the best of himself. Who tried. Who loved you." Merely to pronounce the word "love" made him tremble.

"Ah," she said with a sharp breath. "Now we're coming to it. How did you imagine it was going to be—big shot? Everything made smooth for you? I thought you were leading up to this."

She had not, perhaps, intended to reply as harshly as she did, but she brooded a great deal and now she could not forbear to punish him and make him feel pains like those she had to undergo.

He struck the wall again, this time with his knuckles, and he had scarcely enough air in his lungs to speak in a whisper, because his heart pushed upward with a frightful pressure. He got up and stamped his feet in the narrow enclosure.

"Haven't I always done my best?" he yelled, though his voice sounded weak and thin to his own ears. "Everything comes from me and nothing back again to me. There's no law that'll punish this, but you are committing a crime against me. Before God—and that's no joke. I mean that. Before God! Sooner or later the boys will know it."

In a firm tone, levelly, Margaret said to him, "I won't stand to be howled at. When you can speak normally and have something sensible to say I'll listen. But not to this." She hung up.

Wilhelm tried to tear the apparatus from the wall. He ground his teeth and seized the black box with insane digging fingers and made a stifled cry and pulled. Then he saw an elderly lady staring through the glass door, utterly appalled by him, and he ran from the booth, leaving a large amount of change on the shelf. He hurried down the stairs and into the street.

On Broadway it was still bright afternoon and the gassy air

was almost motionless under the leaden spokes of sunlight, and sawdust footprints lay about the doorways of butcher shops and fruit stores. And the great, great crowd, the inexhaustible current of millions of every race and kind pouring out, pressing round, of every age, of every genius, possessors of every human secret, antique and future, in every face the refinement of one particular motive or essence—*I labor, I spend, I strive, I design, I love, I cling, I uphold, I give way, I envy, I long, I scorn, I die, I hide, I want*. Faster, much faster than any man could make the tally. The sidewalks were wider than any causeway; the street itself was immense, and it quaked and gleamed and it seemed to Wilhelm to throb at the last limit of endurance. And although the sunlight appeared like a broad tissue, its actual weight made him feel like a drunkard.

"I'll get a divorce if it's the last thing I do," he swore. "As for Dad— As for Dad— I'll have to sell the car for junk and pay the hotel. I'll have to go on my knees to Olive and say, 'Stand by me a while. Don't let her win. Olive!'" And he thought, I'll try to start again with Olive. In fact, I must. Olive loves me. Olive—

Beside a row of limousines near the curb he thought he saw Dr. Tamkin. Of course he had been mistaken before about the hat with the cocoa-colored band and didn't want to make the same mistake twice. But wasn't that Tamkin who was speaking so earnestly, with pointed shoulders, to someone under the canopy of the funeral parlor? For this was a huge funeral. He looked for the singular face under the dark gray, fashionable hatbrim. There were two open cars filled with flowers, and a policeman tried to keep a path open to pedestrians. Right at the canopy-pole, now wasn't that that damned Tamkin talking away with a solemn face, gesticulating with an open hand?

"Tamkin!" shouted Wilhelm, going forward. But he was pushed to the side by a policeman clutching his nightstick at both ends, like a rolling pin. Wilhelm was even farther from Tamkin now, and swore under his breath at the cop who continued to press him back, back, belly and ribs, saying, "Keep it moving there, please," his face red with impatient sweat, his brows like red fur. Wilhelm said to him haughtily, "You shouldn't push people like this."

The policeman, however, was not really to blame. He had been ordered to keep a way clear. Wilhelm was moved forward by the pressure of the crowd.

He cried, "Tamkin!"

But Tamkin was gone. Or rather, it was he himself who was carried from the street into the chapel. The pressure ended inside, where it was dark and cool. The flow of fan-driven air dried his face, which he wiped hard with his handkerchief to stop the slight salt itch. He gave a sigh when he heard the organ notes that stirred and breathed from the pipes and he saw people in the pews. Men in formal clothes and black homburgs strode softly back and forth on the cork floor, up and down the center aisle. The white of the stained glass was like mother-of-pearl, the blue of the Star of David like velvet ribbon.

Well, thought Wilhelm, if that was Tamkin outside I might as well wait for him here where it's cool. Funny, he never mentioned he had a funeral to go to today. But that's just like the guy.

But within a few minutes he had forgotten Tamkin. He stood along the wall with others and looked toward the coffin and the slow line that was moving past it, gazing at the face of the dead. Presently he too was in this line, and slowly, slowly, foot by foot, the beating of his heart anxious, thick, frightening, but somehow also rich, he neared the coffin and paused for his turn, and gazed down. He caught his breath when he looked at the corpse, and his face swelled, his eyes shone hugely with instant tears.

The dead man was gray-haired. He had two large waves of gray hair at the front. But he was not old. His face was long, and he had a bony nose, slightly, delicately twisted. His brows were raised as though he had sunk into the final thought. Now at last he was with it, after the end of all distractions, and when his flesh was no longer flesh. And by this meditative look Wilhelm was so struck that he could not go away. In spite of the tinge of horror, and then the splash of heartsickness that he felt, he could not go. He stepped out of line and remained beside the coffin; his eyes filled silently and through his still tears he studied the man as the line of visitors moved with veiled looks past the satin coffin toward the standing bank of lilies, lilacs, roses. With great stifling sorrow, almost admiration, Wilhelm nodded and nodded.

On the surface, the dead man with his formal shirt and his tie and silk lapels and his powdered skin looked so proper; only a little beneath so—black, Wilhelm thought, so fallen in the eyes.

Standing a little apart, Wilhelm began to cry. He cried at first softly and from sentiment, but soon from deeper feeling. He sobbed loudly and his face grew distorted and hot, and the tears stung his skin. A man—another human creature, was what first went through his thoughts, but other and different things were torn from him. What'll I do? I'm stripped and kicked out. . . . Oh, Father, what do I ask of you? What'll I do about the kids—Tommy, Paul? My children. And Olive? My dear! Why, why, why—you must protect me against that devil who wants my life. If you want it, then kill me. Take, take it, take it from me.

Soon he was past words, past reason, coherence. He could not stop. The source of all tears had suddenly sprung open within him, black, deep, and hot, and they were pouring out and convulsed his body, bending his stubborn head, bowing his shoulders, twisting his face, crippling the very hands with which he held the handkerchief. His efforts to collect himself were useless. The great knot of ill and grief in his throat swelled upward and he gave in utterly and held his face and wept. He cried with all his heart.

He, alone of all the people in the chapel, was sobbing. No one knew who he was.

One woman said, "Is that perhaps the cousin from New Orleans they were expecting?"

"It must be somebody real close to carry on so."

"Oh my, oh my! To be mourned like that," said one man and looked at Wilhelm's heavy shaken shoulders, his clutched face and whitened fair hair, with wide, glinting, jealous eyes.

"The man's brother, maybe?"

"Oh, I doubt that very much," said another bystander. "They're not alike at all. Night and day."

The flowers and lights fused ecstatically in Wilhelm's blind, wet eyes; the heavy sea-like music came up to his ears. It poured into him where he had hidden himself in the center of a crowd by the great and happy oblivion of tears. He heard it and sank deeper than sorrow, through torn sobs and cries toward the consummation of his heart's ultimate need.

TOPICS FOR PAPERS AND DISCUSSION

1. *The theme of love.* What does Tommy Wilhelm really want from his father and apparently the world? Recall Maurice Venice's fantasy: "You become a lover to the whole world." Consider Tommy's statement that "a man is only as good as what he loves," and relate it to the many references to love, both positive and negative involving Margaret, Olive, Dr. and Mrs. Adler, Tamkin, etc. Is there any evidence that Tommy is capable of reciprocating or, to the contrary, that he is deluding himself? Relate his overt statements to scenes in which the theme is rendered but not openly expressed. Be sure to include the final scene. Consider Tommy and his "love" at various levels: as son, husband, father, lover, friend, etc.
2. *"Sunk though he be beneath the wat'ry floor."* Analyze the full range of possible meanings of the important motif of water and everything related to it. Discuss the motif of sinking, descending, and falling. Examine references to eyes and sight and the multiple variations on them. How are water, sinking, and eyes related? How do the motifs overlap, repeat, extend, reinforce, or even stand in contrast to each other as a group of related ideas? Analyze closely those passages in which they are united.
3. *Thematic polarities.* This novel is densely packed with dramatic tensions, opposing ideas, counterthemes. One of the most important is "fathers and sons," as it is borne out in the relationship between Dr. Adler and Tommy. Examine this conflict in detail as it reflects the theme. Consider any one of the other thematic subjects: aging and death, deformity or sickness and health, animality and humanity, communication and noncommunication, youth and age, sadism and masochism, innocence and guilt, city and country, alienation and accommodation, wasting one's life and seizing an elusive day, freedom and suppression, the individual and the crowd, need and denial, inward cravings and environmental frustrations.
4. *Suffering-loss-redemption.* Discuss this ancient pattern of initiation and/or salvation as a paradigm for Tommy's life during the few hours covered by the novel. Describe the range and function of the motifs of pain, destruction, and reward. For instance, these three may be physical, psychological, or spiritual. Recall what Tommy thinks he might be dedicated to. Relate his mistakes and those of the other characters to this pattern. Show the significance of the conversations and thoughts about hell, purgatory, and paradise.
5. *Pretense and authenticity.* How are these conditions related to Bellow's concerns in *Seize the Day*? What do they show about his treatment of the business world, the entertainment industry, and personal relationships? What do veracity and mendacity signify?

Are they a variation of a more inclusive theme? What is the function of the many references to clothing, especially clothes worn by Tommy, Dr. Adler, and Tamkin? How are disguise-concealment-withholding and honesty-openness-disclosure related to pretense and authenticity? Discuss this question in terms of the "pretender soul" and "true soul."

6. *Tamkin's poem.* Analyze the poem and relate it to the major concerns of the story, among them the thematic duality of construction and destruction. What is the tone of Tommy's often conflicting responses to the poem? Why is he outraged by it when ostensibly he has remembered whole passages from the poets of the past? How is Tamkin's partial explication relevant not only to the world of the novel generally, but also to Tommy particularly? Is the rest of the poem relevant to Tommy's problem? What words does he unconsciously remember and repeat later? What is the significance of these words to his character?
7. *"One of those subway things . . . ."* Ponder the meaning of the passage on universal brotherhood (p. 456) in which Tommy temporarily embraces the corporate body of mankind. How does it make the subway in which it occurs metaphorical and even thematic? Link the passage to the characters portrayed as saviors and healers, such as Tamkin, Dr. Adler, and Tommy. What is its relationship to the "subway" of the massage room? How do these "underground" experiences relate to the funeral parlor and the emotional responses of Tommy to the death there? Is it fair to say that he has followed, often unconsciously, a "subway" from the beginning of his "day of reckoning"? Review the Theseus myth and relate it psychologically to Tommy's "subways."
8. *Success and money.* How do the principles and pressures of materialism affect Tommy? In what different ways do they affect everyone within the money-oriented society of this story? Relate to these broader ideas: (1) the implicit American dictum "to be is to succeed," (2) the American "dream of success" and the "nightmare of failure." Would money actually solve Tommy's existential crisis? Given the symbolic role played by money, why is it necessary that he be wiped out in the commodities market? What is the relationship of success, money, and Tommy's particular financial problems to Tamkin's poem and to some of his stories, whether or not they are truthful?
9. *Eating, thinness, and fatness.* What do the scenes of eating point to beyond themselves as moments of dramatic encounter? What relationship, process, or inevitable course of events is being worked out in these scenes? Determine how fatness, lard, and other pertinent references are united around a core of particular characters and ideas. In contrast, a number of characters are remarkably thin, or they are figuratively "reduced" physically, financially, or psy-

chologically. What comparison and contrast in ideas and characters is Bellow rendering through this fatness-thinness dichotomy? What has this symbolic contrast to do with success, and what is its relationship to the concept of "the two souls"?

10. *Wilhelm as antihero and hero.* Beginning with the idea that Tommy is a dirty slob and a resounding failure, gather evidence until you have exhausted the case against him. Then proceed from the opposite direction and list his worthwhile attributes. What are the qualities of his mind, emotions, aspirations, and relationships that might contribute to a revised opinion of him? In what complex ways does he view himself and others? Consider his father, Perls, and Tamkin. Account for the repeated identification with toys, and the repetition of his childlike characteristics. Also do not overlook the significance of his Jewishness, whether "wrong kind" or "right kind," and the use of his four names. Consider his need to distinguish himself and his need to be liked by and to like others—are these positive aspects of Tommy as hero?
11. *The functions of "doubling."* How is the technique of "doubling" used in general and in this novel particularly? How do Maurice Venice and Tamkin serve as doubles for Tommy? In what way could the unknown dead man serve the same purpose? Examine the text carefully for examples of doubling. Include images, metaphors, ideas, characters, settings, games, documents, etc. Relate them to Tommy's crises, to his past life, and to the world in which he lives. What ideals, aspirations, and beliefs widen the split in Tommy and his world, whether schizoid or not, implied by the technique of doubling?
12. *Human responsibility.* Describe Tommy's concern or lack of concern for others on this day of multiple crises. What is thus revealed about his sense of responsibility to himself and others? With whom and what does he sympathize most deeply? Analyze his search for identity, his silent plea for transformation, and his quest for salvation as related to his sense of responsibility. How do the other characters, notably Dr. Adler and Tamkin, meet or evade responsibility? How does the theme of responsibility color the ending?
13. *Tamkin—his character and his function.* What is to be made of the enigmatic Tamkin who appears profoundly wise and thoroughly deceptive? Consider the physical description of him. What is the significance of his appearance precisely at this crucial point in Tommy's life? Read Carl Jung's essay "The Phenomenology of the Spirit in Fairy Tales" and relate it to Tamkin's role in Tommy's affairs. How does he serve as surrogate father to Tommy? Explain how Tamkin can be a spur to creative thought, even a savior, and yet find it necessary to render Tommy penniless in the lard and rye deal. Does the character of Tamkin need to be more fully developed, as Bellow himself once suggested? Explain.

14. *Parallelism in characters.* The roles of Maurice Venice, Margaret Wilhelm, and Tamkin have certain similar features. For example, Tommy is tempted by them. Discuss the nature and importance of these temptations. What other aspects of character do they share which are important to Tommy's fate? Given his character, why is it necessary that the three encounters with these people end in similar ways? It should be noted too that Tommy's mother tried to put a stop to the Hollywood venture, and that Dr. Adler claims prior wisdom by warning him about Margaret and Tamkin. How do these parental attempts to restrict Tommy reflect his own intuitions and actions?
15. *Minor characters.* Explain the roles of the unseen women who figure in Tommy's life. What is the relationship of 'Nita Christenberry and Olive, if any? Why is Tommy so disturbed that his father has apparently forgotten his mother's death, and that the bench by her grave has been broken? What common element do almost all the women share in their relationship with Tommy? How do the minor male characters function to reveal aspects of his character? Consider Rubin, the German manager, the old men like Perls and Rappaport, and Artie, the cousin. In addition, how is the dog Scissors important to the story?
16. *Symbolic setting and expressive structure.* What does the novel reveal about conditions of urban life, particularly New York's upper Broadway, where all the present action occurs? Analyze the symbolic use of the Gloriana Hotel, its public and private rooms, both above and below ground, including the movie house underneath the lobby. Then move outward to the streets, to the Ansonia Hotel, to the brokerage office, etc. What is the significance of places beyond New York and in the past: Penn State, the talent scout's office, Southern California, Cuba, Florida, the war front. Why are many of them identified by theater imagery (i.e., the Chinese theater brokerage office)? Comment upon the important references to Roxbury. Connect the settings and Tommy's activities to the seven-part structure of the novel. Look up the meaning of the number seven as a traditional symbol. Work back and forth from the pivotal fourth chapter. How does it encapsulate the world of *Seize the Day* and govern Bellow's interpretation of experience?
17. *Digressive passages.* Discuss the thematic function of Tamkin's apparently outrageous stories about his own adventures, the affairs of his patients, and his personal life. How would you defend the inclusion of his theories about the psychology of the stock market in this group? Contrast those stories with his philosophy of life, if it can be called that. In what manner, if at all, do the stories dramatize his philosophy? What relationship do his digressions have to Tommy's problems? Examine other digressions and relate them to the central concerns of the novel.

18. *The art of allusion.* Examine the text carefully for titles of books and literary allusions to Jesus, Plato, Donne, Shakespeare, Milton, Shelley, Wilde, Yeats, and others. Explain how the original context of the allusions sheds light on their context within *Seize the Day* itself. Determine whether each allusion reinforces the new context, whether it enlarges the situation, whether it is symbolic, whether it is analytical, or whether it serves profound thematic ends. How might each allusion function as a device of characterization and of tone?
19. *The end of* Seize the Day. The ending of the novel is quite ambiguous and provokes critical controversy. The major issue is whether the ending is to be taken as affirmative or negative. How are many of the strands of the story focused in the final scene, including the motifs of dying and death, of water and tears, of hypocrisy and genuineness, of vain love and true love, etc.? Read Ferdinand's remarks and Ariel's song in Shakespeare's *The Tempest* beginning, "This music crept by me on the waters" (I, ii, 391–402). How does this passage dealing with death by water and a transformation to a higher order of being provide a clue to one interpretation of the novel's ending? Defend your own interpretation, whether it be optimistic or pessimistic. Also, what is meant by the novel's final words "the consummation of his heart's ultimate need"?
20. *The Bellow style and voice.* Describe the Bellow style as concretely as possible. Is it an adequate instrument to convey the weighty psychological and philosophical content of Tommy's (and maybe mankind's) story? Could the style be considered labyrinthine at times? Find examples for analysis. Comment on the maze of conflicting tones and what they convey of emotions and characters. Analyze some of those passages in which Bellow's voice is didactic, objective, ambiguous, or lyrical. Attempt to determine what is gained by this flexibility of voice.

Of Mice and Men

JOHN STEINBECK

A few miles south of Soledad, the Salinas River drops in close to the hillside bank and runs deep and green. The water is warm too, for it has slipped twinkling over the yellow sands in the sunlight before reaching the narrow pool. On one side of the river the golden foothill slopes curve up to the strong and rocky Gabilan mountains, but on the valley side the water is lined with trees—willows fresh and green with every spring, carrying in their lower leaf junctures the debris of the winter's flooding; and sycamores with mottled, white, recumbent limbs and branches that arch over the pool. On the sandy bank under the trees the leaves lie deep and so crisp that a lizard makes a great skittering if he runs among them. Rabbits come out of the brush to sit on the sand in the evening, and the damp flats are covered with the night tracks of 'coons, and with the spread pads of dogs from the ranches, and with the split-wedge tracks of deer that come to drink in the dark.

There is a path through the willows and among the sycamores, a path beaten hard by boys coming down from the ranches to swim in the deep pool, and beaten hard by tramps who come wearily down from the highway in the evening to jungle-up near water. In front of the low horizontal limb of a giant sycamore there is an ash pile made by many fires; the limb is worn smooth by men who have sat on it.

Evening of a hot day started the little wind to moving among the leaves. The shade climbed up the hills toward the top. On the sand banks the rabbits sat as quietly as little gray, sculptured stones. And then from the direction of the state highway came the sound of footsteps on crisp sycamore leaves. The rabbits hurried noiselessly for cover. A stilted heron labored up into the air and pounded down river. For a moment the place was lifeless, and then two men emerged from the path and came into the opening by the green pool.

They had walked in single file down the path, and even in the open one stayed behind the other. Both were dressed in denim trousers and in denim coats with brass buttons. Both wore black, shapeless hats and both carried tight blanket rolls slung over their shoulders. The first man was small and quick, dark of face, with restless eyes and sharp, strong features. Every part of him was defined: small, strong hands, slender arms, a thin and bony nose. Behind him walked his opposite, a huge man, shapeless of face, with large, pale eyes, with wide, sloping shoulders; and he walked heavily, dragging his feet a little, the way a bear drags his paws. His arms did not swing at his sides, but hung loosely.

The first man stopped short in the clearing, and the follower nearly ran over him. He took off his hat and wiped the sweatband with his forefinger and snapped the moisture off. His huge companion dropped his blankets and flung himself down and drank from the surface of the green pool; drank with long gulps, snorting into the water like a horse. The small man stepped nervously beside him.

"Lennie!" he said sharply. "Lennie, for God' sakes don't drink so much." Lennie continued to snort into the pool. The small man leaned over and shook him by the shoulder. "Lennie. You gonna be sick like you was last night."

Lennie dipped his whole head under, hat and all, and then he sat up on the bank and his hat dripped down on his blue coat and ran down his back. "Tha's good," he said. "You drink some, George. You take a good big drink." He smiled happily.

George unslung his bindle and dropped it gently on the bank. "I ain't sure it's good water," he said. "Looks kinda scummy."

Lennie dabbled his big paw in the water and wiggled his fingers so the water arose in little splashes; rings widened across the pool to the other side and came back again. Lennie watched them go. "Look, George. Look what I done."

George knelt beside the pool and drank from his hand with quick scoops. "Tastes all right," he admitted. "Don't really seem to be running, though. You never oughta drink water when it ain't running, Lennie," he said hopelessly. "You'd drink out of a gutter if you was thirsty." He threw a scoop of water into his face and rubbed it about with his hand, under his chin and around the back of his neck. Then he replaced his hat, pushed himself back from the river, drew up his knees and embraced them. Lennie, who had been watching, imitated George exactly. He pushed himself back, drew up his knees, embraced them, looked over to George to see whether he had it just right. He pulled his hat down a little more over his eyes, the way George's hat was.

George stared morosely at the water. The rims of his eyes were red with sun glare. He said angrily, "We could just as well of rode clear to the ranch if that bastard bus driver knew what he was talkin' about. 'Jes' a little stretch down the highway,' he says. 'Jes' a little stretch.' God damn near four miles, that's what it was! Didn't wanta stop at the ranch gate, that's what. Too God damn lazy to pull up. Wonder he isn't too damn good to stop in Soledad at all. Kicks us out and says, 'Jes' a little stretch down the road.' I bet it was *more* than four miles. Damn hot day."

Lennie looked timidly over to him. "George?"

"Yeah, what ya want?"

"Where we goin', George?"

The little man jerked down the brim of his hat and scowled over at Lennie. "So you forgot that awready, did you? I gotta tell you again, do I? Jesus Christ, you're a crazy bastard!"

"I forgot," Lennie said softly. "I tried not to forget. Honest to God I did, George."

"O.K.—O.K. I'll tell ya again. I ain't got nothing to do. Might jus' as well spen' all my time tellin' you things and then you forget 'em, and I tell you again."

"Tried and tried," said Lennie, "but it didn't do no good. I remember about the rabbits, George."

"The hell with the rabbits. That's all you ever can remember is them rabbits. O.K.! Now you listen and this time you got to remember so we don't get in no trouble. You remember settin' in that gutter on Howard street and watchin' that blackboard?"

Lennie's face broke into a delighted smile. "Why sure, George,

I remember that . . . but . . . what'd we do then? I remember some girls come by and you says . . . you say . . ."

"The hell with what I says. You remember about us goin' into Murray and Ready's, and they give us work cards and bus tickets?"

"Oh, sure, George. I remember that now." His hands went quickly into his side coat pockets. He said gently, "George . . . I ain't got mine. I musta lost it." He looked down at the ground in despair.

"You never had none, you crazy bastard. I got both of 'em here. Think I'd let you carry your own work card?"

Lennie grinned with relief. "I . . . I thought I put it in my side pocket." His hand went into the pocket again.

George looked sharply at him. "What'd you take outa that pocket?"

"Ain't a thing in my pocket," Lennie said cleverly.

"I know there ain't. You got it in your hand. What you got in your hand—hidin' it?"

"I ain't got nothin', George. Honest."

"Come on, give it here."

Lennie held his closed hand away from George's direction. "It's on'y a mouse, George."

"A mouse? A live mouse?"

"Uh-uh. Jus' a dead mouse, George. I didn' kill it. Honest! I found it. I found it dead."

"Give it here!" said George.

"Aw, leave me have it, George."

"Give it here!"

Lennie's closed hand slowly obeyed. George took the mouse and threw it across the pool to the other side, among the brush. "What you want of a dead mouse, anyways?"

"I could pet it with my thumb while we walked along," said Lennie.

"Well, you ain't petting no mice while you walk with me. You remember where we're goin' now?"

Lennie looked startled and then in embarrassment hid his face against his knees. "I forgot again."

"Jesus Christ," George said resignedly. "Well—look, we're gonna work on a ranch like the one we come from up north."

"Up north?"

"In Weed."

"Oh, sure' I remember. In Weed."

"That ranch we're goin' to is right down there about a quarter mile. We're gonna go in an' see the boss. Now, look—I'll give him the work tickets, but you ain't gonna say a word. You jus' stand there and don't say nothing. If he finds out what a crazy bastard you are, we won't get no job, but if he sees ya work before he hears ya talk, we're set. Ya got that?"

"Sure, George. Sure I got it."

"O.K. Now when we go in to see the boss, what you gonna do?"

"I . . . I," Lennie thought. His face grew tight with thought. "I . . . ain't gonna say nothin'. Jus' gonna stan' there."

"Good boy. That's swell. You say that over two, three times so you sure won't forget it."

Lennie droned to himself softly, "I ain't gonna say nothin' . . . I ain't gonna say nothin' . . . I ain't gonna say nothin'."

"O.K.," said George. "An' you ain't gonna do no bad things like you done in Weed, neither."

Lennie looked puzzled. "Like I done in Weed?"

"Oh, so ya forgot that too, did ya? Well, I ain't gonna remind ya, fear ya do it again."

A light of understanding broke on Lennie's face. "They run us outa Weed," he exploded triumphantly.

"Run us out, hell," said George disgustedly. "We run. They was lookin' for us, but they didn't catch us."

Lennie giggled happily. "I didn't forget that, you bet."

George lay back on the sand and crossed his hands under his head, and Lennie imitated him, raising his head to see whether he were doing it right. "God, you're a lot of trouble," said George. "I could get along so easy and so nice if I didn't have you on my tail. I could live so easy and maybe have a girl."

For a moment Lennie lay quiet, and then he said hopefully, "We gonna work on a ranch, George."

"Awright. You got that. But we're gonna sleep here because I got a reason."

The day was going fast now. Only the tops of the Gabilan mountains flamed with the light of the sun that had gone from the valley. A water snake slipped along on the pool, its head held up like a little periscope. The reeds jerked slightly in the current.

Far off toward the highway a man shouted something, and another man shouted back. The sycamore limbs rustled under a little wind that died immediately.

"George—why ain't we goin' on to the ranch and get some supper? They got supper at the ranch."

George rolled on his side. "No reason at all for you. I like it here. Tomorra we're gonna go to work. I seen thrashin' machines on the way down. That means we'll be bucking grain bags, bustin' a gut. Tonight I'm gonna lay right here and look up. I like it."

Lennie got up on his knees and looked down at George. "Ain't we gonna have no supper?"

"Sure we are, if you gather up some dead willow sticks. I got three can of beans in my bindle. You get a fire ready. I'll give you a match when you get the sticks together. Then we'll heat the beans and have supper."

Lennie said, "I like beans with ketchup."

"Well, we ain't got no ketchup. You go get wood. An' don't you fool around. It'll be dark before long."

Lennie lumbered to his feet and disappeared in the brush. George lay where he was and whistled softly to himself. There were sounds of splashings down the river in the direction Lennie had taken. George stopped whistling and listened. "Poor bastard," he said softly, and then went on whistling again.

In a moment Lennie came crashing back through the brush. He carried one small willow stick in his hand. George sat up. "Awright," he said brusquely. "Gi'me that mouse!"

But Lennie made an elaborate pantomime of innocence. "What mouse, George? I ain't got no mouse."

George held out his hand. "Come on. Give it to me. You ain't puttin' nothing over."

Lennie hesitated, backed away, looked wildly at the brush line as though he contemplated running for his freedom. George said coldly, "You gonna give me that mouse or do I have to sock you?"

"Give you what, George?"

"You know God damn well what. I want that mouse."

Lennie reluctantly reached into his pocket. His voice broke a little. "I don't know why I can't keep it. It ain't nobody's mouse. I didn't steal it. I found it lyin' right beside the road."

George's hand remained outstretched imperiously. Slowly, like a terrier who doesn't want to bring a ball to its master, Lennie approached, drew back, approached again. George snapped his fingers sharply, and at the sound Lennie laid the mouse in his hand.

"I wasn't doin' nothing bad with it, George. Jus' strokin' it."

George stood up and threw the mouse as far as he could into the darkening brush, and then he stepped to the pool and washed his hands. "You crazy fool. Don't you think I could see your feet was wet where you went acrost the river to get it?" He heard Lennie's whimpering cry and wheeled about. "Blubberin' like a baby! Jesus Christ! A big guy like you." Lennie's lip quivered and tears started in his eyes. "Aw, Lennie!" George put his hand on Lennie's shoulder. "I ain't takin' it away jus' for meanness. That mouse ain't fresh, Lennie; and besides, you've broke it pettin' it. You get another mouse that's fresh and I'll let you keep it a little while."

Lennie sat down on the ground and hung his head dejectedly. "I don't know where there is no other mouse. I remember a lady used to give 'em to me—ever' one she got. But that lady ain't here."

George scoffed. "Lady, huh? Don't even remember who that lady was. That was your own Aunt Clara. An' she stopped givin' 'em to ya. You always killed 'em."

Lennie looked sadly up at him. "They was so little," he said, apologetically. "I'd pet 'em, and pretty soon they bit my fingers and I pinched their heads a little and then they was dead—because they was so little."

"I wish't we'd get the rabbits pretty soon, George. They ain't so little."

"The hell with the rabbits. An' you ain't to be trusted with no live mice. Your Aunt Clara give you a rubber mouse and you wouldn't have nothing to do with it."

"It wasn't no good to pet," said Lennie.

The flame of the sunset lifted from the mountaintops and dusk came into the valley, and a half darkness came in among the willows and the sycamores. A big carp rose to the surface of the pool, gulped air and then sank mysteriously into the dark water again, leaving widening rings on the water. Overhead the leaves whisked again and little puffs of willow cotton blew down and landed on the pool's surface.

"You gonna get that wood?" George demanded. "There's plenty right up against the back of that sycamore. Floodwater wood. Now you get it."

Lennie went behind the tree and brought out a litter of dried leaves and twigs. He threw them in a heap on the old ash pile and went back for more and more. It was almost night now. A dove's wings whistled over the water. George walked to the fire pile and lighted the dry leaves. The flame cracked up among the twigs and fell to work. George undid his bindle and brought out three cans of beans. He stood them about the fire, close in against the blaze, but not quite touching the flame.

"There's enough beans for four men," George said.

Lennie watched him from over the fire. He said patiently, "I like 'em with ketchup."

"Well, we ain't got any," George exploded. "Whatever we ain't got, that's what you want. God a'mighty, if I was alone I could live so easy. I could go get a job an' work, an' no trouble. No mess at all, and when the end of the month come I could take my fifty bucks and go into town and get whatever I want. Why, I could stay in a cat house all night. I could eat any place I want, hotel or any place, and order any damn thing I could think of. An' I could do all that every damn month. Get a gallon of whisky, or set in a pool room and play cards or shoot pool." Lennie knelt and looked over the fire at the angry George. And Lennie's face was drawn with terror. "An' whatta I got," George went on furiously. "I got you! You can't keep a job and you lose me ever' job I get. Jus' keep me shovin' all over the country all the time. An' that ain't the worst. You get in trouble. You do bad things and I got to get you out." His voice rose nearly to a shout. "You crazy son-of-a-bitch. You keep me in hot water all the time." He took on the elaborate manner of little girls when they are mimicking one another. "Jus' wanted to feel that girl's dress—jus' wanted to pet it like it was a mouse——Well, how the hell did she know you jus' wanted to feel her dress? She jerks back and you hold on like it was a mouse. She yells and we got to hide in a irrigation ditch all day with guys lookin' for us, and we got to sneak out in the dark and get outta the country. All the time somethin' like that—all the time. I wisht I could put you in a cage with about a million mice an' let you have fun." His anger left him suddenly. He looked across the fire at Lennie's anguished face, and then he looked ashamedly at the flames.

It was quite dark now, but the fire lighted the trunks of the trees and the curving branches overhead. Lennie crawled slowly and cautiously around the fire until he was close to George. He sat back on his heels. George turned the bean cans so that another side faced the fire. He pretended to be unaware of Lennie so close beside him.

"George," very softly. No answer. "George!"

"Whatta you want?"

"I was only foolin', George. I don't want no ketchup. I wouldn't eat no ketchup if it was right here beside me."

"If it was here, you could have some."

"But I wouldn't eat none, George. I'd leave it all for you. You could cover your beans with it and I wouldn't touch none of it."

George still stared morosely at the fire. "When I think of the swell time I could have without you, I go nuts. I never get no peace."

Lennie still knelt. He looked off into the darkness across the river. "George, you want I should go away and leave you alone?"

"Where the hell could you go?"

"Well, I could. I could go off in the hills there. Some place I'd find a cave."

"Yeah? How'd you eat. You ain't got sense enough to find nothing to eat."

"I'd find things, George, I don't need no nice food with ketchup. I'd lay out in the sun and nobody'd hurt me. An' if I foun' a mouse, I could keep it. Nobody'd take it away from me."

George looked quickly and searchingly at him. "I been mean, ain't I?"

"If you don' want me I can go off in the hills an' find a cave. I can go away any time."

"No—look! I was jus' foolin', Lennie. 'Cause I want you to stay with me. Trouble with mice is you always kill 'em." He paused. "Tell you what I'll do, Lennie. First chance I get I'll give you a pup. Maybe you wouldn't kill *it*. That'd be better than mice. And you could pet it harder."

Lennie avoided the bait. He had sensed his advantage. "If you don't want me, you only jus' got to say so, and I'll go off in those hills right there—right up in those hills and live by myself. An' I won't get no mice stole from me."

George said, "I want you to stay with me, Lennie. Jesus Christ, somebody'd shoot you for a coyote if you was by yourself. No, you stay with me. Your Aunt Clara wouldn't like you running off by yourself, even if she is dead."

Lennie spoke craftily, "Tell me—like you done before."

"Tell you what?"

"About the rabbits."

George snapped, "You ain't gonna put nothing over on me."

Lennie pleaded, "Come on, George. Tell me. Please, George. Like you done before."

"You get a kick outta that, don't you? Awright, I'll tell you, and then we'll eat our supper. . . ."

George's voice became deeper. He repeated his words rhythmically as though he had said them many times before. "Guys like us, that work on ranches, are the loneliest guys in the world. They got no family. They don't belong no place. They come to a ranch an' work up a stake and then they go inta town and blow their stake, and the first thing you know they're poundin' their tail on some other ranch. They ain't got nothing to look ahead to."

Lennie was delighted. "That's it—that's it. Now tell how it is with us."

George went on. "With us it ain't like that. We got a future. We got somebody to talk to that gives a damn about us. We don't have to sit in no bar room blowin' in our jack jus' because we got no place else to go. If them other guys gets in jail they can rot for all anybody gives a damn. But not us."

Lennie broke in. "*But not us! An' why? Because . . . because I got you to look after me, and you got me to look after you, and that's why.*" He laughed delightedly. "Go on now, George!"

"You got it by heart. You can do it yourself."

"No, you. I forget some a' the things. Tell about how it's gonna be."

"O.K. Someday—we're gonna get the jack together and we're gonna have a little house and a couple of acres an' a cow and some pigs and——"

"*An' live off the fatta the lan'*," Lennie shouted. "An have *rabbits*. Go on, George! Tell about what we're gonna have in the garden and about the rabbits in the cages and about the rain in the winter and the stove, and how thick the cream is on the milk like you can hardly cut it. Tell about that, George."

"Why'n't you do it yourself? You know all of it."

"No . . . you tell it. It ain't the same if I tell it. Go on . . . George. How I get to tend the rabbits."

"Well," said George, "we'll have a big vegetable patch and a rabbit hutch and chickens. And when it rains in the winter, we'll just say the hell with goin' to work, and we'll build up a fire in the stove and set around it an' listen to the rain comin' down on the roof—Nuts!" He took out his pocket knife. "I ain't got time for no more." He drove his knife through the top of one of the bean cans, sawed out the top and passed the can to Lennie. Then he opened a second can. From his side pocket he brought out two spoons and passed one of them to Lennie.

They sat by the fire and filled their mouths with beans and chewed mightily. A few beans slipped out of the side of Lennie's mouth. George gestured with his spoon. "What you gonna say tomorrow when the boss asks you questions?"

Lennie stopped chewing and swallowed. His face was concentrated. "I . . . I ain't gonna . . . say a word."

"Good boy! That's fine, Lennie! Maybe you're gettin' better. When we get the coupla acres I can let you tend the rabbits all right. 'Specially if you remember as good as that."

Lennie choked with pride. "I can remember," he said.

George motioned with his spoon again. "Look, Lennie. I want you to look around here. You can remember this place, can't you? The ranch is about a quarter mile up that way. Just follow the river?"

"Sure," said Lennie. "I can remember this. Di'n't I remember about not gonna say a word?"

"'Course you did. Well, look. Lennie—if you jus' happen to get in trouble like you always done before, I want you to come right here an' hide in the brush."

"Hide in the brush," said Lennie slowly.

"Hide in the brush till I come for you. Can you remember that?"

"Sure I can, George. Hide in the brush till you come."

"But you ain't gonna get in no trouble, because if you do, I won't let you tend the rabbits." He threw his empty bean can off into the brush.

"I won't get in no trouble, George. I ain't gonna say a word."

"O.K. Bring your bindle over here by the fire. It's gonna be nice sleepin' here. Lookin' up, and the leaves. Don't build up no more fire. We'll let her die down."

They made their beds on the sand, and as the blaze dropped from the fire the sphere of light grew smaller; the curling branches disappeared and only a faint glimmer showed where the tree trunks were. From the darkness Lennie called, "George—you asleep?"

"No. Whatta you want?"

"Let's have different color rabbits, George."

"Sure we will," George said sleepily. "Red and blue and green rabbits, Lennie. Millions of 'em."

"Furry ones, George, like I seen in the fair in Sacramento."

"Sure, furry ones."

"'Cause I can jus' as well go away, George, an' live in a cave."

"You can jus' as well go to hell," said George. "Shut up now."

The red light dimmed on the coals. Up the hill from the river a coyote yammered, and a dog answered from the other side of the stream. The sycamore leaves whispered in a little night breeze.

The bunk house was a long, rectangular building. Inside, the walls were whitewashed and the floor unpainted. In three walls there were small, square windows, and in the fourth, a solid door with a wooden latch. Against the walls were eight bunks, five of them made up with blankets and the other three showing their burlap ticking. Over each bunk there was nailed an apple box with the opening forward so that it made two shelves for the personal belongings of the occupant of the bunk. And these shelves were loaded with little articles, soap and talcum powder, razors and those Western magazines ranch men love to read and scoff at and secretly believe. And there were medicines on the shelves, and little vials, combs; and from nails on the box sides, a few neckties. Near one wall there was a black cast-iron stove, its stovepipe going straight up through the ceiling. In the middle of the room stood a big square table littered with playing cards, and around it were grouped boxes for the players to sit on.

At about ten o'clock in the morning the sun threw a bright dust-laden bar through one of the side windows, and in and out of the beam flies shot like rushing stars.

The wooden latch raised. The door opened and a tall, stoop-shouldered old man came in. He was dressed in blue jeans and he carried a big push-broom in his left hand. Behind him came George, and behind George, Lennie.

"The boss was expectin' you last night," the old man said. "He was sore as hell when you wasn't here to go out this morning." He pointed with his right arm, and out of the sleeve came a round stick-like wrist, but no hand. "You can have them two beds there," he said, indicating two bunks near the stove.

George stepped over and threw his blankets down on the burlap sack of straw that was a mattress. He looked into his box shelf and then picked a small yellow can from it. "Say. What the hell's this?"

"I don't know," said the old man.

"Says 'positively kills lice, roaches and other scourges.' What the hell kind of bed you giving us, anyways. We don't want no pants rabbits."

The old swamper shifted his broom and held it between his elbow and his side while he held out his hand for the can. He studied the label carefully. "Tell you what—" he said finally, "last guy that had this bed was a blacksmith—hell of a nice fella and as clean a guy as you want to meet. Used to wash his hands even *after* he ate."

"Then how come he got graybacks?" George was working up a slow anger. Lennie put his bindle on the neighboring bunk and sat down. He watched George with open mouth.

"Tell you what," said the old swamper. "This here blacksmith —name of Whitey—was the kind of guy that would put that stuff around even if there wasn't no bugs—just to make sure, see? Tell you what he used to do—At meals he'd peel his boil' potatoes, an' he'd take out ever' little spot, no matter what kind, before he'd eat it. And if there was a red splotch on an egg, he'd scrape it off. Finally quit about the food. That's the kinda guy he was—clean. Used ta dress up Sundays even when he wasn't going no place, put on a necktie even, and then set in the bunk house."

"I ain't so sure," said George skeptically. "What did you say he quit for?"

The old man put the yellow can in his pocket, and he rubbed his bristly white whiskers with his knuckles. "Why . . . he . . . just quit, the way a guy will. Says it was the food. Just wanted to move. Didn't give no other reason but the food. Just says 'gimme my time' one night, the way any guy would."

George lifted his tick and looked underneath it. He leaned over and inspected the sacking closely. Immediately Lennie got up and did the same with his bed. Finally George seemed satisfied. He unrolled his bindle and put things on the shelf, his razor and bar of soap, his comb and bottle of pills, his liniment and leather wristband. Then he made his bed up neatly with blankets. The old man said, "I guess the boss'll be out here in a minute. He was sure burned when you wasn't here this morning. Come right in when we was eatin' breakfast and says, 'Where the hell's them new men?' An' he give the stable buck hell, too."

George patted a wrinkle out of his bed, and sat down. "Give the stable buck hell?" he asked.

"Sure. Ya see the stable buck's a nigger."

"Nigger, huh?"

"Yeah. Nice fella too. Got a crooked back where a horse kicked him. The boss gives him hell when he's mad. But the stable buck don't give a damn about that. He reads a lot. Got books in his room."

"What kind of a guy is the boss?" George asked.

"Well, he's a pretty nice fella. Gets pretty mad sometimes, but he's pretty nice. Tell ya what—know what he done Christmas? Brang a gallon of whisky right in here and says, 'Drink hearty boys. Christmas comes but once a year.'"

"The hell he did! Whole gallon?"

"Yes sir. Jesus, we had fun. They let the nigger come in that night. Little skinner name of Smitty took after the nigger. Done pretty good, too. The guys wouldn't let him use his feet, so the nigger got him. If he coulda used his feet, Smitty says he woulda killed the nigger. The guys said on account of the nigger's got a crooked back, Smitty can't use his feet." He paused in relish of the memory. "After that the guys went into Soledad and raised hell. I didn't go in there. I ain't got the poop no more."

Lennie was just finishing making his bed. The wooden latch raised again and the door opened. A little stocky man stood in the open doorway. He wore blue jean trousers, a flannel shirt, a black, unbuttoned vest and a black coat. His thumbs were stuck in his belt, on each side of a square steel buckle. On his head was a soiled brown Stetson hat, and he wore high-heeled boots and spurs to prove he was not a laboring man.

The old swamper looked quickly at him, and then shuffled to the door rubbing his whiskers with his knuckles as he went. "Them guys just come," he said, and shuffled past the boss and out the door.

The boss stepped into the room with the short, quick steps of a fat-legged man. "I wrote Murray and Ready I wanted two men this morning. You got your work slips?" George reached into his pocket and produced the slips and handed them to the boss. "It wasn't Murray and Ready's fault. Says right here on the slip that you was to be here for work this morning."

George looked down at his feet. "Bus driver give us a bum steer," he said. "We hadda walk ten miles. Says we was here when we wasn't. We couldn't get no rides in the morning."

The boss squinted his eyes. "Well, I had to send out the grain teams short two buckers. Won't do any good to go out now till after dinner." He pulled his time book out of his pocket and opened it where a pencil was stuck between the leaves. George scowled meaningfully at Lennie, and Lennie nodded to show that he understood. The boss licked his pencil. "What's your name?"

"George Milton."

"And what's yours?"

George said, "His name's Lennie Small."

The names were entered in the book. "Le's see, this is the twentieth, noon the twentieth." He closed the book. "Where you boys been working?"

"Up around Weed," said George.

"You, too?" to Lennie.

"Yeah, him too," said George.

The boss pointed a playful finger at Lennie. "He ain't much of a talker, is he?"

"No, he ain't, but he's sure a hell of a good worker. Strong as a bull."

Lennie smiled to himself. "Strong as a bull," he repeated.

George scowled at him, and Lennie dropped his head in shame at having forgotten.

The boss said suddenly, "Listen, Small!" Lennie raised his head. "What can you do?"

In a panic, Lennie looked at George for help. "He can do anything you tell him," said George. "He's a good skinner. He can rassel grain bags, drive a cultivator. He can do anything. Just give him a try."

The boss turned on George. "Then why don't you let him answer? What you trying to put over?"

George broke in loudly, "Oh! I ain't saying he's bright. He ain't. But I say he's a God damn good worker. He can put up a four hundred pound bale."

The boss deliberately put the little book in his pocket. He hooked his thumbs in his belt and squinted one eye nearly closed. "Say—what you sellin'?"

"Huh?"

"I said what stake you got in this guy? You takin' his pay away from him?"

"No, 'course I ain't. Why ya think I'm sellin' him out?"

"Well, I never seen one guy take so much trouble for another guy. I just like to know what your interest is."

George said, "He's my . . . cousin. I told his old lady I'd take care of him. He got kicked in the head by a horse when he was a kid. He's awright. Just ain't bright. But he can do anything you tell him."

The boss turned half away. "Well, God knows he don't need any brains to buck barley bags. But don't you try to put nothing over, Milton. I got my eye on you. Why'd you quit in Weed?"

"Job was done," said George promptly.

"What kinda job?"

"We . . . we was diggin' a cesspool."

"All right. But don't try to put nothing over, 'cause you can't get away with nothing. I seen wise guys before. Go on out with the grain teams after dinner. They're pickin' up barley at the threshing machine. Go out with Slim's team."

"Slim?"

"Yeah. Big tall skinner. You'll see him at dinner." He turned abruptly and went to the door, but before he went out he turned and looked for a long moment at the two men.

When the sound of his footsteps had died away, George turned on Lennie. "So you wasn't gonna say a word. You was gonna leave your big flapper shut and leave me do the talkin'. Damn near lost us the job."

Lennie stared hopelessly at his hands. "I forgot, George."

"Yeah, you forgot. You always forget, an' I got to talk you out of it." He sat down heavily on the bunk. "Now he's got his eye on us. Now we got to be careful and not make no slips. You keep your big flapper shut after this." He fell morosely silent.

"George."

"What you want now?"

"I wasn't kicked in the head with no horse, was I, George?"

"Be a damn good thing if you was," George said viciously. "Save ever'body a hell of a lot of trouble."

"You said I was your cousin, George."

"Well, that was a lie. An' I'm damn glad it was. If I was a relative of yours I'd shoot myself." He stopped suddenly, stepped to the open front door and peered out. "Say, what the hell you doin' listenin'?"

The old man came slowly into the room. He had his broom in his hand. And at his heels there walked a dragfooted sheep dog, gray of muzzle, and with pale, blind old eyes. The dog struggled lamely to the side of the room and lay down, grunting softly to himself and licking his grizzled, moth-eaten coat. The swamper watched him until he was settled. "I wasn't listenin'. I was jus' standin' in the shade a minute scratchin' my dog. I jus' now finished swampin' out the wash house."

"You was pokin' your big ears into our business," George said. "I don't like nobody to get nosey."

The old man looked uneasily from George to Lennie, and then back. "I jus' come there," he said. "I didn't hear nothing you guys was sayin'. I ain't interested in nothing you was sayin'. A guy on a ranch don't never listen nor he don't ast no questions."

"Damn right he don't," said George, slightly mollified, "not if he wants to stay workin' long." But he was reassured by the swamper's defense. "Come on in and set down a minute," he said. "That's a hell of an old dog."

"Yeah. I had 'im ever since he was a pup. God, he was a good sheep dog when he was younger." He stood his broom against the wall and he rubbed his white bristled cheek with his knuckles. "How'd you like the boss?" he asked.

"Pretty good. Seemed awright."

"He's a nice fella," the swamper agreed. "You got to take him right."

At that moment a young man came into the bunk house; a thin young man with a brown face, with brown eyes and a head of tightly curled hair. He wore a work glove on his left hand, and, like the boss, he wore high-heeled boots. "Seen my old man?" he asked.

The swamper said, "He was here jus' a minute ago, Curley. Went over to the cook house, I think."

"I'll try to catch him," said Curley. His eyes passed over the new men and he stopped. He glanced coldly at George and then at Lennie. His arms gradually bent at the elbows and his hands closed into fists. He stiffened and went into a slight crouch. His glance was at once calculating and pugnacious. Lennie squirmed under the look and shifted his feet nervously. Curley stepped gingerly close to him. "You the new guys the old man was waitin' for?"

"We just come in," said George.

"Let the big guy talk."

Lennie twisted with embarrassment.

George said, "S'pose he don't want to talk?"

Curley lashed his body around. "By Christ, he's gotta talk when he's spoke to. What the hell are you gettin' into it for?"

"We travel together," said George coldly.

"Oh, so it's that way."

George was tense, and motionless. "Yeah, it's that way."

Lennie was looking helplessly to George for instruction.

"An' you won't let the big guy talk, is that it?"

"He can talk if he wants to tell you anything." He nodded slightly to Lennie.

"We jus' come in," said Lennie softly.

Curley stared levelly at him. "Well, nex' time you answer when you're spoke to." He turned toward the door and walked out, and his elbows were still bent out a little.

George watched him out, and then he turned back to the swamper. "Say, what the hell's he got on his shoulder? Lennie didn't do nothing to him."

The old man looked cautiously at the door to make sure no one was listening. "That's the boss's son," he said quietly. "Curley's pretty handy. He done quite a bit in the ring. He's a lightweight, and he's handy."

"Well, let him be handy," said George. "He don't have to take after Lennie. Lennie didn't do nothing to him. What's he got against Lennie?"

The swamper considered. . . . "Well . . . tell you what. Curley's like a lot of little guys. He hates big guys. He's alla time picking scraps with big guys. Kind of like he's mad at 'em because he ain't a big guy. You seen little guys like that, ain't you? Always scrappy?"

"Sure," said George. "I seen plenty tough little guys. But this Curley better not make no mistakes about Lennie. Lennie ain't handy, but this Curley punk is gonna get hurt if he messes around with Lennie."

"Well, Curley's pretty handy," the swamper said skeptically. "Never did seem right to me. S'pose Curley jumps a big guy an' licks him. Ever'body says what a game guy Curley is. And s'pose he does the same thing and gets licked. Then ever'body says the big guy oughtta pick somebody his own size, and maybe they gang up on the big guy. Never did seem right to me. Seems like Curley ain't givin' nobody a chance."

George was watching the door. He said ominously, "Well, he better watch out for Lennie. Lennie ain't no fighter, but Lennie's strong and quick and Lennie don't know no rules." He walked to the square table and sat down on one of the boxes. He gathered some of the cards together and shuffled them.

The old man sat down on another box. "Don't tell Curley I said none of this. He'd slough me. He just don't give a damn. Won't ever get canned 'cause his old man's the boss."

George cut the cards and began turning them over, looking at each one and throwing it down on a pile. He said, "This guy Curley sounds like a son-of-a-bitch to me. I don't like mean little guys."

"Seems to me like he's worse lately," said the swamper. "He got married a couple of weeks ago. Wife lives over in the boss's house. Seems like Curley is cockier'n ever since he got married."

George grunted, "Maybe he's showin' off for his wife."

The swamper warmed to his gossip. "You seen that glove on his left hand?"

"Yeah. I seen it."

"Well, that glove's fulla vaseline."

"Vaseline? What the hell for?"

"Well, I tell ya what—Curley says he's keepin' that hand soft for his wife."

George studied the cards absorbedly. "That's a dirty thing to tell around," he said.

The old man was reassured. He had drawn a derogatory statement from George. He felt safe now, and he spoke more confidently. "Wait'll you see Curley's wife."

George cut the cards again and put out a solitaire lay, slowly and deliberately. "Purty?" he asked casually.

"Yeah. Purty . . . but——"

George studied his cards. "But what?"

"Well—she got the eye."

"Yeah? Married two weeks and got the eye? Maybe that's why Curley's pants is full of ants."

"I seen her give Slim the eye. Slim's a jerkline skinner. Hell of a nice fella. Slim don't need to wear no high-heeled boots on a grain team. I seen her give Slim the eye. Curley never seen it. An' I seen her give Carlson the eye."

George pretended a lack of interest. "Looks like we was gonna have fun."

The swamper stood up from his box. "Know what I think?" George did not answer. "Well, I think Curley's married . . . a tart."

"He ain't the first," said George. "There's plenty done that."

The old man moved toward the door, and his ancient dog lifted his head and peered about, and then got painfully to his feet to follow. "I gotta be settin' out the wash basins for the guys. The teams'll be in before long. You guys gonna buck barley?"

"Yeah."

"You won't tell Curley nothing I said?"

"Hell no."

"Well, you look her over, mister. You see if she ain't a tart." He stepped out the door into the brilliant sunshine.

George laid down his cards thoughtfully, turned his piles of three. He built four clubs on his ace pile. The sun square was on the floor now, and the flies whipped through it like sparks. A sound of jingling harness and the croak of heavy-laden axles sounded from outside. From the distance came a clear call. "Stable Buck—ooh, sta-able Buck!" And then, "Where the hell is that God damn nigger?"

George stared at his solitaire lay, and then he flounced the cards together and turned around to Lennie. Lennie was lying down on the bunk watching him.

"Look, Lennie! This here ain't no set up. I'm scared. You gonna have trouble with that Curley guy. I seen that kind before. He was kinda feelin' you out. He figures he's got you scared and he's gonna take a sock at you the first chance he gets."

Lennie's eyes were frightened. "I don't want no trouble," he said plaintively. "Don't let him sock me, George."

George got up and went over to Lennie's bunk and sat down on it. "I hate that kinda bastard," he said. "I seen plenty of 'em. Like the old guy says, Curley don't take no chances. He always wins." He thought for a moment. "If he tangles with you, Lennie, we're gonna get the can. Don't make no mistake about that. He's the boss's son. Look, Lennie. You try to keep away from him, will you? Don't never speak to him. If he comes in here you move clear to the other side of the room. Will you do that, Lennie?"

"I don't want no trouble," Lennie mourned. "I never done nothing to him."

"Well, that won't do you no good if Curley wants to plug himself up for a fighter. Just don't have nothing to do with him. Will you remember?"

"Sure, George. I ain't gonna say a word."

The sound of the approaching grain teams was louder, thud of big hooves on hard ground, drag of brakes and the jingle of trace chains. Men were calling back and forth from the teams. George, sitting on the bunk beside Lennie, frowned as he thought. Lennie asked timidly, "You ain't mad, George?"

"I ain't mad at you. I'm mad at this here Curley bastard. I hoped we was gonna get a little stake together—maybe a hundred dollars." His tone grew decisive. "You keep away from Curley, Lennie."

"Sure I will, George. I won't say a word."

"Don't let him pull you in—but—if the son-of-a-bitch socks you—let 'im have it."

"Let 'im have what, George?"

"Never mind, never mind. I'll tell you when. I hate that kind of a guy. Look, Lennie, if you get in any kind of trouble, you remember what I told you to do?"

Lennie raised up on his elbow. His face contorted with thought. Then his eyes moved sadly to George's face. "If I get in any trouble, you ain't gonna let me tend the rabbits."

"That's not what I meant. You remember where we slep' last night? Down by the river?"

"Yeah, I remember. Oh, sure I remember! I go there an' hide in the brush."

"Hide till I come for you. Don't let nobody see you. Hide in the brush by the river. Say that over."

"Hide in the brush by the river, down in the brush by the river."

"If you get in trouble."

"If I get in trouble."

A brake screeched outside. A call came, "Stable—Buck. Oh! Sta-able Buck."

George said, "Say it over to yourself, Lennie, so you won't forget it."

Both men glanced up, for the rectangle of sunshine in the doorway was cut off. A girl was standing there looking in. She had full, rouged lips and wide-spaced eyes, heavily made up. Her fingernails were red. Her hair hung in little rolled clusters, like sausages. She wore a cotton house dress and red mules, on the insteps of which were little bouquets of red ostrich feathers. "I'm lookin' for Curley," she said. Her voice had a nasal, brittle quality.

George looked away from her and then back. "He was in here a minute ago, but he went."

"Oh!" She put her hands behind her back and leaned against the door frame so that her body was thrown forward. "You're the new fellas that just come, ain't ya?"

"Yeah."

Lennie's eyes moved down over her body, and though she did not seem to be looking at Lennie she bridled a little. She looked at her fingernails. "Sometimes Curley's in here," she explained.

George said brusquely, "Well he ain't now."

"If he ain't, I guess I better look some place else," she said playfully.

Lennie watched her, fascinated. George said, "If I see him, I'll pass the word you was looking for him."

She smiled archly and twitched her body. "Nobody can't blame a person for lookin'," she said. There were footsteps behind her, going by. She turned her head. "Hi, Slim," she said.

Slim's voice came through the door. "Hi, Good-lookin'."

"I'm tryin' to find Curley, Slim."

"Well, you ain't tryin' very hard. I seen him goin' in your house."

She was suddenly apprehensive. "'Bye, boys," she called into the bunk house, and she hurried away.

George looked around at Lennie. "Jesus, what a tramp," he said. "So that's what Curley picks for a wife."

"She's purty," said Lennie defensively.

"Yeah, and she's sure hidin' it. Curley got his work ahead of him. Bet she'd clear out for twenty bucks."

Lennie still stared at the doorway where she had been. "Gosh, she was purty." He smiled admiringly. George looked quickly down at him and then he took him by an ear and shook him.

"Listen to me, you crazy bastard," he said fiercely. "Don't you even take a look at that bitch. I don't care what she says and what she does. I seen 'em poison before, but I never seen no piece of jail bait worse than her. You leave her be."

Lennie tried to disengage his ear. "I never done nothing, George."

"No, you never. But when she was standin' in the doorway showin' her legs, you wasn't lookin' the other way, neither."

"I never meant no harm, George. Honest I never."

"Well, you keep away from her, 'cause she's a rat-trap if I ever seen one. You let Curley take the rap. He let himself in for it. Glove fulla vaseline," George said disgustedly. "An' I bet he's eatin' raw eggs and writin' to the patent medicine houses."

Lennie cried out suddenly—"I don' like this place, George. This ain't no good place. I wanna get outa here."

"We gotta keep it till we get a stake. We can't help it, Lennie. We'll get out jus' as soon as we can. I don't like it no better than you do." He went back to the table and set out a new solitaire hand. "No, I don't like it," he said. "For two bits I'd shove out of here. If we can get jus' a few dollars in the poke we'll shove off and go up the American River and pan gold. We can make maybe a couple of dollars a day there, and we might hit a pocket."

Lennie leaned eagerly toward him. "Le's go, George. Le's get outta here. It's mean here."

"We gotta stay," George said shortly. "Shut up now. The guys'll be comin' in."

From the washroom nearby came the sound of running water and rattling basins. George studied the cards. "Maybe we oughtta wash up," he said. "But we ain't done nothing to get dirty."

A tall man stood in the doorway. He held a crushed Stetson hat under his arm while he combed his long, black, damp hair straight back. Like the others he wore blue jeans and a short denim jacket. When he had finished combing his hair he moved into the room, and he moved with a majesty only achieved by royalty and master craftsmen. He was a jerkline skinner, the prince of the ranch, capable of driving ten, sixteen, even twenty mules with a single line to the leaders. He was capable of killing a fly on the wheeler's butt with a bull whip without touching the mule. There was a gravity in his manner and a quiet so profound that all talk stopped when he spoke. His authority was so great that his word was taken on any subject, be it politics or love. This was Slim, the jerkline skinner. His hatchet face was ageless. He might have been thirty-five or fifty. His ear heard more than was said to him, and his slow speech had overtones not of thought, but of understanding beyond thought. His hands, large and lean, were as delicate in their action as those of a temple dancer.

He smoothed out his crushed hat, creased it in the middle and put it on. He looked kindly at the two in the bunk house. "It's brighter'n a bitch outside," he said gently. "Can't hardly see nothing in here. You the new guys?"

"Just come," said George.

"Gonna buck barley?"

"That's what the boss says."

Slim sat down on a box across the table from George. He studied the solitaire hand that was upside down to him. "Hope you get on my team," he said. His voice was very gentle. "I gotta pair of punks on my team that don't know a barley bag from a blue ball. You guys ever bucked any barley?"

"Hell, yes," said George. "I ain't nothing to scream about, but that big bastard there can put up more grain alone than most pairs can."

Lennie, who had been following the conversation back and forth with his eyes, smiled complacently at the compliment. Slim looked approvingly at George for having given the compliment. He leaned over the table and snapped the corner of a loose card. "You guys travel around together?" His tone was friendly. It invited confidence without demanding it.

"Sure," said George. "We kinda look after each other." He indicated Lennie with his thumb. "He ain't bright. Hell of a good worker, though. Hell of a nice fella, but he ain't bright. I've knew him for a long time."

Slim looked through George and beyond him. "Ain't many guys travel around together," he mused. "I don't know why. Maybe ever'body in the whole damn world is scared of each other."

"It's a lot nicer to go around with a guy you know," said George.

A powerful, big-stomached man came into the bunk house.

His head still dripped water from the scrubbing and dousing. "Hi, Slim," he said, and then stopped and stared at George and Lennie.

"These guys jus' come," said Slim by way of introduction.

"Glad ta meet ya," the big man said. "My name's Carlson."

"I'm George Milton. This here's Lennie Small."

"Glad ta meet ya," Carlson said again. "He ain't very small." He chuckled softly at his joke. "Ain't small at all," he repeated. "Meant to ask you, Slim—how's your bitch? I seen she wasn't under your wagon this morning."

"She slang her pups last night," said Slim. "Nine of 'em. I drowned four of 'em right off. She couldn't feed that many."

"Got five left, huh?"

"Yeah, five. I kept the biggest."

"What kinda dogs you think they're gonna be?"

"I dunno," said Slim. "Some kinda shepherds, I guess. That's the most kind I seen around here when she was in heat."

Carlson went on, "Got five pups, huh. Gonna keep all of 'em?"

"I dunno. Have to keep 'em a while so they can drink Lulu's milk."

Carlson said thoughtfully, "Well, looka here, Slim. I been thinkin'. That dog of Candy's is so God damn old he can't hardly walk. Stinks like hell, too. Ever' time he comes into the bunk house I can smell him for two, three days. Why'n't you get Candy to shoot his old dog and give him one of the pups to raise up? I can smell that dog a mile away. Got no teeth, damn near blind, can't eat. Candy feeds him milk. He can't chew nothing else."

George had been staring intently at Slim. Suddenly a triangle began to ring outside, slowly at first, and then faster and faster until the beat of it disappeared into one ringing sound. It stopped as suddenly as it had started.

"There she goes," said Carlson.

Outside, there was a burst of voices as a group of men went by.

Slim stood up slowly and with dignity. "You guys better come on while they's still something to eat. Won't be nothing left in a couple of minutes."

Carlson stepped back to let Slim precede him, and then the two of them went out the door.

Lennie was watching George excitedly. George rumpled his cards into a messy pile. "Yeah!" George said, "I heard him, Lennie. I'll ask him."

"A brown and white one," Lennie cried excitedly.

"Come on. Le's get dinner. I don't know whether he got a brown and white one."

Lennie didn't move from his bunk. "You ask him right away, George, so he won't kill no more of 'em."

"Sure. Come on now, get up on your feet."

Lennie rolled off his bunk and stood up, and the two of them started for the door. Just as they reached it, Curley bounced in.

"You seen a girl around here?" he demanded angrily.

George said coldly, " 'Bout half an hour ago maybe."

"Well what the hell was she doin'?"

George stood still, watching the angry little man. He said insultingly, "She said—she was lookin' for you."

Curley seemed really to see George for the first time. His eyes flashed over George, took in his height, measured his reach, looked at his trim middle. "Well, which way'd she go?" he demanded at last.

"I dunno," said George. "I didn't watch her go."

Curley scowled at him, and turning, hurried out the door.

George said, "Ya know, Lennie, I'm scared I'm gonna tangle with that bastard myself. I hate his guts. Jesus Christ! Come on. They won't be a damn thing left to eat."

They went out the door. The sunshine lay in a thin line under the window. From a distance there could be heard a rattle of dishes.

After a moment the ancient dog walked lamely in through the open door. He gazed about with mild, half-blind eyes. He sniffed, and then lay down and put his head between his paws. Curley popped into the doorway again and stood looking into the room. The dog raised his head, but when Curley jerked out, the grizzled head sank to the floor again.

Although there was evening brightness showing through the windows of the bunk house, inside it was dusk. Through the open door came the thuds and occasional clangs of a horseshoe game, and now and then the sound of voices raised in approval or derision.

Slim and George came into the darkening bunk house together. Slim reached up over the card table and turned on the tin-shaded electric light. Instantly the table was brilliant with light, and the cone of the shade threw its brightness straight downward, leaving the corners of the bunk house still in dusk. Slim sat down on a box and George took his place opposite.

"It wasn't nothing," said Slim. "I would of had to drowned most of 'em anyways. No need to thank me about that."

George said, "It wasn't much to you, maybe, but it was a hell of a lot to him. Jesus Christ, I don't know how we're gonna get him to sleep in here. He'll want to sleep right out in the barn with 'em. We'll have trouble keepin' him from getting right in the box with them pups."

"It wasn't nothing," Slim repeated. "Say, you sure was right about him. Maybe he ain't bright, but I never seen such a worker. He damn near killed his partner buckin' barley. There ain't nobody can keep up with him. God awmighty I never seen such a strong guy."

George spoke proudly. "Jus' tell Lennie what to do an' he'll do it if it don't take no figuring. He can't think of nothing to do himself, but he sure can take orders."

There was a clang of horseshoe on iron stake outside and a little cheer of voices.

Slim moved back slightly so the light was not on his face. "Funny how you an' him string along together." It was Slim's calm invitation to confidence.

"What's funny about it?" George demanded defensively.

"Oh, I dunno. Hardly none of the guys ever travel together. I hardly never seen two guys travel together. You know how the hands are, they just come in and get their bunk and work a month, and then they quit and go out alone. Never seem to give a damn about nobody. It jus' seems kinda funny a cuckoo like him and a smart little guy like you travelin' together."

"He ain't no cuckoo," said George. "He's dumb as hell, but he ain't crazy. An' I ain't so bright neither, or I wouldn't be buckin' barley for my fifty and found. If I was bright, if I was even a little bit smart, I'd have my own little place, an' I'd be bringin' in my own crops, 'stead of doin' all the work and not getting what comes up outa the ground." George fell silent. He wanted to talk. Slim neither encouraged nor discouraged him. He just sat back quiet and receptive.

"It ain't so funny, him an' me goin' aroun' together," George said at last. "Him and me was both born in Auburn. I knowed his Aunt Clara. She took him when he was a baby and raised him up. When his Aunt Clara died, Lennie just come along with me out workin'. Got kinda used to each other after a little while."

"Umm," said Slim.

George looked over at Slim and saw the calm, God-like eyes fastened on him. "Funny," said George. "I used to have a hell of a lot of fun with 'im. Used to play jokes on 'im 'cause he was too dumb to take care of 'imself. But he was too dumb even to know he had a joke played on him. I had fun. Made me seem God damn smart alongside of him. Why he'd do any damn thing I tol' him. If I tol' him to walk over a cliff, over he'd go. That wasn't so damn much fun after a while. He never got mad about it, neither. I've beat the hell outa him, and he coulda bust every bone in my body jus' with his han's, but he never lifted a finger against me." George's voice was taking on the tone of confession. "Tell you what made me stop that. One day a bunch of guys was standin' around up on the Sacramento River. I was feelin' pretty smart. I turns to Lennie and says, 'Jump in.' An' he jumps. Couldn't swim a stroke. He damn near drowned before we could get him. An' he was so damn nice to me for pullin' him out. Clean forgot I told him to jump in. Well, I ain't done nothing like that no more."

"He's a nice fella," said Slim. "Guy don't need no sense to be a nice fella. Seems to me sometimes it jus' works the other way around. Take a real smart guy and he ain't hardly ever a nice fella."

George stacked the scattered cards and began to lay out his solitaire hand. The shoes thudded on the ground outside. At the windows the light of the evening still made the window squares bright.

"I ain't got no people," George said. "I seen the guys that go around on the ranches alone. That ain't no good. They don't have no fun. After a long time they get mean. They get wantin' to fight all the time."

"Yeah, they get mean," Slim agreed. "They get so they don't want to talk to nobody."

"'Course Lennie's a God damn nuisance most of the time," said George. "But you get used to goin' around with a guy an' you can't get rid of him."

"He ain't mean," said Slim. "I can see Lennie ain't a bit mean."

"'Course he ain't mean. But he gets in trouble alla time because he's so God damn dumb. Like what happened in Weed——" He stopped, stopped in the middle of turning over a card. He looked alarmed and peered over at Slim. "You wouldn't tell nobody?"

"What'd he do in Weed?" Slim asked calmly.

"You wouldn' tell? . . . No, 'course you wouldn'."

"What'd he do in Weed?" Slim asked again.

"Well, he seen this girl in a red dress. Dumb bastard like he is, he wants to touch ever'thing he likes. Just wants to feel it. So he reaches out to feel this red dress an' the girl lets out a squawk, and that gets Lennie all mixed up, and he holds on 'cause that's the only thing he can think to do. Well, this girl squawks and squawks. I was jus' a little bit off, and I heard all the yellin', so I comes running, an' by that time Lennie's so scared all he can think to do is jus' hold on. I socked him over the head with a fence picket to make him let go. He was so scairt he couldn't let go of that dress. And he's so God damn strong, you know."

Slim's eyes were level and unwinking. He nodded very slowly. "So what happens?"

George carefully built his line of solitaire cards. "Well, that girl rabbits in an' tells the law she been raped. The guys in Weed start a party out to lynch Lennie. So we sit in a irrigation ditch under water all the rest of that day. Got on'y our heads sticking outa water, an' up under the grass that sticks out from the side of the ditch. An' that night we scrammed outa there."

Slim sat in silence for a moment. "Didn't hurt the girl none, huh?" he asked finally.

"Hell, no. He just scared her. I'd be scared too if he grabbed me. But he never hurt her. He jus' wanted to touch that red dress, like he wants to pet them pups all the time."

"He ain't mean," said Slim. "I can tell a mean guy a mile off."

"'Course he ain't, and he'll do any damn thing I——"

Lennie came in through the door. He wore his blue denim coat over his shoulders like a cape, and he walked hunched way over.

"Hi, Lennie," said George. "How you like the pup now?"

Lennie said breathlessly, "He's brown an' white jus' like I wanted." He went directly to his bunk and lay down and turned his face to the wall and drew up his knees.

George put down his cards very deliberately. "Lennie," he said sharply.

Lennie twisted his neck and looked over his shoulder. "Huh? What you want, George?"

"I tol' you you couldn't bring that pup in here."

"What pup, George? I ain't got no pup."

George went quickly to him, grabbed him by the shoulder and rolled him over. He reached down and picked the tiny puppy from where Lennie had been concealing it against his stomach.

Lennie sat up quickly. "Give 'um to me, George."

George said, "You get right up an' take this pup back to the nest. He's gotta sleep with his mother. You want to kill him? Just born last night an' you take him out of the nest. You take him back or I'll tell Slim not to let you have him."

Lennie held out his hands pleadingly. "Give 'um to me, George. I'll take 'um back. I didn't mean no harm, George. Honest I didn't. I jus' wanted to pet 'um a little."

George handed the pup to him. "Awright. You get him back there quick, and don' you take him out no more. You'll kill him, the first thing you know." Lennie fairly scuttled out of the room.

Slim had not moved. His calm eyes followed Lennie out the door. "Jesus," he said. "He's jes' like a kid, ain't he."

"Sure he's jes' like a kid. There ain't no more harm in him than a kid neither, except he's so strong. I bet he won't come in here to sleep tonight. He'd sleep right alongside that box in the barn. Well—let 'im. He ain't doin' no harm out there."

It was almost dark outside now. Old Candy, the swamper, came in and went to his bunk, and behind him struggled his old dog. "Hello, Slim. Hello, George. Didn't neither of you play horse-shoes?"

"I don't like to play ever' night," said Slim.

Candy went on, "Either you guys got a slug of whisky? I gotta gut ache."

"I ain't," said Slim. "I'd drink it myself if I had, an' I ain't got a gut ache neither."

"Gotta bad gut ache," said Candy. "Them God damn turnips give it to me. I knowed they was going to before I ever eat 'em."

The thick-bodied Carlson came in out of the darkening yard. He walked to the other end of the bunk house and turned on the second shaded light. "Darker'n hell in here," he said. "Jesus, how that nigger can pitch shoes."

"He's plenty good," said Slim.

"Damn right he is," said Carlson. "He don't give nobody else a chance to win——" He stopped and sniffed the air, and still sniffing, looked down at the old dog. "God awmighty, that dog stinks. Get him outa here, Candy! I don't know nothing that stinks as bad as an old dog. You gotta get him out."

Candy rolled to the edge of his bunk. He reached over and patted the ancient dog, and he apologized, "I been around him so much I never notice how he stinks."

"Well, I can't stand him in here," said Carlson. "That stink hangs around even after he's gone." He walked over with his heavy-legged stride and looked down at the dog. "Got no teeth," he said. "He's all stiff with rheumatism. He ain't no good to you, Candy. An' he ain't no good to himself. Why'n't you shoot him, Candy?"

The old man squirmed uncomfortably. "Well—hell! I had him so long. Had him since he was a pup. I herded sheep with him." He said proudly, "You wouldn't think it to look at him now, but he was the best damn sheep dog I ever seen."

George said, "I seen a guy in Weed that had an Airedale could herd sheep. Learned it from the other dogs."

Carlson was not to be put off. "Look, Candy. This ol' dog jus' suffers hisself all the time. If you was to take him out and shoot him right in the back of the head—" he leaned over and pointed, "—right there, why he'd never know what hit him."

Candy looked about unhappily. "No," he said softly. "No, I couldn' do that. I had 'im too long."

"He don't have no fun," Carlson insisted. "And he stinks to beat hell. Tell you what. I'll shoot him for you. Then it won't be you that does it."

Candy threw his legs off his bunk. He scratched the white stubble whiskers on his cheek nervously. "I'm so used to him," he said softly. "I had him from a pup."

"Well, you ain't bein' kind to him keepin' him alive," said Carlson. "Look, Slim's bitch got a litter right now. I bet Slim would give you one of them pups to raise up, wouldn't you, Slim?"

The skinner had been studying the old dog with his calm eyes. "Yeah," he said. "You can have a pup if you want to." He seemed to shake himself free for speech. "Carl's right, Candy. That dog ain't no good to himself. I wisht somebody'd shoot me if I get old an' a cripple."

Candy looked helplessly at him, for Slim's opinions were law. "Maybe it'd hurt him," he suggested. "I don't mind takin' care of him."

Carlson said, "The way I'd shoot him, he wouldn't feel nothing. I'd put the gun right there." He pointed with his toe. "Right back of the head. He wouldn't even quiver."

Candy looked for help from face to face. It was quite dark outside by now. A young laboring man came in. His sloping shoulders were bent forward and he walked heavily on his heels, as though he carried the invisible grain bag. He went to his bunk and put his hat on his shelf. Then he picked a pulp magazine from his shelf and brought it to the light over the table. "Did I show you this, Slim?" he asked.

"Show me what?"

The young man turned to the back of the magazine, put it down on the table and pointed with his finger. "Right there, read that."

Slim bent over it. "Go on," said the young man. "Read it out loud."

"'Dear Editor:'" Slim read slowly. "'I read your mag for six years and I think it is the best on the market. I like stories by Peter Rand. I think he is a whing-ding. Give us more like the Dark Rider. I don't write many letters. Just thought I would tell you I think your mag is the best dime's worth I ever spent.'"

Slim looked up questioningly. "What you want me to read that for?"

Whit said, "Go on. Read the name at the bottom."

Slim read, "'Yours for success, William Tenner.'"
He glanced up at Whit again. "What you want me to read that for?"

Whit closed the magazine impressively. "Don't you remember Bill Tenner? Worked here about three months ago?"

Slim thought. . . . "Little guy?" he asked. "Drove a cultivator?"

"That's him," Whit cried. "That's the guy!"

"You think he's the guy wrote this letter?"

"I know it. Bill and me was in here one day. Bill had one of them books that just come. He was lookin' in it and he says, 'I wrote a letter. Wonder if they put it in the book!' But it wasn't there. Bill says, 'Maybe they're savin' it for later.' An' that's just what they done. There it is."

"Guess you're right," said Slim. "Got it right in the book."

George held out his hand for the magazine. "Let's look at it?"

Whit found the place again, but he did not surrender his hold on it. He pointed out the letter with his forefinger. And then he went to his box shelf and laid the magazine carefully in. "I wonder if Bill seen it," he said. "Bill and me worked in that patch of field peas. Run cultivators, both of us. Bill was a hell of a nice fella."

During the conversation Carlson had refused to be drawn in. He continued to look down at the old dog. Candy watched him uneasily. At last Carlson said, "If you want me to, I'll put the old devil out of his misery right now and get it over with. Ain't nothing left for him. Can't eat, can't see, can't even walk without hurtin'."

Candy said hopefully, "You ain't got no gun."

"The hell I ain't. Got a Luger. It won't hurt him none at all."

Candy said, "Maybe tomorra. Le's wait till tomorra."

"I don't see no reason for it," said Carlson. He went to his bunk, pulled his bag from underneath it and took out a Luger pistol. "Let's get it over with," he said. "We can't sleep with him stinkin' around in here." He put the pistol in his hip pocket.

Candy looked a long time at Slim to try to find some reversal. And Slim gave him none. At last Candy said softly and hopelessly, "Awright—take 'im." He did not look down at the dog at all. He lay back on his bunk and crossed his arms behind his head and stared at the ceiling.

From his pocket Carlson took a little leather thong. He stooped over and tied it around the old dog's neck. All the men except Candy watched him. "Come boy. Come on, boy," he said gently. And he said apologetically to Candy, "He won't even feel it." Candy did not move nor answer him. He twitched the thong. "Come on, boy." The old dog got slowly and stiffly to his feet and followed the gently pulling leash.

Slim said, "Carlson."

"Yeah?"

"You know what to do."

"What ya mean, Slim?"

"Take a shovel," said Slim shortly.

"Oh, sure! I get you." He led the dog out into the darkness.

George followed to the door and shut the door and set the latch gently in its place. Candy lay rigidly on his bed staring at the ceiling.

Slim said loudly, "One of my lead mules got a bad hoof. Got to get some tar on it." His voice trailed off. It was silent outside. Carlson's footsteps died away. The silence came into the room. And the silence lasted.

George chuckled, "I bet Lennie's right out there in the barn with his pup. He won't want to come in here no more now he's got a pup."

Slim said, "Candy, you can have any one of them pups you want."

Candy did not answer. The silence fell on the room again. It came out of the night and invaded the room. George said, "Anybody like to play a little euchre?"

"I'll play out a few with you," said Whit.

They took places opposite each other at the table under the light, but George did not shuffle the cards. He rippled the edge of the deck nervously, and the little snapping noise drew the eyes of all the men in the room, so that he stopped doing it. The silence fell on the room again. A minute passed, and another minute. Candy lay still, staring at the ceiling. Slim gazed at him for a moment and then looked down at his hands; he subdued one hand with the other, and held it down. There came a little gnawing sound from under the floor and all the men looked down toward it gratefully. Only Candy continued to stare at the ceiling.

"Sounds like there was a rat under there," said George. "We ought to get a trap down there."

Whit broke out, "What the hell's takin' him so long? Lay out some cards, why don't you? We ain't going to get no euchre played this way."

George brought the cards together tightly and studied the backs of them. The silence was in the room again.

A shot sounded in the distance. The men looked quickly at the old man. Every head turned toward him.

For a moment he continued to stare at the ceiling. Then he rolled slowly over and faced the wall and lay silent.

George shuffled the cards noisily and dealt them. Whit drew a scoring board to him and set the pegs to start. Whit said, "I guess you guys really come here to work."

"How do ya mean?" George asked.

Whit laughed. "Well, ya come on a Friday. You got two days to work till Sunday."

"I don't see how you figure," said George.

Whit laughed again. "You do if you been around these big ranches much. Guy that wants to look over a ranch comes in Sat'day afternoon. He gets Sat'day night supper an' three meals on Sunday, and he can quit Monday mornin' after breakfast without turning his hand. But you come to work Friday noon. You got to put in a day an' a half no matter how you figure."

George looked at him levelly. "We're gonna stick aroun' a while," he said. "Me an' Lennie's gonna roll up a stake."

The door opened quietly and the stable buck put in his head;

a lean negro head, lined with pain, the eyes patient. "Mr. Slim."

Slim took his eyes from old Candy. "Huh? Oh! Hello, Crooks. What's'a matter?"

"You told me to warm up tar for that mule's foot. I got it warm."

"Oh! Sure, Crooks. I'll come right out an' put it on."

"I can do it if you want, Mr. Slim."

"No. I'll come do it myself." He stood up.

Crooks said, "Mr. Slim."

"Yeah."

"That big new guy's messin' around your pups out in the barn."

"Well, he ain't doin' no harm. I give him one of them pups."

"Just thought I'd tell ya," said Crooks. "He's takin' 'em outa the nest and handlin' them. That won't do them no good."

"He won't hurt 'em," said Slim. "I'll come along with you now."

George looked up. "If that crazy bastard's foolin' around too much, jus' kick him out, Slim."

Slim followed the stable buck out of the room.

George dealt and Whit picked up his cards and examined them. "Seen the new kid yet?" he asked.

"What kid?" George asked.

"Why, Curley's new wife."

"Yeah, I seen her."

"Well, ain't she a looloo?"

"I ain't seen that much of her," said George.

Whit laid down his cards impressively. "Well, stick around an' keep your eyes open. You'll see plenty. She ain't concealin' nothing. I never seen nobody like her. She got the eye goin' all the time on everybody. I bet she even gives the stable buck the eye. I don't know what the hell she wants."

George asked casually, "Been any trouble since she got here?"

It was obvious that Whit was not interested in his cards. He laid his hand down and George scooped it in. George laid out his deliberate solitaire hand—seven cards, and six on top, and five on top of those.

Whit said, "I see what you mean. No, they ain't been nothing yet. Curley's got yella-jackets in his drawers, but that's all so far. Ever' time the guys is around she shows up. She's lookin' for Curley, or she thought she lef' somethin' layin' around and she's lookin' for it. Seems like she can't keep away from guys. An'

Curley's pants is just crawlin' with ants, but they ain't nothing come of it yet."

George said, "She's gonna make a mess. They's gonna be a bad mess about her. She's a jail bait all set on the trigger. That Curley got his work cut out for him. Ranch with a bunch of guys on it ain't no place for a girl, specially like her."

Whit said, "If you got idears, you ought ta come in town with us guys tomorra night."

"Why? What's doin'?"

"Jus' the usual thing. We go in to old Susy's place. Hell of a nice place. Old Susy's a laugh—always crackin' jokes. Like she says when we come up on the front porch las' Sat'day night. Susy opens the door and then she yells over her shoulder, 'Get yor coats on, girls, here comes the sheriff.' She never talks dirty, neither. Got five girls there."

"What's it set you back?" George asked.

"Two an' a half. You can get a shot for two bits. Susy got nice chairs to set in, too. If a guy don't want a flop, why he can just set in the chairs and have a couple or three shots and pass the time of day and Susy don't give a damn. She ain't rushin' guys through and kickin' 'em out if they don't want a flop."

"Might go in and look the joint over," said George.

"Sure. Come along. It's a hell of a lot of fun—her crackin' jokes all the time. Like she says one time, she says, 'I've knew people that if they got a rag rug on the floor an' a kewpie doll lamp on the phonograph they think they're running a parlor house.' That's Clara's house she's talkin' about. An' Susy says, 'I know what you boys want,' she says. 'My girls is clean,' she says, 'an' there ain't no water in my whisky,' she says. 'If any you guys wanta look at a kewpie doll lamp an' take your own chance gettin' burned, why you know where to go.' An' she says, 'There's guys around here walkin' bow-legged 'cause they like to look at a kewpie doll lamp.'"

George asked, "Clara runs the other house, huh?"

"Yeah," said Whit. "We don't never go there. Clara gets three bucks a crack and thirty-five cents a shot, and she don't crack no jokes. But Susy's place is clean and she got nice chairs. Don't let no goo-goos in, neither."

"Me an' Lennie's rollin' up a stake," said George. "I might

go in an' set and have a shot, but I ain't puttin' out no two and a half."

"Well, a guy got to have some fun sometime," said Whit.

The door opened and Lennie and Carlson came in together. Lennie crept to his bunk and sat down, trying not to attract attention. Carlson reached under his bunk and brought out his bag. He didn't look at old Candy, who still faced the wall. Carlson found a little cleaning rod in the bag and a can of oil. He laid them on his bed and then brought out the pistol, took out the magazine and snapped the loaded shell from the chamber. Then he fell to cleaning the barrel with the little rod. When the ejector snapped, Candy turned over and looked for a moment at the gun before he turned back to the wall again.

Carlson said casually, "Curley been in yet?"

"No," said Whit. "What's eatin' on Curley?"

Carlson squinted down the barrel of his gun. "Lookin' for his old lady. I seen him going round and round outside."

Whit said sarcastically, "He spends half his time lookin' for her, and the rest of the time she's lookin' for him."

Curley burst into the room excitedly. "Any you guys seen my wife?" he demanded.

"She ain't been here," said Whit.

Curley looked threateningly about the room. "Where the hell's Slim?"

"Went out in the barn," said George. "He was gonna put some tar on a split hoof."

Curley's shoulders dropped and squared. "How long ago'd he go?"

"Five—ten minutes."

Curley jumped out the door and banged it after him.

Whit stood up. "I guess maybe I'd like to see this," he said. "Curley's just spoilin' or he wouldn't start for Slim. An' Curley's handy, God damn handy. Got in the finals for the Golden Gloves. He got newspaper clippings about it." He considered. "But jus' the same, he better leave Slim alone. Nobody don't know what Slim can do."

"Thinks Slim's with his wife, don't he?" said George.

"Looks like it," Whit said. "'Course Slim ain't. Least I don't think Slim is. But I like to see the fuss if it comes off. Come on, le's go."

George said, "I'm stayin' right here. I don't want to get mixed up in nothing. Lennie and me got to make a stake."

Carlson finished the cleaning of the gun and put it in the bag and pushed the bag under his bunk. "I guess I'll go out and look her over," he said. Old Candy lay still, and Lennie, from his bunk, watched George cautiously.

When Whit and Carlson were gone and the door closed after them, George turned to Lennie. "What you got on your mind?"

"I ain't done nothing, George. Slim says I better not pet them pups so much for a while. Slim says it ain't good for them; so I come right in. I been good, George."

"I coulda told you that," said George.

"Well, I wasn't hurtin' 'em none. I jus' had mine in my lap pettin' it."

George asked, "Did you see Slim out in the barn?"

"Sure I did. He tol' me I better not pet that pup no more."

"Did you see that girl?"

"You mean Curley's girl?"

"Yeah. Did she come in the barn?"

"No. Anyways I never seen her."

"You never seen Slim talkin' to her?"

"Uh-uh. She ain't been in the barn."

"O.K.," said George. "I guess them guys ain't gonna see no fight. If there's any fightin', Lennie, you keep out of it."

"I don't want no fights," said Lennie. He got up from his bunk and sat down at the table, across from George. Almost automatically George shuffled the cards and laid out his solitaire hand. He used a deliberate, thoughtful, slowness.

Lennie reached for a face card and studied it, then turned it upside down and studied it. "Both ends the same," he said. "George, why is it both end's the same?"

"I don't know," said George. "That's jus' the way they make 'em. What was Slim doin' in the barn when you seen him?"

"Slim?"

"Sure. You seen him in the barn, an' he tol' you not to pet the pups so much."

"Oh, yeah. He had a can a' tar an' a paint brush. I don't know what for."

"You sure that girl didn't come in like she come in here today?"

"No. She never come."

George sighed. "You give me a good whore house every time," he said. "A guy can go in an' get drunk and get ever'thing outa his system all at once, an' no messes. And he knows how much it's gonna set him back. These here jail baits is just set on the trigger of the hoosegow."

Lennie followed his words admiringly, and moved his lips a little to keep up. George continued, "You remember Andy Cushman, Lennie? Went to grammar school?"

"The one that his old lady used to make hot cakes for the kids?" Lennie asked.

"Yeah. That's the one. You can remember anything if there's anything to eat in it." George looked carefully at the solitaire hand. He put an ace up on his scoring rack and piled a two, three and four of diamonds on it. "Andy's in San Quentin right now on account of a tart," said George.

Lennie drummed on the table with his fingers. "George?"

"Huh?"

"George, how long's it gonna be till we get that little place an' live on the fatta the lan'—an' rabbits?"

"I don't know," said George. "We gotta get a big stake together. I know a little place we can get cheap, but they ain't givin' it away."

Old Candy turned slowly over. His eyes were wide open. He watched George carefully.

Lennie said, "Tell about that place, George."

"I jus' tol' you, jus' las' night."

"Go on—tell again, George."

"Well, it's ten acres," said George. "Got a little win'mill. Got a little shack on it, an' a chicken run. Got a kitchen, orchard, cherries, apples, peaches, 'cots, nuts, got a few berries. They's a place for alfalfa and plenty water to flood it. They's a pig pen——"

"An' rabbits, George."

"No place for rabbits now, but I could easy build a few hutches and you could feed alfalfa to the rabbits."

"Damn right, I could," said Lennie. "You God damn right I could."

George's hands stopped working with the cards. His voice was growing warmer. "An' we could have a few pigs. I could build a smoke house like the one gran'pa had, an' when we kill a pig we can smoke the bacon and the hams, and make sausage an' all like that. An' when the salmon run up river we could catch a hundred of 'em an' salt 'em down or smoke 'em. We could have them for breakfast. They ain't nothing so nice as smoked salmon. When the fruit come in we could can it—and tomatoes, they're easy to can. Ever' Sunday we'd kill a chicken or a rabbit. Maybe we'd have a cow or a goat, and the cream is so God damn thick you got to cut it with a knife and take it out with a spoon."

Lennie watched him with wide eyes, and old Candy watched him too. Lennie said softly, "We could live offa the fatta the lan'."

"Sure," said George. "All kin's a vegetables in the garden, and if we want a little whisky we can sell a few eggs or something, or some milk. We'd jus' live there. We'd belong there. There wouldn't be no more runnin' round the country and gettin' fed by a Jap cook. No, sir, we'd have our own place where we belonged and not sleep in no bunk house."

"Tell about the house, George," Lennie begged.

"Sure, we'd have a little house an' a room to ourself. Little fat iron stove, an' in the winter we'd keep a fire goin' in it. It ain't enough land so we'd have to work too hard. Maybe six, seven hours a day. We wouldn't have to buck no barley eleven hours a day. An' when we put in a crop, why, we'd be there to take the crop up. We'd know what come of our planting."

"An' rabbits," Lennie said eagerly. "An' I'd take care of 'em. Tell how I'd do that, George."

"Sure, you'd go out in the alfalfa patch an' you'd have a sack. You'd fill up the sack and bring it in an' put it in the rabbit cages."

"They'd nibble an' they'd nibble," said Lennie, "the way they do. I seen 'em."

"Ever' six weeks or so," George continued, "them does would throw a litter so we'd have plenty rabbits to eat an' to sell. An' we'd keep a few pigeons to go flyin' around the win'mill like they done when I was a kid." He looked raptly at the wall over Lennie's head. "An' it'd be our own, an' nobody could can us. If we don't like a guy we can say, 'Get the hell out,' and by God he's got to do it. An' if a fren' come along, why we'd have an extra bunk, an' we'd say, 'Why don't you spen' the night?' an' by God he would. We'd have a setter dog and a couple stripe cats, but you gotta watch out them cats don't get the little rabbits."

Lennie breathed hard. "You jus' let 'em try to get the rabbits. I'll break their God damn necks. I'll . . . I'll smash 'em with a stick." He subsided, grumbling to himself, threatening the future cats which might dare to disturb the future rabbits.

George sat entranced with his own picture.

When Candy spoke they both jumped as though they had been caught doing something reprehensible. Candy said, "You know where's a place like that?"

George was on guard immediately. "S'pose I do," he said. "What's that to you?"

"You don't need to tell me where it's at. Might be any place."

"Sure," said George. "That's right. You couldn't find it in a hundred years."

Candy went on excitedly, "How much they want for a place like that?"

George watched him suspiciously. "Well—I could get it for six hundred bucks. The ol' people that owns it is flat bust an' the ol' lady needs an operation. Say—what's it to you? You got nothing to do with us."

Candy said, "I ain't much good with on'y one hand. I lost my hand right here on this ranch. That's why they give me a job swampin'. An' they give me two hunderd an' fifty dollars 'cause I los' my hand. An' I got fifty more saved up right in the bank, right now. Tha's three hunderd, and I got fifty more comin' the end a the month. Tell you what——" He leaned forward eagerly. "S'pose I went in with you guys. Tha's three hunderd an' fifty bucks I'd put in. I ain't much good, but I could cook and tend the chickens and hoe the garden some. How'd that be?"

George half-closed his eyes. "I gotta think about that. We was always gonna do it by ourselves."

Candy interrupted him, "I'd make a will an' leave my share to you guys in case I kick off, 'cause I ain't got no relatives nor nothing. You guys got any money? Maybe we could do her right now?"

George spat on the floor disgustedly. "We got ten bucks between us." Then he said thoughtfully, "Look, if me an' Lennie work a month an' don't spen' nothing, we'll have a hunderd bucks. That'd be four fifty. I bet we could swing her for that. Then you an' Lennie could go get her started an' I'd get a job an' make up the res', an' you could sell eggs an' stuff like that."

They fell into a silence. They looked at one another, amazed. This thing they had never really believed in was coming true. George said reverently, "Jesus Christ! I bet we could swing her." His eyes were full of wonder. "I bet we could swing her," he repeated softly.

Candy sat on the edge of his bunk. He scratched the stump of his wrist nervously. "I got hurt four years ago," he said. "They'll can me purty soon. Jus' as soon as I can't swamp out no bunk houses they'll put me on the county. Maybe if I give you guys my money, you'll let me hoe in the garden even after I ain't no good at it. An' I'll wash dishes an' little chicken stuff like that. But I'll be on our own place, an' I'll be let to work on our own place." He said miserably, "You seen what they done to my dog tonight? They says he wasn't no good to himself nor nobody else. When they can me here I wisht somebody'd shoot me. But they won't do nothing like that. I won't have no place to go, an' I can't get no more jobs. I'll have thirty dollars more comin', time you guys is ready to quit."

George stood up. "We'll do her," he said. "We'll fix up that little old place an' we'll go live there." He sat down again. They all sat still, all bemused by the beauty of the thing, each mind was popped into the future when this lovely thing should come about.

George said wonderingly, "S'pose they was a carnival or a circus come to town, or a ball game, or any damn thing." Old Candy nodded in appreciation of the idea. "We'd just go to her," George said. "We wouldn't ask nobody if we could. Jus' say, 'We'll go to her,' an' we would. Jus' milk the cow and sling some grain to the chickens an' go to her."

"An' put some grass to the rabbits," Lennie broke in. "I wouldn't never forget to feed them. When we gon'ta do it, George?"

"In one month. Right squack in one month. Know what I'm gon'ta do? I'm gon'ta write to them old people that owns the place that we'll take it. An' Candy'll send a hunderd dollars to bind her."

"Sure will," said Candy. "They got a good stove there?"

"Sure, got a nice stove, burns coal or wood."

"I'm gonna take my pup," said Lennie. "I bet by Christ he likes it there, by Jesus."

Voices were approaching from outside. George said quickly, "Don't tell nobody about it. Jus' us three an' nobody else. They li'ble to can us so we can't make no stake. Jus' go on like we was gonna buck barley the rest of our lives, then all of a sudden some day we'll go get our pay an' scram outa here."

Lennie and Candy nodded, and they were grinning with delight. "Don't tell nobody," Lennie said to himself.

Candy said, "George."

"Huh?"

"I ought to of shot that dog myself, George. I shouldn't ought to of let no stranger shoot my dog."

The door opened. Slim came in, followed by Curley and Carlson and Whit. Slim's hands were black with tar and he was scowling. Curley hung close to his elbow.

Curley said, "Well, I didn't mean nothing, Slim. I just ast you."

Slim said, "Well, you been askin' me too often. I'm gettin' God damn sick of it. If you can't look after your own God damn wife, what you expect me to do about it? You lay offa me."

"I'm jus' tryin' to tell you I didn't mean nothing," said Curley. "I jus' thought you might of saw her."

"Why'n't you tell her to stay the hell home where she belongs?" said Carlson. "You let her hang around bunk houses and pretty soon you're gonna have som'pin on your hands and you won't be able to do nothing about it."

Curley whirled on Carlson. "You keep outta this les' you wanta step outside."

Carlson laughed. "You God damn punk," he said. "You tried to throw a scare into Slim, an' you couldn't make it stick. Slim throwed a scare inta you. You're yella as a frog belly. I don't care if you're the best welter in the country. You come for me, an' I'll kick your God damn head off."

Candy joined the attack with joy. "Glove fulla vaseline," he said disgustedly. Curley glared at him. His eyes slipped on past and lighted on Lennie; and Lennie was still smiling with delight at the memory of the ranch.

Curley stepped over to Lennie like a terrier. "What the hell you laughin' at?"

Lennie looked blankly at him. "Huh?"

Then Curley's rage exploded. "Come on, ya big bastard. Get up on your feet. No big son-of-a-bitch is gonna laugh at me. I'll show ya who's yella."

Lennie looked helplessly at George, and then he got up and tried to retreat. Curley was balanced and poised. He slashed at Lennie with his left, and then smashed down his nose with a right. Lennie gave a cry of terror. Blood welled from his nose. "George," he cried. "Make 'um let me alone, George." He backed until he was against the wall, and Curley followed, slugging him in the face. Lennie's hands remained at his sides; he was too frightened to defend himself.

George was on his feet yelling, "Get him, Lennie. Don't let him do it."

Lennie covered his face with his huge paws and bleated with terror. He cried, "Make 'um stop, George." Then Curley attacked his stomach and cut off his wind.

Slim jumped up. "The dirty little rat," he cried, "I'll get 'um myself."

George put out his hand and grabbed Slim. "Wait a minute," he shouted. He cupped his hands around his mouth and yelled, "Get 'im, Lennie!"

Lennie took his hands away from his face and looked about for George, and Curley slashed at his eyes. The big face was covered with blood. George yelled again, "I said get him."

Curley's fist was swinging when Lennie reached for it. The next minute Curley was flopping like a fish on a line, and his closed fist was lost in Lennie's big hand. George ran down the room. "Leggo of him, Lennie. Let go."

But Lennie watched in terror the flopping little man whom

he held. Blood ran down Lennie's face, one of his eyes was cut and closed. George slapped him in the face again and again, and still Lennie held on to the closed fist. Curley was white and shrunken by now, and his struggling had become weak. He stood crying, his fist lost in Lennie's paw.

George shouted over and over, "Leggo his hand, Lennie. Leggo. Slim, come help me while the guy got any hand left."

Suddenly Lennie let go his hold. He crouched cowering against the wall. "You tol' me to, George," he said miserably.

Curley sat down on the floor, looking in wonder at his crushed hand. Slim and Carlson bent over him. Then Slim straightened up and regarded Lennie with horror. "We got to get him in to a doctor," he said. "Looks to me like ever' bone in his han' is bust."

"I didn't wanta," Lennie cried. "I didn't wanta hurt him."

Slim said, "Carlson, you get the candy wagon hitched up. We'll take 'um into Soledad an' get 'um fixed up." Carlson hurried out. Slim turned to the whimpering Lennie. "It ain't your fault," he said. "This punk sure had it comin' to him. But—Jesus! He ain't hardly got no han' left." Slim hurried out, and in a moment returned with a tin cup of water. He held it to Curley's lips.

George said, "Slim, will we get canned now? We need the stake. Will Curley's old man can us now?"

Slim smiled wryly. He knelt down beside Curley. "You got your senses in hand enough to listen?" he asked. Curley nodded. "Well, then listen," Slim went on. "I think you got your han' caught in a machine. If you don't tell nobody what happened, we ain't going to. But you jus' tell an' try to get this guy canned and we'll tell ever'body, an' then will you get the laugh."

"I won't tell," said Curley. He avoided looking at Lennie.

Buggy wheels sounded outside. Slim helped Curley up. "Come on now. Carlson's gonna take you to a doctor." He helped Curley out the door. The sound of wheels drew away. In a moment Slim came back into the bunk house. He looked at Lennie, still crouched fearfully against the wall. "Le's see your hands," he asked.

Lennie stuck out his hands.

"Christ awmighty, I hate to have you mad at me," Slim said.

George broke in, "Lennie was jus' scairt," he explained. "He didn't know what to do. I told you nobody ought never to fight him. No, I guess it was Candy I told."

Candy nodded solemnly. "That's jus' what you done," he said. "Right this morning when Curley first lit intil your fren', you says. 'He better not fool with Lennie if he knows what's good for 'um.' That's jus' what you says to me."

George turned to Lennie. "It ain't your fault," he said. "You don't need to be scairt no more. You done jus' what I tol' you to. Maybe you better go in the wash room an' clean up your face. You look like hell."

Lennie smiled with his bruised mouth. "I didn't want no trouble," he said. He walked toward the door, but just before he came to it, he turned back. "George?"

"What you want?"

"I can still tend the rabbits, George?"

"Sure. You ain't done nothing wrong."

"I di'n't mean no harm, George."

"Well, get the hell out and wash your face."

Crooks, the negro stable buck, had his bunk in the harness room; a little shed that leaned off the wall of the barn. On one side of the little room there was a square four-paned window, and on the other, a narrow plank door leading into the barn. Crooks' bunk was a long box filled with straw, on which his blankets were flung. On the wall by the window there were pegs on which hung broken harness in process of being mended; strips of new leather; and under the window itself a little bench for leather-working tools, curved knives and needles and balls of linen thread, and a small hand riveter. On pegs were also pieces of harness, a split collar with the horsehair stuffing sticking out, a broken hame, and a trace chain with its leather covering split. Crooks had his apple box over his bunk, and in it a range of medicine bottles, both for himself and for the horses. There were cans of saddle soap and a drippy can of tar with its paint brush sticking over the edge. And scattered about the floor were a number of personal possessions; for, being alone, Crooks could leave his things about, and being a stable buck and a cripple, he was more permanent than the other men, and he had accumulated more possessions than he could carry on his back.

Crooks possessed several pairs of shoes, a pair of rubber boots, a big alarm clock and a single-barreled shotgun. And he had books, too; a tattered dictionary and a mauled copy of the California civil code for 1905. There were battered magazines and a few dirty books on a special shelf over his bunk. A pair of large gold-rimmed spectacles hung from a nail on the wall above his bed.

This room was swept and fairly neat, for Crooks was a proud, aloof man. He kept his distance and demanded that other people keep theirs. His body was bent over to the left by his crooked spine, and his eyes lay deep in his head, and because of their depth seemed to glitter with intensity. His lean face was lined with deep black wrinkles, and he had thin, pain-tightened lips which were lighter than his face.

It was Saturday night. Through the open door that led into the barn came the sound of moving horses, of feet stirring, of teeth champing on hay, of the rattle of halter chains. In the stable buck's room a small electric globe threw a meager yellow light.

Crooks sat on his bunk. His shirt was out of his jeans in back. In one hand he held a bottle of liniment, and with the other he rubbed his spine. Now and then he poured a few drops of the liniment into his pink-palmed hand and reached up under his shirt to rub again. He flexed his muscles against his back and shivered.

Noiselessly Lennie appeared in the open doorway and stood there looking in, his big shoulders nearly filling the opening. For a moment Crooks did not see him, but on raising his eyes he stiffened and a scowl came on his face. His hand came out from under his shirt.

Lennie smiled helplessly in an attempt to make friends.

Crooks said sharply, "You got no right to come in my room. This here's my room. Nobody got any right in here but me."

Lennie gulped and his smile grew more fawning. "I ain't doing nothing," he said. "Just come to look at my puppy. And I seen your light," he explained.

"Well, I got a right to have a light. You go on get outta my room. I ain't wanted in the bunk house, and you ain't wanted in my room."

"Why ain't you wanted?" Lennie asked.

"'Cause I'm black. They play cards in there, but I can't play because I'm black. They say I stink. Well, I tell you, you all of you stink to me."

Lennie flapped his big hands helplessly. "Ever'body went into town," he said. "Slim an' George an' ever'body. George says I gotta stay here an' not get in no trouble. I seen your light."

"Well, what do you want?"

"Nothing—I seen your light. I thought I could jus' come in an' set."

Crooks stared at Lennie, and he reached behind him and took down the spectacles and adjusted them over his pink ears and stared again. "I don't know what you're doin' in the barn anyway," he complained. "You ain't no skinner. They's no call for a bucker to come into the barn at all. You ain't no skinner. You ain't got nothing to do with the horses."

"The pup," Lennie repeated. "I come to see my pup."

"Well, go see your pup, then. Don't come in a place where you're not wanted."

Lennie lost his smile. He advanced a step into the room, then remembered and backed to the door again. "I looked at 'em a little. Slim says I ain't to pet 'em very much."

Crooks said, "Well, you been takin' 'em out of the nest all the time. I wonder the old lady don't move 'em someplace else."

"Oh, she don't care. She lets me." Lennie had moved into the room again.

Crooks scowled, but Lennie's disarming smile defeated him. "Come on in and set a while," Crooks said. "'Long as you won't get out and leave me alone, you might as well set down." His tone was a little more friendly. "All the boys gone into town, huh?"

"All but old Candy. He just sets in the bunk house sharpening his pencil and sharpening and figuring."

Crooks adjusted his glasses. "Figuring? What's Candy figuring about?"

Lennie almost shouted, "'Bout the rabbits."

"You're nuts," said Crooks. "You're crazy as a wedge. What rabbits you talkin' about?"

"The rabbits we're gonna get, and I get to tend 'em, cut grass an' give 'em water, an' like that."

"Jus' nuts," said Crooks. "I don't blame the guy you travel with for keepin' you outa sight."

Lennie said quietly, "It ain't no lie. We're gonna do it. Gonna get a little place an' live on the fatta the lan'."

Crooks settled himself more comfortably on his bunk. "Set down," he invited. "Set down on the nail keg."

Lennie hunched down on the little barrel. "You think it's a lie," Lennie said, "But it ain't no lie. Ever' word's the truth, an' you can ast George."

Crooks put his dark chin into his pink palm. "You travel aroun' with George, don't ya?"

"Sure. Me an' him goes ever' place together."

Crooks continued. "Sometimes he talks, and you don't know what the hell he's talkin' about. Ain't that so?" He leaned forward, boring Lennie with his deep eyes. "Ain't that so?"

"Yeah . . . sometimes."

"Jus' talks on, an' you don't know what the hell it's all about?"

"Yeah . . . sometimes. But . . . not always."

Crooks leaned forward over the edge of the bunk. "I ain't a southern negro," he said. "I was born right here in California. My old man had a chicken ranch, 'bout ten acres. The white kids come to play at our place, an' sometimes I went to play with them, and some of them was pretty nice. My ol' man didn't like that. I never knew till long later why he didn't like that. But I know now." He hesitated, and when he spoke again his voice was softer. "There wasn't another colored family for miles around. And now there ain't a colored man on this ranch an' there's jus' one family in Soledad." He laughed. "If I say something, why it's just a nigger sayin' it."

Lennie asked, "How long you think it'll be before them pups will be old enough to pet?"

Crooks laughed again. "A guy can talk to you an' be sure you won't go blabbin'. Couple of weeks an' them pups'll be all right. George knows what he's about. Jus' talks, an' you don't understand nothing." He leaned forward excitedly. "This is just a nigger talkin', an' a busted-back nigger. So it don't mean nothing, see? You couldn't remember it anyways. I seen it over an' over —a guy talkin' to another guy and it don't make no difference if he don't hear or understand. The thing is, they're talkin', or they're settin' still not talkin'. It don't make no difference, no difference." His excitement had increased until he pounded his knee with his hand. "George can tell you screwy things, and it don't matter. It's just the talking. It's just bein' with another guy. That's all." He paused.

His voice grew soft and persuasive. "S'pose George don't come back no more. S'pose he took a powder and just ain't coming back. What'll you do then?"

Lennie's attention came gradually to what had been said. "What?" he demanded.

"I said s'pose George went into town tonight and you never heard of him no more." Crooks pressed forward some kind of private victory. "Just s'pose that," he repeated.

"He won't do it," Lennie cried. "George wouldn't do nothing like that. I been with George a long time. He'll come back tonight ——" But the doubt was too much for him. "Don't you think he will?"

Crooks' face lighted with pleasure in his torture. "Nobody can't tell what a guy'll do," he observed calmly. "Le's say he wants to come back and can't. S'pose he gets killed or hurt so he can't come back."

Lennie struggled to understand. "George won't do nothing like that," he repeated. "George is careful. He won't get hurt. He ain't never been hurt, 'cause he's careful."

"Well, s'pose, jus' s'pose he don't come back. What'll you do then?"

Lennie's face wrinkled with apprehension. "I don' know. Say, what you doin' anyways?" he cried. "This ain't true. George ain't got hurt."

Crooks bored in on him. "Want me ta tell ya what'll happen? They'll take ya to the booby hatch. They'll tie ya up with a collar, like a dog."

Suddenly Lennie's eyes centered and grew quiet, and mad. He stood up and walked dangerously toward Crooks. "Who hurt George?" he demanded.

Crooks saw the danger as it approached him. He edged back on his bunk to get out of the way. "I was just supposin'," he said. "George ain't hurt. He's all right. He'll be back all right."

Lennie stood over him. "What you supposin' for? Ain't nobody goin' to suppose no hurt to George."

Crooks removed his glasses and wiped his eyes with his fingers. "Jus' set down," he said. "George ain't hurt."

Lennie growled back to his seat on the nail keg. "Ain't nobody goin' to talk no hurt to George," he grumbled.

Crooks said gently, "Maybe you can see now. You got George. You *know* he's goin' to come back. S'pose you didn't have nobody. S'pose you couldn't go into the bunk house and play rummy 'cause you was black. How'd you like that? S'pose you had to sit out here an' read books. Sure you could play horseshoes till it got dark, but then you got to read books. Books ain't no good. A guy needs somebody—to be near him." He whined, "A guy goes nuts if he ain't got nobody. Don't make no difference who the guy is, long's he's with you. I tell ya," he cried, "I tell ya a guy gets too lonely an' he gets sick."

"George gonna come back," Lennie reassured himself in a frightened voice. "Maybe George come back already. Maybe I better go see."

Crooks said, "I didn't mean to scare you. He'll come back. I was talkin' about myself. A guy sets alone out here at night, maybe readin' books or thinkin' or stuff like that. Sometimes he gets thinkin', an' he got nothing to tell him what's so an' what ain't so. Maybe if he sees somethin', he don't know whether it's right or not. He can't turn to some other guy and ast him if he sees it too. He can't tell. He got nothing to measure by. I seen things out here. I wasn't drunk. I don't know if I was asleep. If some guy was with me, he could tell me I was asleep, an' then it would be all right. But I jus' don't know." Crooks was looking across the room now, looking toward the window.

Lennie said miserably, "George wun't go away and leave me. I know George wun't do that."

The stable buck went on dreamily, "I remember when I was a little kid on my old man's chicken ranch. Had two brothers. They was always near me, always there. Used to sleep right in the same room, right in the same bed—all three. Had a strawberry patch.

Had an alfalfa patch. Used to turn the chickens out in the alfalfa on a sunny morning. My brothers'd set on a fence rail an' watch 'em—white chickens they was."

Gradually Lennie's interest came around to what was being said. "George says we're gonna have alfalfa for the rabbits."

"What rabbits?"

"We're gonna have rabbits an' a berry patch."

"You're nuts."

"We are too. You ast George."

"You're nuts." Crooks was scornful. "I seen hunderds of men come by on the road an' on the ranches, with their bindles on their back an' that same damn thing in their heads. Hunderds of them. They come, an' they quit an' go on; an' every damn one of 'em's got a little piece of land in his head. An' never a God damn one of 'em ever gets it. Just like heaven. Ever'body wants a little piece of lan'. I read plenty of books out here. Nobody never gets to heaven, and nobody gets no land. It's just in their head. They're all the time talkin' about it, but it's jus' in their head." He paused and looked toward the open door, for the horses were moving restlessly and the halter chains clinked. A horse whinnied. "I guess somebody's out there," Crooks said. "Maybe Slim. Slim comes in sometimes two, three times a night. Slim's a real skinner. He looks out for his team." He pulled himself painfully upright and moved toward the door. "That you, Slim?" he called.

Candy's voice answered. "Slim went in town. Say, you seen Lennie?"

"Ya mean the big guy?"

"Yeah. Seen him around any place?"

"He's in here," Crooks said shortly. He went back to his bunk and lay down.

Candy stood in the doorway scratching his bald wrist and looking blindly into the lighted room. He made no attempt to enter. "Tell ya what, Lennie. I been figuring out about them rabbits."

Crooks said irritably, "You can come in if you want."

Candy seemed embarrassed. "I do' know. 'Course, if ya want me to."

"Come on in. If ever'body's comin' in, you might just as well." It was difficult for Crooks to conceal his pleasure with anger.

Candy came in, but he was still embarrassed. "You got a nice cozy little place in here," he said to Crooks. "Must be nice to have a room all to yourself this way."

"Sure," said Crooks. "And a manure pile under the window. Sure, it's swell."

Lennie broke in, "You said about them rabbits."

Candy leaned against the wall beside the broken collar while he scratched the wrist stump. "I been here a long time," he said. "An' Crooks been here a long time. This's the first time I ever been in his room."

Crooks said darkly, "Guys don't come into a colored man's room very much. Nobody been here but Slim. Slim an' the boss."

Candy quickly changed the subject. "Slim's as good a skinner as I ever seen."

Lennie leaned toward the old swamper. "About them rabbits," he insisted.

Candy smiled. "I got it figured out. We can make some money on them rabbits if we go about it right."

"But I get to tend 'em," Lennie broke in. "George says I get to tend 'em. He promised."

Crooks interrupted brutally. "You guys is just kiddin' yourself. You'll talk about it a hell of a lot, but you won't get no land. You'll be a swamper here till they take you out in a box. Hell, I seen too many guys. Lennie here'll quit an' be on the road in two, three weeks. Seems like ever' guy got land in his head."

Candy rubbed his cheek angrily. "You God damn right we're gonna do it. George says we are. We got the money right now."

"Yeah?" said Crooks. "An' where's George now? In town in a whore house. That's where your money's goin'. Jesus, I seen it happen too many times. I seen too many guys with land in their head. They never get none under their hand."

Candy cried, "Sure they all want it. Everybody wants a little bit of land, not much. Jus' som'thin' that was his. Somethin' he could live on and there couldn't nobody throw him off of it. I never had none. I planted crops for damn near ever'body in this state, but they wasn't my crops, and when I harvested 'em, it wasn't none of my harvest. But we gonna do it now, and don't you make no mistake about that. George ain't got the money in town. That money's in the bank. Me an' Lennie an' George. We gonna have a room to ourself. We're gonna have a dog an' rabbits an' chickens. We're gonna have green corn an' maybe a cow or a goat." He stopped, overwhelmed with his picture.

Crooks asked, "You say you got the money?"

"Damn right. We got most of it. Just a little bit more to get. Have it all in one month. George got the land all picked out, too."

Crooks reached around and explored his spine with his hand. "I never seen a guy really do it," he said. "I seen guys nearly crazy with loneliness for land, but ever' time a whore house or a blackjack game took what it takes." He hesitated. ". . . If you . . . guys would want a hand to work for nothing—just his keep, why I'd come an' lend a hand. I ain't so crippled I can't work like a son-of-a-bitch if I want to."

"Any you boys seen Curley?"

They swung their heads toward the door. Looking in was Curley's wife. Her face was heavily made up. Her lips were slightly parted. She breathed strongly, as though she had been running.

"Curley ain't been here," Candy said sourly.

She stood still in the doorway, smiling a little at them, rubbing the nails of one hand with the thumb and forefinger of the other. And her eyes traveled from one face to another. "They left all the weak ones here," she said finally. "Think I don't know where they all went? Even Curley. I know where they all went."

Lennie watched her, fascinated; but Candy and Crooks were scowling down away from her eyes. Candy said, "Then if you know, why you want to ast us where Curley is at?"

She regarded them amusedly. "Funny thing," she said. "If I catch any one man, and he's alone, I get along fine with him. But just let two of the guys get together an' you won't talk. Jus' nothing but mad." She dropped her fingers and put her hands on her hips. "You're all scared of each other, that's what. Ever' one of you's scared the rest is goin' to get something on you."

After a pause Crooks said, "Maybe you better go along to your own house now. We don't want no trouble."

"Well, I ain't giving you no trouble. Think I don't like to talk to somebody ever' once in a while? Think I like to stick in that house alla time?"

Candy laid the stump of his wrist on his knee and rubbed it

gently with his hand. He said accusingly, "You gotta husban'. You got no call foolin' aroun' with other guys, causin' trouble."

The girl flared up. "Sure I gotta husban'. You all seen him. Swell guy, ain't he? Spends all his time sayin' what he's gonna do to guys he don't like, and he don't like nobody. Think I'm gonna stay in that two-by-four house and listen how Curley's gonna lead with his left twict, and then bring in the ol' right cross? 'One-two' he says. 'Jus the ol' one-two an' he'll go down.'" She paused and her face lost its sullenness and grew interested. "Say—what happened to Curley's han'?"

There was an embarrassed silence. Candy stole a look at Lennie. Then he coughed. "Why . . . Curley . . . he got his han' caught in a machine, ma'am. Bust his han'."

She watched for a moment, and then she laughed. "Baloney! What you think you're sellin' me? Curley started som'pin' he didn' finish. Caught in a machine—baloney! Why, he ain't give nobody the good ol' one-two since he got his han' bust. Who bust him?"

Candy repeated sullenly, "Got it caught in a machine."

"Awright," she said contemptuously. "Awright, cover 'im up if ya wanta. Whatta I care? You bindle bums think you're so damn good. Whatta ya think I am, a kid? I tell ya I could of went with shows. Not jus' one, neither. An' a guy tol' me he could put me in pitchers. . . ." She was breathless with indignation. "—Sat'iday night. Ever'body out doin' som'pin'. Ever'body! An' what am I doin'? Standin' here talkin' to a bunch of bindle stiffs —a nigger an' a dum-dum and a lousy ol' sheep—an' likin' it because they ain't nobody else."

Lennie watched her, his mouth half open. Crooks had retired into the terrible protective dignity of the negro. But a change came over old Candy. He stood up suddenly and knocked his nail keg over backward. "I had enough," he said angrily. "You ain't wanted here. We told you you ain't. An' I tell ya, you got floozy idears about what us guys amounts to. You ain't got sense enough in that chicken head to even see that we ain't stiffs. S'pose you get us canned. S'pose you do. You think we'll hit the highway an' look for another lousy two-bit job like this. You don't know that we got our own ranch to go to, an' our own house. We ain't got to stay here. We gotta house and chickens an' fruit trees an' a place a hunderd time prettier than this. An' we got fren's, that's what we got. Maybe there was a time when we was scared of gettin' canned, but we ain't no more. We got our own lan', and it's ours, an' we c'n go to it."

Curley's wife laughed at him. "Baloney," she said. "I seen too many you guys. If you had two bits in the worl', why you'd be in gettin' two shots of corn with it and suckin' the bottom of the glass. I know you guys."

Candy's face had grown redder and redder, but before she was done speaking, he had control of himself. He was the master of the situation. "I might of knew," he said gently. "Maybe you just better go along an' roll your hoop. We ain't got nothing to say to you at all. We know what we got, and we don't care whether you know it or not. So maybe you better jus' scatter along now, 'cause Curley maybe ain't gonna like his wife out in the barn with us 'bindle stiffs.'"

She looked from one face to another, and they were all closed against her. And she looked longest at Lennie, until he dropped his eyes in embarrassment. Suddenly she said, "Where'd you get them bruises on your face?"

Lennie looked up guiltily. "Who—me?"

"Yeah, you."

Lennie looked to Candy for help, and then he looked at his lap again. "He got his han' caught in a machine," he said.

Curley's wife laughed. "O.K., Machine. I'll talk to you later. I like machines."

Candy broke in. "You let this guy alone. Don't you do no messing aroun' with him. I'm gonna tell George what you says. George won't have you messin' with Lennie."

"Who's George?" she asked. "The little guy you come with?"

Lennie smiled happily. "That's him," he said. "That's the guy, an' he's gonna let me tend the rabbits."

"Well, if that's all you want, I might get a couple rabbits myself."

Crooks stood up from his bunk and faced her. "I had enough," he said coldly. "You got no rights comin' in a colored man's room. You got no rights messing around in here at all. Now you jus' get out, an' get out quick. If you don't, I'm gonna ast the boss not to ever let you come in the barn no more."

She turned on him in scorn. "Listen, Nigger," she said. "You know what I can do to you if you open your trap?"

Crooks stared hopelessly at her, and then he sat down on his bunk and drew into himself.

She closed on him. "You know what I could do?"

Crooks seemed to grow smaller, and he pressed himself against the wall. "Yes, ma'am."

"Well, you keep your place then, Nigger. I could get you strung up on a tree so easy it ain't even funny."

Crooks had reduced himself to nothing. There was no personality, no ego—nothing to arouse either like or dislike. He said, "Yes, ma'am," and his voice was toneless.

For a moment she stood over him as though waiting for him to move so that she could whip at him again; but Crooks sat perfectly still, his eyes averted, everything that might be hurt drawn in. She turned at last to the other two.

Old Candy was watching her, fascinated. "If you was to do that, we'd tell," he said quietly. "We'd tell about you framin' Crooks."

"Tell an' be damned," she cried. "Nobody'd listen to you, an' you know it. Nobody'd listen to you."

Candy subsided. "No . . ." he agreed. "Nobody'd listen to us."

Lennie whined, "I wisht George was here. I wisht George was here."

Candy stepped over to him. "Don't you worry none," he said. "I jus' heard the guys comin' in. George'll be in the bunk house right now, I bet." He turned to Curley's wife. "You better go home now," he said quietly. "If you go right now, we won't tell Curley you was here."

She appraised him coolly. "I ain't sure you heard nothing."

"Better not take no chances," he said. "If you ain't sure, you better take the safe way."

She turned to Lennie. "I'm glad you bust up Curley a little bit. He got it comin' to him. Sometimes I'd like to bust him myself." She slipped out the door and disappeared into the dark barn. And while she went through the barn, the halter chains rattled, and some horses snorted and some stamped their feet.

Crooks seemed to come slowly out of the layers of protection he had put on. "Was that the truth what you said about the guys come back?" he asked.

"Sure. I heard 'em."

"Well, I didn't hear nothing."

"The gate banged," Candy said, and he went on, "Jesus Christ, Curley's wife can move quiet. I guess she had a lot of practice, though."

Crooks avoided the whole subject now. "Maybe you guys better go," he said. "I ain't sure I want you in here no more. A colored man got to have some rights even if he don't like 'em."

Candy said. "That bitch didn't ought to of said that to you."

"It wasn't nothing," Crooks said dully. "You guys comin' in an' settin' made me forget. What she says is true."

The horses snorted out in the barn and the chains rang and a voice called, "Lennie. Oh, Lennie. You in the barn?"

"It's George," Lennie cried. And he answered, "Here, George. I'm right in here."

In a second George stood framed in the door, and he looked disapprovingly about. "What you doin' in Crooks' room. You hadn't ought to be in here."

Crooks nodded. "I tol' 'em, but they come in anyways."

"Well, why'n't you kick 'em out?"

"I di'n't care much," said Crooks. "Lennie's a nice fella."

Now Candy aroused himself. "Oh, George! I been figurin' and figurin'. I got it doped out how we can even make some money on them rabbits."

George scowled. "I thought I tol' you not to tell nobody about that."

Candy was crestfallen. "Didn't tell nobody but Crooks."

George said, "Well you guys get outta here. Jesus, seems like I can't go away for a minute."

Candy and Lennie stood up and went toward the door. Crooks called, "Candy!"

"Huh?"

"'Member what I said about hoein' and doin' odd jobs?"

"Yeah," said Candy. "I remember."

"Well, jus' forget it," said Crooks. "I didn' mean it. Jus' foolin'. I wouldn' want to go no place like that."

"Well, O.K., if you feel like that. Goodnight."

The three men went out of the door. As they went through the barn the horses snorted and the halter chains rattled.

Crooks sat on his bunk and looked at the door for a moment, and then he reached for the liniment bottle. He pulled out his shirt in back, poured a little liniment in his pink palm and, reaching around, he fell slowly to rubbing his back.

One end of the great barn was piled high with new hay and over the pile hung the four-taloned Jackson fork suspended from its pulley. The hay came down like a mountain slope to the other end of the barn, and there was a level place as yet unfilled with the new crop. At the sides the feeding racks were visible, and between the slats the heads of horses could be seen.

It was Sunday afternoon. The resting horses nibbled the remaining wisps of hay, and they stamped their feet and they bit the wood of the mangers and rattled the halter chains. The afternoon sun sliced in through the cracks of the barn walls and lay in bright lines on the hay. There was the buzz of flies in the air, the lazy afternoon humming.

From outside came the clang of horseshoes on the playing peg and the shouts of men, playing, encouraging, jeering. But in the barn it was quiet and humming and lazy and warm.

Only Lennie was in the barn, and Lennie sat in the hay beside a packing case under a manger in the end of the barn that had not been filled with hay. Lennie sat in the hay and looked at a little dead puppy that lay in front of him. Lennie looked at it for a long time, and then he put out his huge hand and stroked it, stroked it clear from one end to the other.

And Lennie said softly to the puppy, "Why do you got to get killed? You ain't so little as mice. I didn't bounce you hard." He bent the pup's head up and looked in its face, and he said to it, "Now maybe George ain't gonna let me tend no rabbits, if he fin's out you got killed."

He scooped a little hollow and laid the puppy in it and covered it over with hay, out of sight; but he continued to stare at the mound he had made. He said, "This ain't no bad thing like I got to go hide in the brush. Oh! no. This ain't. I'll tell George I foun' it dead."

He unburied the puppy and inspected it, and he stroked it from ears to tail. He went on sorrowfully, "But he'll know. George always knows. He'll say, 'You done it. Don't try to put nothing over on me.' An' he'll say, 'Now jus' for that you don't get to tend no rabbits!'"

Suddenly his anger arose. "God damn you," he cried. "Why do you got to get killed? You ain't so little as mice." He picked up the pup and hurled it from him. He turned his back on it. He sat bent over his knees and he whispered, "Now I won't get to tend the rabbits. Now he won't let me." He rocked himself back and forth in his sorrow.

From outside came the clang of horseshoes on the iron stake, and then a little chorus of cries. Lennie got up and brought the puppy back and laid it on the hay and sat down. He stroked the pup again. "You wasn't big enough," he said. "They tol' me and tol' me you wasn't. I di'n't know you'd get killed so easy." He worked his fingers on the pup's limp ear. "Maybe George won't care," he said. "This here God damn little son-of-a-bitch wasn't nothing to George."

Curley's wife came around the end of the last stall. She came very quietly, so that Lennie didn't see her. She wore her bright cotton dress and the mules with the red ostrich feathers. Her face was made up and the little sausage curls were all in place. She was quite near to him before Lennie looked up and saw her.

In a panic he shoveled hay over the puppy with his fingers. He looked sullenly up at her.

She said, "What you got there, sonny boy?"

Lennie glared at her. "George says I ain't to have nothing to do with you—talk to you or nothing."

She laughed. "George giving you orders about everything?"

Lennie looked down at the hay. "Says I can't tend no rabbits if I talk to you or anything."

She said quietly, "He's scared Curley'll get mad. Well, Curley got his arm in a sling—an' if Curley gets tough, you can break his other han'. You didn't put nothing over on me about gettin' it caught in no machine."

But Lennie was not to be drawn. "No, sir. I ain't gonna talk to you or nothing."

She knelt in the hay beside him. "Listen," she said. "All the guys got a horseshoe tenement goin' on. It's on'y about four o'clock. None of them guys is goin' to leave that tenement. Why can't I talk to you? I never get to talk to nobody. I get awful lonely."

Lennie said, "Well, I ain't supposed to talk to you or nothing."

"I get lonely," she said. "You can talk to people, but I can't talk to nobody but Curley. Else he gets mad. How'd you like not to talk to anybody?"

Lennie said, "Well, I ain't supposed to. George's scared I'll get in trouble."

She changed the subject. "What you got covered up there?"

Then all of Lennie's woe came back on him. "Jus' my pup," he said sadly. "Jus' my little pup." And he swept the hay from on top of it.

"Why, he's dead," she cried.

"He was so little," said Lennie. "I was jus' playin' with him . . . an' he made like he's gonna bite me . . . an' I made like I was gonna smack him . . . an' . . . an' I done it. An' then he was dead."

She consoled him. "Don't you worry none. He was jus' a mutt. You can get another one easy. The whole country is fulla mutts."

"It ain't that so much," Lennie explained miserably. "George ain't gonna let me tend no rabbits now."

"Why don't he?"

"Well, he said if I done any more bad things he ain't gonna let me tend the rabbits."

She moved closer to him and she spoke soothingly. "Don't you worry about talkin' to me. Listen to the guys yell out there. They got four dollars bet in that tenement. None of them ain't gonna leave till it's over."

"If George sees me talkin' to you he'll give me hell," Lennie said cautiously. "He tol' me so."

Her face grew angry. "Wha's the matter with me?" she cried. "Ain't I got a right to talk to nobody? Whatta they think I am, anyways? You're a nice guy. I don't know why I can't talk to you. I ain't doin' no harm to you."

"Well, George says you'll get us in a mess."

"Aw, nuts!" she said. "What kinda harm am I doin' to you? Seems like they ain't none of them cares how I gotta live. I tell you I ain't used to livin' like this. I coulda made somethin' of myself." She said darkly, "Maybe I will yet." And then her words tumbled out in a passion of communication, as though she hurried before her listener could be taken away. "I lived right in Salinas," she said. "Come there when I was a kid. Well, a show come through, an' I met one of the actors. He says I could go with that show. But my ol' lady wouldn't let me. She says because I was on'y fifteen. But the guy says I coulda. If I'd went, I wouldn't be livin' like this, you bet."

Lennie stroked the pup back and forth. "We gonna have a little place—an' rabbits," he explained.

She went on with her story quickly, before she should be interrupted. "'Nother time I met a guy, an' he was in pitchers. Went out to the Riverside Dance Palace with him. He says he was gonna put me in the movies. Says I was a natural. Soon's he got back to Hollywood he was gonna write to me about it." She looked closely at Lennie to see whether she was impressing him. "I never got that letter," she said. "I always thought my ol' lady stole it. Well, I wasn't gonna stay no place where I couldn't get nowhere or make something of myself, an' where they stole your letters. I ast her if she stole it, too, an' she says no. So I married Curley. Met him out to the Riverside Dance Palace that same night." She demanded, "You listenin?"

"Me? Sure."

"Well, I ain't told this to nobody before. Maybe I ought'n to. I don' *like* Curley. He ain't a nice fella." And because she had confided in him, she moved closer to Lennie and sat beside him. "Coulda been in the movies, an' had nice clothes—all them nice clothes like they wear. An' I coulda sat in them big hotels, an' had pitchers took of me. When they had them previews I coulda went to them, an' spoke in the radio, an' it wouldn'ta cost me a cent because I was in the pitcher. An' all them nice clothes like they wear. Because this guy says I was a natural." She looked up at Lennie, and she made a small grand gesture with her arm and hand to show that she could act. The fingers trailed after her leading wrist, and her little finger stuck out grandly from the rest.

Lennie sighed deeply. From outside came the clang of a horseshoe on metal, and then a chorus of cheers. "Somebody made a ringer," said Curley's wife.

Now the light was lifting as the sun went down, and the sun streaks climbed up the wall and fell over the feeding racks and over the heads of the horses.

Lennie said, "Maybe if I took this pup out and throwed him away George wouldn't never know. An' then I could tend the rabbits without no trouble."

Curley's wife said angrily, "Don't you think of nothing but rabbits?"

"We gonna have a little place," Lennie explained patiently. "We gonna have a house an' a garden and a place for alfalfa, an' that alfalfa is for the rabbits, an' I take a sack and get it all fulla alfalfa and then I take it to the rabbits."

She asked, "What makes you so nuts about rabbits?"

Lennie had to think carefully before he could come to a conclusion. He moved cautiously close to her, until he was right against her. "I like to pet nice things. Once at a fair I seen some of them long-hair rabbits. An' they was nice, you bet. Sometimes I've even pet mice, but not when I could get nothing better."

Curley's wife moved away from him a little. "I think you're nuts," she said.

"No I ain't," Lennie explained earnestly. "George says I ain't. I like to pet nice things with my fingers, sof' things."

She was a little bit reassured. "Well, who don't?" she said. "Ever'body likes that. I like to feel silk an' velvet. Do you like to feel velvet?"

Lennie chuckled with pleasure. "You bet, by God," he cried happily. "An' I had some, too. A lady give me some, an' that lady was—my own Aunt Clara. She give it right to me—'bout this big a piece. I wisht I had that velvet right now." A frown came over his face. "I lost it," he said. "I ain't seen it for a long time."

Curley's wife laughed at him. "You're nuts," she said. "But you're a kinda nice fella. Jus' like a big baby. But a person can see kinda what you mean. When I'm doin' my hair sometimes I jus' set an' stroke it 'cause it's so soft." To show how she did it, she ran her fingers over the top of her head. "Some people got kinda coarse hair," she said complacently. "Take Curley. His hair is jus' like wire. But mine is soft and fine. 'Course I brush it a lot. That makes it fine. Here—feel right here." She took Lennie's hand and put it on her head. "Feel right aroun' there an' see how soft it is."

Lennie's big fingers fell to stroking her hair.

"Don't you muss it up," she said.

Lennie said, "Oh! That's nice," and he stroked harder. "Oh, that's nice."

"Look out, now, you'll muss it." And then she cried angrily, "You stop it now, you'll mess it all up." She jerked her head sideways, and Lennie's fingers closed on her hair and hung on. "Let go," she cried. "You let go!"

Lennie was in a panic. His face was contorted. She screamed then, and Lennie's other hand closed over her mouth and nose. "Please don't," he begged. "Oh! Please don't do that. George'll be mad."

She struggled violently under his hands. Her feet battered on the hay and she writhed to be free; and from under Lennie's hand came a muffled screaming. Lennie began to cry with fright. "Oh! Please don't do none of that," he begged. "George gonna say I done a bad thing. He ain't gonna let me tend no rabbits." He moved his hand a little and her hoarse cry came out. Then Lennie grew angry. "Now don't," he said. "I don't want you to yell. You gonna get me in trouble jus' like George says you will. Now don't you do that." And she continued to struggle, and her eyes were wild with terror. He shook her then, and he was angry with her. "Don't you go yellin'," he said, and he shook her; and her body flopped like a fish. And then she was still, for Lennie had broken her neck.

He looked down at her, and carefully he removed his hand from over her mouth, and she lay still. "I don't want ta hurt you," he said, "but George'll be mad if you yell." When she didn't answer nor move he bent closely over her. He lifted her arm and let it drop. For a moment he seemed bewildered. And then he whispered in fright, "I done a bad thing. I done another bad thing."

He pawed up the hay until it partly covered her.

From outside the barn came a cry of men and the double clang of shoes on metal. For the first time Lennie became conscious of the outside. He crouched down in the hay and listened. "I done a real bad thing," he said. "I shouldn't of did that. George'll be mad. An' . . . he said . . . an' hide in the brush till he come. He's gonna be mad. In the brush till he come. Tha's what he said." Lennie went back and looked at the dead girl. The puppy lay close to her. Lennie picked it up. "I'll throw him away," he said. "It's bad enough like it is." He put the pup under his coat, and he crept to the barn wall and peered out between the cracks, toward the horseshoe game. And then he crept around the end of the last manger and disappeared.

The sun streaks were high on the wall by now, and the light was growing soft in the barn. Curley's wife lay on her back, and she was half covered with hay.

It was very quiet in the barn, and the quiet of the afternoon was on the ranch. Even the clang of the pitched shoes, even the voices of the men in the game seemed to grow more quiet. The air in the barn was dusky in advance of the outside day. A pigeon flew in through the open hay door and circled and flew out again. Around the last stall came a shepherd bitch, lean and long, with heavy hanging dugs. Halfway to the packing box where the puppies were she caught the dead scent of Curley's wife, and the hair rose along her spine. She whimpered and cringed to the packing box, and jumped in among the puppies.

Curley's wife lay with a half-covering of yellow hay. And the meanness and the plannings and the discontent and the ache for attention were all gone from her face. She was very pretty and simple, and her face was sweet and young. Now her rouged cheeks and her reddened lips made her seem alive and sleeping very lightly. The curls, tiny little sausages, were spread on the hay behind her head, and her lips were parted.

As happens sometimes, a moment settled and hovered and remained for much more than a moment. And sound stopped and movement stopped for much, much more than a moment.

Then gradually time awakened again and moved sluggishly on. The horses stamped on the other side of the feeding racks and the halter chains clinked. Outside, the men's voices became louder and clearer.

From around the end of the last stall old Candy's voice came. "Lennie," he called. "Oh, Lennie! You in here? I been figuring some more. Tell you what we can do, Lennie." Old Candy appeared around the end of the last stall. "Oh, Lennie!" he called again; and then he stopped, and his body stiffened. He rubbed his smooth wrist on his white stubble whiskers. "I di'n't know you was here," he said to Curley's wife.

When she didn't answer, he stepped nearer. "You oughten to sleep out here," he said disapprovingly; and then he was beside her and—"Oh, Jesus Christ!" He looked about helplessly, and he rubbed his beard. And then he jumped up and went quickly out of the barn.

But the barn was alive now. The horses stamped and snorted, and they chewed the straw of their bedding and they clashed the chains of their halters. In a moment Candy came back, and George was with him.

George said, "What was it you wanted to see me about?"

Candy pointed at Curley's wife. George stared. "What's the matter with her?" he asked. He stepped closer, and then he echoed Candy's words. "Oh, Jesus Christ!" He was down on his knees beside her. He put his hand over her heart. And finally, when he stood up, slowly and stiffly, his face was as hard and tight as wood, and his eyes were hard.

Candy said, "What done it?"

George looked coldly at him. "Ain't you got any idear?" he asked. And Candy was silent. "I should of knew," George said hopelessly. "I guess maybe way back in my head I did."

Candy asked, "What we gonna do now, George? What we gonna do now?"

George was a long time in answering. "Guess . . . we gotta tell the . . . guys. I guess we gotta get 'im an' lock 'im up. We can't let 'im get away. Why, the poor bastard'd starve." And he tried to reassure himself. "Maybe they'll lock 'im up an' be nice to 'im."

But Candy said excitedly, "We oughtta let 'im get away. You don't know that Curley. Curley gon'ta wanta get 'im lynched.

Curley'll get 'im killed."

George watched Candy's lips. "Yeah," he said at last, "that's right, Curley will. An' the other guys will." And he looked back at Curley's wife.

Now Candy spoke his greatest fear. "You an' me can get that little place, can't we, George? You an' me can go there an' live nice, can't we, George? Can't we?"

Before George answered, Candy dropped his head and looked down at the hay. He knew.

George said softly, "—I think I knowed from the very first. I think I knowed we'd never do her. He usta like to hear about it so much I got to thinking maybe we would."

"Then—it's all off?" Candy asked sulkily.

George didn't answer his question. George said, "I'll work my month an' I'll take my fifty bucks an' I'll stay all night in some lousy cat house. Or I'll set in some poolroom till ever'body goes home. An' then I'll come back an' work another month an' I'll have fifty bucks more."

Candy said, "He's such a nice fella. I didn' think he'd do nothing like this."

George still stared at Curley's wife. "Lennie never done it in meanness," he said. "All the time he done bad things, but he never done one of 'em mean." He straightened up and looked back at Candy. "Now listen. We gotta tell the guys. They got to bring him in, I guess. They ain't no way out. Maybe they won't hurt 'im." He said sharply, "I ain't gonna let 'em hurt Lennie. Now you listen. The guys might think I was in on it. I'm gonna go in the bunk house. Then in a minute you come out and tell the guys about her, and I'll come along and make like I never seen her. Will you do that? So the guys won't think I was in on it?"

Candy said, "Sure, George. Sure I'll do that."

"O.K. Give me a couple minutes then, and you come runnin' out an' tell like you jus' found her. I'm going now." George turned and went quickly out of the barn.

Old Candy watched him go. He looked helplessly back at Curley's wife, and gradually his sorrow and his anger grew into words. "You God damn tramp," he said viciously. "You done it, di'n't you? I s'pose you're glad. Ever'body knowed you'd mess things up. You wasn't no good. You ain't no good now, you lousy tart." He sniveled, and his voice shook. "I could of hoed in the garden and washed dishes for them guys." He paused, and then went on in a singsong. And he repeated the old words: "If they was a circus or a baseball game . . . we would of went to her . . . jus' said 'ta hell with work,' an' went to her. Never ast nobody's say so. An' they'd of been a pig and chickens . . . an' in the winter . . . the little fat stove . . . an' the rain comin' . . . an' us jus' settin' there." His eyes blinded with tears and he turned and went weakly out of the barn, and he rubbed his bristly whiskers with his wrist stump.

Outside the noise of the game stopped. There was a rise of voices in question, a drum of running feet and the men burst into the barn. Slim and Carlson and young Whit and Curley, and Crooks keeping back out of attention range. Candy came after them, and last of all came George. George had put on his blue denim coat and buttoned it, and his black hat was pulled down low over his eyes. The men raced around the last stall. Their eyes found Curley's wife in the gloom, they stopped and stood still and looked.

Then Slim went quietly over to her, and he felt her wrist. One lean finger touched her cheek, and then his hand went under her slightly twisted neck and his fingers explored her neck. When he stood up the men crowded near and the spell was broken.

Curley came suddenly to life. "I know who done it," he cried. "That big son-of-a-bitch done it. I know he done it. Why—ever'body else was out there playin' horseshoes." He worked himself into a fury. "I'm gonna get him. I'm going for my shotgun. I'll kill the big son-of-a-bitch myself. I'll shoot 'im in the guts. Come on, you guys." He ran furiously out of the barn. Carlson said, "I'll get my Luger," and he ran out too.

Slim turned quietly to George. "I guess Lennie done it, all right," he said. "Her neck's bust. Lennie coulda did that."

George didn't answer, but he nodded slowly. His hat was so far down on his forehead that his eyes were covered.

Slim went on, "Maybe like that time in Weed you was tellin' about."

Again George nodded.

Slim sighed. "Well, I guess we got to get him. Where you think he might of went?"

It seemed to take George some time to free his words. "He—would of went south," he said. "We come from north so he would of went south."

"I guess we gotta get 'im," Slim repeated.

George stepped close. "Couldn' we maybe bring him in an' they'll lock him up? He's nuts, Slim. He never done this to be mean."

Slim nodded. "We might," he said. "If we could keep Curley in, we might. But Curley's gonna want to shoot 'im. Curley's still mad about his hand. An' s'pose they lock him up an' strap him down and put him in a cage. That ain't no good, George."

"I know," said George. "I know."

Carlson came running in. "The bastard's stole my Luger," he shouted. "It ain't in my bag." Curley followed him, and Curley carried a shotgun in his good hand. Curley was cold now.

"All right, you guys," he said. "The nigger's got a shotgun. You take it, Carlson. When you see 'um, don't give 'im no chance. Shoot for his guts. That'll double 'im over."

Whit said excitedly, "I ain't got a gun."

Curley said, "You go in Soledad an' get a cop. Get Al Wilts, he's deputy sheriff. Le's go now." He turned suspiciously on George. "You're comin' with us, fella."

"Yeah," said George. "I'll come. But listen, Curley. The poor bastard's nuts. Don't shoot 'im. He di'n't know what he was doin'."

"Don't shoot 'im?" Curley cried. "He got Carlson's Luger. 'Course we'll shoot 'im."

George said weakly, "Maybe Carlson lost his gun."

"I seen it this morning," said Carlson. "No, it's been took."

Slim stood looking down at Curley's wife. He said, "Curley—maybe you better stay here with your wife."

Curley's face reddened. "I'm goin'," he said. "I'm gonna shoot the guts outa that big bastard myself, even if I only got one hand. I'm gonna get 'im."

Slim turned to Candy. "You stay here with her then, Candy. The rest of us better get goin'."

They moved away. George stopped a moment beside Candy and they both looked down at the dead girl until Curley called, "You George! You stick with us so we don't think you had nothin' to do with this."

George moved slowly after them, and his feet dragged heavily.

And when they were gone, Candy squatted down in the hay and watched the face of Curley's wife. "Poor bastard," he said softly.

The sound of the men grew fainter. The barn was darkening gradually and, in their stalls, the horses shifted their feet and rattled the halter chains. Old Candy lay down in the hay and covered his eyes with his arm.

The deep green pool of the Salinas River was still in the late afternoon. Already the sun had left the valley to go climbing up the slopes of the Gabilan mountains, and the hilltops were rosy in the sun. But by the pool among the mottled sycamores, a pleasant shade had fallen.

A water snake glided smoothly up the pool, twisting its periscope head from side to side; and it swam the length of the pool and came to the legs of a motionless heron that stood in the shallows. A silent head and beak lanced down and plucked it out by the head, and the beak swallowed the little snake while its tail waved frantically.

A far rush of wind sounded and a gust drove through the tops of the trees like a wave. The sycamore leaves turned up their silver sides, the brown, dry leaves on the ground scudded a few feet. And row on row of tiny wind waves flowed up the pool's green surface.

As quickly as it had come, the wind died, and the clearing was quiet again. The heron stood in the shallows, motionless and waiting. Another little water snake swam up the pool, turning its periscope head from side to side.

Suddenly Lennie appeared out of the brush, and he came as silently as a creeping bear moves. The heron pounded the air with its wings, jacked itself clear of the water and flew off down river. The little snake slid in among the reeds at the pool's side.

Lennie came quietly to the pool's edge. He knelt down and drank, barely touching his lips to the water. When a little bird skittered over the dry leaves behind him, his head jerked up and he strained toward the sound with eyes and ears until he saw the bird, and then he dropped his head and drank again.

When he was finished, he sat down on the bank, with his side to the pool, so that he could watch the trail's entrance. He embraced his knees and laid his chin down on his knees.

The light climbed on out of the valley, and as it went, the tops of the mountains seemed to blaze with increasing brightness.

Lennie said softly, "I di'n't forget, you bet, God damn. Hide in the brush an' wait for George." He pulled his hat down low over his eyes. "George gonna give me hell," he said. "George gonna wish he was alone an' not have me botherin' him." He turned his head and looked at the bright mountain tops. "I can go right off there an' find a cave," he said. And he continued sadly, "—an' never have no ketchup—but I won't care. If George don't want me . . . I'll go away. I'll go away."

And then from out of Lennie's head there came a little fat old woman. She wore thick bull's-eye glasses and she wore a huge gingham apron with pockets, and she was starched and clean. She stood in front of Lennie and put her hands on her hips, and she frowned disapprovingly at him.

And when she spoke, it was in Lennie's voice. "I tol' you an' tol' you," she said. "I tol' you, 'Min' George because he's such a nice fella an' good to you.' But you don't never take no care. You do bad things."

And Lennie answered her, "I tried, Aunt Clara, ma'am. I tried and tried. I couldn't help it."

"You never give a thought to George," she went on in Lennie's voice. "He been doin' nice things for you alla time. When he got a piece a pie you always got half or more'n half. An' if they was any ketchup, why he'd give it all to you."

"I know," said Lennie miserably. "I tried, Aunt Clara, ma'am. I tried and tried."

She interrupted him. "All the time he coulda had such a good time if it wasn't for you. He woulda took his pay an' raised hell in a whore house, and he coulda set in a pool room an' played snooker. But he got to take care of you."

Lennie moaned with grief. "I know, Aunt Clara, ma'am. I'll go right off in the hills an' I'll fin' a cave an' I'll live there so I won't be no more trouble to George."

"You jus' say that," She said sharply. "You're always sayin' that, an' you know sonofabitching well you ain't never gonna do it. You'll jus' stick around an' stew the b'Jesus outa George all the time."

Lennie said, "I might jus' as well go away. George ain't gonna let me tend no rabbits now."

Aunt Clara was gone, and from out of Lennie's head there came a gigantic rabbit. It sat on its haunches in front of him, and it waggled its ears and crinkled its nose at him. And it spoke in Lennie's voice too.

"Tend rabbits," it said scornfully. "You crazy bastard. You ain't fit to lick the boots of no rabbit. You'd forget 'em and let 'em go hungry. That's what you'd do. An' then what would George think?"

"I would *not* forget," Lennie said loudly.

"The hell you wouldn'," said the rabbit. "You ain't worth a greased jack-pin to ram you into hell. Christ knows George done ever'thing he could to jack you outa the sewer, but it don't do no good. If you think George gonna let you tend rabbits, you're even crazier'n usual. He ain't. He's gonna beat hell outa you with a stick, that's what he's gonna do."

Now Lennie retorted belligerently, "He ain't neither. George won't do nothing like that. I've knew George since—I forget when—and he ain't never raised his han' to me with a stick. He's nice to me. He ain't gonna be mean."

"Well he's sick of you," said the rabbit. "He's gonna beat hell outa you an' then go away an' leave you."

"He won't," Lennie cried frantically. "He won't do nothing like that. I know George. Me an' him travels together."

But the rabbit repeated softly over and over, "He gonna leave you, ya crazy bastard. He gonna leave ya all alone. He gonna leave ya, crazy bastard."

Lennie put his hands over his ears. "He ain't, I tell ya he ain't." And he cried, "Oh! George—George—George!"

George came quietly out of the brush and the rabbit scuttled back into Lennie's brain.

George said quietly, "What the hell you yellin' about?"

Lennie got up on his knees. "You ain't gonna leave me, are ya, George? I know you ain't."

George came stiffly near and sat down beside him. "No."

"I knowed it," Lennie cried. "You ain't that kind."

George was silent.

Lennie said, "George."

"Yeah?"

"I done another bad thing."

"It don't make no difference," George said, and he fell silent again.

Only the topmost ridges were in the sun now. The shadow in the valley was blue and soft. From the distance came the sound of men shouting to one another. George turned his head and listened to the shouts.

Lennie said, "George."

"Yeah?"

"Ain't you gonna give me hell?"

"Give ya hell?"

"Sure, like you always done before. Like, 'If I di'n't have you I'd take my fifty bucks——' "

"Jesus Christ, Lennie! You can't remember nothing that happens, but you remember ever' word I say."

"Well, ain't you gonna say it?"

George shook himself. He said woodenly, "If I was alone I could live so easy." His voice was monotonous, had no emphasis. "I could get a job an' not have no mess." He stopped.

"Go on," said Lennie. "An' when the enda the month come——"

"An' when the end of the month come I could take my fifty bucks an' go to a . . . cat house. . . ." He stopped again.

Lennie looked eagerly at him. "Go on, George. Ain't you gonna give me no more hell?"

"No," said George.

"Well, I can go away," said Lennie. "I'll go right off in the hills an' find a cave if you don't want me."

George shook himself again. "No," he said. "I want you to stay with me here."

Lennie said craftily—"Tell me like you done before."

"Tell you what?"

"'Bout the other guys an' about us."

George said, "Guys like us got no fambly. They make a little stake an' then they blow it in. They ain't got nobody in the worl' that gives a hoot in hell about 'em——"

"But not us," Lennie cried happily. "Tell about us now."

George was quiet for a moment. "But not us," he said.

"Because——"

"Because I got you an'——"

"An' I got you. We got each other, that's what, that gives a hoot in hell about us," Lennie cried in triumph.

The little evening breeze blew over the clearing and the leaves rustled and the wind waves flowed up the green pool. And the shouts of men sounded again, this time much closer than before.

George took off his hat. He said shakily, "Take off your hat, Lennie. The air feels fine."

Lennie removed his hat dutifully and laid it on the ground in front of him. The shadow in the valley was bluer, and the evening came fast. On the wind the sound of crashing in the brush came to them.

Lennie said, "Tell how it's gonna be."

George had been listening to the distant sounds. For a moment he was business-like. "Look acrost the river, Lennie, an' I'll tell you so you can almost see it."

Lennie turned his head and looked off across the pool and up the darkening slopes of the Gabilans. "We gonna get a little place," George began. He reached in his side pocket and brought out Carlson's Luger; he snapped off the safety, and the hand and gun lay on the ground behind Lennie's back. He looked at the back of Lennie's head, at the place where the spine and skull were joined.

A man's voice called from up the river, and another man answered.

"Go on," said Lennie.

George raised the gun and his hand shook, and he dropped his hand to the ground again.

"Go on," said Lennie. "How's it gonna be. We gonna get a little place."

"We'll have a cow," said George. "An' we'll have maybe a pig an' chickens . . . an' down the flat we'll have a . . . little piece alfalfa——"

"For the rabbits," Lennie shouted.

"For the rabbits," George repeated.

"And I get to tend the rabbits."

"An' you get to tend the rabbits."

Lennie giggled with happiness. "An' live on the fatta the lan'."

"Yes."

Lennie turned his head.

"No, Lennie. Look down there acrost the river, like you can almost see the place."

Lennie obeyed him. George looked down at the gun.

There were crashing footsteps in the brush now. George turned and looked toward them.

"Go on, George. When we gonna do it?"

"Gonna do it soon."

"Me an' you."

"You . . . an' me. Ever'body gonna be nice to you. Ain't gonna be no more trouble. Nobody gonna hurt nobody nor steal from 'em."

Lennie said, "I thought you was mad at me, George."

"No," said George. "No, Lennie. I ain't mad. I never been mad, an' I ain't now. That's a thing I want ya to know."

The voices came close now. George raised the gun and listened to the voices.

Lennie begged, "Le's do it now. Le's get that place now."

"Sure, right now. I gotta. We gotta."

And George raised the gun and steadied it, and he brought the muzzle of it close to the back of Lennie's head. The hand shook violently, but his face set and his hand steadied. He pulled the trigger. The crash of the shot rolled up the hills and rolled down again. Lennie jarred, and then settled slowly forward to the sand, and he lay without quivering.

George shivered and looked at the gun, and then he threw it from him, back up on the bank, near the pile of old ashes.

The brush seemed filled with cries and with the sound of running feet. Slim's voice shouted, "George. Where you at, George?"

But George sat stiffly on the bank and looked at his right hand that had thrown the gun away. The group burst into the clearing, and Curley was ahead. He saw Lennie lying on the sand. "Got him, by God." He went over and looked down at Lennie, and then he looked back at George. "Right in the back of the head," he said softly.

Slim came directly to George and sat down beside him, sat very close to him. "Never you mind," said Slim. "A guy got to sometimes."

But Carlson was standing over George. "How'd you do it?" he asked.

"I just done it," George said tiredly.

"Did he have my gun?"

"Yeah. He had your gun."

"An' you got it away from him and you took it an' you killed him?"

"Yeah. Tha's how." George's voice was almost a whisper. He looked steadily at his right hand that had held the gun.

Slim twitched George's elbow. "Come on, George. Me an' you'll go in an' get a drink."

George let himself be helped to his feet. "Yeah, a drink."

Slim said, "You hadda, George. I swear you hadda. Come on with me." He led George into the entrance of the trail and up toward the highway.

Curley and Carlson looked after them. And Carlson said, "Now what the hell ya suppose is eatin' them two guys?"

TOPICS FOR PAPERS AND DISCUSSION

1. *George and Lennie.* One critic has written that these two characters share "the kind of love that joins master and dog." Do you agree? Select Candy and his dog as the epitome of that relationship and compare George and Lennie with them. In what ways does George need Lennie as much as Lennie needs him? Cite particular scenes which validate these needs. Expand on the idea of "need" to include friendship, loyalty, and human brotherhood. Where precisely are these ideas stated, and where are they enacted? What is to be made of Slim's final action and the response of the others?

2. *Slim and Lennie—polarities of humanity.* As the troubles begin to gather around Lennie, Slim with increasing frequency is paired with George. Describe Slim and Lennie as opposites. What images are used to reveal both men? Analyze and comment on those actions and themes which form the patterns of their experiences. What seems to be intended? What are we supposed to see in the new equation: Slim and George? Consider the significance of their climbing "up toward the highway" at the end.
3. *Women in Steinbeck's world.* What functions do women serve in the lives of George, Lennie, and the other men? While obviously the role of Curley's wife is an important one, why didn't Steinbeck give her a name? What is meant by calling her "jail bait" and "rat-trap"? Is the trap a subtle link to Lennie? Even though she is referred to as "a tramp," a "trouble" maker, and "a tart," Curley's wife is not entirely unsympathetic. Explain. Does she share any dreams in common with George and Lennie? Consider Whit's distinctions between Susy and Clara and the way they run their whorehouses. How is Aunt Clara's role different as a woman out of the past? What is her function near the end of the novel?
4. *The Darwinian theme.* Attempt to interpret the novel by use of Charles Darwin's major theories of evolution. Examine the conflicts among the characters, even those who are most compatible. Analyze each situation for evidence of biological and social or economic Darwinism. Discuss natural selection, survival of the fittest, etc., as they apply or do not apply to the world depicted in *Of Mice and Men.* What elements are not influenced by Darwin? How do they actually harmonize with Steinbeck's use of Darwinian theories?
5. *Freedom and enslavement as themes.* Show how these two abstractions are concretely carried out in the story. What different kinds of freedom and slavery are depicted? Which of the freedoms are only apparently "free"? Which are necessary? Which can be dispensed with? Deal with enslavement in the same manner. In spite of the evident racism around him, are there ways in which Crooks is freer than the more independent characters? How might the terms *freedom* and *enslavement* be modified to become more directly applicable to experiences in the novel?
6. *Sensory motifs.* Notice the almost compulsive references to hands and feet in Steinbeck's novel. How do they function thematically? Determine the relevance of light and darkness, fire and water, noise and silence to the theme. Also consider other sensory motifs based upon seeing, touching, hearing, tasting, and smelling. Why are the senses so important in Steinbeck's writing?
7. *Nature and civilization.* Are these two themes supposed to be poles apart in the novel? How does the primitiveness of Steinbeck's characters affect this polarization? Are "men" and "mice" alike? Con-

sider the motif of animal imagery which permeates the story—does it serve to erase the differences between human and beast? If not, why? Notice the various authorial uses of certain animals, and especially those of different sizes. What raises the men above the bestial? Why is the crucial killing scene set in the barn among animals? With respect to this topic, what is the function of the Edenic farm? Compare the imagined life on it with the activities among men and animals in the grove by the river, and with the activities of town and city.

8. *Agrarianism and social protest.* In what way is agrarian doctrine important to the novel? How does agrarianism relate to the dream of land ownership? Seemingly the dream has been destroyed, but how does Steinbeck reconcile the clash between the ideal and the practical? From another point of view, are we supposed to see the farm laborers as an exploited proletariat? Is the novel a study of "have-nots" in a society of "haves"? In what way is the novel a protest against conditions of the Depression which produced bindle stiffs? Defend or refute the statement that "Steinbeck's work is not specifically about the failure of agrarianism or the perniciousness of capitalism; rather it is a work of art which uses those references for more important ends."
9. *Religious ritual and mythology.* Examine any evidence of ritualizing in the novel. What forms of litany are related to the rituals? The many references to Jesus Christ seem to indicate that Steinbeck is interested in conveying the story from a perspective of Christian myth. Discuss this idea and its function in what appears to be a demythologized world, one fallen, damned, and even hellish. In what way is the impossible dream linked to the submerged myth? Is it even perhaps the heart of the myth? Account for the death of Lennie, and the subsequent actions of George and Slim in light of the question: "In a world bereft of religious sanctions, who or what is divine?"
10. *Narrative structure—its expressive dimension.* The novel is divided into seven sections. Explain how the first three episodes lead logically and dramatically to the events in the long central chapter, and how the final three lead logically away from it to the inevitability of the resolution. Examine the idea that "the central chapter contains the novel in miniature." What is gained by focusing all the harmonious and conflicting material in the center of the novel? What is intended by ending the novel where it began? Could a geometric design be used to illustrate this structuring? What kind(s)?
11. *Significant patterning of events.* Examine Steinbeck's careful patterning of events. For instance, in the third part, George repeatedly tells Lennie where to hide if trouble arises; the phrase "Stable Buck" is called out; a dangerous woman appears in the doorway; Slim enters and almost immediately brings into the foreground the

idea of survival through solidarity; and, shortly after, Carlson decides to shoot Candy's dog. What overtones emerge from the pattern of these events? Explain how other overtones are generated by means of similar patterning. Also, show how this patterning of events relates to Steinbeck's original working title for the novel: *Something That Happened*. What does the final title contribute? Is the apparently logical and inevitable design anywhere diverted by unexpected countermovement, accident, contradiction, inconsistency? Explain.

12. *The special use of language.* Examine the linguistic phenomenon displayed by the curses of the characters. The various expletives represent radically opposed intentions and meanings, according to who utters them and in what situation. For instance, George speaks of "that bastard bus driver" and intends one thing; yet a moment later he calls Lennie "a crazy bastard" and intends something quite different. What do the expletives reveal of the condition of the world in which the men live? What do they show about the relationships between friends and acquaintances, bosses and employees? What do the expletives expose about the personalities of those who use them?
13. *Novel and drama.* After reviewing standard techniques of drama, examine those that are evident in the novel, such as the termination of an act or scene right after the action has built to a climactic moment or the creation of functionally expressive entrances and exits, etc. Describe the effectiveness of a number of the many dramatic techniques that Steinbeck utilizes. Explain how the techniques of the two different genres may function harmoniously. Steinbeck readily changed the novel into a play because, as he said, *Of Mice and Men* was "an attempt to write a novel in three acts to be played from the lines." How does this dramatic structure affect the narrative structure?
14. *The sense of place.* Compare varying ideas of "place." Take into consideration the ranch, the distant Gabilan mountains, the "cat houses," the grove of sycamores with its clearing and its pool, Lennie's references to the cave, and George's references to the poolroom. Consider the different cities mentioned, especially Weed. How does the dream of "a place" figure in the lives of the men? In what ways does the idea of a golden land vary from character to character, especially Curley's wife?
15. *The symbolic density of the novel.* Some of Steinbeck's symbols are relatively simple; some are mythological, archetypal, or biblical; and some spring from literary history, such as the pigeon that flies in and out of the barn where Curley's wife lies dead. Explain what each of the following contributes in meaning: grove and pool, heron and snake, heights and depths, path and highway, the "far rush of wind" which suddenly dies in the final section. What is the meaning of George's woodenness and stiffness before and

after Lennie's death, and Slim's leading "George into the entrance of the trail"?

16. *Space as a symbolic dimension.* In fiction, drama, and films, space and volume are often manipulated to achieve dramatic and symbolic expression. Explain what Steinbeck achieves by his frequent expansion and contraction of spatial dimensions. What events take place in confined, narrow, and enclosed spaces or in free, broad, and open spaces? What symbolic differences are there, for example, among the bunkhouse, Crooks' room, and the barn? Examine larger, more voluminous spaces in the same way.
17. *Minor episodes as thematic enrichment.* Show how the following minor episodes are related to the major concerns of the story: Whitey's fear of lice, as it relates to George; the meeting with the boss; William Tenner's letter in the pulp magazine; the first appearance of Curley in the bunkhouse; Lennie's "conversations" with Aunt Clara and the "gigantic rabbit" toward the end. The fifth section consists entirely of the gathering in Crooks' room—in what ways is it a major episode? Evaluate the significance of the description of nature which opens the novel and the one which begins the final section.
18. *An appraisal of weaknesses and strengths.* The novel has been criticized because of its sentimentality, its use of stock characters, its contrivance and predictability of plot, the faultiness of Lennie's hallucinations at the end, and the emphasis upon pathological behavior. Analyze and discuss these putative weaknesses. Are there any others? Why must the dream of "the good place" end with the death of Curley's wife and Lennie? Review the conversation between George and Candy in the barn. If indeed there are weaknesses, what are the compensating strengths? Why, for so many readers, does the novel seem "right," a deeply moving experience?
19. *Universalities.* Steinbeck described *Of Mice and Men* as a "microcosm" and as "a study of the dreams and pleasures of everyone." Lennie embodied "the inarticulate and powerful yearnings of all men." How does the novel support this theory of a miniature world full of universal relevance? Consider again the time it portrays, and the economic and social conditions of the characters. Do they permit Steinbeck to fulfill his theory? Can you cite specific aspects of his handling of the materials which expand the novel beyond its own time and place in history?
20. *The end of the novel.* Although it seems clear enough, the ending is ambiguous. Describe as fully as possible the various ways of reading it. Which would you choose as compatible with the materials developed in the story? Defend your choice. Compare the end with the beginning. What natural or cosmic changes have occurred since Lennie and George are first introduced entering "the opening by the green pool"? Comment on several of the oblique biblical

echoes such as "the shadow in the valley was blue" and "look acrost the river, Lennie." Explain how Slim is used to comment on and set straight the ethical questions involved in George's killing of Lennie, especially Slim's tragic words: "You hadda, George. I swear you hadda."

The Violent Bear It Away

FLANNERY O'CONNOR

From the days of John the Baptist until now,
the kingdom of heaven suffereth violence, and
the violent bear it away. MATTHEW 11:12

ONE

I

Francis Marion Tarwater's uncle had been dead for only half a day when the boy got too drunk to finish digging his grave and a Negro named Buford Munson, who had come to get a jug filled, had to finish it and drag the body from the breakfast table where it was still sitting and bury it in a decent and Christian way, with the sign of its Saviour at the head of the grave and enough dirt on top to keep the dogs from digging it up. Buford had come along about noon and when he left at sundown, the boy, Tarwater, had never returned from the still.

The old man had been Tarwater's great-uncle, or said he was, and they had always lived together so far as the child knew. His uncle had said he was seventy years of age at the time he had rescued and undertaken to bring him up; he was eighty-four when he died. Tarwater figured this made his own age fourteen. His uncle had taught him Figures, Reading, Writing, and History beginning with Adam expelled from the Garden and going on down through the presidents to Herbert Hoover and on in speculation toward the Second Coming and the Day of Judgment. Besides giving him a good education, he had rescued him from his only other connection, old Tarwater's nephew, a schoolteacher who had no child of his own at the time and wanted this one of his dead sister's to raise according to his own ideas.

The old man was in a position to know what his ideas were. He had lived for three months in the nephew's house on what he had thought at the time was Charity but what he said he had found out was not Charity or anything like it. All the time he had lived there, the nephew had secretly been making a study of him. The nephew, who had taken him in under the name of Charity, had at the same time been creeping into his soul by the back door, asking him questions that meant more than one thing, planting traps around the house and watching him fall into them, and finally coming up with a written study of him for a schoolteacher magazine. The stench of his behaviour had reached heaven and the Lord Himself had rescued the old man. He had sent him a rage of vision, had told him to fly with the orphan boy to the farthest part of the backwoods and raise him up to justify his Redemption. The Lord had assured him a long life and he had snatched the baby from under the schoolteacher's nose and taken him to live in the clearing, Powderhead, that he had a title to for his lifetime.

The old man, who said he was a prophet, had raised the boy to expect the Lord's call himself and to be prepared for the day he would hear it. He had schooled him in the evils that befall prophets; in those that come from the world, which are trifling, and those that come from the Lord and burn the prophet clean; for he himself had been burned clean and burned clean again. He had learned by fire.

He had been called in his early youth and had set out for the city to proclaim the destruction awaiting a world that had abandoned its Saviour. He proclaimed from the midst of his fury that the world would see the sun burst in blood and fire and while he raged and waited, it rose every morning, calm and contained in itself, as if not only the world, but the Lord Himself had failed to hear the prophet's message. It rose and set, rose and set on a world that turned from green to white and green to white and green to white again. It rose and set and he despaired of the Lord's listening. Then one morning he saw to his joy a finger of fire coming out of it and before he could turn, before he could shout, the finger had touched him and the destruction he had been waiting for had fallen in his own brain and his own body. His own blood had been burned dry and not the blood of the world.

Having learned much by his own mistakes, he was in a position to instruct Tarwater—when the boy chose to listen—in the hard facts of serving the Lord. The boy, who had ideas of his own, listened with an impatient conviction that he would not make any mistakes himself when the time came and the Lord called him.

That was not the last time the Lord had corrected the old man with fire, but it had not happened since he had taken Tarwater from the schoolteacher. That time his rage of vision had been clear. He had known what he was saving the boy from and it was saving and not destruction he was seeking. He had learned enough to hate the destruction that had to come and not all that was going to be destroyed.

Rayber, the schoolteacher, had shortly discovered where they were and had come out to the clearing to get the baby back. He had had to leave his car on the dirt road and walk a mile through the woods on a path that appeared and disappeared before he came to the corn patch with the gaunt two-story shack standing in the middle of it. The old man had been fond of recalling for Tarwater the red sweating bitten face of his nephew bobbing up and down through the corn and behind it the pink flowered hat of a welfare-woman he had brought along with him. The corn was planted up to four feet from the porch that year and as the nephew came out of it, the old man appeared in the door with his shotgun and shouted that he would shoot any foot that touched his step and the two stood facing each other while the welfare-woman bristled out of the corn, ruffled like a peahen upset on the nest. The old man said if it hadn't been for the welfare-woman, his nephew wouldn't have taken a step. Both their faces were scratched and bleeding from thorn bushes and a switch of blackberry bush hung from the sleeve of the welfare-woman's blouse.

She had only to let out her breath slowly as if she were releasing the last patience on earth and the nephew lifted his foot and planted it on the step and the old man shot him in the leg. He recalled for the boy's benefit the nephew's expression of outraged righteousness, a look that had so infuriated him that he had raised the gun slightly higher and shot him again, this time taking a wedge out of his right ear. The second shot flushed the righteousness off his face and left it blank and white, revealing that there was nothing underneath it, revealing, the old man sometimes admitted, his own failure as well, for he had tried and failed, long ago, to rescue the nephew. He had kidnapped him when the child was seven and had taken him to the backwoods and baptized him and instructed him in the facts of his Redemption, but the instruction had lasted only a few years; in time the child had set himself a different course. There were moments when the thought that he might have helped the nephew on to his new course himself became so heavy in the old man that he would stop telling the story to Tarwater, stop and stare in front of him as if he were looking into a pit which had opened up before his feet.

At such times he would wander into the woods and leave Tarwater alone in the clearing, occasionally for days, while he thrashed out his peace with the Lord, and when he returned, bedraggled and hungry, he would look the way the boy thought a prophet ought to look. He would look as if he had been wrestling a wildcat, as if his head were still full of the visions he had seen in its eyes, wheels of light and strange beasts with giant wings of fire and four heads turned to the four points of the universe. These were the times that Tarwater knew that when he was called, he would say, "Here I am, Lord, ready!" At other times when there was no fire in his uncle's eye and he spoke only of the sweat and stink of the cross, of being born again to die, and of spending eternity eating the bread of life, the boy would let his mind wander off to other subjects.

The old man's thought did not always move at the same rate of speed through every point in his story. Sometimes, as if he did not want to think of it, he would speed over the part where he shot the nephew and race on, telling how the two of them, the nephew and the welfare-woman (whose very name was comical—Bernice Bishop) had scuttled off, making a disappearing rattle in the corn, and how the welfare-woman had screamed, "Why didn't you tell me? You knew he was crazy!" and how when they came out of the corn on the other side, he had noted from the upstairs window where he had run that she had her arm around the nephew and was holding him up while he hopped into the woods. Later he learned that he had married her though she was twice his age and he could only possibly get one child out of her. She had never let him come back again.

And the Lord, the old man said had preserved the one child he had got out of her from being corrupted by such parents. He had preserved him in the only possible way: the child was dim-witted. The old man would pause here and let the weight of this mystery sink in on Tarwater. He had made, since he learned of that child's existence, several trips into town to try to kidnap him so that he could baptize him, but each time he had come back unsuccessful. The schoolteacher was on his guard and the old man was too fat and stiff now to make an agile kidnapper.

"If by the time I die," he had said to Tarwater, "I haven't got him baptized, it'll be up to you. It'll be the first mission the Lord sends you."

The boy doubted very much that his first mission would be to baptize a dim-witted child. "Oh no it won't be," he said. "He don't mean for me to finish up your leavings. He has other things in mind for me." And he thought of Moses who struck water from a rock, of Joshua who made the sun stand still, of Daniel who stared down lions in the pit.

"It's no part of your job to think for the Lord," his great-uncle said. "Judgment may rack your bones."

The morning the old man died, he came down and cooked the breakfast as usual and died before he got the first spoonful to his mouth. The downstairs of their house was all kitchen, large and dark, with a wood stove at one end of it and a board table drawn up to the stove. Sacks of feed and mash were stacked in the corners and scrapmetal, woodshavings, old rope, ladders, and other tinder were wherever he or Tarwater had let them fall. They had slept in the kitchen until a bobcat sprang in the window one night and frightened his uncle into carrying the bed upstairs where there were two empty rooms. The old man prophesied at the time that the stairsteps would take ten years off his life. At the moment of his death, he sat down to his breakfast and lifted his knife in one square red hand halfway to his mouth, and then with a look of complete astonishment, he lowered it until the hand rested on the edge of the plate and tilted it up off the table.

He was a bull-like old man with a short head set directly into his shoulders and silver protruding eyes that looked like two fish straining to get out of a net of red threads. He had on a putty-colored hat with the brim turned up all around and over his undershirt a grey coat that had once been black. Tarwater, sitting across the table from him, saw red ropes appear in his face and a tremor pass over him. It was like the tremor of a quake that had begun at his heart and run outward and was just reaching the surface. His mouth twisted down sharply on one side and he remained exactly as he was, perfectly balanced, his back a good six inches from the chair back and his stomach caught just under the edge of the table. His eyes, dead silver, were focused on the boy across from him.

Tarwater felt the tremor transfer itself and run lightly over him. He knew the old man was dead without touching him and he continued to sit across the table from the corpse, finishing his breakfast in a kind of sullen embarrassment as if he were in the presence of a new personality and couldn't think of anything to say. Finally he said in a querulous tone, "Just hold your horses. I already told you I would do it right." The voice sounded like a stranger's voice, as if the death had changed him instead of his great-uncle.

He got up and took his plate out the back door and set it down on the bottom step and two long-legged black game roosters tore across the yard and finished what was on it. He sat down on a long pine box on the back porch and his hands began absently to unravel a length of rope while his long face stared ahead beyond the clearing over the woods that ran in grey and purple folds until they touched the light blue fortress line of trees set against the empty morning sky.

Powderhead was not simply off the dirt road but off the wagon track and footpath, and the nearest neighbors, colored not white, still had to walk through the woods, pushing plum branches out of their way to get to it. Once there had been two houses; now there was only the one house with the dead owner inside and the living owner outside on the porch, waiting to bury him. The boy knew he would have to bury the old man before anything would begin. It was as if there would have to be dirt over him before he would be thoroughly dead. The thought seemed to give him respite from something that pressed on him.

A few weeks before, the old man had started an acre of corn to the left and had run it beyond the fenceline almost up to the house on one side. The two strands of barbed-wire ran through the middle of the patch. A line of fog, hump-shaped, was creeping toward it like a white hound dog ready to crouch under and crawl across the yard.

"I'm going to move that fence," Tarwater said. "I ain't going to have any fence I own in the middle of a patch." The voice was loud and strange and disagreeable. Inside his head it continued: you ain't the owner. The schoolteacher owns it.

I own it, Tarwater said, because I'm here and can't nobody get me off. If any schoolteacher comes to claim the property, I'll kill him.

The Lord may send you off, he thought. There was a complete stillness over everything and the boy felt his heart begin to swell. He held his breath as if he were about to hear a voice from on high. After a few moments he heard a hen scratching beneath him under the porch. He ran his arm fiercely under his nose and gradually his face paled again.

He had on a faded pair of overalls and a grey hat pulled down over his ears like a cap. He followed his uncle's custom of never taking off his hat except in bed. He had always followed his uncle's customs up to this date but: if I want to move that fence before I bury him, it wouldn't be a soul to hinder me, he thought; no voice will be uplifted.

Bury him first and get it over with, the loud stranger's disagreeable voice said. He got up and went to look for the shovel.

The pine box he had been sitting on was his uncle's coffin but he didn't intend to use it. The old man was too heavy for a thin boy to hoist over the side of a box and though old Tarwater had built it himself a few years before, he had said that if it wasn't feasible to get him into it when the time came, then just to put him in the hole as he was, only to be sure the hole was deep. He wanted it ten foot, he said, not just eight. He had worked on the box a long time and when he finished it, he had scratched on the lid, MASON TARWATER, WITH GOD, and had climbed into it where it stood on the back porch, and had lain there for some time, nothing showing but his stomach which rose over the top like over-leavened bread. The boy had stood at the side of the box, studying him. "This is the end of us all," the old man said with satisfaction, his gravel voice hearty in the coffin.

"It's too much of you for the box," Tarwater said. "I'll have to sit on the lid to press you down or wait until you rot a little."

"Don't wait," old Tarwater had said. "Listen. If it ain't feasible to use the box when the time comes, if you can't lift it or whatever, just get me in the hole but I want it deep. I want it ten foot, not just eight, ten. You can roll me to it if nothing else. I'll roll. Get two boards and set them down the steps and start me rolling and dig where I stop and don't let me roll over into it until it's deep enough. Prop me with some bricks so I won't roll into it and don't let the dogs nudge me over the edge before it's finished. You better pen up the dogs," he said.

"What if you die in bed?" the boy asked. "How'm I going to get you down the stairs?"

"I ain't going to die in bed," the old man said. "As soon as I hear the summons, I'm going to run downstairs. I'll get as close to the door as I can. If I should get stuck up there, you'll have to roll me down the stairs, that's all."

"My Lord," the child said.

The old man sat up in the box and brought his fist down on the edge of it. "Listen," he said. "I never asked much of you. I taken you and raised you and saved you from that ass in town and now all I'm asking in return is when I die to get me in the ground where the dead belong and set up a cross over me to show I'm there. That's all in the world I'm asking you to do. I ain't even asking you to go for the niggers and try to get me in the plot with my daddy. I could ask you that but I ain't. I'm doing everything to make it easy for you. All I'm asking you is to get me in the ground and set up a cross."

"I'll be doing good if I get you in the ground," Tarwater said. "I'll be too wore out to set up any cross. I ain't bothering with trifles."

"Trifles!" his uncle hissed. "You'll learn what a trifle is on the day those crosses are gathered! Burying the dead right may be the only honor you ever do yourself. I brought you out here to raise you a Christian, and more than a Christian, a prophet!" he hollered, "and the burden of it will be on you!"

"If I don't have the strength to do it," the child said, watching him with a careful detachment, "I'll notify my uncle in town and he can come out and take care of you. The schoolteacher," he drawled, observing that the pockmarks in his uncle's face had already turned pale against the purple. "He'll tend to you."

The threads that restrained the old man's eyes thickened. He gripped both sides of the coffin and pushed forward as if he were going to drive it off the porch. "He'd burn me," he said hoarsely. "He'd have me cremated in an oven and scatter my ashes. 'Uncle,' he said to me, 'you're a type that's almost extinct!' He'd be willing to pay the undertaker to burn me to be able to scatter my ashes," he said. "He don't believe in the Resurrection. He don't believe in the Last Day. He don't believe in the bread of life . . ."

"The dead don't bother with particulars," the boy interrupted.

The old man grabbed the front of his overalls and pulled him up against the side of the box and glared into his pale face. "The world was made for the dead. Think of all the dead there are," he said, and then as if he had conceived the answer for all the insolence in the world, he said, "There's a million times more dead than living and the dead are dead a million times longer than the living are alive," and he released him with a laugh.

The boy had shown only by a slight quiver that he was shaken by this, and after a minute he had said, "The schoolteacher is my uncle. The only blood connection with good sense I'll have and a living man and if I wanted to go to him, I'd go; now."

The old man looked at him silently for what seemed a full minute. Then he slammed his hands flat on the sides of the box and roared, "Whom the plague beckons, to the plague! Whom the sword to the sword! Whom fire to fire!" And the child trembled visibly.

"I saved you to be free, your own self!" he had shouted, "and not a piece of information inside his head! If you were living with him, you'd be information right now, you'd be inside his head, and what's furthermore," he said, "you'd be going to school."

The boy grimaced. The old man had always impressed on him his good fortune in not being sent to school. The Lord had seen fit to guarantee the purity of his up-bringing, to preserve him from contamination, to preserve him as His elect servant, trained by a prophet for prophecy. While other children his age were herded together in a room to cut out paper pumpkins under the direction of a woman, he was left free for the pursuit of wisdom, the companions of his spirit Abel and Enoch and Noah and Job, Abraham and Moses, King David and Solomon, and all the prophets, from Elijah who escaped death, to John whose severed head struck terror from a dish. The boy knew that escaping school was the surest sign of his election.

The truant officer had come only once. The Lord had told the old man to expect it and what to do and old Tarwater had instructed the boy in his part against the day when, as the devil's emissary, the officer would appear. When the time came and they saw him cutting across the field, they were ready. The child got behind the house and the old man sat on the steps and waited. When the officer, a thin bald-headed man with red galluses, stepped out of the field onto the packed dirt of the yard, he greeted old Tarwater warily and commenced his business as if he had not come for it. He sat down on the steps and spoke of poor weather and poor health. Finally, gazing out over the field, he said, "You got a boy, don't you, that ought to be in school?"

"A fine boy," the old man said, "and I wouldn't stand in his way if anybody thought they could teach him. You boy!" he called. The boy didn't come at once. "Oh you boy!" the old man shouted.

In a few minutes Tarwater appeared from around the side of the house. His eyes were open but not well-focused. His head rolled uncontrollably on his slack shoulders and his tongue lolled in his open mouth.

"He ain't bright," the old man said, "but he's a mighty good boy. He knows to come when you call him."

"Yes," the truant officer said, "well yes, but it might be best to leave him in peace."

"I don't know, he might take to schooling," the old man said. "He ain't had a fit for going on two months."

"I speck he better stay at home," the officer said. "I wouldn't want to put a strain on him," and he commenced to speak of other things. Shortly he took his leave and the two of them watched with satisfaction as the diminishing figure moved back across the field and the red galluses were finally lost to view.

If the schoolteacher had got hold of him, right now he would have been in school, one among many, indistinguishable from the herd, and in the schoolteacher's head, he would be laid out in parts and numbers. "That's where he wanted me," the old man said, "and he thought once he had me in that schoolteacher magazine, I would be as good as in his head." The schoolteacher's house had had little in it but books and papers. The old man had not known when he went there to live that every living thing that passed through the nephew's eyes into his head was turned by his brain into a book or a paper or a chart. The schoolteacher had appeared to have a great interest in his being a prophet, chosen by the Lord, and had asked numerous questions, the answers to which he had sometimes scratched down on a pad, his little eyes lighting every now and then as if in some discovery.

The old man had fancied he was making progress in convincing the nephew again of his Redemption, for he at least listened though he did not *say* he believed. He seemed to delight to talk about the things that interested his uncle. He questioned him at length about his early life, which old Tarwater had practically forgotten. The old man had thought this interest in his forebears would bear fruit, but what it bore, what it bore, stench and shame, were dead words. What it bore was a dry and seedless fruit, incapable even of rotting, dead from the beginning. From time to time, the old man would spit out of his mouth, like gobbets of poison, some of the idiotic sentences from the schoolteacher's piece. Wrath had burned them on his memory, word for word. "His fixation of being called by the Lord had its origin in insecurity. He needed the assurance of a call, and so he called himself."

"Called myself!" the old man would hiss, "called myself!" This so enraged him that half the time he could do nothing but repeat it. "Called myself. I called myself. I, Mason Tarwater, called myself! Called myself to be beaten and tied up. Called myself to be spit on and snickered at. Called myself to be struck down in my pride. Called myself to be torn by the Lord's eye. Listen boy," he would say and grab the child by the straps of his overalls and shake him slowly, "even the mercy of the Lord burns." He would let go the straps and allow the boy to fall back into the thorn bed of that thought, while he continued to hiss and groan.

"Where he wanted me was inside that schoolteacher magazine. He thought once he got me in there, I'd be as good as inside his head and done for and that would be that, that would be the end of it. Well. that wasn't the end of it! Here I sit. And there you sit. In freedom. Not inside anybody's head!" and his voice would run away from him as if it were the freest part of his free self and were straining ahead of his heavy body to be off. Something of his great-uncle's glee would take hold of Tarwater at that point and he would feel that he had escaped some mysterious prison. He even felt he could smell his freedom, pine-scented, coming out of the woods, until the old man would continue, "You were born into bondage and baptized into freedom, into the death of the Lord, into the death of the Lord Jesus Christ."

Then the child would feel a sullenness creeping over him, a slow warm rising resentment that this freedom had to be connected with Jesus and that Jesus had to be the Lord.

"Jesus is the bread of life," the old man said.

The boy, disconcerted, would look off into the distance over the dark blue treeline where the world stretched out, hidden and at its ease. In the darkest, most private part of his soul, hanging upsidedown like a sleeping bat, was the certain, undeniable knowledge that he was not hungry for the bread of life. Had the bush flamed for Moses, the sun stood still for Joshua, the lions turned aside before Daniel only to prophesy the bread of life? Jesus? He felt a terrible disappointment in that conclusion, a dread that it was true. The old man said that as soon as he died, he would hasten to the banks of the Lake of Galilee to eat the loaves and fishes that the Lord had multiplied.

"Forever?" the horrified boy asked.

"Forever," the old man said.

The boy sensed that this was the heart of his great-uncle's madness, this hunger, and what he was secretly afraid of was that it might be passed down, might be hidden in the blood and might strike some day in him and then he would be torn by hunger like the old man, the bottom split out of his stomach so that nothing would heal or fill it but the bread of life.

He tried when possible to pass over these thoughts, to keep his vision located on an even level, to see no more than what was in front of his face and to let his eyes stop at the surface of that. It was as if he were afraid that if he let his eye rest for an instant longer than was needed to place something—a spade, a hoe, the mule's hind quarters before his plow, the red furrow under him—that the thing would suddenly stand before him, strange and terrifying, demanding that he name it and name it justly and be judged for the name he gave it. He did all he could to avoid this threatened intimacy of creation. When the Lord's call came, he wished it to be a voice from out of a clear and empty sky, the trumpet of the Lord God Almighty, untouched by any fleshly hand or breath. He expected to see wheels of fire in the eyes of unearthly beasts. He had expected this to happen as soon as his great-uncle died. He turned his mind off this quickly and went to get the shovel. The schoolteacher is a living man, he thought as he went, but he'd better not come out here and try to get me off this property because I'll kill him. Go to him and be damned, his uncle had said. I've saved you from him this far and if you go to him the minute I'm in the ground there's nothing I can do about it.

The shovel lay against the side of the hen house. "I'll never set my foot in the city again," the boy said to himself aloud. I'll never go to him. Him nor nobody else will ever get me off this place.

He decided to dig the grave under the fig tree because the old man would be good for the figs. The ground was sandy on top and solid brick underneath and the shovel made a clanging sound when he struck it in the sand. Two hundred pounds of dead mountain to bury, he thought, and stood with one foot on the shovel, leaning forward, studying the white sky through the leaves of the tree. It would take all day to get a hole big enough out of this rock and the schoolteacher would burn him in a minute.

Tarwater had seen the schoolteacher once from a distance of about twenty feet and he had seen the dim-witted child closer up. The little boy somewhat resembled old Tarwater except for his eyes which were grey like the old man's but clear, as if the other side of them went down and down into two pools of light. It was plain to look at him that he did not have any sense. The old man had been so shocked by the likeness and the unlikeness that the time he and Tarwater had gone there, he had only stood in the door staring at the little boy and rolling his tongue around outside his mouth as if he had no sense himself. That had been the first time he had seen the child and he could not forget him. "Married her and got one child out of her and that without sense," he would murmur. "The Lord preserved him and now He means to see he's baptized."

"Well whyn't you get on with it then?" the boy asked, for he wanted something to happen, wanted to see the old man in action, wanted him to kidnap the child and have the schoolteacher have to come after him so that he could get a closer look at his other uncle. "What ails you?" he asked. "What makes you tarry so long? Why don't you make haste and steal him?"

"I take my directions from the Lord God," the old man said, "Who moves in His own time. I don't take them from you."

The white fog had eased through the yard and disappeared into the next bottom and the air was clear and blank. His mind continued to dwell on the schoolteacher's house. "Three months there," his great-uncle had said. "It shames me. Betrayed for three months in the house of my own kin and if when I'm dead you want to turn me over to my betrayer and see my body burned, go ahead! Go ahead, boy," he had shouted, sitting up splotch-faced in his box. "Go ahead and let him burn me but watch out for the Lord's lion after that. Remember the Lord's lion set in the path of the false prophet! I been leavened by the yeast he don't believe in," he had said, "and I won't be burned! And when I'm gone, you'll be better off in these woods by yourself with just as much light as the sun wants to let in than you'll be in the city with him."

He kept on digging but the grave did not get any deeper. "The dead are poor," he said in the voice of the stranger. You can't be any poorer than dead. He'll have to take what he gets. Nobody to bother me, he thought. Ever. No hand uplifted to hinder me from anything; except the Lord's and He ain't said anything. He ain't even noticed me yet.

A sand-colored hound beat its tail on the ground nearby and a few black chickens scratched in the raw clay he was turning up. The sun had slipped over the blue line of trees and circled by a haze of yellow was moving slowly across the sky. "Now I can do anything I want to," he said, softening the stranger's voice so that he could stand it. Could kill off all those chickens if I had a mind to, he thought, watching the worthless black game bantams that his uncle had been fond of keeping.

He favored a lot of foolishness, the stranger said. The truth is he was childish. Why, that schoolteacher never did him any harm. You take, all he did was to watch him and write down what he seen and heard and put it in a paper for schoolteachers to read. Now what was wrong in that? Why nothing. Who cares what a schoolteacher reads? And the old fool acted like he had been killed in his very soul. Well he wasn't so near dead as he thought he was. Lived on fourteen years and raised up a boy to bury him, suitable to his own taste.

As Tarwater slashed at the ground with the shovel, the stranger's voice took on a kind of restrained fury and he kept repeating, you got to bury him whole and completely by hand and that schoolteacher would burn him in a minute.

After he had dug for an hour or more, the grave was only a foot deep, not as deep yet as the corpse. He sat down on the edge of it for a while. The sun was like a furious white blister in the sky.

The dead are a heap more trouble than the living, the stranger said. That schoolteacher wouldn't consider for a minute that on the last day all the bodies marked by crosses will be gathered. In the rest of the world they do things different than what you been taught.

"I been there once," Tarwater muttered. "Nobody has to tell me."

His uncle two or three years before had gone to call on the lawyers to try to get the property unentailed so that it would skip the schoolteacher and go to Tarwater. Tarwater had sat at the lawyer's twelfth-story window and looked down into the pit of the street while his uncle transacted the business. On the way from the railroad station he had walked tall in the mass of moving metal and concrete speckled with the very small eyes of people. The glitter of his own eyes was shaded under the stiff roof-like brim of a new grey hat, balanced perfectly straight on his buttressing ears. Before coming he had read facts in the almanac and he knew that there were 75,000 people here who were seeing him for the first time. He wanted to stop and shake hands with each of them and say his name was F. M. Tarwater and that he was here only for the day to accompany his uncle on business at a lawyer's. His head jerked backwards after each passing figure until they began to pass too thickly and he observed that their eyes didn't grab at you like the eyes of country people. Several people bumped into him and this contact that should have made an acquaintance for life, made nothing because the hulks shoved on with ducked heads and muttered apologies that he would have accepted if they had waited.

Then he had realized, almost without warning, that this place was evil—the ducked heads, the muttered words, the hastening away. He saw in a burst of light that these people were hastening away from the Lord God Almighty. It was to the city that the prophets came and he was here in the midst of it. He was here enjoying what should have repelled him. His lids narrowed with caution and he looked at his uncle who was rolling on ahead of him, no more concerned with it all than a bear in the woods. "What kind of prophet are you?" the boy hissed.

His uncle paid him no attention, did not stop.

"Call yourself a prophet!" he continued in a high rasping carrying voice.

His uncle stopped and turned. "I'm here on bidnis," he said mildly.

"You always said you were a prophet," Tarwater said. "Now I see what kind of prophet you are. Elijah would think a heap of you."

His uncle thrust his head forward and his eyes began to bulge. "I'm here on bidnis," he said. "If you been called by the Lord, then be about your own mission."

The boy paled slightly and his gaze shifted. "I ain't been called *yet*," he muttered. "It's you that's been called."

"And I know what times I'm called and what times I ain't," his uncle said and turned and paid him no more attention.

At the lawyer's window, he knelt down and let his face hang out upsidedown over the floating speckled street moving like a river of tin below and watched the glints on it from the sun which drifted pale in a pale sky, too far away to ignite anything. When he was called, on that day when he returned, he would set the city astir, he would return with fire in his eyes. You have to do something particular here to make them look at you, he thought. They ain't going to look at you just because you're here. He considered his uncle with renewed disgust. When I come for good, he said to himself, I'll do something to make every eye stick on me, and leaning forward, he saw his new hat drop down gently, lost and casual, dallied slightly by the breeze on its way to be smashed in the tin river below. He clutched at his bare head and fell back inside the room.

His uncle was in argument with the lawyer, both hitting the desk that separated them, bending their knees and hitting their fists at the same time. The lawyer, a tall dome-headed man with an eagle's nose, kept repeating in a restrained shriek, "But I didn't make the will. I didn't make the law," and his uncle's gravel voice grated, "I can't help it. My daddy wouldn't have seen a fool inherit his property. That's not how he intended it."

"My hat is gone," Tarwater said.

The lawyer threw himself backwards into his chair and screaked it toward Tarwater and saw him without interest from pale blue eyes and screaked it forward again and said to his uncle, "There's nothing I can do. You're wasting your time and mine. You might as well resign yourself to this will."

"Listen," old Tarwater said, "at one time I thought I was finished, old and sick and about to die and no money, nothing, and I accepted his hospitality because he was my closest blood connection and you could have called it his duty to take me, only I thought it was Charity, I thought . . ."

"I can't help what you thought or did or what your connection thought or did," the lawyer said and closed his eyes.

"My hat fell," Tarwater said.

"I'm only a lawyer," the lawyer said, letting his glance rove over the lines of clay-colored books of law that fortressed his office.

"A car is liable to have run over it by now."

"Listen," his uncle said, "all the time he was studying me for this paper. Taking secret tests on me, his own kin, crawling into my soul through the back door and then says to me, 'uncle, you're a type that's almost extinct!' Almost extinct!" the old man piped barely able to force a thread of sound from his throat. "You see how extinct I am!"

The lawyer closed his eyes again and smiled into one cheek.

"Other lawyers," the old man growled and they had left and visited three more, without stopping, and Tarwater had counted eleven men who might have had on his hat or might not. Finally when they came out of the fourth lawyer's office, they sat down on the window ledge of a bank building and his uncle felt in his pocket for some biscuits he had brought and handed one to Tarwater. The old man unbuttoned his coat and allowed his stomach to ease forward and rest on his lap while he ate. His face worked wrathfully; the skin between the pockmarks appeared to jump from one spot to another. Tarwater was very pale and his eyes glittered with a peculiar hollow depth. He had an old work kerchief tied around his head, knotted at the four corners. He didn't observe the passing people who observed him now. "Thank God we're finished and can go home," he muttered.

"We ain't finished here," the old man said and got up abruptly and started down the street.

"My Lord!" the boy groaned, jumping to catch up with him. "Can't we sit down for one minute? Ain't you got any sense? They all tell you the same thing. It's only one law and it's nothing you can do about it. I got sense enough to get that; why ain't you? What's the matter with you?"

The old man strode on with his head thrust forward as if he were smelling out an enemy.

"Where we going?" Tarwater asked after they had walked out of the business streets and were passing between rows of grey bulbous houses with sooty porches that overhung the sidewalks. "Listen," he said, hitting at his uncle's hip, "I never ast to come."

"You would have ast to come soon enough," the old man muttered. "Get your fill now."

"I never ast for no fill. I never ast to come at all. I'm here before I knew this here was here."

"Just remember," the old man said, "just remember that I told you to remember when you ast to come that you never liked it when you were here," and they kept on going, crossing one length of sidewalk after another, row after row of overhanging houses with half-open doors that let a little dried light fall on the stained passageways inside. Finally they came out into another section where the houses were clean and squat and almost identical and each had a square of grass in front of it. After a few blocks Tarwater dropped down on the sidewalk and said, "I ain't going no further. I don't even know where I'm going and I ain't going no further." His uncle didn't stop or look back. In a second he jumped up and followed him again in a panic lest he be left.

The old man kept straining forward as if his blood scent were leading him closer and closer to the place where his enemy was hiding. He suddenly turned up the short walk of a pale yellow brick house and moved rigidly to the white door, his heavy shoulders hunched as if he were going to crash through it. He struck the wood with his fist, ignoring a polished brass knocker. At that instant Tarwater realized that this was where the schoolteacher lived, and he stopped where he was and remained rigid, his eye on the door. He knew by some obscure instinct that the door was going to open and reveal his destiny. In his mind's eye, he saw the schoolteacher about to appear in it, lean and evil, waiting to engage whom the Lord would send to conquer him. The boy clamped his teeth together to keep them from chattering. The door opened.

A small pink-faced boy stood in it with his mouth hung in a silly smile. He had white hair and a knobby forehead. He wore steel-rimmed spectacles and had pale silver eyes like the old man's except that they were clear and empty. He was gnawing on a brown apple core.

The old man stared at him, his lips parting slowly until his mouth hung open. He looked as if he beheld an unspeakable mystery. The little boy made an unintelligible noise and pushed the door almost shut, hiding himself all but one spectacled eye.

Suddenly a tremendous indignation seized Tarwater. He eyed the small face peering from the crack. He searched his mind fiercely for the right word to hurl at it. Finally he said in a slow emphatic voice, "Before you was here, *I* was here."

The old man caught his shoulder and pulled him back. "He don't have good sense," he said. "Can't you see he don't have good sense? He don't know what you're talking about."

The boy grew more furious than ever. He swung around on his heel to leave.

"Wait," his uncle said and caught him. "Get behind that hedge yonder and hide yourself. I'm going in there and baptize him."

Tarwater's mouth was agape.

"Get behind there like I told you," he said and gave him a push toward the hedge. Then the old man braced himself. He turned and went back to the door. Just as he reached it, it was flung open and a lean young man with heavy black-rimmed spectacles stood in it, his head thrust forward, glaring at him.

Old Tarwater raised his fist. "The Lord Jesus Christ sent me to baptize that boy!" he shouted. "Stand aside. I mean to do it!"

Tarwater's head popped up from behind the hedge. Breathlessly he took the schoolteacher in—the narrow boney face slanting backwards from the jutting jaw, the hair that receded from the high forehead, the eyes encircled in glass. The white-haired child had caught hold of his father's leg and was hanging onto it. The schoolteacher pushed him back inside the house. Then he stepped outside and slammed the door behind him and continued to glare at the old man as if he dared him to take a step.

"That boy cries out for his baptism," the old man said. "Precious in the sight of the Lord even an idiot!"

"Get off my property," the nephew said in a tight voice as if he were keeping it calm by force. "If you don't, I'll have you put back in the asylum where you belong."

"You can't touch the servant of the Lord!" the old man hollered.

"You get away from here!" the nephew shouted, losing control of his voice. "Ask the Lord why He made him an idiot in the first place, uncle. Tell him I want to know why!"

The boy's heart was beating so fast he was afraid it was going to gallop out of his chest and disappear forever. He was head and shoulders out of the shrubbery.

"Yours not to ask!" the old man shouted. "Yours not to question the mind of the Lord God Almighty. Yours not to grind the Lord into your head and spit out a number!"

"Where's the boy?" the nephew asked, looking around suddenly as if he had just thought of it. "Where's the boy you were going to raise into a prophet to burn my eyes clean?" and he laughed.

Tarwater lowered his head into the bush again, instantly disliking the schoolteacher's laugh which seemed to reduce him to the least importance.

"His day is going to come," the old man said. "Either him or me is going to baptize that child. If not me in my day, him in his."

"You'll never lay a hand on him," the schoolteacher said. "You could slosh water on him for the rest of his life and he'd still be an idiot. Five years old for all eternity, useless forever. Listen," he said, and the boy heard his taut voice turn low with a kind of subdued intensity, a passion equal and opposite to the old man's, "he'll never be baptized—just as a matter of principle, nothing else. As a gesture of human dignity, he'll never be baptized."

"Time will discover the hand that baptizes him," the old man said.

"Time will discover it," the nephew said and opened the door behind him and stepped back inside and slammed it on himself.

The boy had risen from the shrubbery, his head swirling with excitement. He had never been back there again, never seen his cousin again, never seen the schoolteacher again, and he hoped to God, he told the stranger digging the grave along with him now that he would never see him again though he had nothing against him himself and he would dislike to have to kill him but if he came out here, messing in what was none of his business except by law, then he would be obliged to.

Listen, the stranger said, what would he want to come out here for—where there's nothing?

Tarwater didn't answer. He didn't search out the stranger's face but he knew by now that it was sharp and friendly and wise, shadowed under a stiff broad-brimmed panama hat that obscured the color of his eyes. He had lost his dislike for the thought of the voice. Only every now and then it sounded like a stranger's voice to him. He began to feel that he was only just now meeting himself, as if as long as his uncle had lived, he had been deprived of his own acquaintance. I ain't denying the old man was a good one, his new friend said, but like you said: you can't be any poorer than dead. They have to take what they can get. His soul is off this mortal earth now and his body is not going to feel the pinch, of fire or anything else.

"It was the last day he was thinking of," Tarwater murmured.

Well now, the stranger said, don't you think any cross you set up in the year 1952 would be rotted out by the year the Day of Judgment comes in? Rotted to as much dust as his ashes if you reduced him to ashes? And lemme ast you this: what's God going to do with sailors drowned at sea that the fish have et and the fish that et them et by other fish and they et by yet others? And what about people that get burned up naturally in house fires? Burnt up one way or another or lost in machines until they're pulp? And all those sojers blasted to nothing? What about all those that there's nothing left of to burn or bury?

If I burnt him, Tarwater said, it wouldn't be natural, it would be deliberate.

Oh I see, the stranger said. It ain't the Day of Judgment for him you're worried about. It's the Day of Judgment for you.

That's my bidnis, Tarwater said.

I ain't buttin into your bidnis, the stranger said. It don't mean a thing to me. You're left by yourself in this empty place. Forever by yourself in this empty place with just as much light as that dwarf sun wants to let in. You don't mean a thing to a soul as far as I can see.

"Redeemed," Tarwater muttered.

Do you smoke? the stranger asked.

Smoke if I want to and don't if I don't, Tarwater said. Bury if need be and don't if don't.

Go take a look at him and see if he's fell off his chair, his friend suggested.

Tarwater let the shovel drop in the grave and returned to the house. He opened the front door a crack and put his face to it. His uncle glared slightly to the side of him like a judge intent upon some terrible evidence. The boy shut the door quickly and went back to the grave, cold in spite of the sweat that stuck his shirt to his back. He began digging again.

The schoolteacher was too smart for him, that's all, the stranger said presently. You remember well enough how he said he kidnapped him when the schoolteacher was seven years of age. Gone to town and persuaded him out of his own backyard and brought him out here and baptized him. And what come of it? Nothing. The schoolteacher don't care now if he's baptized or if he ain't. It don't mean a thing to him one way or the other. Don't care if he's Redeemed or not neither. He only spent four days out here; you've spent fourteen years and now got to spend the rest of your life.

You see he was crazy all along, he continued. Wanted to make a prophet out of that schoolteacher too, but the schoolteacher was too smart for him. He got away.

He had somebody to come for him, Tarwater said. His daddy came and got him back. Nobody came and got me back.

The schoolteacher himself come after you, the stranger said, and got shot in the leg and the ear for his trouble.

I was not yet one year old, Tarwater said. A baby can't walk off and leave.

You ain't a baby now, his friend said.

The grave did not appear to get any deeper though he continued to dig. Look at the big prophet, the stranger jeered, and watched him from the shade of the speckled tree shadows. Lemme hear you prophesy something. The truth is the Lord ain't studying about you. You ain't entered His Head.

Tarwater turned around abruptly and worked from the other side and the voice continued from behind him. Anybody that's a prophet has got to have somebody to prophesy to. Unless you're just going to prophesy to yourself, he amended—or go baptize that dim-witted child, he added in a tone of high sarcasm.

The truth is, he said after a minute, the truth is that you're just as smart, if you ain't actually smarter, than the schoolteacher. Because he had somebody—his daddy and his mother—to tell him the old man was crazy, whereas you ain't had anybody and yet you've figured it out for yourself. Of course, it's taken you longer, but you've come to the right conclusion: you know he was a crazy man even when he wasn't in the asylum, even those last years.

Or if he wasn't actually crazy, he was the same thing in a different way: he didn't have but one thing on his mind. He was a one-notion man. Jesus. Jesus this and Jesus that. Ain't you in all your fourteen years of supporting his foolishness fed up and sick to the roof of your mouth with Jesus? My Lord and Saviour, the stranger sighed, I am if you ain't.

After a pause he continued. The way I see it, he said, you can do one of two things. One of them, not both. Nobody can do both of two things without straining themselves. You can do one thing or you can do the opposite.

Jesus or the devil, the boy said.

No no no, the stranger said, there ain't no such thing as a devil. I can tell you that from my own self-experience. I know that for a fact. It ain't Jesus or the devil. It's Jesus or *you*.

Jesus or me, Tarwater repeated. He put the shovel down for a rest and thought: he said the schoolteacher was glad to come. He said all he had to do was go out in the schoolteacher's back yard where he was playing and say, Let's you and me go to the country for a while—you have to be born again. The Lord Jesus Christ sent me to see to it. And the schoolteacher got up and took hold of his hand without a word and came with him and all the four days while he was out here he said the schoolteacher was hoping they wouldn't come for him.

Well that's all the sense a seven-year-old boy's got, the stranger said. You can't expect no more from a child. He learned better as soon as he got back to town; his daddy told him the old man was crazy and not to believe a word of what all he had learnt him.

That's not the way he told it, Tarwater said. He said that when the schoolteacher was seven years old, he had good sense but later it dried up. His daddy was an ass and not fit to raise him and his mother was a whore. She ran away from here when she was eighteen years old.

It took her that long? the stranger said in an incredulous tone. My, she was kind of a ass herself.

My great-uncle said he hated to admit it that his own sister was a whore but he had to say it to say the truth, the boy said.

Shaw, you know yourself that it give him great satisfaction to admit she was a whore, the stranger said. He was always admitting somebody was an ass or a whore. That's all a prophet is good for—to admit somebody else is an ass or a whore. And anyway, he asked slyly, what do you know about whores? Where have you ever run up on one of them?

Certainly I know what one of them is, the boy said.

The Bible was full of them. He knew what they were and to what they were liable to come, and just as Jezebel was discovered by dogs, an arm here and a foot there, so said his great-uncle, it had almost been with his own mother and grandmother. The two of them, along with his grandfather, had been killed in an automobile crash, leaving only the schoolteacher alive in that family, and Tarwater himself, for his mother (unmarried and shameless) had lived just long enough after the crash for him to be born. He had been born at the scene of the wreck.

The boy was very proud that he had been born in a wreck. He had always felt that it set his existence apart from the ordinary one and he had understood from it that the plans of God for him were special, even though nothing of consequence had happened to him so far. Often when he walked in the woods and came upon some bush a little removed from the rest, his breath would catch in his throat and he would stop and wait for the bush to burst into flame. It had not done it yet.

His uncle had never seemed to be aware of the importance of the way he had been born, only of how he had been born again. He would often ask him why he thought the Lord had rescued him out of the womb of a whore and let him see the light of day at all, and then why, having done it once, He had gone and done it again, allowing him to be baptized by his great-uncle into the death of Christ, and then having done it twice, gone on and done it a third time, allowing him to be rescued by his great-uncle from the schoolteacher and brought to the backwoods and given a chance to be brought up according to the truth. It was because, his uncle said, the Lord meant him to be trained for a prophet, even though he was a bastard, and to take his great-uncle's place when he died. The old man compared their situation to that of Elijah and Elisha.

All right, the stranger said, I suppose you know what one of them is. But there's a heap else you don't know. You go ahead and put your feet in his shoes. Elisha after Elijah like he said. But just lemme ast you this: where is the voice of the Lord? I haven't heard it. Who's called you this morning? Or any morning? Have you been told what to do? You ain't even heard the sound of natural thunder this morning. There ain't a cloud in the sky. The trouble with you, I see, he concluded, is that you ain't got but just enough sense to believe every word he told you.

The sun was directly overhead, apparently dead still, holding its breath, waiting out the noontime. The grave was about two feet deep. Ten foot now, remember, the stranger said and laughed. Old men are selfish. You got to expect the least of them. The least of everybody, he added and let out a flat sigh that was like a gust of sand raised and dropped suddenly by the wind.

Tarwater looked up and saw two figures cutting across the field, a colored man and woman, each dangling an empty vinegar jug by a finger. The woman, tall and Indianlike, had on a green sun hat. She stooped under the fence without pausing and came on across the yard toward the grave; the man held the wire down and swung his leg over and followed at her elbow. They kept their eyes on the hole and stopped at the edge of it, looking down into the raw ground with shocked satisfied expressions. The man, Buford, had a crinkled face, darker than his hat. "Old man passed," he said.

The woman lifted her head and let out a slow sustained wail, piercing and formal. She set her jug down on the ground and crossed her arms and then lifted them in the air and wailed again.

"Tell her to shut up that," Tarwater said. "I'm in charge here now and I don't want no nigger-mourning."

"I seen his spirit for two nights," she said. "Seen him two nights and he was unrested."

"He ain't been dead but since this morning," Tarwater said. "If you all want your jugs filled, give them to me and dig while I'm gone."

"He'd been predicting his passing for many years," Buford said. "She seen him in her dream several nights and he wasn't rested. I known him well. I known him very well indeed."

"Poor sweet sugar boy," the woman said to Tarwater, "what you going to do here now by yourself in this lonesome place?"

"Mind my bidnis," the boy said, jerking the jug out of her hand. He started off so quickly that he almost fell. He stalked across the back field toward the rim of trees that surrounded the clearing.

The birds had gone into the deep woods to escape the noon sun and one thrush, hidden some distance ahead of him, called the same four notes again and again, stopping each time after them to make a silence. Tarwater began to walk faster, then he began to lope, and in a second he was running like something hunted, sliding down slopes waxed with pine needles and grasping the limbs of trees to pull himself, panting, up the slippery inclines. He crashed through a wall of honeysuckle and lept across a sandy near-dry stream bed and fell down against the high clay bank that formed the back wall of a cove where the old man kept his extra liquor hidden. He hid it in a hollow of the bank, covered with a large stone. Tarwater began to fight at the stone to pull it away, while the stranger stood over his shoulder panting, he was crazy! He was crazy! That's the long and short of it, he was crazy!

Tarwater got the stone away and pulled out a black jug and sat down against the bank with it. Crazy! the stranger hissed, collapsing by his side.

The sun appeared, a furious white, edging its way secretly behind the tops of the trees that rose over the hiding place.

A man, seventy years of age, to bring a baby out into the backwoods to raise him right! Suppose he had died when you were four years old instead of fourteen? Could you have toted mash to the still then and supported yourself? I never heard of no four-year-old running a still.

Never did I hear of that, he continued. You weren't anything to him but something that would grow big enough to bury him when the time came and now that he's dead, he's shut of you but you got two hundred and fifty pounds of him to put below the face of the earth. And don't think he wouldn't heat up like a coal stove to see you take a drop of liquor, he added. Though he had a weakness for it himself. When he couldn't stand the Lord one instant longer, he got drunk, prophet or no prophet. Hah. He might say it would hurt you but what he meant was you might get so much you wouldn't be in no fit condition to bury him. He said he brought you out here to raise you according to principle and that was the principle: that you should be fit when the time came to bury him so he would have a cross to mark where he was at.

A prophet with a still! He's the only prophet I ever heard of making liquor for a living.

After a minute he said in a softer tone as the boy took a long swallow from the black jug, well, a little won't interfere. Moderation never hurt no one.

A burning arm slid down Tarwater's throat as if the devil were already reaching inside him to finger his soul. He squinted at the angry sun creeping behind the topmost fringe of trees.

Take it easy, his friend said. Do you remember them nigger gospel singers you saw one time, all drunk, all singing, all dancing around that black Ford automobile? Jesus, they wouldn't have been near so glad they were Redeemed if they hadn't had that liquor in them. I wouldn't pay too much attention to my Redemption if I was you. Some people take everything too hard.

Tarwater drank more slowly. He had been drunk only one time before and that time his uncle had beat him with a piece of crate for it, saying liquor would dissolve a child's gut, another of his lies because his gut had not dissolved.

It should be clear to you, his kind friend said, how all your life you been tricked by that old man. You could have been a city slicker for the last fourteen years. Instead, you been deprived of any company but his, you been living in a two-story barn in the middle of this earth's bald patch, following behind a mule and plow since you were seven. And how do you know the education he give you is true to the facts? Maybe he taught you a system of figures nobody else uses? How do you know that two added to two makes four? Four added to four makes eight? Maybe other people don't think so. How do you know if there was an Adam or if Jesus eased your situation any when He redeemed you? Or how do you know if He actually done it? Nothing but that old man's word and it ought to be obvious to you by now that he was crazy. And as for Judgment Day, the stranger said, every day is Judgment Day.

Ain't you old enough to have learnt that yet for yourself? Don't everything you do, everything you have ever done, work itself out right or wrong before your eye and usually before the sun has set? Have you ever got by with anything? No you ain't nor ever thought you would. You might as well drink all that liquor since you've already drunk so much. Once you pass the moderation mark you've passed it, and that gyration you feel working down from the top of your brain, he said, that's the Hand of God laying a blessing on you. He has given you your release. That old man was the stone before your door and the Lord has rolled it away. He ain't rolled it quite far enough, of course. You got to finish up yourself but He's done the main part. Praise Him.

Tarwater had ceased to have any feeling in his legs. He dozed for a while, his head hanging to the side and his mouth open and the liquor trickling slowly down the side of his overalls where the jug had overturned in his lap. Eventually there was only a drip at the neck of the bottle, forming and filling and dropping, silent and measured and sun-colored. The bright even sky began to fade, coarsening with clouds until every shadow had gone in. He woke with a wrench forward, his eyes focusing and unfocusing on something that looked like a burnt rag hanging close to his face.

Buford said, "This ain't no way for you to act. Old man don't deserve this. There's no rest until the dead is buried." He was squatting on his heels, one hand gripped around Tarwater's arm. "I gone yonder to the door and seen him sitting there at the table, not even laid out on a cooling board. He ought to be laid out and have some salt on his bosom if you mean to keep him overnight."

The boy's lids pinched together to hold the image steady and in a second he made out two small red blistered eyes.

"He deserves to lie in a grave that fits him," Buford said. "He was deep in this life, he was deep in Jesus' misery."

"Nigger," the child said, working his strange swollen tongue, "take your hand off me."

Buford lifted his hand. "He needs to be rested," he said.

"He'll be rested all right when I get through with him," Tarwater said vaguely. "Go on and lea' me to my bidnis."

"Nobody going to bother you," Buford said, standing up. He waited a minute, bent, looking down at the limp figure sprawled against the bank. The boy's head was tilted backwards over a root that jutted out of the clay wall. His mouth hung open and his turned-up hat cut a straight line across his forehead, just over his half-open unseeing eyes. His cheekbones protruded, narrow and thin like the arms of a cross, and the hollows under them had an ancient look as if the child's skeleton beneath were as old as the world. "Nobody going to bother you," the Negro muttered, pushing through the wall of honeysuckle without looking back. "That going to be your trouble."

Tarwater closed his eyes again.

Some night bird complaining close by woke him up. It was not a screeching noise, only an intermittent hump-hump as if the bird had to recall his grievance each time before he repeated it. Clouds were moving convulsively across a black sky and there was a pink unsteady moon that appeared to be jerked up a foot or so and then dropped and jerked up again. This was because, as he observed in an instant, the sky was lowering, coming down fast to smother him. The bird screeched and flew off in time and Tarwater lurched into the middle of the stream bed and crouched on his hands and knees. The moon was reflected like pale fire in the few spots of water in the sand. He sprang at the wall of honeysuckle and began to tear through it, confusing the sweet familiar odor with the weight coming down on him. When he stood up on the other side, the black ground swung slowly and threw him down again. A flare of pink lightning lit the woods and he saw the black shapes of trees pierce out of the ground all around him. The night bird began to hump again from a thicket where he had settled.

He got up and began to move in the direction of the clearing, feeling his way from tree to tree, the trunks very cold and dry to his touch. There was distant thunder and a continuous flicker of pale lightning firing one section of woods and then another. Finally he saw the shack, standing gaunt-black and tall in the middle of the clearing, with the pink moon trembling directly over it. His eyes glittered like open pits of light as he moved across the sand, dragging his crushed shadow behind him. He didn't turn his head to that side of the yard where he had started the grave. He stopped at the far back corner of the house and squatted down on the ground and looked underneath at the litter there, chicken crates and barrels and old rags and boxes. He had a small box of wooden matches in his pocket.

He crawled under and began to set small fires, building one from another, and working his way out at the front porch, leaving the fire behind him eating greedily at the dry tinder and the floor boards of the house. He crossed the front side of the yard and went through the rutted field without looking back until he reached the edge of the opposite woods. Then he glanced over his shoulder and saw that the pink moon had dropped through the roof of the shack and was bursting and he began to run, forced on through the woods by two bulging silver eyes that grew in immense astonishment in the center of the fire behind him. He could hear it moving up through the black night like a whirling chariot.

Toward midnight he came out on the highway and caught a ride with a salesman who was a manufacturer's representative, selling copper flues throughout the Southeast, and who gave the silent boy what he said was the best advice he could give any young fellow setting out to find himself a place in the world.

While they sped forward on the black untwisting highway, watched on either side by a dark wall of trees, the salesman said that it had been his personal experience that you couldn't sell a copper flue to a man you didn't love. He was a thin fellow with a narrow face that appeared to have been worn down to the sharpest possible depressions. He wore a broad-brimmed stiff grey hat of the kind used by businessmen who would like to look like cowboys. He said love was the only policy that worked 95% of the time. He said when he went to sell a man a flue, he asked first about that man's wife's health and how his children were. He said he had a book that he kept the names of his customer's families in and what was wrong with them. A man's wife had cancer, he put her name down in the book and wrote *cancer* after it and inquired about her every time he went to that man's hardware store until she died; then he scratched out the word *cancer* and wrote *dead* there. "And I say thank God when they're dead," the salesman said; "that's one less to remember."

"You don't owe the dead anything," Tarwater said in a loud voice, speaking for almost the first time since he had got in the car.

"Nor they you," said the stranger. "And that's the way it ought to be in this world—nobody owing nobody nothing."

"Look," Tarwater said suddenly, sitting forward, his face close to the windshield, "we're headed in the wrong direction. We're going back where we came from. There's the fire again. There's the fire we left!"

Ahead of them in the sky there was a faint glow, steady, and not made by lightning. "That's the same fire we came from!" the boy said in a high voice.

"Boy, you must be nuts," the salesman said. "That's the city we're coming to. That's the glow from the city lights. I reckon this is your first trip anywhere."

"You're turned around," the child said; "it's the same fire."

The stranger twisted his rutted face sharply. "I've never been turned around in my life," he said. "And I didn't come from any fire. I come from Mobile. And I know where I'm going. What's the matter with you?"

Tarwater sat staring at the glow in front of him. "I was asleep," he muttered. "I'm just now waking up."

"You should have been listening to me," the salesman said. "I been telling you things you ought to know."

II

If the boy had actually trusted his new friend, Meeks, the copper flue salesman, he would have accepted Meeks' offer to take him directly to his uncle's door and let him out. Meeks had turned on the car light and told him to climb over onto the back seat and root around until he found the telephone book and when Tarwater had climbed back with it, he had showed him how to find his uncle's name in the book. Tarwater wrote the address and the telephone number down on the back of one of Meeks' cards. Meeks' telephone number was on the other side and he said any time Tarwater wanted to contact him for a little loan or any assistance, not to be afraid to use it. What Meeks had decided after about a half hour of the boy was that he was just enough off in the head and just ignorant enough to be a very hard worker, and he wanted a very ignorant energetic boy to work for him. But Tarwater was evasive. "I got to contact this uncle of mine, my only blood connection," he said.

Meeks could look at this boy and tell that he was running away from home, that he had left a mother and probably a sot-father and probably four or five brothers and sisters in a two-room shack set in a brush-swept bare-ground clearing just off the highway and that he was hightailing it for the big world, having first, from the way he reeked, fortified himself with stump liquor. He didn't for a minute believe he had any uncle at any such respectable address. He thought the boy had set his finger down on the name, Rayber, by chance and said, "That's him. A schoolteacher. My uncle."

"I'll take you right to his door," Meeks had said, fox-like. "We pass there going through town. We pass right by there."

"No," Tarwater said. He was sitting forward on the seat, looking out the window at a hill covered with old used-car bodies. In the indistinct darkness, they seemed to be drowning into the ground, to be about half-submerged already. The city hung in front of them on the side of the mountain as if it were a larger part of the same pile, not yet buried so deep. The fire had gone out of it and it appeared settled into its unbreakable parts.

The boy did not intend to go to the schoolteacher's until daylight and when he went he intended to make it plain that he had not come to be beholden or to be studied for a schoolteacher magazine. He began trying to remember the schoolteacher's face so that he could stare him down in his mind before he actually faced him. He felt that the more he could recall about him the less advantage the new uncle would have over him. The face had not been one that held together in his mind, though he remembered the sloping jaw and the black-rimmed glasses. What he could not picture were the eyes behind the glasses. He had no memory of them and there was every kind of contradiction in the rubble of his great-uncle's descriptions. Sometimes the old man had said the nephew's eyes were black and sometimes brown. The boy kept trying to find eyes that fit mouth, nose that fit chin, but every time he thought he had a face put together, it fell apart and he had to begin on a new one. It was as if the schoolteacher, like the devil, could take on any look that suited him.

Meeks was telling him about the value of work. He said that it had been his personal experience that if you wanted to get ahead, you had to work. He said this was the law of life and it was no way to get around it because it was inscribed on the human heart like love thy neighbor. He said these two laws were the team that worked together to make the world go round and that any individual who wanted to be a success and win the pursuit of happiness, that was all he needed to know.

The boy was beginning to see a consistent image for the schoolteacher's eyes and was not listening to this advice. He saw them dark grey, shadowed with knowledge, and the knowledge moved like tree reflections in a pond where far below the surface shadows a snake may glide and disappear. He had made a habit of catching his great-uncle in contradictions about the schoolteacher's appearance.

"I forget what color eyes he's got," the old man would say, irked. "What difference does the color make when I know the look? I know what's behind it."

"What's behind it?"

"Nothing. He's full of nothing."

"He knows a heap," the boy said. "I don't reckon it's anything he don't know."

"He don't know it's anything he can't know," the old man said. "That's his trouble. He thinks if it's something he can't know then somebody smarter than him can tell him about it and he can know it just the same. And if you were to go there, the first thing he would do would be to test your head and tell you what you were thinking and howcome you were thinking it and what you ought to be thinking instead. And before long you wouldn't belong to your self no more, you would belong to him."

The boy had no intention of allowing this to happen. He knew enough about the schoolteacher to be on his guard. He knew two complete histories, the history of the world, beginning with Adam, and the history of the schoolteacher, beginning with his mother, old Tarwater's own and only sister who had run away from Powderhead when she was eighteen years old and had become—the old man said he would mince no words, even with a child—a whore, until she had found a man by the name of Rayber who was willing to marry one. At least once a week, beginning at the beginning, the old man had reviewed this history through to the end.

His sister and this Rayber had brought two children into the world, one the schoolteacher and one a girl who had turned out to be Tarwater's mother and who, the old man said, had followed in the natural footsteps of her own mother, being already a whore by the time she was eighteen.

The old man had a great deal to say about Tarwater's conception, for the schoolteacher had told him that he himself had got his sister this first (and last) lover because he thought it would contribute to her *self-confidence*. The old man would say this, imitating the schoolteacher's voice and making it sillier than the boy felt it probably was. The old man was thrown into a fury of exasperation that there was not enough scorn in the world to cast upon this idiocy. Finally he would give up trying. The lover had shot himself after the accident, which was a relief to the schoolteacher for he wanted to bring up the baby himself.

The old man said that with the devil having such a heavy role in his beginning, it was little wonder that he should have an eye on the boy and keep him under close surveillance during his time on earth, in order that the soul he had helped call into being might serve him forever in hell. "You are the kind of boy," the old man said, "that the devil is always going to be offering to assist, to give you a smoke or a drink or a ride, and to ask you your bidnis. You had better mind how you take up with strangers. And keep your bidnis to yourself." It was to foil the devil's plans for him that the Lord had seen to his upbringing.

"What line you going to get into?" Meeks asked.

The boy didn't appear to hear.

Whereas the schoolteacher had led his sister into evil, with success, old Tarwater had made every attempt to lead his own sister to repentance, without success. Through one means or another, he had managed to keep up with her after she ran away from Powderhead; but even after she married, she would not listen to any word that had to do with her salvation. He had twice been thrown out of her house by her husband—each time with the assistance of the police because the husband was a man of no force—but the Lord had prompted him constantly to go back, even in the face of going to jail. When he could not get inside the house, he would stand outside it and shout and then she would let him in lest he attract the attention of the neighbors. The neighborhood children would gather to listen to him and she would have to let him in.

It was not to be wondered at, the old man would say, that the schoolteacher was no better than he was with such a father as he had. The man, an insurance salesman, wore a straw hat on the side of his head and smoked a cigar and when you told him his soul was in danger, he offered to sell you a policy against any contingency. He said he was a prophet too, a prophet of life insurance, for every right-thinking Christian, he said, knew that it was his Christian duty to protect his family and provide for them in the event of the unexpected. There was no use treating with him, the old man said; his brain was as slick as his eyeballs and the truth would no more soak into it than rain would penetrate tin. The schoolteacher, with Tarwater blood in him, at least had his father's strain diluted. "Good blood flows in his veins," the old man said. "And good blood knows the Lord and there ain't a thing he can do about having it. There ain't a way in the world he can get rid of it."

Meeks abruptly poked the boy in the side with his elbow. He said if it was one thing a person needed to learn it was to pay attention to older people than him when they gave him good advice. He said he himself had graduated from the School of Experience with an H.L.L. degree. He asked the boy if he knew what was an H.L.L. degree. Tarwater shook his head. Meeks said the H.L.L. degree was the Hard Lesson from Life degree. He said it was the quickest got and that it stayed learnt the longest.

The boy turned his head to the window.

One day the old man's sister had worked a perfidy on him. He had been in the habit of going on Wednesday afternoon because on that afternoon the husband played a golf game and he could find her alone. On this particular Wednesday, she did not open the door but he knew she was inside because he heard footsteps. He beat on the door a few times to warn her and when she wouldn't open it, he began to shout, for her and for all who would hear.

While he was telling this to Tarwater, he would jump up and begin to shout and prophesy there in the clearing the same way he had done it in front of her door. With no one to hear but the boy, he would flail his arms and roar, "Ignore the Lord Jesus as long as you can! Spit out the bread of life and sicken on honey. Whom work beckons, to work! Whom blood to blood! Whom lust to lust! Make haste, make haste. Fly faster and faster. Spin yourselves in a frenzy, the time is short! The Lord is preparing a prophet. The Lord is preparing a prophet with fire in his hand and eye and the prophet is moving toward the city with his warning. The prophet is coming with the Lord's message. 'Go warn the children of God,' saith the Lord, 'of the terrible speed of justice.' Who will be left? Who will be left when the Lord's mercy strikes?"

He might have been shouting to the silent woods that encircled them. While he was in his frenzy, the boy would take up the shotgun and hold it to his eye and sight along the barrel, but sometimes as his uncle grew more and more wild, he would lift his face from the gun for a moment with a look of uneasy alertness, as if while he had been inattentive, the old man's words had been dropping one by one into him and now, silent, hidden in his bloodstream, were moving secretly toward some goal of their own.

His uncle would prophesy until he exhausted himself and then he would fall with a thud on the swayback step and sometimes it would be five or ten minutes before he could go on and relate how the sister had worked the perfidy on him.

Whenever he came to this part of the story, his breath would at once come short as if he were struggling to run up a hill. His face would get redder and his voice thinner and sometimes it would give out completely and he would sit there on the step, beating the porch floor with his fist while he moved his lips and no sound came out. Finally he would pipe, "They grabbed me. Two. From behind. The door behind. Two."

His sister had had two men and a doctor behind the door, listening, and the papers made out to commit him to the asylum if the doctor thought he was crazy. When he understood what was happening, he had raged through her house like a blinded bull, everything crashing behind him, and it had taken two of them and the doctor and two neighbors to get him down. The doctor had said he was not only crazy but dangerous and they had taken him to the asylum in a strait jacket.

"Ezekiel was in the pit for forty days," he would say, "but I was in it for four years," and he would stop at that point and warn Tarwater that the servants of the Lord Jesus could expect the worse. The boy could see that this was so. But no matter how little they had now, his uncle said, their reward in the end was the Lord Jesus Himself, the bread of life!

The boy would have a hideous vision of himself sitting forever with his great-uncle on a green bank, full and sick, staring at a broken fish and a multiplied loaf.

His uncle had been in the asylum four years because it had taken him four years to understand that the way for him to get out was to stop prophesying on the ward. It had taken him four years to discover what the boy felt he himself would have discovered in no time at all. But at least in the asylum the old man had learned caution and when he got out, he put everything he had learned to the service of his cause. He proceeded about the Lord's business like an experienced crook. He had given the sister up but he intended to help her boy. He planned to kidnap the child and keep him long enough to baptize him and instruct him in the facts of his Redemption and he mapped out his plan to the last detail and carried it out exactly.

Tarwater liked this part best because in spite of himself he had to admire his uncle's craft. The old man had persuaded Buford Munson to send his daughter in to get a job cooking for the sister and with the girl once in the house, he had been able to find out what he needed to know. He learned that there were two children now instead of one and that his sister sat in her nightgown all day drinking whiskey out of a medicine bottle. While Luella Munson washed and cooked and took care of the children, his sister lay on the bed sipping from the bottle and reading books that she had to buy fresh every night from the drugstore. But the principal reason the kidnapping had been so easy was because his great-uncle had had the full cooperation of the schoolteacher himself, a thin boy with a boney pale face and a pair of gold-rimmed spectacles that were always falling down his nose.

The two of them, the old man said, had liked each other from the first. The day he had gone to do the kidnapping, the husband was away on business and the sister, shut up in her room with the bottle, didn't even know the time of day. All the old man had done was to walk in and tell Luella Munson that his nephew was going off to spend a few days with him in the country and then he had gone out to the back yard and spoken to the schoolteacher who had been digging holes and lining them with broken glass.

He and the schoolteacher had taken the train as far as the junction and had walked the rest of the way to Powderhead. The old man had explained to him that he was not taking him on this trip for pleasure but because the Lord had sent him to do it, to see that he was born again and instructed in his Redemption. All these facts were new to the schoolteacher, for his parents had never taught him anything, old Tarwater said, except not to wet the bed.

In four days the old man taught him what was necessary to know and baptized him. He made him understand that his true father was the Lord and not the simpleton in town and that he would have to lead a secret life in Jesus until the day came when he would be able to bring the rest of his family around to repentance. He had made him understand that on the last day it would be his destiny to rise in glory in the Lord Jesus. Since this was the first time anybody had bothered to tell these facts to the schoolteacher, he could not hear too much of them, and as he had never seen woods before or been in a boat or caught a fish or walked on roads that were not paved, they did all those things too and, his uncle said, he even allowed him to plow. His sallow face had become bright in four days. At this point Tarwater would begin to weary of the story.

The schoolteacher had spent four days in the clearing because his mother had not missed him for three days and when Luella Munson had mentioned where he had gone, she had to wait another day before his father came home and she could send him after the child. She would not come herself, the old man said, for fear the wrath of God would strike her at Powderhead and she would not be able to get back to the city again. She had wired the schoolteacher's father and when the simpleton arrived at the clearing, the schoolteacher was in despair at having to leave. The light had left his eyes. He had gone but the old man insisted that he had been able to tell by the look on his face that he would never be the same boy again.

"If he didn't say he didn't want to go, you can't be sure he didn't," Tarwater would say contentiously.

"Then why did he try to come back?" the old man asked. "Answer me that. Why one week later did he run away and try to find his way back and got his picture in the paper when the state patrol found him in the woods? I ask you why. Tell me that if you know so much."

"Because here was less bad than there," Tarwater said. "Less bad don't mean good, it only means better-than."

"He tried to come back," his uncle said slowly, emphasizing each word, "to hear more about God his Father, more about Jesus Christ Who had died to redeem him and more of the Truth I could tell him."

"Well go on," Tarwater would say irritably, "get on with the rest of it." The story always had to be taken to completion. It was like a road that the boy had travelled on so often that half the time he didn't look where they were going, and when at certain points he would become aware where they were, he would be surprised to see that the old man had not got farther on with it. Sometimes his uncle would lag at one point as if he didn't want to face what was coming and then when he finally came to it, he would try to get past it in a rush. At such points, Tarwater plagued him for details. "Tell about when he came when he was fourteen years old and had already decided none of it was true and he give you all that sass."

"Bah," the old man would say. "He was living in confusion. I don't say it was his fault then. They told him I was a crazy man. But I'll tell you one thing: he never believed them neither. They kept him from believing me but I kept him from believing them and he never took on none of their ways though he took on worse ones. And when he got shut of the three of them in that crash, nobody was gladder than he was. Then he turned his mind to raising you. Said he was going to give you every advantage, every advantage." The old man snorted. "You have me to thank for saving you from those advantages."

The boy looked off into the distance as though he were staring blankly at his invisible advantages.

"When he got shut of the three of them in that crash, this was the first place he came. On the very day they were killed he came out here to tell me. Straight out here. Yes sir," the old man said with the greatest satisfaction, "straight out here. He hadn't seen me in years but this is where he came. I was the one he came to. I was the one he wanted to see. Me. I had never left his mind. I had taken my seat in it."

"You skipped all that part about how he came when he was fourteen and give you all that sass," Tarwater said.

"It was sass he had got from them," the old man said. "Just parrot-mouthing all they had ever said about how I was a crazy man. The truth was even if they told him not to believe what I had taught him, he couldn't forget it. He never could forget that there was a chance that that simpleton was not his only father. I planted the seed in him and it was there for good. Whether anybody liked it or not."

"It fell amongst cockles," Tarwater said. "Say the sass."

"It fell in deep," the old man said, "or else after that crash he wouldn't have come out here hunting me."

"He only wanted to see if you were still crazy," the boy offered.

"The day may come," his great-uncle said slowly, "when a pit opens up inside you and you know some things you never known before," and he would give him such a prescient piercing look that the child would turn his face away, scowling fiercely.

His great-uncle had gone to live with the schoolteacher and as soon as he had got there, he had baptized Tarwater, practically under the schoolteacher's nose and the schoolteacher had made a blasphemous joke of it. But the old man could never tell this straight through. He always had to back up and tell why he had gone to live with the schoolteacher in the first place. He had gone for three reasons. One, he said, because he knew the schoolteacher wanted him. He was the only person in the schoolteacher's life who had ever taken two steps out of his way in his behalf. And two, because his nephew was the proper person to bury him and he wanted to have it understood with him how he wanted it done. And three, because the old man meant to see that Tarwater was baptized.

"I know all that," the boy would say, "get on with the rest of it."

"After the three of them perished and the house was his, he cleared it out," old Tarwater said. "He moved every stick of furniture out of it except a table and a chair or two and a bed or two and the crib he bought for you. Taken down all the pictures and all the curtains and taken up all the rugs. Even burned up all his mother's and sister's and the simpleton's clothes, didn't want a thing of theirs around. It wasn't anything left but books and papers that he had collected. Papers everywhere," the old man said. "Every room looked like the inside of a bird's nest. I came a few days after the crash and when he saw me standing there, he was glad to see me. His eyes lit up. He was glad to see me. 'Ha,' he said, 'my house is swept and garnished and here are the seven other devils, all rolled into one!'" The old man slapped his knee with pleasure.

"It don't sound to me like . . ."

"No, he didn't say so," the uncle said, "but I ain't an idiot."

"If he didn't say so you can't be sure."

"I'm as sure," his uncle said, "as I am that this here," and he held up his hand, every short thick finger stretched rigid in front of Tarwater's face, "is my hand and not yours." There was something final in this that always made the boy's impudence subside.

"Well get on with it," he would say. "If you don't make haste, you'll never get to where he blasphemed at."

"He was glad to see me," his uncle said. "He opened the door with all that house full of paper-trash behind him and there I stood and he was glad to see me. It was all underneath his face."

"What did he say?" Tarwater asked.

"He looked at my satchel," the old man said, "and he said, 'Uncle, you can't live with me. I know exactly what you want but I'm going to raise this child my way.'"

These words of the schoolteacher's had always caused a quick charge of excitement to race through Tarwater, an almost sensuous satisfaction. "It might have sounded to you like he was glad to see you," he said. "It don't sound that way to me."

"He wasn't but twenty-four years old," the old man said. "His expression hadn't even set on his face yet. I could still see the seven-year-old boy that had gone off with me, except that now he had a pair of black-rimmed glasses and a nose big enough to hold them up. The size of his eyes had shrunk because his face had grown but it was the same face all right. You could see behind it to what he really wanted to say. When he came out here later to get you back after I had stolen you, it was already set. It was as set then as the outside of a penitentiary but not now when I'm telling you about. Then it wasn't set and I could see he wanted me. Else why had he come out to Powderhead to tell me they were all dead? I ask you that? He could have let me alone."

The boy couldn't answer.

"Anyway," the old man said, "what all he gone on and done proved he wanted me right then because he took me in. He looked at my satchel and I said, 'I'm on your charity,' and he said, 'I'm sorry, Uncle. You can't live with me and ruin another child's life. This one is going to be brought up to live in the real world. He's going to be brought up to expect exactly what he can do for himself. He's going to be his own saviour. He's going to be free!'" The old man turned his head to the side and spit. "Free," he said. "He was full of such-like phrases. But then I said it. I said what changed his mind."

The boy sighed at this. The old man considered it his master stroke. He had said, "I never come to live with you. I come to die!"

"And you should have seen his face," he said. "He looked like he'd been pushed all of a sudden from behind. He hadn't cared if the other three were wiped out but when he thought of me going, it was like he was losing somebody for the first time. He stood there staring at me." And once, only once, the old man had leaned forward and said to Tarwater, in a voice that could no longer contain the pleasure of its secret, "He loved me like a daddy and he was ashamed of it!"

The boy's face had remained unmoved. "Yes," he said, "and you had told him a bare-face lie. You never had no intention of dying."

"I was sixty-nine years of age," his uncle said. "I could have died the next day as well as not. No man knows the hour of his death. I didn't have my life in front of me. It was not a lie, it was only a speculation. I told him, I said, 'I may live two months or two days.' And I had on my clothes that I bought to be buried in—all new."

"Ain't it that same suit you got on now?" the boy asked indignantly, pointing to the threadbare knee. "Ain't it that one you got on yourself right now?"

"I may live two months or two days, I said to him," his uncle said.

Or ten years or twenty, Tarwater thought.

"Oh it was a shock to him," the old man said.

It might have been a shock, the boy thought, but he wasn't all that sorry about it. The schoolteacher had merely said, "So I'm to put you away, Uncle? All right, I'll put you away. I'll do it with pleasure. I'll put you away for good and all," but the old man insisted that his words were one thing and his actions and the look on his face another.

His great-uncle had not been in the nephew's house ten minutes before he had baptized Tarwater. They had gone into the room where the crib was with Tarwater in it and as the old man looked at him for the first time—a wizened grey-faced scrawny sleeping baby—the voice of the Lord had come to him and said: HERE IS THE PROPHET TO TAKE YOUR PLACE. BAPTIZE HIM.

That? the old man had asked, that wizened grey-faced . . . and then as he wondered how he could baptize him with the nephew standing there, the Lord had sent the paper boy to knock on the door and the schoolteacher had gone to answer it.

When he came back in a few minutes, his uncle was holding Tarwater in one hand and with the other he was pouring water over his head out of the bottle that had been on the table by the crib. He had pulled off the nipple and stuck it in his pocket. He was just finishing the words of baptism as the schoolteacher came back in the door and he had had to laugh when he looked up and saw his nephew's face. It looked hacked, the old man said. Not even angry at first, just hacked.

Old Tarwater had said, "He's been born again and there ain't a thing you can do about it," and then he had seen the rage rise in the nephew's face and had seen him try to conceal it.

"Time has passed you by, Uncle," the nephew said. "That can't even irritate me. That only makes me laugh," and he laughed, a short forced bark, but the old man said his face was mottled. "Just as well you did it now," he said. "If you had got me when I was seven days instead of seven years, you might not have ruined my life."

"If it's ruined," the old man said, "it wasn't me that ruined it."

"Oh yes it was," the nephew said, advancing across the room, his face very red. "You're too blind to see what you did to me. A child can't defend himself. Children are cursed with believing. You pushed me out of the real world and I stayed out of it until I didn't know which was which. You infected me with your idiot hopes, your foolish violence. I'm not always myself, I'm not al . . ." but he stopped. He wouldn't admit what the old man knew. "There's nothing wrong with me," he said. "I've straightened the tangle you made. Straightened it by pure will power. I've made myself straight."

"You see," the old man said, "he admitted himself the seed was still in him."

Old Tarwater had laid the baby back in the crib but the nephew took him out again, a peculiar smile, the old man said, stiffening on his face. "If one baptism is good, two will be better," he said and he had turned Tarwater over and poured what was left in the bottle over his bottom and said the words of baptism again.

Old Tarwater had stood there, aghast at this blasphemy. "Now Jesus has a claim on both ends," the nephew said.

The old man had roared, "Blasphemy never changed a plan of the Lord's!"

"And the Lord hasn't changed any of mine either," said the nephew coolly and put the baby back.

"And what did I do?" Tarwater asked.

"You didn't do nothing," the old man said as if what he did or didn't do was of no consequence whatsoever.

"It was me that was the prophet," the boy said sullenly.

"You didn't even know what was going on," his uncle said.

"Oh yes I did," the child said. "I was laying there thinking."

His uncle would ignore this and go on. He had thought for a while that by living with the schoolteacher, he might convince him again of all that he had convinced him of when he had kidnapped him as a child and he had had hope of it up until the time when the schoolteacher showed him the study he had written of him for the magazine. Then the old man had realized at last that there was no hope of his doing anything for the schoolteacher. He had failed the schoolteacher's mother and he had failed the schoolteacher, and now there was nothing to do but try to save Tarwater from being brought up by a fool. In this he had not failed.

The boy felt that the schoolteacher could have made more of an effort to get him back. He had come out and got shot in the leg and the ear but if he had used his head, he might have avoided that and got him back at the same time. "Why didn't he bring the law out here and get me back?" he had asked.

"You want to know why?" his uncle said. "Well I'll tell you why. I'll tell you exactly why. It was because he found you a heap of trouble. He wanted it all in his head. You can't change a child's pants in your head."

The boy would think: but if the schoolteacher hadn't written that piece on him, we might all three be living in town right now.

When the old man had read the piece in the schoolteacher magazine, he had at first not recognized who it was the schoolteacher was writing about, who the type was that was almost extinct. He had sat down to read the piece, full of pride that his nephew had succeeded in having a composition printed in a magazine. He had handed it carelessly to his uncle and said he might want to glance over it and the old man had sat down at once at the kitchen table and commenced to read it. He recalled that the schoolteacher had kept passing by the kitchen door to witness how he was taking the piece.

About the middle of it, old Tarwater had begun to think that he was reading about someone he had once known or at least someone he had dreamed about, for the figure was strangely familiar. "This fixation of being called by the Lord had its origin in insecurity. He needed the assurance of a call and so he called himself," he read. The schoolteacher kept passing by the door, passing and repassing, and finally he came in and sat down quietly on the other side of the small white metal table. When the old man looked up, the schoolteacher smiled. It was a very slight smile, the slightest that would do for any occasion. The old man knew from the smile who it was he had been reading about.

For the length of a minute, he could not move. He felt he was tied hand and foot inside the schoolteacher's head, a space as bare and neat as the cell in the asylum, and was shrinking, drying up to fit it. His eyeballs swerved from side to side as if he were pinned in a strait jacket again. Jonah, Ezekiel, Daniel, he was at that moment all of them—the swallowed, the lowered, the enclosed.

The nephew, his smile still fixed, reached across the table and put his hand on the old man's wrist in a gesture of pity. "You've got to be born again, Uncle," he said, "by your own efforts, back to the real world where there's no saviour but yourself."

The old man's tongue lay in his mouth like a stone but his heart began to swell. His prophet's blood surged in him, surged to floodtide for a miraculous release, though his face remained shocked, expressionless. The nephew patted his huge clenched fist and got up and left the kitchen, bearing away his smile of triumph.

The next morning when he went to the crib to give the baby his bottle, he found nothing in it but the blue magazine with the old man's message scrawled on the back of it: THE PROPHET I RAISE UP OUT OF THIS BOY WILL BURN YOUR EYES CLEAN.

"It was me could act," the old man said, "not him. He could never take action. He could only get everything inside his head and grind it to nothing. But I acted. And because I acted, you sit here in freedom, you sit here a rich man, knowing the Truth, in the freedom of the Lord Jesus Christ."

The boy would move his thin shoulder blades irritably as if he were shifting the burden of Truth like a cross on his back. "He came out here and got shot to get me back," he said obstinately.

"If he had really wanted you back, he could have got you," the old man said. "He could have had the law out here after me or got me put back in the asylum. There was plenty he could have done, but what happened to him was that welfare-woman. She persuaded him to have one of his own and let you go, and he was easy persuaded. And that one," the old man would say, beginning to brood on the schoolteacher's child again, "that one—the Lord gave him one he couldn't corrupt." And then he would grip the boy's shoulder and put a fierce pressure on it. "And if I don't get him baptized, it'll be for you to do," he said. "I enjoin you to do it, boy."

Nothing irritated the boy so much as this. "I take my orders from the Lord," he would say in an ugly voice, trying to pry the fingers out of his shoulder. "Not from you."

"The Lord will give them to you," the old man said, gripping his shoulder tighter.

"He had to change that one's pants and he done it," Tarwater muttered.

"He had the welfare-woman to do it for him," his uncle said. "She had to be good for something, but you can bet she ain't still around there. Bernice Bishop!" he said as if he found this the most idiotic name in the language. "Bernice Bishop!"

The boy had sense enough to know that he had been betrayed by the schoolteacher and he did not mean to go to his house until daylight, when he could see behind and before him. "I ain't going there until daylight," he said suddenly to Meeks. "You needn't to stop there because I ain't getting out there."

Meeks leaned casually against the door of the car, driving with half his attention and giving the other half to Tarwater. "Son," he said, "I'm not going to be a preacher to you. I'm not going to tell you not to lie. I ain't going to tell you nothing impossible. All I'm going to tell you is this: don't lie when you don't have to. Else when you do have to, nobody'll believe you. You don't have to lie to me. I know exactly what you done." A shaft of light plunged through the car window and he looked to the side and saw the white face beside him, staring up with soot-colored eyes.

"How do you know?" the boy asked.

Meeks smiled with pleasure. "Because I done the same thing myself once," he said.

Tarwater caught hold of the sleeve of the salesman's coat and gave it a quick pull. "On the Day of Judgment," he said, "me and you will rise and say we done it!"

Meeks looked at him again with one eyebrow cocked at the same angle he wore his hat. "Will we?" he asked. Then he said, "What line you gonna get into, boy?"

"What line?"

"What you going to do? What kind of *work*?"

"I know everything but the machines," Tarwater said, sitting back again. "My great-uncle learnt me everything but first I have to find out how much of it is true." They were entering the dilapidated outskirts of the city where wooden buildings leaned together and an occasional dim light lit up a faded sign advertising some remedy or other.

"What line was your great-uncle in?" Meeks asked.

"He was a prophet," the boy said.

"Is that right?" Meeks asked and his shoulders jumped several times as if they were going to leap over his head. "Who'd he prophesy to?"

"To me," Tarwater said. "Nobody else would listen to him and there wasn't anybody else for me to listen to. He grabbed me away from this other uncle, my only blood connection now, so as to save me from running to doom."

"You were a captive audience," Meeks said. "And now you're coming to town to run to doom with the rest of us, huh?"

The boy didn't answer at once. Then he said in a guarded tone, "I ain't said what I'm going to do."

"You ain't sure about what all this great-uncle of yours told you, are you?" Meeks asked. "You figure he might have got aholt to some misinformation."

Tarwater looked away, out the window, at the brittle forms of the houses. He was holding both arms close to his sides as if he were cold. "I'll find out," he said.

"Well how now?" Meeks asked.

The dark city was unfolding on either side of them and they were approaching a low circle of light in the distance. "I mean to wait and see what happens," he said after a moment.

"And suppose nothing don't happen?" Meeks asked.

The circle of light became huge and they swung into the center of it and stopped. It was a gaping concrete mouth with two red gas pumps set in front of it and a small glass office toward the back. "I say suppose nothing don't happen?" Meeks repeated.

The boy looked at him darkly, remembering the silence after his great-uncle's death.

"Well?" Meeks said.

"Then I'll make it happen," he said. "I can act."

"Attaboy," Meeks said. He opened the car door and put his leg out while he continued to observe his rider. Then he said, "Wait a minute. I got to call my girl."

A man was asleep in a chair tilted against the outside wall of the glass office and Meeks went inside without waking him up. For a minute Tarwater only craned his neck out the window. Then he got out and went to the office door to watch Meeks use the machine. It sat, small and black, in the center of a cluttered desk which Meeks sat down on as if it had been his own. The room was lined with automobile tires and had a concrete and rubber smell. Meeks took the machine in two parts and held one part to his head while he circled with his finger on the other part. Then he sat waiting, swinging his foot, while the horn buzzed in his ear. After a minute an acid smile began to eat at the corners of his mouth and he said, drawing in his breath, "Heythere, Sugar, hyer you?" and Tarwater, from where he stood in the door, heard an actual woman's voice, like one coming from beyond the grave, say, "Why Sugar, is that reely you?" and Meeks said it was him in the same old flesh and made an appointment with her in ten minutes.

Tarwater stood awestruck in the doorway. Meeks put the telephone together and then he said in a sly voice, "Now why don't you call your uncle?" and watched the boy's face change, the eyes swerve suspiciously to the side and the flesh drop around the boney mouth.

"I'll speak with him soon enough," he muttered, but he kept looking at the black coiled machine, fascinated. "How do you use it?" he asked.

"You dial it like I did. Call your uncle," Meeks urged.

"No, that woman is waiting on you," Tarwater said.

"Let 'er wait," Meeks said. "That's what she knows how to do best."

The boy approached it, taking out the card he had written the number on. He put his finger on the dial and began gingerly to turn it.

"Great God," Meeks said and took the receiver off the hook and put it in his hand and thrust his hand to his ear. He dialed the number for him and then pushed him down in the office chair to wait but Tarwater stood up again, slightly crouched, holding the buzzing horn to his head, while his heart began to kick viciously at his chest wall.

"It don't speak," he murmured.

"Give him time," Meeks said, "maybe he don't like to get up in the middle of the night."

The buzzing continued for a minute and then stopped abruptly. Tarwater stood speechless, holding the earpiece tight against his head, his face rigid as if he were afraid that the Lord might be about to speak to him over the machine. All at once he heard what sounded like heavy breathing in his ear.

"Ask for your party," Meeks prompted. "How do you expect to get your party if you don't ask for him?"

The boy remained exactly as he was, saying nothing.

"I told you to ask for your party," Meeks said irritably. "Ain't you got good sense?"

"I want to speak with my uncle," Tarwater whispered.

There was a silence over the telephone but it was not a silence that seemed to be empty. It was the kind where the breath is drawn in and held. Suddenly the boy realized that it was the schoolteacher's child on the other side of the machine. The white-haired, blunted face rose before him. He said in a furious shaking voice, "I want to speak with my uncle. Not you!"

The heavy breathing began again as if in answer. It was a kind of bubbling noise, the kind of noise someone would make who was struggling to breathe in water. In a second it faded away.

The horn of the machine dropped out of Tarwater's hand. He stood there blankly as if he had received a revelation he could not yet decipher. He seemed to have been stunned by some deep internal blow that had not yet made its way to the surface of his mind.

Meeks picked up the earpiece and listened but there was no sound. He put it back on the hook and said, "Come on. I ain't got this kind of time." He gave the stupefied boy a shove and they left, driving off into the city again. Meeks told him to learn to work every machine he saw. The greatest invention of man, he said, was the wheel and he asked Tarwater if he had ever thought how things were before it was a wheel, but the boy didn't answer him. He didn't even appear to be listening. He sat slightly forward and from time to time his lips moved as if he were speaking silently with himself.

"Well, it was terrible," Meeks said sourly. He knew the boy didn't have any uncle at any such respectable address and to prove it, he turned down the street the uncle was supposed to live on and drove slowly past the small shapes of squat houses until he found the number, visible in phosphorescent letters on a small stick set on the edge of the grass plot. He stopped the car and said, "Okay, kiddo, that's it."

"That's what?" Tarwater mumbled.

"That's your uncle's house," Meeks said.

The boy grabbed the edge of the window with both hands and stared out at what appeared to be only a black shape crouched in a greater darkness a little distance away. "I told you I wasn't going there until daylight," he said angrily, "go on."

"You're going there right now," Meeks said. "Because I ain't getting stuck with you. You can't go with me where I'm going."

"I ain't getting out here," the boy said.

Meeks reached across him and opened the car door. "So long, son," he said, "if you get real hungry by next week, you can contack me from that card and we might make a deal."

The boy gave him one white-faced outraged look and flung himself from the car. He moved up the short concrete walk to the doorstep and sat down abruptly, absorbed into the darkness. Meeks pulled the car door shut. His face hung for a moment watching the barely visible outline of the boy's shape on the step.

Then he drew back and drove on. He won't come to no good end, he said to himself.

III

Tarwater sat in the corner of the doorstep, scowling in the dark as the car disappeared down the block. He did not look up at the sky but he was unpleasantly aware of the stars. They seemed to be holes in his skull through which some distant unmoving light was watching him. It was as if he were alone in the presence of an immense silent eye. He had an intense desire to make himself known to the schoolteacher at once, to tell him what he had done and why and to be congratulated by him. At the same time, his deep suspicion of the man continued to work in him. He tried to bring the schoolteacher's face again to mind, but all he could manage was the face of the seven-year-old boy the old man had kidnapped. He stared at it boldly, hardening himself for the encounter.

Then he rose and faced the heavy brass knocker on the door. He touched it and jerked his hand away, burnt by a metallic coldness. He looked quickly over his shoulder. The houses across the street formed a dark jagged wall. The quiet seemed palpable, waiting. It seemed almost to be waiting patiently, biding its time until it should reveal itself and demand to be named. He turned back to the cold knocker and grabbed it and shattered the silence as if it were a personal enemy. The noise filled his head. He was aware of nothing but the racket he was making.

He beat louder and louder, bamming at the same time with his free fist until he felt he was shaking the house. The empty street echoed with his blows. He stopped once to get his breath and then began again, kicking the door frenziedly with the blunt toe of his heavy work shoe. Nothing happened. Finally he stopped and the implacable silence descended around him, immune to his fury. A mysterious dread filled him. His whole body felt hollow as if he had been lifted like Habakkuk by the hair of his head, borne swiftly through the night and set down in the place of his mission. He had a sudden foreboding that he was about to step into a trap laid for him by the old man. He half-turned to run.

At once the glass panels on either side of the door filled with light. There was a click and the knob turned. Tarwater jerked his hands up automatically as if he were pointing an invisible gun and his uncle, who had opened the door, jumped back at the sight of him.

The image of the seven-year-old boy disappeared forever from Tarwater's mind. His uncle's face was so familiar to him that he might have seen it every day of his life. He steadied himself and shouted, "My great-uncle is dead and burnt, just like you would have burnt him yourself!"

The schoolteacher remained absolutely still as if he thought that by looking long enough his hallucination would disappear. He had been roused by the vibration in the house and had run, half-asleep, to the door. His face was like the face of a sleep-walker who wakes and sees some horror of his dreams take shape before him. After a moment he muttered, "Wait here, deaf," and turned and went quickly out of the hall. He was barefooted and in his pajamas. He came back almost at once, plugging something into his ear. He had thrust on the black-rimmed glasses and he was sticking a metal box into the waist-band of his pajamas. This was joined by a cord to the plug in his ear. For an instant the boy had the thought that his head ran by electricity. He caught Tarwater by the arm and pulled him into the hall under a lantern-shaped light that hung from the ceiling. The boy found himself scrutinized by two small drill-like eyes set in the depths of twin glass caverns. He drew away. Already he felt his privacy imperilled.

"My great-uncle is dead and burnt," he said again. "I was the only one there to do it and I done it. I done your work for you," and as he said the last, a perceptible trace of scorn crossed his face.

"Dead?" the schoolteacher said. "My uncle? The old man's dead?" he asked in a blank unbelieving tone. He caught Tarwater abruptly by the arms and stared into his face. In the depths of his eyes, the boy, shocked, saw an instant's stricken look, plain and awful. It vanished at once. The straight line of the schoolteacher's mouth began turning into a smile. "And how did he go—with his fist in the air?" he asked. "Did the Lord arrive for him in a chariot of fire?"

"He didn't have no warning," Tarwater said, suddenly breathless. "He was eating his breakfast and I never moved him from the table. I set him on fire where he was and the house with him."

The schoolteacher said nothing but the boy read in his look a doubt that this had happened, a suspicion that he dealt with an interesting liar.

"You can go there and see for yourself," Tarwater said. "He was too big to bury. I done it the quickest way."

His uncle's eyes had the look now of being trained on a fascinating problem. "How did you get here? How did you know this was where you belonged?" he asked.

The boy had expended all his energy announcing himself. He was suddenly blank and stunned and he remained stupidly silent. He had never been this tired before. He felt he was about to fall.

The schoolteacher waited, searching his face impatiently. Then his expression changed again. He tightened his grip on Tarwater's arm and his eyes turned, glowering, toward the front door, which was still open. "Is he out there?" he asked in a low enraged voice. "Is this one of his tricks? Is he out there waiting to sneak in a window and baptize Bishop while you're here baiting me? Is that his senile game this time?"

The boy blanched. In his mind's eye he saw the old man, a dark shape standing behind the corner of the house, restraining his wheezing breath while he waited impatiently for him to baptize the dim-witted child. He stared shocked at the schoolteacher's face. There was a wedge-shaped gash in his new uncle's ear. The sight of it brought old Tarwater so close that the boy thought he could hear him laugh. With a terrible clarity he saw that the schoolteacher was no more than a decoy the old man had set up to lure him to the city to do his unfinished business.

His eyes began to burn in his fierce fragile face. A new energy seized him. "He's dead," he said. "You can't be any deader than he is. He's reduced to ashes. He don't even have a cross set up over him. If it's anything left of him, the buzzards wouldn't have it and the bones the dogs'll carry off. That's how dead he is."

The schoolteacher winced, but almost at once he was smiling again. He held Tarwater's arms tightly and peered into his face as if he were beginning to see a solution, one that intrigued him with its symmetry and rightness. "It's a perfect irony," he murmured, "a perfect irony that you should have taken care of the matter in that way. He got what he deserved."

The boy's pride swelled. "I done the needful," he said.

"Everything he touched he warped," the schoolteacher said. "He lived a long and useless life and he did you a great injustice. It's a blessing he's dead at last. You could have had everything and you've had nothing. All that can be changed now. Now you belong to someone who can help you and understand you." His eyes were alight with pleasure. "It's not too late for me to make a man of you!"

The boy's face darkened. His expression hardened until it was a fortress wall to keep his thoughts from being exposed; but the schoolteacher did not notice any change. He gazed through the actual insignificant boy before him to an image of him that he held fully developed in his mind.

"You and I will make up for lost time," he said. "We'll get you started now in the right direction."

Tarwater was not looking at him. His neck had suddenly snapped forward and he was staring straight ahead over the schoolteacher's shoulder. He heard a faint familiar sound of heavy breathing. It was closer to him than the beating of his own heart. His eyes widened and an inner door in them opened in preparation for some inevitable vision.

The small white-haired boy shambled into the back of the hall and stood peering forward at the stranger. He had on the bottoms to a pair of blue pajamas drawn up as high as they would go, the string tied over his chest and then again, harness-like, around his neck to keep them on. His eyes were slightly sunken beneath his forehead and his cheekbones were lower than they should have been. He stood there, dim and ancient, like a child who had been a child for centuries.

Tarwater clenched his fists. He stood like one condemned, waiting at the spot of execution. Then the revelation came, silent, implacable, direct as a bullet. He did not look into the eyes of any fiery beast or see a burning bush. He only knew, with a certainty sunk in despair, that he was expected to baptize the child he saw and begin the life his great-uncle had prepared him for. He knew that he was called to be a prophet and that the ways of his prophecy would not be remarkable. His black pupils, glassy and still, reflected depth on depth his own stricken image of himself, trudging into the distance in the bleeding stinking mad shadow of Jesus, until at last he received his reward, a broken fish, a multiplied loaf. The Lord out of dust had created him, had made him blood and nerve and mind, had made him to bleed and weep and think, and set him in a world of loss and fire all to baptize one idiot child that He need not have created in the first place and to cry out a gospel just as foolish. He tried to shout, "NO!" but it was like trying to shout in his sleep. The sound was saturated in silence, lost.

His uncle put a hand on his shoulder and shook him slightly to penetrate his inattention. "Listen boy," he said, "getting out from under the old man is just like coming out of the darkness into the light. You're going to have a chance now for the first time in your life. A chance to develop into a useful man, a chance to use your talents, to do what you want to do and not what he wanted—whatever idiocy it was."

The boy's eyes were focussed beyond him, the pupils dilated. The schoolteacher turned his head to see what it was that was keeping him from being responsive. His own face tightened. The little boy was creeping forward, grinning.

"That's only Bishop," he said. "He's not all right. Don't mind him. All he can do is stare at you and he's very friendly. He stares at everything that way." His hand tightened on the boy's shoulder and his mouth stretched painfully. "All the things that I would do for him—if it were any use—I'll do for you," he said. "Now do you see why I'm so glad to have you here?"

The boy heard nothing he said. The muscles in his neck stood out like cables. The dim-witted child was not five feet from him and was coming every instant closer with his lop-sided smile. Suddenly he knew that the child *recognized* him, that the old man himself had primed him from on high that here was the forced servant of God come to see that he was born again. The little boy was sticking out his hand to touch him.

"Git!" Tarwater screamed. His arm shot out like a whip and knocked the hand away. The child let out a bellow startlingly loud. He clambered up his father's leg, pulling himself up by the schoolteacher's pajama coat until he was almost on his shoulder.

"All right, all right," the schoolteacher said, "there, there, shut up, it's all right, he didn't mean to hit you," and he righted the child on his back and tried to slide him off but the little boy hung on, thrusting his head against his father's neck and never taking his eyes off Tarwater.

The boy had a vision of the schoolteacher and his child as inseparably joined. The schoolteacher's face was red and pained. The child might have been a deformed part of himself that had been accidentally revealed.

"You'll get used to him," he said.

"No!" the boy shouted.

It was like a shout that had been waiting, straining to burst out. "I won't get used to him! I won't have anything to do with him!" He clenched his fist and lifted it. "I won't have anything to do with him!" he shouted and the words were clear and positive and defiant like a challenge hurled in the face of his silent adversary.

TWO

IV

After four days of Tarwater, the schoolteacher's enthusiasm had passed. He would admit no more than that. It had passed the first day and had been succeeded by determination, and while he knew that determination was a less powerful tool, he thought that in this case, it was the one best fitted for the job. It had taken him barely half a day to find out that the old man had made a wreck of the boy and that what was called for was a monumental job of reconstruction. The first day enthusiasm had given him energy but ever since, determination had exhausted him.

Although it was only eight o'clock in the evening, he had put Bishop to bed and had told the boy that he could go to his room and read. He had bought him books, among other things still ignored. Tarwater had gone to his room and had closed the door, not saying whether he intended to read or not, and Rayber was in bed for the night, lying too exhausted to sleep, watching the late evening light fade through the hedge that grew in front of his window. He had left his hearing aid on so that if the boy tried to escape, he would hear and could go after him. For the last two days he had looked poised to leave, and not simply to leave but to be gone, silently and in the night when he would not be followed. This was the fourth night and the schoolteacher lay thinking, with a wry expression on his face, how it differed from the first.

The first night he had sat until daylight by the side of the bed where, still dressed, the boy had fallen. He had sat there, his eyes shining, like a man who sits before a treasure he is not yet convinced is real. His eyes had moved over and over the sprawled thin figure which had appeared lost in an exhaustion so profound that it seemed doubtful it would ever move again. As he followed the outline of the face, he had realized with an intense stab of joy that his nephew looked enough like him to be his son. The heavy work shoes, the worn overalls, the atrocious stained hat filled him with pain and pity. He thought of his poor sister. The only real pleasure she had had in her life was the time she had had the lover who had given her this child, the hollow-cheeked boy who had come from the country to study divinity but whose mind Rayber (a graduate student at the time) had seen at once was too good for that. He had befriended him, had helped him to discover himself and then to discover her. He had engineered their meeting purposely and then had observed to his delight how it prospered and how the relationship developed them both. If there had been no accident, he felt sure the boy would have become completely stable. As it was, after the calamity he had killed himself, a prey to morbid guilt. He had come to Rayber's apartment and had stood confronting him with the gun. He saw again the long brittle face as raw red as if a blast of fire had singed the skin off it and the eyes that had seemed burnt too. He had not felt they were entirely human eyes. They were the eyes of repentance and lacked all dignity. The boy had looked at him for what seemed an age but was perhaps only a second, then he had turned without a word and left and killed himself as soon as he reached his own room.

When Rayber had first opened the door in the middle of the

night and had seen Tarwater's face—white, drawn by some unfathomable hunger and pride—he had remained for an instant frozen before what might have been a mirror thrust toward him in a nightmare. The face before him was his own, but the eyes were not his own. They were the student's eyes, singed with guilt. He had left the door hurriedly to get his glasses and his hearing aid.

As he sat that first night by the bed, he had recognized something rigid and recalcitrant about the boy even in repose. He lay with his teeth bared and the hat clenched in his fist like a weapon. Rayber's conscience smote him that all these years he had left him to his fate, that he had not gone back and saved him. His throat had tightened, his eyes had begun to ache. He had vowed to make it up to him now, to lavish on him everything he would have lavished on his own child if he had had one who would have known the difference.

The next morning while Tarwater was still asleep, he had rushed out and bought him a decent suit, a plaid shirt, socks, and a red leather cap. He wanted him to have new clothes to wake up to, new clothes to indicate a new life.

After four days they were still untouched in the box on a chair in the room. The boy had looked at them as if the suggestion he put them on were equal to asking that he appear naked.

It was apparent from everything he did and said exactly who had brought him up. At every turn an almost uncontrollable fury would rise in Rayber at the brand of independence the old man had wrought—not a constructive independence but one that was irrational, backwoods, and ignorant. After Rayber had rushed back with the clothes, he had gone to the bed and put his hand on the still sleeping boy's forehead and decided that he had a fever and should not get up. He had prepared a breakfast on a tray and brought it to the room. When he appeared in the door with it, Bishop at his side, Tarwater was sitting up in the bed, in the act of shaking out his hat and putting it on. Rayber had said, "Don't you want to hang up your hat and stay a while?" and had given him such a smile of welcome and good will as he thought had possibly never been turned on him before.

The boy, with no look of appreciation or even interest, had

pulled the hat down farther on his head. His gaze had turned with a peculiar glare of recognition to Bishop. The child had on a black cowboy hat and he was gaping over the top of a trash-basket that he clasped to his stomach. He kept a rock in it. Rayber remembered that Bishop had caused the boy some disturbance the night before and he pushed him back with his free hand so that he could not get in. Then stepping into the room, he closed the door and locked it. Tarwater looked at the closed door darkly as if he continued to see the child through it, still clasping his trashbasket.

Rayber set the tray down across his knees and stood back scrutinizing him. The boy seemed barely aware that he was in the room. "That's your breakfast," his uncle said as if he might not be able to identify it. It was a bowl of dry cereal and a glass of milk. "I thought you'd better stay in bed today," he said. "You don't look too chipper." He pulled up a straight chair and sat down. "Now we can have a real talk," he said, his smile spreading. "It's high time we got to know each other."

No expression of approval or pleasure lightened the boy's face. He glanced at the breakfast but did not pick up the spoon. He began to look around the room. The walls were an insistent pink, the color chosen by Rayber's wife. He used it now for a store room. There were trunks in the corners with crates piled on top of them. On the mantel, besides medicine bottles and dead electric lightbulbs and some old match boxes, was a picture of her. The boy's attention paused there and the corner of his mouth twitched slightly as if in some kind of comic recognition. "The welfare woman," he said.

His uncle reddened. The tone he detected under this was old Tarwater's exactly. Without warning, irritation mounted in him. The old man might suddenly have obtruded his presence between them. He felt the same familiar fantastic anger, out of all proportion to its cause, that his uncle had always been able to stir in him. With an effort, he forced it out of his way. "That's my wife," he said, "but she doesn't live with us anymore. This is her old room you're in."

The boy picked up the spoon. "My great-uncle said she wouldn't hang around long," he said and began to eat rapidly as if he had established enough independence by this remark to eat somebody else's food. It was apparent from his expression that he found the quality of it poor.

Rayber sat and watched him, saying to himself in an effort to calm his irritation: this child hasn't had a chance, remember he hasn't had a chance. "God only knows what the old fool has told you and taught you!" he said with a sudden explosive force. "God only knows!"

The boy stopped eating and looked at him sharply. Then after a second he said, "He ain't had no effect on me," and returned to his eating.

"He did you a terrible injustice," Rayber said, wishing to impress this on him as often as he could. "He kept you from having a normal life, from getting a decent education. He filled your head with God knows what rot!"

Tarwater continued to eat. Then with a stoney deliberateness, he looked up and his gaze fastened on the gash in his uncle's ear. Somewhere in the depths of his eyes a glint appeared. "Shot yer, didn't he?" he said.

Rayber took a package of cigarets from his shirt pocket and lit one, his motions inordinately slow from the effort he was making to calm himself. He blew the smoke straight into the boy's face. Then he tilted back in the chair and gave him a long hard look. The cigaret hanging from the corner of his mouth trembled. "Yes, he shot me," he said.

The glint in the boy's eyes followed the wires of the hearing aid down to the metal box stuck in his belt. "What you wired for?" he drawled. "Does your head light up?"

Rayber's jaw snapped and then relaxed. After a moment, after extending his arm stiffly and knocking the ash off his cigaret onto the floor, he replied that his head did not light up. "This is a hearing aid," he said patiently. "After the old man shot me I began to lose my hearing. I didn't have a gun when I went to get you back. If I'd stayed he would have killed me and I wouldn't have done you any good dead."

The boy continued to study the machine. His uncle's face might have been only an appendage to it. "You ain't done me no good alive neither," he remarked.

"Do you understand me?" Rayber persisted. "I didn't have a gun. He would have killed me. He was a mad man. The time when I can do you good is beginning now, and I want to help you. I want to make up for all those years."

For an instant the boy's eyes left the hearing aid and rested on his uncle's eyes. "Could have got you a gun and come back terreckly," he said.

Stricken by the distinct sound of betrayal in his voice, Rayber could not say a word. He looked at him helplessly. The boy returned to his eating.

Finally Rayber said, "Listen." He took hold of the fist with the spoon in it and held it. "I want you to understand. He was crazy and if he had killed me, you wouldn't have this place to come to now. I'm no fool. I don't believe in senseless sacrifice. A dead man is not going to do you any good, don't you know that? Now I can do something for you. Now I can make up for all the time we've lost. I can help correct what he's done to you, help you to correct it yourself." He kept hold of the fist all the while it was being drawn insistently back. "This is our problem together," he said, seeing himself so clearly in the face before him that he might have been beseeching his own image.

With a quick yank, Tarwater managed to free his hand. Then he gave the schoolteacher a long appraising look, tracing the line of his jaw, the two creases on either side of his mouth, the forehead extending into skull until it reached the pie-shaped hairline. He gazed briefly at the pained eyes behind his uncle's glasses, appearing to abandon a search for something that could not possibly be there. The glint in his eye fell on the metal box half-sticking out of Rayber's shirt. "Do you think in the box," he asked, "or do you think in your head?"

His uncle had wanted to tear the machine out of his ear and fling it against the wall. It's because of you I can't hear!" he said, glaring at the impassive face. "It's because once I tried to help you!"

"You never helped me none."

"I can help you now," he said.

After a second he sank back in his chair. "Perhaps you're right," he said, letting his hands fall in a helpless gesture. "It was my mistake. I should have gone back and killed him or let him kill me. Instead I let something in you be killed."

The boy put down his milk glass. "Nothing in me has been killed," he said in a positive voice, and then he added, "And you needn't to worry. I done your work for you. I tended to him. It was me put him away. I was drunk as a coot and I tended to him." He said it as if he were recalling the most vivid point in his history.

Rayber heard his own heart, magnified by the hearing aid, suddenly begin to pound like the works of a gigantic machine in his chest. The boy's delicate defiant face, his glowering eyes still shocked by some violent memory, brought back instantly to him the vision of himself when he was fourteen and had found his way to Powderhead to shout imprecations at the old man.

An insight came to him that he was not to question until the end. He understood that the boy was held in bondage by his great-uncle, that he suffered a terrible false guilt for burning and not burying him, and he saw that he was engaged in a desperate heroic struggle to free himself from the old man's ghostly grasp. He leaned forward and said in a voice so full of feeling that it was barely balanced, "Listen, listen Frankie," he said, "you're not alone any more. You have a friend. You have more than a friend now." He swallowed. "You have a father."

The boy turned very white. His eyes were blackened by the shadow of some unspeakable outrage. "I ain't ast for no father," he said and the sentence struck like a whip across his uncle's face. "I ain't ast for no father," he repeated. "I'm out of the womb of a whore. I was born in a wreck." He flung this forth as if he were declaring a royal birth. "And my name ain't Frankie. I go by Tarwater and . . ."

"Your mother was not a whore," the schoolteacher said angrily. "That's just some rot he's taught you. She was a good healthy American girl, just beginning to find herself when she was struck down. She was . . ."

"I ain't fixing to hang around here," the boy said, looking about him as if he might throw over the breakfast tray and jump out the window. "I only come to find out a few things and when I find them out, then I'm going."

"What did you come to find out?" the schoolteacher asked

evenly. "I can help you. All I want to do is help you any way I can."

"I don't need noner yer help," the boy said, looking away.

His uncle felt something tightening around him like an invisible strait jacket. "How do you mean to find out if you don't have help?"

"I'll wait," he said, "and see what happens."

"And suppose," his uncle asked, "nothing happens?"

An odd smile, like some strange inverted sign of grief, came over the boy's face. "Then I'll make it happen," he said, "like I done before."

In four days nothing had happened and nothing had been made to happen. They had simply covered—the three of them—the entire city, walking and all night Rayber rewalked the same territory backwards in his sleep. It would not have been so tiring if he had not had Bishop. The child dragged backwards on his hand, always attracted by something they had already passed. Every block or so he would squat down to pick up a stick or a piece of trash and have to be pulled up and along. Whereas Tarwater was always slightly in advance of them, pushing forward on the scent of something. In four days they had been to the art gallery and the movies, they had toured department stores; ridden escalators, visited the supermarkets, inspected the water works, the post office, the railroad yards and the city hall. Rayber had explained how the city was run and detailed the duties of a good citizen. He had talked as much as he had walked, and the boy for all the interest he showed might have been the one who was deaf. Silent, he viewed everything with the same noncommittal eye as if he found nothing here worth holding his attention but must keep moving, must keep searching for whatever it was that appeared just beyond his vision.

Once he had paused at a window where a small red car turned slowly on a revolving platform. Seizing on the display of interest, Rayber had said that perhaps when he was sixteen, he could have a car of his own. It might have been the old man who had replied that he could walk on his two feet for nothing without being beholden. Rayber had never, even when Old Tarwater had lived under his roof, been so conscious of the old man's presence.

Once the boy had stopped suddenly in front of a tall building and had stood glaring up at it with a peculiar ravaged look of recognition. Puzzled, Rayber said, "You look as if you've been here before."

"I lost my hat there," he muttered.

"Your hat is on your head," Rayber said. He could not look at the object without irritation. He wished to God there were some way to get it off him.

"My first hat," the boy said. "It fell," and he had rushed on, away from the place as if he could not stand to be near it.

Only one other time had he shown a particular interest. He had stopped with a kind of lurch backwards in front of a large grimey garage-like structure with two yellow and blue painted windows in the front of it, and had stood there, precariously balanced as if he were arresting himself in the middle of a fall. Rayber recognized the place for some kind of pentecostal tabernacle. Over the door was a paper banner bearing the words, UNLESS YE BE BORN AGAIN YE SHALL NOT HAVE EVERLASTING LIFE. Beneath it a poster showed a man and woman and child holding hands. "Hear the Carmodys for Christ!" it said. "Thrill to the Music, Message, and Magic of this team!"

Rayber was well enough aware of the boy's trouble to understand the sinister pull such a place would have on his mind. "Does this interest you?" he asked drily. "Does it remind you of something in particular?"

Tarwater was very pale. "Horse manure," he whispered.

Rayber smiled. Then he laughed. "All such people have in life," he said, "is the conviction they'll rise again."

The boy steadied himself, his eyes still on the banner but as if he had reduced it to a small spot a great distance away.

"They won't rise again?" he said. The statement had the lilt of a question and Rayber realized with an intense thrill of pleasure that his opinion, for the first time, was being called for.

"No," he said simply, "they won't rise again." There was a profound finality in his tone. The grimey structure might have been the carcass of a beast he had just brought down. He put his hand experimentally on the boy's shoulder. It was suffered to remain there.

In a voice unsteady with the sudden return of enthusiasm he said, "That's why I want you to learn all you can. I want you to be educated so that you can take your place as an intelligent man in the world. This fall when you start school . . ."

The shoulder was roughly withdrawn and the boy, throwing him one dark look, removed himself to the farthest edge of the sidewalk.

He wore his isolation like a mantle, wrapped it around himself as if it were a garment signifying the elect. Rayber had intended to keep notes on him and write up his most important observations but each night his energy had been too depleted to permit him to do any work. He had dropped off every night into a restless sleep, afraid that he would wake up and find the boy gone. He felt he had hastened his urge to leave by confronting him with the test. He had intended giving him the standard ones, intelligence and aptitude, and then going on to some he had perfected himself dealing with emotional factors. He had thought that in this way he could ferret to the center of the emotional infection. He had laid a simple aptitude test out on the kitchen table—the printed book and a few newly sharpened pencils. "This is a kind of game," he said. "Sit down and see what you can make of it. I'll help you begin."

The expression that came over the boy's face was very peculiar. His eyelids lowered just slightly; his mouth failed a smile by only a fraction; his look was compounded of fury and superiority. "Play with it yourself," he said. "I ain't taking no *test*," and he spit the word out as if it were not fit to pass between his lips.

Rayber sized up the situation. Then he said, "Maybe you don't really know how to read and write. Is that the trouble?"

The boy thrust his head forward. "I'm free," he hissed. "I'm outside your head. I ain't in it. I ain't in it and I ain't about to be."

His uncle laughed. "You don't know what freedom is," he said, "you don't . . ." but the boy turned and strode off.

It was no use. He could no more be reasoned with than a jackal. Nothing gave him pause—except Bishop, and Rayber knew that the reason Bishop gave him pause was because the child reminded him of the old man. Bishop looked like the old man grown backwards to the lowest form of innocence, and Rayber observed that the boy strictly avoided looking him in the eye. Wherever the child happened to be standing or sitting or walking seemed to be for Tarwater a dangerous hole in space that he must keep away from at all costs. Rayber was afraid that Bishop would drive him away with his friendliness. He was always creeping up to touch him and when the boy was aware of his being near, he would draw himself up like a snake ready to strike and hiss, "Git!" and Bishop would scurry off to watch him again from behind the nearest piece of furniture.

The schoolteacher understood this too. Every problem the boy had he had had himself and had conquered, or had for the most part conquered, for he had not conquered the problem of Bishop. He had only learned to live with it and had learned too that he could not live without it.

When he had got rid of his wife, he and the child had begun living together in a quiet automatic fashion like two bachelors whose habits were so smoothly connected that they no longer needed to take notice of each other. In the winter he sent him to a school for exceptional children and he had made great strides. He could wash himself, dress himself, feed himself, go to the toilet by himself and make peanut butter sandwiches though sometimes he put the bread inside. For the most part Rayber lived with him without being painfully aware of his presence but the moments would still come when, rushing from some inexplicable part of himself, he would experience a love for the child so outrageous that he would be left shocked and depressed for days, and trembling for his sanity. It was only a touch of the curse that lay in his blood.

His normal way of looking on Bishop was as an "x" signifying the general hideousness of fate. He did not believe that he himself was formed in the image and likeness of God but that Bishop was he had no doubt. The little boy was part of a simple equation that required no further solution, except at the moments when with little or no warning he would feel himself overwhelmed by the horrifying love. Anything he looked at too long could bring it on. Bishop did not have to be around. It could be a stick or a stone, the line of a shadow, the absurd old man's walk of a starling crossing the sidewalk. If, without thinking, he lent himself to it, he would feel suddenly a morbid surge of the love that terrified him—powerful enough to throw him to the ground in an act of idiot praise. It was completely irrational and abnormal.

He was not afraid of love in general. He knew the value of it and how it could be used. He had seen it transform in cases where nothing else had worked, such as with his poor sister. None of this had the least bearing on his situation. The love that would overcome him was of a different order entirely. It was not the kind that could be used for the child's improvement or his own. It was love without reason, love for something futureless, love that appeared to exist only to be itself, imperious and all demanding, the kind that would cause him to make a fool of himself in an instant. And it only began with Bishop. It began with Bishop and then like an avalanche covered everything his reason hated. He always felt with it a rush of longing to have the old man's eyes—insane, fish-coloured, violent with their impossible vision of a world transfigured—turned on him once again. The longing was like an undertow in his blood dragging him backwards to what he knew to be madness.

The affliction was in the family. It lay hidden in the line of blood that touched them, flowing from some ancient source, some desert prophet or pole-sitter, until, its power unabated, it appeared in the old man and him and, he surmised, in the boy. Those it touched were condemned to fight it constantly or be ruled by it. The old man had been ruled by it. He, at the cost of a full life, staved it off. What the boy would do hung in the balance.

He had kept it from gaining control over him by what amounted to a rigid ascetic discipline. He did not look at anything too long, he denied his senses unnecessary satisfactions. He slept in a narrow iron bed, worked sitting in a straight-backed chair, ate frugally, spoke little, and cultivated the dullest for friends. At his high school he was the expert on testing. All his professional decisions were prefabricated and did not involve his participation. He was not deceived that this was a whole or a full life, he only knew that it was the way his life had to be lived if it were going to have any dignity at all. He knew that he was the stuff of which fanatics and madmen are made and that he had turned his destiny as if with his bare will. He kept himself upright on a very narrow line between madness and emptiness, and when the time came for him to lose his balance, he intended to lurch toward emptiness and fall on the side of his choice. He recognized that in silent ways he lived an heroic life. The boy would go either his way or old Tarwater's and he was determined to save him for the better course. Although Tarwater claimed to believe nothing the old man had taught him, Rayber could see clearly that there was still a backdrag of belief and fear in him keeping his responses locked.

By virtue of kinship and similarity and experience, Rayber was the person to save him, yet something in the boy's very look drained him, something in his very look, something starved in it, seemed to feed on him. With Tarwater's eyes on him, he felt subjected to a pressure that killed his energy before he had a chance to exert it. The eyes were the eyes of the crazy student father, the personality was the old man's, and somewhere between the two, Rayber's own image was struggling to survive and he was not able to reach it. After three days of walking, he was numb with fatigue and plagued with a sense of his own ineffectiveness. All day his sentences had not quite connected with his thought.

That night they had eaten at an Italian restaurant, dark and not crowded, and he had ordered ravioli for them because Bishop liked it. After each meal the boy removed a piece of paper and a stub of pencil from his pocket and wrote down a figure—his estimate of what the meal was worth. In time he would pay back the total sum, he had said, as he did not intend to be beholden. Rayber would have liked to see the figures and learn what his meals were valued at—the boy never asked the price. He was a finicky eater, pushing the food around on his plate before he ate it and putting each forkful in his mouth as if he suspected it was poisoned. He had pushed the ravioli about, his face drawn. He ate a little of it and then put the fork down.

"Don't you like that?" Rayber had asked. "You can have something else if you don't."

"It all come out the same slop bucket," the boy said.

"Bishop is eating his," Rayber said. Bishop had it smeared all over his face. Occasionally he would feed a spoonful into the sugar bowl or touch the tip of his tongue to the dish.

"That's what I said," Tarwater said, and his glance grazed the top of the child's head, "—a hog might like it."

The schoolteacher put his fork down.

Tarwater was glaring at the dark walls of the room. "He's like a hog," he said. "He eats like a hog and he don't think no more than a hog and when he dies, he'll rot like a hog. Me and you too," he said, looking back at the schoolteacher's mottled face, "will rot like hogs. The only difference between me and you and a hog is me and you can calculate, but there ain't any difference between him and one."

Rayber appeared to be gritting his teeth. Finally he said, "Just forget Bishop exists. You haven't been asked to have anything to do with him. He's just a mistake of nature. Try not even to be aware of him."

"He ain't my mistake," the boy muttered. "I ain't having a thing to do with him."

"Forget him," Rayber said in a short harsh voice.

The boy looked at him oddly as if he were beginning to perceive his secret affliction. What he saw or thought he saw seemed grimly to amuse him. "Let's leave out of here," he said, "and get to walking again."

"We are not going to walk tonight," Rayber said. "We are going home and go to bed." He said it with a firmness and finality he had not used before. The boy had only shrugged.

As Rayber lay watching the window darken, he felt that all his nerves were stretched through him like high tension wire. He began trying to relax one muscle at a time as the books recommended, beginning with those in the back of his neck. He emptied his mind of everything but the just visible pattern of the hedge against the screen. Still he was alert for any sound. Long after he lay in complete darkness, he was still alert, unrelaxed, ready to spring up at the least creak of a floor board in the hall. All at once he sat up, wide awake. A door opened and closed. He leapt up and ran across the hall into the opposite room. The boy was gone. He ran back to his own room and pulled his trousers on over his pajamas. Then grabbing his coat, he went out the house by way of the kitchen, barefooted, his jaw set.

V

Keeping close to his side of the hedge, he crept through the dark damp grass toward the street. The night was close and very still. A light went on in a window of the next house and revealed, at the end of the hedge, the hat. It turned slightly and Rayber saw the sharp profile beneath it, the set thrust of a jaw very like his own. The boy was stopped still, most likely taking his bearings, deciding which direction to walk in.

He turned again and again Rayber saw only the hat, intransigently ground upon his head, fierce-looking even in the dim light. It had the boy's own defiant quality, as if its shape had been formed over the years by his personality. It had been the first thing that Rayber had seen must go. It suddenly moved out of the light and vanished.

Rayber slipped through the hedge and followed, soundless on his bare feet. Nothing cast a shadow. He could barely make out the boy a quarter of a block in front of him, except when occasionally light from a window outlined him briefly. Since Rayber didn't know whether he thought he was leaving for good or only going for a walk on his own, he decided not to shout and stop him but to follow silently and observe. He turned off his hearing aid and pursued the dim figure as if in a dream. The boy walked even faster at night than in the day time and was always on the verge of vanishing.

Rayber felt the accelerated beat of his heart. He took a handkerchief out of his pocket and wiped his forehead and inside the neck of his pajama top. He walked over something sticky on the sidewalk and shifted hurriedly to the other side, cursing under his breath. Tarwater was heading toward town. Rayber thought it likely he was returning to see something that had secretly interested him. He might discover tonight what he would have found by testing if the boy had not been so pig-headed. He felt the insidious pleasure of revenge and checked it.

A patch of sky blanched, revealing for a moment the outlines of the housetops. Tarwater turned suddenly to the right. Rayber cursed himself for not stopping long enough to get his shoes. They had come into a neighborhood of large ramshackle boarding houses with porches that abutted the sidewalks. On some of them late sitters were rocking and watching the street. He felt eyes in the darkness move on him and he turned on the hearing aid again. On one porch a woman rose and leaned over the banister. She stood with her hands on her hips, looking him over, taking in his bare feet, the striped pajama coat under his seersucker suit. Irritated, he glanced back at her. The thrust of her neck indicated a conclusion formed. He buttoned his coat and hurried on.

The boy stopped on the next corner. His lean shadow made by a street light slanted to the side of him. The hat's shadow, like a knob at the top of it, turned to the right and then the left. He appeared to be considering his direction. Rayber's muscles felt suddenly weighted. He was not conscious of his fatigue until the pace slackened.

Tarwater turned to the left and Rayber began angrily to move again. They went down a street of dilapidated stores. When Rayber turned the next corner, the gaudy cave of a movie house yawned to the side of him. A knot of small boys stood in front of it. "Forgot yer shoes!" one of them chirruped. "Forgot yer shirt!"

He began a kind of limping lope.

The chorus followed him down the block. "Hi yo Silverwear, Tonto's lost his underwear! What in the heck do we care?"

He kept his eye wrathfully on Tarwater who was turning to the right. When he reached the corner and turned, he saw the boy stopped in the middle of the block, looking in a store window. He slipped into a narrow entrance a few yards farther on where a flight of steps led upward into darkness. Then he looked out.

Tarwater's face was strangely lit from the window he was standing before. Rayber watched curiously for a few moments. It looked to him like the face of someone starving who sees a meal he can't reach laid out before him. At last, something he *wants*, he thought, and determined that tomorrow he would return and buy it. Tarwater reached out and touched the glass and then drew his hand back slowly. He hung there as if he could not take his eyes off what it was he wanted. A pet shop, perhaps, Rayber thought. Maybe he wants a dog. A dog might make all the difference. Abruptly the boy broke away and moved on.

Rayber stepped out of the entrance and made for the window he had left. He stopped with a shock of disappointment. The place was only a bakery. The window was empty except for a loaf of bread pushed to the side that must have been overlooked when the shelf was cleaned for the night. He stared, puzzled, at the empty window for a second before he started after the boy again. Everything a false alarm, he thought with disgust. If he had eaten his dinner, he wouldn't be hungry. A man and woman strolling past looked with interest at his bare feet. He glared at them, then glanced to the side and saw his bloodless wired reflection in the glass of a shoe shop. The boy disappeared all at once into an alley. My God, Rayber thought, how long is this going on?

He turned into the alley, which was unpaved and so dark that he could not see Tarwater in it at all. He was certain that any minute he would cut his feet on broken glass. A garbage can materialized in his path. There was a noise like the collapse of a tin house and he found himself sitting up with his hand and one foot in something unidentifiable. He scrambled up and limped on, hearing his own curses like the voice of a stranger broadcast through his hearing aid. At the end of the alley, he saw the lean figure in the middle of the next block, and with a sudden fury he began to run.

The boy turned into another alley. Doggedly Rayber ran on. At the end of the second alley, the boy turned to the left. When Rayber reached the street, Tarwater was standing still in the middle of the next block. With a furtive look around him, he vanished, apparently into the building he had been facing. Rayber dashed forward. As he reached the place, singing burst flatly against his eardrums. Two blue and yellow windows glared at him in the darkness like the eyes of some Biblical beast. He stopped in front of the banner and read the mocking words, UNLESS YE BE BORN AGAIN. . . .

That the boy's corruption was this deep did not surprise him. What unstrung him was the thought that what Tarwater carried into the atrocious temple was his own imprisoned image. Enraged, he started around the building to locate a window he could look through and see the boy's face among the crowd. When he saw him, he would roar at him to come out. The windows near the front were all too high but toward the back, he found a lower one. He pushed through a straggly shrub beneath it and, his chin just above the ledge, looked into what appeared to be a small ante-room. A door on the other side of it opened onto a stage and there a man in a bright blue suit was standing in a spotlight, leading a hymn. Rayber could not see into the main body of the building where the people were. He was about to move away when the man brought the hymn to a close and began to speak.

"Friends," he said, "the time has come. The time we've all been waiting for this evening. Jesus said suffer the little children to come unto Him and forbid them not and maybe it was because He knew that it would be the little children that would call others to Him, maybe He knew, friends, maybe He hadda hunch."

Rayber listened angrily, too exhausted to move away once he had stopped.

"Friends," the preacher said, "Lucette has travelled the world over telling people about Jesus. She's been to India and China. She's spoken to all the rulers of the world. Jesus is wonderful, friends. He teaches us wisdom out of the mouths of babes!"

Another child exploited, Rayber thought furiously. It was the thought of a child's mind warped, of a child led away from reality that always enraged him, bringing back to him his own childhood's seduction. Glaring at the spotlight, he saw the man there as a blur which he looked through, down the length of his life until what confronted him were the old man's fish-coloured eyes. He saw himself taking the offered hand and innocently walking out of his own yard, innocently walking into six or seven years of unreality. Any other child would have thrown off the spell in a week. He could not have. He had analysed his case and closed it. Still, every now and then he would live over the five minutes it had taken his father to snatch him away from Powderhead. Through the blur of the man on the stage, as if he were looking into a transparent nightmare, he had the experience again. He and his uncle sat on the steps of the house at Powderhead watching his father emerge from the woods and sight them across the field. His uncle leaned forward, squinting, his hand cupped over his eyes, and he sat with his hands clenched between his knees, his heart threshing from side to side as his father moved closer and closer.

"Lucette travels with her mother and daddy and I want you to meet them because a mother and daddy have to be unselfish to share their only child with the world," the preacher said. "Here they are, friends—Mr. and Mrs. Carmody!"

While a man and woman moved into the light, Rayber had a

clear vision of plowed ground, of the shaded red ridges that separated him from the lean figure approaching. He had let himself imagine that the field had an undertow that would drag his father backwards and suck him under, but he came on inexorably, only stopping every now and then to put a finger in his shoe and push out a clod of dirt.

"He's going to take me back with him," he said.

"Back with him where?" his uncle growled. "He ain't got any place to take you back to."

"He can't take me back with him?"

"Not where you were before."

"He can't take me back to town?"

"I never said nothing about town," his uncle said.

He saw vaguely that the man in the spotlight had sat down but that the woman was still standing. She became a blur and he saw his father again, getting closer and closer and he had one impulse to dart up and run through his uncle's house and tear out the back to the woods. He would have raced along the path, familiar to him then, and sliding and slipping over the waxy pine needles, he would have run down and down until he reached the thicket of bamboo and would have pushed through it and out onto the other side and would have fallen into the stream and lain there, panting and wheezing and safe where he had been born again, where his head had been thrust by his uncle into the water and brought up again into a new life. Sitting on the step, his leg muscles twitched as if they were ready for him to spring up but he remained absolutely still. He could see the line of his father's mouth, the line that had gone past the point of exasperation, past the point of loud wrath to a kind of stoked rage that would feed him for months.

While the woman evangelist, tall and raw-boned, was speaking of the hardships she had endured, he watched his father as he reached the edge of the yard and stepped onto the packed dirt, his face a slick pink from the exertion of crossing a field. He was drawing short hard breaths. For an instant he seemed about to reach forward and snatch him but he remained where he was. His pale eyes moved carefully over the rock-like figure watching him steadily from the steps, at the red hands knotted on the heavy thighs and then at the gun lying on the porch. He said, "His mother wants him back, Mason. I don't know why. For my part you could have him but you know how she is."

"A drunken whore," his uncle growled.

"Your sister, not mine," his father said, and then said, "All right boy, snap it up," and nodded curtly to him.

He explained in a high reedy voice the exact reason he could not go back, "I've been born again."

"Great," his father said, "great." He took a step forward and grabbed his arm and yanked him to his feet. "Glad you got him fixed up, Mason," he said. "One bath more or less won't hurt the bugger."

He had had no chance to see his uncle's face. His father had already lept into the plowed field and was dragging him across the furrows while the pellets pierced the air over their heads. His shoulders, just under the window ledge, jumped. He shook his head to clear it.

"For ten years I was a missionary in China," the woman was saying, "for five years I was a missionary in Africa, and one year I was a missionary in Rome where minds are still chained in priestly darkness; but for the last six years, my husband and I have travelled the world over with our daughter. They have been years of trial and pain, years of hardship and suffering." She had on a long dramatic cape, one side of which was turned backward over her shoulder to reveal a red lining.

His father's face was suddenly very close to his own. "Back to the real world, boy," he was saying, "back to the real world. And that's me and not him, see? Me and not him," and he heard himself screaming, "It's him! Him! Him and not you! And I've been born again and there's not a thing you can do about it!"

"Christ in hell," his father said, "believe it if you want to. Who cares? You'll find out soon enough."

The woman's tone had changed. The sound of something grasping drew his attention again. "We have not had an easy time. We have been a hard-working team for Christ. People have not always been generous to us. Only here are the people really generous. I am from Texas and my husband is from Tennessee but we have travelled the world over. We know," she said in a deepened softened voice, "where the people are really generous."

Rayber forgot himself and listened. He felt a relief from his pain, recognizing that the woman was only after money. He could hear the beginning click of coins falling in a plate.

"Our little girl began to preach when she was six. We saw that she had a mission, that she had been called. We saw that we could not keep her to ourselves and so we have endured many hardships to give her to the world, to bring her to you tonight. To us," she said, "you are as important as the great rulers of the world!" Here she lifted the end of her cape and holding it out as a magician would made a low bow. After a moment she lifted her head, gazed in front of her as if at some grand vista, and disappeared from view. A little girl hobbled into the spotlight.

Rayber cringed. Simply by the sight of her he could tell that she was not a fraud, that she was only exploited. She was eleven or twelve with a small delicate face and a head of black hair that looked too thick and heavy for a frail child to support. A cape like her mother's was turned back over one shoulder and her skirt was short as if better to reveal the thin legs twisted from the knees. She held her arms over her head for a moment. "I want to tell you people the story of the world," she said in a loud high child's voice. "I want to tell you why Jesus came and what happened to Him. I want to tell you how He'll come again. I want to tell you to be ready. Most of all," she said, "I want to tell you to be ready so that on the last day you'll rise in the glory of the Lord."

Rayber's fury encompassed the parents, the preacher, all the idiots he could not see who were sitting in front of the child, parties to her degradation. She believed it, she was locked tight in it, chained hand and foot, exactly as he had been, exactly as only a child could be. He felt the taste of his own childhood pain laid again on his tongue like a bitter wafer.

"Do you know who Jesus is?" she cried. "Jesus is the Word of God and Jesus is love. The Word of God is love and do you know what love is, you people? If you don't know what love is you won't know Jesus when He comes. You won't be ready. I want to tell you people the story of the world, how it never known when love come, so when love comes again, you'll be ready."

She moved back and forth across the stage, frowning as if she were trying to see the people through the fierce circle of light that followed her. "Listen to me, you people," she said, "God was angry with the world because it always wanted more. It wanted as much as God had and it didn't know what God had but it wanted it and more. It wanted God's own breath, it wanted His very Word and God said, 'I'll make my Word Jesus, I'll give them my Word for a king, I'll give them my very breath for theirs.'"

"Listen you people," she said and flung her arms wide, "God told the world He was going to send it a king and the world waited. The world thought, a golden fleece will do for His bed. Silver and gold and peacock tails, a thousand suns in a peacock's tail will do for His sash. His mother will ride on a four-horned white beast and use the sunset for a cape. She'll trail it behind her over the ground and let the world pull it to pieces, a new one every evening."

To Rayber she was like one of those birds blinded to make it sing more sweetly. Her voice had the tone of a glass bell. His pity encompassed all exploited children—himself when he was a child, Tarwater exploited by the old man, this child exploited by parents, Bishop exploited by the very fact he was alive.

"The world said, 'How long, Lord, do we have to wait for this?' And the Lord said, 'My Word is coming, my Word is coming from the house of David, the king.'" She paused and turned her head to the side, away from the fierce light. Her dark gaze moved slowly until it rested on Rayber's head in the window. He stared back at her. Her eyes remained on his face for a moment. A deep shock went through him. He was certain that the child had looked directly into his heart and seen his pity. He felt that some mysterious connection was established between them.

"'My Word is coming,'" she said, turning back to face the glare, "'my Word is coming from the house of David, the king.'"

She began again in a dirge-like tone. "Jesus came on cold straw, Jesus was warmed by the breath of an ox. 'Who is this?' the world said, 'who is this blue-cold child and this woman, plain as the winter? Is this the Word of God, this blue-cold child? Is this His will, this plain winter-woman?'

"Listen you people!" she cried, "the world knew in its heart, the same as you know in your hearts and I know in my heart. The world said, 'Love cuts like the cold wind and the will of

God is plain as the winter. Where is the summer will of God? Where are the green seasons of God's will? Where is the spring and summer of God's will?'

"They had to flee into Egypt," she said in a low voice and turned her head again and this time her eyes moved directly to Rayber's face in the window and he knew they sought it. He felt himself caught up in her look, held there before the judgment seat of her eyes.

"You and I know," she said turning again, "what the world hoped then. The world hoped old Herod would slay the right child, the world hoped old Herod wouldn't waste those children, but he wasted them. He didn't get the right one. Jesus grew up and raised the dead."

Rayber felt his spirit borne aloft. But not those dead! he cried, not the innocent children, not you, not me when I was a child, not Bishop, not Frank! and he had a vision of himself moving like an avenging angel through the world, gathering up all the children that the Lord, not Herod, had slain.

"Jesus grew up and raised the dead," she cried, "and the world shouted, 'Leave the dead lie. The dead are dead and can stay that way. What do we want with the dead alive?' Oh you people!" she shouted, "they nailed Him to a cross and run a spear through His side and then they said, 'Now we can have some peace, now we can ease our minds.' And they hadn't but only said it when they wanted Him to come again. Their eyes were opened and they saw the glory they had killed.

"Listen world," she cried, flinging up her arms so that the cape flew out behind her, "Jesus is coming again! The mountains are going to lie down like hounds at His feet, the stars are going to perch on His shoulder and when He calls it, the sun is going to fall like a goose for His feast. Will you know the Lord Jesus then? The mountains will know Him and bound forward, the stars will light on His head, the sun will drop down at His feet, but will you know the Lord Jesus then?"

Rayber saw himself fleeing with the child to some enclosed garden where he would teach her the truth, where he would gather all the exploited children of the world and let the sunshine flood their minds.

"If you don't know Him now, you won't know Him then. Listen

to me, world, listen to this warning. The Holy Word is in my mouth!

"The Holy Word is in my mouth!" she cried and turned her eyes again on his face in the window. This time there was a lowering concentration in her gaze. He had drawn her attention entirely away from the congregation.

Come away with me! he silently implored, and I'll teach you the truth, I'll save you, beautiful child!

Her eyes still fixed on him, she cried, "I've seen the Lord in a tree of fire! The Word of God is a burning Word to burn you clean!" She was moving in his direction, the people in front of her forgotten. Rayber's heart began to race. He felt some miraculous communication between them. The child alone in the world was meant to understand him. "Burns the whole world, man and child," she cried, her eye on him, "none can escape." She stopped a little distance from the end of the stage and stood silent, her whole attention directed across the small room to his face on the ledge. Her eyes were large and dark and fierce. He felt that in the space between them, their spirits had broken the bonds of age and ignorance and were mingling in some unheard of knowledge of each other. He was transfixed by the child's silence. Suddenly she raised her arm and pointed toward his face. "Listen you people," she shrieked, "I see a damned soul before my eye! I see a dead man Jesus hasn't raised. His head is in the window but his ear is deaf to the Holy Word!"

Rayber's head, as if it had been struck by an invisible bolt, dropped from the ledge. He crouched on the ground, his furious spectacled eyes glittering behind the shrubbery. Inside she continued to shriek, "Are you deaf to the Lord's Word? The Word of God is a burning Word to burn you clean, burns man and child, man and child the same, you people! Be saved in the Lord's fire or perish in your own! Be saved in . . ."

He was groping fiercely about him, slapping at his coat pockets, his head, his chest, not able to find the switch that would cut off the voice. Then his hand touched the button and he snapped it. A silent dark relief enclosed him like shelter after a tormenting wind. For a while he sat limp behind the bush. Then the reason for his being here returned to him and he experienced a moment of loathing for the boy that earlier would have made him shudder.

He wanted nothing but to get back home and sink into his own bed, whether the boy returned or not.

He got out of the shrubbery and started toward the front of the building. As he turned onto the sidewalk, the door of the tabernacle flew open and Tarwater flung himself out. Rayber stopped abruptly.

The boy stood confronting him, his face strangely mobile as if successive layers of shock were settling on it to form a new expression. After a moment he raised his arm in an uncertain gesture of greeting. The sight of Rayber seemed to afford him relief amounting to rescue.

Rayber's face had the wooden look it wore when his hearing aid was off. He did not see the boy's expression at all. His rage obliterated all but the general lines of his figure and he saw them moulded in an irreversible shape of defiance. He grabbed him roughly by the arm and started down the block with him. Both of them walked rapidly as if neither could leave the place fast enough. When they were well down the block, Rayber stopped and swung him around and glared into his face. Through his fury he could not discern that for the first time the boy's eyes were submissive. He snapped on his hearing aid and said fiercely, "I hope you enjoyed the show."

Tarwater's lips moved convulsively. Then he murmured, "I only gone to spit on it."

The schoolteacher continued to glare at him. "I'm not so sure of that."

The boy said nothing. He seemed to have suffered some shock inside the building that had permanently slowed his tongue.

Rayber turned and they walked away in silence. At any point along the way, he could have put his hand on the shoulder next to his and it would not have been withdrawn, but he made no gesture. His head was churning with old rages. The afternoon he had learned the full extent of Bishop's future had sprung to his mind. He saw himself rigidly facing the doctor, a man who had made him think of a bull, impassive, insensitive, his brain already on the next case. He had said, "You should be grateful his health is good. In addition to this, I've seen them born blind as well, some without arms and legs, and one with a heart outside."

He had lurched up, almost ready to strike the man. "How can

I be grateful," he had hissed, "when one—just one—is born with a heart outside?"

"You'd better try," the doctor had said.

Tarwater walked slightly behind him and Rayber did not cast a glance back at him. His fury seemed to be stirring from buried depths that had lain quiet for years and to be working upward, closer and closer, toward the slender roots of his peace. When they reached the house he went in and straight to his bed without turning to look at the boy's white face which, drained but expectant, lingered a moment at the threshold of his door as if waiting for an invitation to enter.

VI

The next day, too late, he had the sense of opportunity missed. Tarwater's face had hardened again and the steely gleam in his eye was like the glint of a metal door sealed against an intruder. Rayber felt afflicted with a peculiar chilling clarity of mind in which he saw himself divided in two—a violent and a rational self. The violent self inclined him to see the boy as an enemy and he knew that nothing would hinder his progress with the case so much as giving in to such an inclination. He had waked up after a wild dream in which he chased Tarwater through an interminable alley that twisted suddenly back on itself and reversed the roles of pursuer and pursued. The boy had overtaken him, given him a thunderous blow on the head, and then disappeared. And with his disappearance there had come such an overwhelming feeling of release that Rayber had waked up with a pleasant anticipation that his guest would be gone. He was at once ashamed of the feeling. He settled on a rational, tiring plan for the day and by ten o'clock the three of them were on their way to the natural history museum. He intended to stretch the boy's mind by introducing him to his ancestor, the fish, and to all the great wastes of unexplored time.

They passed part of the territory they had walked over the night before but nothing was said about that trip. Except for the circles under Rayber's eyes, there was nothing about either of them to indicate it had been made. Bishop stumped along, squatting every now and then to pick up something off the sidewalk, while Tarwater, to avoid contamination with them, walked a good four feet to the other side and slightly in advance. I must have infinite patience, I must have infinite patience, Rayber kept repeating to himself.

The museum lay on the other side of the city park which they had not crossed before. As they approached it, the boy paled as if he were shocked to find a wood in the middle of the city. Once inside the park, he stopped and stood glaring about him at the huge trees whose ancient rustling branches intermingled overhead. Patches of light sifting through them spattered the concrete walks with sunshine. Rayber observed that something disturbed him. Then he realized that the place reminded him of Powderhead.

"Let's sit down," he said, wanting both to rest and to observe the boy's agitation. He sat down on a bench and stretched his legs in front of him. He suffered Bishop to climb into his lap. The child's shoelaces were untied and he tied them, for the moment ignoring the boy who was standing there, his face furiously impatient. When he finished tying the shoes, he continued to hold the child, sprawled and grinning, in his lap. The little boy's white head fitted under his chin. Above it Rayber looked at nothing in particular. Then he closed his eyes and in the isolating darkness, he forgot Tarwater's presence. Without warning his hated love gripped him and held him in a vice. He should have known better than to let the child onto his lap.

His forehead became beady with sweat; he looked as if he might have been nailed to the bench. He knew that if he could once conquer this pain, face it and with a supreme effort of his will refuse to feel it, he would be a free man. He held Bishop rigidly. Although the child started the pain, he also limited it, contained it. He had learned this one terrible afternoon when he had tried to drown him.

He had taken him to the beach, two hundred miles away, intending to effect the accident as quickly as possible and return bereaved. It had been a beautiful calm day in May. The beach, almost empty, had stretched down into the gradual swell of ocean. There was nothing to be seen but an expanse of sea and sky and sand and an occasional figure, stick-like, in the distance. He had taken him out on his shoulders and when he was chest deep in the water, had lifted him off, swung the delighted child high in the air and then plunged him swiftly below the surface on his back and held him there, not looking down at what he was doing but up, at an imperturbable witnessing sky, not quite blue, not quite white.

A fierce surging pressure had begun upward beneath his hands and grimly he had exerted more and more force downward. In a second, he felt he was trying to hold a giant under. Astonished, he let himself look. The face under the water was wrathfully contorted, twisted by some primeval rage to save itself. Automatically he released his pressure. Then when he realized what he had done, he pushed down again angrily with all his force until the struggle ceased under his hands. He stood sweating in the water, his own mouth as slack as the child's had been. The body, caught by an undertow, almost got away from him but he managed to come to himself and snatch it. Then as he looked at it, he had a moment of complete terror in which he envisioned his life without the child. He began to shout frantically. He plowed his way out of the water with the limp body. The beach which he had thought empty before had become peopled with strangers converging on him from all directions. A bald-headed man in red and blue Roman striped shorts began at once to administer artificial respiration. Three wailing women and a photographer appeared. The next day there had been a picture in the paper, showing the rescuer, striped bottom forward, working over the child. Rayber was beside him on his knees, watching with an agonized expression. The caption said, OVERJOYED FATHER SEES SON REVIVED.

The boy's voice broke in on him harshly. "All you got to do is nurse an idiot!"

The schoolteacher opened his eyes. They were bloodshot and vague. He might have been returning to consciousness after a blow on the head.

Tarwater was glaring to the side of him. "Come on if you're coming," he said, "and if you ain't, I'm going on about my bidnis."

Rayber didn't answer.

"So long," Tarwater said.

"And where would your business be?" Rayber asked sourly. "At another tabernacle?"

The boy reddened. He opened his mouth and said nothing.

"I nurse an idiot that you're afraid to look at," Rayber said. "Look him in the eye."

Tarwater shot a glance at the top of Bishop's head and left it there an instant like a finger on a candle flame. "I'd as soon be afraid to look at a dog," he said and turned his back. After a moment, as if he were continuing the same conversation, he muttered, "I'd as soon baptize a dog as him. It would be as much use."

"Who said anything about baptizing anybody?" Rayber said. "Is that one of your fixations? Have you taken that bug up from the old man?"

The boy whirled around and faced him. "I told you I only gone there to spit on it," he said tensely. "I ain't going to tell you again."

Rayber watched him without saying anything. He felt that his own sour words had helped him recover himself. He pushed Bishop off and stood up. "Let's get going," he said. He had no intentions of discussing it further, but as they moved on silently, he thought better of it.

"Listen Frank," he said, "I'll grant that you went to spit on it. I've never for a second doubted your intelligence. Everything you've done, your very presence here proves that you're above your background, that you've broken through the ceiling the old man set for you. After all, you escaped from Powderhead. You had the courage to attend to him the quickest way and then get out of there. And once out, you came directly to the right place."

The boy reached up and picked a leaf from a tree branch and bit it. A wry expression spread over his face. He rolled the leaf into a ball and threw it away. Rayber continued to speak, his voice detached, as if he had no particular interest in the matter, and his were merely the voice of truth, as impersonal as air.

"Say that you went to spit on it," he said, "the point is this: there's no need to spit on it. It's not worth spitting on. It's not that important. You've somehow enlarged the significance of it in your mind. The old man used to enrage me until I learned better. He wasn't worth my hate and he's not worth yours. He's only worth our pity." He wondered if the boy were capable of the steadiness of pity. "You want to avoid extremes. They are for violent people and you don't want . . ." —he broke off abruptly as Bishop let loose his hand and galloped away.

They had come out into the center of the park, a concrete circle with a fountain in the middle of it. Water rushed from the mouth of a stone lion's head into a shallow pool and the little boy was flying toward it, his arms flailing like a windmill. In a second he was over the side and in. "Too late, goddammit," Rayber muttered, "he's in." He glanced at Tarwater.

The boy stood arrested in the middle of a step. His eyes were on the child in the pool but they burned as if he beheld some terrible compelling vision. The sun shone brightly on Bishop's white head and the little boy stood there with a look of attention. Tarwater began to move toward him.

He seemed to be drawn toward the child in the water but to be pulling back, exerting an almost equal pressure away from what attracted him. Rayber watched, puzzled and suspicious, moving along with him but somewhat to the side. As he drew closer to the pool, the skin on the boy's face appeared to stretch tighter and tighter. Rayber had the sense that he was moving blindly, that where Bishop was he saw only a spot of light. He felt that something was being enacted before him and that if he could understand it, he would have the key to the boy's future. His muscles were tensed and he was prepared somehow to act. Suddenly his sense of danger was so great that he cried out. In an instant of illumination he understood. Tarwater was moving toward Bishop to baptize him. Already he had reached the edge of the pool. Rayber sprang and snatched the child out of the water and set him down, howling, on the concrete.

His heart was beating furiously. He felt that he had just saved the boy from committing some enormous indignity. He saw it all now. The old man *had* transferred his fixation to the boy, *had* left him with the notion that he must baptize Bishop or suffer some terrible consequence. Tarwater put his foot down on the marble edge of the pool. He leaned forward, his elbow on his knee, looking over the side at his broken reflection in the water. His lips moved as if he were speaking silently to the face forming in the pool. Rayber said nothing. He realized now the magnitude of the boy's affliction. He knew that there was no way to appeal to him with reason. There was no hope of discussing it sanely with him, for it was a compulsion. He saw no way of curing him except perhaps through some shock, some sudden concrete confrontation with the futility, the ridiculous absurdity of performing the empty rite.

He squatted down and began to take off Bishop's wet shoes. The child had stopped howling and was crying quietly, his face red and hideously distorted. Rayber turned his eyes away.

Tarwater was walking off. He was past the pool, his back strangely bent as if he were being driven away with a whip. He was moving off onto one of the narrow tree-shaded paths.

"Wait!" Rayber shouted. "We can't go to the museum now. We'll have to go home and change Bishop's shoes."

Tarwater could not have failed to hear but he kept on walking and in a second was lost to view.

Goddam backwoods imbecile, Rayber said under his breath. He stood looking at the path where the boy had disappeared. He felt no urge to go after him for he knew that he would be back, that he was held by Bishop. His feeling of oppression was caused now by the certain knowledge that there was no way to get rid of him. He would be with them until he had either accomplished what he came for, or until he was cured. The words the old man had scrawled on the back of the journal rose before him: THE PROPHET I RAISE UP OUT OF THIS BOY WILL BURN YOUR EYES CLEAN. The sentence was like a challenge renewed. I will cure him, he said grimly. I will cure him or know the reason why.

VII

The Cherokee Lodge was a two-story converted warehouse, the lower part painted white and the upper green. One end sat on land and the other was set on stilts in a glassy little lake across which were dense woods, green and black farther toward the skyline, grey-blue. The long front side of the building, plastered with beer and cigaret signs, faced the highway, which ran about thirty feet away across a dirt road and beyond a narrow stretch of iron weed. Rayber had passed the place before but had never been tempted to stop.

He had selected it because it was only thirty miles from Powderhead and because it was cheap and he arrived there the next day with the two boys in time for them to take a walk and look around before they ate. The ride up had been oppressively silent, the boy sitting as usual on his side of the car like some foreign dignitary who would not admit speaking the language—the filthy hat, the stinking overalls, worn defiantly like a national costume.

Rayber had hit upon his plan in the night. It was to take him back to Powderhead and make him face what he had done. What he hoped was that if seeing and feeling the place again were a real shock, the boy's trauma might suddenly be revealed. His irrational fears and impulses would burst out and his uncle—sympathetic, knowing, uniquely able to understand—would be there to explain them to him. He had not said they were going to Powderhead. So far as the boy knew, this was to be a fishing trip. He thought that an afternoon of relaxation in a boat before the experiment would help ease the tension, his own as well as Tarwater's.

On the drive up, his thoughts had been interrupted once when he saw Bishop's face rise unorganized into the rearview mirror and then disappear as he attempted to crawl over the top of the front seat and climb into Tarwater's lap. The boy had turned and without looking at him had given the panting child a firm push onto the back seat again. One of Rayber's immediate goals was to make him understand that his urge to baptize the child was a kind of *sickness* and that a sign of returning health would be his ability to begin looking Bishop in the eye. Rayber felt that once he could look the child in the eye, he would have confidence in his ability to resist the morbid impulse to baptize him.

When they got out of the car, he watched the boy closely, trying to discover his first reaction to being in the country again. Tarwater stood for a moment, his head lifted sharply as if he detected some familiar odor moving from the pine forest across the lake. His long face, depending from the bulb-shaped hat, made Rayber think of a root jerked suddenly out of the ground and exposed to the light. The boy's eyes narrowed so that the lake must have been reduced to the width of a knife-blade in his sight. He looked at the water with a peculiar undisguised hostility. Rayber even thought that as his eye fell on it, he began to tremble. At least he was certain that his hands clenched. His glare steadied, then with his usual precipitous gait, he set off around the building without looking back.

Bishop climbed out of the car and thrust his face against his father's side. Absently Rayber put his hand on the little boy's ear and rubbed it gingerly, his fingers tingling as if they touched the sensitive scar of some old wound. Then he pushed the child aside, picked up the bag and started toward the screen door of the lodge. As he reached it, Tarwater came quickly around the side of the building with the distinct look to Rayber of being pursued. His feeling for the boy alternated drastically between compassion for his haunted look and fury at the way he was treated by him. Tarwater acted as if to see him at all required a special effort. Rayber opened the screen door and stepped inside, leaving the two boys to come in or not as they pleased.

The interior was dark. To the left he made out a reception desk with a heavy plain-looking woman behind it, leaning on her elbows. He set the bags down and gave her his name. He had the feeling that though her eyes were on him, they were looking behind him. He glanced around. Bishop was a few feet away, gaping at her.

"What's your name, Sugarpie?" she asked.

"His name is Bishop," Rayber said shortly. He was always irked when the child was stared at.

The woman tilted her head sympathetically. "I reckon you're taking him off to give his mother a little rest," she said, her eyes full of curiosity and compassion.

"I have him all the time," he said and added before he could stop himself, "his mother abandoned him."

"No!" she breathed. "Well," she said, "it takes all kinds of women. I couldn't leave a child like that."

You can't even take your eyes off him, he thought irritably and began to fill out the card. "Are the boats for rent?" he asked without looking up.

"Free for the guests," she said, "but anybody gets drowned, that's their lookout. How about him? Can he sit still in a boat?"

"Nothing ever happens to him," he murmured, finishing the card and turning it around to her.

She read it, then she glanced up and stared at Tarwater. He was standing a few feet behind Bishop, looking around him suspiciously, his hands in his pockets and his hat pulled down. She began to scowl. "That boy there—is yours too?" she asked, pointing the pen at him as if this were inconceivable.

Rayber realized that she must think he was some one hired for a guide. "Certainly, he's mine too," he said quickly and in a voice the boy could not fail to hear. He made it a point to impress on him that he was wanted, whether he cared to be wanted or not.

Tarwater lifted his head and returned the woman's stare. Then he took a stride forward and thrust his face at her. "What do you mean—is his?" he demanded.

"Is his," she said, drawing back. "You don't look it is all." Then she frowned as if, continuing to study him, she began to see a likeness.

"And I ain't it," he said. He snatched the card from her and read it. Rayber had written, "George F. Rayber, Frank and Bishop Rayber," and their address. The boy put the card down on the desk and picked up the pen, gripping it so hard that his fingers turned red at the tips. He crossed out the name *Frank* and underneath in an old man's meticulous hand he began to write something else.

Rayber looked at the woman helplessly and lifted his shoulders as if to say, "I have more than one problem," and shrug it off, but the gesture ended in a violent tremor. To his horror he felt the side of his mouth give a series of quick jerks. He had an instant's premonition that if he wished to save himself, he should leave at once, that the trip was doomed.

The woman handed him the key and, looking at him suspiciously, said, "Up the steps yonder and four doors down to the right. We don't have anybody to tote the bags."

He took the key and started up a rickety flight of steps to the left. Halfway up, he paused and said in a voice in which there was a remnant of authority, "Bring up that bag when you come, Frank."

The boy was finishing his essay on the card and gave no indication of hearing.

The woman's curious gaze followed Rayber up the stairs until he disappeared. She observed as his feet passed the level of her head that he had on one brown sock and one grey. His shoes were not run-down but he might have slept in his seersucker suit every night. He was in bad need of a haircut and his eyes had a peculiar look—like something human trapped in a switch box. Has come here to have a nervous breakdown, she said to herself. Then she turned her head. Her eyes rested on the two boys, who had not moved. And who wouldn't? she asked herself.

The afflicted child looked as if he must have dressed himself. He had on a black cowboy hat and a pair of short khaki pants that were too tight even for his narrow hips and a yellow t-shirt that had not been washed any time lately. Both his brown high-top shoes were untied. The upper part of him looked like an old man and the lower part like a child. The other, the mean-looking one, had picked up the desk card again and was reading over what he had written on it. He was so taken up with it that he did not see the little boy reaching out to touch him. The instant the child touched him, the country boy's shoulders leapt. He snatched his touched hand up and jammed it in his pocket. "Leave off!" he said in a high voice. "Git away and quit bothering me!"

"Mind how you talk to one of them there, you boy!" the woman hissed.

He looked at her as if it were the first time she had spoken to him. "Them there what?" he murmured.

"That there kind," she said, looking at him fiercely as if he had profaned the holy.

He looked back at the afflicted child and the woman was startled by the expression on his face. He seemed to see the little boy and nothing else, no air around him, no room, no nothing, as if his gaze had slipped and fallen into the center of the child's eyes and was still falling down and down and down. The little boy turned after a second and skipped off toward the steps and the country boy followed, so directly that he might have been attached to him by a tow-line. The child began to scramble up the steps on his hands and knees, kicking his feet up on each one. Then suddenly he flipped himself around and sat down squarely in the country boy's way and stuck his feet out in front of him, apparently wanting his shoes tied. The country boy stopped still. He hung over him like some one bewitched, his long arms bent uncertainly.

The woman watched fascinated. He ain't going to tie them, she said, not him.

He leaned over and began to tie them. Frowning furiously, he tied one and then the other and the child watched, completely absorbed in the operation. When the boy finished tying them, he straightened himself and said in a querulous voice, "Now git on and quit bothering me with them laces," and the child flipped over on his hands and feet and scrambled up the stairs, making a great din.

Confused by this kindness, the woman called, "Hey boy."

She had intended to say, "Whose boy are you?" but she said nothing, her mouth opening on a vanished sentence. His eyes as they turned and looked down at her were the color of the lake just before dark when the last daylight has faded and the moon has not risen yet, and for an instant she thought she saw something fleeing across the surface of them, a lost light that came from nowhere and vanished into nothing. For some moments they stared at each other without issue. Finally, convinced she had not seen it, she muttered, "Whatever devil's work you mean to do, don't do it here."

He continued to look down at her. "You can't just say NO," he said. "You got to do NO. You got to show it. You got to show you mean it by doing it. You got to show you're not going to do one thing by doing another. You got to make an end of it. One way or another."

"Don't you do nothing here," she said, wondering what he would do here.

"I never ast to come here," he said. "I never ast for that lake to be set down in front of me," and he turned and moved on up the stairs.

The woman looked in front of her for some time as if she were seeing her own thoughts before her like unintelligible handwriting on the wall. Then she looked down at the card on the counter and turned it over. "Francis Marion Tarwater," he had written. "Powderhead, Tennessee. NOT HIS SON."

VIII

After they had had their lunch, the schoolteacher suggested they get a boat and fish awhile. Tarwater could tell that he was watching him again, his little eyes protected and precise behind his glasses. He had been watching him ever since he came but now he was watching in a different way: he was watching for something that he planned to make happen. The trip was designed to be a trap but the boy had no attention to spare for it. His mind was entirely occupied with saving himself from the larger grander trap that he felt set all about him. Ever since his first night in the city when he had seen once and for all that the schoolteacher was of no significance—nothing but a piece of bait, an insult to his intelligence—his mind had been engaged in a continual struggle with the silence that confronted him, that demanded he baptize the child and begin at once the life the old man had prepared him for.

It was a strange waiting silence. It seemed to lie all around him like an invisible country whose borders he was always on the edge of, always in danger of crossing. From time to time as they had walked in the city, he had looked to the side and seen his own form alongside him in a store window, transparent as a snakeskin. It moved beside him like some violent ghost who had already crossed over and was reproaching him from the other side. If he turned his head the opposite way, there would be the dim-witted boy, hanging onto the schoolteacher's coat, watching him. His mouth hung in a lopsided smile but there was a judging sternness about his forehead. The boy never looked lower than the top of his head except by accident for the silent country appeared to be reflected again in the center of his eyes. It stretched out there, limitless and clear.

Tarwater could have baptized him any one of a hundred times without so much as touching him. Each time the temptation came, he would feel that the silence was about to surround him and he was going to be lost in it forever. He would have fallen but for the wise voice that sustained him—the stranger who had kept him company while he dug his uncle's grave.

Sensations, his friend—no longer a stranger—said. Feelings.

What you want is a sign, a real sign, suitable to a prophet. If you are a prophet, it's only right you should be treated like one. When Jonah dallied, he was cast three days in a belly of darkness and vomited up in the place of his mission. That was a sign; it wasn't no sensation.

It takes all my time to set you straight. Look at you, he said—going to that fancy-house of God, sitting there like an ape letting that girl-child bend your ear. What did you expect to see there? What did you expect to hear? The Lord speaks to prophets personally and He's never spoke to you, never lifted a finger, never dropped a gesture. And as for that strangeness in your gut, that comes from you, not the Lord. When you were a child you had worms. As likely as not you have them again.

The first day in the city he had become conscious of the strangeness in his stomach, a peculiar hunger. The city food only weakened him. He and his great-uncle had eaten well. If the old man had done nothing else for him, he had heaped his plate. Never a morning he had not awakened to the smell of fatback frying. The schoolteacher paid scarce attention to what he put inside him. For breakfast, he poured a bowl of shavings out of a cardboard box; in the middle of the day he made sandwiches out of lightbread; and at night he took them to a restaurant, a different one every night run by a different color of foreigner so that he would learn, he said, how other nationalities ate. The boy did not care how other nationalities ate. He had always left the restaurants hungry, conscious of an intrusion in his works. Since the breakfast he had finished sitting in the presence of his uncle's corpse, he had not been satisfied by food, and his hunger had become like an insistent silent force inside him, a silence inside akin to the silence outside, as if the grand trap left him barely an inch to move in, barely an inch in which to keep himself inviolate.

His friend was adamant that he refuse to entertain hunger as a sign. He pointed out that the prophets had been fed. Elijah had lain down under a juniper tree to die and had gone to sleep and an angel of the Lord had come and waked him and fed him a hearth-cake, had done it moreover twice, and Elijah had risen and gone about his business, lasting on the two hearth-cakes forty days and nights. Prophets did not languish in hunger but were fed from the Lord's bounty and the signs given them were unmistakable. His friend suggested he demand an unmistakable sign, not a pang of hunger or a reflection of himself in a store window, but an unmistakable sign, clear and suitable—water bursting forth from a rock, for instance, fire sweeping down at his command and destroying some site he would point to, such as the tabernacle he had gone to spit on.

His fourth night in the city, after he had returned from listening to the child preach, he had sat up in the welfare-woman's bed and raising his folded hat as if he were threatening the silence, he had demanded an unmistakable sign of the Lord.

Now we'll see what class of prophet you are, his friend said. We'll see what the Lord has in mind for you.

The next day the schoolteacher had taken them into a park where trees were fenced together in a kind of island that cars were not allowed in. They had only but entered it when he felt a hush in his blood and a stillness in the atmosphere as if the air were being purged for the approach of revelation. He would have turned and run but the schoolteacher parked himself on a bench and pretended to go to sleep with the dimwit in his lap. The trees rustled thickly and the clearing rose to his mind's eye. He imagined the blackened spot in the center of it between the two chimneys, and saw rising from the ashes the burnt-out frames of his own and his uncle's bed. He opened his mouth to get air and the schoolteacher woke up and began asking questions.

He prided himself that from the first night he had answered his questions with the cunning of a Negro, giving no information, knowing nothing, and each time he was questioned, raising his uncle's fury until it was observable under his skin in patches of pink and white. A few of his ready answers and the schoolteacher was willing to move on.

They had walked deeper into the park and he began to feel again the approach of mystery. He would have turned and run in the opposite direction but it was all on him in an instant. The path widened and they were faced with an open space in the middle of the park, a concrete circle with a fountain in the center of it. Water rushed out of the mouth of a stone lion's head into a shallow pool below and as soon as the dim-witted boy saw the water, he gave a whoop and galloped off toward it, flapping his arms like something released from a cage.

Tarwater saw exactly where he was heading, knew exactly what he was going to do.

"Too late, goddammit," the schoolteacher muttered, "he's in."

The child stood grinning in the pool, lifting his feet slowly up and down as if he liked the feel of the wet seeping into his shoes. The sun, which had been tacking from cloud to cloud, emerged above the fountain. A blinding brightness fell on the lion's tangled marble head and gilded the stream of water rushing from his mouth. Then the light, falling more gently, rested like a hand on the child's white head. His face might have been a mirror where the sun had stopped to watch its reflection.

Tarwater started forward. He felt a distinct tension in the quiet. The old man might have been lurking near, holding his breath, waiting for the baptism. His friend was silent as if in the felt presence, he dared not raise his voice. At each step the boy exerted a force backward but he continued nevertheless to move toward the pool. He reached the rim of it and lifted his foot to swing it over the side. Just as his shoe touched the water, the schoolteacher bounded forward and snatched the dimwit out. The child split the silence with his bellow.

Slowly Tarwater's lifted foot came down on the edge of the pool and he leaned there, looking into the water where a wavering face seemed trying to form itself. Gradually it became distinct and still, gaunt and cross-shaped. He observed, deep in its eyes, a look of starvation. I wasn't going to baptize him, he said, flinging the silent words at the silent face. I'd drown him first.

Drown him then, the face appeared to say.

Tarwater stepped back, shocked. Scowling, he straightened himself and moved away. The sun had gone in and there were black caves in the tree branches. Bishop was lying on his back, roaring from a red distorted face, and the schoolteacher stood above him, staring at nothing in particular as if it were he who had received a revelation.

Well, that's your sign, his friend said—the sun coming out from under a cloud and falling on the head of a dimwit. Something that could happen fifty times a day without no one being the wiser. And it took that schoolteacher to save you and just in time. Left to yourself you would already have done it and been lost forever. Listen, he said, you have to quit confusing a madness with a mission. You can't spend your life fooling yourself this way. You have to take hold and put temptation behind you. If you baptize once, you'll be doing it the rest of your life. If it's an idiot this time, the next time it's liable to be a nigger. Save yourself while the hour of salvation is at hand.

But the boy was shaken. He scarcely heard the voice as he walked off deeper into the park and down a path he scarcely saw. When he finally took note of his surroundings, he was sitting on a bench, looking down at his feet where two pigeons were moving in drunken circles. On the other side of the bench was a man of a generally grey appearance who had been examining a hole in his shoe when Tarwater sat down but who stopped then and devoted himself to a close scrutiny of the boy. Finally he reached over and plucked Tarwater's sleeve. The boy looked up into two pale yellow-rimmed eyes.

"Be like me, young fellow," the stranger said, "don't let no jackasses tell you what to do." He was grinning wisely and his eyes held a malevolent promise of unwanted friendship. His voice sounded familiar but his appearance was as unpleasant as a stain.

The boy got up and left hastily. An interesting coincident, his friend observed, that he should say the same thing as I've been saying. You think there's a trap laid all about you by the Lord. There ain't any trap. There ain't anything except what you've laid for yourself. The Lord is not studying about you, don't know you exist, and wouldn't do a thing about it if He did. You're alone in the world, with only yourself to ask or thank or judge; with only yourself. And me. I'll never desert you.

The first sight that met his eyes when he got out of the car at the Cherokee Lodge was the little lake. It lay there, glass-like, still, reflecting a crown of trees and an infinite overarching sky. It looked so unused that it might only the moment before have been set down by four strapping angels for him to baptize the child in. A weakness working itself up from his knees, reached his stomach and came upward and forced a tremor in his jaw. Steady, his friend said, everywhere you go you'll find water. It wasn't invented yesterday. But remember: water is made for more than one thing. Hasn't the time come? Don't you have to do something at last, one thing to prove you ain't going to do another? Hasn't your hour of dallying passed?

They ate their lunch in the dark other-end of the lobby where the woman who ran the place served meals. Tarwater ate voraciously. With an expression of intense concentration, he ate six buns filled with barbecue and drank three cans of beer. He might have been preparing himself for a long journey or for some action that would take all his strength. Rayber observed his sudden appetite for the poor food and decided that he was eating compulsively. He wondered if the beer might loosen his tongue, but in the boat he was as glum as ever. He sat hunched over, his hat pulled down, and scowled at the spot where his line disappeared in the water.

They had managed to get the boat away from the dock before Bishop came out of the lodge. The woman had drawn him to an icecooler and produced a green popsickle which she held up for him while she gazed fascinated into his mysterious face. They were in the middle of the lake before he came clattering down the dock, the woman running behind. She snatched him just in time to keep him from plunging over the edge.

Rayber made a frantic grabbing motion in the boat and cried out. Then he reddened and scowled. "Don't look," he said, "she'll take care of him. We need a break."

The boy gazed darkly where the accident had been prevented. The child was a black spot in the glare of his vision. The woman turned him around and started leading him back to the lodge. "It wouldn't have been no great loss if he had drowned," he observed.

Rayber had an instant's picture of himself, standing in the ocean, holding the child's limp body in his arms. With a kind of convulsive motion, he cleared his head of the image. Then he saw that Tarwater had observed his discomposure; he was looking at him with a distinct attention, a peculiar prescient look as if he were about to penetrate some secret.

"Nothing ever happens to that kind of child," Rayber said. "In a hundred years people may have learned enough to put them to sleep when they're born."

Something appeared to be working on the boy's face, struggling there, some war between agreement and outrage.

Rayber's blood burned beneath his skin. He tried to restrain the urge to confess. He leaned forward; his mouth opened and closed and then in a dry voice he said, "Once I tried to drown him," and grinned horribly at the boy.

Tarwater's lips parted as if only they had heard, but he said nothing.

"It was a failure of nerve," Rayber said. The glare on the water gave him the sensation of glancing at white fire each time he looked up or out where it was reflected on the water. He turned down the brim of his hat all the way around.

"You didn't have the guts," Tarwater said as if he would put it in a more accurate way. "He always told me you couldn't do nothing, couldn't act."

The schoolteacher leaned forward and said between his teeth, "I've resisted him. I've done that. What have you done? Maybe you attended to him the quickest way but it takes more than that to go against his will for good. Are you quite sure," he said, "are you quite sure you've overcome him? I doubt it. I think you're chained to him right now. I think you're not going to be free of him without my help. I think you've got problems that you're not capable of solving yourself."

The boy scowled and was silent.

The glare pierced Rayber's eyeballs fiercely. He did not think he could stand an afternoon of this. He felt recklessly compelled to pursue the subject. "How do you like being in the country again?" he growled. "Remind you of Powderhead?"

"I come to fish," the boy said disagreeably.

Goddam you, his uncle thought, all I'm trying to do is save you from being a freak. He was holding his line unbaited in the blinding water. He felt a madness on him to talk about the old man. "I remember the first time I ever saw him," he said. "I was six or seven. I was out in the yard playing and all of a sudden I felt something between me and the sun. Him. I looked up and there he was, those mad fish-coloured eyes looking down at me. Do you know what he said to me—a seven year old child?" He tried to make his voice sound like the old man's. "'Listen boy,' he said, 'the Lord Jesus Christ sent me to find you. You have to be born again.'" He laughed, glaring at the boy with his furious blistered-looking eyes. "The Lord Jesus Christ had my welfare so at heart that he sent a personal representative. Where was the calamity? The calamity was I believed him. For five or six years. I had nothing else but that. I waited on the Lord Jesus. I thought I'd been born again and that everything was going to be different or was different already because the Lord Jesus had a great interest in me."

Tarwater shifted on the seat. He seemed to listen as if behind a wall.

"It was the eyes that got me," Rayber said. "Children may be attracted to mad eyes. A grown person could have resisted. A child couldn't. Children are cursed with believing."

The boy recognized the sentence. "Some ain't," he said.

The schoolteacher smiled thinly. "And some who think they aren't are," he said, feeling that he was back in control. "It's not as easy as you think to throw it off. Do you know," he said, "that there's a part of your mind that works all the time, that you're not aware of yourself. Things go on in it. All sorts of things you don't know about."

Tarwater looked around him as if he were vainly searching for a way to get out of the boat and walk off.

"I think you're basically very bright," his uncle said. "I think you can understand the things that are said to you."

"I never came for no school lesson," the boy said rudely. "I come to fish. I ain't worried what my underhead is doing. I know what I think when I do it and when I get ready to do it, I don't talk no words. I do it." There was a dull anger in his voice. He was becoming aware of how much he had eaten. The food appeared to be sinking like a leaden column inside him and to be pushed back at the same time by the hunger it had intruded upon.

The schoolteacher watched him a moment and then said, "Well anyway, as far as the baptizing went, the old man could have spared himself. I was already baptized. My mother never overcame her upbringing and she had had it done. But the damage to me of having it done at the age of seven was tremendous. It made a lasting scar."

The boy looked up suddenly as if there had been a tug at his line. "Him back there," he said and jerked his head toward the lodge, "he ain't been baptized?"

"No," Rayber said. He looked at him narrowly. He thought that if he could get the right words in now, he might do some good, might give him a painless lesson. "I may not have the guts to drown him," he said, "but I have the guts to maintain my self-respect and not to perform futile rites over him. I have the guts not to become the prey of superstitions. He is what he is and there's nothing for him to be born into. My guts," he finished, "are in my head."

The boy only stared at him, his eyes filmed with a dull cast of nausea.

"The great dignity of man," his uncle said, "is his ability to say: I am born once and no more. What I can see and do for myself and my fellowman in this life is all of my portion and I'm content with it. It's enough to be a man." There was a light ring in his voice. He watched the boy closely to see if he had struck a chord.

Tarwater turned an expressionless face toward the rim of trees that made a paling around the lake. He appeared to stare into emptiness.

Rayber subsided again but he could stand it only a few minutes. He finished the cigaret and lit another. Then he decided to start off on a new tack and leave the morbid alone for a while. "I'll tell you what I've planned for us to do in a couple of weeks," he said in an almost affable tone. "We're going up for a plane ride. How about that?" He had been considering this, holding it in reserve, thinking it would be the greatest marvel he could produce, something that would surely stir the glum child out of himself.

There was no response. The boy's eyes looked glazed.

"Flying is the greatest engineering achievement of man," Rayber said in an irked voice. "Doesn't it stir your imagination even slightly? If it doesn't I'm afraid there's something wrong with you."

"I done flew," Tarwater said and suppressed a belch. He was entirely occupied with his nausea which he could feel minutely rising.

"How could you have flown?" his uncle asked angrily.

"Him and me give a dollar to go up in one at a fair once," he said. "The houses weren't nothing but matchboxes and the people were invisible—like germs. I wouldn't give you nothing for no airplane. A buzzard can fly."

The schoolteacher gripped both sides of the boat and pushed forward. "He's warped your whole life," he said hoarsely. "You're going to grow up to be a freak if you don't let yourself be helped. You still believe all that crap he taught you. You're eaten up with false guilt. I can read you like a book!" The words were out before he could stop them.

The boy did not even look at him. He leaned over the side of the boat and shuddered. The column, released, formed a sweetly sour circle on the water. A wave of dizziness came over him and then his head cleared. A ravenous emptiness raged in his stomach as if it had reestablished its rightful tenure. He washed his mouth out with a handful of the lake and then wiped his face on his sleeve.

Rayber trembled at his recklessness. He felt certain he had produced this by the word *guilt*. He put his hand on the boy's knee and said, "You'll feel better now."

Tarwater said nothing, glaring with his red-lidded wet eyes at the water as if he were glad he had polluted it.

"It's just as much relief," his uncle said, pressing his advantage, "to get something off your mind as off your stomach. When you tell somebody else your troubles, then they don't bother you so much, they don't get in your blood and make you sick. Somebody else shares the weight. God boy," he said, "you need help. You need to be saved right here now from the old man and everything he stands for. And I'm the one who can save you." With his hat turned down all around he looked like a fanatical country preacher. His eyes glistened. "I know what your problem is," he said. "I know and I can help you. Something's eating you on the inside and I can tell you what it is."

The boy looked at him fiercely. "Why don't you shut your big mouth?" he said. "Why don't you pull that plug out of your ear and turn yourself off? I come to fish. I never came to have no traffic with you."

His uncle snapped the cigaret out of his fingers and it hit the water with a hiss. "Every day," he said coldly, "you remind me more of the old man. You're just like him. You have his future before you."

The boy put down his line. With rigid deliberate movements he lifted his right foot and pulled off his shoe, then his left foot and pulled off that shoe. Then he jerked the straps of his overalls off his shoulders and pulled them down, over his bottom and off. He had on a pair of long thin old man's drawers. He pulled his hat tight down on his head so that it would not possibly come off, then he threw himself out of the boat and swam away, smashing the glassy lake with his cupped fists as if he would like to make it sting and bleed.

My God! Rayber thought, I touched a nerve that time! He kept his eye on the hat in the receding spasm of water. The empty overalls lay at his feet. He grabbed them and felt in the pockets. He took out two stones, a nickel, a box of wooden matches and three nails. He had brought along the new suit and shirt and laid them out on a chair.

Tarwater reached the dock and climbed onto it, the drawers clinging to him, the hat still ground down on his forehead. He turned just in time to see his uncle thrust the bundled overalls below the surface of the water.

Rayber felt as if he had just run across a mined field. At once he was afraid he had made a mistake. The thin rigid figure on the dock did not move. It seemed no more than a wraith-like column of fragile white-hot rage, materialized for an instant, the makings of some pure unfathomable passion. The boy turned and started rapidly toward the lodge and Rayber decided it would be best to linger on the lake a while.

When he came in, he was startled to see Tarwater lying on the far cot in his new clothes and to see Bishop sitting on the other end of it, watching him as if he were mesmerized by the steel-like glint that came from the boy's eyes and was directed into his own. In the plaid shirt and new blue trousers, he looked like a changeling, half his old self and half his new, already half the boy he would be when he was rehabilitated.

Rayber's spirits rose cautiously. He was holding the shoes with the contents of the overall pockets in them. He set them down on the bed and said, "No hard feelings about the clothes, old man. That was just my round."

There was a strange suppressed excitement about the boy's whole figure, as if he had settled on an inevitable course of action. He did not get up, did not acknowledge the shoes, but he acknowledged his uncle's presence by shifting the glint in his eyes slightly, on him and then away. The schoolteacher might have been just enough present to be ignored. Then he looked back at Bishop, triumphantly, boldly, into the very center of his eyes.

Rayber stood puzzled in the doorway. "Who wants to go for a ride?" he asked.

Bishop jumped off the bed and was at his side in an instant. Tarwater started at the little boy's abrupt disappearance from his field of vision, but he did not get up or turn his face toward the schoolteacher in the door.

"Well, we'll leave Frank to his meditations," Rayber said and swung the child around by the shoulder and left with him, hastily. He wanted to escape before the boy changed his mind.

IX

The heat was not as intense on the road as it had been on the lake and he drove with a sense of refreshment he had not felt in the five days Tarwater had been with him. Once out of sight of the boy, he felt a pressure had been lifted from the atmosphere. He eliminated the oppressive presence from his thoughts and retained only those aspects of it that could be abstracted, clean, into the future person he envisioned.

The sky was a cloudless even blue and he drove without destination, though he meant before they returned to the lodge to stop and have the car filled for tomorrow's trip to Powderhead. Bishop was hanging out the window, his mouth open, letting the air dry his tongue. Automatically, Rayber reached over and locked the door and pulled him back in by his shirt. The child sat, solemnly taking his hat off his head and putting it on his feet, then taking it off his feet and putting it on his head. After he had done this a while, he climbed over the seat and disappeared into the back of the car.

Rayber continued to think of Tarwater's future, his thoughts rewarding except when every now and then the boy's actual face would lodge in the path of a plan. The sudden intrusion of the face made him think of his wife. He seldom thought of her anymore. She would not divorce him for fear she would be given custody of the child and she was now as far away as she could get, in Japan, in some welfare capacity. He was aware of his good fortune in getting rid of her. It was she who had prevented his going back and getting Tarwater away from the old man. She would have been glad enough to have had him if she had not seen him that day when they went to Powderhead to face the old man down. The baby had crawled into the door behind old Tarwater and had sat there, unblinking, as the old man raised his gun and shot Rayber in the leg and then in the ear. She had seen him; Rayber had not; but she would not forget the face. It was not simply that the child was dirty, thin, and grey; it was that its expression had no more changed when the gun went off than the old man's had. This had affected her deeply.

If there had not been something repellent in its face, she said, her maternal instinct would have made her rush forward and snatch it. She had even had that in mind before they arrived and she would have had the courage to do it in spite of the old man's gun; but the child's look had frozen her. It was the opposite of everything appealing. She could not express her exact revulsion, for her feeling was not logical. It had, she said, the look of an adult, not of a child, and of an adult with immovable insane convictions. Its face was like the face she had seen in some medieval paintings where the martyr's limbs are being sawed off and his expression says he is being deprived of nothing essential. She had had the sense, seeing the child in the door, that if it had known that at that moment all its future advantages were being stolen from it, its expression would not have altered a jot. The face for her had expressed the depth of human perversity, the deadly sin of rejecting defiantly one's own obvious good. He had thought all this was possibly her imagination but he understood now that it was not imagination but fact. She said she could not have lived with such a face; she would have been bound to destroy the arrogant look on it.

He reflected wryly that she had not been able to live with Bishop's face any better though there was no arrogance on it. The little boy had climbed up from the floor of the back seat and was hanging over breathing into his ear. By temperament and training she was ready to handle an exceptional child, but not one as exceptional as Bishop, not one bearing her own family name and the face of "that horrible old man." She had returned once in the last two years and demanded that he put Bishop in an institution because she said he could not adequately care for him —though it was plain from the look of him that he thrived like an air plant. His own behaviour on that occasion was still a source of satisfaction to him. He had knocked her not quite halfway across the room.

He had known by that time that his own stability depended on the little boy's presence. He could control his terrifying love as long as it had its focus in Bishop, but if anything happened to the child, he would have to face it in itself. Then the whole world would become his idiot child. He had thought what he would have to do if anything happened to Bishop. He would have with one supreme effort to resist the recognition; with every nerve and muscle and thought, he would have to resist feeling anything at all, thinking anything at all. He would have to anesthetize his life. He shook his head to clear it of these unpleasant thoughts. After it had cleared, they returned one by one. He felt a sinister pull on his consciousness, the familiar undertow of expectation, as if he were still a child waiting on Christ.

The car apparently of its own volition had turned onto a dirt road which without warning pierced his abstraction with its familiarity. He put on his brakes.

It was a narrow corrugated road sunk between deep red embankments. He looked about him angrily. He had not had the least intention of coming here today. His car was on the crest of a hill and the embankments on either side had the look of forming an entrance to a region he would enter at his peril. The road sloped down a quarter of a mile or so within his sight and then turned to disappear behind an edge of the wood. When he had been on this road the first time, he had ridden it backwards. A Negro with a mule and wagon had met him and his uncle at the junction and they had ridden, their feet dangling from the back of the wagon. He had leaned over most of the way, watching the mule's hoofprints in the dust as they rolled over them.

He decided finally that there would be wisdom in looking at the place today so that there would be no surprises for him when he returned tomorrow with the boy, but for some few moments, he did not move on. The road that lay in front of him he remembered as being four or five miles long. Then there was a stretch through the woods that would have to be walked and then the field to be crossed. He thought with distaste of crossing it twice, today and again tomorrow. He thought with distaste of crossing it at all. Then as if to stop his thinking, he put his foot down hard on the accelerator and took the road defiantly. Bishop jumped up and down, squealing and making unintelligible noises of delight.

The road grew narrower as it approached its end and presently he found himself going over what was no more than a rutted wagon path, his speed reduced to nothing. He stopped the car finally in a little clearing grown up in Johnson grass and blackberry bushes where what was left of the road touched the edge of the wood. Bishop jumped out and made for the blackberry bushes, attracted by the wasps that buzzed over them. Rayber leapt out and grabbed him just before he reached for one. Gingerly he picked the child a blackberry and handed it to him. The little boy studied it and then, with his fallen smile, returned it to him as if they were performing a ceremony. Rayber flung it away and turned to find the trail through the woods.

He took the child by the hand and pulled him along on what he thought might shortly become a path. The forest rose about him, mysterious and alien. Descending to speak with the shade of my uncle, he thought irritably and wondered if the old man's charred bones would be lying in the ashes. At the thought he almost stopped but did not. Bishop could barely walk for gaping. He lifted his face to stare open-mouthed above him as if he were in some vast overwhelming edifice. His hat fell off and Rayber picked it up and clamped it on his head again and pulled him on. Somewhere below them out of the silence a bird sounded four crystal notes. The child stopped, his breath held.

Rayber knew suddenly that alone with Bishop he could not go to the bottom and cross the field. Tomorrow with the other boy, with his brain engaged, he would be able to make it. He remembered that somewhere along here there was a point where one could look out between two trees and see the clearing below. When he had first walked through the wood with his uncle, they had stopped at that place and his uncle had pointed down to where, far across the field, a sagging unpainted house stood in a bare hard-packed yard. "Yonder it is," he had said, "and someday it'll be yours—these woods and that field and that fine house." He remembered that his heart had expanded unbelievably.

Suddenly he realized that the place *was* his. In the stress of having the boy return to him, he had never considered the property. He stopped, astounded by the fact that he owned all of this. His trees stood rising above him, majestic and aloof, as if they belonged to an order that had never budged from its first allegiance in the days of creation. His heart began to beat frenetically. Quickly he reduced the whole wood in probable board feet into a college education for the boy. His spirits lifted. He pulled the child along, intending to find the opening where the house could be seen. A few yards below, a sudden patch of sky indicated the spot. He let Bishop go and strode toward it.

The forked tree was familiar to him or seemed so. He put his hand on one trunk, leaned forward and looked out. His gaze moved quickly and unseeing across the field and stopped abruptly where the house had been. Two chimneys stood there, separated by a black space of rubble.

He stood expressionless, his heart strangely wrenched. If the bones were lying in the ashes he could not see them from this distance, but a vision of the old man, farther away in time, rose before him. He saw him standing on the edge of the yard, one hand lifted in an astounded greeting, while he stood a little way off in the field, his fists clenched, trying to shout, trying to make his adolescent fury come out in clear sensible words. He had only stood there shrilling, "You're crazy, you're crazy, you're a liar, you have a head full of crap, you belong in a nut house!" and then had turned and run, carrying away nothing but the registered change in the old man's expression, the sudden drop into some mysterious misery, which afterwards he had never been able to get out of his mind. He saw it as he stared at the two denuded chimneys.

He felt a pressure on his hand and glanced down, continuing to see the same expression and barely noting that it was Bishop he was looking at now. The child wanted to be lifted up to see. Absently he picked him up and held him in the fork of the tree and let him look out. The dull face, the empty grey eyes seemed to Rayber to reflect the ravaged scene across the field. The little boy turned his head after a moment and gazed instead at him. A dreaded sense of loss came over him. He knew that he could not remain here an instant longer. He turned with the child and went quickly back through the woods the way he had come.

On the highway again, he drove gripping the wheel, his face tense, his mind turned on the problem of Tarwater as if his own and not only the boy's salvation depended on his solving it. He had ruined his plan by going to Powderhead too soon. He knew he could not go there again, that he would have to find another way. He went over the afternoon's experience in the boat. There, he thought, he had been on the right track. He had simply not gone far enough. He decided that he would put the whole thing verbally before the boy. He would not argue with him but only tell him, tell him in so many plain words that he had a compulsion and what it was. Whether he answered, whether he cooperated, he would have to listen. He could not escape knowing that there was someone who knew exactly what went on inside him and who understood it for the good reason that it was understandable. He would go the whole way this time and tell him everything. The boy should at least know that he had no secrets. Casually while they ate their supper, he would lift the compulsion from his mind, expose it to the light, and let him have a good look at it. What he did about it would be his own affair. All at once this seemed to him extremely simple, the way he should have proceeded in the first place. Only time simplifies, he thought.

He stopped for gas at a pink stucco filling station where pottery and whirligigs were sold. While the car was being filled, he got out and looked for something to take as a peace offering, for he wanted the encounter to be pleasant if possible. His eye roved over a shelf of false hands, imitation buck teeth, boxes of simulated dog dung to put on the rug, wooden plaques with cynical mottos burnt on them. Finally he saw a combination corkscrew-bottleopener that fit in the palm of the hand. He bought it and left.

When they returned to the room, the boy was still lying on the cot, his face set in a deadly calm as if his eyes had not moved since they left. Again Rayber had a vision of the face his wife must have seen and he experienced a moment's revulsion for the boy that made him tremble. Bishop climbed onto the bottom of the cot and Tarwater returned the child's gaze steadily. He seemed unaware that Rayber was in the room.

"I could eat a horse," the schoolteacher said. "Let's go down."

The boy turned his head and regarded him evenly, with no interest but with no hostility. "It's what you'll get," he said, "if you eat here."

Rayber, unamused, pulled out the corkscrew-bottleopener and dropped it negligently on his chest. "That might come in handy sometime," he said and turned and began to wash his hands at the basin.

In the mirror, he saw him pick it up gingerly and look at it. He pushed the corkscrew out of the circle and then meditatively pushed it back. He studied it back and front and held it in the palm of his hand where it fit like a halfdollar. Presently he said in a grudging voice, "I don't have no use for it but I thank you," and put it in his pocket.

He returned his attention to Bishop as if this were its natural place. He lifted himself on one elbow and fixed the child with a narrow look. "Git up, you," he said slowly. He might have been commanding a small animal he was successfully training. His voice was steady but experimental. The hostility in it seemed contained and directed toward some planned goal. The little boy was watching with complete fascination.

"Git up now, like I tol' you to," Tarwater repeated slowly.

The child obediently climbed down off the bed.

Rayber felt a twinge of ridiculous jealousy. He stood by, his brows working irritably as the boy moved out of the door without a word and Bishop followed him. After a moment he slung his towel into the basin and walked after them.

The lodge was shaking with the stamping of four couples dancing at the other end of the lobby where the woman who ran the place had a nickelodeon. The three of them sat down at the red tin table and Rayber turned off his hearing aid until the racket should stop. He sat glaring around him, disgruntled at this intrusion.

The dancers were about Tarwater's age but they might have

belonged to a different species entirely. The girls could be distinguished from the boys only by their tight skirts and bare legs; their faces and heads were alike. They danced with a furious stern concentration. Bishop was entranced. He stood up in his chair, watching them, his head hanging forward as if any moment it might drop off. Tarwater, his eyes dark and distant, stared through them. They might have been insects buzzing across the surface of his vision.

When the music whined to a stop, they clambered back to their table and sprawled in their chairs. Rayber turned his hearing aid on and winced as Bishop's bellow blared into his head. The child was jumping up and down in his chair, roaring his disappointment. As soon as the dancers saw him, he stopped making the noise and stood still, devouring them with his gape. An angry silence fell over them. Their look was shocked and affronted as if they had been betrayed by a fault in creation, something that should have been corrected before they were allowed to see it. With pleasure Rayber could have dashed across the room and swung his lifted chair in their faces. They got up and pushed each other out sullenly, packed themselves in a topless automobile and roared off, sending an indignant spray of gravel against the side of the lodge. Rayber let out his breath as if it were sharp and might cut him. Then his eyes fell on Tarwater.

The boy was looking directly at him with an omniscient smile, faint but decided. It was a smile that Rayber had seen on his face before. It seemed to mock him from an ever-deepening inner knowledge that grew in indifference as it came nearer and nearer to a secret truth about him. Without warning its meaning pierced Rayber and he felt such a fury that for the moment all his strength left him. Go, he wanted to shout. Get your damn impudent face out of my sight! Go to hell! Go baptize the whole world!

The woman had been standing for some time at his side, waiting to take their order but she could have been invisible for all the notice he paid her. She began tapping the menu on a glass, then she slid it in front of his face. Without reading it, he said, "Three hamburger plates," and thrust it aside.

When she was gone, he said in a dry voice, "I want to lay some cards on the table." He sought the boy's eyes and steadied himself by the hated glint in them.

Tarwater looked at the table as if waiting for the cards to be laid on it.

"That means I want to talk straight to you," Rayber said, rigidly keeping the exasperation out of his voice. He strove to make his gaze, his tone, as indifferent as his listener's. "I have some things to say to you that you'll have to listen to. What you do about what I have to say is your own business. I have no further interest in telling you what to do. I only intend to put the facts before you." His voice was thin and brittle-sounding. He might have been reading from a paper. "I notice that you've begun to be able to look Bishop in the eye. That's good. It means you're making progress but you needn't think that because you can look him in the eye now, you've saved yourself from what's preying on you. You haven't. The old man still has you in his grip. Don't think he hasn't."

The boy continued to give him the same omniscient look. "It's you the seed fell in," he said. "It ain't a thing you can do about it. It fell on bad ground but it fell in deep. With me," he said proudly, "it fell on rock and the wind carried it away."

The schoolteacher grasped the table as if he were going to push it forward into the boy's chest. "Goddam you!" he said in a breathless harsh voice. "It fell in us both alike. The difference is that I know it's in me and I keep it under control. I weed it out but you're too blind to know it's in you. You don't even know what makes you do the things you do."

The boy looked at him angrily but he said nothing.

At least, Rayber thought, I've shocked that look off his face. He did not say anything for a few moments while he thought how to continue.

The woman returned with the three plates. She set them down slowly, giving herself time for observation. The man's face had a sweaty harassed look and so did the boy's. He threw her an ugly glance. The man began to eat at once as if he wanted to get it over with. The little boy took his bun apart and began to lick the mustard off it. The other boy looked at his as if it were probably bad meat and did not touch it. She left and watched indignantly for a few seconds from the kitchen door. The boy finally picked his hamburger up. He raised it half-way to his mouth and then put it down again. He picked it up and put it down twice without biting into it. Then he pulled his hat down and sat there, his arms folded. She had had enough and closed the door.

The schoolteacher leaned forward across the table, his eyes pin-pointed and very bright. "You can't eat," he said, "because something is eating you. And I intend to tell you what it is."

"Worms," the boy hissed as if his disgust could not be contained an instant longer.

"It takes guts to listen," Rayber said.

Tarwater leaned toward him with a kind of blaring attention. "You ain't got nothing to say to me that I don't have the guts to listen to," he said.

The schoolteacher sat back. "All right," he said, "then listen." He folded his arms and looked at him for an instant before he began. Then he started coldly. "The old man told you to baptize Bishop. You have that order lodged in your head like a boulder blocking your path."

The blood drained from the boy's face but his eyes did not swerve. They looked at Rayber furiously, the glint in them gone.

The schoolteacher spoke slowly, picking his words as if he were looking for the steadiest stones to step on across a rushing stream. "Until you get rid of this compulsion to baptize Bishop, you'll never make any progress toward being a normal person. I said in the boat you were going to be a freak. I shouldn't have said that. I only meant you had the choice. I want you to see the choice. I want you to make the choice and not simply be driven by a compulsion you don't understand. What we understand, we can control," he said. "You have to understand what it is that blocks you. I wonder if you're smart enough to take this in. It's not simple."

The boy's face seemed dry and old as if he had taken it in long ago, and now it was part of him like the current of death in his blood. The schoolteacher was touched by this muteness before the facts. His anger left him. The room was silent. A pink cast had fallen from the windows over the table. Tarwater looked away from his uncle at Bishop. The little boy's hair was pink and lighter than his face. He was sucking his spoon; his eyes were drowned in silence.

"I want to put two solutions before you," Rayber said. "What you do is up to you."

Tarwater looked at him again, with no mockery, no glint in his eye, but with no anticipation either, as if his course were irrevocably set.

"Baptism is only an empty act," the schoolteacher said. "If there's any way to be born again, it's a way that you accomplish yourself, an understanding about yourself that you reach after a long time, perhaps a long effort. It's nothing you get from above by spilling a little water and a few words. What you want to do is meaningless, so the easiest solution would be simply to do it. Right here now, with this glass of water. I would permit it in order to get it out of your mind. As far as I'm concerned, you may baptize him at once." He pushed his own glass of water across the table. His look was patient and ironical.

The boy's glance touched the top of the glass and then bounded off. His hand lying by the side of his plate twitched. He jammed it into his pocket and looked the other way, out the window. His whole aspect seemed shaken as if his integrity had been dangerously challenged.

The schoolteacher pulled back the glass of water. "I knew that would be too cheap for you," he said. "I knew you would refuse to do anything so unworthy of the courage you've already shown." He raised the glass and drank the rest of the water. Then he set it down on the table. He looked tired enough to collapse; his aspect was so weary that he might just have attained the top of a mountain he had been climbing for days.

After an interval he said, "The other way is not so simple. It's the way I've chosen for myself. It's the way you take as a result of being born again the natural way—through your own efforts. Your intelligence." His words had a disconnected sound. "The other way is simply to face it and fight it, to cut down the weed every time you see it appear. Do I have to tell you this? An intelligent boy like you?"

"You don't have to tell me nothing," Tarwater murmured.

"I don't have a compulsion to baptize him," Rayber said. "My own is more complicated, but the principle is the same. The way we have to fight it is the same."

"It ain't the same," Tarwater said. He turned toward his uncle. The glint had reappeared. "I can pull it up by the roots, once and for all. I can do something. I ain't like you. All you can do is think what you would have done if you had done it. Not me. I can do it. I can act." He was looking at his uncle now with a completely fresh contempt. "It's nothing about me like you," he said.

"There are certain laws that determine every man's conduct," the schoolteacher said. "You are no exception." He saw with perfect clarity that the only feeling he had for this boy was hate. He loathed the very sight of him.

"Wait and see," Tarwater said as if it needed only a short time to be proved.

"Experience is a terrible teacher," Rayber said.

The boy shrugged and got up. He walked off, across the room to the screen door where he stood looking out. At once Bishop climbed down off his chair and started after him, putting on his hat as he went. Tarwater stiffened when the child approached but he did not move and Rayber watched as the two of them stood there side by side, looking out the door—the two figures, hatted and somehow ancient, bound together by some necessity of nerve that excluded him. He was startled to see the boy put his hand on Bishop's neck just under his hat, open the door and guide him out of it. It occurred to him that what he meant by "doing something" was to make a slave of the child. Bishop would be at his command like a faithful dog. Instead of avoiding him, he planned to control him, to show who was master.

And I will not permit that, he said. If anyone controlled Bishop, it would be himself. He put his money on the table under the salt-shaker and went out after them.

The sky was a bright pink, casting such a weird light that every color was intensified. Each weed that grew out of the gravel looked like a live green nerve. The world might have been shedding its skin. The two were in front of him half way down the dock, walking slowly, Tarwater's hand still resting just under Bishop's hat; but it seemed to Rayber that it was Bishop who was doing the leading, that the child had made the capture. He thought with a grim pleasure that sooner or later the boy's confidence in his own judgment would be brought low.

When they arrived at the end of the dock, they stood looking down into the water. Then to Rayber's chagrin, the boy lifted the child like a sack under the arms and lowered him over the edge of the dock into the boat that was tied there.

"I haven't given you permission to take Bishop out in the boat," Rayber said.

Tarwater may have heard or he may not; he did not answer. He sat down on the edge of the dock and for a few moments looked across the water at the opposite bank. Part of a red globe hung almost motionless in the far side of the lake as if it were the other end of the elongated sun cut through the middle by a swath of forest. Pink and salmon-colored clouds floated in the water at different depths. Suddenly Rayber wanted nothing so much as a half hour to himself, without sight of either of them. "But you may take him," he said, "if you'll be careful."

The boy didn't move. He was leaning forward, his thin shoulders hunched, his hands gripped on the edge of the dock. He seemed poised there waiting to make a momentous move.

He dropped down into the boat with Bishop.

"You'll look after him?" Rayber asked.

Tarwater's face was like a very old mask, colorless and dry. "I'll tend to him," he said.

"Thanks," his uncle said. He experienced a short feeling of warmth for the boy. He strolled back down the dock to the lodge and when he reached the door, he turned and watched the boat move out into view on the lake. He raised his arm and waved but Tarwater showed no sign of seeing him and Bishop's back was turned. The small black-hatted figure sat like a passenger being borne by the surly oarsman across the lake to some mysterious destination.

Back in his room, Rayber lay on the cot trying to feel the release he had felt when he started out in the car in the afternoon. More than anything else, what he experienced in the boy's presence was the feeling of pressure and when it was taken off for a while, he realized how intolerable it was. He lay there thinking with distaste of the moment when the silent mutinous face would appear again in the door. He imagined the rest of the summer spent coping with the boy's cold intractability. He began to consider the possibility of his leaving of his own accord and after a moment he knew that this was actually what he wanted him to do. He no longer felt any challenge to rehabilitate him. All he wanted now was to get rid of him. He thought with horror of being stuck with him for good and began to consider ways that he might hasten his departure. He knew he would never leave as long as Bishop was around. The thought flew through his mind that he might put Bishop in an institution for a few weeks. He was shaken and turned his mind to other things. For a while he dozed and dreamed that he and Bishop were speeding away in the car, escaping safely from a lowering tornado-like cloud. He awoke to find the room growing dim.

He got up and went to the window. The boat with the two of them in it was near the middle of the lake, almost still. They were sitting there facing each other in the isolation of the water, Bishop small and squat, and Tarwater gaunt, lean, bent slightly forward, his whole attention concentrated on the opposite figure. They seemed to be held still in some magnetic field of attraction. The sky was an intense purple as if it were about to explode into darkness.

Rayber left the window and threw himself on the cot again but he was no longer sleepy. He had a peculiar sense of waiting, of marking time. He lay with his eyes closed as if listening to something he could hear only when his hearing aid was off. He had had this sense of waiting, kin in degree but not in kind, when he was a child and expected any moment that the city would blossom into an eternal Powderhead. Now he sensed that he waited for a cataclysm. He waited for all the world to be turned into a burnt spot between two chimneys.

All he would be was an observer. He waited with serenity. Life had never been good enough to him for him to wince at its destruction. He told himself that he was indifferent even to his own dissolution. It seemed to him that this indifference was the most that human dignity could achieve, and for the moment forgetting his lapses, forgetting even his narrow escape of the afternoon, he felt he had achieved it. To feel nothing was peace.

He watched idly as a round red moon rose into the lower corner of his window. It might have been the sun rising on the upside-down half of the world. He came to a decision. When the boy came back he would say: Bishop and I are returning to town tonight. You may go with us under these conditions: not that you *begin* to cooperate, but that you cooperate, fully and completely, that you change your attitude, that you allow yourself to be tested, that you prepare yourself to enter school in the fall, and that you take that hat off your head right now and throw it out the window into the lake. If you can't meet these requirements, then Bishop and I are leaving by ourselves.

It had taken him five days to reach this state of clarity. He thought of his foolish emotions the night the boy had come, thought of himself sitting by the side of the bed, thinking that at last he had a son with a future. He saw himself again following the boy down back alleys to end finally at a detestable temple, saw the idiot figure of himself standing with his head in the window, listening to the mad child preach. It was unbelievable. Even the plan to take the boy back to Powderhead seemed ridiculous to him now and going to Powderhead this afternoon was the act of an insane person. His indecision, his uncertainty, his eagerness up to now appeared shameful and absurd to him. He felt that he had regained his senses after five days of madness. He could not wait for them to return so that he could deliver his ultimatum.

He closed his eyes and went over the scene in detail, seeing the sullen face at bay, the haughty eyes forced to look down. His power would lie in the fact that he was indifferent now whether the boy stayed or went, or not indifferent for he positively wanted him to leave. He smiled at the thought that his indifference lacked that one perfection. Presently he dozed again, and again he and Bishop were fleeing in the car, the tornado just behind them.

When he awoke again, the moon travelling toward the middle of the window had lost its color. He sat up startled as if it were a face looking in on him, a pale messenger breathlessly arrived.

He got up and went to the window and leaned out. The sky was a hollow black and an empty road of moonlight crossed the lake. He leaned far out, his eyes narrowed, but he could see nothing. The stillness disturbed him. He turned the hearing aid on and at once his head buzzed with the steady drone of crickets and treefrogs. He searched for the boat in the darkness and could see nothing. He waited expectantly. Then an instant before the cataclysm, he grabbed the metal box of the hearing aid as if he were clawing his heart. The quiet was broken by an unmistakable bellow.

He did not move. He remained absolutely still, wooden, expressionless, as the machine picked up the sounds of some fierce sustained struggle in the distance. The bellow stopped and came again, then it began steadily, swelling. The machine made the sounds seem to come from inside him as if something in him were tearing itself free. He clenched his teeth. The muscles in his face contracted and revealed lines of pain beneath harder than bone. He set his jaw. No cry must escape him. The one thing he knew, the one thing he was certain of was that no cry must escape him.

The bellow rose and fell, then it blared out one last time, rising out of its own momentum as if it were escaping finally, after centuries of waiting, into silence. The beady night noises closed in again.

He remained standing woodenly at the window. He knew what had happened. What had happened was as plain to him as if he had been in the water with the boy and the two of them together had taken the child and held him under until he ceased to struggle.

He stared out over the empty still pond to the dark wood that surrounded it. The boy would be moving off through it to meet his appalling destiny. He knew with an instinct as sure as the dull mechanical beat of his heart that he had baptized the child even as he drowned him, that he was headed for everything the old man had prepared him for, that he moved off now through the black forest toward a violent encounter with his fate.

He stood there trying to remember something else before he moved away. It came to him finally as something so distant and vague in his mind that it might already have happened, a long time ago. It was that tomorrow they would drag the pond for Bishop.

He stood waiting for the raging pain, the intolerable hurt that was his due, to begin, so that he could ignore it, but he continued to feel nothing. He stood light-headed at the window and it was not until he realized there would be no pain that he collapsed.

THREE

X

The headlights revealed the boy at the side of the road, slightly crouched, his head turned expectantly, his eyes for an instant lit red like the eyes of rabbits and deer that streak across the highway at night in the path of speeding cars. His pantslegs were wet up to the knees as if he had been through a swamp. The driver, minute in the glassed cab, brought the looming truck to a halt and left the motor idling while he leaned across the empty seat and opened the door. The boy climbed in.

It was an auto-transit truck, huge and skeletal, carrying four automobiles packed in it like bullets. The driver, a wiry man with a nose sharply twisted down and heavy-lidded eyes, gave the rider a suspicious look and then shifted gears and the truck began to move again, rumbling fiercely. "You got to keep me awake or you don't ride, buddy," he said. "I ain't picking you up to do you a favor." His voice, from some other part of the country, curled at the end of each sentence.

Tarwater opened his mouth as if he expected words to come out of it but none came. He remained, staring at the man, his mouth half-open, his face white.

"I'm not kiddin', kid," the driver said.

The boy kept his elbows gripped into his sides to prevent his frame from shaking. "I only want to go as far as where this road joins 56," he said finally. There were queer ups and downs in his voice as if he were using it for the first time after some momentous failure. He appeared to listen to it himself, to be trying to hear beyond the quaver in it to some solid basis of sound.

"Start talking," the driver said.

The boy wet his lips. After a moment he said in a high voice, entirely out of control, "I never wasted my life talking. I always done something."

"What you done lately?" the man asked. "How come your

pantslegs are wet?"

He looked down at his wet pantslegs and kept looking. They seemed to turn his mind entirely from what he had been going to say, to absorb his attention completely.

"Wake up, buddy," the driver said. "I say how come are your pantslegs wet?"

"Because I never took them off when I done it," he said. "I took off my shoes but I never taken off my pants."

"When you done what?"

"I'm going home," he said. "It's a place I get off at on 56 and then down that road a piece I take a dirt road. It's liable to be morning before I get there."

"How come your pantslegs are wet?" the driver persisted.

"I drowned a boy," Tarwater said.

"Just one?" the driver asked.

"Yes." He reached over and caught hold of the sleeve of the man's shirt. His lips worked a few seconds. They stopped and then started again as if the force of a thought were behind them but no words. He shut his mouth, then tried again but no sound came. Then all at once the sentence rushed out and was gone. "I baptized him."

"Huh?" the man said.

"It was an accident. I didn't mean to," he said breathlessly. Then in a calmer voice he said, "The words just come out of themselves but it don't mean nothing. You can't be born again."

"Make sense," the man said.

"I only meant to drown him," the boy said. "You're only born once. They were just some words that run out of my mouth and spilled in the water." He shook his head violently as if to scatter his thoughts. "There's nothing where I'm going but the stall," he began again, "because the house is burnt up but that's the way I want it. I don't want nothing of his. Now it's all mine."

"Of his whose?" the man muttered.

"Of my great-uncle's," the boy said. "I'm going back there. I ain't going to leave it again. I'm in full charge there. No voice will be uplifted. I shouldn't never have left it except I had to prove I wasn't no prophet and I've proved it." He paused and jerked the man's sleeve. "I proved it by drowning him. Even if I did baptize him that was only an accident. Now all I have to do is mind my own bidnis until I die. I don't have to baptize or prophesy."

The man only looked at him, shortly, and then back at the road.

"It's not going to be any destruction or any fire," the boy said. "There are them that can act and them that can't, and them that are hungry and them that ain't. That's all. I can act. And I ain't hungry." The words crowded out as if they were pushing each other forward. Then he was suddenly silent. He seemed to watch the darkness that the headlights pushed in front of them, always at the same distance. Sudden signs would spring up and vanish at the side of the road.

"That don't make sense but make up some more of it," the driver said. "I gotta stay awake. I ain't riding you just for a good time."

"I don't have no more to say," Tarwater said. His voice was thin, as if many more words would destroy it permanently. It seemed to break off after each sound had found its way out. "I'm hungry," he said.

"You just said you weren't hungry," the driver said.

"I ain't hungry for the bread of life," the boy said. "I'm hungry for something to eat here and now. I threw up my dinner and I didn't eat no supper."

The driver began to feel in his pocket. He pulled out half a bent sandwich wrapped in waxed paper. "You can have this," he said. "It don't have but one bite out of it. I didn't like it."

Tarwater took it and held it wrapped in his hand. He didn't open it.

"Okay, eat it!" the driver said in an exasperated voice. "What's the matter with you?"

"When I come to eat, I ain't hungry," Tarwater said. "It's like being empty is a thing in my stomach and it don't allow nothing else to come down in there. If I ate it, I would throw it up."

"Listen," the driver said, "I don't want you puking in here and if you got something catching, you get out right now."

"I'm not sick," the boy said. "I never been sick in my life except sometimes when I over ate myself. When I baptized him it wasn't nothing but words. Back home," he said, "I'll be in charge. I'll have to sleep in the stall until I get to where I can build me back a house. If I hadn't been a big fool I'd have taken him out and burned him up outside. I wouldn't have burned up the house along with him."

"Live and learn," the driver said.

"My other uncle knows everything," the boy said, "but that don't keep him from being a fool. He can't do nothing. All he can do is figure it out. He's got this wired head. There's an electric cord runs into his ear. He can read your mind. He knows you can't be born again. I know everything he knows, only I can do something about it. I did," he added.

"Can't you talk about something else?" the driver asked. "How many sisters you got at home?"

"I was born in a wreck," the boy said.

He took off his hat and rubbed his head. His hair was flat and thin, dark across his white forehead. He held the hat in his lap like a bowl and looked into it. He took out a box of wooden matches and a white card. "I put all this here in my hat when I drowned him," he said. "I was afraid my pockets would get wet." He held up the card close to his eyes and read it aloud. "T. Fawcett Meeks. Southern Copper Parts. Mobile, Birmingham, Atlanta." He stuck the card in the inside band of his hat and put the hat back on his head. He put the box of matches in his pocket.

The driver's head was beginning to roll. He shook it and said, "Talk, dammit."

The boy reached into his pocket and pulled out the combination corkscrew-bottleopener the schoolteacher had given him. "My uncle give me this," he said. "He ain't so bad. He knows a heap. I speck I'll be able to use this thing some time or other," and he looked at it lying compact in the center of his hand. "I speck it'll come in handy," he said, "to open something."

"Tell me a joke," the driver said.

The boy didn't look as if he knew any joke. He didn't look as if he knew what a joke was. "Do you know what the greatest invention of man is?" he asked finally.

"Naw," the driver said, "what?"

He didn't answer. He was staring ahead again into the darkness and seemed to have forgotten the question.

"What's the greatest invention of man?" the truck driver asked irritably.

The boy turned and looked at him without comprehension. There was a choking sound in his throat and then he said, "What?"

The driver glared at him. "What's the matter with you?"

"Nothing," the boy said. "I feel hungry but I ain't."

"You belong in the booby hatch," the driver muttered. "You ride through these states and you see they all belong in it. I won't see nobody sane again until I get back to Detroit."

For a few miles they rode in silence. The truck moved slower and slower. The driver's lids would fall as if they were weighted with lead and he would shake his head to open them. Almost at once they would close again. The truck began to veer. He shook his head once violently and pulled off the road onto a wide shoulder and leaned back and began to snore without once looking at Tarwater.

The boy sat quietly on his side of the cab. His eyes were open wide without the least look of sleep in them. They seemed not to be able to close but to be open forever on some sight that would never leave them. Presently they closed but his body did not relax. He sat rigidly upright, a still alert expression on his face as if under the closed lids an inner eye were watching, piercing out the truth in the distortion of his dream.

They were sitting facing each other in a boat suspended on a soft bottomless darkness only a little heavier than the black air around them, but the darkness was no hindrance to his sight. He saw through it as if it were day. He looked through the blackness and saw perfectly the light silent eyes of the child across from him. They had lost their diffuseness and were trained on him, fish-colored and fixed. By his side, standing like a guide in the boat, was his faithful friend, lean, shadow-like, who had counseled him in both country and city.

Make haste, he said. Time is like money and money is like blood and time turns blood to dust.

The boy looked up into his friend's eyes, bent upon him, and was startled to see that in the peculiar darkness, they were violet-colored, very close and intense, and fixed on him with a peculiar look of hunger and attraction. He turned his head away, unsettled by their attention.

No finaler act than this, his friend said. In dealing with the dead you have to act. There's no mere word sufficient to say NO.

Bishop took off his hat and threw it over the side where it floated right-side-up, black on the black surface of the lake. The boy turned his head, following the hat with his eyes, and saw suddenly that the bank loomed behind him, not twenty yards away, silent, like the brow of some leviathan lifted just above the surface of the water. He felt bodiless as if he were nothing but a head full of air, about to tackle all the dead.

Be a man, his friend counseled, be a man. It's only one dimwit you have to drown.

The boy edged the boat toward a dark clump of bushes and tied it. Then he removed his shoes, put the contents of his pockets into his hat and put the hat into one shoe, while all the time the grey eyes were fixed on him as if they were waiting serenely for a struggle already determined. The violet eyes, fixed on him also, waited with a barely concealed impatience.

This is no time to dwaddle, his mentor said. Once it's done, it's done forever.

The water slid out from the bank like a broad black tongue. He climbed out of the boat and stood still, feeling the mud between his toes and the wet clinging around his legs. The sky was dotted with fixed tranquil eyes like the spread tail of some celestial night bird. While he stood there gazing, for the moment lost, the child in the boat stood up, caught him around the neck and climbed onto his back. He clung there like a large crab to a twig and the startled boy felt himself sinking backwards into the water as if the whole bank were pulling him down.

Sitting upright and rigid in the cab of the truck, his muscles began to jerk, his arms flailed, his mouth opened to make way for cries that would not come. His pale face twitched and grimaced. He might have been Jonah clinging wildly to the whale's tongue.

The silence in the truck was corrugated with the snores of the driver, whose head rolled from side to side. The boy's jerking arms almost touched him once or twice as he struggled to extricate himself from a monstrous enclosing darkness. Occasionally a car would pass, illuminating for an instant his contorted face. He grappled with the air as if he had been flung like a fish on the shores of the dead without lungs to breathe there. The night finally began to fade. A plateau of red appeared in the eastern sky just above the treeline and a dun-colored light began to reveal the fields on either side. Suddenly in a high raw voice the defeated boy cried out the words of baptism, shuddered, and opened his eyes. He heard the sibilant oaths of his friend fading away on the darkness.

He sat trembling in the corner of the cab, exhausted, dizzy, holding his arms tight against his sides. The plateau had widened and was broken by the sun which rose through it majestically with a long red wingspread. With his eyes open, his face began to look less alert. Deliberately, forcefully, he closed the inner eye that had witnessed his dream.

In his hand he was clutching the truck driver's sandwich. His fingers had clenched it through. He loosened them and looked at it as if he had no idea what it was; then he put it in his pocket.

After a second he grabbed the driver's shoulder and shook him violently and the man woke up and grabbed the steering wheel convulsively as if the truck were moving at a high rate of speed. Then he perceived that it was not moving at all. He turned and glared at the boy. "What do you think you're doing in here? Where do you think you're going?" he asked in an enraged voice.

Tarwater's face was pale but determined. "I'm going home," he said. "I'm in charge there now."

"Well get out and go then," the driver said. "I don't ride nuts in the day time."

With dignity the boy opened the door and stepped down out of the cab. He stood, scowling but aloof, by the side of the road and waited until the gigantic monster had grated away and disappeared. The highway stretched in front of him, lean and grey, and he began to walk, putting his feet down hard on the ground. His legs and his will were good enough. He set his face toward the clearing. By sundown he would be there, by sundown he would be where he could begin to live his life as he had elected it, and where, for the rest of his days, he would make good his refusal.

XI

After he had walked about an hour, he took out the truck driver's pierced sandwich which he had stuck, still wrapped, in his pocket. He undid it and let the paper blow behind. The truck driver had bitten off one of the pointed ends. The boy put the unbitten end in his mouth but after a second he took it out again with faint teeth marks in it and put it back in his pocket. His stomach alone rejected it; his face looked violently hungry and disappointed.

The morning had opened up, clear and cloudless and brilliant. He walked on the embankment and did not look over his shoulder as cars came behind him and swiftly passed, but as each one disappeared on the narrowing strip of highway, he felt the distance between himself and his goal grow longer. The ground under him was strange to his feet, as if he were walking on the back of a giant beast which might any moment stretch a muscle and send him rolling into the ditch below. The sky was like a fence of light to keep it in. The glare forced him to lower his lids but on the other side of it, hidden from his daily sight but present to his inner eye that remained rigidly open, there stretched the clear grey borders of the country he had saved himself from crossing into.

He repeated every few yards, to force himself on faster, that he would soon be home, that there was only the rest of the day between him and the clearing. His throat and eyes burned with dryness and his bones felt brittle as if they belonged to a person older than himself and with much experience; and when he considered it—his experience—it was apparent to him that since his great-uncle's death, he had lived the lifetime of a man. It was as no boy that he returned. He returned tried in the fire of his refusal, with all the old man's fancies burnt out of him, with all the old man's madness smothered for good, so that there was never any chance it would break out in him. He had saved himself forever from the fate he had envisioned when, standing in the schoolteacher's hall and looking into the eyes of the dimwitted child, he had seen himself trudging off into the distance in the bleeding stinking mad shadow of Jesus, lost forever to his own inclinations.

The fact that he had actually baptized the child disturbed him only intermittently and each time he thought of it, he reviewed its accidental nature. It was an accident and nothing more. He considered only that the boy was drowned and that he had done it, and that in the order of things, a drowning was a more important act than a few words spilled in the water. He realized that in this small instance the schoolteacher had succeeded where he had failed. The schoolteacher had not baptized him. He recalled his words: "My guts are in my head." My guts are in my head too, the boy thought. Even if by some chance it had not been an accident, what was of no consequence in the first place was of no consequence in the second; and he had succeeded in drowning the child. He had not said NO, he had done it.

The sun, from being only a ball of glare, was becoming distinct like a large pearl, as if sun and moon had fused in a brilliant marriage. The boy's narrowed eyes made a black spot of it. When he was a child he had several times, experimentally, commanded the sun to stand still, and once for as long as he watched it—a few seconds—it had stood still, but when he turned his back, it had moved. Now he would have liked for it to get out of the sky altogether or to be veiled in a cloud. He turned his face enough to rid his vision of it and was aware again of the country which seemed to lie beyond the silence, or in it, stretching off into the distance around him.

Quickly he set his mind again on the clearing. He thought of the burnt spot in the center of it and he imagined with a careful deliberateness how he would pick up any burnt bone that he might find in the ashes of the house and sling it off into the nearest gulley. He envisioned the calm and detached person who would do this, who would clear out the rubble and build back the house. Beyond the glare, he was aware of another figure, a gaunt stranger, the ghost who had been born in the wreck and who had fancied himself destined at that moment to the torture of prophecy. It was apparent to the boy that this person, who paid him no attention, was mad.

As the sun burned brighter, he became more and more thirsty

and his hunger and thirst combined in a pain that shot up and down him and across from shoulder to shoulder. He was about to sit down when ahead in a brush-swept space off the side of the road he saw a Negro's shack. A small coloured boy stood in the yard, alone except for a razor-backed shoat. His eyes were already fixed on the boy coming down the road. As Tarwater came nearer he saw a cluster of coloured children watching him from the shack door. There was a well to the side under a sugarberry tree and he quickened his pace.

"I want me some water," he said, approaching the forward boy. He took the sandwich from his pocket and handed it to him. The child, who was about the size and shape of Bishop, put it to his mouth with the same motion that he took it and never removed his eyes from the boy's face.

"Yonder hit," he said and pointed with the sandwich to the well.

Tarwater went to it and cranked the bucket up level with the rim. There was a dipper but he did not use it. He leaned over and put his face to the water and drank. He drank until be began to feel dizzy. Then he pulled off his hat and thrust his head into the water. As it touched the deeper parts of his face, a shock ran through him, as if he had never been touched by water before. He looked down into a grey clear pool, down and down to where two silent serene eyes were gazing at him. He tore his head away from the bucket and stumbled backwards while the blurred shack, then the hog, then the coloured child, his eyes still fixed on him, came into focus. He slammed his hat down on his wet head and wiped his sleeve across his face and walked hastily away. The little Negroes watched him until he was off the place and had disappeared down the highway.

The vision stuck like a burr in his head and it took him more than a mile to realize he had not seen it. The water had strangely not assuaged his thirst. To take his mind off it, he reached in his pocket and pulled out the schoolteacher's present and began to admire it. It reminded him that he also had a nickel. The first store or filling station he came to, he would buy himself a drink and open it with the opener. The little instrument glittered in the center of his palm as if it promised to open great things for him. He began to realize that he had not adequately appreciated the schoolteacher while he had the opportunity. The lines of his uncle's face had already become less precise in his mind and he began to see again the eyes shadowed with knowledge that he had imagined before he went to the city. He returned the cork-screw-bottleopener to his pocket and held it there in his hand as if henceforth it would be his talisman.

Presently up ahead, he caught sight of the crossroads where 56 joined the highway he was on. The dirt road was not ten miles down from this point. There was a patched-together store and filling station on the far side of the crossroad. He hastened on in anticipation of the drink he was going to buy, his thirst growing by the second. Then as he came closer, he saw the large woman who stood in the door of the place. His thirst increased but his enthusiasm fled. She was leaning against the frame, her arms folded, and she filled almost the whole entrance. She was a black-eyed woman with a granite-like face and a tongue persistent to question. He and his great-uncle had traded at this place on occasion and when the woman was there, the old man had liked to linger and discourse, for he found her as pleasant as a shade tree. The boy had always stood by impatiently, kicking up the gravel, his face dark with boredom.

She spotted him across the highway and although she did not move or raise her hand, he could feel her eyes reeling him in. He crossed the highway and was drawn forward, scowling at a neutral space between her chin and shoulder. After he had arrived and stopped, she did not speak but only looked at him and he was obliged to direct a glance upward at her eyes. They were fixed on him with a black penetration. There was all knowledge in her stony face and the fold of her arms indicated a judgment fixed from the foundations of time. Huge wings might have been folded behind her without seeming strange.

"The niggers told me how you done," she said. "It shames the dead."

The boy pulled himself together to speak. He was conscious that no sass would do, that he was called upon by some force outside them both to answer for his freedom and make bold his acts. A tremor went through him. His soul plunged deep within itself to hear the voice of his mentor at its most profound depths. He opened his mouth to overwhelm the woman and to his horror what rushed from his lips, like the shriek of a bat, was an obscenity he had overheard once at a fair. Shocked, he saw the moment lost.

The woman did not move a muscle. Presently she said, "And now you come back. And who is going to hire out a boy who burns down houses?"

Still aghast at his failure, he said in a shaky voice, "I ain't ast nobody to hire me out."

"And shames the dead?"

"The dead are dead and stay that way," he said, gaining a little strength.

"And scorns the Resurrection and the Life?"

His thirst was like a rough hand clenched in his throat. "Sell me a purple drink," he said hoarsely.

The woman did not move.

He turned and went, his look as dark as hers. There were circles under his eyes and his skin seemed to have shrunk on the frame of his bones from dryness. The obscenity echoed sullenly in his head. The boy's mind was too fierce to brook impurities of such a nature. He was intolerant of unspiritual evils and with those of the flesh he had never truckled. He felt his victory sullied by the remark that had come from his mouth. He thought of turning and going back and flinging the right words at her but he had still not found them. He tried to think of what the schoolteacher would have said to her but no words of his uncle's would rise to his mind.

The sun was behind him now and his thirst had reached the point where it could not get worse. The inside of his throat felt as if it were coated with burning sand. He moved on doggedly. No cars were passing. He made up his mind that he would flag the next car that passed. He hungered now for companionship as much as food and water. He wanted to explain to someone what he had failed to explain to the woman and with the right words to wipe out the obscenity that had stained his thought.

He had gone almost two more miles when a car finally passed him and then slowed down and stopped. He had been trudging absently and had not waved it down but when he saw it stop, he began to run forward. By the time he reached it, the driver had leaned over and opened the door. It was a lavender and cream-colored car. The boy scrambled in without looking at the driver and closed the door and they drove on.

Then he turned and looked at the man and an unpleasant sensation that he could not place came over him. The person who had picked him up was a pale, lean, old-looking young man with deep hollows under his cheekbones. He had on a lavender shirt and a thin black suit and a panama hat. His lips were as white as the cigaret that hung limply from one side of his mouth. His eyes were the same color as his shirt and were ringed with heavy black lashes. A lock of yellow hair fell across his forehead from under his pushed-back hat. He was silent and Tarwater was silent. He drove at a leisurely rate and presently he turned in the seat and gave the boy a long personal look. "Live around here?" he asked.

"Not on this road," Tarwater said. His voice was cracked from dryness.

"Going somewheres?"

"To where I live," the boy croaked. "I'm in charge there now."

The man said nothing else for a few minutes. The window by the boy's side was cracked and patched with a piece of adhesive tape and the handle to lower it had been removed. There was a sweet stale odor in the car and there did not seem enough air to breathe freely. Tarwater could see a pale reflection of himself, eyeing him darkly from the window.

"Don't live on this road, huh?" the man said. "Where do your folks live?"

"No folks," Tarwater said. "It's only me. I take care of myself. Nobody tells me what to do."

"Don't huh?" the man said. "I see it's no flies on you."

"No," the boy said, "there's not."

There was something familiar to him in the look of the stranger but he could not place where he had seen him before. The man put his hand in the pocket of his shirt and brought out a silver case. He snapped it open and passed it over to Tarwater. "Smoke?" he said.

The boy had never smoked anything but rabbit tobacco and he did not want a cigaret. He only looked at them.

"Special," the man said, continuing to hold out the case. "You don't get one of this kind every day, but maybe you ain't had much experience smoking."

Tarwater took the cigaret and hung it in the corner of his mouth, exactly as the man's was hung. Out of another pocket, the man produced a silver lighter and flashed the flame over to him. The cigaret didn't light the first time but the second time he pulled in his breath, it lit and his lungs were unpleasantly filled with smoke. The smoke had a peculiar odor.

"Got no folks, huh?" the man said again. "What road do you live on?"

"It ain't even a road to it," the boy said. "I lived with my great-uncle but he's dead, burnt up, and now it's only me." He began to cough violently.

The man reached across the dashboard and opened the glove compartment. Inside, lying on its side was a flat bottle of whiskey. "Help yourself," he said. "It'll kill that cough."

It was an old-looking stamped bottle without the paper front on it and with a bitten-off cork in the top. "I get that special too," the man said. "If there's flies on you, you can't drink it."

The boy grasped the bottle and began to pull at the cork, and simultaneously there came into his head all his great-uncle's warnings about poisonous liquor, all his idiot restrictions about riding with strangers. The essence of all the old man's foolishness flooded his mind like a rising tide of irritation. He grasped the bottle the more firmly and pulled at the cork, which was too far in, with his fingers. He put the bottle between his knees and took the schoolteacher's corkscrew-bottleopener out of his pocket.

"Say, that's nifty," the man said.

The boy smiled. He pushed the corkscrew in the cork and pulled it out. Never a thought of the old man's but he would change it now. "This here thing will open anything," he said.

The stranger was driving slowly, watching him.

He lifted the bottle to his lips and took a long swallow. The liquid had a deep barely concealed bitterness that he had not expected and it appeared to be thicker than any whiskey he had ever had before. It burned his throat savagely and his thirst raged anew so that he was obliged to take another and fuller swallow. The second was worse than the first and he perceived that the stranger was watching him with what might be a leer.

"Don't like it, huh?" he said.

The boy felt a little dizzy but he thrust his face forward and said,

"It's better than the Bread of Life!" and his eyes glittered.

He sat back and took the cork off the opener and put it back on the bottle and returned the bottle to the compartment. Already his motions seemed to be slowing down. It took him some time to get his hand back in his lap. The stranger said nothing and Tarwater turned his face to the window.

The liquor lay like a hot rock in the pit of his stomach, heating his whole body, and he felt himself pleasantly deprived of responsibility or of the need for any effort to justify his actions. His thoughts were heavy as if they had to struggle up through some dense medium to reach the surface of his mind. He was looking into thick unfenced woods. The car moved almost slow enough for him to count the outside trunks and he began to count them, one, one, one, until they began to merge and flow together. He leaned his head against the glass and his heavy lids closed.

After a few minutes the stranger reached over and pushed his shoulder but he did not stir. The man then began to drive faster. He drove about five miles, speeding, before he espied a turnoff into a dirt road. He took the turn and raced along for a mile or two and then pulled his car off the side of the road and drove down into a secluded declivity near the edge of the woods. He was breathing rapidly and sweating. He got out and ran around the car and opened the other door and Tarwater fell out of it like a loosely-filled sack. The man picked him up and carried him into the woods.

Nothing passed on the dirt road and the sun continued to move with a brilliant blandness on its way. The woods were silent except for an occasional trill or caw. The air itself might have been drugged. Now and then a large silent floating bird would glide into the treetops and after a moment rise again.

In about an hour, the stranger emerged alone and looked furtively about him. He was carrying the boy's hat for a souvenir and also the corkscrew-bottleopener. His delicate skin had acquired a faint pink tint as if he had refreshed himself on blood. He got quickly into his car and sped away.

When Tarwater woke up, the sun was directly overhead, very small and silver, sifting down light that seemed to spend itself before it reached him. He saw first his thin white legs stretching in front of him. He was propped up against a log that lay across a small open space between two very tall trees. His hands were loosely tied with a lavender handkerchief which his friend had thought of as an exchange for the hat. His clothes were neatly piled by his side. Only his shoes were on him. He perceived that his hat was gone.

The boy's mouth twisted open and to the side as if it were going to displace itself permanently. In a second it appeared to be only a gap that would never be a mouth again. His eyes looked small and seedlike as if while he was asleep, they had been lifted out, scorched, and dropped back into his head. His expression seemed to contract until it reached some point beyond rage or pain. Then a loud dry cry tore out of him and his mouth fell back into place.

He began to tear savagely at the lavender handkerchief until he had shredded it off. Then he got into his clothes so quickly that when he finished he had half of them on backwards and did not notice. He stood staring down at the spot where the displaced leaves showed him to have lain. His hand was already in his pocket bringing out the box of wooden matches. He kicked the leaves together and set them on fire. Then he tore off a pine branch and set it on fire and began to fire all the bushes around the spot until the fire was eating greedily at the evil ground, burning every spot the stranger could have touched. When it was a roaring blaze, he turned and ran, still holding the pine torch and lighting bushes as he went.

He barely noticed when he ran out of the woods onto the bare red road. It streaked beneath him like fire hardened and only gradually as his breath choked him did he slow down and begin to take his bearings. The sky, the woods on either side, the ground beneath him, came to a halt and the road assumed direction. It swung down between high red embankments and then mounted a flat field plowed to its edges on either side. Off in the distance a shack, sunk a little on one side, seemed to be afloat on the red folds. Down the hill the wooden bridge lay like the skeleton of some prehistoric beast across the stream bed. It was the road home, ground that had been familiar to him since his infancy but now it looked like strange and alien country.

He stood clenching the blackened burnt-out pine bough. Then after a moment he began to move forward again slowly. He knew that he could not turn back now. He knew that his destiny forced him on to a final revelation. His scorched eyes no longer looked hollow or as if they were meant only to guide him forward. They looked as if, touched with a coal like the lips of the prophet, they would never be used for ordinary sights again.

XII

The broad road began to narrow until it was no more than a rutted rain-washed gulley which disappeared finally into a blackberry thicket. The sun, red and mammoth, was about to touch the treeline. Tarwater paused an instant here. His glance passed over the ripening berries, turned sharply and pierced into the wood which lay dark and dense before him. He drew in his breath and held it a second before he plunged forward, blindly following the faint path that led down through the wood to the clearing. The air was laden with the odor of honeysuckle and the sharper scent of pine but he scarcely recognized what they were. His senses were stunned and his thought too seemed suspended. Somewhere deep in the wood a woodthrush called and as if the sound were a key turned in the boy's heart, his throat began to tighten.

A faint evening breeze had begun to stir. He stepped over a tree fallen across his path and plunged on. A thorn vine caught in his shirt and tore it but he didn't stop. Farther away the woodthrush called again. With the same four formal notes it trilled its grief against the silence. He was heading straight for a gap in the wood where, through a forked birch, the clearing could be seen below, down the long hill and across the field. Always when he and his great-uncle were returning from the road, they would stop there. It had given the old man the greatest satisfaction to look out over the field and in the distance see his house settled between its chimneys, his stall, his lot, his corn. He might have been Moses glimpsing the promised land.

As Tarwater approached the tree, his shoulders were set high and tense. He seemed to be preparing himself to sustain a blow. The tree, forked a few feet from the ground, loomed in his way. He stopped and with a hand on either trunk, he leaned forward through the fork and looked out at an expanse of crimson sky. His gaze, like a bird that flies through fire, faltered and dropped. Where it fell, two chimneys stood like grieving figures guarding the blackened ground between them. His face appeared to shrink as he looked.

He remained motionless except for his hands. They clenched and unclenched. What he saw was what he had expected to see, an empty clearing. The old man's body was no longer there. His dust would not be mingling with the dust of the place, would not be washed by the seeping rains into the field. The wind by now had taken his ashes, dropped them and scattered them and lifted them up again and carried each mote a different way around the curve of the world. The clearing was burned free of all that had ever oppressed him. No cross was there to say that this was ground that the Lord still held. What he looked out upon was the sign of a broken covenant. The place was forsaken and his own. As he looked, his dry lips parted. They seemed to be forced open by a hunger too great to be contained inside him. He stood there open-mouthed, as if he had no further power to move.

He felt a breeze on his neck as light as a breath and he half-turned, sensing that some one stood behind him. A sibilant shifting of air dropped like a sigh into his ear. The boy turned white.

Go down and take it, his friend whispered. It's ours. We've won it. Ever since you first begun to dig the grave, I've stood by you, never left your side, and now we can take it over together, just you and me. You're not ever going to be alone again.

The boy shuddered convulsively. The presence was as pervasive as an odor, a warm sweet body of air encircling him, a violet shadow hanging around his shoulders.

He shook himself free fiercely and grabbed the matches from his pocket and tore off another pine bough. He held the bough under his arm and with a shaking hand struck a match and held it to the needles until he had a burning brand. He plunged this into the lower branches of the forked tree. The flames crackled up, snapping for the drier leaves and rushing into them until an arch of fire blazed upward. He walked backwards from the spot pushing the torch into all the bushes he was moving away from, until he had made a rising wall of fire between him and the grinning presence. He glared through the flames and his spirits rose as he saw that his adversary would soon be consumed in a roaring blaze. He turned and moved on with the burning brand tightly clenched in his fist.

The path twisted downward through reddened tree trunks that gradually grew darker as the sun sank out of sight. From time to time he plunged the torch into a bush or tree and left it blazing behind him. The wood became less dense. Suddenly it opened and he stood at its edge, looking out on the flat cornfield and far across to the two chimneys. Planes of purpling red above the treeline stretched back like stairsteps to reach the dusk. The corn the old man had left planted was up about a foot and moved in wavering lines of green across the field. It had been freshly plowed. The boy stood there, a small rigid, hatless figure, holding the blackened pine bough.

As he looked, his hunger constricted him anew. It appeared to be outside him, surrounding him, almost as if it were visible before him, something he could reach out for and not quite touch. He sensed a strangeness about the place as if there might already be an occupant. Beyond the two chimneys, his eyes moved over the stall, grey and weathered, and crossed the back field and stopped at the far black wall of woods. A deep filled quiet pervaded everything. The encroaching dusk seemed to come softly in deference to some mystery that resided here. He stood, leaning slightly forward. He appeared to be permanently suspended there, unable to go forward or back. He became conscious of the very breath he drew. Even the air seemed to belong to another.

Then near the stall he saw a Negro mounted on a mule. The mule was not moving; the two might have been made out of rock. He started forward across the field boldly, raising his fist in a gesture that was half-greeting and half-threat, but after a second his hand opened. He waved and began to run. It was Buford. He would go home with him and eat.

Instantly at the thought of food, he stopped and his muscles contracted with nausea. He blanched with the shock of a terrible premonition. He stood there and felt a crater opening inside him, and stretching out before him, surrounding him, he saw the clear grey spaces of that country where he had vowed never to set foot. Mechanically he began to move forward. He came out on the hard ground of the yard a few feet from the fig tree, but his eyes took the far circuit to it, lingering above the stall and moving beyond it to the far treeline and back. He knew that the next sight to meet his eyes would be the half-dug gaping grave, almost at his feet.

The Negro was watching him steadily. He began to move forward on the mule. When the boy finally forced his eyes to move again, he saw the mule's hooves first and then Buford's feet hanging at its sides. Above, the brown crinkled face was looking down at him with a scorn that could penetrate any surface.

The grave, freshly mounded, lay between them. Tarwater lowered his eyes to it. At its head, a dark rough cross was set starkly in the bare ground. The boy's hands opened stiffly as if he were dropping something he had been clutching all his life. His gaze rested finally on the ground where the wood entered the grave.

Buford said, "It's owing to me he's resting there. I buried him while you were laid out drunk. It's owing to me his corn has been plowed. It's owing to me the sign of his Saviour is over his head."

Nothing seemed alive about the boy but his eyes and they stared downward at the cross as if they followed below the surface of the earth to where its roots encircled all the dead.

The Negro sat watching his strange spent face and grew uneasy. The skin across it tightened as he watched and the eyes, lifting beyond the grave, appeared to see something coming in the distance. Buford turned his head. The darkening field behind him stretched downward toward the woods. When he looked back again, the boy's vision seemed to pierce the very air. The Negro trembled and felt suddenly a pressure on him too great to bear. He sensed it as a burning in the atmosphere. His nostrils twitched. He muttered something and turned the mule around and moved off, across the back field and down to the woods.

The boy remained standing there, his still eyes reflecting the field the Negro had crossed. It seemed to him no longer empty but peopled with a multitude. Everywhere, he saw dim figures seated on the slope and as he gazed he saw that from a single basket the throng was being fed. His eyes searched the crowd for a long time as if he could not find the one he was looking for. Then he saw him. The old man was lowering himself to the ground. When he was down and his bulk had settled, he leaned forward, his face turned toward the basket, impatiently following its progress toward him. The boy too leaned forward, aware at last of the object of his hunger, aware that it was the same as the old man's and that nothing on earth would fill him. His hunger was so great that he could have eaten all the loaves and fishes after they were multiplied.

He stood there, straining forward, but the scene faded in the gathering darkness. Night descended until there was nothing but a thin streak of red between it and the black line of earth but still he stood there. He felt his hunger no longer as a pain but as a tide. He felt it rising in himself through time and darkness, rising through the centuries, and he knew that it rose in a line of men whose lives were chosen to sustain it, who would wander in the world, strangers from that violent country where the silence is never broken except to shout the truth. He felt it building from the blood of Abel to his own, rising and engulfing him. It seemed in one instant to lift and turn him. He whirled toward the treeline. There, rising and spreading in the night, a red-gold tree of fire ascended as if it would consume the darkness in one tremendous burst of flame. The boy's breath went out to meet it. He knew that this was the fire that had encircled Daniel, that had raised Elijah from the earth, that had spoken to Moses and would in the instant speak to him. He threw himself to the ground and with his face against the dirt of the grave, he heard the command. GO WARN THE CHILDREN OF GOD OF THE TERRIBLE SPEED OF MERCY. The words were as silent as seeds opening one at a time in his blood.

When finally he raised himself, the burning bush had disappeared. A line of fire ate languidly at the treeline and here and there a thin crest of flame rose farther back in the woods where a dull red cloud of smoke had gathered. The boy stooped and picked up a handful of dirt off his great-uncle's grave and smeared it on his forehead. Then after a moment, without looking back he moved across the far field and off the way Buford had gone.

By midnight he had left the road and the burning woods behind him and had come out on the highway once more. The moon, riding low above the field beside him, appeared and disappeared, diamond-bright, between patches of darkness. Intermittently the boy's jagged shadow slanted across the road ahead of him as if it cleared a rough path toward his goal. His singed eyes, black in their deep sockets, seemed already to envision the fate that awaited him but he moved steadily on, his face set toward the dark city, where the children of God lay sleeping.

TOPICS FOR PAPERS AND DISCUSSION

1. *The calling of the prophet.* First, conduct some research into prophets, especially from the Old Testament. Differentiate among kinds of prophecy. What are some characteristics of a religious prophet? Can a divinely compelled "man of God" also be a critic of the social order? Compare old Tarwater and Tarwater as prophets. If this novel is about a boy choosing his "vocation," to use O'Connor's word, why is he so resistant to God's calling?
2. *The devil and his forms.* How does the devil figure in this story? Consider Baudelaire's remark that the devil's greatest wile is to persuade us that he does not exist. In what ways is Tarwater affected by the voice of his "friend," the "stranger"? While obviously the homosexual rapist is intended to be diabolic, how about other characters, for example, Meeks, the copper flue salesman? Does Tarwater rid himself of the devil? How?
3. *"Grotesque," "violence," and "redemption."* These three words are seminal in any study of the O'Connor canon. "For me the meaning of life is centered in our Redemption by Christ," O'Connor wrote in an essay, adding that "writers who see by the light of their Christian faith will have, in these times, the sharpest eyes for the grotesque, for the perverse, and for the unacceptable." Do you find her statements to be contradictory or puzzling? The actions of Tarwater, a fourteen-year-old boy, are grotesque and violent. How do you reconcile the constructiveness of his achieved spiritual state and the destructiveness of his actions? What is the significance of the epigraph from Matthew?
4. *Setting as symbol.* The narrative occurs in three major and distinctly different places, and "on the road" between them. How do the three major settings symbolize opposing forces in Rayber and in Tarwater? Why is it fitting that Tarwater should return at last to "the dark city, where the children of God lay sleeping"? Examine the various metaphors and images the author uses for landscape. How does the three-part structure of the novel relate to setting? You might next consider how the structure and setting relate to the basic triangular conflict: old Tarwater-Rayber-Tarwater.

5. *The "mystery" of things.* Relate O'Connor's belief in religious mystery to "hierophany," defined by Mircia Eliade as: "the manifestation of the sacred in some ordinary object, a stone or a tree." Contrast this principle with its opposite, "desacralization," which merges profaneness with apathy. At this extreme, "things" are so taken for granted that they have no significance beyond themselves; essential mysteries are thus met by indifference. How are these antithetical ideas reflected in the novel? Try to apprehend the meaning of such "things" as the hearing aid, the hat, the loaf of bread in the bakery window, the partly eaten sandwich, the corkscrew.
6. *The character of Rayber.* In commenting on the novel, the author called Rayber "the typical modern man." Is he? What is implied in her designation? Connect Rayber to the following: atheism, reason, science, existentialism, nihilism. O'Connor also has said that old Tarwater "is the hero . . . and I'm right behind him 100 percent." However vital he may be, he is already dead at the beginning, and the author devotes the entire long middle section to Rayber. Why? Is Rayber a victim of modern society or of his own martyr-like self-delusion? Is he reprehensible or sympathetic? If he is divided between the demands of love and emotionalism on one hand and the need for emptiness and apathy on the other, why does he intend "to lurch toward emptiness"? Analyze him in depth.
7. *Evidences of archetypes.* The novel contains numerous archetypes of characters, of situations, of symbols and associations. Trace some in each of these categories. For example, consider these situations as archetypes: Tarwater embarks on a "journey," he is assigned a "task," he has a "quest," he undergoes an "initiation," he suffers a "fall," we are made aware of "death-rebirth."
8. *The nature of southern fundamentalism.* Ponder O'Connor's position—a devout Roman Catholic writing in the predominantly Protestant South. Furthermore, much of her fictional concern was with backwoods evangelism. Where do Catholicism and primitive Protestantism part company? How are they linked, for example, to the rite of baptism? The author referred to old Tarwater as "a sort of crypto-Catholic." What did she mean? What is the author trying to say about "the Bible Belt"? Could the action of the novel take place anywhere else except in the South?
9. *Motifs and leitmotifs.* Frequently physical objects are related to ambiguous and sometimes contradictory actions and meanings: water with baptism or death, earth with burial or fecundity, bread with hunger or regeneration, etc. Analyze these symbolic elements. On three occasions Tarwater sets fires. Why? What is the full import of fire as a motif? Explain the symbology based upon old clothes and new clothes, eyes, names, tied shoelaces, machines and vehicles, chance encounters, biblical allusions.

10. *Analysis of a single episode.* Concentrate upon the opening breakfast table scene or the drowning or the rape scene. Consider the significance of the revival meeting held at a "pentecostal tabernacle" by "the Carmodys for Christ" when both Tarwater and Rayber hear Lucette. Why does the author go to such lengths to quote the child evangelist's sermon? What happens in the next scene when Tarwater and Rayber meet outside, and why are their actions so important at this point? Examine in detail word choice, sentence structure, tone, and characterization.
11. *The meaning of freedom.* Contrast old Tarwater's view of freedom with Rayber's. Old Tarwater says to his great-nephew: "You were born into bondage and baptized into freedom . . . ." Explain. Is a prophet free to act in "bondage"? In reply to a question about the novel O'Connor stated that "Tarwater is certainly free and meant to be," in spite of his apparent compulsion to be a prophet. Distinguish between free actions and those which seem predestined or dictated by fate. Also, review the circumstances under which old Tarwater was put into a mental institution, and the way he obtained his freedom from it.
12. *The hearing aid as thematic symbol.* After being shot by old Tarwater, Rayber loses his hearing. His deafness and "the box" take on many meanings. Trace the use and nonuse of "the box" by Rayber. Recall Tarwater's question: "Do you think in the box, or do you think in your head?" Is the hearing aid a marvel of science and engineering, an artificial contrivance, a screen provided by technology, a distorter of reality, or a mechanical representation of Rayber? Could it be some or all of these?
13. *Bishop as focus.* The idiot child never says a word, yet his role is crucial. Why? How is he regarded by his father? by Tarwater? In the same way that Tarwater resembles Rayber, Bishop resembles old Tarwater. Why this odd inversion? In what ways is Bishop's defective mentality important to the theological underpinning of the story? Most importantly, why does Bishop become the victim of a ritual murder? Is "ritual murder" the wrong terminology? If so, correct it.
14. *The Tarwater legacy.* Account for Tarwater's unusual birth and background. Why does the boy pride himself on being born in "a wreck"? Trace the geneology of three generations, beginning in "past time" with the grandparents. Fix upon important nephew-uncle relationships. What parallel patterns emerge? Women are conspicuous by their absence in this novel. Among others, Bernice Bishop Rayber is seen only briefly. Why?
15. *The significance of baptism and/or burial.* Why does old Tarwater object to cremation? Why is baptism of such great import to him? Since for "the general run of readers, baptism is a meaningless

rite," O'Connor has spoken of having to imbue baptism "with an awe and terror which will suggest its awful mystery" and "which will jar the reader into some kind of emotional recognition of its significance." Does she succeed in her purpose? You might also consider the use of theological paradox (or, from another viewpoint, literary oxymoron), such as "seeing, when your eyes are burned clean" and "salvation by drowning."

16. *Education and ignorance.* Why is Rayber repeatedly referred to as "the schoolteacher"? Does he actually teach? What do the many references to education, teaching, and school suggest about theme? Early in the novel the following passage appears: "The old man had always impressed on him his good fortune in not being sent to school. The Lord had seen fit to guarantee the purity of his up-bringing to preserve him from contamination, to preserve him as His elect servant, trained by a prophet for prophecy." Does education contaminate? Does the novel support ignorance?
17. *The concern for Christ.* In an essay O'Connor observed that "while the South is hardly Christ-centered, it is most certainly Christ-haunted." In the novel "the stranger" serves to implement this idea during the grave digging when "speaking" to Tarwater about the old man: "He was a one-notion man. Jesus. Jesus this and Jesus that." Is the South depicted in the novel Christ-centered or Christ-haunted? Distinguish between religious belief and religious obsession. One critic considers this novel rare in modern writing because it gives us a sense of "what it feels like, to believe that Christian belief means everything." Do you agree with this judgment? Try to assess the position of Christ in the novel. Does that position bear upon an area as large and diverse as the South, or is O'Connor's statement to be held in question as an insupportable generalization?
18. *The conflict of head and heart.* Pascal wrote that "the heart has its reasons which reason knows nothing of." Apply this notion to the main characters. Why does Rayber's published psychological analysis of Mason Tarwater bother the old man so much? Consider other polarities as thematic subjects: religious belief and disbelief, past and present, great expectations and disappointments, sin or evil and redemption, love and withdrawal from love, acceptance or rejection of grace, secular and sacred life, commitment and denial, entrapment and escape.
19. The Violent Bear It Away *as a comic novel.* Does it seem unusual for a religious book to be funny? Analyze the scene in which old Tarwater gives advance instructions on his burial as he lies in his coffin. Examine the scenes depicting the visit of the truant officer and the chance encounters with Meeks and with the anonymous truck driver. Analyze the "kidnaping" and shooting scenes. Is this humor farcical? ironical? satirical? Do the comic scenes add to or

detract from the overall effectiveness of the novel? Are they intrusive as mere comic relief, or are they woven into the very texture of the narrative?

20. *Defects of narration and vision.* This novel is not without its detractors. It has been criticized for a variety of reasons: its characters are too fanatical; the first half is better than the second half; the religious ideas are muddled; the rape scene is artificial and melodramatic; Rayber is not a convincing intellectual; there is too much (or not enough) authorial control; the novel is fragmented by its multiple points of view; it is too long; it is dull, and so on. Present a convincing argument for or against some of these so-called defects.

Comparative Studies

The following topics may suggest ideas for long papers or may serve as subjects for panel discussions or may provide projects for independent study. Numerous additional topics could be devised, and we encourage their development. The titles of other works offered here as examples are only partial, to say the least. Furthermore, we have limited titles to fiction, but comparisons could be extended to other genres wherever appropriate.

The tripartite arrangement of topics reflects a progression of study. Within the first group, comparisons are restricted to the anthology itself and are primarily critical. In the second section, we direct students to expand their reading and research to include other works by the individual writers represented in the anthology. Finally, the third group gives suggestions for more general comparisons with outside works and other writers.

INTERNAL COMPARISONS AMONG THE NOVELS

1. *The plight of "the outsider."* The alienation of the individual in modern society is a prominent and compelling subject of recent fiction. Examine its thematic coherence in some or all of the seven novels in the collection.
2. *Urban life and rural life.* Compare city living as shown in *Slaughterhouse-Five; Goodbye, Columbus;* and *Seize the Day.* Show how a sense of rural America is captured by *Noon Wine, The Ballad of the Sad Café, Of Mice and Men,* and *The Violent Bear It Away.*
3. *Physical and mental infirmities.* Draw comparisons among Helton and Lennie and Bishop. Contrast Crooks with Lymon, or Rayber's deafness with Rappaport's blindness. Why are the authors so concerned with mental defectives, cripples, and other handicapped characters?
4. *The American experience.* What could a foreigner learn from these novels about our national character and the superiority or inferiority of American life? Show how some of the novels transcend place to represent universal experience.

COMPARATIVE WORK IN INDIVIDUAL AUTHORS

Kurt Vonnegut, Jr.

5. *Science fiction and fantasy.* How do the elements of science fiction and fantasy in *Slaughterhouse-Five* relate to other Vonnegut novels and stories? On a larger scale, how does Vonnegut fit into the context of science-fiction writing from Jonathan Swift to Robert A. Heinlein?
6. *Reappearing motifs.* As a writer, Vonnegut has created a cosmos of his own that is, if not in design or achievement, at least functionally similar to Faulkner's Yoknapatawpha County as a source for fictive materials. Trace incidents, places, ideas, and characters that are used again and again, for example: the Dresden fire-bombing; Tralfamadore and Ilium, New York; the effects of scientific technology; characters like Kilgore Trout, the Rumfoords, Eliot Rosewater, and Howard W. Campbell, Jr. Besides *Slaughterhouse-Five,* be sure to deal with *The Sirens of Titan, Mother Night,* and *God Bless You, Mr. Rosewater.*
7. *Becoming.* "When I write I simply become what I seemingly must become," Vonnegut wrote in the preface to *Welcome to the Monkey House.* What has he become? Sort out these critical ascriptions of him: humanist, pessimist, social surrealist, fabulator, fantasist, science-fiction writer, moral crusader, black humorist, satirist,

absurdist, metafictionist. Can some be combined? Trace his progress from *Player Piano* (1952) to the present.

Carson McCullers

8. *Symbolic values of grotesquerie.* Since the motif of the grotesque is central to all of McCullers' work, compare its use in *The Ballad of the Sad Café* with grotesquerie to be found in *Reflections in a Golden Eye, The Heart Is a Lonely Hunter,* and *Clock Without Hands.* What does grotesquerie reveal symbolically?
9. *The poetic element.* Demonstrate and defend the author's susceptibility to poetic qualities in many passages of her novels and short stories. Attack or support the criticism that her poetic style fails because (as one commentator has written of *Reflections in a Golden Eye*) "the people are caricatures and the narrator's commentary is a triumph of adjectives over analysis, reminiscent of the worst of Poe . . . ."
10. *The elemental world of legend and romance.* How is this world used in *The Member of the Wedding,* the short stories, and the other McCullers novels? Does this world represent mere escapism for the characters, or does it have some deeply hidden symbolic functions?

Philip Roth

11. *Roth's career.* Trace the course of Roth's development from the beginnings with *Goodbye, Columbus* to the present time. Compare his work that deals with American Jewish themes and characters to his work about other subjects.
12. *Males and females.* Compare Neil Klugman with other Roth protagonists like Gabe Wallach, Alex Portnoy, David Alan Kepesh, Peter Tarnopol. How does Brenda compare with other important women in his novels?
13. *Images of the Jew in America.* Compare Roth with other prominent American Jewish writers like Bernard Malamud, Saul Bellow, Norman Mailer, Isaac Bashevis Singer, etc. In what ways are his fictional concerns similar and different?

Katherine Anne Porter

14. *"A Southerner by tradition and inheritance."* In addition to this self-appraisal, Porter has also said of herself, "I have a very profound feeling for the South." Do these feelings emerge in a story like *Noon Wine*? Compare it with other Porter stories set in the South, such as "The Source," "The Witness," "The Old Order," "The Last Leaf," "The Grave," "The Jilting of Granny Weatherall," and *Old*

Mortality. Other than their geographical setting, what makes them typically "southern"?

15. *The foreign element*. Porter has written extensively about foreigners and foreign countries. Compare this work with her fiction set in America, which deals with both native Americans and immigrants to America. Examine uses of foreign locales in "The Martyr," "Flowering Judas," "Hacienda," "That Tree," "Mariá Concepción," "The Leaning Tower," and *Ship of Fools*.
16. *"A very firm foundation in actual human experience."* This phrase reflects Porter's vital concern in her writing with the importance of personal experience, either what she underwent herself, or what she saw or heard about. Review primary and secondary sources concerning her life and career, and then trace autobiographical elements in her fiction. Determine how she modified her varied real experiences to suit her artistic purposes.

Saul Bellow

17. *The dangers of the contemporary world*. Discuss this recurrent theme in Bellow's fiction. Along with *Seize the Day* examine such other novels as *Herzog*, *The Victim*, and *Mr. Sammler's Planet*. What transformations of authentic personality, what deformations and distortions of philosophy, and what misrepresentations of relationships result from the pressures of contemporary life?
18. *Love*. The redemptive power of love is another recurrent theme in Bellow's work. Show its importance from *Dangling Man* to *The Adventures of Augie March* to *Mr. Sammler's Planet*.
19. *The "intellectual" novelist*. What is meant by the description of Bellow as a "novelist of the intellectuals"? Does such terminology result from the many expressed ideas in his work, or from his intellectual approach to life, or is it because he has written about intellectuals like Moses Herzog and Artur Sammler? Is such categorization warranted or accurate? See Bellow's essay "Where Do We Go From Here," which deals in part with the "novel of ideas."

John Steinbeck

20. *California as locale*. Compare *Of Mice and Men* with Steinbeck's other fiction about California, for example, *The Long Valley*, *Tortilla Flat*, *In Dubious Battle*, and pertinent parts of *The Grapes of Wrath*. Measure Steinbeck's California fiction against the later work set elsewhere, for example, *The Winter of Our Discontent*.
21. *The "buddy" novel*. Contrast Lennie and George in *Of Mice and Men* and Mac and Jim of *In Dubious Battle*. Then branch outward to compare the two novels with other modern works based upon close

male friendships, of which there have been many, like Jack Kerouac's *On the Road*, Mark Harris' *Bang the Drum Slowly*, Truman Capote's *In Cold Blood*, Hermann Hesse's *Narcissus and Goldmund*, etc.

22. *Endings.* Compare the endings of *In Dubious Battle, Of Mice and Men*, and *The Grapes of Wrath*. Account for the varying merits or faults of these endings. Is each appropriate to the context of the work itself? Are they equally successful?

Flannery O'Connor

23. *Variations on a theme.* Start with O'Connor's short story "You Can't Be Any Poorer Than Dead," which she revised and rewrote as the opening chapter of *The Violent Bear It Away*. How do the two versions compare? Next read her short story "The Lame Shall Enter First," which tells a somewhat different story, but with a similar cast of characters. Compare Rayber with Sheppard, Tarwater with Rufus, Bishop with Norton. How are the triangular conflicts of the characters and the themes of the stories alike and different? Other O'Connor fiction helpful for comparison includes "The River" and *Wise Blood*.
24 *A religious pair.* Compare the preoccupation with religious matters in the work of O'Connor and another Catholic writer, such as J. F. Powers (American), Graham Greene (British), Frank O'Connor (Irish), or Francǫis Mauriac (French).
25. *Images of the South.* From a substantial amount of O'Connor's fiction, derive a portrait of the South. Choose another southern writer for purposes of contrast: among women, Ellen Glasgow, Carson McCullers, Katherine Anne Porter, Caroline Gordon, Eudora Welty; among men, William Faulkner, Robert Penn Warren, Thomas Wolfe, Erskine Caldwell, Jesse Stuart, William Styron.

EXTERNAL COMPARISONS WITH OTHER WORKS

26. *Novels in other media.* At least five of these novels have been presented in other media. Compare these adaptations with the original: *Slaughterhouse-Five* as a movie; *Noon Wine* as a TV drama; *The Ballad of the Sad Café* as a play; *Goodbye, Columbus* as a movie; *Of Mice and Men* as a play, a movie, and a TV drama.
27. *Bildungsroman.* Find elements of "the novel of growth or development" in *Goodbye, Columbus; The Violent Bear It Away;* and *Slaughterhouse-Five.* Compare these findings with elements of the *bildungsroman* in another American novel, such as J. D. Salinger's *The Catcher in the Rye*, Ralph Ellison's *Invisible Man*, or Mark

Twain's *Huckleberry Finn*. In addition, numerous European novels could be used for comparison, such as Charles Dickens' *Great Expectations*, Thomas Mann's *Tonio Kröger*, Joseph Conrad's *Lord Jim*, Hermann Hesse's *Demian*, James Joyce's *Portrait of the Artist as a Young Man*, Bohumil Hrabal's *Closely Watched Trains*, or Gabriel Fielding's *In The Time of Greenbloom*.

28. *"The double."* Review the use of doubles in *Goodbye, Columbus*, *The Violent Bear It Away*, *Noon Wine*, and *Seize the Day*. Compare these with other fiction about the double, like Fyodor Dostoevsky's *The Double*, Joseph Conrad's *The Secret Sharer*, Robert Louis Stevenson's *Dr. Jekyll and Mr. Hyde*, Saul Bellow's *The Victim*, Vladimir Nabokov's *Pale Fire*, Jorge Luis Borges' *Labyrinths*.
29. *Family ties*. Compare various kinds of familial themes, such as "marriage" in *Noon Wine* and Gustave Flaubert's *Madame Bovary*; "fathers and sons" in *Seize the Day* and Franz Kafka's *The Metamorphosis*; "family disaffection" in *Goodbye, Columbus* and Elizabeth Bowen's *The Death of the Heart*; or "family heritage" in *The Violent Bear It Away* and Nathaniel Hawthorne's *The Scarlet Letter*.
30. *Influences and/or similarities*. Show the influence of Nathanael West or Teilhard de Chardin upon Flannery O'Connor. Make a study of the friendship of John Steinbeck and marine biologist Ed Ricketts to show how Ricketts' work and personal character made their way into Steinbeck's writing. Find evidences of the thought of German philosopher Arthur Schopenhauer in the work of Saul Bellow, or show similarities in the fictional techniques of Bellow and James Joyce. Compare Joseph Heller's *Catch-22* and *Slaughterhouse-Five* as antiwar novels.

Biographical Notes

KURT VONNEGUT, JR., was born on Armistice Day, November 11, 1922, in Indianapolis, Indiana. His father and grandfather were prominent Indiana architects, and his older brother is a distinguished scientist.

Vonnegut attended four universities, including Cornell where he was a student of chemistry from 1940 to 1942, and the University of Chicago where, from 1945 to 1947, he studied anthropology. During World War II he served as an infantryman in Europe. Captured in the Battle of the Bulge, he was among a group of American POW's interned in Dresden, Germany, when it was bombed by American and British planes in February, 1945. After brief stints as a news reporter in Chicago and a public-relations man for General Electric in Schenectady, New York, Vonnegut began full-time writing in 1950. Living on Cape Cod with his wife Jane and their large family, he managed to make a living writing for the paperback market and for popular magazines like *Collier's, Cosmopolitan,* and the *Saturday Evening Post.* The emergent success of Vonnegut is traceable through two decades: from obscurity and mislabeling as "science-fiction writer" to recognition as a youth-cult figure to national stature and overdue critical acceptance as a serious artist. He has written seven novels: *Player Piano* (1952), *The Sirens of Titan* (1959), *Mother Night* (1961), *Cat's Cradle* (1963), *God Bless You, Mr. Rosewater* (1965), *Slaughterhouse-Five* (1969), and *Breakfast of Champions* (1973); two collections of short stories, *Canary in a Cat House* (1961) and *Welcome to the Monkey House* (1968); several plays, including *Happy Birthday, Wanda June,* produced on Broadway in 1971, and *Between Time and Timbuktu,* written for TV in 1972; and approximately sixty stories, reviews, and articles, some of which have been collected in *Wampeters, Foma & Grandfalloons* (1974). He taught at the Writers' Workshop at The University of Iowa for two years and also later held a guest lectureship at Harvard. He was awarded a Guggenheim Fellowship to Germany in 1967, and in 1973 was elected a member of the National Institute of Arts and Letters. He now resides in New York City.

CARSON (SMITH) MCCULLERS was born in Columbus, Georgia, February 19, 1917. Unlike many other Southern writers, notably William Faulkner and Flannery O'Connor, she chose to live away from her native region. However, the South remained the principal setting of her fiction. As a teenager, she went to New York to pursue a career in music, and New York was to remain her home for most of her adult life. After brief attendance at Columbia University and New York University, she was married in 1937 to Reeves McCullers. (He took his life in 1953.) Although music seemed to engage her at first, she expressed an early interest in writing. Her first novel, *The Heart Is a Lonely Hunter,* was published when she was only twenty-three. She produced four more novels: *Reflections in a Golden Eye* (1941), *The Member of the Wedding* (1946), and *Clock Without Hands* (1961); *The Ballad of the Sad Café,* which appeared in 1943 in *Harper's Bazaar,* became part of a distinguished collection of stories published in 1951 under the same title.

Her other works include *The Square Root of Wonderful* (1958) and a volume of children's rhymes, *Sweet as a Pickle and Clean as a Pig* (1964). Mrs. McCullers also met success as a playwright, adapting her novel *The Member of the Wedding* for the Broadway stage; it won the New York Critics Award as the best play of 1950. In 1963 she assisted Edward Albee with his stage adaptation of *The Ballad of the Sad Café*. A volume of previously uncollected writings, entitled *The Mortgaged Heart*, appeared posthumously in 1971. Like her fellow Georgian Flannery O'Connor, she was plagued by ill health, writing for many years handicapped by partial paralysis. She died at the age of fifty on September 29, 1967, in Nyack, New York. A slow, meticulous worker, she produced a small body of work that is limited in range, but marked by its skillful control, strength of characterization, and profound vision.

PHILIP ROTH was born March 19, 1933, in Newark, New Jersey. He graduated from Bucknell University in 1954 and took a master's degree from the University of Chicago in 1955. After Army service, he taught English at the University of Chicago from 1956 to 1958. He has been a visiting instructor of writing at several universities: Iowa, Princeton, Pennsylvania, and SUNY at Stony Brook. Roth burst into prominence in 1959 with the publication of *Goodbye, Columbus and Five Short Stories*, a collection which won the National Book Award for fiction the following year. In the 1960s, he produced three novels: *Letting Go* (1962), *When She Was Good* (1967), and *Portnoy's Complaint* (1969), which became a best seller. His work of the early 1970s was wide-ranging in subject matter and, as augured by *Portnoy's Complaint*, became more exaggerative and satiric in tone. In 1971 Roth unleashed a biting satire of the Nixon administration entitled *Our Gang (Starring Tricky and His Friends)*. It was followed in 1972 by *The Breast* whose hero, David Alan Kepesh, finds himself turned into a giant female breast. His next novel, *The Great American Novel* (1973), is a comic fable about baseball in America. In his eighth work of fiction, *My Life as a Man* (1974), Roth returns to a more realistic, though still comic, vein. In this novel an unusual narrative structure is employed for the first-person account of the protagonist, Peter Tarnopol, a Jewish writer and intellectual. Roth is an accomplished writer of short fiction, and his short stories have frequently appeared in annual collections of *Best American Short Stories*. He has published articles, reviews, and stories in such magazines as *Commentary*, the *New Yorker*, *Esquire*, *The New York Review of Books*, and *Harper's*, and he has been a frequent contributor to the *New American Review*. Roth was a Guggenheim Fellowship recipient in 1960, and in 1970, at the age of 37, he was elected a member of the National Institute of Arts and Letters.

Katherine Anne Porter was born May 15, 1890, in Indian Creek, Texas. After the death of her grandmother, the family farm was sold and the Porters moved to San Antonio in 1904. She attended convent schools, was married at 16, divorced at 19, and went to Chicago where she worked for a newspaper. From 1917 until a trip to Mexico in 1920 to study art, she worked for the Fort Worth *Critic* and the Denver *Rocky Mountain News;* she also served as a ghost-writer in New York. After her return to Fort Worth in 1921, she was employed by a trade magazine and in 1922 published her first story, "María Concepción." For seven years (1922–1929) she traveled, reviewed books, and worked on a biography of Cotton Mather. In 1930 her most famous volume of stories, *Flowering Judas,* was published. The following year, she received a Guggenheim Fellowship to Mexico; later she traveled to Europe. Her second marriage in 1933 ended in divorce. An enlarged edition of *Flowering Judas* appeared in 1935, followed in 1939 by *Pale Horse, Pale Rider,* a collection of three short novels including *Noon Wine.* She became a member of the National Institute of Arts and Letters in 1942, and afterward served as a Fellow of Regional American Literature of the Library of Congress. *The Leaning Tower and Other Stories* was published in 1944. From 1949 to 1962 she lectured and taught at many colleges and universities in the United States and abroad. A volume of essays and reviews, *The Days Before,* was published in 1952. *Ship of Fools,* a long-awaited first novel, appeared in 1962 and was widely read and discussed. In 1966 her *Collected Short Stories* won the National Book Award for fiction and the Pulitzer Prize. The following year she was awarded the National Institute of Arts and Letters Gold Medal for fiction. *The Collected Essays and Occasional Writings* appeared in 1970.

Saul Bellow, the son of Russian-Jewish immigrants, was born in Lachine, Quebec, July 10, 1915, and grew up in Chicago. He attended the University of Chicago from 1933 to 1935 and graduated from Northwestern University in 1937. For a three-year period in the 1940s, he was a member of the editorial department of *Encyclopaedia Britannica,* and he also saw service as a merchant seaman during World War II. He has taught at several colleges and universities, including Bard, Princeton, Minnesota, and most recently has served as a professor with the Committee on Social Thought at the University of Chicago. Bellow was made a Guggenheim Fellow in 1948 and 1955. He received the National Book Award for fiction in 1953 and 1965, a Ford Foundation grant in 1959, and the International Literature Prize in 1965. He is also a member of the American Institute of Arts and Letters. Bellow's first published story appeared in 1940, and since then he has written seven novels: *Dangling Man* (1944), *The Victim* (1947), *The Adventures of Augie March* (1953), *Seize the Day* (1956), *Henderson the Rain King*

(1959), *Herzog* (1964), and *Mr. Sammler's Planet* (1970). Four of these novels were selected in *Book Week*'s poll of the "Twenty Best Books" published by American fiction writers from 1945 to 1965. Bellow has also written short stories, plays, essays, and reviews. A collection of his shorter fiction, *Mosby's Memoirs and Other Stories*, was published in 1968. Among his best-known stories are "A Father-to-Be," "Looking for Mr. Green," "A Sermon by Dr. Pep," and "The Mexican General." The essays include "Deep Readers of the Word, Beware," "Distractions of a Fiction Writer," "Facts That Put Fancy to Flight," and "The Future of Fiction." *The Last Analysis*, a play, was produced in 1964, and in 1966 the three short plays, *Out from Under, Orange Soufflé*, and *The Wen*, were produced. Bellow also edited the literary journal *The Noble Savage*.

JOHN STEINBECK was born in Salinas, California, February 27, 1902. He entered Stanford University in 1920 and, after intermittent study, left in 1925 without taking a degree. While learning the craft of fiction writing, he worked briefly as a reporter on a New York newspaper and at a series of odd jobs on both the East and West Coasts. His first novel, *Cup of Gold* (1929), attracted little notice. Similar critical neglect awaited his second and third novels, *The Pastures of Heaven* (1932) and *To a God Unknown* (1933). Steinbeck's first critical and public success, *Tortilla Flat*, was published in 1935. His fifth novel, *In Dubious Battle* (1936), dealt with a strike during a California fruit harvest. The following year *Of Mice and Men* appeared as a novel and a play. The 1938 collection of short fiction, *The Long Valley*, treats various aspects of life in the Salinas Valley, the locale of much of his best writing. One of its memorable selections was the previously published short novel *The Red Pony*. His masterpiece *The Grapes of Wrath* (1939) won the Pulitzer Prize and made Steinbeck world famous. Afterward he produced novels of markedly differing length and theme: *The Moon Is Down* (1942), *Cannery Row* (1945), *The Pearl* (1947), *The Wayward Bus* (1947), *Burning Bright* (1950), *East of Eden* (1952), *Sweet Thursday* (1954), *The Short Reign of Pippin IV* (1957), and *The Winter of Our Discontent* (1961). He worked on film and television scripts, wrote or collaborated on several plays and one musical. He also produced a considerable body of expository prose, including personal reports of World War II and the war in Vietnam, and travel reportage of sea expeditions, a trip to Russia, and (in *Travels with Charley*, 1962) a cross-country tour of the United States. An interesting posthumous work is *Journal of a Novel* (1969), consisting of letters to his editor on the writing of *East of Eden*. Steinbeck married three times and was the father of two sons. Although many critics contend that the quality of his fiction began to decline in the early 1940s, Steinbeck's rank as a major American writer has remained firm. His international prominence was recognized and permanently assured when he was awarded the Nobel Prize for Literature in 1962. He died at the age of 66 on December 20, 1968, in New York.

FLANNERY O'CONNOR was born in Savannah, Georgia, March 25, 1925. When she was about thirteen, she moved with her parents to Milledgeville, Georgia, where her family had lived since before the Civil War. She died there August 3, 1964, of disseminated lupus from which she had suffered recurrent attacks since her mid-twenties. (The disease had also claimed her father's life in 1941.) She graduated from the Woman's College of Georgia in 1945 and received a master's degree in fine arts from The University of Iowa in 1947, after study in the Writers' Workshop. Except for her graduate work, brief residence in New York and Connecticut, a trip to Europe, and travels for addresses, participation in symposiums, and the like, she spent most of her life in her native Georgia. Her avocation was raising peacocks at her farm home, Andalusia, near Milledgeville. She never married. Her writing talent was recognized early, and she won numerous awards and grants during her brief career. Her output was limited: a few essays (gathered into the posthumous collection *Mystery and Manners,* 1969); two short novels, *Wise Blood* (1952) and *The Violent Bear It Away* (1960); and two collections of short stories, *A Good Man Is Hard to Find* (1955) and *Everything That Rises Must Converge* (published posthumously in 1965). Most of her stories and parts of the novels were originally published in distinguished literary journals and magazines. *The Complete Stories,* a total of 31 stories including apprentice fiction contained in her master's thesis, was published in 1971 and was awarded the National Book Award for fiction the following year. Even though her work was cut short by an early death at 39, her literary reputation is assured. She is considered by many critics to be the leading writer of short fiction in postwar America. As testament, in the decade since her death scores of articles and a dozen books about her work have appeared. Miss O'Connor was a devout Catholic. A sense of profound religious mystery lies at the heart of much of her writing, in spite of its apparent preoccupation with the grotesque, the comic, and the violent.

1 2 3 4 5 6 7 8 9 10 -GB- 80 79 78 77 76 75 74